THE EMPIRE OF BONES SAGA VOLUME THREE

TERRY MIXON

The Empire of Bones Saga Volume 3

Published by Yowling Cat Press ®

Digital edition date: 6/21/2023

Print ISBN: 978-1947376427

Individual Works

Behind Enemy Lines Copyright © 2017 by Terry Mixon

Print ISBN: 978-1947376007

The Terra Gambit Copyright © 2018 by Terry Mixon

Print ISBN: 978-1947376083

Hidden Enemies Copyright © 2018 by Terry Mixon

Print ISBN: 978-1947376120

Cover art - image copyrights as follows:

Thanapol Sinsrang | Dreamstime.com

Luca Oleastri

Donna Mixon

Cover design and composition by Donna Mixon

Print design and layout by Terry Mixon

Audio edition performed and produced by Veronica Giguere

Reach her at: v@voicesbyveronica.com

ALSO BY TERRY MIXON

You can always find the most up to date listing of Terry's titles on his Amazon Author Page.

Note: the links below (ebook only, obviously) redirect you to my website where you can click a button to go to Amazon. This allows me to participate in Amazon's associates program and earn a little more. Sorry for any inconvenience.

The Last Hunter

The Last Hunter

Bonds of Blood

Alpha Strike

The Enemy Revealed

Command Authority

The Grand Conspiracy

Shield of Humanity

Fog of War

Ships of the Line

Operation Liberty

The Empire of Bones Saga

Empire of Bones

Veil of Shadows

Command Decisions

Ghosts of Empire

Paying the Price

Recon in Force

Behind Enemy Lines

The Terra Gambit

Hidden Enemies

Race to Terra

Ruined Terra

Victory on Terra

When Luck Runs Out

Gunboat Diplomacy

The Imperial Marines Saga

Spoils of War

Imperial Recruit

Enemy Action

The Humanity Unlimited Saga

Liberty Station

Freedom Express

Tree of Liberty

Blood of Patriots

Single Novels

Scorched Earth

Storm Divers

The Vigilante Series with Glynn Stewart

Heart of Vengeance

Oath of Vengeance

Bound By Law

Bound By Honor

Bound By Blood

Box Sets

The Empire of Bones Saga Volume 1

The Empire of Bones Saga Volume 2

The Empire of Bones Saga Volume 3

The Empire of Bones Saga Volume 4

Humanity Unlimited Publisher's Pack 1

Humanity Unlimited Publisher's Pack 2

Want to get updates from Terry about new books and other general nonsense going on in his life? He promises there will be cats. Go to TerryMixon.com/Mailing-List and sign up.

DEDICATION

This book would not be possible without the love and support of my beautiful wife.
Donna, I love you more than life itself.

ACKNOWLEDGMENTS

Once again, the people who read my books before you see them have saved me. Thanks to Tracy Bodine, Michael Falkner, Cain Hopwood, Kristopher Neidecker, Bob Noble, Jon Paul Olivier, and Jason Young for making me look good.

I also want to thank my readers for putting up with me. You guys are great.

BEHIND ENEMY LINES

BOOK SEVEN

Cut off from home, Princess Kelsey Bandar needs a place to hide from the vengeful Rebel Empire.

The secrets she stole give her people a fighting chance in the war that brought down the original Terran Empire. If she gets them home. If her prisoners cooperate.

Should that prove impossible, she must then convince a long-hidden people to help her. After she finds them, of course.

1

"Why the hell did you sneak aboard one of our ships?" Kelsey Bandar shouted once she had her mother alone in her office on *Persephone*. "We're at war!"

Justine Bandar sat without asking, smirking as she lounged in a chair in front of her daughter's desk. "I'm making certain that we have the opportunity to talk without you using your supposed duty as an excuse to avoid me."

She'd even had the nerve to use air quotes when she'd said "supposed."

Kelsey rubbed her face tiredly. "You've lost your mind. Do you even understand the situation you've inserted yourself into?"

Her mother made a pooh-poohing gesture. "I'm certain it's not nearly as dire as you'd have me believe. In any case, I refuse to let you go away angry. You're my daughter. I'm not going to allow you to deny me."

The woman leaned forward a little. "I've known you all your life, baby girl. You can't fool me. You're hurting inside, and you need your mother." Her expression allowed a little distaste to show through. "That has to be what's behind some of your more questionable choices recently."

Kelsey counted slowly to ten in her head before she spoke. "As hard as this may be to believe, you're not my biggest problem right now. Let me lay it out for you, Mother. While you've been hiding aboard *Audacious*, we've traveled deep inside the Rebel Empire.

"At this very moment, there's probably an enemy fleet trying to find and kill us. Let me emphasize that a little bit, just in case it's too subtle. They're going to try to *kill* us."

Her mother huffed. "Don't be so dramatic. I'm sure the situation isn't nearly as bad as you'd like me to believe. You're trying to distract me from this unhealthy mind-set of yours."

Kelsey slapped her hand on the desk and stood. As short as she was, that wasn't nearly as impressive as she'd prefer. Still, it would have to do.

"It's *exactly* that dire, Mother. Forget Jared Mertz. He's the least of your worries right now. We're currently behind enemy lines, and I just stole an entire Rebel Empire research station. One I'm sure they're desperate to keep out of our hands.

"Once they figure out how I did it, they're going to come after us. If they catch us, they're not going to politely ask me to give it back. They're going to start shooting."

For the first time since they'd discovered her mother hiding aboard the carrier, Justine Bandar looked a bit less certain. She squirmed in her seat. "What's a research station? Why are you taking it?"

"That's the kind of thing I don't have the time or patience to explain right now, Mother. The *only* purpose of this meeting is to tell you how badly you've screwed up.

"Until I have more time, I'm going to see that you get housing that's more suitable to your current circumstances."

Her mother smiled a little. "That little room *was* on the small side, and I can think of a few furnishings that would make life a little easier. These ships of yours are so… functional. Fleet should hire a few interior decorators. Add some soothing colors and make things a little more comfortable."

"I don't have time for this." Kelsey signaled for the marines through her implants. The door to her office slid open, and two hulking men stepped inside.

She pointed at her mother. "Justine Bandar is under arrest. Take her to the brig."

Her mother shot to her feet. "You can't arrest me! I'm your *mother*!"

"Oh, allow me to assure you, I can. Let's start with your unauthorized presence on a Fleet carrier. You've already admitted to that crime. I'm sure there are plenty of other regulations you've violated, but that will do for now.

"Once I'm certain we're in a relatively safe place, we'll have that little chat you so desperately want. Until then, you can contemplate your sins in a cell. If I have to, I'll send someone down to explain precisely how bad your situation is.

"In fact, that's a great idea. You *should* speak to someone in the Fleet Judge Advocate General's office. They can explain the severity of your crimes to you in exquisite detail. I'm sure the legal officer on *Audacious* can help you out. Marines, take her away."

The two men firmly grasped the ex-empress by her arms and dragged her gently from Kelsey's office. Her mother struggled and ordered them to release her until the hatch slid closed behind them. Kelsey was certain the woman would scream, demand, and promise retribution all the way to her new accommodations.

She slowly sat back down and rubbed the bridge of her nose. How in the hell had her mother even gotten on board the carrier? Obviously, someone had helped smuggle her aboard, but that didn't explain how she'd managed to stay hidden for two weeks. No, someone had been providing ongoing support.

It really didn't surprise Kelsey that some people in Fleet still saw her mother as an authority figure. After all, the woman had ruled the Empire at her father's side for decades. For many people, she still had that aura of command. Or they thought she could give them something in return for their support.

They needed to learn the error of their ways in the strongest of terms.

"*Persephone*, signal *Audacious* for me. I want to speak to Commodore Anderson."

"Signaling now, Colonel."

Kelsey's father—Emperor Karl Bandar—had decided that she needed to be a marine to command marines. So, he'd worked with Admiral Yeats to make that happen.

Her ship—*Persephone*—was a Marine Raider vessel from the Old Empire. Its computer would allow only someone with the appropriate codes and Marine Raider implants to command it. Kelsey was the only person in the New Terran Empire that met those criteria.

That wouldn't be true for very much longer, though. Her executive officer, Major Angela Ellis, was almost halfway through the implant procedures required to become a Marine Raider. She'd had the requisite cranial implants already. Last week, she'd gotten the pharmacology unit, ocular, auditory, and olfactory enhancements.

Over the next three weeks, she'd go through additional procedures to coat her bones with layers of graphene and weave artificial muscles through her natural ones. They'd start with her legs, and then move to her arms and upper body over two additional sessions. That would give the woman time to master her upgraded body.

Learning to use the new muscles was going to be challenging, but Kelsey had no doubt the marine would master them quickly. If a pampered little princess could do it, Angela Ellis could.

"This unit has Commodore Anderson on the line for you, Colonel," *Persephone* said.

"On my screen."

An image of Zia Anderson appeared on Kelsey's screen. The young woman smiled wryly. "Have you gotten your unexpected guest comfortably situated?"

"You could say that. I just had the marines take her down to the brig."

Zia's eyes widened. "Seriously? You locked your *mother* in the brig?"

"Damned right I did. She's got to learn that she can't just throw her weight around like that anymore."

"You mean she's got to learn she can't mess with you like that, don't you?"

"That too," Kelsey said with a grimace. "I'm going to put the fear of God into her. It'll do her good to sweat for a while.

"But that's not why I called. Someone on *Audacious* aided and abetted her. If they're willing to stash an ex-empress on your ship for two weeks, what else might they do?"

"That's a good question," Zia said. "I've already told Brandon to find them, though he has other things going on. He'll eventually get to the bottom of this."

Brandon Levy was a by-the-book kind of guy. Kelsey expected he'd find the people who'd hidden Justine Bandar. He'd make them suffer for it too.

"We'll let him take care that, then," Kelsey said. "I'd prefer administrative punishment."

"That pretty much sums up the orders I've already given him."

Technically, Zia was the senior Imperial officer in their task force, so that was really her call to make. Kelsey could make big picture decisions, but if she meddled in the details, Zia would have every right to smack her hand. Like she'd just delicately done.

"Right. Sorry. They're your people to discipline. I do, however, insist you leave my mother to me."

"You'll get no argument from me," Zia said solemnly. "I'd prefer not to tangle with her."

Kelsey nodded. "We have a deal, then. I want you to send your legal officer over, though. He needs to explain the regulations my mother violated and tell her the penalties she faces for breaking them. I think she needs a wake-up call."

"I'll talk to him as soon as we're done," Zia said with a nod. "He can come over with Carl."

She frowned. "Why is Carl coming over?"

Zia shrugged. "I'm not sure. Something about Ned Quincy."

"Maybe that means he's figured out how to relocate the program. That would be awesome. Having some privacy would be nice."

Ned Quincy had been an officer in the Marine Raiders before the Fall. He'd saved a lot of memories using an as-yet-unknown method devised by one of his people.

When Kelsey had taken those memories into her implants and allowed Marcus—the sentient AI in command of Jared's flagship—to change the operational program to enable her to search the memories, Ned had come to pseudo-life.

He wasn't quite a person, but he was far more than a computer program. He seemed to have genuine emotions.

Unfortunately, he lived in Kelsey's head. Which made going to the bathroom awkward, to say the least.

They'd come to an agreement about him accessing her implants, but it wasn't the same as being alone.

Carl had been working on some secret project to relocate the programs in a manner that kept them active. Perhaps his visit was to get that rolling.

"Ned is in hibernation at the moment," Kelsey said. "He doesn't sleep like a real person, but we found out that he had to have downtime every week or so. So, I can freely say that I'll be damned happy to have him out of my head.

"I like him, but no one needs to have someone potentially looking over her shoulder all the damned time. Or actually hearing the more focused thoughts in your head. That's too intimate."

"I can't imagine why it hasn't driven you crazy. Or Talbot."

Kelsey laughed. "Who says it hasn't? In any case, don't let my mother distract you from finding us a hidey-hole. That has to be your first priority."

She rose from behind her desk. "I'm certainly not going to let her distract me. Maybe I can help find us a weak flip point so we can get the hell out of here."

* * *

MAJOR RUSS TALBOT tried not to hover as Carl Owlet hunched over the main computer in the captured research center. "What's taking so long? I thought you were the master of breaking into computers."

The young scientist glanced back peevishly. "I'd be done a lot faster if you'd stop asking me that every five minutes. This kind of work takes time under the best of circumstances. Which, I'll point out, this isn't."

Since Talbot really didn't know anything about computer hacking, so he couldn't dispute any of that.

"Why is this one so much harder?" he asked. "You've gotten into a lot of Old Empire computers before. Don't you have a bunch of tools to make this easy?"

Carl set the tablet he was using onto the locked console and turned to face him. "I *do* have tools, but I've had zero luck breaking into every military computer we've captured from the Rebel Empire. Whoever programs them is paranoid, and I mean that literally.

"I only got into the AI at Harrison's World because Kelsey killed its power so abruptly. It didn't have time to lock its memory. The storage was still accessible. If the AI had sent a command to lock it up, I'd be banging my head there too.

"This computer contains classified research the Rebel Empire doesn't want anyone to have. Not even its own people. Remember, the AIs don't exactly trust humans, particularly the ones they use as slaves.

"Honestly, the fact that they require humans to do this research in the first place tells us something very interesting about how they work. Or rather, how they don't work. I'm shocked they didn't shoot the researchers as soon as we attacked."

"I suspect that had to do with the fact we surprised them so badly," Talbot said. "We literally dumped a brigade's worth of marines onto them with no warning. First, we snuck into a system that they were certain they had locked down, then we used the transport rings to get our people onto the orbital without them having a chance to see us coming.

"Last, we set off your jammers and blew a nice big hole into their secure area. Our people were all over them before they had a chance to figure out what was happening, much less act on it. I'm sure that shutting down all the fusion plants within a couple of minutes had something to do with our success too."

The young man nodded. "Overwhelming surprise was the goal. I'm just stunned that it worked so well. Frankly, far too many of your wife's plans go astray for my comfort. Then she blows up a lot of things to make up for lost ground."

Talbot laughed. "A surprising number of things get blown up even when things go according to her plans too. I'll admit this mission resulted in less devastation than most. With discretion being the better part of valor, we'll just keep that opinion to ourselves.

"Maybe it would help to step back a bit and look at the big picture," he told the young scientist after a moment. "What precisely do we have our hands on?"

Carl sighed. "If we're just talking about the research facility, we've got five major labs doing work on various projects. One of them is some kind of missile-enhancement program. We're talking bigger warheads, faster drives, and more endurance. Possibly making them smarter and harder to hit. They're also looking at more powerful beams and stronger battle screens.

"Then there's the production area for the Raider implants. That's not technically research, but extremely restricted. I suspect the people running it are more like factory workers. They probably didn't know what they were producing.

"Stealing the orbital and the minds that made all this possible is going to have a profound impact on the Rebel Empire's research programs. We took their research, hardware, and the minds that made it happen. They won't be able to replace any of that very quickly, and this isn't the kind of knowledge the AIs want on the loose."

Talbot snorted. "They'd probably give any retiring worker a private send-off without a suit."

Carl winced. "Ouch. Based on the plans I saw on paper, it looks as though they only used the Raider implant equipment whenever they needed a fresh batch for the crazy AI on Erorsi.

"That points to the probability that the Rebel Empire doesn't have any attack forces outfitted with Marine Raider implants, which we already suspected. That's good news for us."

Talbot nodded. "Then there's the AI production line that Annette Vitter said was going to kick off soon."

The crazy fighter pilot had bluffed her way into the restricted area on the orbital and parleyed a case of mistaken identity into access to a briefing about the AI project. Talk about huge brass balls. The woman would've made a hell of a marine.

"Not exactly," Carl disagreed. "They already had a facility here to produce the hardware. The plans that Captain Vitter had seen there had revolved around expanding that. If I had to guess, I'd wager that this was a backup production center for AI hardware that they wanted to make more productive."

"Are you making any progress in understanding how to produce that hardware?"

Carl gave him a flat look. "In case it escaped your notice, there are a lot of competing priorities vying for my attention. It'll take several days just to figure out what we have our hands on, and if they find a weak flip point, I'll have to drop everything and work on that."

"I really wish we brought more of your people along for this mission," Talbot grumbled. "We're really short in the scientist department this time."

His young friend smiled wryly. "To be fair, we'd only planned on snagging some equipment and running for it. Nobody in their right mind thought Princess Kelsey would steal an entire orbital or run *away* from our support ships."

The untimely arrival of a Rebel Empire fleet had forced them to run in the opposite direction. All they had with them now was the carrier *Audacious*, the Marine Raider ship *Persephone*, a freighter whose contents they were still trying to pin down, and a recovery ship they were using to move the captured orbital along at a snail's pace.

Not enough force to deal with a determined pursuer, and circumstances had trapped them in a series of systems running deeper into the Rebel Empire.

The enemy would've already chased them down if they hadn't made it look as though the orbital had exploded. It wouldn't be long before the Rebel Empire commander saw through that ruse. Then he'd figure out that one of the battle stations guarding the system's flip points wasn't communicating. Neither were the destroyers that had been backing it up.

He'd likely assume that whoever had blown up the orbital had come in that way, killing the ships and station on the way in. Once they realized the orbital was gone, he'd be after them at top speed.

The New Terran Empire's forces only had one chance. They needed to find a weak flip point and slip away.

The Rebel Empire didn't know weak flip points existed. If his team found one, they'd get the breathing room they needed to solve their current problems. If not, well, things would get very, very ugly.

Carl proved his thoughts were roaming along those lines when he spoke again. "Any word on the search for weak flip points? All of this is going to be for nothing if we don't get off the path the Rebel Empire expects us to be on. Once they figure out that wasn't their orbital that blew up."

"Commodore Anderson hasn't mentioned anything. We still have probes and fighters out searching this system. No luck yet."

Their forces had fled through the first empty system without looking for weak flip points. Kelsey had wanted to be completely certain they'd gotten clear before any Rebel Empire ships came looking for them. They were in the second system now. If they didn't find anything here, they'd move onto the third.

"Well, do the best you can," Talbot finally said. "Once we have the prisoners settled into the area of the orbital we've cleared for them, I'll have you talk with the scientists. Perhaps you can form some kind of bond. You know, geek to geek."

Carl chuckled. "I'll certainly do my best. How long do you think that's going to take?"

He shrugged. "We're talking about roughly ten thousand people. Just determining who everyone is will take days. They're not exactly cooperating. It would help if we had access to the personnel files."

The young scientist picked up his tablet glumly. "I still have a few ideas to try. If all of else fails, we might be able to trick one of them into logging in."

Talbot considered that and smiled. "You know, that's a really good idea. I'll let you get back to work while I see if I can come up with a plan."

2

To Kelsey's joy, it turned out that Carl had indeed figured out how to extract Ned Quincy from her implants without harming him. The equipment the young scientist had brought over managed the task without incident, after she woke Ned and he gave his consent.

That didn't mean Carl was going to be putting Ned into something else right away, though. He had a lot of work remaining to design a computer that could correctly mimic having Raider implants.

When he managed that, Ned would be back in some form. She hoped that happened soon, but they had other things on their plates.

Such as the scanner readings from the far-flung probes. It only took a few hours after Carl had extracted Ned before one of them found something.

"I've found a weak flip point," Carl said from his borrowed console on *Persephone*'s bridge.

Relief flooded through her. She'd been afraid they wouldn't find one before they had to flee this system. Now they had a chance.

"What can we tell about it?" she asked.

He shrugged. "Not much. The probe is still too far away from the flip point to take any measurements."

That's about what Kelsey had expected. "Have the task force change course toward the flip point. It might cost us some time, but I'd rather have everybody close by."

Time crawled as the ships slowly made their way toward the newly discovered flip point. It wasn't very far away from the regular flip point they'd need to use if this new one was unsuitable. They could resume their headlong flight with only a few hours lost if they had to.

"Is the flip point going to be large enough for the orbital?" she asked him once they'd drawn near the potential escape hatch.

"I'll need to send a probe through to get readings from the other side before I can be sure."

"I'm sorry if I seem a bit abrupt," she said, "but I'm worried we'll have company very soon. I'd really like to get away before they arrive."

"Couldn't we just move to the outer system? If we cut our power to standby, they'll go right past us."

"Yes, but they'd be in front of us then. If this flip point doesn't work out, we'd probably run into them when we try the next system. I'd rather avoid that."

The young scientist sighed. "I see your point. The probe is getting some better readings now. Once I've precisely isolated the flip point, we can send it through. When it comes back, I should be able to tell what the relative strength is and whether or not we can transit safely."

"What kind of timeframe are we talking about?" she asked.

"Half an hour or so. Maybe less."

Kelsey forced herself to wait. That involved an inordinate amount of pacing.

Twenty minutes later, he grunted. "The flip point is strong enough to allow the ships through, even *Audacious*. I'm not sure about the recovery ship while it's holding the orbital, though."

"We can't just leave it behind," she said. "This is a package deal. We all have to make it through."

He sighed. "I understand, but I can't command physics. We should focus on seeing what's on the other side."

"Send the probe. We also need to make sure we're not running into something like the nova where Omega lives."

"Good point. I'm sending the instructions to flip it now. It'll go over, take readings for about ten minutes, and then return. If you don't mind, I'm going to get a sandwich while it does that. It's been a while since I ate."

"That's something I can take care of." A quick message to the galley had food on the way for all of them.

The probe flipped out of the system just as their food arrived. Someone had made extra sandwiches for Kelsey, for which she was grateful. It no longer bothered her that she was always eating something to feed her enhanced body.

They had enough time to take the edge off their hunger before the probe returned and began transmitting data.

"The other side looks safe enough," Carl said after a moment. "It's a normal system with no obvious radio, grav, or power sources detected on passive scans. The probe didn't stay long enough to note anything subtle, so it might still be occupied in some smaller fashion."

"What about the flip point?" Kelsey asked. "Is it going to be strong enough to allow the recovery ship to make it through with the orbital?"

"It's close. The only way to find out for sure is to try. On the negative side, the far end is not as strong as this side. If we go across, the orbital is definitely too large to come back. Probably not *Audacious*, either. We'd be committed."

She sighed. "Tell me again what happens if the recovery ship comes apart midflip? Those arms aren't really all that secure, since the orbital is far too big to fit inside them in their normal configuration."

"I'm not really sure, but it can't be good. Best case, the recovery ship arrives in the other system but is unable to move the orbital any farther."

"What's the worst case?" She already had a fairly good idea of what it was, but she wanted to hear him say it.

His lips compressed. "Just about as bad as you'd imagine. The stress of flipping distorts the field generated by the arms, and the orbital comes apart. I'm not sure if that's preflip or on the other side."

Kelsey rubbed her face. If they passed this flip point by, they might not find another before the Rebel Empire caught up with them. On the other hand, if they tried to use the flip point and failed, thousands of people could die.

"Well, it's not as if we really have a choice," she finally said. "We'll go take a look around. If things look promising, we'll give it a try."

* * *

ANNETTE VITTER MADE a show of struggling against the two marines as they hauled her through the hatch. They weren't being gentle, so she didn't even have to act very hard.

"Let me go, you cretins!" she shouted.

Of course, they didn't release her. They had their own roles to play.

They manhandled her another few meters into the compartment and shoved her forward, just as planned.

She stumbled, turned, and shot a glare at their retreating backs as they marched back out. "I don't know who you bastards think you are, but you'll never get away with this."

The hatch slid shut and she turned with a huff to face the prisoners. She'd met most of them at the meeting she'd attended just before Kelsey and the marines had captured the orbital.

The only people she knew by name were Commander Edward Irons and Commodore Murdock. The former was friendly, and the latter was a droning bore. They, of course, knew her as Commander Violet Renner, a role she'd continue playing for the moment.

They'd stashed the real Commander Renner in a special holding cell. Princess Kelsey had decided early on to keep the woman isolated from everyone else so that Annette could use her identity if she had to.

Annette wasn't sure Talbot's plan would work, but she was willing to give it a try. He'd be monitoring the situation via a camera above the main hatch to the cafeteria they were using to house the senior prisoners.

Under other circumstances, they could've used her implants to see and hear what she did, but they had to jam everyone to keep the prisoners from communicating. In any case, the odds were good that no one was going to assault her.

If they did, she'd be able to handle herself until help arrived. One didn't fly marines around without picking up a few things.

Irons rose from the table where he'd been sitting and headed her way. "Commander Renner! We were worried. Are you all right?"

"I'm fine," she said, rubbing her forehead. "I've got a killer headache, though."

Stunners did that to people. They'd knock you out for a couple of hours and leave you with a splitting headache. Not that she'd been stunned this time, of course, but everyone else had. They'd know intimately what she was talking about.

He nodded sympathetically. "That's pretty much how the rest of us feel too. Did they question you?"

"Commander Irons," Commodore Emilia Murdock said from a table off in a corner by herself. "Please escort Commander Renner to me. You'll have time to chitchat later."

The woman's tone was one of irritation. Annette couldn't tell if that was because she was impatient because Irons was delaying Annette or if Murdock always sounded that way. Based on the meeting Annette had attended, she was betting on the latter.

Irons managed a contrite expression. "Of course, Commodore. Right away." He made a show of escorting Annette to the Commodore's table before returning to his associates.

Since the only chair at the table was the one the Commodore was using, Annette decided she'd just stand at attention. "Commander Renner reporting, Commodore."

"At ease, Commander. Report."

Annette allowed herself to relax fractionally. The older woman didn't seem to be the type that wanted her subordinates to be at ease.

"Yes, ma'am. I was on my way to my quarters when all hell broke loose. I heard explosions and then ran into a squad of marines in powered armor. They were shooting everybody in sight with stunners. I tried to get out of the way, but one of them hit me.

"I woke up in a small compartment with other Fleet personnel. Once I was finally able to get someone's attention, I convinced them to bring me here with the other senior officers. All I know for certain is that there are a lot of marines and Fleet personnel among our attackers."

"I was able to get into my office and take a look at the monitors before they captured the primary control center," the older woman said. "There must've been hundreds of marines in armor. I have no idea where they came from, but their surprise was total.

"Whoever the traitors are, they had help smuggling people onto this orbital. Inside help. There's absolutely no way that many unknown personnel could've gotten past our security. Also, someone with the appropriate access codes had to disable their armor's self-destruct systems."

Annette made a show of agreeing without saying anything. She could see how it would be confusing to the older woman. The Rebel Empire didn't allow their marines to use powered armor or heavy weapons without strict supervision. Marines and enlisted personnel didn't have cranial implants, so the armor had to be manually controlled.

Which meant that an officer with implants had to unlock it for their use. Those same officers could remotely detonate explosive charges hidden inside the armor. She wondered if that engendered trust issues with the Rebel Empire marines.

"Whoever it was, ma'am, they knew what they were doing," Annette said. "The fact that we're still sitting here means they disabled all the self-destruct charges. They have everything."

"Not quite," Murdock said. "They're undoubtedly after our research, but it's not going to do them much good. The computers are locked down, and only our top people have the codes."

The older woman smiled. "And they're not going to have very much time to consolidate their gains. They don't know it yet, but they're going to have visitors very soon. Much sooner than they'd planned for, I imagine."

That would be the fleet of ships that had come into Dresden space right after Princess Kelsey had captured the orbital. They were still probably trying to figure out what had happened. Annette hoped they found a weak flip point so they could escape before those vessels came after them.

The senior Rebel Empire officer shook her head. "No, our captors aren't going to be pleased at all. Meanwhile, we need to come up with plans to escape our confinement and free our fellow officers. I'm not going to sit on my butt waiting for someone to come rescue me. We'll get out of here on our own.

"I want you to join Commander Irons and assist him in any way that he requires. He's much more familiar with the orbital layout than you are. After all, you've only been here a few hours."

The older woman sighed. "You're not seeing us at our best, Commander Renner, but that's about to change. Dismissed."

Annette came to attention and saluted. She spun on her heel and walked over to the table where Irons was sitting with several other senior officers. She'd seen most of them at the briefing, but hadn't learned their names.

Their conversation ceased as she stepped up beside the table. Irons gestured for her to take the open seat beside him.

"Everyone, this is Violet Renner. As you might remember, she arrived just before the current unpleasantness.

"Commander Renner, allow me to introduce the rest of the command staff. To my right is Commander Andrew Gomez. He's our hardware guru."

The slender Hispanic man inclined his head.

"Across from you is Jeannette Martin. She's the civilian computer specialist that oversees all aspects of our research computers. She'd normally have our chief scientist with her, but our captors have her somewhere else."

Martin was a somewhat overweight brunette woman with a darker complexion. She smiled at Annette shyly.

"Finally," Irons said, "the man you were here to replace. Commander Raul Castille is our senior security officer, of course."

The tall man smiled coolly. "Commander Renner. I'm sorry we didn't have an opportunity to get together before the Commodore's briefing, but I had other tasks that kept me occupied. I must say that the image in your personnel file doesn't do you justice."

Oh, crap.

3

Kelsey tapped in to the scanner feed as soon as they were through the flip point. As the probe had said, the new system seemed deserted at first glance, but they were only operating off passive scanners.

That meant they'd pick up active fusion plants eventually, if the people that built them hadn't shielded them well enough. If there were any ships moving out there, they'd spot them if they were moving fast enough.

That's where the risk came in. The system might have a Rebel Empire picket force that they wouldn't notice right away. They had to go slow and be careful.

"Take us out of the flip point," she ordered. "Launch a dozen stealthed probes and get them scanning the rest of the system. If there's something out there, I want to know about it."

The process of thoroughly vetting an unknown system could take days. They didn't have time for that, so she'd just have to do the best she could. If after three hours, they hadn't detected signs of people, she'd declare it safe enough for them to move forward.

"Colonel," Lieutenant Jack Thompson—her helm officer—said. "The computer has generally located this system in relation to the Old Empire maps we have. If the estimate is accurate, the Old Empire wasn't aware of it."

Kelsey smiled at the man. "That's good news. It might mean we have some breathing room to get ourselves in order. It also means that the system might have flip points that lead somewhere useful. Like taking us partway home."

If they could avoid going into the Rebel Empire, that would be amazingly good luck. Now that they knew her people existed, it wouldn't be so easy to slip home again without them noticing.

"What do we know about the system?" she asked.

"It has a main sequence G-class star, and we're picking up indications of several planets," Angela said from her console. "We won't know for a while if any are in the habitable zone. It's roughly three hundred light years from the system we just left."

A habitable planet would be good. It would allow them the luxury of moving their prisoners to a location where they'd be both more comfortable and less dangerous. As long as they continued housing the prisoners on the station, there was always the chance they might stage a breakout.

"Take us into the system at half speed," she told Jack. "Continue scanning with passives. If you pick up anything unusual—no matter how small—I want to know immediately."

"Aye, ma'am."

While her ship and the probes began fanning out into the new system, she resumed considering how she was going to deal with her mother. Justine Bandar was a complication that Kelsey really didn't have time for, but the woman wasn't going away. Unfortunately.

From what Kelsey had heard, her mother hadn't stopped yelling at the poor lieutenant tasked with guarding her. *Persephone* was too small to have a brig. She'd used the word with her mother to make a point, but she'd really housed her in the smallest stateroom on the ship.

Having recently occupied several different cells, Kelsey knew her mother was just fine. A brig would only have a bunk, a desk, and a chair that didn't move. Oh, and a toilet that only barely protected someone's modesty from the guards.

Kelsey wondered how ex-Empress Justine Bandar would react to someone tossing her into a real cell. The mind boggled.

The next three hours proceeded without incident or unexpected discovery. *Persephone* edged deeper into the system, all her electronic senses straining to detect anything unusual. All they found was a seemingly empty system.

Kelsey drummed her fingers on her armrest and considered the situation. "We don't have time to search every corner of the system just now. Leave the probes in place, and take us back to the flip point."

"Aye, ma'am."

The Raider ship turned in a tight arc and returned to the flip point. When she was in place, Kelsey gave the order to flip. They appeared back in the original system without any problem. At least *Persephone* could flip back.

The latest information from Carl indicated that nothing much larger could go back. The weak flip point was one way for ships of any real size.

Kelsey opened a channel to *Audacious*. An image of Zia Anderson appeared. The other woman looked a little worn around the edges.

"Give me some news, Highness."

"Initial scans show the target system is probably empty."

Zia visibly relaxed. "Oh, thank God. I've been sitting here worrying that we were jumping out of the frying pan and into the fire. If this flip point had led to a heavily occupied system deeper inside the Rebel Empire, we'd have been screwed."

"I was a little worried about that myself," Kelsey admitted. "That doesn't mean all the news is good, though. The flip point is one way for ships larger than *Persephone*."

The other woman sighed. "It could be the other way around. That would suck."

"Agreed. Any sign of our friends?"

The Fleet officer shook her head. "The probes we left watching the flip point leading back toward Dresden are still clear. No sign of any pursuit. That won't last much longer."

That was true. They needed to get a move on, if they hoped to escape unnoticed.

"So, what's the plan?" Kelsey asked.

"We're going to take a chance and attempt to send the recovery ship through," Zia said. "I don't think we can risk hoping for a better option in the next system."

Kelsey thought so too. Sooner or later, their luck was going to run out.

"How are we going do this?" she asked. "Do we want to send some ships through first to wait on the other side, or send the recovery ship first? Also, what about the prisoners? Do we evacuate those we can, or does everyone take their chances together?"

The Fleet officer seemed to consider that for a moment. "I think we'll send *Persephone* through again, and then the recovery ship. We'll leave the prisoners aboard the orbital. We don't have room to house them anywhere else.

"Even if we could, moving them would take too long. We need to do this now. Head back over and wait for the recovery ship."

Cain Hopwood and his team of specialists were crewing the recovery ship for her. Their eclectic skills actually made them well-suited to handle it. If anyone could get the orbital through, they would.

"Roger that. We'll let you know as soon as the recovery ship arrives."

Kelsey killed the channel and turned toward her helm officer. "Take us back through."

It only took a few minutes to flip *Persephone* back to the other system and move away from the flip point far enough to be safe. The next few minutes were nerve-racking, but the recovery ship appeared without obvious signs of damage.

Kelsey let out the breath she hadn't realized she'd been holding, and then signaled the crew manning the recovery ship. A quick response indicated that everything looked good on their end.

She grinned. "We're going to pull this off. Send a probe back to *Audacious*. Let them know that everything went just fine."

Five minutes later, the rest of their ships appeared through the flip point.

They'd escaped the Rebel Empire's clutches. Now all they had to do was find another way home.

* * *

Raul Castille considered the woman sitting beside him. One thing was certain: she wasn't Violet Renner. If someone only had a basic description of Renner, she'd fool them, but he'd seen the real woman's personnel file.

From the look in her eyes, the imposter realized the game was up too. It would be interesting to see how she responded.

What had her plan been? Whom did she truly represent? Did he actually want to unmask her now?

After a moment's contemplation, he decided to keep his discovery to himself.

The revelation of her true identity would probably spark a small-scale riot. Her compatriots were undoubtedly ready to rush in and save her. His companions would likely attack her as well. Predictable and boring.

It would be much more entertaining to let this play out a little further. The life of a security officer was often one of drudgery. This was a rare opportunity for him to play at the top of his game.

"Yes, indeed," he continued coolly. "Your picture doesn't do you justice, Commander Renner. Then again, official pictures rarely do."

He smiled, being certain to show his teeth. "I can't begin to tell you how much I'm looking forward to working with you. Particularly under the circumstances we find ourselves in. This should be utterly fascinating."

The woman quickly regrouped and cleared her throat. "I agree, Commander Castille. This is going to be a unique experience."

"I couldn't have said it better myself. And I *insist* you call me Raul." He turned his attention to Irons. "I believe you were running down our options to escape confinement, Commander. Please continue."

Irons nodded, completely unaware of the byplay between Castille and the spy among them.

"Right. We can't be certain what conditions the rest of our people are being held in, but no matter how many marines they brought with them, these people can't have everyone covered as well as they'd like. All we have to do is look for an opportunity to escape.

"If we can get to one of the armories, we'll turn this around. Even a small number of armed personnel can free others. Once we start a breakout, they won't be able to stop us without killing everyone."

Castille allowed himself a small smile. "What makes you think they won't be willing to do precisely that? Obviously, these people planned long and hard for this operation. Simply acquiring the restricted weapons and powered armor must've taken years and an incredible amount of money. Surely they will kill to obtain what they want."

He glanced at "Renner" as he said the last bit.

Her presence actually argued against what he'd just said. If the enemy was willing to send a spy among them, they still needed something. Most likely access to the restricted computer systems.

"What are they really after?" he continued. "Considering the effort required to seize a classified research station like this, they must believe the return is worth a lot of blood and treasure. As we all know, the work we do here is not something one can sell on the open market.

"That means they have a backer. Someone in the upper reaches of the higher orders, I'd wager. Someone in a position of power that believes they can use this technology to advance their cause, whatever it is."

"I can't see that," Jeanette Martin said. "So much of what we're doing here is oriented toward Fleet. There's absolutely no way the lords will allow anyone in the higher orders to have that type of technology."

Well, that was certainly true, Raul conceded. The lords would not allow *anyone* to obtain the technical specifications for an artificial intelligence. Perhaps that was what the woman and her compatriots sought.

If so, it wouldn't do them one bit of good. They'd locked the information down tightly enough that not even he could access it alone.

Only Commodore Murdock, Jeanette Martin, and he acting in concert could access the computers controlling the manufacturing process for the artificial intelligence hardware. The lords had instituted that level of protection to be certain that this type of situation never occurred.

He suspected, however, that their attackers were unaware of this. They probably believed that they could just waltz in, take whatever they wanted, and escape before anyone noticed. That wasn't going to happen.

Truly, that was another reason to play this out and give them hope. He'd overheard Commodore Murdock mention the expected Fleet reinforcements to the false officer. She was aware their time was quite limited. What the woman didn't know was that the odds of her escaping were almost zero.

When the orders had come to send their protective force on their current mission, he'd argued against them. Not that he'd truly had a chance of amending the System Lord's instructions in any way. At least Murdock had arranged for a new protective force. They'd only been uncovered for a few weeks and that was coming to an end in the next day or so.

With the battle stations covering every exit to Dresden, these people would be pinned like bugs as soon as the Fleet vessels arrived. The longer he could delay them, the better this would work out.

"Well, they certainly came for something," he assured the computer specialist. "And they certainly wouldn't have brought the forces they did if they didn't expect to capture something worth their time. What else could they be looking for?"

"Perhaps they came for the restricted implant upgrades," Irons said. "That type of enhancement could prove very useful under certain circumstances."

Castille considered that. "Perhaps. That does seem to be the only technology that would be of use to someone in the higher orders, though

I'm certain the lords would take drastic action to exterminate anyone that possessed it."

He turned his eyes toward the spy among them. "Do you think they came for the supplies on hand or the manufacturing equipment, Violet? I think your point of view would be quite helpful in this situation."

The woman shook her head. "I can't say that I'm familiar with the upgrades you're speaking of. Commodore Murdock didn't cover that during the briefing."

Raul nodded. It was possible she didn't know anything about the illegal upgrades. In any case, it would be educational to brief her on them and see how she reacted.

"Of course," he said smoothly. "The enhancements we're speaking of are restricted technology from the dictatorship. The old Emperor used illegal enhancements on his personal guard to increase their strength and combat ability to a mind-boggling degree. When the lords overthrew him, they banned this technology.

"It was quite invasive and irreversible. I'm told that it increased their strength tenfold and made them killing machines. It also used drugs that turned them into mindless monsters, forced to obey every command given to them.

"That dehumanizing aspect is perhaps why the lords have forbidden this technology. Would you ever want to see someone turned into a monster like that, Violet?"

"That sounds horrible. Of course I wouldn't. No one would. That said, these attackers had many armed marines already in their group. This technology would make them much more powerful."

The spy looked at each of them in turn. "What if they don't work for the higher orders? What if they're ghosts?"

Castille opened his mouth to reject the idea, but stopped. If one of their captors suggested the idea, he should at least consider it. Could they be ghosts?

No one really knew anything about the ghosts, but he'd read the classified briefings. They were undoubtedly some remnant of the dictatorship. No one knew precisely where they based themselves, but old ships occasionally attacked shipping or isolated warships.

What could someone like the ghosts gain from this research facility? Quite a lot, he decided. It wouldn't help them build more ships, but it might make the ones they clearly possessed deadlier.

"That's an interesting idea," he said after a moment. "I think it's worth exploring in more detail, but that doesn't really answer the question of how we can turn the tables on our captors. Tell me, Violet, if you were leading us, how would you break out of this compartment?"

The woman smiled. "If you can't find an opportunity to overwhelm the guards, you need to manufacture one. Or you have to give up."

"Giving up is not an option," Irons said. "I refuse to sit on my ass until Fleet comes in and rescues us."

The woman shrugged. "I'm not sure what to tell you. We have no weapons and no real way to get any. Without them, we're stuck here."

"All true," Castille said. "I suppose it doesn't really matter. Fleet will arrive in force shortly. When they do, these people will run away like cockroaches in the light. All we have to do is wait."

He watched the other woman closely to see how she responded to that. She didn't seem concerned, which worried him a little. What did she know that he didn't?

4

Talbot watched Commodore Anderson as she monitored the prisoner's compartment with more than a hint of concern. He'd finally decided that he needed to tell her what he was doing. She'd arrived a few moments ago and now stood there shaking her head.

"This is insane," she said. "If Annette slips up, they're going to be all over her."

"There *is* a hint of risk," he admitted, "but we have a team of marines ready to rush in if there's any problem whatsoever."

The commodore looked unconvinced. "Did it ever occur to you to run this past me first? Hell, even Princess Kelsey would've told you no."

Talbot doubted that, but it would be impolite to burst the woman's bubble.

"She's been in there for over an hour, ma'am. If they were going to discover that she was a fraud, they'd have done so by now. She's convinced them that she's the real deal."

"All it takes is one slip-up," Zia disagreed. "We know next to nothing about these people. Not even the most basic things."

She sighed. "Okay, let's say that you're right. What is your endgame?"

"We want to engineer a breakout, but under our control. If we can make them think they're really escaping, I believe we can get them to give us the access codes to their computers."

"No way," Zia said. "You'd have to give them virtually complete access to the orbital so they could get there. This cafeteria is nowhere near the research center."

"It doesn't need to be. Once they're outside the compartment, they'll be able to use their implants to access the orbital's systems. We're almost certain they'll try to erase the restricted computers. If they do, the system will block them but capture the passwords."

She seemed to consider the plan, but shook her head. "Those computers aren't just isolated from physical access. They'll have made certain that no one can use implants to get into them."

"Carl said there were triggers to wipe the drives that can be accessed from anywhere on the orbital. I'd wager several people inside that compartment acting in unison could set them off."

"Let's say they do. I'm sure Carl's programing is good, but what if they somehow managed to get past the blocks? We can't risk them actually damaging the research computers. We *need* that data."

"Carl said the drives are heavily encrypted, but he's made multiple copies," Talbot said. "He also took the precaution of cloning the drives and putting the original cores on *Audacious*. The automated backups too. Even if the prisoners manage to wipe the drives, we've lost nothing, and we'll have their codes."

"I don't want to be the downer here, but I think you're underestimating these people. I'm willing to bet a dinner at any place you'd care to name that this plan fails."

"That's kind of negative," Talbot grumbled. "If we can't trick them, we're no worse off than we were before."

"You're not thinking of the big picture, Talbot. What if we missed a self-destruct device? What if they have a mad plan of their own?"

She gestured to the vid feed. "Obviously, it's too late for me to stop this harebrained scheme, but I'm putting my foot down about allowing them into the orbital's systems."

He rubbed his face. "I understand your concerns, ma'am, but if we can't get the prisoners to give us access, we might never be able to build artificial intelligences for ourselves."

"Well, you certainly won't be able to if you allow them to blow up the orbital. I'm not going to pull Annette out of there, but you're going to have to come up with some way to let her know your plans have changed."

"I suppose we could start pulling prisoners out to question," he said. "If we start with Commodore Murdock and work our way down, we should be able to get her in the first three or four people without raising suspicion. It also allows us to establish our bona fides with the prisoners. If we don't open a dialogue soon, they're going to get suspicious."

Zia watched the vid feed for a while longer. "What exactly do they imagine is going to happen? We popped out of nowhere and captured their orbital, but they think they have the Dresden system locked down tight. They've got to be wondering what we're doing."

"Surely they'll have figured that out now that they felt the orbital flip twice," Talbot said. "That's not easy to miss."

"Three times," Zia said. "We flipped into the new system an hour ago."

Talbot stared at her. "I didn't feel a thing. How is that possible?"

"It's probably the mass of the station," she said. "The larger the vessel, the less effect a flip has on the crew. You can feel them a little, even on a superdreadnought or a carrier, but this orbital is larger.

"Also, since the flip drives aren't actually inside the station, a lot of the disruption is channeled into the recovery ship. They get a pretty rough ride."

Talbot sighed. "Well, I suppose I need to start pulling the prisoners out for interrogation. Sorry, ma'am."

Zia clapped him on the shoulder. "It was a bold plan, Major. Your wife will be proud. Now, if you'll excuse me, I need to get back over to *Audacious*. This system seems empty, but we all know how quickly things like that can change."

* * *

COMMANDER VERONICA GIGUERE fought the urge to stalk her cell. The close confinement and isolation were getting to her. It had been three weeks, and her patience was long gone.

She understood that she didn't have any leverage, but she was going crazy. Ever since she'd surrendered, she'd had to do what her captors said. That changed now.

She was going to see her people, and she wanted answers to the questions that had been building up in her mind. Being locked into a cell certainly gave one time to think.

She'd presented her demands to the polite jailor two hours ago, and her self-imposed deadline was just about up. If someone didn't come to talk to her in ten minutes, she'd start her very own riot.

The hatch to her cell slid aside without warning. Standing on the other side was the officer that had separated her from the rest of her crew. After, of course, he'd done something to her head. Something he'd better be prepared to explain in detail.

"Commander Giguere," he said. "I understand you wished to speak with me."

"I demand to see my crew." She poured a fair amount of aggressiveness into her tone. She didn't want to sound like she was begging. This situation required strength.

He seemed to consider her request for a moment and then nodded. "That can be arranged, but I believe it's time we had a talk first. I'm certain you have many questions. You deserve to have some answers."

She eyed him suspiciously. "That's very accommodating of you, Captain Levy, if I remember your name correctly."

"I'm acknowledging the reality of the situation," he said. "You and your crew aren't going to get back to your people anytime soon, so it's not going to hurt if you understand the scope of what's happening.

"Quite frankly, I should've explained this to you weeks ago. Let's just say that I've had a lot on my mind. Now that we have time to take a breath, I'll rectify that."

"I'm not certain why, but that fills me with dread," she said suspiciously. "Fine. If you're going to answer my questions, let's start with this. Who the hell are you people?"

He smiled slightly. "We're Fleet."

"Bull. Fleet doesn't implant their enlisted personnel. You're rebels. Or something."

"I suspect it's going to take quite a bit of time for us to determine which labels are appropriate. In the meanwhile, allow me to suggest that we move somewhere that allows us to sit down more comfortably. Perhaps you'd care for something to eat or drink."

"To my shock, the quality of the food and drink has been more than acceptable," she said. "However, going somewhere with a little bit more leg room would be very nice."

He nodded sharply. "Then we'll do so. You'll forgive me if I'm not quite ready to accept your parole, so we'll have some marine guards to make sure that you don't wander off."

Levy stepped back and gestured for her to exit her cell.

The brig had a wide central area with a circular console. The lieutenant behind it watched her without expression. Four marine guards stood at varying points inside the compartment, each in unpowered armor and equipped with a stun rifle.

There were a dozen cells, each with their hatches closed. She imagined her senior officers were behind them. She itched to demand that Levy open them up right away, but she restrained herself. If he was going to give her some answers, she wanted to hear them first.

When the hatch to the corridor slid open, she saw two additional marines waiting for them. Unlike the others, these two were unarmored. They'd also exchanged their rifles for more discreet stunners on their hips.

Captain Levy gestured for her to precede him down the hall. He stepped up next to her, and the marines fell in behind them. Close enough to intervene if need be, but too far away for her to attack with any hope of success.

"What kind of ship is this?" she asked. "This is the big one, right?"

"She's a carrier," the man said. "The fighters you engaged are based here."

Those damned little things. Commodore Crabtree—the deputy fleet commander in charge of her portion of the task force—had dismissed them as a distraction. That proved a fatal mistake for him and far too many of her comrades.

Their part of the task force had started with six light cruisers and fourteen destroyers. By the time the fighting ended, they'd lost five light cruisers and five destroyers. Most of the rest were wrecked beyond repair, she suspected.

She'd never seen anything like the little bastards. They'd bob and weave, and then blast a ship with an intensely powerful short-ranged missile. Nothing like what a real ship carried, but more than enough—in sufficient numbers—to drop the battle screens on the cruisers. Without them, the larger ships were just as vulnerable as the destroyers.

The loss of life had been hideous. She'd spent the last three weeks grieving for the friends she'd never see again. Far too many of them had died at the hands of those little fighters. A type of craft that she knew Fleet didn't have.

"It's things like that that convince me you're lying," she said. "Fleet doesn't have anything like those devils."

"There lies the heart of our story. I'd normally take the lift, but the marines insist we use the stairs. The officers' mess is three decks down. We'll order something to eat, and I'll explain everything. Well, minus a few classified details, but you'll get the big picture."

"Why are you doing this?"

He smiled. "Because I need for you to understand just what your situation is. Everything you thought you understood is completely wrong. It's going to be very difficult for you to accept that. It would be impossible if I didn't give you as much information as I could."

"I have absolutely no idea what the hell you're talking about," she assured him. "Whatever game you're playing, I'm not buying."

"Well, then, lunch should be fascinating."

5

Kelsey took a deep breath when she arrived outside of her mother's cabin. She'd rather be doing just about anything else right now, but she couldn't let this situation fester too long.

She smiled at the guard and opened the hatch to find her mother sitting on the couch and reading a tablet. She stepped inside and allowed the hatch to close. "I understand you wanted to speak to me. Start talking, but be pithy. I have zero patience for you right now."

"Haven't you ever heard of signaling?" Justine asked acerbically. "What if I'd been naked?"

Her mother rose from the couch gracefully and gestured at the compartment. "And couldn't you find a larger room? I can barely breathe in here."

"When is this going to sink in, Mother? You're a prisoner. You don't have a right to privacy any longer. The guard can come into this room at any moment without any notice whatsoever."

"You're being ridiculous," her mother huffed. "How long are we going to play this game?"

"You see, that's the problem. You think this is a trick. It's not. You broke the law and put people's lives at risk. There are consequences.

"I realize you haven't been subject to limitations on your behavior for a long time, but you've crossed the line. Unless you change your attitude, you're going to find yourself in front of a military tribunal. Did your lawyer explain the penalties you'd face?"

Her mother sneered. "Yes, that little stuffed shirt 'explained' it all to me. More like he droned on and on and on. Could you send someone with a personality next time?"

Kelsey sat on the edge of the couch. "You're a real piece of work. I don't think I've ever met anyone as full of themselves as you are. You think you can do no wrong, and that someone will provide everything you desire.

"Honestly, I've met rulers from an oppressive feudal society that treat people with more respect than you do. Since it's probably escaped your mind already, let me remind you that sneaking aboard a Fleet vessel could earn you a minimum of ten years in a military prison.

"In case it wasn't obvious, this cabin is not a cell. It's actually someone's quarters. Someone that had to move out so I could put you in here. A real cell is far smaller and significantly less comfortable."

Her mother snorted daintily. "Surely you aren't delusional enough to think I actually believe you'd do any such thing. This is just you trying to make a point.

"I'm your mother. I refuse to play. I've already wasted enough of my time hiding in that other room for weeks so that I could talk to you. All because you wouldn't take the time to sit down with me on Avalon. This is your fault."

"Amazing. Can anything get through that bulletproof skull of yours? Contrary to what you seem to believe, you don't get to disrupt everyone's lives because they don't dance to your tune. Not anymore. You gave that right up when you divorced my father."

Her mother threw her hands up. "And here we go. I was absolutely justified in divorcing Karl. Even if I weren't, that's between the two of us."

"Wrong," Kelsey said hotly. "You made it my business when you cheated on him like you did. When you dared to hold a grudge against Jared Mertz because my father cheated, just like you. A mistake he confessed and paid the price for, I might add.

"How many men did you cheat with while you were married? Let's see, at least eighteen that I'm aware of. You probably managed to sneak more in some other way. Or perhaps they were already there. How many Imperial Guardsmen have you slept with? Palace staff? Visiting dignitaries? Surely, the grand total is far greater than eighteen.

"You don't even have the threadbare cover of retaliating for Father's infidelity. According to the time stamps, you started cheating long before that. No, you don't get to shift the blame to other people this time."

"My sex life is none of your business," her mother said coldly. "As for Jared Mertz, the little toad thinks that because my ex-husband slept with the help, that makes him something special. Well, it doesn't."

"I agree," Kelsey said at once. "His parentage has nothing to do with him being special. He managed that all on his own, *in spite of* his parentage. And before you attempt to tell me how wrong I am, have you bothered to read anything about what happened on the exploratory mission?"

Her mother shrugged. "I wasn't really looking for news on the little bastard. I wanted to hear about my daughter, and let me tell you, there was almost nothing to learn. So, I came to see for myself."

Kelsey felt her jaw clench. "It's as if you're going out of your way to piss me off. I'm not twelve anymore, Mother. You don't get to declare whom I can be friends with. In fact, you don't get to dictate any part of my life anymore.

"Let me fill you in about a few facts. Jared Mertz isn't the only bastard in this family. So am I, but you already knew that. The more I think about it, the angrier I get. You're unbelievable. Are you even human? I ask because I've met an alien that has more human decency than you."

Her mother's eyes flashed. "How *dare* you speak to me that way? I should slap your face. I don't care how you feel. You don't get to disrespect me that way, little girl."

Kelsey grunted. "I've only begun understanding that you don't care how *anyone* feels. You also have peculiar expectations about the way the world works. You think you get to be a screaming jerk to whomever you like, but everyone else is supposed to be nice to you.

"Perhaps that's the way it used to be, but you have to *earn* my respect now. That isn't going to happen as long as you insist on being a selfish child throwing temper tantrums. I'm not a little girl that you can intimidate anymore, Mother. I've been through things in the last eighteen months that would make you run howling in terror. I mean that literally, by the way.

"I've survived things that you cannot possibly imagine. The kind of things that nightmares are made of. In fact, I still have far too many nights where I wake up screaming. That's my burden to bear, the price I pay for my own stupidity. My own arrogance."

Kelsey slowly stood. "When you're ready to speak civilly, tell the guard. If all you want to do is bitch, don't bother. If I come down here again and run head-on into your arrogance, I won't be so quick to come back again."

She walked out of the compartment without glancing back. The hatch closed in her mother's face.

"I want you to check on the prisoner at random intervals over the next shift," she told the guard. "Twice, I think. If she complains—which she will—ignore her. Stun her if she gets physical."

The man looked a shade uncertain.

"I'm trying to get her to understand the gravity of her situation," she added. "If I don't teach her some limits, she's going to be a jerk the entire time we're out here. Don't go overboard, but put her firmly in her place."

The marine nodded. "Aye, ma'am. She uses the door com to ask for you all the time. I've been ignoring that as you ordered. Should I start responding?"

"Yes. If she behaves civilly, tell her you'll pass along the message. If she's a jackass, tell her she can rot. If she's a monumental pain in the ass, I'll send her over to *Audacious* to spend some quality time in a *real* cell."

The man sighed. "This is harder than I'd imagined, ma'am. She was the empress when I grew up. The urge to obey is strong."

"Yes, and she uses that sentiment ruthlessly. Be strong. You're actually doing her a service. One she's likely to curse you for, but a real one nonetheless."

Kelsey started to walk away, but stopped and turned. "As distasteful as this is for me to say, she's probably going to try to seduce you. I don't want to come back later and find you tied up in her closet."

The man looked offended. "First, Colonel, I'd never do anything like that with a prisoner. Second, I'm a little harder to overpower than you seem to think."

"Probably," she agreed, "but don't play her game. I don't want to have to have that particular debriefing. There are some things a daughter doesn't need to hear about."

He chuckled a little. "I suppose not, Colonel. No worries. I'll keep everything safe and secure here, including my trousers."

"Good man. Carry on."

Carl was waiting for her on the bridge when she made it back. He sat beside Angela. The two of them had been speaking softly. He sat up straighter and waited for her to take a seat before speaking.

"I have bad news," he said. "There isn't another flip point in the system. A regular one anyway. We won't have finished searching for weak flip points for a few more days."

"That can't be possible," she said. "There has to be another flip point."

He shrugged. "Not that the probes have discovered. As far as I can tell, the only way in or out of this system is through the weak flip point we used."

She stared at the master plot. The various probes were filling in details about the system, but they still knew so very little about it. At least according to the icons she could see.

"I have a tremendous amount of respect for you, Carl, but how can you possibly know that? We've been here less than a day."

"I understand that. To be clear, this is only a preliminary status report. We might find a flip point buried in the data. I just wanted to alert you to the probability that there isn't one so you can plan.

"There are plenty of systems that have only one flip point. We call them cul-de-sacs. If that's possible with regular flip points, why would it be less likely with a weak flip point? Hell, there are undoubtedly many star systems that have no flip points of any kind."

She sighed. "It's more like I don't *want* to believe it. The weak flip point is too small to allow us back out. If there isn't something in this system, we're screwed.

"What about the theory Doctor Leonard had about using weak flip points for multiple destinations? Have you gotten anywhere with that?"

Carl shook his head. "Flip physics was never my specialty," he admitted. "I've read the papers, but I can't say I really understand the theoretical aspects. Not at the level I need to make that kind of breakthrough happen."

She scowled at the young man. "That's unacceptable. It would be wonderful to have Doctor Leonard here to figure out the answer for us, but he's not. You're going to have to buckle down and figure this out. If it's possible to utilize a weak flip point to go elsewhere—and with bigger ships—we need to know about it.

"I realize you've been trying to break into the research computers, but I want you to focus every bit of your attention on this problem. Take the theory apart and come up with something we can use. We're not going anywhere until you do."

He sighed. "I'll get right to work on it."

Kelsey watched him depart and worried. That was a lot of weight to carry on those young shoulders, but she'd seen him come through before. He was smarter than he thought. He'd find a solution to their problems.

Meanwhile, she needed to focus on their new home. While the probes had been unsuccessful at finding any other flip points, they'd gotten a good read on the normal matter in the system.

It was a fairly average place. Ten major bodies orbiting a normal star. Many of the outer ones were gaseous in nature, but the inner ones were solid. One of them was inside the goldilocks zone and might be habitable. They'd have to go a lot closer to be sure.

Nothing she'd seen had indicated there was any hostile presence inside the system. As far as she was concerned, the time for hiding was over. They needed to see what they were dealing with.

"Signal the other ships," she told Angela. "Set course for the planet inside the habitable zone. Let's go see if anyone is home."

6

Annette was more than a bit relieved when Talbot finally pulled her out of the compartment. The security man was creeping her out.

The marine officer eyed her. "You okay?"

"I'm am now. I was really worried they were going to jump me."

"You seemed like you were doing fine," Talbot said. "You must be hell at the poker table."

She grinned. "I can hold my own. Still, there's a guy in there that I wouldn't want to play against. Raul Castille, their security man. He made me right away."

The marine's eyes widened. "He *made* you? How could he have made you? You sat there and talked with them for hours."

"He was playing with me. He flat out said that he'd seen Violet Renner's personnel file. He knows what she looks like. He made several coy statements that the others never picked up on, but I knew he was poking at me."

"That is kind of creepy," Talbot said. "Well, it's pretty clear my plan isn't going to work. They have to know what we're up to.

"The commodore was down checking on you, too. She was pissed that I hadn't run this by her, and she thinks it's too dangerous. So, we're pulling the plug."

Annette nodded. "I was pretty much afraid of that. I saw that you pulled Commodore Murdock out for questioning. Has she said anything useful?"

The marine grimaced. "She's had plenty to say, none of it useful. I swear to God, I thought I'd never meet anybody more officious and condescending than Wallace Breckenridge. Boy, was I wrong.

"How the hell can that woman run a place like the research center?

She'd be up in everyone's business. No one would be able to get anything done."

Annette laughed. "I suspect that most of the other prisoners would quietly agree with you. She's a real piece of work. If we're not going to get into the computers by trickery, how are we going to do it?"

Talbot shrugged. "Carl needs to find a tech solution. Or, he's just going to have to reverse engineer the manufacturing equipment based on the hardware we have. It might take longer, but he'll find a way."

"Speaking of finding a way, are we any closer to finding our way out of this system?" she asked.

"Last I heard they haven't found any other flip points. While they figure out that problem, we'll have to deal with the prisoners."

"Are we authorized to do that? I'm not exactly military intelligence."

"We're what we have," he said. "There are still a lot of questions we need answered. For example, why was the research facility located at Dresden, of all places? That wasn't precisely an easy-to-access location for the Rebel Empire. Why not somewhere more centrally located?

"And why did they send a fleet to take out the Erorsi AI now? Why not five hundred years ago? What was the trigger? Was it something we did?"

"Probably," she said. "I'd also like to know why they aren't using the Raider implants for themselves. Or are they? That kind of information is critical to our ultimate survival. Also, is this the only location that makes Raider implants? If it is, we might have caught a break."

"Where do you want to start?" Talbot asked. "The security guy?"

Annette smiled. "Surprisingly, yes. I think he might let some information slip. He seems to think he's smarter than everyone else. Maybe he is. If so, he won't be able to resist playing with us."

"How do you want to handle this?"

"I'm going to open up to him. Carl overwrote the viral code in the senior prisoner's implants while they were out, so there's no danger of a programmed reaction. If I give him some information, he may give me some back. If I answer some questions, so might he.

"Another thing I'd like to find out about is those ghosts they've mentioned. Who are they? What does the Rebel Empire know about them? What do they suspect? There's so much that we don't know."

"And even more that we don't know we're ignorant of," Talbot agreed. "We're using the compartment next to this one for questioning the individual officers. Commodore Murdock is in there now. Once my guy finishes with her, you can take his place, and I'll bring Castille to you."

* * *

Raul nodded toward Commodore Murdock as the guards took him out of the cafeteria and brought her in. She looked indignant. As though their captors had offended her by asking questions. The woman never ceased to amaze him.

Once into the corridor, the guards walked him to the compartment next door. Inside he found the fake Violet Renner waiting for him. Only now she wore captain's tabs.

"Goodness," he said with mock surprise. "Promotions happen without any warning around here."

The woman smiled thinly. "Have a seat, Commander. Since you took great joy in making sure that I knew you'd seen through my impersonation, I'm sure it won't shock you that I'm done playing that game. Instead, I'm going to ask you some direct questions. Ones that I'm willing to pay for."

He pulled out the chair and draped himself across it. The two marines stood in the back corners of the compartment. They were well positioned to restrain him, if he decided to become aggressive. He wouldn't bother.

"I must say I like this game better. I'm not a conventional man, Captain… I'm afraid we haven't been formally introduced. Whom am I addressing?"

"My name is Annette Vitter."

"So, you are a Fleet officer. I wasn't sure."

Her smile widened a little bit. "Oh, I'm a Fleet officer all right. Just not in the way you mean. I'm not a renegade officer. None of us are."

"Ah. I see. You're going to tell me that you're operating under orders."

"Absolutely."

"I find that difficult to believe. Let me tell you what I think. I believe you *are* Fleet, but a renegade. You're working for someone in the higher orders. Probably the coordinator of one of the major worlds.

"Somehow, you found out about the work we're doing here, and that coordinator wants it for him or herself. Your mission is to make that happen."

He grinned. "Unfortunately, that's very unlikely to happen. I'm sorry to have to inform you, but you're going to be trapped in this system."

If the news bothered her, she hid it very well. In fact, she looked completely unperturbed.

"I have some bad news for you. The fleet you sent to take out the renegade ship's computer and attack the holdout system it was keeping bottled up won't be coming back. As for the replacement fleet you're expecting, it's already arrived."

He laughed. "You'd like me to believe that you're part of the replacement fleet? Somehow, I doubt that very much. I'm not completely certain how you know where we dispatched the original fleet to, though. Perhaps you'd care to explain that in more detail?"

"As a gesture of goodwill, certainly. We were lying in wait for your ships. They won't be coming back at all, I'm afraid. You see, while I'm completely truthful in saying that I'm Fleet, it's not the same Fleet you serve. It's the one that came before."

Now he guffawed. "Please, tell me another one. I don't know what your game is, Annette, but this is *very* entertaining. You don't mind if I call you Annette, do you?"

"Feel free," she said with a magnanimous gesture. "You want to be entertained? Let's see if I can manage that. One of the things you manufacture here is for use by the computer at Erorsi. You did know that that's the name of the system where the computer is located, right?

"Back before the AIs overthrew the Old Empire, Erorsi was home to billions of people. Now it's a wasteland filled with savage human beings the computer enhanced against their wills using equipment produced here. Specifically, Marine Raider implants."

Raul sat up, all his amusement gone. "Where did you hear that name?"

Annette smiled. "From a different ship's computer. One on a Marine Raider ship. It confirmed many things we suspected about those enhancements."

He shook his head. "I'm sure you'd like me to believe that. You're fishing for information. It's not playing by the rules you set up, Annette."

"Ah, but I *am* playing by the rules," she said with a cool grin. "What's more, I'm willing to prove it. This compartment is shielded, so you can utilize your implants without me having to worry about you doing something naughty. Allow me to share with you what I know about Marine Raider implants."

When his implants received a connection request, he cautiously accepted it. As a security officer, he had special filters to be sure nothing malicious made it into his system, but these were interesting times.

The communication had a file attached to it. He opened it and was astonished to see a very detailed scan analysis of an individual with the implants they manufactured here on the orbital. It only took a moment to grasp that they were authentic.

"Where did you get this?" he demanded flatly.

The woman leaned forward and whispered conspiratorially. "I'll tell you that in exchange for a few answers of my own. Take a moment to examine what I sent to you. Are you going to try to tell me they aren't what we're speaking of?"

"No. It's obvious that you've somehow obtained extremely classified data. I'm not sure how you made them up to look as though they'd been implanted inside a real person, but that's very clever.

"Yes, these implants are manufactured here, and the old dictatorship called them Marine Raider implants. They're forbidden technology. Merely possessing knowledge about them is a death sentence. Which saddens me, since I kind of like you."

"That makes me feel all warm and fuzzy inside," she said. "I'm not worried about any death sentences. You see, I wasn't joking when I said I come from a different Fleet."

She leaned even farther forward. "Your precious lords missed a planet. That's all it took. Now we're back, looking to restore the Empire."

He eyed her suspiciously. This had to be a joke. One in admittedly poor taste.

"So, you're trying to tell me that you're a ghost? You really need to work on being more convincing."

"I can see that I'll have to do something drastic to convince you that I'm telling the truth. Very well."

She reached into a bag sitting beside the table and pulled out a headband with a chinstrap. She tossed it onto the table in front of him. "Put this on. Once you've secured it, it takes a special key to take it back off."

He examined it without touching it. "What is it?"

"An implant jammer. While you're wearing it, you'll be unable to interact with anything through your implants. As I said, I don't want you doing anything naughty. You have the choice of putting it on yourself or my associates will assist you."

Well, if those were his options, he'd do it himself. He picked the headset up and put it on. The chinstrap tightened comfortably, but wouldn't back off. By design, he supposed.

Annette rose from her seat, came around the table, and snugged the strap even further. "There we go. I don't want you slipping out of this unexpectedly. You seem very resourceful to me."

He gave her a toothy grin. "One does try. So, where are you taking me?"

"On a sightseeing tour. Take my word, the view will be *very* educational."

The two marines gripped his arms as she exited the compartment. She might be willing to pretend to trust him a little, but they weren't taking any chances. He'd have no opportunity to tear loose from their grasp. Certainly not after he noted the other marines that trailed them at a distance in the corridor.

She led him down to the docking level where an unfamiliar small craft awaited them. It had aggressive lines and only two places to sit. One of them was situated far forward on the craft and the other was immediately behind it. Both had raised canopies.

He stopped and examined the craft closely. He'd never seen anything like it.

"What is this?"

"This is a Mark Five Raptor," she said. "A space superiority fighter. You'll be in front. Normally, we'd both be in flight suits, but I'm not going to do anything fancy. Just a little stroll in the park. Get in."

He had to admit, this was not where he'd expected things to go. He utilized the handholds built into the side of the little craft and climbed up to the acceleration couch. He didn't have very much experience with small craft.

In fact, he'd never been inside the cockpit of one before. He'd expected more controls, though. As in more than blank, featureless panels.

The canopy above his head lowered and locked into place. He heard the woman climb into the area behind him, and her canopy lowered as well.

The small craft came to life and lifted off the deck. It turned and flew through the protective field into space at a gentle pace.

As soon as they cleared the bay, he noticed there was something attached to the orbital's hull. Some type of metal band. A large, thick one.

"What is that?"

"You ask a lot of questions without giving me any interesting answers of your own, but I'll let you put them on account. Keep watching. It'll become obvious in a moment."

As the fighter craft drew away from the orbital, he started getting a better look at the metal band. It was attached to a ship that nestled against the orbital. One that looked vaguely familiar.

"Is that…"

"The recovery ship you've been using to transport ore? It is, indeed. It took a little bit of modification, but it managed to move your orbital just fine too."

A chill ran through his body. He turned and scanned the heavens.

"Are you looking for a planet?" she asked helpfully. "I'm afraid we've left Dresden far behind."

The small craft began rotating slowly, giving him a look at everything around them. There was no planet. They had taken the orbital out of Dresden orbit.

"I'll grant you that's clever," he said, "but it's not going to make any difference when Fleet arrives. They'll keep looking until they find us."

"I'm certain you're right. Unfortunately, they'll still be looking in the Dresden system for a while. We're no longer there."

The chill became ice that settled at the base of his spine. "What do you mean?"

"I think you can piece it together. That ship is more than capable of flipping with a huge cargo. It was designed to move superdreadnoughts and larger freighters from system to system in the Old Empire.

"It took a little bit of work to expand the arms to encompass the orbital, but we managed. We've departed and taken the entire orbital with us."

"That is quite a claim. One that I'm not willing to believe. Even though there weren't many ships in this system, each of the flip points is guarded. You didn't just sneak out with our orbital in tow."

Annette laughed. "We absolutely did. Though, I admit it took some force to get past the battle station and three destroyers at our target flip point."

The little craft turned again. What it exposed took his breath away. It was a Fleet warship unlike any he'd ever seen. Sitting near a large freighter of a class that seemed familiar, it looked much bigger than the rare heavy cruiser that had passed through Dresden. Certainly larger than the light cruisers that normally led their guard forces.

"What you're seeing is our flagship," she said before he asked. "That is the Fleet Carrier *Audacious*. She's a modified superdreadnought hull. I realize that the AIs aren't forthcoming about larger vessels, so you might not have seen one before."

He eyed the ship worriedly as it grew larger in front of them. "Superdreadnought? What is a superdreadnought?"

"Let's just say that it's the next size up from the battlecruiser," she said with some amusement. "And if you haven't heard of those, they're significantly larger than heavy cruisers. *Audacious* dates from before the Fall. We've put her back into service, and that's where this fighter came from.

"Full disclosure, my actual duties are to command the fighter wings aboard that ship. You see, Raul, I'm not lying to you. We've come to retake what's ours. If you want to know more about that ship and us, you're going to have to answer a few questions on my terms."

As the massive vessel grew larger before them, he decided that he had no choice but to believe she was telling him some version of the truth. If so, this wasn't a game anymore. Or perhaps it was. Just a significantly more dangerous one.

He allowed himself a small smile. Well, he'd always told himself that he could play at any level. Now was the time to prove it.

7

"The probe is starting to pick up readings from the planet," Angela said.

Kelsey turned her attention away from the system schematic she'd been studying. According to the latest update, they still hadn't found any flip points in the system. That was worrying.

She could've checked the scanner readings for herself, but what was the point of having a crew if you did everything? She was forcing herself to delegate.

"What have we got?" she asked.

Her XO threw a scanner image up on the main screen. "I think there might be a ship in orbit."

That made Kelsey sit up and take notice. She tapped into the feed the probe was sending back. The new object might be a ship, but if so, it wasn't under power. There were no detectable fusion plants.

It could just be a captured asteroid, but she didn't think so. Not with their luck.

"I assume there's no indication of scanners from the bogie?" Kelsey asked.

"No. If it's looking, it's only using passive scanners."

Kelsey knew the odds of any vessel detecting one of their probes with passive scanners was insignificant, but that didn't mean impossible. She'd best be cautious.

"Launch two more probes and bracket the planet. I want to be sure there aren't any other surprises in orbit."

The probes approached the planet slowly and carefully. Once the first had made it into close range, it was apparent the object *was* a ship in a stable geosynchronous orbit. Still no fusion plants. The ship was probably a derelict.

One that certainly seemed to have discovered the weak flip points long ago, if there truly were no other exits from this system.

"Bring us into orbit, Jack. Keep us on the other side of the planet from the derelict. Can you identify what kind of ship that is, Angela?"

"It's in the Imperial database," she said. "It's a Capella-class cruise liner. Top of the line back in the Old Empire. She could move ten thousand passengers in style. Maybe twice that if you packed them in. Even more if you strained life support to the breaking point."

That wasn't what she'd expected to find out here. The stories of the ghosts had led her to expect an Old Empire Fleet ship.

A few minutes later, they had a visual. It looked undamaged and unpowered. The probe's passive scanners indicated that it was cold and lifeless. Its passengers and crew had either died or departed.

"What can you tell me about the planet?" Kelsey asked.

"It looks as though it might be habitable, if you stretch the definition a bit. Somewhat cold for my taste, but beggars can't be choosers, I suppose. At the moment, most of the planet is experiencing heavy winter.

"Only the equator is relatively warm. We don't have enough information on the planet's orbit to determine if it goes closer during part of the year or perhaps even farther away, but there's almost no axial tilt. If the orbit is relatively circular, this place is an icebox"

Kelsey watched the images of the planet slowly rotating beneath them. There was some green—mostly around the equator. She didn't know what temperature was more prevalent closer to the poles, but it certainly looked cold.

"Any radio transmissions or power signatures?"

"No, ma'am. Everything quiet on that front."

"Okay," Kelsey said. "Task two probes with mapping the planet. If there's something man-made down there, I want to know about it. Keep the third probe watching that ship.

"Then I want you to take a team over to examine the ship. I want to know how it got here and what happened to the passengers and crew."

Angela raised an eyebrow. "I'm shocked that you aren't insisting on leading the expedition yourself."

"Oh, I want to, but I just can't justify it. Being an adult sucks. As boring as it sounds, I need to keep an eye on the big picture."

Somehow, someone on that cruise liner had figured out how to use the weak flip points. If they'd had good luck, their descendants were living on the planet below. If not, then they'd all died in orbit.

"How long until we know if the planet is habitable?"

"I can give you a little bit more information now. The atmosphere seems breathable. It looks as though the equatorial temperature is above the freezing point of water. I suspect most places on the equator are pretty comfortable right now."

"What about the poles?"

"Damned cold. We're talking Arctic freeze. There's evidence of glaciers coming pretty far down into the two hemispheres. If I had to make a wager, I think the money is on this being a chilly place to live."

Kelsey nodded slowly at the picture. "You don't think it gets much warmer than this?"

"Further observation might change that, but I'm not inclined to think so."

"How much landmass on the equator are we talking about?"

Angela shrugged. "There are a number of scattered islands—some of them pretty big—and one sizable continent. Plenty of room for survivors."

"Focus your attention there, then. I want to know if we have any people living down there."

"The continent is heavily forested. We may not be able to easily spot them."

"Do the best you can."

Kelsey composed a message to Zia Anderson and attached the scanner readings they had of the cruise liner. By the time they had more information, the other ships would be to the planet. One way or the other, she hoped the ship had an interesting story to tell.

* * *

VERONICA GIGUERE TRIED to listen to Levy without calling him a liar to his face, but it was hard. He kept insisting on telling her nonsense stories about survivors of the old dictatorship and how the artificial intelligences behind overthrowing the dictator were evil.

Please. She was a Fleet officer. She knew who the lords were and how they maintained and nurtured the Empire. That didn't mean they kept humanity in a state of slavery and ignorance. That was simply bull. They kept society orderly and efficient.

Were there problems? Of course. Where human beings lived together, there were always problems. For the most part, the lords kept humanity from eating its own entrails. One only had to look at the dregs of society to see that.

"How can you say any of that with a straight face?" she asked when he'd finished. "I'd call it propaganda, but even someone from the lower orders would recognize that stuff couldn't possibly be true. Those are the paranoid ravings of a lunatic.

"Why don't you tell me the truth? Someone subverted Fleet. Which world is funding your little outing? More importantly, what do you actually hope to accomplish by ambushing your fellow officers like this? You know I'll never rest until I take you down."

The man shook his head. "To be honest, you're something of a long-term project, Commander Giguere. You've lived in your society your entire life, so I don't expect change to come easily. In fact, I suspect that convincing you I'm telling the truth is going to be a long and difficult process."

He sipped his coffee. "Why do you find it so difficult to believe me? I can present any number of my fellow officers that will tell you exactly the same thing. I can even find crewmen that will tell you so. Thousands of people. Surely we're not all deluded."

She looked around the officers' mess and once again examined the men and women dining around them. They looked so normal, but she knew that was a lie. They couldn't be. Every single one was a traitor.

How had Levy or his masters convinced so many people to betray their oaths? Was Fleet really that rotten?

Veronica knew Fleet wasn't perfect. There was entirely too much politicking and currying of favor for her taste. Add to that the fact that larger commands were rare, and you had an environment that was almost toxically cutthroat. About the only thing off-limits was actually planting a knife in someone else's back.

Yet that was life. Nothing worthwhile came without fighting for it.

The man shrugged when she said nothing. "As I said, I don't expect this process to go quickly or even to be successful in every case. All I can do is try. My intention is to expose you to the truth and let you draw your own conclusions."

She gave him a cool smile. "That seems a little difficult considering I'm locked away in a cell all by myself."

"That changes today. I'm relocating you and your senior officers to new quarters. They may not be much more spacious than the brig, but they'll allow you to interact with each other in a more comfortable environment. I'm also giving you access to the ship's computer. The library is quite extensive."

She sighed. "So you're going to give me unfettered access to your propaganda? Why bother? We can't trust anything you people say or the documents you provide."

"Once you see the sheer volume of information, I think you might change your mind. If nothing else, perhaps it will be entertaining for you to dissect the 'propaganda' I'm providing for you.

"With the exception of military secrets, I'm also going to make certain you have an opportunity to question either myself or someone else of your choosing about what you find. You'll have complete access to your crew to be certain that we're seeing to their needs, too. Surely that's better than sitting alone in your cell twiddling your thumbs."

She couldn't very well argue with that. Three weeks being by herself had almost driven her mad. Of course, she was also familiar with Stockholm Syndrome. The longer he kept telling them his story, the more likely that some of them begin believing parts of it.

Not that she was certain how anybody could give any credence to the story he was putting out.

"Since you're going to be answering my questions, I have one for you," she said. "I saw several of your people with implants pretending to be marines that first day. Why would you have your officers pretend to be crewmen?"

"We're not pretending. Every single human being on our ships has implants. Crewmen, officers, and civilians. Only one person that I'm aware of doesn't have them, and she's a special case. Does that sound like your Fleet to you?"

It sounded like insanity. Only idiots trusted the lower orders with a loaded weapon, and she included implant access in that list.

"I can question anyone I like?" she asked.

"Pick anyone in this compartment or we can walk anywhere you'd like on board this ship. You can stop anyone you like and asked them whatever strikes your fancy. If it's classified, I'll make the decision on whether or not they can answer, but I won't put words in their mouths.

"In fact, I suggest you ask unusual questions. What they do for living. Why they're fighting against the Rebel Empire. That's what we call you, by the way. It's because we consider ourselves to be the true Terran Empire."

Well, if he was going to be so forthcoming, it shouldn't be very hard to trip someone up. All she needed to do was get away from the people he had groomed to give his false answers. Someone from the lower orders—as the crewmen would be—certainly weren't sophisticated enough to deceive her.

"Very well. Let's play your game."

8

Talbot stuck his head into Carl's lab and knocked on the frame of the hatch. "How's it going?"

The young scientist looked a bit frazzled when he turned from his screen. He held up his fist. "I swear to God, the next person to ask me that is going to catch this on the nose."

Talbot laughed. "So that's the way it is. They told you we found a ship, right?"

Carl's expression brightened. "They did? That's excellent news, though I'm certain Doctor Leonard is going to be very disappointed to learn that someone else discovered weak flip points."

"It doesn't count if you don't make it back," Talbot said. "Your girlfriend is searching the ship right now, but it certainly doesn't look as though anyone is living there. Either they're living on the planet, they died off, or they went back where they came."

"No. I'm just about certain these weak flip points actually do lead to other locations, but not without technology the Old Empire didn't have. Do you understand anything about how flip drives work?"

The marine nodded. "A little. The engines express energy along a certain frequency that triggers a weakness in the space-time continuum. The ship moves from one end of a wormhole to the other."

"That's right, as far as it goes. What Doctor Leonard suspects—and what I've come to believe is probably true—is that we can focus the energy even more precisely along certain wavelengths. That may open up other potential destinations. In effect, a weak flip point is actually one with multiple wormholes terminating in the same volume of space."

He cleared away a spot on the table. "Think of it this way. This cup is a weak flip point. If we come along and express energy in a broad spectrum as we currently do, we can trigger it to take us to my stylus. If we do the same at my stylus, it will take us back to my cup.

"However, there might be other wormholes present, and the distorted gravitic reading comes from some kind of harmonic dissonance as they try to express themselves. If we can narrow the energy frequency to most closely link to one of the secondary wormholes, perhaps it will open a wormhole leading to this data chip."

Talbot sighed. "I hear you talking, but it doesn't make sense to me. How is that even possible?"

Carl's face told him that he wouldn't understand the answer, but the young scientist gamely tried to tell him anyway.

"I could give you lots justifications, but it boils down to an educated guess based on the evidence. The only way to be sure is to make it work. Tell me about this ship."

"At this point, we only know that it's some kind of passenger liner. It's cold and dark, so nobody's been on it for a while. Maybe we'll be able to salvage its computer and figure out how they got here, though."

"That would be good. It would be even better to know how they discovered the weak flip point in the first place. I suppose we need a better name than weak flip points. If the theory is correct, that's an inaccurate term. Maybe I should call them multiflip points."

The marine smiled. "It doesn't really matter what you call it, so long as it works. Another angle they're looking at is the planet. One of the continents and several islands sit on the equator. From what they tell me, it's a cold place. Even living on the equator would be hard going if it gets colder."

"If the ship really did come through during the Fall, none of the people down there is going to be able to tell us anything first hand. Civilians with nanites have long lifespans, but that potential gets much shorter under primitive conditions. You'll lose people to accidents and violence. It's probably a safe bet that none of the original survivors lasted more than a hundred years."

Talbot shrugged. "People tell stories. We'll find out something about how they got here, though it might be garbled. If, of course, there's anyone here in the first place."

"How did playing a spy work out for Captain Vitter?" Carl asked.

He grimaced. "Not so well. Apparently, somebody figured out who she was right away. The guy spent two hours tormenting her with innuendo. If we're going to get the specifications and manufacturing techniques for the artificial intelligence systems and Raider implants, you'll have to come up with another plan."

The younger man sighed. "I was afraid of that. Given enough time, we'll eventually work out the specifics of creating each individual part. Just having the equipment itself will make that a lot easier."

Talbot clapped his friend on the shoulder. "You'll figure it out. I'll leave you to your work and go find some other trouble to get into."

He'd barely made it into the corridor before he received a message from Commodore Anderson.

"Yes, ma'am?"

She smiled at him through the implant feed. "We have good news, for once. The probes have picked up signs of primitive settlements on the equatorial continent. Somebody's down there. I want you to gather up a scouting team and check it out."

He grinned. "I'll get rolling."

* * *

RAUL FELT as though he were stumbling along when the marines put him back into the mess compartment. The events of the last few hours had shaken him to the core.

"Commander Castille," Commodore Murdock said sternly. "Where have you been?"

He shook his head in a futile attempt to clear it. "I've been getting an education on precisely how screwed we are, Commodore."

The woman frowned. "Get your ass over here and explain that to me."

The confused jumble of feelings in his gut narrowed to irritation. Murdock was the worst choice for a senior officer in a situation like this. Not only was she completely clueless, she was going to make any action the rest of them took that much harder.

His annoyance grew when he saw that she still didn't have another chair at her table. That was just the kind of petty nonsense the woman had a reputation for.

Well, perhaps he should do something about that.

He came to attention. "My apologies, Commodore. The information I just obtained is shocking. Our situation is graver than we'd believed. I need to brief all the senior officers so that we can coordinate an organized response to this new threat."

Her frown deepened. "I'll make the decision about who needs to know what, as well as what our response will be, *Commander*." She emphasized his title, no doubt to remind him that she was a flag officer and he was not.

"Are you familiar with the security protocols for the research station?" he asked politely.

"It's a little early to start a court of inquiry into how you should've stopped this attack before it ever started, Commander. Let's focus on turning the tables first."

He smiled blandly. "While I no doubt hold most of the blame in this, you're right this isn't the time. My point is that the security of the Empire is at stake. I'm declaring a state of emergency and assuming command of this facility and its personnel so I can effectively deal with it."

Commodore Murdock surged to her feet. "I will not tolerate you attempting to usurp my command, Castille. You're under arrest." She raised her voice. "Commander Irons, come here."

The other officer hurried over from his table. "Yes, Commodore?"

She pointed at Raul. "Commander Castille is under arrest. See that he is secured in whatever manner you see fit."

Raul smiled at Irons. "That won't be necessary, Commander. Under the research facility's emergency security protocols, I've just assumed command of this facility and all its personnel. I assume you're familiar with them?"

The other officer nodded. "Of course. What are your orders, sir?"

"What the hell are you doing?" Murdock demanded. "You will do as I instructed, or you'll find yourself under arrest as well, Commander Irons."

The man looked contrite. "I'm sorry, Commodore. The security protocols give Commander Castille the authority to assume command."

He turned to Raul. "We don't have access to more private accommodations for a prisoner, sir. Particularly one of flag rank. What you have in mind?"

"This is mutiny," Murdock snarled. "I'll have you both shot for this."

"I suppose we'll need to keep her at this table for now," Raul said, ignoring her. "It's not as though she's been mingling with anyone else up to this point. Find a pair of officers that will obey your instructions and make sure that she stays here and behaves herself."

"That shouldn't be too difficult," the other officer said with a glance at the fuming Commodore.

A few minutes later, two scowling officers flanked the Commodore. Raul supposed they would keep her in line, but if they didn't, he could deal with her more harshly.

He joined Commander Irons and Jeanette Martin at their table. He then filled them in on the things he'd seen when Annette Vitter took him on her little tour of the carrier *Audacious*. He wrapped up with the revelation that they weren't in the Dresden system any longer.

Jeanette held up a hand. "Hold on. You're telling me that they *stole* the orbital? As in, they've absconded with us?"

Her choice of words made him smile. "I'm afraid that's exactly what I'm saying. As the imposter was bringing me back, we were just entering orbit around a planet.

"I saw this world with my own eyes. It's in the habitable zone, but it wasn't Dresden. I haven't got the faintest idea where we are, but our assumption that Fleet was coming to rescue us is incorrect."

Irons rubbed his forehead. "That changes everything. This is a disaster, and this is all my fault."

"That's an epic declaration, Commander. Considering the number of ships and those fighters they brought with them, I'm somewhat at a loss as to how you bear any responsibility. Perhaps you'd care to explain it to me."

The other officer slumped dejectedly. "I brought her into the restricted area. I thought she was Renner, and I bypassed every bit of security we had in place to keep hostile personnel out."

Raul laughed. Not a little chuckle, but a fuller laugh. "Frankly, Edward, I don't think it made the slightest bit of difference whether you brought her to that meeting or not. They were still on the station, and they had overwhelming force.

"No. If you'd realized you were dealing with an imposter—which has to be the ballsiest move I've ever seen—then the most you'd have been able to do was force them to advance their timetable. That would've changed nothing."

He considered telling them the woman's ludicrous claims about being minions of the despot that escaped the revolution, but decided that would only muddy the waters. The ploy had to be a bizarre disinformation campaign anyway.

After a moment, he sighed and leaned back in his chair. "What's obvious to me is that this operation was meticulously planned and took advantage of weaknesses in our security that we didn't even know were there.

"Frankly, I'm convinced this had to be some kind of inside job. Someone smoothed the way for these intruders. There's just no other way to explain how they got so many people on board the orbital without being discovered."

"What do we do now?" Jeanette asked. "We can't get to the computers to purge them, but they're not going to break into them by brute force, either. They're going to have to dissect every bit of equipment in the research area to gain any kind of advantage.

"Do we have any idea which world is financing this operation? Or is it some type of mutiny inside Fleet itself?"

Raul shrugged. "I'm not sure. We need to stymie them in a way that won't provoke them into torturing us. They have us completely at their mercy."

Whatever the enemy's plans were, he felt certain they'd be coming along to execute them before very much longer. Once they had more information, he and his compatriots could formulate a plan to resist them.

While Raul would never have willingly chosen for these events to occur, he felt invigorated. This was going to be the most fun he'd had in years.

9

Kelsey exited the pinnace into the cruise liner's landing bay. The magnetic boots of her armor clicked on the deck as she walked. Angela had portable lights scattered about, so the compartment was not in total gloom.

She could've used the miniature grav drive her armor boasted, but for such a short distance, it didn't seem worthwhile.

It had taken her executive officer less than an hour to determine that the derelict was completely lifeless and harmless. In fact, it probably hadn't been fit for occupation in centuries.

The evidence was all around her as she made her way toward engineering. The deck plans in her implants guided her past stripped compartments. Even the hatches and grav plates were gone.

The ship would never be useful as an interstellar vessel ever again. It probably wouldn't ever support life on its own. They'd even taken a number of hull plates, exposing the interior to open space.

She found Angela and several engineers standing in the gloomy cavern that had been engineering. At least it was gloomy until the rear end lit up with bluish light. The aft quadrant was gone, and Kelsey could see the planet they were orbiting.

Someone had ripped all of the consoles out. The only notable object in the room was the flip drive. For some reason, they'd left it behind.

"What have we got?" Kelsey asked as she stepped up beside her executive officer.

The marine's expression was wry inside her helmet. "We've got a whole lot of nothing. In fact, we have so much nothing that it means something. Someone stripped this derelict of anything useful, and when I say anything, I really mean *everything*."

Kelsey gestured toward the flip drive. "That doesn't look like nothing."

"I'll let Jake explain that."

The engineering technician took that as his cue. "That might look like a flip drive, Colonel, but it isn't really. At least, not anymore. It's completely fried. As far as I can tell, there's not a single salvageable part left. Seriously, it actually caught *fire*."

"Any idea what might've caused that?" Kelsey asked.

"Whatever it was, it happened a long time ago. Based on the age of the scorch marks, probably sometime around the Fall."

Kelsey nodded. "It's always possible this happened when they used the weak flip point. Our military drives are more robust than civilian models. What about the rest of the ship? Is there *anything* useful left?"

"Someone spent a lot of man-hours stripping this ship down to the decks, and then taking most of the decks too. The computers are gone, and every bit of electronics is missing. They even took the wiring. Basically, this liner is ready for the scrapyard. There's nothing we can recover from it that will tell us anything."

Kelsey sighed. "Well, that's disappointing. Somehow, this ship used the weak flip point, arrived here in orbit, and then the crew and passengers vanished, taking with them anything that might tell us something useful."

"Maybe that's intentional," Angela said. "If I wanted to be certain that no one could figure out where I'd gone, I'd either strip the ship down or destroy it. Frankly, I think these folks probably needed every bit of technology they could get their hands on, so dumping it into the sun didn't make as much sense."

"Talbot is almost ready to check out the inhabited area we spotted below," Kelsey said. "Basically, all we can see from orbit is the fact that they have some cultivated fields. The area is heavily forested, so any dwellings are probably underneath the trees."

"If I had to guess," Angela said, "they're not intentionally trying to hide from anyone. Otherwise, they'd have destroyed the ship. They'd also be a bit more cautious about hiding any cultivated areas."

Kelsey agreed with that assessment. Whoever was down there—if anyone was down there—wasn't concerned about someone spotting them. Not really.

The fact that they didn't have any high-tech dwellings might very well mean that the descendants of the survivors were living a very primitive lifestyle. Probably nothing like the Pale Ones, but definitely something more agrarian.

"I'm going to have Jake ship the flip drive over to Carl," Angela said. "If anyone can figure something out with this piece of junk, he can."

"Did the ship even have a name?" Kelsey asked. "Maybe it's in our databases."

"*Radiant Dawn*. We only know that because it's written on the hull. Our databases have listings of Fleet vessels, but not civilian ones. We've got nothing on this ship."

Kelsey grunted. "Pity. Maybe Talbot will be able to find out something. We'll just have to keep working with what we have up here."

"Speaking of working with what we have, how are things going with your mother?"

Kelsey gave the tall woman a sour look. "I went down and talked with her. Things did not go well. Did you know that her picture is in the Imperial dictionary next to the word 'entitled'? That woman thinks that the universe revolves around her. It's maddening."

"This should not be a shock to you. You've known her your entire life. Surely, she behaved the same way when you were growing up."

Kelsey sighed. "Of course she did. It's not that I expect her to be different, but I've changed. I don't have the tolerance to deal with her bull. I have so many other priorities that I just want to leave her down there in that little cabin until we get back home, however long it takes."

Angela laughed. "That's a nice pipe dream, but you're going to have to deal with her sooner rather than later. That is one situation that won't be improved by putting it off."

"I don't know what to say. I've been through things that she will never understand. Her petty prejudices make my teeth hurt. I just want to shake her."

"Maybe you should, if you think it will serve your end goal. Since she's here and you have to deal with her, what is the optimum outcome of your interaction with her?"

Kelsey thought about that. "I want her to respect me for who I am. I want her to respect Jared as my brother. And I want her to recognize how bad her behavior is."

Angela shook her head. "One of the things they taught me when I became an officer was that some things are outside your control. If your mother is ever going to realize that what she did is wrong, it's going to have to be on her own time.

"Kelsey, she's been behaving this way longer than you've been alive. One thing everyone needs to understand about relationships is that you can't change the other person if they don't want to change."

"So I should dial back my expectations and just let her get away with it?"

"I wouldn't say you're letting her get away with anything. You're accepting that it isn't your problem to fix. Give her the cold shoulder all you like, just don't expect it to make her change who she is unless she wants to.

"As for Admiral Mertz, that's also tied up in her past with your father. Nothing you do is going to change how she feels. Maybe one day she'll be forced to sit down with Jared and learn what kind of person he really is. If so, that's Jared's fight. You need to focus on what's critical for you."

Kelsey smiled a little. "So it's all about me, then?"

"Yes, it is. The only thing you can work out with your mother is your relationship. If she doesn't respect you, grind her face into it. Make her decide to change."

"I suppose that's true," Kelsey said slowly. "I just don't want to talk to her right now."

"Putting something painful off only makes it more difficult. When you find yourself having to do something difficult, grit your teeth and do it. Every time she disrespects you, yank her up short. If she wants to discuss your life, make it clear that you have the final say in all the decisions about your personal life. If she doesn't like that, tough."

"I kind of started that already."

Angela clapped Kelsey on the shoulder. "Then go finish it."

* * *

Veronica walked around *Audacious* for almost two hours. To her shock, Levy allowed her to dictate their direction of travel and didn't even deter her from going into sensitive areas.

For example, when she wanted to go to engineering, he allowed it. He had to know she was looking their engines over and seeing how they powered the ship, but he didn't seem concerned.

She had to admit the big ship intimidated her. As a junior officer, she'd served aboard a heavy cruiser. At the time, she couldn't have imagined a more powerful warship.

Audacious could swat that ship down with zero effort. Hell, it could do the same for several of them, even without its fighters. Her little destroyer wouldn't have had a chance.

It didn't take her long to forget about their surroundings, though. The more people she spoke with, the more confused she became. She followed Levy's advice and asked a wide array of questions about people's backgrounds and origins. She asked them what they knew about the fall of the dictatorship.

Their answers were not what she expected. As with any group of people, there wasn't a lot of consistency in the wording they used, and some even made contradictory statements. Just like she'd have found asking people back home about the fall of the dictatorship.

Yet these people all seemed to believe that Levy's version of the truth was what had really happened. More chillingly, even the lowest ranking of the crewmen spoke like someone born to the middle orders.

They seemed educated and bright. Even more unusually, they didn't have the general fear of officers that Fleet seemed to inoculate them with. Everyone she spoke to seemed reserved, but unawed by her, or even Captain Levy.

It was surreal and more than a bit frightening.

He allowed her to see her crew. He didn't take her in to speak with them, but he did show her the large cargo spaces his people were using to hold them. They seemed to have everything they needed and were in good spirits.

After watching her people interact with one another without

interference from Levy's people, she allowed him to lead her back to her new accommodations without comment.

Two marines with rifles stood outside the hatch. They stepped clear to allow her access while still covering the doorway.

She turned to Levy before she entered the suite. "I'm still not certain what you're playing at. I'll tell my officers what you've said and what I've heard, but I don't expect any of us to believe this pile of horse manure."

He shrugged. "I can't control what you believe. All I can do is make sure that you have enough data to make an informed decision.

"Once you've slept on it, you might consider looking at some of the records available in the ship's library. Then we can speak again."

She nodded and went into the suite. The hatch slid closed behind her.

They'd already relocated her senior officers to the suite. They gathered around her and started asking questions.

She held up a hand. "Let me sit down for a second. I need to get this straight in my head, and then I'll brief you on what happened. The good news is that our crew is safe. I've seen them, and they're in good spirits."

A lot of senior Fleet officers didn't care how the lower orders fared, even under good conditions, but she'd surrounded herself with men and women who cared about the people under them. She was convinced that was why her efficiency rates for ship performance were so high.

Someone brought her a cool drink, and she took a sip. After a moment, she set it on the coffee table and launched into a concise description of everything that had happened while she was gone.

It would take a while, but the discussion afterward should be damned interesting.

10

Talbot guided the pinnaces down to an isolated spot. He'd sent drones ahead to be certain their landing zone was clear, so all he had to do was redirect them toward the cultivated fields after the pinnaces landed.

The temperature outside hovered somewhere between cool and cold. There were no crops currently growing in the fields, but there was evidence that someone had tilled them recently. There were people around somewhere.

He dispatched two squads to set up a perimeter around the pinnaces and then sent the drones farther afield.

It only took twenty minutes to locate a village. The people were dressed in rough, homespun cloth. Their grooming was on the unkempt side. Definitely not an advanced people.

The only people in sight were male. That seemed somewhat odd. Perhaps the women were inside the buildings, such as they were.

The locals had used roughly hewn logs and stone to build their dwellings. A few of them looked somewhat lopsided. Definitely not put together by professionals.

The drones were low profile, so he didn't expect any of the locals to notice them. That gave him plenty of time to record them in their natural setting.

That's when the first of the incongruities appeared. Once he had the long-range microphones on them, he realized that their basic conversation didn't match the technological level at which they were living. They spoke standard and occasionally mentioned things that were technological. Tablets mostly. They seemed to miss them.

Talbot eventually decided that he wasn't going to learn any more without approaching them. He weighed the pros and cons of appearing on foot or bringing one of the pinnaces in for a landing near the village.

Since they seemed to have some understanding of high technology, he decided on the latter. There were fewer chances for misunderstandings that way.

He did take the opportunity to relocate his marines closer to the village beforehand. If one of the locals tried something, he wanted his snipers in position to take them out safely.

Once everyone was in position, he had the pilot bring his pinnace around and landed beside one of the fields nearest the village. He dropped the ramp and walked down it slowly.

The air smelled of vegetation, and the wind bit at him through his uniform. He should've brought a jacket.

The people in the village noticed the pinnace landing, of course. It only took a few minutes for a small delegation of men to approach. Their expressions were closed, their faces hostile. This didn't look promising.

"What do you want?" one of the men asked. "You've already collected your damned bounty for the year."

"I just want to talk," Talbot said, his hands out to his sides a little. "There's no need for trouble."

The men glanced at one another in evident confusion. The man who'd spoken seemed to consider Talbot's words and then stepped forward. "Very well. Talk."

"Whoever you think I am, you're mistaken. I just want to find out who you people are."

The man blinked in obvious surprise. "You know who we are. You come every year to take the crops you demand we raise for you. Why are you playing this game?"

Talbot shrugged. "I don't know what to tell you. We just arrived in this system and found the derelict ship in orbit. I have no idea who you people are."

His words caused more consternation amongst the men. They had a brief, emphatic discussion in hushed tones before the first man once more turned to face Talbot.

"You're telling me that you're not one of those rebel bastards?"

"Maybe if we start with a simple question. How did you people get here?"

For the first time, Talbot saw something that looked like interest or excitement on the man's face. "You're truly not one of them? Are you with Fleet?"

"I'm Major Russel Talbot, Imperial Marines."

The man took two steps forward and fell to his knees. "Thank the gods. We thought no one would ever rescue us."

Talbot smiled. "Well, we've found you now. Who are you, and how did you get here?"

The man wiped tears from his face. "My name is Arthur Craig. I was a civil servant on Gibraltar before those bastards captured the freighter I was traveling on. They banished me here. They said all the higher orders were banished here."

Talbot checked the man. He had implants. They all did. Based on what he'd just heard, they were nobles from the Rebel Empire. Or at least wealthy families. They sure didn't look like it now.

The princess had chanced across a planet where someone—likely the ghosts—were putting their high-ranking prisoners. These people wouldn't be at all happy to learn whom he represented. In fact, their corrupted implant code would force them to attack him if they knew.

"I see. The people that captured you live somewhere else but force you to grow food for them. Is that right?"

"Yes," the man said. "It's those damned ghosts. The gods only know how long they've been doing this. We've had contact with other villages where none of the original prisoners is still alive. Some of the villages claim they've been here since the despot was overthrown. Have you come to take us home? Please tell me you've come to take us home."

Talbot hedged his bets. "Since we've just found you, I can't speak for my commanding officers about what's going to happen next. We never expected to find anyone here, so they'll need to devise a plan. I feel certain that they'll wish to speak with someone to get more information."

The man surged to his feet. "I'll go with you. I'll explain everything. I even have some information about the ghosts. Critical information." The desperation in his voice was painful to hear.

The marine nodded slowly. "Very well. I can take you up to our ship, but I can't say when you'd be coming back."

"I hope I never come back," the man snarled. "This place is hell. A frozen hell."

Talbot sent instructions for the marines to regroup at the other pinnace and then gestured for the man to come with him. "I'll take you up now. If your people have any specific needs that we might be able to meet, such as medical care, I'll see to it as soon as we get to the ship."

"Thank you," the man said, tears streaming down his face. "I thought this nightmare would never end. They make us live like animals just to feed them. They make sure to tell us about the warm, beautiful worlds where they take the women and the lower orders just to torment us."

The ghosts sounded like a bunch of asses. Or pirates.

That explained why Talbot wasn't seeing any women. The marine kept an eye on the rest of the men as he led Craig into the pinnace. He didn't want them to rush him. He only spoke again once he'd safely closed the ramp.

"Well, I can assure you that we'll get to the bottom of this," Talbot said. "Let's get you strapped in and start up, shall we?"

* * *

ANNETTE WALKED into a compartment and eyed the researchers gathered there. It had taken her a while to figure out where the marines had stashed them. With over ten thousand people under lock and key, it wasn't easy to keep track of specific individuals.

Unlike the last set of people that she'd dealt with, these were all civilians. In fact, she couldn't imagine a more diverse set of people. They ranged from young to old, male and female, and any number of body types. Many of them reminded her of Carl Owlet. She supposed that wasn't surprising.

This compartment had originally been a storage area, but they'd moved all the crates against the bulkheads. Someone had scrounged up a few tables and chairs to go with the bedding on the floor. They really needed to come up with a better way of housing so many people.

She cleared her throat. "May I have your attention? My name is Annette Vitter, and I wish to speak with the most senior person."

A middle-aged woman with dark skin and curly hair rose from one of the tables. "I suppose that would be me. Jacqueline Parker. Is someone finally going to tell us what's going on?"

Annette gestured for the two marines at her heels to stay where they were and walked forward with her hand extended. "Yes, ma'am. I'll do what I can to explain everything and try to reduce the stress that you're undoubtedly under. Might we sit somewhere?"

The woman gestured to the table that she'd risen from. "Join me. Who are you people? What's going on?"

Annette verified the woman had implants as she sat. She couldn't tell her the unvarnished truth until they'd scrubbed the code. "I just need to verify some facts first. Once I've done that, we'll give you an examination to be sure you're healthy. Then I'll explain why we're here and what we intend to do.

"Let me begin by assuring you that we mean you no harm. We are not going to hurt any of you. In fact, we'd prefer to be your friends."

The woman gave her a lopsided smile. "You certainly have an odd way of showing friendship. Well, it seems I have some time available in my schedule, so go ahead and ask your questions."

"Are you all scientists and researchers?" Annette asked.

"Yes, though not all of the researchers are here," the woman said, her expression strained. "Are they all right? No one's been hurt, have they?"

"No one has been harmed," Annette said. "We just didn't have room to place everyone together, and I'm afraid we didn't realize we had missed some of you. If I could get a list of names, I'll have them moved here so that you can all be housed together."

"That would be good," Parker said. "It would take a lot of the strain off of my shoulders."

"What precisely do you do here?" Annette asked.

"I work in the gamma lab. I'm responsible for the people there and the research that we conduct."

"What are you researching?"

The woman smiled wanly. "It's classified. I may be your prisoner, but I still can't reveal the secrets of what we're working on."

Annette smiled. "We're going to find out one way or the other. Why don't you make it easy on yourself and just tell us?"

"Because I'd like to live," the woman said.

"It may not be readily apparent, but you're safe now. No one is going to harm you."

"I don't think you understand," Parker said. "We physically cannot tell you any aspect of what we're working on. To even attempt to do so would mean death."

Annette gestured around them. "No one can get to you here. You're safe."

"You definitely don't understand. We have explosive devices implanted in our skulls. If any one of us attempts to speak about classified projects with someone not cleared to hear the information, the explosive device will quite literally blow our heads off."

That information flabbergasted Annette. That was a new low, even for the Rebel Empire.

Now she was afraid to ask the woman any further questions. She couldn't risk someone with critical information blowing up in front of her very eyes.

"I assume that it's somehow linked with your implants," Annette said. "Would it object to a medical examination? In other words, can we look at it?"

Parker shrugged. "No one has ever had problems with an examination before, but these are new waters. None of us is particularly happy to have devices like that ready to snuff our lives at a moment's notice. I'll volunteer on one condition."

"What's that?" Annette asked.

The woman smiled widely. "I want us to get better food and some strong drink. It's been a tough couple of days."

11

Kelsey stood in *Audacious*'s landing bay as the cutter transporting the senior prisoners from the orbital landed. She'd decided it was time to relocate them. She had to admit she really wanted to meet this Castille. He sounded like quite the character.

The marines escorted the prisoners off the cutter and herded them into a small group in front of her. She stepped forward and cleared her throat.

"May I have your attention, please? My name is Kelsey, and I'm going to see you situated. I'd welcome you aboard *Audacious*, but that feels a little pushy. You didn't exactly have a choice about coming over."

Commander Raul Castille stepped forward to meet her with his hand extended. "My name is Raul. I'd say it's a pleasure to meet you, but the circumstances are less than ideal. In any case, I suppose we're at your disposal."

"Has anyone told you that you're refreshingly honest, Commander?" Kelsey shook his hand. "Well, we might be enemies, but there's no reason we can't be civil. Perhaps even cordial."

He inclined his head. "This is also true. What do you have in mind for us? Forgive me, but I don't know your rank. Or even your last name."

She smiled. "We'll get to that in due time. First, let's get you to the suite of rooms we've set aside for you. I assure you, they're much more comfortable than the officers' mess on the orbital.

"Also, since you're no longer aboard the orbital, we can remove the jamming devices that were blocking your implant access. The unclassified portions of our ship's library are now available to you."

The other male senior prisoner stepped up to join them. "Forgive me if I seem to be butting in. My name is Edward Irons, and as the operations officer in charge of—or formerly in charge of— the Dresden Orbital, I must ask what you intend to do with the remaining prisoners.

"The conditions that they're being kept in are not conducive to good health. They need to be able to get out and move around."

Kelsey inclined her head toward him. "Commander Irons. We find ourselves in agreement. I want to move all the prisoners that we can, but it will take time to prepare accommodations that are more spacious.

"I can assure you that our medical personnel will continue examining them and make absolutely certain that they are in the best health possible as we work on that."

The third member of the senior officers' cabal stepped forward. "My name is Jeanette Martin. What are you going to do with us? How long are we to be your prisoners? When can I see the people I'm responsible for?"

Kelsey held her hands out. "I will answer those questions as soon as we get you settled into your new quarters."

She looked over to where Commodore Murdock stood glaring at them. "It's my understanding that you have placed some type of restriction upon Commodore Murdock. While it's unusual for prisoners to have prisoners, we've decided to allow that.

"One set of rooms in the suite can be secured from the common area. So long as you do not attempt to harm the commodore, we'll continue to allow you to restrict her movement."

Kelsey gestured for the marines at her side to lead the way. The prisoners fell in beside her while the other guards brought up the rear.

Once they arrived at the suite of rooms, Kelsey went inside, but instructed the marines to wait in the corridor.

Castille raised an eyebrow. "Don't you think you're being a little too trusting? We are, after all, your prisoners. What if we seize you and present a set of demands?"

Kelsey smiled. "I suppose that's part of the conversation that we need to have. I'm not concerned that you're going to take me prisoner. You might try, but you wouldn't succeed.

"Perhaps you should examine your accommodations? Then we can settle in before I broach the subjects. I suspect this is going to be an intense conversation. If you don't mind, I'd rather do it over food. I'm feeling a bit peckish."

He laughed. "Considering that we were living in a cafeteria, I feel confident that these rooms are significantly better than what we had." He glanced at Commander Irons. "Edward, please look everything over."

The other man nodded and began walking through the rooms attached to the common area.

Kelsey pointed at the far door. "That's the compartment reserved for Commodore Murdock. You can secure the manual lock from the outside. Over on the right, you can see the communal kitchen. If you want to continue this conversation, that's where I'll be."

It only took Kelsey a few minutes to make some iced tea and put a selection of meats and cheeses beside stacked bread. The condiments were on the side. Everyone could build a sandwich to their taste.

Once she was ready, the four of them sat at one of the tables. Kelsey put together a sandwich with a little bit of everything on it and dug in.

Castille waited for her to finish her sandwich before he spoke again. "We appreciate your seeing us to better-quality quarters. However, I believe it's time we put our cards on the table. Who are you, and what do you want with us?"

Kelsey smiled. "I believe you know who we are. Captain Vitter said that she was very clear about it."

Irons and Martin glanced at one another, confusion evident on their faces. Castille inclined his head toward them.

"I didn't think her story truthful, so I didn't pass it on to my associates. If that's going to be your official line, perhaps you should restate it. My apologies, Jeanette, Edward."

"I can see where this would be hard to accept," Kelsey said. "Our story isn't easy to believe. That doesn't make it untrue, however.

"I'm sure you've all heard about the Empire's civil war. I'm not going to get into the weeds about it, but what you've been taught is incomplete."

Commander Irons frowned at her. "Incomplete in what way?"

"It doesn't take into account the fact that some of the people your ancestors fought against escaped. They got away and settled a world outside your reach. Over the last five hundred years, those people have gathered their strength. I should say, my people. Now we've returned."

Jeanette shook her head. "That's preposterous. The lords completely overthrew the old dictatorship. Surely, you're not going to try to convince us that we're still fighting that war. It's settled."

"That's where things get complicated," Kelsey said. "My full name is Kelsey Bandar. I have two titles. The first is colonel because I'm the senior officer in the newly reconstituted Marine Raider division."

Castille laughed. "That's ridiculous. You expect me to believe that you command detachments of unstoppable war machines? I can bend you into a pretzel with one hand. If there is anyone less likely to be a warrior in this compartment, I do not see them."

"I can understand your reservations," Kelsey said. "I agree that I don't look very intimidating, but that doesn't change the facts."

She dabbed at the corners of her lips to make sure she hadn't left any mustard and dropped her napkin onto her plate. Then she rose to her feet, stepped over to the couch, and picked it up. It took a moment for her to find its balance, but she raised it almost to the ceiling.

Everyone stared at her, their eyes wide and mouths open. Silence ruled.

Once she was certain that she'd made her point, Kelsey set the couch back onto the deck. She brushed her hands off and returned to her seat.

"Commander Vitter told me she showed you a scan of someone with Raider implants. That was me."

Castille's mouth snapped shut. "This is an unexpected and somewhat frightening turn of events. How is this even possible? We control the manufacture of those things. How could you possibly have them if you've been separated from the Empire for so long?"

Kelsey smiled without humor. "Do you remember the computer you sent that fleet to destroy? Well, you've been sending it Raider implants for centuries. It followed the same instructions given to all the other subverted ships during the civil war.

"In case you don't know, they took anyone that they captured, corrupted their implants, and forcibly made them into fighting machines. They became prisoners in their own bodies, compelled to slaughter their friends and family.

"How do I know this? Because until very recently, it was still doing exactly that. I had the very great misfortune of straying into its grasp, and that computer put these things inside me. I still have nightmares about it, and I probably always will."

She took a deep breath and forced the terrible thoughts back into their mental lockbox.

"I believe that establishes my credentials on the Marine Raider front," she said brightly. "Let's get my other title settled. It's actually more relevant to our current discussion anyway.

"My father is the sitting emperor of the New Terran Empire. His lineage goes all the way back to Lucien, the boy emperor who escaped your grasp. Marcus's son. So, in nonmilitary settings, I have to deal with people calling me Crown Princess Kelsey Bandar, heir to the Imperial Throne."

Kelsey smiled at their shocked expressions. "We're not some greedy group from inside your Empire trying to take all of your secret research for profit. We're the people your ancestors failed to exterminate. You see, Commander, the war is far from settled."

Needless to say, they didn't believe her. She answered their questions and argued with them for a while, but finally hit her limit an hour later.

She stood slowly. "I think we've accomplished as much as one can reasonably expect. As I said earlier, you have access to the ship's library. I urge you to explore it deeply. You'll certainly learn a lot. Perhaps even understand what really happened all those years ago. We'll speak again soon."

Kelsey exited the compartment and gave the marine guards more detailed instructions. Once she was satisfied things were well in hand, she headed for Carl's main lab on the carrier.

Surprisingly, he wasn't sitting at his computer. He stood beside the recovered flip drive from the liner.

He smiled at her as she stepped up beside him. "You look tired."

"I feel tired. Give me some good news."

Carl gestured toward the drive. "I've just finished looking this over. It's just as fried as they'd said, but it has a nonstandard modification. It has a frequency tuner."

She eyed his satisfied expression warily. "You say that as if it means something. What is a frequency tuner?"

His expression fell. "What is with the education these days? A frequency tuner is a device that restricted the flip drive to a certain range of output. Or perhaps one of several ranges."

"You think they used it to refine their destinations through the weak flip point? Like what you were discussing as an option for us?"

"Yes," he said. "It's not possible to determine which particular range of frequencies the device might once have preferred, but that's what it did."

"How difficult will it be to duplicate?" she asked. "And how dangerous? Something burned out this flip drive. We absolutely cannot afford to have something like that happen to us."

"This is a civilian drive, built to far less robust standards than what you'll find on our ships. Even the recovery ship has military drives. I can't say for sure that it's completely safe, but we can be careful. Since there isn't another flip point in this system, we're going to have to take chances."

"You're sure of that?"

"I'm afraid so," he said softly. "The probes have scoured the system. There are no other flip points. The only way out is the way we came."

12

Talbot knew he probably should run this visit past his wife, but he wanted to have an unmonitored conversation with her mother. This was likely to get ugly, and he'd rather spare Kelsey that. This conversation needed to happen no matter how nasty it got, though.

The marine guard nodded at him as he instructed the hatch to signal his presence. Perhaps a little bit of common courtesy would make this easier. Talbot wasn't going to hold his breath, but one never knew.

The hatch slid open, and Justine Bandar stared up at him imperiously. Her already sour expression took a turn for the worse.

"Well, that just about makes this day perfect. What do you want?"

"I'd like to talk about your daughter. Believe it or not, it's in my best interest to see the two of you reconciled."

He figured the odds were about fifty-fifty that she'd close the hatch in his face. He could see the calculation behind her gaze.

She stepped back and gestured for him to enter. "Well then, by all means, come in. This should be fascinating."

Her quarters were standard Fleet issue. She undoubtedly saw them as a step down.

His mother-in-law walked to the couch and sat. "I'd offer you some refreshments, but I don't believe you'll be staying that long.

"Why would you want to see my daughter and me reconciled? In case it escaped your notice, I am not in favor of your marriage."

While the woman hadn't offered him a seat, he took one anyway. Standing while she sat gave her too much power over him.

"We've never been formally introduced," he said. "I'm Major Russel Talbot, Imperial Marines. Call me Talbot. Everyone does."

"I know your name. Russel. You left out a few titles. Let me be clear.

Your position doesn't change one thing between us. You're a commoner trying to climb the ladder into high society, and I will not allow it."

He laughed. "I couldn't give squat about my position in society. Frankly, I thought the knighthood was far too much. The rest of those titles? If you can convince your ex-husband to take them back, I'm perfectly fine with that. I have no desire to see myself included in the nobility. Bunch of puffed-up stuffed shirts."

Justine raised an eyebrow. "That's the first interesting thing you've said. I'm shocked that we find ourselves in agreement about anything."

"I don't know why," he said. "In any case, I'm not here to talk about me. I'm here to talk about Kelsey."

The woman sneered at him. "What can you possibly tell me about my daughter that I don't already know? She thinks something has changed that makes her incomprehensible to me. She's wrong. And if you think you're going to take me to task for my sex life, you'd better think again."

"I couldn't care less about your sex life. Bang whomever you choose. Knock yourself right out. As far as how Kelsey feels about that, that's between you two. All I'm here for is to give you some information that your daughter isn't going to give you."

The woman's eyes narrowed. "What information might that be?"

"The fact that she's been through hell. Literally, through hell. She's changed in ways both mental and physical that you cannot comprehend unless I explain it to you in words with less than three syllables."

He held up a hand when she started to respond hotly. Miraculously, she shut up.

"Rather than argue, why don't you let me explain it to you? If you have questions, then you can ask them. If you don't, then I can leave. I'm not here to fight with you. That's your daughter's job."

Justine leaned back and crossed her arms over her chest. "Why do both of you think that I cannot understand my daughter has been through something terrible? I'm sure the mission she was on was ghastly. Just look at the company she had to keep."

"Sometimes ignorance is bliss," he said. "It's going to give me great pleasure to educate you. And by company, I assume you mean Jared Mertz. He's also outside the scope of our discussion.

"Focus on your daughter. Kelsey went through something horrific. Something that has changed her irrevocably. Not just mentally—though it has certainly given her nightmares—but physically.

"Let me stress that again. It's been more than a year since the events in question, and she still has nightmares almost every night. She wakes up screaming in terror and pain. Is that getting through that thick skull of yours?"

A look of unease flitted across the ex-empress's face. "Nightmares? What could possibly have happened to her to give Kelsey nightmares?"

He leaned forward. "The information I'm about to pass on to you is classified. Your ex-husband has declared it an Imperial secret. Technically,

I'm in violation of quite a few laws in mentioning this to you, but I suspect he'll grant me an exemption.

"Your daughter was captured by a group of individuals we call the Pale Ones. They implanted machines in her body. Not just the implants you might've heard about. I'm talking about much more significant changes, and this was not a voluntary or painless process."

He used his implants to send a signal to the vid monitor on the wall. It began playing one of the marines' helmet videos from the rescue. He'd selected the clip from after they'd arrived aboard *Courageous*. The team was on their way to the medical center.

He froze it so that Kelsey's face was framed on the monitor. The terrible red scars of the implant surgery cut across her face.

Justine Bandar sucked in a horrified breath. "Oh my God."

"They didn't use anesthesia or any form of regeneration. She had scars just like that across her entire body. I was a prisoner in the next compartment while they did it. I could hear her screaming for over an hour as they cut her open."

He made the image go away. "I could show you everything they did to her, but I'm going to do you a kindness that I'm not sure you'd do me under similar circumstances. I'm not going to show you something you can *never* forget.

"They coated her bones in a substance called graphene to strengthen them. They wove artificial muscles through her normal muscles. They implanted equipment to dispense combat drugs into her. They turned her into the deadliest killing machine that Imperial science could build."

His mother-in-law stared at him in horror. "No. That's not possible. She doesn't look like that at all."

"Regeneration fixed the physical scars, in combination with something called medical nanites. She has millions of tiny machines scattered throughout her body to repair damage. The only lingering injuries she has are inside her mind.

"And that brings me to the second half of her situation. She's had to kill people. Not just by giving orders, not just with guns, but also with her bare hands. I'm not sure I can put a number on how many lives she's ended to save her friends and herself. Oh, and the Empire. Let's not forget that."

He started the second video. The one taken at the Parliament building on Pentagar. He didn't watch the events on the monitor. He'd seen those innumerable times. Instead, he watched his mother-in-law's expression of horror grow deeper.

When the video finished, he allowed the silence to drag on. When she continued to stare at the monitor as though it were still playing, he continued.

"While your daughter isn't a murderer, she's most assuredly a killer. She's one of the deadliest fighters I've ever seen. All of this trauma has brought out one factor you've never seen in your daughter. One that's been hiding in plain sight all this time.

"Kelsey has a will of steel. She will do whatever is necessary for the Empire. The little girl that you could bully around died in an operating theater on board a space station that no longer exists. The woman you see may look like her, but she won't knuckle under to bullies. Not even to you."

He rose to his feet. "I'll leave you to think about that in whatever peace you can find. I'll also give you some free advice. If you want to reconcile with your daughter, you're going to have to give up any thought of dominating her. Trust me, the worst you can do doesn't even come close to what she's been through."

Talbot left her in the compartment, still staring at the blank monitor. He hoped she could come to grips with this information and change how she interacted with her daughter. If she couldn't, well, he'd done his best.

* * *

ANNETTE STAYED with Jacqueline Parker throughout the entire process of scanning the woman's implants. She could see the woman's nervousness.

Audacious's chief medical officer, Zac Zoboroski, walked the scientist through the process without explaining any of the details that would have caused a negative reaction. Annette was impressed with his bedside manner and soothing voice.

The process of overwriting the corrupted code took several hours. The doctor passed this off as a deep scan mapping out the explosive device and how precisely it was placed.

He stepped over beside Annette while the machine in the medical center overwrote the corrupted code. "That's a despicable device. I have no idea what the software triggers are, but the amount of explosive is easily enough to completely shatter her skull and sever her spine."

Annette grimaced. "She said that the programming monitored them and what they said. If they knowingly revealed classified information to someone that wasn't cleared to hear it, it would set off the device. There has to be some extra code inside the implant that monitors that somehow."

The man shrugged. "I've captured the code, and I'll pass it on to Sir Carl. He'll be able to figure out precisely what's different. Under normal circumstances, the device would be relatively simple to remove, but I'm pretty sure it has an antitampering device. Without the appropriate codes to disarm it, I suspect it would go off if I tried."

Annette considered that. "Is there any kind of remote activator?"

The doctor nodded. "Almost certainly. Overwriting the implant code will probably make it safe for her to speak, but I'm not sure what to do about remote signals. Those will continue to be a danger."

"Something else for Sir Carl to work on. Who knows? We might be able to get the researchers working on fixing the problem themselves. There's a kind of symmetry in that."

She went over and exchanged small talk with the scientist for the next two hours. That was challenging, considering she knew very little about the woman's society as a whole or the life of a restricted researcher in particular.

The theme that emerged was that while Jacqueline's education was quite broad and, in specific fields, very deep, she didn't get out much. It seemed that she and the other scientists kept each other's company more often than not.

Basically, they were prisoners. If Annette was right in her guess, this had been true for the woman's entire life. Considering that they hadn't found any retired scientists, the Rebel Empire probably disposed of them once they couldn't work. Dead women told no tales.

Annette excused herself and went for sandwiches and tea. She figured the other woman would be hungry by the time this was all done.

The procedure was complete by the time she returned. She set up the food in the closest break room and brought Jacqueline Parker to join her.

"Okay, let me start off by telling you what we were really doing," Annette said.

The other woman smiled a little. "I figured that was taking too long for any kind of realistic scan."

"Since the device is rigged to be controlled by your implants, we overwrote the code with the base version that doesn't have the interfaces to do anything with it," Annette said. "In other words, the code running your implants now has no idea the explosives are there or what should set them off.

"The doctor is uncertain if they can be safely removed, but nothing we discuss should pose any danger to you at this point. One other piece of bad news is that they may also be remotely controllable. While we have everyone on lockdown, I think it might be best if we bring all of your people off the orbital just to be safe."

"I think that's a great idea," Parker said. "You have no idea how it feels to have them watching you all the time. To know that if you made a mistake, you'd be dead before you realized it."

"I can't imagine how they recruit people for this kind of job," Annette said. "If they don't let you out to talk to anyone else, the whole concept of pay seems ludicrous."

"We aren't paid for our work," the woman said bluntly. "We never had a choice about what we wanted to do with our lives. All of us were brought in as children and trained for this work. But even with all the negatives, it's still better than where we came from."

Annette frowned a little. "I don't think I understand."

"We all came from an exceptionally primitive society. One where we were taken as very young children and separated from what amounted to savages. Thankfully, most of our memories of that time aren't very clear, but it was a brutal life."

Everything suddenly clicked, and Annette knew where these people came from. The tithes of children the computer at Erorsi had been trading for the high-tech gear from the Rebel Empire. That had to be where the scientists had come from.

She wondered if the Rebel Empire had done so because no one would miss those people. Now wasn't the time to ask, but it did call for some deeper research later.

Based on what she'd seen, Annette thought the woman was understating the benefits of living on the orbital in comparison to being a Pale One. The woman didn't even know what was done to those that stayed as they grew older.

"I might be able to provide a little information about where you came from," Annette said. "If my guesses are correct in any case. What I need to know is if you're willing to have a frank discussion with me about what you were working on. Now that it's safe to do so."

Jacqueline Parker smiled coldly. "I've been under a death sentence my entire life. I'll tell you everything I know if you can get my people out of this place."

13

Veronica sat alone in her quarters trying to wrap her mind around just how screwed they really were. She and her people had stayed up late into the evening discussing their situation and looking through the massive library of data that their captors had made available to them.

It hadn't taken long to realize the sheer volume of information available —exabytes of material—meant that not all of it could be fake.

The library dated back literally centuries. Millions of hours of vids, news shows, and more. Billions of articles, books, textbooks and academic journals for restricted research subjects, and more.

And a mind-boggling amount of virtual-reality porn stashed in various hidden repositories. Even some ancient pieces which looked to be live action with actual participants. Which begged the obvious question. Why would anyone include something like that?

She'd set her people to reading different articles about the war against the old dictatorship.

After a few hours, a disturbing trend appeared. What they were reading did not match up with what she had learned in school. Of course, this could all be propaganda. If so, someone had invested an incredible amount of work to trick people that couldn't do anything about it in the first place.

It made no sense. These people had already demonstrated they had enough firepower to take out an entire Fleet task force. Why try to convince her the lords had been playing some kind of game with humanity?

She stayed awake late, picking random historical areas to poke her nose into. It made her sick to her stomach, having to read the lies about the old dictatorship. And they had to be lies. She refused to believe that the lords had overthrown humanity and now oppressed them in a slavery so pervasive they couldn't even recognize it.

It was later than normal when she woke. She dressed and ate breakfast with her senior officers in the little kitchen their suite shared.

Many of them had burned the midnight oil as well. All of them seemed uneasy.

She laid out the areas she'd researched more closely and listened to them as they detailed their own finds.

Her chief engineer, Lieutenant Graham Bakersfield, summed up her thoughts in his usual blunt manner. "Something stinks."

Lieutenant Commander Armand Fuller, her executive officer, glared at the engineer. "Watch yourself."

The younger officer raised an eyebrow. "About what, Commander? It's all laid out for anyone to see. They don't have any reason to lie to us. It's not as though we can do anything. They destroyed our entire task force."

Veronica rapped the table with her knuckles. "Let's restrain ourselves. We don't have any idea what their true plans are. Let's not make assumptions."

She added her helm officer, Lieutenant Candice Wells, and her tactical officer, Lieutenant Brent Kowalski, into her instructions with a pointed glance.

"What I want each of you to do today is divide up the various areas we've already looked at and start reading everything you can about them. I want an assessment of how authentic these documents look. As Graham said, there's far too much material here for them to have just created everything out of whole cloth. I want to know if it feels consistent."

She gave them all a stern look. "What I don't want is for there to be any fighting amongst ourselves. We're already in enough trouble."

After sending each of them off to their own corners, she again dug into every bit of information she could about the dictator, Marcus Bandar. From everything she'd learned in school, the man had been a monster. Surely, they couldn't whitewash him so completely.

By lunch, she was feeling much less certain of that viewpoint. Of course, she'd been certain going into this that they would censor anything negative about the man. The narrative she'd learned as a child didn't suit this story at all.

Yet she found plenty of criticism. Any number of people seemed to object to some aspect of the man's rulings. It seemed, based on the record she had in front of her, that anyone could criticize the man about anything. Not just privately, but on what passed for news programs.

Diving down the rabbit hole of watching news programs to see if they seemed real had caused her to question everything she'd believed. Just one of the news programs went back many decades before the rebellion against the old dictatorship. She had copies of every evening newscast.

There was absolutely no way that someone had spent the time to fake everything in it, not even the lords.

She picked dozens of news items at random. Both good and bad. Most times, she was able to verify through other sources that the events the news programs covered were consistent with what was being presented in them.

Oh, the opinions of the people on the shows might be at odds with the facts, but it wasn't difficult to discern their individual agendas. Anyone that served in Fleet had to play politics, even if they detested being anywhere near the higher orders.

By the time her stomach informed her that she needed something to eat, she wasn't sure she wanted to. She felt ill. No wonder Captain Levy seemed so confident and serene. She was finding it difficult to refute the evidence.

That still didn't mean it was true. It could be some elaborate ruse used to dupe Levy and his people. If so, someone had gone to an insane amount of trouble to fake the historical record for these people. That seemed even more far-fetched. Why?

She wasn't sure what to believe anymore.

Rather than dine with the rest of her people, she decided to see if she could get another trip to the officers' mess. She signaled at the hatch and smiled at the marine who opened it.

He stood far enough back that he wasn't in danger of being rushed, and his companions had them covered from farther down the corridor.

"Yes, ma'am?"

"I was wondering if it is acceptable for me to take lunch at the officers' mess, Corporal."

The marine nodded. "Captain Levy left orders that allow it, ma'am. If you'll stay inside, I'll summon two marines to escort you. Do you want me to notify the captain to join you?"

She shook her head. "No, Corporal. I think I'd rather dine alone. I just want to see and hear the people around me."

"Understood, ma'am. Please step back into your quarters."

Ten minutes later, the hatch opened again. Two new marines stood waiting for her. "This way, ma'am," one of them said politely. The woman gestured for Veronica to precede her.

They escorted her to the officers' mess. It looked pretty much as it had the last time she'd been there. A fairly chaotic room of people dining and talking.

One person stood out, however. A man with commander's tabs dining at a table against the wall, with a pair of marine guards of his own.

She stopped and eyed him. She knew all the senior officers of her task force. He wasn't one of them.

"Who is that man?" she asked the marine at her side.

"One of the new prisoners. They just came aboard yesterday. He's from the orbital at Dresden."

Veronica stared at the woman in shock. None of them had explicitly said where the task force had come from. This had to be some trick to try to get information from her.

Only, how was that supposed to work?

"I've changed my mind," Veronica said. "I think I'll dine with him. Unless of course, you have an objection." She stared challengingly at the marine.

The woman shrugged. "Nothing in my orders precludes that, ma'am. After you."

* * *

RAUL WAS ABOUT HALFWAY through his meal when he saw the woman stalking toward him with a determined step. She was new. Her rank tabs indicated she was a commander, and marines flanked her.

Under other circumstances, he might think she was coming to arrest him. That seemed somewhat redundant at this point.

He put his fork down and focused his attention politely on her. "Yes?"

"Might I join you, Commander?"

He gestured toward the seat across from him. "Be my guest. Might I suggest the steak? It's quite good."

Once the woman had seated herself, the marines that had been accompanying her joined those watching him. Curious.

"I don't believe we've met. I'm Raul Castille."

She extended her hand. "Veronica Giguere. Commanding officer of the destroyer *R-7322*."

That prompted him to check his implant storage. That was one of the destroyers formally assigned to guard Dresden. It was one of the ships that had departed a few weeks before the intruders had showed up.

As the orbital's security officer, he had files on all the senior officers assigned in the system. Indeed, he had hers.

It only took a few moments for him to conclude she was the real deal. Her personnel file had a number of images that his captors would not have been able to alter.

He smiled. "I'm actually familiar with you, Commander. I am—rather, I used to be—the chief security officer for the Dresden orbital. We never personally met, but I have reviewed your file. I'm surprised to see you here."

"I'm not even sure where here is, Commander. My crew and I have been prisoners aboard this ship for three weeks. Are we at Dresden?"

"I'm not certain where we are, either," Raul said. "The only thing I can say for sure is that I don't believe we need to be so formal with one another. We're both prisoners together, you and I. Call me Raul. May I call you Veronica?"

"I suppose so."

The same man who'd taken his order stepped up to the table and offered Veronica a menu. She shook her head. "I'll take what he's having."

Once the server had departed, she stared at Raul. "How did they get you? Were you traveling on some ship they ambushed? They seem to be quite good at ambushes."

He gave her a wan smile. "On that point, I believe we agree. No. They captured the orbital entirely. Then they proceeded to steal it. What about the task force you were with? Did they only get your ship? Were some of the others able to get away?"

Veronica stared at him, her mouth open for a moment before she snapped it shut. "You've got to be kidding me! How could they possibly steal the Dresden orbital? The system is guarded! There are battle stations at every flip point. Surely you saw them coming."

He laughed. "Yes, well, I'd imagine my next performance evaluation is going to be a trial. Probably quite literally. I'm still not certain how they managed it, but they snuck into the system without anyone being the wiser. It was as though they magically appeared on the orbital. There were marines in powered armor *everywhere*.

"We never had a chance. Once they were inside our guard, they stunned everyone with the orbital's antiboarding weapons. They took the ship we used for moving ore, modified it to hold the orbital, and somehow got away with it. I was unconscious at the time, so I'm not sure how they managed that, but they did it. What about your task force? What happened?"

Veronica sighed and sagged a little in her chair. "We made it to the target system. The one with the crazy computer. Commodore Wilson split the task force and led the smaller portion to ambush the computer. Commodore Crabtree—his deputy—led the larger portion to take the system next door. My ship was with the latter group.

"Only they were waiting for us. They took out the pickets we left behind to keep the exit open, and then ships inside the computer's system jumped the freighter and its escort. Commodore Wilson went after them, but they took him out."

She rubbed her forehead. "I didn't see it happen. Commodore Crabtree pushed forward and flipped into the other system. They were supposed to be primitive, relatively speaking. Only they weren't. They had a fleet bigger than ours waiting on the other side. Huge ships. Modern ships. A lot of them.

"They had old battle stations guarding the flip point that absorbed our initial fire. I think they were decoys. Only two light cruisers and six destroyers made it back out."

He let that sink in. "I see. And what did you find when you got back to the computer's system?"

"They destroyed Commodore Wilson's section of the task force. They were waiting for us too. Commodore Crabtree died during the assault on that third system. The two remaining light cruisers died trying to take out this carrier.

"All six of the destroyers that were left were damaged and obviously outclassed. When they offered to accept our surrender, I gave in. As a security officer, that's probably not what you wanted to hear."

He allowed himself to shrug. "I'm not precisely in a position to judge. Only six destroyers survived? That's terrible. You mentioned other ships. How many and of what classes?"

"They had a fifty percent numerical advantage," the woman said, pain written across her face. "They also had a number of significantly larger ships. Not only heavy cruisers, but also things they call battlecruisers and two monster ships the same size as this carrier they called superdreadnoughts. We never stood a chance."

Raul leaned back in his chair masking his shock. The carrier had been a terrible surprise to him, but this news undercut everything he thought he knew. He'd been toying with the idea that his captors were lying to him. Now he could no longer afford to delude himself.

If they possessed fleets of that caliber—ones they hadn't felt the need to use at Dresden—then their story must be true. Some version of it anyway. They must actually be a splinter group of the old dictatorship that escaped the rebellion.

The Empire was in serious trouble. He wasn't sure what he could do, but he had to come up with some kind of plan. He couldn't just sit back and let them get away with this.

The classified research they'd stolen not only helped them, but its loss hurt the Empire. As far as Raul knew, Dresden was the only place that manufactured Raider implants. Those would be terrible in battle.

Worse yet, while other locations were probably able to produce the hardware required by the lords, allowing lackeys of the dictatorship to build lords of their own would be a catastrophe.

He leaned forward. "This is shocking, terrible news. I'm afraid that I'm going to add to your sorrows."

Raul proceeded to tell her about some of the things the enemy had stolen with the Dresden orbital. With any luck, the two of them could come up with some kind of plan to turn the situation around.

Considering how isolated they were, that seemed unlikely, but he had a duty to try.

14

Kelsey rapped her knuckles on the briefing room table. "If I could have your attention, we need to get this show on the road."

She'd gathered all her top people to get an update on the various threads they were each working on. They'd been in this new system for a full day now.

"Zia, what's the status of the prisoners?" she asked.

"The ones on the orbital or the ones on the planetary surface?"

Kelsey grimaced. "Let's stick with the ones that we brought to the party."

Their surveys had located dozens of farming and ranching villages. Based on the testimony of the one man they'd brought up from the surface, everyone below was likely to be either someone from the higher orders of the Rebel Empire or descended from them.

These ghosts—whoever they were—occasionally dropped off new people, but mostly left the prisoners to whatever lives they could build for themselves. Not exactly kind considering the climate, but not brutal, either.

They'd finally pinned the planet's orbit down. It was deep winter for the inhabitants now, but it appeared that everything would warm up to an acceptable level for summer. So, as long as they didn't leave the equator, existence wouldn't be overly harsh.

"We finished going through everyone and getting names," Zia said. "We've isolated the purely civilian side from the Fleet crewmen and officers. The vast majority of them are still on board the orbital, and there's no way to change that. We don't have the space to house them anywhere else."

There had been over ten thousand people on the orbital when they'd captured it. She really needed to come up with something else very soon.

Just guarding the various areas were straining their manpower to the very limit.

"I've been thinking about that," Kelsey said. "I think we need to tear out every bit of equipment that we're interested in and turn them loose."

Brandon Levy looked skeptical. "With that many people together, they're going to come up with some kind of mischief to get into. Is that really what we want?"

"Do we have a choice? How long are we going to drag them with us? Once we take the manufacturing equipment and the research computers off the orbital, we don't need it anymore."

"So, you're just planning on leaving it here?" Annette Vitter asked. "Isn't that just asking for trouble? If they get back through the weak flip point, then the Rebel Empire will know all about the hole in their maps. That would be a disaster."

"So, let's tear out all the manufacturing capability," Carl said. "If they have no way to build a flip drive, it doesn't matter what they do."

"That's too risky," Zia said. "People are more resourceful than you give them credit for. Maybe somebody on the planet's surface used to be a whiz at manufacturing or is a flip drive physicist. We can't know what would happen, other than to say the chances would be unacceptably high."

Kelsey sighed. "You're probably right. All it would take is them cobbling together some type of probe with a makeshift flip drive. I guess that's off the table."

"Maybe not," Carl said. "To build a flip drive requires several extremely rare and hard to refine elements. That's what kept us on Avalon for so long. Yes, I understand that we didn't know how to build one, but the refining process took decades to perfect once we actually located enough of the exotic elements.

"Pentagar had knowledge of how to build flip drives, but because their system didn't have any of these elements, they were trapped. Basically, it doesn't matter what these people know if we can keep them from accessing any of those exotic elements."

"That's all fine and good," Kelsey said, "but you haven't said whether or not those elements are present here. Are they?"

He shrugged. "We'd have to look a lot harder—and in many more places—for me to answer that question. I think the takeaway from this should be that we could make it impossible for them to build a flip drive.

"There's a lot of similarity in how they build the AI computer systems. The basic manufacturing gear that they have outside of the research facility just isn't capable of performing the tasks required."

Zia slowly nodded. "Add in the fact that they don't even have detectors to find the weak flip points, and that should keep them pretty well pinned down for a long time. Besides, somebody else is responsible for the people in this system. They'll be back long before the new guys figure out a way to escape."

Kelsey wasn't convinced. "I'm going to have to think on that for a while. It might be better to shuttle them down to the surface. We can move some limited manufacturing capability down and allow them to build a higher tech civilization without giving them access to a space-based platform."

She looked over at Annette. "What about the research scientists? How goes the process of making friends?"

"Exceedingly well. Now that we've disabled the explosives in their heads, they've become a very friendly bunch. *Very* helpful. I have a list of all the research projects they were working on and access to their files.

"Unlike the two manufacturing units, the chief researcher has access to her people's computers. We've already copied all the files. Of course, I'm not a scientist, so I have no idea how useful it's going to be, but it sounds promising. Virtually everything is aimed toward some kind of improvement on Fleet vessels and weapons."

"I've glanced over some of it, and I think a number of items are revolutionary," Carl said. "They were working on upgraded computers for the missile systems. The potential increase in targeting ability and range are going to be more shocking to us than the Old Empire missiles were to our compatriots back on Avalon."

"That's quite a statement," Kelsey said. "I look forward to hearing about it."

"One other thing," Annette said. "I found out what happened to the children from Erorsi. The Rebel Empire brought them to Dresden, and they became researchers."

Kelsey blinked. "You're telling me that the scientists here are all kids taken from the Pale Ones? That's amazing."

"I couldn't agree more," Annette said. "I haven't told them all the details, yet. I figured there'd always be time to have that conversation when you decided the time was right."

"Excellent. I think that can wait until we get the hell out of here. Speaking of getting out of here, what's the status on your research, Carl?"

"I've already begun modifying some of our probes. The frequency tuner that I'm installing onto their flip drives should restrict the power output to ranges similar to what that liner used.

"I suggest that we send one of *Persephone*'s stealthed probes back to the system that we came from before we test these. There's always a possibility that one of them will flip into that first system, and if the drive malfunctions, it might be detectable by ships there. So, let's be sure no one is home before we start playing around with this."

"Agreed," Kelsey said. "We'll wait until we're certain the other system is empty before we test any of your prototypes. Let's set this up for tomorrow morning. Can you be ready by then?"

"Absolutely."

Kelsey turned her attention to Brandon. "I have a few questions for you. First up, have you located who helped my mother?"

One side of his mouth quirked up. "They weren't nearly as clever as they'd thought they were. Once I identified who was bringing her food, it was child's play to get them to turn on one another.

"It seems that there were four of them. Someone in Fleet Personnel convinced them that he could give them orders to do this. I'd imagine Admiral Yeats will strenuously disagree once we get home."

"What's going to happen to them?" Kelsey asked.

"While I could bring them up on charges, I've decided to handle it administratively. I figure a year or two of scut work will satisfy me."

Kelsey laughed. "Perfect. The other question is about Commander Giguere. I understand that you've been trying to ease her into the mindset that the AIs lied to them. How's that going?"

He shrugged. "She's fairly closed-mouthed. All I've heard her express is skepticism. As I recall, you said it took months for Commander Richards to come around. I don't think we'll benefit by rushing this situation, either.

"There has been one interesting development. She's linked up with Commander Castille from the Dresden orbital. They've had their heads down over lunch for almost two hours now."

Annette chuckled. "Man, I'd love to listen in on that conversation. That guy is devious. I'm not sure that allowing them to mingle is going to help our cause."

"Probably not," Brandon agreed. "It might convince him that we're telling the truth, though."

"Come again? He's a hard-core Rebel Empire officer. What makes you think he's susceptible to being turned?"

"I'm not certain that he'll be turned into a supporter. More like a believer. Even if we convince him that he's been lied to his entire life, he has a lot invested in their system. He might just continue supporting it. In any case, the discussions will be fascinating."

Zia sighed. "This is all getting very convoluted. Let's say that we do leave the majority of our prisoners here. Who are we keeping with us and why?"

"We need to keep the researchers," Kelsey said. "We also need to have the top management people from the orbital, both civilian and Fleet. All of them might have useful information. Given enough time, some of them will come over to our side.

"Here's what I think we'll do. We need to strip out the equipment and computers we intend to take with us when we leave. Then we can pick an area down below and start setting up housing for the prisoners. We can turn construction over to them.

"Considering that everyone else here has been getting by with only primitive tools, these folks should be able to make perfectly serviceable and comfortable housing. They could then trade those skills with the other prisoners to get food and knowledge. The technology would spread to the other villages eventually. A win-win situation."

Carl stared off into space. "It will take us a couple of days to strip the orbital of all the useful equipment. Moving the manufacturing gear is going to be the most time-consuming. Then we have to parse out what equipment is acceptable to move to the planet's surface. That'll take longer."

"Indeed, it will," Zia agreed. "Transporting that many people is going to take a while. I figure at least a week."

"Then we'd best get started," Kelsey said. "Round up some of the civilians that have the most construction experience and take them down to select their new home. Get them started building the initial shelters.

"I want to keep their population sizes similar to what we're seeing now. Spread them out. Separate the Fleet people from the rest. I'd imagine the Fleet personnel will still manage to dominate them in the end, but that's not our problem.

"I want to complete the relocation of prisoners and stripping the orbital within seven days. That might be tight, but let's try to make it happen."

Once she saw the agreement in everyone's eyes, Kelsey stood slowly. "When we find a way out of the system, we'll drop the orbital into the sun. That'll keep anyone here from being able to use it, even if they eventually get off the planet's surface."

"I think that's a bad idea," Zia said. "Why don't you save it as a bargaining chip? Once we finally locate these ghosts, I'd imagine they might be able to find a use for an orbital like that and a ship to move it around. We're going to need to build some goodwill."

Kelsey considered that and slowly nodded. "Okay. Once we've stripped it clean of things we're taking with us, we'll relocate it into the outer system. That way they can't just come back here and locate it while we're out searching for them. Keep me informed about all these projects. Dismissed."

15

The next morning Annette stopped by Carl Owlet's lab just after breakfast. She found the young scientist already hard at work.

From all appearances, he and his people had disassembled the flip drive that they'd found on the disabled liner. It lay scattered across several tables with the remainder sitting in a pile at the rear bulkhead.

She'd brought Jacqueline Parker with her so that the two could become acquainted. The woman looked around the lab curiously.

"What are you researching here?"

Annette smiled. "We'll get to that. First, I want you to meet someone."

She led the woman over to where Carl was furiously typing on a keyboard, hunched over a large monitor. She cleared her throat. "Good morning, Carl."

The young man looked up, apparently startled by her voice. He rose to his feet. "Sorry. I didn't hear you come in."

Annette wasn't surprised. By all accounts, the scientist was very single-minded.

"Carl Owlet, allow me to introduce Jacqueline Parker. Jacqueline is the lead researcher from the Dresden orbital. Jacqueline, Carl is our senior researcher."

The woman looked a little skeptical. "Forgive me, but you seem a little young for the lead position."

Carl smiled. "I get that a lot. Frankly, I'd be a lot more comfortable with someone else in charge too. For some reason, they've decided that I'm the best guy they're going to get for this position. Particularly on this mission."

"Don't let him fool you," Annette said. "This is the same man who discovered and perfected faster-than-light communication."

Jacqueline's eyes widened. "That's impossible. Nothing goes faster than the speed of light."

Carl gave Annette a look. "Isn't that supposed to be classified?"

"Actually, I've already spoken with Princess Kelsey and Commodore Anderson. Jacqueline and her people were prisoners on the orbital, forced to work against their will. They've cooperated fully with us, and the computer is satisfied that she is a free agent willing to work with us.

"In fact, I would suggest that she and her research team might be of great use to you in figuring out our current problem. Nothing against your assistants, but we didn't bring a large scientific contingent along with us on this mission. You can use all the help you can get."

She turned to Jacqueline. "I wouldn't let his youth lull you into a false sense of who he is. He's very humble, so he'd probably never tell you this, but he won the Terran Empire's highest award for scientific achievement: the Lucien Prize. The emperor knighted him for his contributions to science."

The older woman searched her face for a moment, as though she were trying to determine if Annette was pulling a prank on her. "Well, if you say he's done all this, then I suppose I best learn a little bit more about him."

The woman focused her attention on Carl. "Faster-than-light communication? Exactly how does that work?"

Carl stood. "Basically, the communication device uses entangled photons in large numbers to transmit information from one place to another. That unfortunately means that the units are paired.

"That results in information passed from one unit to another at faster-than-light speed, regardless of the distance between them. In fact, the effect works through a flip point.

"Not more than one hop, but once is enough. That means we can place units on either side of the flip point and get real-time information sent from one to the other without a vessel having to traverse the flip point."

Jacqueline looked skeptical. "You're talking about Einstein's theory, right? Spooky action at a distance? You've actually managed to build hardware that utilizes this principle reliably?"

"I have," the young scientist said. "When I have time, I intend to work on FTL buoys we can sit at flip points scattered throughout the Empire. They'd be linked with ones on the other side of flip points, with main worlds in the system, and any Fleet installations.

"If it works as I hope, someone on one side of the Empire could send a message from their world to the flip-point buoy, which would then retransmit it through the flip point and across to any destination. If it were a multisystem jump, one buoy would communicate across to another buoy that would then send the information along.

"Theoretically, a person on one side of the Empire could send a message to a friend on the other side with a transmission delay measured in minutes.

"It would depend on the load of the buoy. If no one else was using it, or if its processing power was strong enough, the actual transmission of a single message could span the distance in less than a minute."

Silence reigned for a moment. "I want to see this."

"We're not in a position to devote the resources to that research right now," Annette said. "We've got higher-priority work that has to be done first. That's why I brought you down to meet Carl. Or perhaps I should say, Sir Carl. The emperor did knight the man, after all."

Jacqueline considered them both. "Okay, I'll bite. What projects are you working on now, if I can ask? How could my people or I help you? Does it revolve around some of the research we were doing at Dresden?"

Carl shook his head. "It doesn't. While all the work you've done appears fascinating, this revolves around flip-point physics. Have they explained to you where we are or how we got here?"

"No."

"You might as well pull up a chair. This is going to take a while."

Once the women had seated themselves, he continued. "One of the first things that we discovered when we explored the old Empire was that there was a different kind of flip point. One that was extremely difficult to detect but led to places that we'd never visited before.

"We've utilized one of them to get to a place that is safe for the moment. However, we believe that these new flip points have a special property that potentially allows for transit to multiple destinations, depending on the specific frequency of the output."

He gestured toward the disassembled parts. "Someone utilized this flip drive to do exactly that. We have to figure out how they did it and where they went from here."

"I'm not a flip-point physicist, but what you're saying is impossible."

Carl grinned. "Not really. In fact, we're going to send some probes through to verify the theory very shortly. Let me explain this in more detail. Get ready to have your mind blown."

Annette sat back and listened as he began explaining the physics behind the weak flip points to the disbelieving scientist. While much of the explanation was going to fly far over her head, she was pleased to see that the two were already working together. This was going to work out.

* * *

TALBOT ESCORTED a civilian survey team from the Dresden orbital down to the surface of the planet. To keep things simple, he chose a large island a good distance from where the other prisoners lived. Perhaps "prisoners" was the wrong term. "Unwilling colonists" might be more appropriate.

Since he was feeling a bit puckish, he dubbed the island Atlantis. After all, it was going to be the home of the high-tech civilization among the primitives.

The civilians doing the survey were a surly lot. He couldn't blame them.

They were completely uprooting these people and stranding them on an unknown world. Likely for the rest of their lives.

Considering what the Rebel Empire stood for, his sympathy was limited. If his side won this war, they'd come back and relocate these people. If they didn't win, well, at least they'd survive.

Once he had the construction people surveying the island to find a location for their new home, he set out to get detailed scans of the entire island and its surroundings. He'd chosen a large harbor as the primary city location for Atlantis. That way, when they built oceangoing vessels, it would be handy.

Commodore Anderson had ordered him to get decent scans of every island within striking distance of Atlantis. Other teams were busy scanning all the other potentially habitable landmasses. They wanted to be sure that they knew the location of every single group of colonists. It wouldn't do to have some folks isolated and left to suffer.

It only took a few hours for something to pop up as unusual. They were flying over a moderately sized landmass centered on an extinct or dormant volcano when the scanners read something artificial. This place was far away from where any other colonists had been located, so he was curious.

Talbot ordered the pilot to bring them around for a closer pass. The target was camouflaged fairly well.

Sitting along the western side of the island were the remains of a moderately large town. The vegetation had encroached completely into the area, making it look like a wilderness. He could see why he hadn't seen it from orbit.

He zoomed the scanner in and examined one of the buildings. It was roughly done, but obviously made of modern materials. Imperial materials. The style was also one he was moderately familiar with from his time on Harrison's World. He'd seen similar structures when visiting some of the small towns.

"Find us a good place to land near that town," Talbot instructed the pilot.

"Aye, sir."

The cutter pilot brought them down into a clearing about half a kilometer away from the ruined town.

Talbot knew that he should probably let someone know where he was going, but he wanted to take a good look at the place first. No one had occupied this place for a very long time, so it should be relatively safe.

He dug out some unpowered armor from one of the storage bins and verified that he had plenty of flechettes for the pistol he always carried. Just to be safe, he grabbed the flechette rifle kept with the armor. He doubted there were any wild animals that could hurt him, based on their previous scans of the planet, but he'd play it safe.

"Take the cutter back up over the town and circle around," he told the pilot. "I'll stay in communication with you every ten minutes. If you can't get ahold of me, call for backup."

He exited the cutter and headed toward the town. The vegetation he was crossing through was very similar to what he'd found on the other islands. All of the separate landmasses must've been connected at one point. Everything was too homogenous to have developed separately.

With the rough terrain, it took him about twenty minutes to get to the outskirts of the town. Some buildings were made of plascrete, though roughly done. Barring serious damage, they'd last a long, long time.

Not all the buildings around him were that sturdy, though. Many of them were made of local materials and had collapsed. He could see trees growing out of what had once been buildings made of wood or stone.

Talbot resisted the urge to go inside any of them. He'd save that for the larger ones near the center of town.

Large was a relative term. The tallest structure looked to be about eight or nine stories. Maybe ten, at most. It was also made of plascrete, but someone had taken the time to make it actually look good.

Even after all this time, the walls were still bright white, and he could see inlaid pieces in the plascrete that gave it darker accents. It looked very sleek and completely out of place in this wilderness.

The doors leading into the front of the building were closed but not locked. With his pistol in hand, he cautiously went inside. The bottom floor appeared to be mainly a large lobby. A wide desk with places for half a dozen people stood in front of the bank of elevators.

The wall behind the desk had the Fleet emblem across its entire width, with the almost-unnecessary words below it: Fleet Headquarters.

It seems he'd found where the ghosts had set up shop after they'd fled through the weak flip point.

16

Raul Castille looked around to see if anyone was sitting close enough to overhear what he was about to say to Veronica. Realistically, he knew that the enemy could be monitoring them closely, but the other diners were making enough noise to perhaps shield what he was about to say.

"I think I've come up with an escape plan."

She raised an eyebrow. "Where would we go? Are you planning to steal one of the flip-capable warships? That seems a little bit of a stretch."

"No. I'm smart enough to realize we don't have the manpower or access for something like that. I'm talking about hiding until these people are gone. They're not going to stay here in this system forever. Once they've left, the Empire will eventually come and find us."

The woman gave him a look that said she was not convinced. "I'm not sure that's the best idea. In fact, I'm not sure of anything at this point."

He frowned. "What does that mean?"

She gestured at the people around them. "My people and I have been doing research on what they say happened during the revolution. I went into that project with the full expectation that we'd quickly find the forgeries. Now, I'm not so sure."

"Of course they're feeding us lies," he said derisively. "You can't possibly believe that fiction they're spouting. That the lords have enslaved us? You are a Fleet officer. You should know better."

"We've done a lot of reading," she said quietly. "Their library of books is quite extensive. I'm talking exabytes of data. It can't all be faked. Looking back at the time of the revolution, none of what they have indicates anything like what they taught us in history class."

Raul rubbed his forehead. "I can't believe we're even having this conversation. How could you possibly believe anything you're reading?"

She shrugged. "One of my officers picked a few books that he'd read before. Heirlooms handed down through his family since the revolution. Actual, physical books.

"He was only passingly familiar with a few of them, but some he knew by heart. There's no way these people could know which books to leave in the same condition as what my officer had read. None."

"And you're saying that these books your officer knew were precisely as he remembered? Please. No one has that good of a memory."

"His memory is pretty good. If he says that he can't find anything in that particular volume that looks different, I believe him. If one book is accurate, I have to wonder how many others are."

He shook his head strongly. "That kind of talk is treason. I suggest for your own well-being that you reconsider what you're saying."

"Don't be an idiot. I'm not disloyal to the Empire. The problem is that I'm not a rubber-stamping yes woman, either. If we ever hope to understand who these people really are, we have to understand our own history, and we need to be sure that it's true. At this point, I'm not convinced it is."

He stared at her coolly. "So you're saying that you have no intention of trying to escape with me?"

"That's not what I'm saying at all. We have a duty to escape. If you have a plan with a reasonable chance of success, I'll do whatever I can to make it happen."

He relaxed a little. He hadn't realized he'd tensed up. "Good. Good. I've overheard a number of people talking about the planet we're orbiting. Apparently, it's where the ghosts have been keeping the people they've captured during their raids. Mostly the higher orders.

"They've also located the island used by the ghosts before they departed this world. Details are sketchy about both groups, but if we can escape to the surface of the planet, we can hide among the people that are already down there. They will help us.

"Eventually, someone will come looking. When that happens, we can all get off this planet and take the knowledge we've gained with us. The lords need to know what we've found out about these people."

Her eyes turned toward the guards leaning against the wall. "How do you intend to get past our armed watchers?"

He smiled. "That's all a matter of timing. You see, my guards keep watch on me, and your guards keep watch on you. They're not working as a concerted whole, but as two separate entities. We can use that lack of communication to our advantage."

"Sounds tricky. As soon as we attack, alarms will go off throughout the ship. How are we going to get to the docking bay, steal a cutter, dodge the fighters these people have, and land on a planet without them knowing where we've gone?"

"That sounds like defeatism. You need to trust that we're going to have some luck fall our way."

She grunted. "The problem with luck is that it comes in two flavors: good and bad. I'm certain we're going to have some kind of luck. I just suspect some of it is not going to be the kind we want. How do you want to do this?"

"Here's what I have in mind..."

* * *

KELSEY LOOKED around the massive lobby with amazement. "How in the world did people running for their lives build something like this?"

Talbot shrugged. "I have no idea. They had the liner with them, so they might have had some skilled construction people they could tap. Maybe even some equipment. Or they could have built this place a hundred years later.

"I've had my people sweep the building from top to bottom. The previous occupants stripped all the computers out. We haven't found a single electronic device of any kind. Nothing with any writing at all. Someone scrubbed this building."

"Surely they couldn't have done that to the whole town."

"You might be surprised. We selected a few buildings at random and turned up very similar results. The town appears as though they abandoned it in a very orderly fashion.

"They swept it from one end to the other looking for anything they'd missed. If it were me, I'd have had multiple teams. One group to sweep behind the first. Perhaps even a third."

"It's not very helpful," she said sourly. "This is obviously where the survivors from Fleet set up shop. The thing is, I'm not really sure why. They had their ships. They're obviously using them to harass the Rebel Empire. This world is okay, but why pick it?"

"I'm going to bet it took time for them to figure out how to use the weak flip points," Talbot said. "If they didn't have someone like Carl along, it might have taken them years to grasp what they were dealing with. Fleet engineers are pretty bright people, but there are limits to what they can do.

"If I had to wager a guess, they used the liner to test out their first-generation flip modulator. It failed spectacularly. That would make them slow down."

That made sense. If they didn't have someone to work out the theory, it might have taken them decades to work it out. That more than explained the town they were standing in.

"Well, we need to be thorough," she said. "I want you and your people to search every building that seems safe to enter. Leave no stone unturned. Pick a few that aren't safe and see about having the engineers help move the rubble. Perhaps something was left there."

"I'm not holding out too much hope," he said. "These people were pretty damned thorough."

Once he'd left, Kelsey stared up at the Fleet emblem on the wall. What must it have been like for those people? They'd obviously fled during the height of the rebellion. This place must've seemed like a godsend. No pursuit and a chance to live out their lives in peace.

But at some point, they'd made the discovery they could use the weak flip point to travel to other systems. Ones not occupied by the Rebel Empire.

They'd relocated. From the rumors that she'd heard, these people attacked the Rebel Empire where they could and then vanished as if they had never been.

It had to drive the AIs nuts.

They'd undoubtedly lost ships along the way. They'd probably never had very many to begin with. If she had to guess, the ghosts probably came from a single task group assigned to escort the liner, and perhaps a few other vessels they'd picked up along the way.

She imagined that the discovery of multiple destinations through the weak flip points had inspired them to move on and then to use them to attack their enemies. Guerrilla warfare.

Now they lurked in the dark, striking out at their enemies from the shadows, and then vanishing without a trace. No wonder the Rebel Empire called them ghosts. The supernatural overtones were almost inevitable.

It fell to her and her people to find out where these descendants of loyalists lived now. They'd obviously decided to use the first world they'd discovered to house the prisoners they'd captured. The ones they didn't like anyway. That meant they'd found more desirable worlds that they lived on now.

They took the lower orders elsewhere. Hypothetically, there were probably several other strata to the society that had formed around these ghosts.

Based on this building, Fleet service might be one of them. Certainly, it had to be important to them. Even more important than it had been for the Old Empire. Fleet was all that stood between them and death.

Kelsey sighed. This wasn't getting them any closer to solving the mysteries. If they were going to find a way to track these ghosts, then it was going to fall to Carl and his people. There were obviously more destinations to be discovered using the weak flip point. Her friend just needed to find them.

She supposed she needed to stop using the phrase "weak flip point." Carl had been tossing around a new name. Multiflip point. That was a hell of a lot more descriptive, so it was time for her to endorse its use. She'd spread the word once she got back into orbit.

Finding this town had excited her so much. She'd figured that they could finally get answers to some of her questions. Yet the people they were following had proved cautious and thorough. It was going to take a lot more work to track them down.

Once she did, then the delicate dance would begin. These people had no reason to trust anyone. They'd been at war for five hundred years. It would be all too easy for them to assume that her task group was a Rebel Empire unit and attack.

Whenever they found these people, she was going to need to proceed very, *very* carefully. They needed allies, not more enemies.

These ghosts had absolutely no reason to trust her people. She needed to come up with a reason why they should. So far, that had eluded her.

After taking one last look at the wall, Kelsey headed toward her cutter. It was time to get back to work.

17

Even after thinking about Castille's plan overnight, Veronica still thought he was insane, but she really didn't have a choice. He was a security officer. If she didn't follow his instructions, the end result would not be pretty. Once the lords found them again—which they would—it would be the end of her. Perhaps literally.

Timing was going to be key in making this work. If the two of them were not precisely where they needed to be at exactly the right moment, it couldn't happen.

Thankfully, cranial implants made keeping precise time a simple task. She gathered her officers and informed their guards they were going to eat lunch as a group.

Even with the larger number of prisoners, the two guards still felt they had control of the situation with their stunners. They followed along somewhat behind Veronica and her officers to keep them at a safe distance.

On a ship of this size, with as many people as were around them, that would normally be perfectly adequate. Unfortunately for them, Raul Castille had taken this behavior into account. At a predetermined cross corridor, he stepped out at just the right moment to surprise her guards.

She had to admit he made quick work of them. They had no chance to stop his explosive attack.

Not that she had time to watch. She whirled and threw herself at his guards. All of her hand-to-hand training came to her rescue with a spinning back kick that caught one of them in the head. He dropped without a sound.

Two of her officers took out the final man just as quickly.

Veronica expected the overhead alarms to begin screaming, but they were silent. The guards had not gotten an alert out before they'd gone down. That was an unexpected bit of good luck. The original plan had called for them to retreat as quickly as possible while the ship searched for them.

Castille shot all four men with the stunner he'd appropriated. They quickly stashed the unconscious marines in a handy compartment. He'd chosen a section of the ship with less traffic, and fortune had favored them with no inconvenient witnesses.

"Where is the Commodore?" she asked.

"She won't be joining us. She and the rest of the orbital staff will be staying here. Don't worry. They'll keep their mouths shut."

That might mean a number of different things. Veronica hoped it was just mulishness on the commodore's part and not something more sinister.

Still, she had to admit that she felt some relief at avoiding close quarters with the obnoxious woman. A single visit had convinced her that she wanted nothing to do with Murdock.

Since they all wore Fleet uniforms, no one raised an eyebrow as they headed for the landing bay. She could only barely suppress her paranoia. Everyone they passed seemed to be staring at them.

Castille stepped next to her. "That went well."

"Better than I'd expected," she admitted. "I hope we're able to appropriate a cutter before they discover we've escaped."

"Me too," he admitted. "From everything I've heard they're busy exploring the planet below us. There are a number of cutters going up and down. We should be able to insert ourselves into the traffic without too much trouble."

"I love your confidence."

Unfortunately, she didn't share it. The odds of them being able to hijack a cutter without the pilot giving an alarm were low. In that case, they'd have to make a run for it anyway, but they'd have other ships in pursuit. There would be no chance to hide themselves on the planet's surface.

The landing bay was just as large as she'd remembered. It obviously serviced a lot of small craft.

It only took a moment to pick out a cutter that was just coming in for a landing near them. She gestured for the pilot to open the boarding ramp as he settled down, and he nodded.

She led her people up the ramp as if she belonged there. Two marines stood in the center of the cutter, bracketing a well-dressed woman. Based upon the restraints, she was a prisoner.

Interestingly, Veronica didn't detect cranial implants in the woman. She was obviously of the lower orders. Why was she here? What did she know?

One of the marines pushed the woman a step forward. "We'll turn her over to you, Commander."

"Yes, you will." She shot him with her stunner.

Her executive officer took out his partner before the first man even finished collapsing.

The woman opened her mouth to say something, but Veronica shot her too.

Castille sprinted toward the cockpit and stunned the pilot. A quick search of the cutter verified that no one else was aboard.

Veronica stepped back out to the cutter and looked around. No one seemed to be paying any attention to them. Excellent.

She made her way to the cockpit as they secured the prisoners and closed the cutter up. A query of her implants revealed the cutter wasn't locked.

"It's not secured," she said through the open hatch. "The good luck just keeps coming. I've accessed the communications log. I have their call sign."

With a deep breath, she initiated communications with flight control.

"Control, this is foxtrot seven five two requesting departure."

"Stand by, foxtrot seven five two."

For a moment, she worried the man had realized it wasn't the same person speaking to him. Then he continued. "You are cleared for outbound departure, foxtrot seven five two."

"Copy that. Thank you, Control."

She deftly lifted the cutter off the deck and turned it toward the exit. A gentle application of acceleration slid them smoothly outside of the ship. They were in space.

Other cutters were moving back and forth between the ships and the planet. It seemed that their destination was on the other side of the planet. That was good enough for her. She fell in behind one of the other cutters and followed it around.

Many of the cutters headed toward a series of islands, but she saw one rising from a much larger island that was significantly farther away from the first cluster. Perfect.

Based on the level of traffic, that other location would be a much better hiding place. It also had a large volcano near the center of the island. It must've been inactive, because there was a large lake filling it.

Even better.

Once the cutter she'd seen departing the island was out of scanner range, she changed course and darted toward the volcano.

It had experienced a significant eruption at some point in the distant past. One side of the caldera had blown out. The lake that filled the interior came up right to the edge.

Her scanners couldn't detect how deep the water was, but that was kind of the point. Once she submerged, no one would find them that easily. They could hide out at the bottom and wait for their enemies to depart.

The interior of the volcano was interesting. It seemed as though they were not the only visitors. Someone had taken the time to carve a deep ledge at the base of the caldera near the water line.

With the missing side, the water would never rise high enough to flood it. Interestingly, the pocket was deep enough to land a cutter in. With all the stone all around it, no external signals would be able to reach the cutter.

That meant their enemies would be unable to detect or control the cutter remotely. It only took a moment for her to make the decision to change their course.

She brought the cutter inside the large landing area—for that was exactly what it appeared to be—and settled on the flat stone.

She shut down the cutter's systems and ordered her officers to locate and disconnect the power supplies from all systems. That way no signals would go out, and it wouldn't respond to remote commands.

The ramp lowered. A minute later, the consoles went dark. They were safe.

She smiled at Castille as she came into the back. "I didn't think we'd pull it off. Congratulations. Your plan was brilliant."

He grinned back at her. "I wish I could say that I hadn't had my own doubts, but I'd be lying. What is this place?"

Veronica shrugged. "The only way to know for sure is to go take a look. Our guests will be out for a few more hours."

To say the interior of the landing area was gloomy would be something of an understatement. The reflected sunlight cast some illumination inside the hollowed-out landing area, but not nearly enough to see much detail.

She searched the compartments inside the cutter until she found a stash of handheld lights. Once everyone had taken one for themselves, she stepped out onto the landing pad.

It was obviously man-made. The stone was far too smooth to be natural. The scuff marks indicated other vessels had landed here in the past.

The rear of the landing area had a standard Imperial hatch imbedded in the wall. The mystery deepened. What the hell was this place?

* * *

"WHAT DO you mean they've escaped?" Talbot demanded.

He'd barely had time to step on board *Audacious* to brief the commodore when the marine acting as the head of the carrier's security element cornered him.

Lieutenant Yvonne Gutierrez shrank a little. "We don't know yet, Major. Their guards went to relieve the duty marines and couldn't find them. An implant search led to a compartment near the officers' mess. We're searching the ship. We'll find them."

The woman took a deep breath. "They didn't all escape. Commander Castille killed the senior staff from the orbital. Commodore Murdock was the only survivor. He broke her neck, but she was still alive.

"I called an emergency medical team, and they managed to resuscitate her. No word on if she'll make it, but someone wanted them all dead."

He resisted the impulse to curse. It wouldn't help. No matter how good it might feel. "I want to know the moment you find them. Get more marines to the flight deck too."

"Aye, sir."

He headed for the lift. This was just terrific. How in the world had they managed to turn the tables on their guards?

There'd been a risk of trouble when they'd agreed to allow them to access to the ship. Never in his wildest dreams had he envisioned them actually escaping.

He sighed. Well, there was no getting around it. He needed to explain this to the commodore.

Minutes later, he arrived to find the flag bridge in a state of almost chaos. Zia turned to him. "Do we know what happened?"

"Not precisely. It seems they overpowered all four guards without an alarm getting out."

Commodore Anderson said something not suitable for a senior officer. "I'm looking at the flight logs now. We've had a lot of cutters land and take off. With ferrying people away from the Dresden orbital, a lot of boats stop here to pick up things to take down to the surface."

One of her officers raised his head. "Ma'am, I've identified a cutter than never returned to base. It's not answering any of our calls, and I'm not getting a transponder ping."

Talbot checked the information through his implants. "It looks like the cutter came from *Persephone*."

The commodore frowned. "What the heck would they be doing here? I'll ping them."

After a few moments, her face paled. "Oh crap. They were bringing Kelsey's mother. Apparently, she'd raised hell, so they were sending her over to spend a few days in a real cell."

He stared at the planet on the main display. "They have her, then. Somewhere down there. Kelsey is going to go ballistic."

"And with every reason," Zia said. "We'll get every boat we have searching for them. We'll find them."

Talbot wished he believed that, but he didn't. They'd underestimated the prisoners. Now they'd pay the price for their arrogance.

18

Kelsey stared at Zia through the communications screen on her desk. "What do you mean they've kidnapped my mother?"

Her voice was so calm that it felt as if she were watching her reaction from the sidelines.

Zia's mouth turned downward. "It seems that our prisoners came up with a grand plan to take out one another's guards. Commander Castille and Commander Giguere arrived at a certain cross corridor at the same moment. That allowed each group to attack the other's guards.

"We didn't foresee this level of coordination. We should have had more stringent monitoring and additional guards."

Kelsey let out a long, slow breath. "There'll be plenty of time to lose my temper later. How long have they been gone?"

"Over an hour. Closer to two. All indications are that they've gone to ground on the planet. The landing zones were on the other side of the planet from *Audacious*, so we didn't see precisely where they went.

"I've diverted all available cutters to begin an in-depth search. If it were me, I'd have submerged the cutter in water just off a coast. That would eliminate the possibility that our scanners would pick them up. All they have to do at this point is wait. Sooner or later, we're going to leave."

Kelsey felt her lips compress. "I'm not going anywhere without my mother. She might be a huge pain in my ass, but she's my *mother*. Deploy as many marines as you feel comfortable with down to the surface. I want every island scoured from one end to the other. Leave no cranny unexplored."

Zia nodded. "Already in progress. Kelsey, I'm really sorry."

The princess sighed. "The precautions sounded reasonable to me too. It's easy to forget that we're not the only people that can pull off miraculous escapes. They didn't hurt their guards, so it's unlikely they'll hurt my mother.

"We'll find them. It's just going to be a matter of searching for a needle in a haystack. Do the best you can and keep me informed."

"Aye, ma'am," Zia said. "*Audacious* out."

Kelsey buried her face in her hands. Oh God. How could one little woman cause her so much trouble?

Intellectually, she knew that her mother wasn't to blame for this particular incident. That didn't stop her from blaming her emotionally. That was unfair, but it was going to take Kelsey a long time before she saw her mother differently.

Her implants chimed with another incoming call. This time from Carl. She put him on the screen.

"You better not have bad news," she said bluntly.

He raised an eyebrow. "Why? Are you getting lots of bad news right now? Anything I should know about?"

"You first."

"Okay. We think we've got the flip tuner worked out. I have a prototype installed on a regular probe that we can test. If, of course, you think that's okay."

She sat up straighter. "That's good news. The probes we left in the other system say it's empty right now. How do we need to do this? How does this even work?"

The young scientist seemed to consider for a moment how to phrase his answer. "In a general sense, the flip tuner focuses the energy put out by the flip drive into a narrow band of frequencies. With a regular flip point, that's not necessary. It only has one destination.

"With a multiflip point, there are alternate paths that—supposedly—a ship can transit. We have to fine-tune where the energy resonates. The frequency of the vibration is what I believe makes one path more likely than another."

Kelsey didn't pretend to know much at all about flip-point physics. "If you say so. Are we even certain that there are multiple destinations available to us?"

Carl shrugged. "Theoretically, yes. Practically? We won't know until we find one. At this point, I have no way of scanning a multiflip point to determine how many potential destinations it has or even what frequencies would work to get us there. The science is too immature. Perhaps once we've used this one, the process will become clearer."

"We'll double check with the probes on guard in the other system first. We absolutely do not want to transit something they might detect through that flip point."

"Got it," he said. "Now, what bad news is raining on your parade?"

"The senior officers from the destroyer and Commander Castille from the orbital escaped. They're somewhere on the planet. Worse, they got their hands on my mother, two marines, and a cutter pilot."

Carl winced. "Okay, that's bad news. Do you think they're in any danger?"

"Realistically? No. Of course, all that changes if my mother won't shut up. They might just shoot her to keep her quiet."

The young man laughed a little. "They may not be our Fleet, but I think they have the restraint to avoid something like that. Particularly since they're probably worried we'll find them."

"Do you have anything in your bag of tricks that might allow us to find them more easily?"

"Nothing springs to mind, but I'll give it a little bit of thought. Also, I have one other bit of good news. The researchers that we liberated are working with me to help bypass the lockouts on the manufacturing equipment. No guarantees, but they're a pretty smart bunch. We might manage to get everything working in spite of the lockout."

"If there's anything that I can do to help, just let me know," Kelsey said. "What about an AI? Did they have enough equipment on the orbital to actually build one?"

"I sent some of the engineering people from *Audacious* to look, but they didn't find anything. Well, not AI hardware like we've seen before anyway. They did find some equipment that might be connected with the AI project, but I'm not ready to talk about it until I'm sure what I have. It might prove useful, but it might just be a curiosity too."

"Understood. Great work."

The young man smiled. "Thank you. Which ship am I going out to the flip point on? *Persephone* or *Audacious*?"

As much as she wanted to stay close by, Kelsey knew that Zia could conduct the search more effectively than she could.

"I'll take you out there. I need something to distract me. I'll call the bridge and get us moving."

Once Kelsey finished talking with him, she got the ship under way and leaned back in her chair. Why did life have to be so complicated?

* * *

Annette brought her fighter into a flat arc over the island Talbot had found. The scanners registered a number of ships and people, but tagged them all as friendlies. The missing cutter was nowhere in sight.

That meant it was either somewhere under the water or on another island entirely.

Frankly, "island" was the wrong word to use in describing this place. It might be smaller than a continent, but it was certainly larger than what she considered an island. If they had to search it closely, they'd be working for months.

The escaped prisoners had an entire planet to hide on. There was no way they were going to discover them unless they got lucky.

With a sigh, she brought up a plot of the general area and looked at how the squadron was deployed. Some of the fighters were covering other portions of the island, while the rest scanned as deeply into the water as they could, looking for any anomalies.

She made a wide circle around the volcano at the center of the island. It was a little too prominent to be the escaped prisoners' chosen hideout, but it paid to be thorough.

The scanners penetrated the rock deeply enough to be certain that it was natural stone. A few lava tubes were large enough to show up on the scans. No unusual metals.

Annette made one pass over the top of the volcano, looking down as she inverted her fighter. There was water down inside the caldera. Her scanners couldn't penetrate to the bottom. It was as impenetrable as the ocean.

She weighed the option of going down and immersing her fighter, but decided it wasn't worth it. It would take her hours to search the water inside that thing. Time better spent looking for the prisoners over a wider area.

* * *

RAUL WATCHED the fighter arc across the sky from his hiding place in a deep crevice near the excavated landing pad. Once it vanished, he waited for it to come back. If the pilot had spotted anything out of the ordinary, he'd come back for a second look.

Nothing.

He had to admit that he was surprised. Even with the positive face he put on for Commander Giguere, he'd secretly expected their enemies to recapture them quickly. This type of convenient escape only happened in fiction.

Once he'd convinced himself that they were still safe, he made his way up the crack until he could see down into the caldera from a small ledge. Whoever had built the concealed landing area had done so in a way that made it invisible from above. Based on the coating they'd found on the rock inside it, it was shielded against scanners.

Someone had wanted to be absolutely certain that no one knew about this hidden facility.

He made his way back down the crevice and to the landing area. He walked past the powered-down cutter and stopped where the rest of them had gathered next to the sealed hatch.

Lieutenant Bakersfield—Commander Giguere's engineering officer—was still working on it. Personally, he was about ready to suggest something more forceful. Living out of a cutter would be uncomfortable enough, even if it had power. Without power, it would be horrible.

"Are you certain that you're going to be able to open that hatch, Commander?" he asked politely.

The man nodded. "I've already got access to the control panel, sir. I'm just trying to figure out which sequence of codes will trigger the hatch to unlock. This isn't a very difficult entry. It really wasn't meant to keep people out."

Raul raised an eyebrow. "Truly? It seems to me that locks are made specifically for keeping people out."

"Perhaps it would be better to say that this lock is only meant to keep honest people honest. Anyone could force their way in without much difficulty. We're only working this carefully in an attempt to keep the hatch intact."

Moments later, the light above the lock turned green, and they all heard the sound of bolts retracting.

The man grinned at Raul. "See? Piece of cake."

Those of them with stunners raised them as the hatch slid open. The short corridor just inside was initially dark, but the overhead lights came on as soon as Commander Giguere stepped inside.

"It still has power," she said. "That can't be good. An operating fusion plant will lead them right to us."

Raul shook his head. "I think not. While I was outside, I saw a fighter fly overhead. If it had detected either the cutter or a fusion plant, it would've come back. Whatever is down here, it's well shielded. That makes it very interesting to me. I love secrets. Especially when they belong to other people."

The woman smiled a bit. "Then let's go see what they're hiding."

19

Kelsey watched Carl work at his borrowed console. The young scientist was always so focused. Once he'd settled in, it seemed as though he'd forgotten the rest of them were on the bridge.

He'd tried to explain some of the mathematics and flip physics to her, but she'd waved him off. She knew her limitations.

The probes they'd posted in the Rebel Empire system showed no enemy traffic. Of course, that could change at a moment's notice. She'd taken the precaution of positioning a probe on the other side of the multiflip point and two more watching that system's regular flip points.

The distant probes would send their information back to them at light speed, so it was always possible that someone would arrive in the system while they were conducting the test. That was a risk, but one they'd have to take.

This would be the perfect time to use one of Carl's FTL coms, but she still worried that a passing Rebel Empire ship would detect something. The temptation was strong, but she resisted the impulse.

She turned toward Carl. "It looks as though the system is clear. Proceed with the test."

"Yes, ma'am."

Carl manipulated his controls, and the probe she was watching through her implants vanished. It had successfully flipped, but they wouldn't know for another minute if it went to the system they knew about or somewhere completely new.

The timer counted down, and the probe reappeared on their scanners. It began streaming data immediately.

Kelsey didn't even need to wait for Carl to speak to know that his frequency tuner had worked. The system the probe had arrived in wasn't the one they'd fled through. This one was occupied.

"The probe appears to have gone to a different system," he said after a moment. "I'm detecting radio transmissions. Lots of them."

"So I see. Congratulations. What can you tell me about this new system?"

He turned in his seat to face her. "Even at a glance, it's easy to tell that it's heavily occupied. I'm detecting hundreds of grav drives moving around. There are also signals coming from multiple areas of the system as well.

"Based on this information, I believe this new system is more heavily occupied than any Rebel Empire system we've seen to date. Ma'am, I think this might be a core world."

"It's far too early to make that kind of assessment," she said. "We'll continue examining the data and allow the facts to lead us where they do. Make sure to shunt all this to operations. I want our intelligence staff combing through what you've picked up.

"A minute's worth of data isn't enough to make any kind of assessment. Was there anything close enough to the multiflip point to detect the probe?"

"No. The multiflip point is far enough off the beaten path to prevent anyone from detecting a ship flipping in. The probe is completely safe."

"It's a little early to send a ship, but that's good information to have. Get the probe back on station and have it monitor for an hour. That should give us a better baseline of how many ships are in the system, whose they are, and which system it is."

He nodded. "The system is definitely occupied by humans. The unencrypted traffic is in Standard. I may be able to identify it based on the visible stars.

"That's not something that the Old Empire needed to do, but I've made progress updating their flip charts to consider the most prominent stellar masses in our section of the explored galaxy. At the very least, I should be able to roughly place which sector the system lies in."

"Do that," she said. "Now that you've proved your theory is correct, can you tell if this is the only other possible destination?"

"Not without trying a number of additional test flips. The theory I'm working under says that energy inside a specific range should lead to a single destination. We need to determine how wide a window of energy is required for a specific branch.

"Theoretically, there could be as many as a dozen more. I suspect there will be fewer. The fact that its gravitational energy signature is so much weaker on this side indicates that it has more branches from this side than in the Rebel Empire system. Say five on this side, three on the other.

"Those are just numbers I've thrown out for comparison. I won't be able to make an educated guess of how many branches there are until I have an adequate baseline. That means we need to find more multiflip points to examine."

"I'm certain that we'll find more as we proceed, but we might not have the time to examine them as thoroughly as you'd like," Kelsey said. "Do the best you can in figuring this one out while we don't have someone breathing down our necks.

"You said you had other probes prepared. Just how long do you think it will take you to figure out how many branches this multiflip point has?"

"I'll be able to define the window of frequencies that leads to this new system inside half an hour. We might discover other destinations in the process. Once I have that information, it should only take three or four hours to probe all the potential windows.

"It's possible that some energy ranges won't actually take the probe anywhere. They might be dead zones of some kind. The theory indicates that's possible too. Also, based on the size of the window, it should allow me to determine whether or not a ship is capable of flipping to the target system."

Kelsey frowned. "I thought that once we had the ability to tune our flip drives, we would be able to pass through to any of the destinations."

He made an ambivalent gesture. "That assumes we'll be able to successfully incorporate these tuners into our flip drives. I'm extremely hesitant to recommend modifications to our existing hardware. It's just too dangerous.

"It looks as if the ghosts tried to build a tuner into the liner's flip drive. It burned out. There are significant limits to how much we can affect the frequency ranges on existing drives. The ship's overall mass plays a role too.

"Eventually, we'll be able to build new flip drives that have built-in tuners. Then we should be able to access all the possible branches in these multiflip points. Until then, our options might be limited."

She felt herself sighing. He was right. They absolutely couldn't take a chance of stranding one of their ships.

So, they'd be restricted to exploring systems that the carrier could transit to—if any. Thankfully, they didn't have to take the Dresden orbital any farther. Once they finished transferring the prisoners down to the surface, they could move it into the outer system.

"Are you going to be able to guess at the tonnage a particular destination will allow?" she asked. "Or if a ship's drive is even capable of reaching that system?"

He nodded. "*Persephone* has a very robust flip drive. While I can't say it's tunable, we can focus the output a little more tightly. That should allow her to make the flip into most of the systems on the other side of the multiflip point.

"I'm pretty sure the same is not true of *Audacious*. The more multiflip points I examine—and the more we transit—the better my future guess will be. I'll also need to attempt designing an external frequency tuner for *Audacious*. If I can, that might open up some possible destinations the carrier can reach."

"The ghosts probably had large ships. Maybe not in the same class as

Audacious, but that means it's possible. Back to work and find us a way home. We don't transit unless you find something interesting."

With the search for the escaped prisoners showing no signs of immediate success, Kelsey knew they had time to examine this multiflip point in detail. Frankly, she was looking forward to learning more about the new system. It would distract her from worrying.

* * *

"They're not on this island," Talbot told Annette. "I'd hoped it would be that easy, but we'll have to expand the search."

The two of them sat in the temporary building the marines had erected on the island. The fighter pilot rubbed her face. "This is going to give me ulcers. How in the world did this happen? We had them locked down on a ship full of our people. Not only did they knock out their guards, they waltzed right down to the flight deck and stole a cutter. Who does that?"

He felt his lips quirk into a wry smile. "I seem to remember my wife pulling off a few stunts like this. We underestimated them.

"Look on the positive side. They didn't kill any of our people, so her mother is probably safe. As an added bonus, they have to listen to her bitch about everything. You can insert the obligatory mother-in-law joke here."

She gave him a quelling stare. "I wouldn't let your wife hear you say that. Logically, I know you're probably right, but that doesn't help.

"We have to do something. We can't just leave her here. Lord knows what she could tell them. Probably nothing militarily significant, but she knows the name of our home world. The marines and the pilot definitely know too much.

"If the Rebel Empire figures out where to come looking for us, they'll exterminate us. We absolutely cannot leave without recovering every single prisoner that escaped. Heaven help us if they've spread any classified information to the people down here. If they have, I don't know what we'll do."

"We've had ships ferrying people down to all the populated locations," he said. "The missing cutter is not anywhere near the colonists."

"They could be moving underwater," Annette said. "Their speed shouldn't be tremendous, but they could be in any number of hidden locations at the bottom of the ocean by now."

"We've dropped listening buoys all around the islands," he said. "Cutters normally don't have to worry about making noise. Their engines vibrate in a manner that will produce a detectable signal of their passage, if they come close enough to a buoy.

"With them scattered all around the occupied islands, our escapees are not going to be able to come close to the colonists. As we clear each island, we can focus more of our forces on the rest. We'll very shortly know that the landmasses are clear.

"Then it becomes a waiting game. Their supplies aren't infinite. The cutter isn't designed to keep their air clean indefinitely or carry enough food and water for an extended hide. They're going to have to find a place on the surface. One where the colonists have planted food they can eat. When they do, we'll find them."

Talbot rubbed his face. "I just hope nobody finds us before we do."

20

It took several hours to satisfy Veronica that they'd examined every square centimeter of the abandoned base. By her estimation, the hidden facility had housed roughly a thousand people. It hadn't done so in quite some time, though. A thick layer of dust coated everything.

That made it very easy to determine that no one had been inside the base in hundreds of years.

In fact, the dust was so extreme that it made exploring the facility a filthy, choking experience. Clouds of the damned stuff rose any time someone dared step on it.

They'd retreated to the cutter and scavenged some emergency breathing masks. Those at least allowed them to both breathe and see.

Once they'd finished exploring the base, she sent her officers off to the edge of the lake to clean up. That required loosening some of the uniform constraints. It wasn't as though they'd brought any luggage. They only had the clothes on their backs.

Each of them washed their uniform and hung it from the cutter to dry. That left them sitting around in their underwear. Not exactly something Command would be pleased about.

Too bad.

Commander Castille bit into a survival bar. "I expected more from this place. You know, a secret lair filled with sharks wearing lasers. That sort of thing."

She chuckled. "Well, the joke's on us, then. This damned place is uninhabitable. If there's anything hidden, it's under a pile of dust."

"Why do you think they built it?"

She shrugged. "My guess is that the people running from the revolution built it. They wanted to avoid paying for their crimes. They shielded the fusion plant and this landing area damned well."

"They left a number of computers. Have we tried accessing them yet?"

"I tried to get into a few, but they're all locked," she said. "That isn't to say my people can't gain access. They're just going to need time to work on them."

Castille smiled sardonically. "We seem to have an abundance of time. Until we can be certain that our erstwhile captors have departed, we're stuck here. Judging from the amount of dirt inside that place, preparing quarters for our use is going to be a time-consuming, thankless job."

Veronica had to agree. She hated housecleaning on the best of days. This took it to a whole new level.

"While we couldn't gain access to the computers, that doesn't mean we didn't find any information," she said. "We picked up a number of tablets the builders left behind. We plugged them in. Once they've recharged, we'll see if there's anything worth recovering."

She gestured toward their still-unconscious prisoners. "What about them?"

Castille considered the four. "The marines won't talk. The pilot probably won't, either. The woman is a possibility, though."

"She's going to wake up soon. Do you think she'll have useful information?"

He shrugged. "I have personnel files from the station in my implant storage, and she's not anywhere in them. She doesn't look anything like a freighter crewman, so I doubt very much they picked her up off one of the in-system craft.

"Based on her clothing, she's someone of substance. Since she doesn't have implants, I might venture someone from a powerful mercantile family. We don't have many people on Dresden that fit into that category, and they'd all have implants. Her identity is a mystery."

One look at the woman's fingernails confirmed she hadn't worked a day in her life. No, she was wealthy. Most likely powerful too. At least until their captors got their hands on her.

Perhaps they'd captured her on the way to Dresden. It wasn't as though they had any insight into the roster of captives these people had. It was almost certain that they hadn't intended for Veronica to see this woman at all.

It was going to be interesting watching Commander Castille interrogate her. While wearing nothing but his underclothing.

She gestured toward the ceiling. "How long do you think they'll continue looking for us?"

"A long time," he said with a grunt. "We know things about them that they probably wouldn't like our superiors hearing.

"We don't know any of the important parts, yet. Where they're from being the biggest question. Somehow, I don't believe that they come from the system the crazy computer had pinned down.

"Not only are they too powerful, but they seem too knowledgeable. If they'd had access to even a portion of this technology, that mad computer would never have been able to hold them."

About that time, one of the marines twitched. The stunner effects were wearing off.

Castille stood and gestured toward the ramp. "Everyone out. Take the military prisoners with you. Stash them in a compartment on the base. I want to control what the woman sees when she wakes up. A bunch of mostly naked people will give her the wrong impression of what's going on."

Veronica raised an eyebrow as she stood. "And what kind of impression are you going to give in your underwear?"

He grinned. "A good one, from all accounts. However, I'm going to dress before she wakes up, even if it's still damp. If she's used to being in control, she's going to resist. Most of those types think Fleet officers are jumped-up proles. I can't afford to feed into the mind-set."

She walked down the ramp with him. He probably did cut a wide swath through the ladies. He wasn't her type, though. Not even close.

After he'd dressed and gone back inside the cutter, she stared out over the water. No matter what Castille believed, she strongly suspected the contents of the tablets—and even the computers themselves—would horrify the security officer, as they would her, if for different reasons.

Based on the long-abandoned state of this facility, if they could find any information at all, she'd be willing to trust that it was accurate.

She wondered what she would do if their captors had been truthful with her. What if the AIs truly were the monsters those people said? What if her entire life had been a lie?

At this point, did it really matter? She'd served the Empire for decades. Was she going to stop now?

Would Castille even let them stop? Would he want to? Security officers were intensely dedicated to the Empire. He'd keep fighting, even if the truth was ugly.

That raised an interesting question. Did he already know the answers to the questions she'd been asking herself? Did he willingly serve things like Levy thought the AIs were?

She sighed. No matter how this played out, their lives were changing. She could feel it in her bones.

* * *

Raul sat near where the prisoner lay on one of the acceleration couches. He'd left her hands bound in front of her, so she'd be fairly comfortable. He might have to change that if she proved uncooperative.

The woman's eyelids flickered momentarily and then flew open. She raised her hands to her head and groaned.

He sympathized. Stunners left the most obnoxious headaches.

"My apologies for the rough manner in which you've been treated," he said.

She glared at him. "What the hell is going on here? Who the hell are you?"

"My name is Raul Castille. I'm afraid that you're still a prisoner, but you've traded up for a better class of captor."

The woman rubbed her temples with her fingertips. "That remains to be seen."

He spread his hands with a smile. "Now that you're awake, why don't we get to know one another? While it's true that I have you at a disadvantage, our situation is not all one-sided. For example, I don't know who you are. Perhaps you could enlighten me."

"How could you possibly *not* know who I am? Were you born in a cave?"

He blinked, nonplussed. "Apparently so. I take it that you believe yourself to be someone important. You're going to have to give me a few pointers if you expect me to grovel appropriately."

The woman managed to draw herself up haughtily. "I am Justine Bandar."

"You're related to Kelsey Bandar? Why did she have you in custody?"

The woman stared at him as though he were an imbecile. "I'm Justine Bandar, ex-wife to the Terran emperor, mother to the crown princess. One of the most powerful nobles in the Empire."

She sounded so arrogant that he had no difficulty believing that she was telling the truth. Except for the fact that he wasn't ready to buy into this story that there was another Empire.

"Ah. I see the problem. I'm not from the Empire. At least, not *your* Empire."

Her eyes narrowed. "Seriously? I thought my daughter was making that up."

Raul opened his mouth to say something, but closed it again. He wasn't quite certain how to respond. He'd expected defiance or fear, not whatever this was.

"Well," he said after a moment. "This is going to be a refreshing change of pace for me. Why was your daughter holding you prisoner? Did you break some law?"

"If I'm not going to give my daughter the satisfaction of cooperating with this absurd charade, what makes you think I'm going to behave any differently toward you? I did nothing wrong."

Yes, this was going to be significantly different from his normal interrogation technique. The woman wasn't going to be much of a physical threat, so perhaps he should lead with the carrot.

He rose to his feet and stepped toward her. "Now that you're awake and I have a better idea of who I'm dealing with, I think it's safe enough to unlock those restraints."

She wasted no time in extending her hands toward him.

Once he removed the cuffs, she rubbed her wrists. "At least this is a step in the right direction. That doesn't make up for you giving me this beastly headache.

"My daughter has kept me locked in a dreary little room since she caught me. I was never one to pay much attention to the news. I honestly have no idea who you are."

Raul had worked almost exclusively with Fleet personnel for the last decade. His experience in dealing with civilians—particularly those belonging to the higher orders—was strictly limited. That's what this woman was, though she probably used different words to describe her social class.

"It sounds as though your daughter did you a great injustice," he said, making certain to have a compassionate tone.

"You have no idea. This is all so much more complicated than it needed to be."

"It turns out that I have time to listen, and I'm told that I have a sympathetic ear."

Justine Bandar considered him for a moment. "Perhaps the two of us do have the potential to exchange information. I'll tell you my story, if you tell me yours. And I want some water and a pain pill."

He had absolutely no idea what they were going to discuss, but if it gave him insight into the enemy, it was more than worth the time to be chatty. It only took him a moment to get her some water and a pain pill.

Raul handed them to her and leaned back in his chair. "You have my word that I will share information as freely as you do. Why don't you begin?"

This was going to be fascinating.

21

It only took Carl about fifteen minutes to identify the occupied system. The maps they had of the old Terran Empire called it Archibald.

Kelsey thought that was one hell of a name. Archibald was one of the original core worlds. *Persephone*'s database listed it as once having a population above ten billion.

Of course, that was before the Fall. Based on the space traffic they'd observed and the sheer number of communications they'd intercepted, that was probably still accurate.

It's population undoubtedly dwarfed Avalon's. She'd seen the recordings of Imperial City in the old days. Cities like that probably covered Archibald.

While the historical data available to her was interesting, Kelsey sat on pins and needles waiting for the probe to return with more information. It arrived on schedule without any issues and began streaming what it had captured into their systems.

It was going to take time to make sense of all the details. All she wanted from the initial readings was a feel for how dangerous this place was going to be for them.

Carl looked up from his console. "Based on the communications the probe intercepted, I can confirm that this is Archibald."

Kelsey stood and walked over to him. "That's nice, but it doesn't really get us where we need to go."

"I agree," he said. "Several of the other probes we've sent out have found other flip branches that are potentially more useful. Both are empty systems that aren't on any Imperial map that I've discovered."

"Any sign of the ghosts?"

"Nothing yet. That doesn't mean they didn't use those systems, though.

They had to go somewhere. Also, I need to check the multiflip point from the other side."

Kelsey cocked her head. "You mean the two sides might access different systems?"

The young scientist nodded. "Almost certainly. Just because it links to the system we're in with one branch doesn't mean that all of its available branches will go to the same locations as this side. We're going to have to do a thorough check to be sure."

Kelsey supposed that made sense. Exploring these new multiflip points was going to be incredibly complex. If she understood correctly, it was theoretically possible to flip from one side to the other, pick another branch flip to a new system, perhaps many times. All without traveling across any of the systems they visited.

That allowed a traveler to visit a ridiculous number of systems in an extremely short period of time, but only after they had mapped out the frequencies required to transition to those systems.

The ghosts might be only hours away, though perhaps any number of unmapped flips stood between them.

"Are those two systems the only other possible branches from this multiflip point?" Kelsey finally asked.

"Probably not. I still need to figure out the frequency boundaries and probe each zone to be certain."

Carl bent down. "In fact, one of the probes just visited a fourth system. Hm. I'm picking up a few radio signals. There's definitely somebody there, but they aren't spread throughout the system. All the transmissions appear to be coming from the same area of space."

"Send the probe back to get us more information. That might be where the ghosts went."

Another hour passed. Kelsey spent some of the nervous energy building inside her by getting food for everyone on the bridge. They'd just finished eating when the probe returned.

"I don't think this is a ghost system," Carl said slowly.

"Why not?" Kelsey asked.

He wordlessly threw an image onto the screen.

Kelsey wasn't certain if this was a news program or some other kind of entertainment, but the person centered in the video was definitely not human. Very close, but with some startling differences.

The being was tall and slender with pale turquoise skin. Based on the being's prominently displayed assets, the speaker was female.

The similarities between these beings and humans were incredible. She had two eyes, a nose, and a mouth in the same locations as a human woman. As were her breasts.

Her eyes seemed larger, though not by much. Her nose was slender and short. Her mouth wider. Unless Kelsey was mistaken, her teeth seemed a tad pointed too.

Kelsey thought she looked exotic, but beautiful. "Well, I didn't expect to find aliens. Can you explain why they look so much like us?"

The young scientist shrugged. "I have no idea. The only other aliens we've encountered were radically different."

The race of beings that had built Omega station in the Nova system and traveled to a different dimension had been aquatic.

Their study of the Omega race was still in its infancy. What she knew for certain was that anything was possible when it came to alien life. The Omega race was nothing like humanity in physical shape.

Kelsey frowned. "You tapped into their video pretty easily. Shouldn't figuring out their transmission protocols have taken you a while?"

"You'd think so. Here's another mystery for you. They're using standard Imperial frequencies and encoding."

She blinked. "Excuse me? These are aliens. How is that even possible?"

"I haven't got the faintest idea. What I can tell you is that they're only located on one planet in the system. It's in the habitable zone, though far outside the range this probe can pick up. They may not be as advanced as this makes them seem."

Kelsey rubbed her forehead. "We don't have time to investigate all these mysteries. We need to find the ghosts, not aliens that somehow got their hands on Imperial technology."

"What makes you think the two aren't connected?" Angela asked from her console. "Perhaps the ghosts traded with the natives. If they were advanced enough to make use of Imperial technology, they might have provided something useful in return."

"Isn't there some kind of rule that forbids interfering with aliens? Some kind of prime directive?"

"You've been watching too many of those old prespaceflight entertainment vids. The Old Empire never met an alien species. Why would they have a rule against uplifting them?

"Even if they did, these ghosts were desperate. I think they'd be willing to break that particular rule if it gave them an advantage they needed to survive."

Kelsey shook her head. "Dispatch three stealthed probes into the system to gather more information. In fact, send probes into all the empty systems as well. Start mapping them. We'll leave the one probe at the Archibald multiflip point to continue gathering data.

"Carl, I need to know how many potential branches this side of the multiflip point has. I want probes in every single one of them within the next hour. You can spend time after that doing your experiments to narrow down the frequency bands, but I need to know what we're dealing with.

"Until we find out more information, we'll designate this system as Pandora, so we have a name to call it. Besides, the alien's skin color makes me think of that old movie where they used the name."

"On it," Carl said.

Kelsey returned to her seat and gestured for Angela to join her. "This is spinning out of control. The number of systems we can potentially access is going to keep growing exponentially."

"That's a lot better than having no potential destinations," the tall marine said reasonably. "At least we might find another system that leads us back to Pentagar or Harrison's World. Potentially even home."

"If we're lucky. If not, we'll need to find the ghosts. They went somewhere. It would be very useful to make friendly contact with them."

The marine clapped Kelsey on the shoulder. "You're still new at this. Just be glad no one is shooting at you."

Kelsey supposed that was true. Things could always be worse.

Of course, things could always get better too. Maybe Talbot would find the escapees quickly. She might not like her mother very much right now, but she wanted her safe. Fast.

* * *

Once her uniform dried, Veronica began examining the tablets they'd been charging inside the abandoned facility. Most of the contents seemed innocuous. Their owners had used them for everyday tasks, and there were no files worthy of further study.

That was until she found a journal. That proved both fascinating and horrifying.

The fascination stemmed from the fact that the man who wrote it—Commander Frank Beaumont—had obviously been keeping a record of his daily activities and thoughts for years. The entries spanned five decades.

The earliest entries gave her a flavor of what it was like growing up on an agricultural world far from the center of the Empire. It documented how his family raised food for more populous systems.

Frank's father hadn't been pleased when he'd joined Fleet. That didn't seem to bother Frank all that much. The two of them seemed to have issues.

Veronica only skimmed the entries, but it quickly became clear that this man hadn't lived under anything like the old dictatorship as she knew it.

Then came the revolution. That's where things became horrifying.

Once fighting broke out, he documented everything. She no longer nursed any doubts that Captain Levy had told her the unvarnished truth. The AIs had lied. The horrors she read made her physically ill.

She forced herself to continue reading until his ship—the battlecruiser *Infamous*—escaped an ambush while escorting a number of civilian ships filled with refugees near Dresden.

He documented how the AI-controlled ships had mercilessly vaporized the defenseless civilian vessels where they could. That alone told her the truth. It was monstrous.

The commodore commanding the protective task force had rallied and counterattacked. She'd defeated the attackers, but reinforcements attacked the pickets she'd left at Dresden. That forced her into hiding.

Their task force didn't have supplies to stay in the outer system forever, but it was too dangerous to travel farther. They repaired what they could and waited.

His account didn't specify how he'd gotten to this system. Perhaps he didn't know.

She set the tablet down on the dirty console and rubbed her eyes. She could continue reading, but his story had already answered the most important questions she'd had. She knew who'd built the base and why they'd concealed it so well.

How could this be happening? How could everything she knew be a lie?

And what the hell could she do about it?

Castille wouldn't accept this. She knew it. He'd either declare it to be some kind of trick or find a reason to disregard the story. What he'd probably done to Commodore Murdock made it clear the lengths he was willing to go for the Empire.

Thankfully, she didn't have to make a decision about how to proceed right now. He was still busy questioning the female prisoner. Whatever they were discussing must've been fascinating. He'd been in the cutter for hours.

The two marines and the cutter pilot had woken shortly after the woman. Her people had them in an old conference room. She'd resisted the urge to question them. Maybe that had been the wrong call.

She went in search of cleaning supplies. Once she had enough basic equipment, she had Graham take it all to the conference room.

Armand stood outside the hatch with a stunner strapped to his waist.

"I'm going in to talk to them," she said without any preamble. "Alone."

"I don't think that's a good idea, ma'am. There are three of them and only one of you. Even with a stunner, they could take you."

She smiled. "That's why you'll need to be down at the other end of the corridor, so you can shoot them as they come out."

Veronica held up her hand when he started to object again. "I've made my decision, Commander. By all means, keep Graham here with you. If I call for help, you can come in. Carefully."

"At least allow us to make sure they don't jump you," Graham said. "You know, push them back into a corner."

"Fine. Just try not to shoot anybody. I want to talk to them."

At Armand's nod, Graham set the supplies on the deck and opened the hatch. The three prisoners sat around the filthy conference table.

When they started to rise, Veronica stepped into the compartment, her stunner raised. "Up against the bulkhead, gentleman. I'd rather not have to stun you again."

The two marines looked to the cutter pilot for guidance. When he raised his hands slightly and stepped over to the bulkhead, they grudgingly followed.

Veronica glanced at her men. "Bring the cleaning supplies inside and put them on the table. Wait outside. If I call for assistance, come in shooting. Stun everyone, including me."

Once Graham had placed the box of cleaning supplies on the table, Veronica closed the hatch.

She smiled at the three men. "I realize we've gotten off to a terrible start, but I think we have a lot to discuss. I'm Commander Veronica Giguere, in case you hadn't guessed."

"We're not going to tell you anything," the pilot said with a stony face.

"Oh, I think you will. First, I'm going to tell you a story. Then you can explain to me what it means."

The men glanced at one another. "I have no idea what you're talking about," the pilot said after a long moment.

Veronica pointed to the box. "This place is a mess, and you're going to be here a while. Take the supplies and start cleaning the other end of the compartment. While you do, I'll pass on a story that I just read. I think you'll find it fascinating. It's about a man who fought the AIs."

She moved a chair to the corner and sat. "Let me introduce you to Frank Beaumont. He grew up on a farm. Maybe it's just me, but that sounds like a dirty, smelly place. Anyone here know about that?"

When they shook their heads, she launched into his story.

22

Annette decided that riding out a flip on *Persephone*'s hull was even worse than when she'd hidden in her fighter while they invaded the Dresden system.

The Raider ship's lower mass provided almost no protection. Even with her implants, it took her almost a minute to regain full control of her stomach.

Still, she understood why they had to go through like this. *Audacious* was too large to go through the multiflip point, so that meant they'd had to strap the fighters onto *Persephone*'s hull.

If they were going to make a habit of this, Annette was going to get Carl Owlet to design some magnetic clamps the pilots could release from inside the cockpit. In fact, that wasn't a bad idea at all.

It took a few minutes for the crewmen in vacuum suits to release her fighter. She used her grav drive on its lowest setting to edge away from the ship. They released the other five fighters over the next fifteen minutes.

That definitely wouldn't work if they needed to do this again.

Once her scouting group had formed around her, they headed deeper into the Pandora system. Fighters were hard to detect—even when traveling quickly—so they could accelerate faster than a larger ship.

According to the plan, *Persephone* would monitor the system via her probes while Annette scouted the planet where the signals originated. If there were any trouble, the princess would come hauling butt and give them some cover.

The probe that they'd originally sent to the alien world had provided an interesting mix of information. The majority of the planet wasn't industrialized. The night-side view showed very little in the way of alien-made lighting, even inside what were obviously major cities. Electricity was uncommon, it seemed.

Yet there were those troubling transmissions.

She took control of the probes that *Persephone* had just launched and sent them ahead. They'd arrive in planetary orbit several hours before her. She could task them to look at anything they determined to be interesting once she arrived.

Annette brought up a map of the planet over her implants. She started studying the rough layout of the major cities and trying to determine what political entities they might fit into. If these people were as underdeveloped as they appeared, the odds of them having a single planetary government were nonexistent.

A closer examination of some of the urban centers brought something unusual to her attention. They'd laid one of the larger cities out in a very unusual pattern. It wasn't near a river, either. She couldn't imagine why they'd put so many people there.

It wasn't prudent to send a signal to the probe from this far away. The risk of detection was too high. She'd have to send one of her probes to take a closer look when they got there.

Frankly, she had no idea what she'd find.

* * *

As much as he wanted to focus on the search for the escaped prisoners, Talbot had other problems that desperately required his attention. They had to relocate the prisoners from the orbital to the planet's surface. That meant the construction of the shelters was on a very tight schedule.

Unfortunately, the crews he'd brought to the surface were slowing things down. He needed to get them moving again if he was going to meet Kelsey's deadline.

He took a pinnace from the search area to the island they'd selected for the primary construction. The landmass was about as far away from the original villages as possible. He didn't want the female population here causing a war with the all-male original settlers.

As he'd expected, no one was working when he landed.

Talbot settled his light armor, checked his stunner, and motioned for his escort to follow him down the ramp. He didn't need a lot of backup, but he wanted to make a point.

It seemed as though the construction personnel had elected one of themselves as their leader. The tall, heavily muscled man had a bird of some kind tattooed on his arm. He showed Talbot a smug expression as the marine walked toward him, but said nothing.

Talbot stopped about two meters away. "Are we really going to do this?"

The other man smiled, showing a lot of teeth. "I'm not sure what you mean."

"Oh, don't be coy. You think you're going to stand there telling me that you and your people aren't going to do the work. I'll complain that you're delaying everything. Then you tell me what you want before you get back to work.

"That isn't going to happen. All you're doing is putting yourselves into a hard spot."

The man's grin widened, and he spread his hands. "If I'm wrong, tell me what's going to happen. The way I see it, you Fleet bastards don't have a lot of choice. No buildings? People are going to freeze."

"That's about what I expected you to say. Here's where things go south for you. We're going to keep bringing people down no matter what you do. If you want to screw your own people, go right ahead. Anything that happens from that point forward is on you."

The man looked uncertain but didn't say anything.

Talbot turned on his heel and headed back into the pinnace. Either these idiots would get back to work, or they'd have to deal with the crisis they'd created.

The weather wasn't terrible. Chilly was a more appropriate description than cold, so no one was in serious physical danger. He'd provide more than enough cold-weather gear to keep them alive no matter what the idiots did.

That didn't mean they'd be happy, though. Not his problem. He needed to get back to the search.

* * *

Raul spoke with Justine Bandar far longer than he'd intended. The woman was fascinating. Just as arrogant as anyone he'd met from the higher orders but delightfully easy to converse with.

And very informative. She'd shared what he considered classified information with wild abandon. All he had to do was get her complaining about either her daughter, her ex-husband's bastard, or the situation she'd found herself in.

It was easy to manufacture the compassion required to get her rolling. Once she started talking, there didn't seem to be any governor on what she'd discuss. By the time they'd been together just a few hours, he had a good overview of this supposed New Terran Empire.

Thankfully, even with all the ships that Veronica had seen, it didn't appear that these people were as great a threat as he'd feared. They only occupied a small area of space, and their population was sparse. Their basic technology level was also far inferior to the Empire.

Best of all, he had the name of their capital: Avalon. He had no doubt that he'd be able to locate them on a map. Once the Empire knew where to send their warships, they'd end this problem in very short order.

He walked down the cutter's ramp, leaving the woman under guard behind him. He'd already made the decision to house her separately from the other prisoners. He didn't want them convincing her to shut her exceptionally pretty mouth.

It took about twenty minutes to locate Veronica. She was working in one of the compartments inside the old base. She seemed to be cleaning what had obviously been personal quarters, so perhaps she was arranging a less dusty place to stay. Smart.

He rapped on the hatch to get her attention. When she'd turned her head, saw who he was, and set her rag down on the table, he stepped inside.

"My apologies for interrupting," he said. "I've completed questioning the woman. Her story is very interesting."

Veronica nodded. "I'm sure it is. We've discovered a few things too. One of the tablets had a journal. It covered about fifty years from start to finish, so we're far from being able to say that we've read every word, but it has raised some disturbing questions."

Raul picked up the rag and cleaned off a handy chair. He settled comfortably and crossed one leg over the other. "Surely you're not going to tell me that it implicates the lords as being homicidal maniacs bent on human domination."

She stepped over and closed the hatch. "That's exactly what I'm telling you. The story was from five hundred years ago, written during the events in question. The account paints a very different picture of the old Empire too.

"I need to be frank. The old emperor doesn't sound at all like the despot they taught us about in school. In fact, I'm convinced the people that captured us are more correct than we are about the AIs."

He kept his expression pleasant, but his mind was racing. Their circumstances were dire. He couldn't afford to have this kind of disruption in the middle of an already chancy escape.

"I'll need to read the relevant journal entries myself, but let's assume that you've interpreted them correctly just for the sake of the discussion. So what? The past is done. We can't change it.

"We have to live in the world as it exists. The lords are our masters. Did they do terrible things to gain that mastery? Perhaps. Nevertheless, they are the ones we serve."

Her eyes narrowed. "I'm a Fleet officer. I know where my loyalties lie, but have you been playing some kind of game all this time? Do you security people already know all of this? I just want to know."

Raul laughed, though there wasn't much humor in the situation. "Oh no. I'm hearing this for the first time. If anyone in the Empire knows, I'm not aware of it. Perhaps I don't have the clearance.

"I do know this, though. It changes nothing. These people want to destroy our way of life. Worse yet, even if they offer a better society—and I'm willing to provisionally entertain the possibility—they don't have the military force needed to overthrow the AIs. Not even with everything that they've captured at Dresden."

Veronica sat in another of the chairs. "Tell me what you know."

"The woman's name is Justine Bandar. She's the mother of the woman who greeted us on the carrier. The ex-empress of the supposed New Terran

Empire. She's given us everything we need to stop these people. We just have to find a way to get the word back to our superiors."

He considered her for a long moment. "I sympathize, Veronica. I truly do. There are many things wrong with the Empire. Things I wish worked differently. Perhaps in time we can change them.

"If our former captors told us the truth as they saw it, the AIs can obviously learn. Things have improved since they overthrew the old dictatorship. If that's even the right word."

When she didn't add anything, he continued. "Obviously, terrible things were done, if their stories are accurate. But do you truly believe these people can create change for the better? Or would it just be for the worse? If the AIs are as bad they told us, then they will react very strongly to this threat.

"And not just toward the New Terran Empire. Do you really want to have them repress our people too? That's a real possibility."

He leaned back in his chair and watched her. She obviously had mixed feelings. The question was, would she end up supporting him and the Empire, or go in the direction he suspected her heart tugged her?

He'd have to watch her closely. He'd regret it if he had to act against her as he had Commodore Murdock and the rest, but he knew his duty. Hopefully she was smart enough to know hers.

23

"I have some more information," Carl said.

Kelsey looked over from the main screen where she'd been examining some of the images the aliens were transmitting. "Give it to me."

The young scientist stood and walked over. "We're still working on the language, but I can tell you that there are less than a dozen transmission sites.

"They're not transmitting continuously, either. Sometimes signals last for a couple of hours, but other times only for a few minutes. I don't think they're news programs or even entertainment."

"What are they?"

"I think this is message traffic. Back on Terra before they had the ability to transmit radio signals, everything had to go through something called telegraph lines with physical wires.

"If you needed to get information to someone a long distance away, you'd deliver a message to a transmission station, and they'd send it on. It might need to go through several retransmissions to reach the final destination, but the recipient eventually got it.

"I believe we're seeing something very much like that. The delivery style and the fact that the transmissions only take place intermittently indicate they're only communicating when there's something to say."

Kelsey considered that. "Once Annette gets on station, she should be able to help clarify the situation."

"Agreed," he said. "None of the transmissions have had a human being in it. That may mean there are no humans on this planet."

She certainly hoped that wasn't the case. It would be a lot easier if they could find a representative of these elusive ghosts to negotiate with. If they chanced across one of their ships in space, there was the very likely possibility that they'd shoot first and never bother asking questions.

"I understand that I'm asking you to guess, but do you think it's worth our time and effort to contact these people?"

Carl considered her question for a moment. "Honestly? No. I'd say these people are preindustrial. Perhaps even feudal. Of course, they're aliens. It might not be that simple.

"Would they make good friends? Possibly, but we're not out here to make friends. We have to get the information we have back to the Empire. That has to be our first priority."

That's about what she'd thought, but she'd wanted to hear someone else say it.

"How long until Annette is on station?" she asked.

"Less than an hour now."

"Keep going through those transmissions. I'd love it if you could figure out some type of translation program."

He gave her a skeptical look. "That's not likely. The language isn't even close to Standard. I'll need better understanding of common words and concepts to develop a translation program. These transmissions have people talking but no context. The video shots are just of the people speaking.

"The individual we call Omega was different. He'd interacted with humans before and had a lot of computing power to throw at improving his translation code. Just being able to speak to these folks is going to prove impossible in the short run, I suspect."

Omega hadn't just known humans before. He'd known Carl. Several of him, in fact. True, they'd come from alternate realities, but that had to give the alien some insight when it came to interacting with this one particular human.

The station that Omega was part of had been a gateway to other universes. He'd become part of the ring they'd discovered in the Nova system so that he could facilitate the evacuation of his species to avoid extinction at the hands of their errant star.

Something about the nova—not just in their universe, but also in numerous others—had somehow linked many of the stations in ways that she didn't understand. They'd become one on the inside. Omega was the same in all of those universes. A living bridge between them.

The idea of other realities boggled her mind. Yet one more thing she didn't have time to distract herself with.

"I know you're probably right, but how often do we meet an alien species?" she finally asked. "Even counting Omega, this is only the second time. And no offense to him, but he's only a single being trapped on a station in an extremely inhospitable system.

"Pandora is a planet full of people. Think of how much we could learn from them. Not technologically obviously, but this is important. Perhaps it's not our most pressing issue, but I don't want to let this opportunity slip past."

"I get that," Carl said. "We still have five days before Talbot finishes removing the prisoners from the Dresden orbital. If you don't mind, I'll start using my probes on this side of the multiflip point and see if there's any overlap in destinations. I honestly don't expect to find much, but we should look."

"That's a good idea," she agreed. "I think we can assume the Pandorans won't see us all the way out here. Let's poke around the multiflip point and map out the places it leads. It's conceivable that one of the links will provide us with something useful."

She sent him back to his console just as Angela came out of the lift. The tall marine had gone to get sandwiches for the bridge crew. Something they all appreciated.

Her executive officer handed her a small pile of them. "Here you go."

Kelsey accepted the plate gratefully. "Thank God. I'm starving."

When she'd taken the edge off her hunger, she focused her attention on Angela. "I've decided that we're going to flip back to the system with the orbital for a bit. I think it's time to send you to *Audacious* for the next implant procedure."

Her tall friend scowled. "Seriously? We just brought my boyfriend on board, and you're sending me off?"

Kelsey laughed. "You're not going to be getting frisky for a bit. You might pull something important off him."

The marine snorted. "Don't tell him that, or I'll never get any. Kelsey, we're in an alien star system hunting for potentially hostile ships. I hardly think this is the time to remove your executive officer from the equation."

"I think it's pretty safe to say that we're not going to run into anyone in this system. While it does have at least two regular flip points, there's no sign that the ghosts visit on any regular schedule, and this is obviously not one of their home systems.

"If you want to become a full-blown Marine Raider, you've got to keep going with the procedures. This next one is for your legs. Once Doctor Zoboroski finishes, you can come back. As my executive officer, you can do your job sitting down."

That didn't seem to make the marine any happier. "If I have to move somewhere, I'm going to fall on my face. I saw you after your procedure. It's going to take me days to figure out how to walk again, isn't it?"

"Probably," Kelsey agreed. "That still doesn't change anything. It's not going to be as bad as you think, Angela. I had to recover from everything all at once and had no one to guide me through the process. You do.

"By the time we're ready to leave this system, you'll have recovered to the point where they can do the left half of your torso. You're almost there. Don't keep looking for excuses to put it off."

Angela scowled. "Yes, ma'am. I don't have to like it, though."

Kelsey smiled a little. "I think you'll like it just fine once you're done. Imagine what a badass you'll be. You'll be able to tie me into a pretzel when we spar."

The marine smiled. "You sure know how to make a girl feel better."

* * *

ANNETTE EDGED CAREFULLY into orbit around the planet Princess Kelsey had dubbed Pandora. The probes hadn't discovered any artificial satellites, but she needed to be cautious.

After half an hour, her fighters had circled the globe several times and determined there was nothing outside the atmosphere. That certainly confirmed the Pandorans were primitive, relatively speaking.

She passed the information to *Persephone*. Nobody down below was going to detect the larger ship, so they could come in and get a better idea of what they were dealing with.

While Annette waited for the ship, she set her people to doing a visual inspection of the planet. She wanted to have a high-resolution map by the time the princess arrived.

Annette focused her attention on the strangely shaped city she'd observed through the probes. As it was in daylight now, she was able to see what made it look so odd.

It wasn't a city at all. It was a debris field.

The strange layout of the lights she'd seen at night was because they'd set up a number of small encampments around what was obviously the wreckage of a crashed ship.

A quick check confirmed that it wasn't broadcasting a distress beacon. It had been there a while and must not have had an operational fusion plant.

They'd need to send drones into the atmosphere to see just what was happening, but it certainly appeared as though a lot of people were combing through the wreckage, based upon the number of buildings.

Annette didn't see any intact sections, so she couldn't identify the ship's class. It was obviously a big one. Significantly larger than *Persephone*, for sure.

The Marine Raider ship was the only Old Empire ship they'd found that was even *capable* of landing on a planet. Anything that produced this much debris shouldn't have been in the atmosphere in the first place.

She started estimating the amount of wreckage. The ship below was at least a heavy cruiser. Perhaps even a battlecruiser.

Based on how contained the wreckage was, someone had managed to keep it together most of the way down. Otherwise, the wreckage would be scattered across many square kilometers.

Annette zoomed the resolution on the probe as far as she could. It felt like she was sitting about ten kilometers up.

The locals were definitely scavenging. A number of large tents surrounded the wreck, and Annette could see people carrying objects into them. A larger ring of permanent structures surrounded them.

Since people didn't build cities in a week, this had been going on for a long time. Years, certainly. Probably decades.

Annette finally broke off her examination when *Persephone* pulled into orbit hours later. She signaled the Marine Raider ship, and Princess Kelsey answered.

Using her implants to communicate made it seem as though she were standing in front of the other woman.

"What have you got for me?" the princess asked.

She laid out everything she'd found.

"That's a big ship," Annette said when she was done. "I have difficulty believing they intended to take her down to the surface. Whoever landed her was one hell of a pilot."

The noblewoman looked skeptical. "Landing? No one walked away from that."

"That's one of the things you learn as a pilot, Highness. Sometimes you don't walk away. That doesn't negate the skill that got them close.

"The locals seem to be scavenging equipment. Based on the number of buildings and the nature of the wreckage, I suspect it's been down there for decades."

Princess Kelsey looked at the view screen in front of her. "The computer is doing some estimations based on the amount of wreckage. It's tentatively identifying it as a battlecruiser. I can't begin to imagine how long it would take a primitive group to strip something that size.

"They certainly didn't figure out how to use the communications gear in a decade or two. Not unless somebody survived to show them how it was done."

Annette couldn't imagine anyone had directly survived the crash, but she supposed it was possible. Miracles did occasionally happen.

"I suspect any survivors abandoned ship via escape pods before the crash," she said. "That would get a lot of people clear in a hurry. Someone obviously stayed on board that ship right up until the very end, though."

The princess nodded. "We're not picking up any distress beacons, so whatever happened took place a long time ago. The pods aren't good for more than a few months of power, but the ship would still be transmitting if any of the fusion plants survived."

"No chance of that," Annette said. "They probably killed most of them before they entered the atmosphere. A crash like this would've blown them for sure."

"Head back home," the princess ordered. "It's going to take a while for the probes to give us a more comprehensive picture. You might as well be comfortable while they do it."

"Aye, ma'am. We're on our way."

Annette sent a signal to her people, and they all turned toward *Persephone*. It would be good to get out of the cockpit, take a hot shower, and get something to eat. By the time she felt human again, they'd have a better idea of what kind of situation they were dealing with.

24

Veronica was just finishing her unappetizing ration bar when Graham rapped his knuckle on the open hatch to her new quarters. She held up a finger while she finished chewing the last bit and swallowed it. She followed that up with a long drink of cold, fresh water.

"What have you got for me, Graham? If it's better food, you have my complete attention."

The young engineering officer laughed. "If only we were so lucky. No, I'm afraid we're stuck with these nasty ration bars for the time being. You have to wonder, why can't anyone make survival rations that actually taste good?"

"It's one of the great mysteries of the universe," she allowed. "I take it you have something interesting for me."

"You could say that. I've gotten into their main computer."

She straightened. "Are you serious? That's great!"

"I won't bore you with all the technical details, but suffice it to say, someone wasn't as conscientious as they should've been with password security. Once I gained access, I managed to compromise the system administrator's login. Sloppy. They should be ashamed."

Veronica laughed. "I'm not going to complain about someone else's failure when it suits our needs. Have you found anything interesting?"

He shook his head. "I literally just finished cracking the system administrator's account. I figured you'd want to know right away."

She stood. "You're damned right. Let's go see if we can find something interesting."

They'd been in the abandoned facility for five days now. She'd stayed on the cutter the first night. That convinced her to clean up some of the abandoned quarters. She still wasn't satisfied with the level of cleanliness.

Still, it could've been worse. Candace Wells—her helm officer—was splitting her time between her quarters and Justine Bandar's. The haughty woman was running her ragged, and Veronica knew the quiet officer was ready to strangle the harpy.

Graham led her deeper into the base. They'd restored one of the lifts to service. It beat using the stairs.

The computer center was at the lowest level. Whoever had built the base had decided it was best to put it right next to the fusion plant. Probably so they'd be certain of destroying it, if they decided the facility had to go.

It turned out her young engineering officer had done a much better job of cleaning out his workspace than she had her quarters. The room was spotless.

She looked around in amazement. "How the hell did you find enough time to clean this place and break into the computer?"

He frowned at her. "I used the cleaning bots."

Veronica put her hands on her hips and gave him a flat stare. "You have the cleaning bots working, and you didn't tell me? I've been busting my ass to get my room in half-decent shape."

"I thought I'd told Commander Fuller. Maybe I only dreamed I did. You should probably take some of them back to your room."

"Graham, you're exasperating. Get your head out of the computer innards and think of other people."

"Sorry, ma'am. I'll try to do better."

He gestured toward the computer console. "I've taken the liberty of adding all of us to the system. You have complete access to everything. The only thing that I've restricted is the computer security protocols. For safety sake, I decided to disable them. We wouldn't want to wipe the system by accident."

She sat at the console. "No, we wouldn't."

Veronica used her implants to access the computer. It readily opened for examination. She initiated a search for classified files.

That brought back a lot of hits. The computer was packed with classified information, at least as far as the people who'd built it were concerned.

The first thing she did was to search for a listing of ships associated with the task force. She found it in the logs created by a Commodore Sanjay. A side query indicated that she was the commanding officer of the task force that had escaped and built this base.

It seems that she'd escaped the revolution with quite a few ships. Three battlecruisers, six heavy cruisers, nine light cruisers, and fourteen destroyers. Quite a strike force.

They'd been escorting a motley mix of civilian vessels packed with refugees. There was a long listing of the ships, but there was no rhyme or reason to them. They'd probably grabbed every bit of shipping that could hold people when they ran. All told, they'd shepherded almost a hundred civilian vessels.

None of which they'd left in this system. Except for an old cruise liner that they'd been doing some type of experimentation with.

She frowned. It took her several minutes to locate the file with information about the modifications done to the cruise liner. It proved unexpectedly enlightening.

Sanjay's task force and the civilians under her protection had escaped the Empire through an unknown kind of flip point. One that turned out to be very difficult to detect.

One of the scanner officers had found the anomaly in the system nearest Dresden. They'd risked sending a probe through and found this system. The one containing the planet she was standing on.

They'd named it Icebox. Apparently, they'd arrived in deep winter.

She'd have to figure out what they'd done here at a later point. Right now, she was just concerned with why they'd modified the cruise liner.

The answer made her laugh. It turned out the anomaly was a one-way ticket. Once they'd arrived, they'd been unable to leave. The system hadn't contained any regular flip points, either.

After quite a bit of research, they'd modified the flip drive on the cruise liner to attempt a transit back to the system they'd fled. It had failed to transit and burned out the flip drive.

Well, that explained why they'd left the ship in orbit. Where had they gone? Had they finally figured out how to use the anomaly? Had they built this place only to return home and die in some unknown battle?

She spooled to the end of Commodore Sanjay's log. That entry was more than two decades after they'd arrived at Icebox. It followed the previous entry by six years.

The commodore had left a brief note that she was leaving a repository of classified files on the computer at this base—which they'd apparently abandoned at some point—and was putting it into hibernation before they left the system.

Veronica searched the commodore's files and found the most recent dispatches. She'd expected to find that they'd perfected a device to modify their flip drives. What she found was far more unexpected.

Apparently, they'd never managed to go back through the anomaly. Instead, they'd settled this planet and built a city down on the coast below the volcano. Shortly before Commodore Sanjay made her final entry, they'd discovered a flip point in this system. One in a location they hadn't expected.

She blinked and stared at Graham. "I think I found us a way out."

"Seriously?" he asked. "That's great."

Veronica smiled wryly. "We'll see. It turns out there's another flip point in this system. One our captors probably don't know about."

He scratched his head and gave her a quizzical look. "Why not?"

"Because it's not positioned where they'd expect to find it. That gives us an opportunity."

* * *

RAUL WAS WASHING his face when Veronica caught up with him. She started to say something but stopped and took a closer look at his face.

"What happened to you?" she asked.

He smiled ruefully. "Believe it or not, I was attacked by one of the prisoners."

She swore. "I knew this was going to happen. It was one of the marines, wasn't it?"

"Justine Bandar. It turns out she's not pleased with the quarters we've provided for her."

Veronica blinked. "Seriously? She hauled off and popped you?"

"Thankfully for my ego, no. However, she has a stellar throwing arm."

To his chagrin, Veronica started laughing. He didn't blame her. It was ludicrous.

Once she'd laughed herself out, he drew himself up with all the dignity he could muster. "If we're finished—and by we, I mean you—what brings you by?"

She smoothed her expression, but he could still see the humor dancing in her eyes. "I just wanted to let you know that Graham managed to access the base computer. Obviously, we're going to have a lot to go over, but I found something I think you need to know about."

He stiffened, his bruised face forgotten. "You have my full attention."

"I found the log belonging to the task force commander who built this base. A Commodore Sanjay. It turns out she and her ships were here for several decades before they left again. That's because they couldn't go back through the anomaly that led them here, and there were no other flip points in this system."

He raised an eyebrow. "So, her people figured out how to go back through the anomaly? Why did it take so long?"

"They never figured out how to go back through the anomaly," Veronica said. "It proved to be a one-way trip. They did, however, discover a flip point that they'd missed in their initial examination of the system."

"Another anomaly? What do we know about them?"

"A regular flip point, actually. They missed it because it's positioned far beyond the orbit of the outermost planet."

He digested that information for a moment. He didn't serve as a ship's officer, so he wasn't familiar with the normal layout of flip points. "And that's unusual?"

"Unheard of. Regular flip points sit between the habitable zone and about the middle of the outer system. The one we're talking about here is significantly farther out. Even a ship going out to the outermost planet—for which there is no conceivable reason—wouldn't have detected it."

"I'll bite. How did they manage to find it?"

She shrugged. "I didn't stop to look. I figured the fact that it existed at all was all that mattered. That said, it doesn't really improve our prospects. We don't happen to have any handy flip-capable ships."

That deflated him a little. "True. It doesn't sound as though our captors are going to find it, either. If they can't go back through the anomaly, I'm not sure what we're going to do. We can hold out for another few months, if we cut our rations, but these people need to leave if we're to have any chance of returning to the Empire."

Veronica pursed her lips. "Maybe. Maybe not. While we were on board the carrier, I overheard several of the officers talking about their operations. They're a bit nervous about the prisoners on the planet getting ahold of the Dresden orbital.

"They planned on using their cutters to shuttle everyone down to the planet's surface. Once the orbital is empty, they intend to move it into the outer system. That means the recovery ship is going to be going about two-thirds of the way toward where we want to be.

"I suppose we should at least consider stealing the freighter they have with them, but it doesn't have a reason to leave orbit. They'd get suspicious fast, even if we could man the ship. The recovery ship is made for a small crew. A freighter isn't."

He felt his eyes narrowing. "Very true about the freighter. The recovery ship does present an opportunity. All we need to do is find a way to take advantage of it."

Veronica nodded. "We need to get back into orbit without them detecting us, sneak aboard the recovery ship, overpower the crew, and waltz right out under their noses. Sounds like a piece of cake."

"Don't be so negative," he said with a smile. "We've already proven very resourceful. We'll need to brainstorm potential plans. Do we have any idea how long before they plan to move the orbital?"

She shrugged. "Not really. I figure it'll take at least a week to get the people off the orbital. Then they need to strip the research and manufacturing equipment you told me about. Ten days, give or take."

"Then we have a little time. Pass my congratulations back to your engineer. Well done. This gives us a fighting chance. If we can escape and get this information back to the Empire, we'll solve the problem of the ghosts and the New Terran Empire."

25

Talbot exited the marine pinnace and entered the Dresden orbital. His was far from the only boat in the large bay. Just about every cutter and pinnace in the task force that wasn't involved in searching for the escapees was transporting people to the surface.

In fact, that's why he was here. He needed them to up the pace if they were going to clear the orbital on schedule.

Major Gabe Collins was waiting for him in the landing bay. Gabe was the commanding officer of *Audacious*'s marine detachment, just like Talbot commanded the marines assigned to *Invincible.*

Admiral Mertz had moved every marine in the task force to *Audacious* for the raid on Dresden and put Talbot in command of the assembled brigade-strength force. That made all this his responsibility until they made it back home.

That meant there was no room to spare in marine country, but he had more than enough trained fighters to take care of any problems. Too bad he didn't have the pinnaces to move them around.

"Things must be bad if you're waiting for me," Talbot said. "Why don't we just go to the conference room and hash this out?"

Collins nodded. "It just felt rude not to be here for your arrival, Talbot. I didn't want you to feel snubbed."

Talbot laughed. "It's good to see you still have a sense of humor. Let's see if I can fix that."

They didn't have to travel far to find a conference room. There was one right off the landing bay. Once inside, they sat at the large table.

Collins grimaced. "We're running about half a day behind. It seems that some of the civilians are getting froggy. They've realized they're being moved and are trying to slow walk us."

"Slow walk?"

"They're not resisting, but they're going very, very slowly. I'm not sure how we can speed them up without physically grabbing them and hustling them onto the cutters. I've considered stunning a few to allow the others to learn by example."

"As satisfying as that might be, I don't think we need to antagonize these people any more than we have to," Talbot said. "Kelsey was very clear that we're to leave them with as positive an opinion of us as possible."

Collins smiled. "I'm not precisely sure how that's supposed to work, considering we're stranding them on a strange planet."

"That is a challenge," Talbot acknowledged. "We can only do the best we can. Does the resistance seem widespread? I thought the prisoners were isolated from one another."

"It took us a while to figure out how they were getting messages back and forth. We used the cafeteria staff for food preparation and then had marines escort them to deliver it. We started watching them more closely, but it was already too late. The damage was done."

Talbot considered that for a moment. "That makes sense. You're telling me that it's going to be roughly twelve hours more than your original target?"

"Things might go more smoothly once we've moved more people, but that sounds about right. On the plus side, with fewer people on the orbital, we have less potential for prison breaks."

That had worried Talbot in the beginning. With over ten thousand prisoners, they'd have been unable to contain a general riot without someone getting hurt.

"And that's the way I'd like to keep it," he said. "I'm authorizing the delay, but try to keep it to a minimum. Kelsey is busy exploring the alien system she discovered, so she may not be back by the deadline anyway."

Collins raised an eyebrow. "I'm surprised you're not raising a stink."

Talbot laughed. "I'm starting to learn that I have very little control over what my wife does. If I want to stay sane, I need to focus on things I can actually control. Major Ellis is keeping an eye on her, so I'll just have to cross my fingers and hope for the best.

"What about the manufacturing equipment? How far along are we on getting it moved over to *Audacious*?"

The other officer smiled. "We're running ahead of schedule on that. We've finished cleaning out the secure labs and shipping everything over. The manufacturing equipment is larger, but we're probably about two-thirds of the way done.

"We could finish it in a day, but I have people going through the cargo manifests and storage areas to make certain we don't miss anything important."

"Don't rush it. It's important we get things right. Are you finding anything interesting in the cargo bays?"

"Actually, yes. Dresden is a major industrial center where they build a lot of Fleet equipment. We can use most of it.

"There's also a lot of raw material for use by the manufacturing machines on the orbital. Lots of rare elements used in the implants and AIs. Even though we don't have the ability to use the equipment right now, it's going to be a boost once we start."

Carl Owlet still hadn't managed to break into the computers controlling the manufacturing machines. To be fair, he hadn't had a lot of time. He'd had to explore the multiflip point and its potential destinations.

Kelsey had brought him back from the alien system when she dropped Angela off for her next implant procedure. The marine had finished and gone back, but Carl had already mapped both sides of the multiflip point, so there was no longer a need to have him in the Pandora system.

His young friend hadn't been pleased that he wasn't with Angela anymore. Ah, young love.

In any case, this side of the multiflip point led to five different systems. One of them was a core world of the Rebel Empire: Archibald. Three were unoccupied and unexplored. The last one was an alien-occupied system Kelsey was currently exploring.

The multiflip point from the alien side led to four systems: the one with the unwilling colonists, Archibald, and two different unoccupied systems. So there was some overlap, but not much.

From what Talbot had heard, *Persephone* could use the multiflip point, but *Audacious* was too large. The recovery ship was an unknown, but it certainly couldn't flip with the Dresden orbital. That made it far too massive.

His young friend had been working hard with the scientists they'd freed from the research station. Talbot still wasn't certain they should be allowing them to work on such critical systems, but Carl had vouched for them.

"If you can finish clearing out the equipment and supplies by the time you've moved the last of the prisoners down to the planet, I'll be satisfied," Talbot said. "If it takes longer, it takes longer. Have you at least broken all the manufacturing equipment down?"

"Most of it is crated," Collins said. "We just have to dedicate the cutter space to move it over to *Audacious*."

"Good. I'm not going to feel completely comfortable until you're done."

A rap at the hatch drew his attention. His pilot stood there.

"Sorry to disturb you, Major. I got a message from *Audacious*. They'd like us to stop by before you head back down to the surface."

"Any idea why?"

The man shrugged. "No idea, sir. It came directly from Commodore Anderson."

"Then we'll drop in and see what she has for us."

He rose to his feet. "Keep up the good work, Gabe. What you're doing here is very important. It's going to make a universe of difference when we get back home."

* * *

KELSEY FELT as though she were about to go insane. Almost a week had passed, and there was still no sign of her mother. It took all her willpower to put her worry into a mental box and focus on the tasks she had to accomplish.

The alien society helped distract her, but if Talbot didn't find her mother soon, she'd go nuts.

They'd put the time they'd spent orbiting the alien world to good use. Angela had deployed a number of probes above the most interesting sites, and they'd dispatched marine pinnaces at night to release drones.

Still no luck in deciphering the alien language, but that would come in time. They were recording every transmission they detected. If they couldn't figure it out now, Marcus could have a go at it when they returned to the New Terran Empire.

Angela was adjusting to her upgraded legs. She only fell over occasionally at this point, and she'd only bounced off the ceiling once.

Kelsey was secretly jealous. The marine had adjusted to the physical changes brought on by the Marine Raider implants a lot better than she had.

"Kelsey, I think I found something," Angela said.

She rose and walked over to Angela's console. The marine had a video display running, and Kelsey immediately grasped the importance of what she was seeing.

The scene was a smaller town. Most of those were agricultural in nature, either hosting many farms in the surrounding area or supporting ranching of native beasts. Often both.

The buildings were made of wood, the roads were unpaved, and the people seemed simple in their lifestyle. That probably included the human male she saw walking in the center of the image.

The man was dressed like the aliens, and he seemed unconcerned at being in their midst. He was in his early twenties. His brown hair and blue eyes stood out in sharp contrast to the aliens around him.

Over the week that they'd been observing the Pandorans, Kelsey had discovered they had a range of skin tones. All of them were blue to some degree, but it seemed that the shades darkened as they aged.

The aliens didn't seem overly disturbed by the man's presence. That wasn't to say they weren't curious or standoffish. They made way to allow him through, and many stared at him as he passed by, but no one seemed overly afraid.

Humans, it seemed, were a known quantity.

"Is he alone, or are there more?" Kelsey asked.

"He's the only one I've seen so far. We can keep track of him now, though. He might lead us to others."

The marine turned in her seat. "Have you decided whether or not we're going to make contact?"

Kelsey nodded. "We don't really have a choice. We need to know what happened here and what they can tell us about the ghosts. His familiarity with the local population leads me to suspect these folks haven't been in contact with the ghosts in some time."

"Maybe. What's your plan?"

"Continue monitoring him for now. Make certain you bring in extra drone coverage so he doesn't slip out the back of some building. We need to know where he goes and who he talks to. If there are other humans in this town, he'll eventually lead us to them.

"If not, he'll leave at some point. Once he's on the road, we should be able to arrange a discreet meeting. One without too much danger for anyone involved."

The natives' method of transportation was as primitive as the rest of their society. The poor walked, those with more means rode beasts similar to horses, and the very wealthy rode in enclosed carriages. None of the latter made their way out to little places like this, though.

Angela gave her a stern look. "You're going to let someone else make contact."

Kelsey smiled. "Don't be ridiculous."

The marine sighed. "I suppose that shouldn't surprise me. Well, let me rain on your parade a little. You're not going down there without a proper escort. If things go sour, we're going to pull you out. That's not open to negotiation."

"Not that I'm negotiating, but I don't expect to run into any trouble I can't handle. These folks aren't exactly the most advanced people in the universe. While we've seen some gunpowder weapons, almost everything they use is muscle powered. I don't think I'm going to run into anything that I can't deal with."

Angela rubbed her face. "Don't confuse primitive with harmless. One of those crossbow bolts can leave you just as dead as a plasma grenade. They also have numbers. If we get them stirred up, they can overwhelm us. Remember that Custer guy you told me about? Don't make this your Little Big Horn."

"Thanks for *that* perspective," Kelsey said dryly. "This doesn't have to be some kind of conflict, Angela. All I'm going to do is talk to the man. If I've worked things right, it'll be in private. Everything will be fine."

Angela didn't seem convinced. "I'm sending Annette down to scout the best landing places ahead of time. I'd go myself, if I could. Be careful, Kelsey."

26

Annette took her fighter down to the surface while it was still dark below. The planet's relatively large moon had set about an hour ago, and the area was so deep into the sleep cycle that very few people could even potentially spot her.

Not that she intended to get close enough to the town for the residents to become aware of her. That wasn't her mission.

Instead, she took her fighter along the road leading from the town at a very low speed. While she wasn't setting up a real ambush, arranging for Princess Kelsey to meet with a traveler wasn't too far off.

The more she examined the rut-filled track, she became convinced "road" wasn't the appropriate word. This was just a big trail. No wonder the rich and their carriages avoided the town.

She imagined it cost a good deal more in time, effort, and money to clear and lay a solid roadway capable of supporting coaches in relative comfort. Just clearing the trees and removing the stumps would be backbreaking.

The path she was following wasn't nearly so refined. It looked as though the people that had cleared it had cut any offending trees off as close to the ground as possible, but the stumps still protruded five to ten centimeters off the ground.

That would cause a serious jolt on some rich guy's butt, she imagined.

In less than an hour, she'd located half a dozen potential spots for a quiet meeting. Time to check them out on foot to be sure they were suitable. She'd start with the most promising.

Annette landed in an isolated clearing relatively near the road and killed the lights inside her cockpit. She sat in the dark for a few minutes while her eyes adjusted.

Once she was certain her eyes had adjusted as much as they were going to, she raised the canopy. The scents of the forest washed over her.

The smell wasn't terrible, but it was unusual. Annette had grown up in a city. Traipsing around the wilderness was not something she'd ever done before. She'd best go slow and watch her step.

There was a wide variety of noises coming from the darkened woods. Small creatures moving about, insects doing whatever bugs did, and other unidentifiable sounds.

It was spooky. She quickly decided that retiring to some place out in the wilds was not for her.

Annette pulled a pair of marine goggles from the compartment beside her knee and put them on. They rendered the outside world a pale green, but the darkness vanished. These high-tech devices took what little ambient light existed and amplified it.

She climbed down the side of her fighter and stepped onto the ground. Fallen leaves crunched under her feet.

The noises coming from the forest stopped. The animals must've heard her. It took a few minutes before they resumed whatever they were doing.

It took her half an hour to make it to the road. The area wasn't anywhere close to the town, really, but it sat between the small community and a larger town up the trail.

The road leading away from the town in the other direction was much more isolated. It was—amazingly—in even worse condition than the one she stood near. Even wagons wouldn't be going that way. It only supported people on foot or riding the local beasts of burden.

If the human they'd spotted took that route out of town, she'd have plenty of time to scout out other potential meeting locations.

Annette found an area adjacent to the road where travelers camped. She could see where they'd cut the vegetation away and dug fire pits. The efforts seemed relatively recent.

She calculated the distance from the town and decided this might be where a traveler on foot camped overnight. If the man were traveling alone, or in a small band of people, this place would be perfect.

They could set a marine pinnace down in the clearing she'd used and quickly move to observe any people resting here.

That didn't mean there wasn't going to be excitement when Kelsey introduced herself. That wasn't Annette's problem, though. She just needed to make sure the area was as secure and isolated as possible.

She'd been standing still for a bit, so she noticed when the local wildlife shut up. The silence made her crouch. She hadn't spooked them this time. Was there something else out there?

A strange sound came from across the road. She edged over far enough to take a look. What she saw surprised her.

A dozen of the natives had slipped into the area on the far side of the road. Based on how easily they moved in the dark, these aliens had better night vision than they'd expected, so she'd best be careful.

Each of them had one of the short-bladed swords they seemed to favor strapped around their waists. They also had the native equivalent of crossbows for ranged attacks. Their clothing seemed fashioned to blend in to the foliage.

Each of the Pandorans began shaping the foliage into something that would conceal them from view. They were setting up an actual ambush.

Suddenly paranoid about her own safety, Annette looked into the woods behind her. To her chagrin, she heard movement between her and the clearing where her fighter sat.

It was too bad Carl Owlet hadn't gotten the improved implant coms into circulation before this mission. If she had one, she'd have been able to communicate with her fighter from several kilometers away.

No use crying over spilt beer.

Annette edged deeper into the woods and a little up the closest hill. She moved slowly and deliberately, watching where she placed her feet. She couldn't risk making any noise.

She found a position where the foliage concealed her. She'd chosen to wear a black flight suit, so there wasn't much danger they'd spot her in the dark. That didn't mean that she was safe, though.

Annette had no idea who these people were or what they intended to do, but they'd probably hear her if she tried to sneak past them.

She had no choice but to settle in and hope that she could slip out of the area as soon as the ambushers settled in. That was going to take a while.

It probably meant that she'd miss her next scheduled report to *Persephone*. That should bring a little attention her way. All she had to do was keep her head down, and she'd be fine.

* * *

Veronica swatted at an unidentifiable bug. She had no idea what it was, but it was huge. They filled the air in the forest that she and Castille were walking through.

"Are you sure this is the best idea?" she asked as she dodged a root that threatened to send her tumbling. Again.

The security officer glanced over his shoulder at her. "Of course I am. How else are we going to find a way to get back up to orbit? The moment we turn on the systems in that cutter, they have the potential to track us."

"Just hold up a minute." She stopped so that she could focus her attention on him without breaking a leg. He obliged her by lowering the machete he was using to forge their path through the thick vegetation.

"Graham can go over every circuit in that cutter," she said. "If there's some type of remote control mechanism, he can disable it. Sneaking onto their landing field seems a little… rash."

Castille smiled. "That's why they'll never expect it. Relax. This is just a scouting mission. I just want to see how they've laid things out in case we come back to retrieve something."

"Like what?"

"A transponder," he said. "Just getting into orbit won't do us much good if they realize our cutter isn't sending a response to their automated traffic control. That'll make them suspicious. We're going to have to slip onto one of their cutters and steal a transponder so we become a known quantity."

She considered that. Grudgingly, she admitted his logic made sense. That didn't make this crazy trip feel any safer.

"If they spot us, it's over," she cautioned him. "Once they realize we're here, they'll bury this island in search parties. They'll find the base."

"Then we need to make certain no one sees us."

He returned to the task of hacking his way through the vegetation, and she fell in behind him.

It took them hours to get near the abandoned town. Once they did, they had to make their way through the foliage without the machete. She'd be covered in scratches by the time they were done.

The slow pace meant it was almost dark by the time they arrived in the overgrown streets of the town.

There were still a few people doing something on the far side of the town, but they were easy to spot by their lights. They apparently didn't want to trip over anything. Smart.

Castille led them deeper into the empty town. They'd discussed going around and approaching the landing area from the forest, but he'd decided against it. The crew that maintained the landing area was too active, and the risk of them hearing the Fleet officers tromping through the wilderness was too high.

Veronica stopped when they arrived at a large building covered in white stone. It was of higher quality than the buildings around it. If she were judging their location correctly, they were also standing at the center of the town.

"That looks important," Castille said. "I wonder what they used it for. A government center of some kind?" He spoke softly so that his voice didn't carry.

She shrugged in the darkness. "Probably. I'm not seeing any lights moving around inside, so why don't we use it while we wait for the rest of these people to go to bed?"

He considered that for a moment and nodded. "Good idea. Let's go in carefully, though. If there is someone inside, I'd rather not announce our presence."

They made their way up the steps to the large doors. Someone had wedged them open. Probably the same people that had swept the debris off the steps.

The interior of the building was lost in gloom. Neither of them dared use a light as they edged inside.

Castille held out a hand to stop her.

Veronica froze, listening closely to see what had alerted him to danger. She didn't hear anything.

"I'm going to use my light on low," he said. "I don't want to trip over something in the dark."

Her heart raced as the light came on. Even at its dimmest setting, it momentarily blinded her. She stood there blinking until her eyes adjusted and she could begin to see what was around them.

The large room that they stood in seemed to be a lobby of some kind. Maybe this was a hotel.

Off to one side, the remains of what had probably once been comfortable chairs sat crumbling on the smooth stone floor. Ahead of them was a long desk, very much like what one would find in a grand hotel.

It took her a few moments to recognize the words on the wall behind the desk. They caused her to suck in a deep breath. Fleet headquarters.

"Well, I suppose we know where they set up shop now," Castille said wryly. "I wonder if they ever expected people like us to find this place."

That seemed like an inane question. Whoever those people had been, they'd probably felt the same way about their Fleet as she felt about hers. Or, perhaps more appropriately, as she had.

The revelation about the AIs had shaken her to her core. The bedrock of her existence now felt like sand under her feet.

There were plenty of things about Fleet that Veronica disliked. The backstabbing between officers vying for the plum positions, the social strata between the officers and the crew, and some of the odious missions they occasionally had to carry out.

Now she wondered if that kind of thing was intentional. Had the AIs set up a series of competing interests inside Fleet to make certain it was never a threat to their rule?

She'd probably never know. Hell, just knowing the truth about the revolt made her death or disappearance much more likely if they made it home.

One more thing she couldn't change.

"If we're going to stay here, we should probably move to one of the upper floors," she said after a moment. "We don't want someone to wander in and find us."

"We'll take the stairs," Castille said. "The second floor should be sufficient for our needs. We'll pick an interior room and take turns getting a few hours of sleep. That should refresh us from our journey."

Some kind soul had wedged the door to the stairs open, so they didn't have to risk making noises that might carry in the night air. They made their way up to the second floor and found a suitable room toward the center.

It had obviously been an office at some point. The plain metal desk that sat inside looked forlorn and abandoned.

Veronica closed the door slowly. It made a low squeaking noise that set her teeth on edge. Thank God, no one was around to hear it.

She opened her pack and pulled out the tape she'd brought along. She tore off a thin strip and covered the gaps. Now they could turn the light up without risking someone seeing anything in the gloom.

Yeah, this office had definitely seen better days. The remains of shelves had crumbled on the outer edges of the room, dumping their contents to the floor. She hoped nothing poisonous was nesting inside the mess.

Castille looked around curiously before pulling a roll of padding out of his pack. He laid it out in the clearest area.

"Take the first break," he said. "I'll keep watch for a few hours and then wake you."

Veronica lay down and tried to relax. Thinking about the people who'd once worked here made that hard. She dreaded going to sleep because she was afraid that she'd dream of the horrors they'd endured.

She might as well just close her eyes and pretend. She didn't want to talk with the security officer right now.

Part of her had begun hoping that the enemy found them. That thought might be traitorous, but she wasn't sure it was the worst option. She needed to know more if she was going to do what was best for her people.

Whatever that was.

Somewhere in the midst of worrying about her problems, she fell into a dreamless sleep.

27

It turned out the reason Commodore Anderson had called Talbot back to *Audacious* was because Commodore Murdock had managed to pull through the emergency surgery to repair her damaged spine.

Perhaps repair wasn't the best description. Commander Castille had done an excellent job. The doctor had privately confided to Talbot that he'd expected the woman to die in spite of everything he could do.

Murdock's long-term prognosis was poor. Even with the advanced medical technology of the Old Empire at their fingertips, nerve repairs were tricky. Particularly the spine.

The odds were high that Murdock would never walk again. She might also never regain the use of her arms. Paraplegics were rare in modern society, but she'd be one of the unlucky few.

Commodore Anderson had instructed Talbot to remain on board the carrier so he could speak with the prisoner when she woke up. Oddly, Murdock had called for him before her surgery.

Not by name. She'd called him "that marine officer" when she demanded to speak to someone during one of her waking moments.

Talbot had eaten dinner and gone to sleep in the quarters he and Kelsey shared when they were aboard the carrier. He'd set the alarm to get him up early.

That proved wise. He'd only just finished breakfast when Zoboroski called him down to the medical center.

Talbot rapped his knuckles on the hatch leading to Zoboroski's office a few minutes later. "Morning, Zac. How's she doing?"

The doctor grimaced. "About as poorly as I expected. She's lost the use of her arms too. They best thing I can say is that I've saved her life."

He shook his head a little. "I'm not certain she's going to thank you for that."

"Living up to my oath to do no harm is sometimes complicated," the doctor admitted. "The odds are very, very high that she's going to be confined to a bed for the rest of her life."

Talbot grunted. "I assume the fact you've called me means she's awake."

Zoboroski nodded. "She's demanded to speak with you again."

"Why me?"

"You're going to have to ask her that."

Talbot sighed. "Then I suppose I'd best get this over with. I assume you've already told her the bad news."

"As if I'd make you do that. I talked with her right before I called you. She knows how unlikely even a partial recovery is going to be."

"Then I'd best go see what she wants."

Zoboroski rose from behind his desk and led Talbot down the corridor. He stopped short of the compartment where Talbot suspected Murdock was waiting for him.

"I'll leave the two of you alone to discuss whatever it is she wants to talk about," Zoboroski said. "The only instructions I'm going to give you are not to push her into a rage. One of the two of you is going to have to be the adult. I'm afraid that's you."

"Has anyone ever told you what a spoilsport you are?"

"It's part of my medical training." Zoboroski clapped him on the shoulder. "Good luck."

Talbot took a deep breath and walked into the compartment.

Commodore Emilia Murdock looked completely different from what Talbot remembered. The supercilious woman had rubbed him the wrong way from the moment he'd met her, but she'd never looked so helpless. So frail. Not even when he'd cornered her in the interrogation room.

Frankly, she looked decades older lying in that bed with her hands neatly arranged on the covers. It was creepy knowing that she was unable to move them from where they lay.

"It's about damned time," the woman said in a hoarse voice. "You'd think my rank would earn me at least a little courtesy."

He pulled up the visitor's chair and sat. "My apologies, Commodore. I wasn't on board when you called. I'm sure someone said this, but we're very sorry for what happened to you."

The woman snorted bitterly. "You're the one that put me under his control. You could've locked me into a cell somewhere else. It would've sucked, but at least I'd be able to move."

"We could have," Talbot said. "We didn't have any reason to expect Castille would attack you. Why did he?"

"He said he had to kill me so that I wouldn't talk."

"You were going to talk? Frankly, I hadn't pegged you as feeling cooperative."

When she didn't say anything, he continued. "He obviously had an escape plan worked out. A successful one, I might add. Why didn't he just take you with him?"

"I don't know," the woman said tiredly. "He didn't even give me the option. One minute I was sitting in my room reading a book and the next he was on top of me with his arm around my neck.

"Bastard had the gall to apologize for what he was about to do. Then he jerked my head back, and it was all over. If I never hear a sound like that again, it'll be too soon."

The best timeline they could put together said that Castille had struck right before he'd left the quarters to go to lunch. As a courtesy, they hadn't had the computer monitoring the prisoners' quarters. That turned out to have been a mistake.

Castille had gone into each person's room and killed them one by one. He'd used some kind of blunt object to crush the mens' skulls, and then he'd strangled the civilian computer specialist. Finally, he'd snapped his commanding officer's neck before coolly leaving the suite as if nothing had happened.

Yeah, Castille was one coldhearted bastard.

"I regret to inform you that you were not the only one he attacked," Talbot said softly. "Commander Castille murdered Commanders Irons, Gomez, and Jeanette Martin before he attacked you."

Murdock closed her eyes. "God. This is a nightmare."

Talbot chose to say nothing. There was nothing he *could* say.

After a minute, Murdock opened her eyes. "I want to make a deal. I'll give you what you want in exchange for asylum and the best medical care you can give me. I understand the odds of me recovering are slim, but I want to live."

Talbot felt his eyebrows rise. "We agree, of course, but we were already going to give you the best care we could. I'm not sure you can give us what we really want, though. I understand that the critical computers on board the orbital require multiple codes in order to access their contents."

Commodore Murdock gave him a nasty smile. "Commander Castille made an error. He tried to kill everyone that had those codes, but he missed someone. It takes two of us to access the system. He left two of us alive."

"Two?" Talbot asked. "Who else did he miss? I thought that Commander Renner hadn't yet received her authorization codes."

"She hadn't. Castille's codes would've expired as soon as she assumed his duties. Besides, she's security. She would never have cooperated with you. She's probably just as bad as he is.

"No. I'm thinking of someone else. You see, we have a number of researchers aboard the orbital. They're prisoners too, so they'd probably be willing to cooperate with you, if you sweet-talk them.

"The woman in charge of them has a code, though she doesn't know it. It's an emergency measure in case some type of accident kills off most of the command staff. It's the same code she uses to manage the research systems."

Talbot smiled. "Well then, I think we have a deal."

"Good," the woman grunted. "I want that bastard to know I stuck a knife in his back after he tried to kill me."

* * *

KELSEY ARRIVED on the bridge less than five minutes after the duty officer woke her. "What's happening?"

The man rose from the command console and allowed her to take her seat.

"Captain Vitter is overdue. I tried calling her, but I haven't received a response. I rerouted some of the drones to cover the area around her. There are a number of Pandorans setting up what certainly looks like an ambush. I found her on a hill nearby. She's pinned down but undiscovered.

"Also, it seems the man you wanted to meet must've eluded the drones we had watching the town. He's traveling alone on the road and moving slowly, but I think he'll reach the ambush point at about dawn. Assuming, of course, that the camping area is his true destination."

Kelsey quickly checked the information he'd gathered. It certainly did appear as though someone had set up a very slick ambush, and the fact the man had felt he needed to sneak out of town was very interesting.

Whom had he offended? His discreet departure and the large number of people sent to kill or capture him meant there was more going on than met the eye.

"Gather the marines," she said. "I'm heading down to the surface shortly. How much danger is there that the ambushers will find her?"

The man shrugged. "I don't know. She's still close to their area of operations, and they have forces between her and her fighter."

She reviewed what the drones were seeing in real-time. There were several dozen aliens concealed in the woods around the camping area. From the way they were moving around, they could see just fine.

While a few of them were taking up positions watching the road, most were building concealment around the camping area. None of them was particularly close to where Annette was hiding, so Kelsey didn't have to come rushing in guns blazing.

The tricky part of this was going to be extracting the pilot without alerting the aliens to her presence.

She called Angela while she considered her options.

"What's wrong?" the marine demanded after only a moment.

"Aren't you supposed to be asleep?" Kelsey asked. "It's the middle of the night."

"Marines learn to sleep with one eye open. You're up, so there must be trouble. Fill me in while I get dressed."

Kelsey briefed her on the situation. She concluded with an overhead map of the area around Annette with little red dots representing the potentially hostile aliens.

"I'm not quite certain how we're going to extract Annette," Kelsey concluded. "This is something you're better suited to figure out."

The doors to the lift slid open, and Angela strode onto the bridge. The com link between them terminated.

"That was quick," Kelsey said. "I think you've pretty well adjusted to your new legs."

Angela sat at her console and brought up several displays. "It's amazing how motivated one gets when a crisis occurs. From what I can see, Annette is safe for the moment. We'll want to get her out before dawn, though.

"The more interesting challenge is our human friend. He's going to walk into an ambush if you don't go tell him. He doesn't seem like the trusting type, so I'm not sure how open he's going to be to you just popping out of the dark."

"That's actually the easier of our two problems. I'm going to have the marines drop me off on the road in front of him. He'll see me when he comes to that stretch. Humans are curious creatures. He'll look around for a trap, but he's going to talk."

Angela gave her a doubtful look. "You're going to meet him all by yourself? Don't you think that's a little risky?"

"I'll be armed. If he gets froggy, I'll stun him. With drones all around us, I'll know where he is at every moment. With my enhanced vision, I'll see him more clearly than he can see me."

Kelsey smiled coolly. "And let's not forget that I'm a Marine Raider. If he wants to fight, I'll be moving a lot faster than him, and I'm one hell of a lot stronger. This isn't nearly as dangerous as it seems at first glance."

Her executive officer nodded reluctantly. "Are you going to have that conversation at the same time we're rescuing Annette?"

"If you can come up with a good plan, yes."

The marine smiled. "That's actually an easy one. The forest canopy is solid, so the aliens won't be able to see the sky very well. We'll take one of the pinnaces over her position and lower a line. It looks as if there's an opening in the trees a few dozen meters from her position. That'll work just fine."

Kelsey had to admit that was a neat solution. "Perfect. Once they get her out of the area, they can join the marines guarding me.

"Just in case the man proves more resourceful than I anticipate, the pinnaces can swoop in and drop marines on top of him in thirty seconds. They'll be in unpowered armor, so I don't think he'll be much of a threat."

That seemed to suit Angela better. "I like it."

"Good. Let me know if the situation down there changes."

Kelsey stepped into the lift and headed down to the tiny part of the ship set aside for marine country.

Finally. A little action.

While she hoped this didn't turn violent, she'd felt as though she'd been boxing at shadows for the last week. She couldn't do anything to resolve the problems besetting them. She'd felt helpless.

That changed now.

28

According to Raul's implants, they had four hours before the sun began lightening the sky. As expected, there wasn't very much happening at the landing field.

That wasn't to say that everything was quiet. A number of people were up and performing various tasks as he and Veronica slipped from the edge of town and into the jungle bordering the area.

Half a dozen people clustered around one of the cutters, performing some kind of maintenance. Everything around them was well lit. That meant they'd be unable to see anything in the darkness beyond the reach of the light.

Three cutters sat in the landing zone, two buttoned up tight. They had small shelters set up nearby. Probably for crew.

Raul stopped behind a stack of crates to observe the workers. Veronica crouched beside him.

He examined the crates with a frown. "What do you think they have inside these?" he asked quietly.

The destroyer commander examined the crates as well as she could but ended up shrugging. "There's no telling. There certainly doesn't seem to be any reason for shipping things down here. Perhaps it's stuff they recovered from inside the town."

"I suppose it doesn't really matter," he said. "Tell me, how difficult would it be to gain access to one of the unoccupied cutters?"

"They can be opened from the outside, but you have to have the right code or be able to bypass the lockout. Graham can do it. Not while people are working on another cutter right next to him, though."

Raul found it hard to argue with that kind of logic. No matter how they played this, they were running a serious risk. They'd have to sneak into the landing area, break into a cutter, and swap out the transponder without anyone realizing they'd ever been there.

The only way his plan had a chance of success was if the enemy never realized they'd made contact with him and his people. If they had to stun any of the workers, that would send up a huge red flag, and searchers would flood the island.

If anyone realized they'd tampered with one of the cutters, they'd be on the lookout for strange vessels. Only through complete obscurity could they waltz right past the enemy warships and steal the Dresden orbital back from them.

"Let's slip around and take a closer look at the sealed cutters," Veronica said. "I know Graham is going to ask me some questions, so I'd prefer to have decent answers for him."

"What kind of questions?" Raul asked.

"The first one is whether or not those cutters are locked. It's entirely possible they just closed them up without a code."

Veronica eyed the workers in their bubble of light and headed over toward the parked cutters. She walked slowly but seemingly made no effort to hide herself.

His heart in his throat, Raul walked after her. Amazingly, they made it to the parked cutters without any issue. No one had seen them.

He stood watching the workers while Veronica stepped up beside the forward landing gear. She climbed one of the struts and meddled with something inside the opening the strut normally occupied.

She climbed back down and stepped over to him. "The maintenance hatch is unsecure. They didn't bother arming the security system, either. I'm going in for a look. Keep an eye out in case anyone comes by."

Veronica scampered nimbly up into the cutter.

The night was so quiet that he could almost hear what the workers were saying to one another. He pondered the risks and then moved away from the cutter until he could hear them clearly.

Once he was close enough, he knelt on the ground and listened.

For the most part, all they were doing was bantering back and forth. Trash talk, basically. He was about to give up on hearing anything interesting when one of the women asked a question.

"Any word on when we're going to wrap up work at this site?"

An unseen companion inside the open cutter responded. "We're supposed to be ready to pull up stakes in forty-eight hours. Word is, that's the earliest we can leave the system. If they finished relocating all the prisoners by then."

"You think they'll really move all those people in two days?"

"Who the hell knows? Once they do, we can get the hell out here. If they can find the empress."

Raul watched the woman shake her head. Based on her expression, the woman didn't think very much of Justine.

"Ex-empress," the woman stressed. "And don't forget that she snuck on board our ship. She's a criminal."

The man inside laughed. "People like her always get away with crap that would land us in prison. She's not a criminal. She's a noble. Get used to it."

The sentiment amused Raul. Apparently, some things were similar in both empires. The rich and the powerful rarely had to face the consequences of their actions.

He was still chuckling to himself when he heard a soft whine somewhere above him.

Shocked, he looked up. A bright star was moving rapidly in the heavens above and growing brighter.

Holy crap. There was a cutter coming in for landing.

Based on the layout of the field, there was a very good chance it was going to land right on top of him.

* * *

ANNETTE FELT PRETTY good about her chances. The aliens seemed to have settled into their various positions. Maybe she'd be able to slip away unnoticed after all.

Her flight suit wasn't the most insulated uniform she'd ever worn, so she was thankful that she'd thrown a jacket on when she'd climbed out of her fighter. It made sitting still in the cooler air tolerable.

Things went well until she heard the aliens between her and her fighter begin moving toward the ambush location. Now they'd pass close by her position.

Annette had pegged them as reinforcements for the people out by the road. If they ran into trouble taking down their prey, no doubt the reserve provided enough force to make sure everything worked out in the end.

She wasn't certain what had signaled them to move forward. None of the aliens overlooking the road had gone to meet them, yet the backup forces were moving forward to join their friends.

Since they were going to pass very close to her location, she made herself even smaller and got closer to the ground. She had a flechette pistol and a stunner, but she'd prefer not having to reveal herself.

That seemed good enough until she heard someone coming up the hill toward her.

Annette moved to the other side of a large tree. Conscious of every sound she made, she held her breath.

Someone came into the clearing where she'd been a moment before. She could see him stealthily moving between branches in the foliage.

She willed the man to keep moving down the hill, but he stopped. The pause was only momentary. He moved forward and started down the hill on the other side of the tree she crouched behind.

Or so she thought until someone grabbed her by the back of her jacket and yanked her off balance.

She pulled her stunner as she fell, but the alien man knocked it from her hand before slamming her to the ground and jabbing the pointy end of a knife to her throat.

Annette lay there, frozen in shock and sudden fear. The man sat on her torso, pinning one hand with his knee while he held the other one down with his free hand.

"Well, I seem to have found a little bird," he said softly. "Don't chirp, or I'll be forced to hurt you."

Astonishingly, he spoke Standard as well as she did.

She'd fallen hard, and the night-vision goggles had come loose during their struggle. They lay somewhere off in the darkness. With them gone, she couldn't clearly see him, but she thought he was the same man who'd been in the clearing.

The two of them stared at one another for what felt like an eternity. She forced herself to relax. There was no way that she was moving him. Surrender was the only option.

"I don't suppose I could convince you to let me up," she said softly. "It's a little hard to breathe down here."

He shook his head with a small smile. "I think not. There's too much risk you'd give me away."

She pondered that for a moment. Give him away to whom?

"You're not with the people down there, are you?" she asked.

"And neither, it appears, are you. This is indeed an intriguing surprise. If you aren't with the Kalorian soldiers, then who are you with?"

"I don't suppose I could plead ignorance?"

He chuckled softly. "You humans. You always think you're so funny. Tell me how you knew Jacob was coming this way tonight."

Her mind raced as she tried to think of what to say. In the end, she decided to be honest.

"Actually, we were hoping to meet Jacob away from prying ears."

"We? Are my men going to find other humans lurking in the woods? I really don't understand what game you think you're playing. People are going to die before the sun comes up. Why are you hiding here in the forest?"

She opened her mouth to respond, but he pressed the knife into her throat a little. "On second thought, I don't think I have time to hear your response right now. Don't struggle. That will only make this hurt worse."

He dropped the knife beside her head and reached into his jacket.

She tried to throw him off but failed. He had her pinned and obviously knew how to fight.

He pulled an object from his belt. Annette only had a moment to recognize the stunner before her world went dark.

29

Talbot left the medical center and went straight to Carl's lab.

As he'd expected, the place was a hive of activity. They were still retrieving equipment from the Dresden orbital, and crewmen were maneuvering much of it into areas inside the massive compartment.

Carl was at the center of the activity, directing where to secure everything. Standing at his side was the former director of research on the Dresden orbital, Doctor Jacqueline Parker.

The dark-skinned woman was still an enigma to Talbot. He couldn't begin to imagine the life she'd lived. Not from her chaotic memories of Erorsi and the savage Pale Ones as a child, to having the Rebel Empire plant explosives in her head.

Carl spotted Talbot when he was almost to them. He raised his hand in greeting. "I thought you were down on the surface looking for Kelsey's mother."

"I was. Hello again, Doctor Parker. Commodore Anderson called me back up to talk to someone."

The young scientist gave him an appraising look. "Must have been important."

"You could say that. Am I remembering rightly that you set up a copy of the manufacturing computers for testing?"

Carl's eyes narrowed. "I did, not that it's helped very much. Why?"

"Because that means we can check something without risking the real cores. I just left Commodore Murdock. She says that she's willing to assist us. Not only that, she told me where we might be able to get the second code required for access."

Parker's jaw dropped. "Are you kidding me? You got that horrible old woman to cooperate with you?"

"Did you hear about the escape, Doctor Parker?" Talbot asked.

Her expression became guarded. "I heard a little bit. The security bastard and some other Fleet officers managed to get off the ship."

"But you didn't hear what happened to Commodore Murdock and the other senior officers from the Dresden orbital?"

She frowned. "No. Why?"

"Because Commander Castille killed everyone except Commodore Murdock. He still managed to paralyze her from the neck down."

The shock on Parker's face was profound. "Oh my God. I might not have liked working for them, but most of those people were relatively decent. Castille and Murdock were the ones I couldn't stand."

"It's a horrible thing," Talbot agreed. "The only bit of good to come out of the situation is that Commodore Murdock gave me her code. Now all we need is the second code to test it."

"If all of them are dead, who has the code?"

He pointed at her. "You do."

The woman started laughing. "That's the most ridiculous thing I've ever heard. Major Talbot, they used explosives in my skull to compel me to work for them. And rest assured, when I finally became a liability, they'd have taken me somewhere and set it off. Those people wouldn't trust me with something like that."

"It makes a crazy kind of sense," he disagreed. "No one would ever expect you to have it. Murdock said you had the code in case no one else was available. It's the same one you use to access your computers as the lead researcher."

Parker didn't look convinced. "If you say so."

Carl gestured toward the side of the lab. "We can verify it easily enough. Let's step over to the manufacturing computers and give it a try."

The three of them walked over to a console and Carl sat. "As I said, the cores are encrypted but I was able to make copies. The originals are safely stored elsewhere. If something goes wrong, these will wipe themselves, but we'll still be able to try again."

The young scientist focused his attention on Parker. "How does this work? Talbot gives a code and then you do?"

Parker nodded. "Try to access the core. It should prompt you for the first code. Major Talbot can enter it at that point. If that code is accepted, it will prompt for a second one. That's where I apparently come in."

Carl stared at the console for a moment and then looked at Talbot. "Ready for you."

Talbot used his implants to access the computer. When he felt its presence, he sent the code that Commodore Murdock had shared with him. The computer immediately indicated the code had been accepted and prompted for the next code.

"It's ready for you, Doctor Parker," Talbot said.

She focused on the computer for a moment before a shocked expression spread across her face. "I'll be damned. It accepted the code!"

Carl frowned in concentration for a moment and then grinned. "We're in! The core is unlocked!"

Talbot stood there and watched for a moment as the young scientist explored the access he had gained to the computer. After several minutes, he tapped Carl on the shoulder to remind him that he was still standing there.

The young scientist's eyes focused on him. "Sorry. I got distracted."

"Did that completely unlock it? I'm going to go report to Commodore Anderson in just a minute, and I'm certain she'll want to know."

Carl smiled widely. "As far as I can tell, your codes gave me complete access. Be sure to send them to me so I can use them again, if need be.

"I've already initiated the copying of the data to a clean computer core. We should be able to access all the information we need to manufacture Marine Raider implants and AI computer hardware. Everything seems to be there."

Talbot hadn't realized he'd been tense until he felt himself relax. "That's great news. I wasn't sure what we were going to do if we couldn't get that information."

His friend shrugged. "We'd have figured something out. We always do."

"The man I have on the orbital said he'd have the last of the hardware to you sometime today. Does that match up with what you're seeing?"

"It does. If anything, he's running ahead of schedule. By my estimation, we should have the last of the manufacturing and research equipment aboard in about six hours. It may take another half a day to move all the supplies that I've flagged as necessary for the manufacturing process, though."

"Excellent," Talbot said. "That's one thing off my plate. As soon as we can get the Dresden orbital cleared, we can move it to the outer system. Then I can focus my attention on finding the escapees and rescuing Kelsey's mother. Good work."

His young friend grinned. "It seems like you did all the hard work."

Talbot waved at Parker and headed for the corridor. He'd stop in to brief Commodore Anderson and then get back down to the planet. The clock was ticking.

* * *

Veronica jumped a little when Castille climbed into the cutter and pushed the hatch closed.

"What's wrong?" she demanded.

"There's another cutter coming in," he said. "I barely got under cover before it turned its landing lights on."

"That tears it," she said. "We need to get out of here, and I don't think we can afford to try sneaking back in again."

He frowned. "What do you mean? We have to come back for the transponder."

"No, we don't. I'm taking it right now."

"That's going to tip them off," he hissed. "We're not ready to make our play yet. I overheard the workers outside saying it was going to be another day or two before they finished getting the prisoners off the orbital."

"Are you going to count on the enemy being punctual? We don't have time to waste coming back here tomorrow night. By then, the schedule will definitely be too tight. We need to be in orbit at that point.

"They're never going to realize there's a problem so long as we keep this cutter from taking off. They'd have no reason to test the transponder if the cutter is grounded for maintenance."

Raul raised an eyebrow. "Is it grounded for maintenance?"

"Give me fifteen minutes, and they won't be flying this thing for a few days. It'll take them that long just to diagnose where the trouble is."

She wasn't an engineering officer, but Veronica knew her way around small craft. She'd started her career as a cutter pilot. That meant she had more than enough experience to know what would disable one. Particularly in a way that was infuriatingly hard to find.

Veronica went into the engine compartment and started digging through the guts of the grav drive controls. The flight-deck officer on her first assignment out of the academy had disabled a cutter by doing exactly what she was doing now.

It had taken her three days to trace the fault. Three infuriating, agonizing days of him staring over her shoulder and belittling her skills while she sweated.

Years later, she'd decided the man had been an evil genius. That one incident had driven her to learn more about cutters than she'd ever dreamed possible. Not that she'd ever forgiven him for putting her through hell. The sadist didn't deserve the credit for any nonexistent good motives.

The thing she liked best about this particular trick was that it disabled access to the avionics compartment along with the grav drive. Even if they tried to ping the transponder, they wouldn't get any reading on it.

Once she had the console open, she unplugged several connections and removed a component. One of the toolboxes attached to the bulkhead provided an instrument that let her send a surge of power that overloaded it.

Frying it only took a moment. She then painstakingly reassembled the console. When the pilots began their preflight, the engines would indicate they had a fault. The maintenance people would dig into them, but they'd be fine.

Only by tracing every bit of diagnostic circuitry would they locate the faulty component. Even with multiple people tearing the system apart, they wouldn't find it for at least two days. Her ego tried to egg her on to three, but that might be pushing it.

When she'd reassembled the console, she dug into the avionics compartment and removed the transponder. If anyone actually looked inside, they'd see the gaping hole where it normally sat.

She didn't expect that, though. Why look at something when you had your implants to tell you its condition? Veronica had met plenty of officers that never bothered physically checking anything. She was willing to bet the maintenance crews and pilots down here would behave the same.

Once she'd put the tool back in the toolbox, she bagged the transponder to keep it from being damaged and returned to the flight deck.

"I've got it," she said. "Let's see if it's safe for us to depart. I'll let you go down to the ground while I secure everything."

Castille still didn't look convinced, but at least he'd stopped arguing.

She unsealed the emergency hatch and lowered her head cautiously until she could see the area around them.

The new cutter had opened its ramp, and a number of people were moving the crates she and Castille had hidden behind on to it. Not only were they focused on their task, but the lighting also made it impossible to see anyone outside their general area.

Moving as quietly as possible, she lowered herself onto the landing gear and edged to the side so Castille could pass her. Once he'd made it to the ground, she sealed the hatch and followed him down.

Now all they had to do was get out of the area without anyone seeing them.

So, of course, someone stepped out of the shelter they were passing. A man in a lieutenant's uniform stared at them from just a few meters away.

"What's going on?" he asked sleepily.

30

The marines dropped Kelsey off on the road about a kilometer in front of where the human was presently walking. In the low light conditions, he'd have to be virtually on top of her before he noted her presence.

She found a convenient place in plain sight and started waiting.

With her enhanced vision, she had no trouble seeing him as he came around the closest bend. He was wearing a dark cloak with its hood up—probably to ward off the chill—but she could still clearly see his face.

He was actually walking beside the road. That made sense. It would be hard to see the ruts in the dim light cast by the stars.

Honestly, she wondered why he was traveling in the dark of night. All it would take was one pothole and he'd break a leg.

To her amazement, he slowed while he was still fairly distant. From the way he was looking around, he'd sensed something.

Kelsey wasn't moving. She had no idea how he could've detected her presence. Yet, something had obviously raised his guard.

Well, she might as well get this over with.

Keeping her pace slow, she began walking down the center of the road toward him. She kept an eye on the ruts to avoid ruining her entrance.

The man quickly focused his attention on her. He seemed as though he might be ready to flee but stopped himself. Perhaps he realized there was only one of her.

"I come in peace," she said as she came to a halt about thirty meters from him. "I mean you no harm."

"Says the person accosting a weary traveler in the middle of the night in the back end of nowhere," he said dryly.

Kelsey couldn't see his hands under the cloak, but she assumed he was holding some type of weapon. Based on the tech level, it was probably the hilt of a sword, but she wasn't going to take unnecessary chances. It was possible he had access to Imperial technology.

"I realize how this looks, but I wanted to warn you there's an ambush set for you ahead."

His head came up sharply. "Really? And out of the goodness of your heart, you've decided to come tell me about it? I can barely see you. How did you know who I was?"

"I'm about to make a light."

No need to be hasty. She didn't want to goad him into intemperate action.

She turned on a camp light that she'd brought with her. It wasn't a tight beam. More of a distributed light source that would allow people to see inside a tent. It didn't illuminate him much, but it would show her quite clearly.

"My name is Kelsey Bandar and, as you can see, I'm quite alone."

The man hesitated a moment and then walked forward until he was only ten meters away. In the light, she could see his expression clearly. He looked shocked.

"I thought myself familiar with all of the humans living in this area. How could I possibly not know you?"

Kelsey smiled. "I'm not from around here."

He eyed her uniform. "No. I'd say not. I'll wager you're not even part of Clan Dauntless."

She raised an eyebrow. "Clan Dauntless? No. I'm not part of any clan. I'm not from this world at all."

The man stared at her for a long moment before shaking his head. "We always knew this day might come, but I never believed it. Not deep down. Why have you come for me?"

"I'm just looking for information. I was completely serious about the ambush too. You probably shouldn't keep traveling along this road. It's not safe."

"No. I imagine not."

Kelsey's enhanced hearing heard a soft click that her combat reflexes identified as likely a safety flipping off. She threw herself to the side, and flechettes tore through the space where she'd been standing moments before.

She landed hard in the deep grass to the side of the road, already drawing her stunner and opening fire.

The man was quick. He ducked low and rolled to the side, still firing at her.

Kelsey heard the pinnace's drives kick into maximum thrust in the darkness above her. Marines in unpowered armor would be on them in seconds.

"Stunners only!" she sent over the combat link. "Don't hurt him!"

For a moment, she thought the man was going to get away into the forest, but she managed to line up a shot at the very last moment. The stunner bolt took him in the back just as he passed into the trees.

Kelsey stood slowly, wary of additional small arms fire. If she'd only clipped him, he might still be awake enough to shoot her.

The pinnace touched down right in front of her, and marines came boiling out. Half a dozen of them raced to the woods while the rest secured the area.

Two of them came back with the man slung limply between them. The corporal accompanying them handed her a Fleet flechette pistol.

Kelsey examined it for a moment before she stared at the unconscious man. "Well, well. Aren't you full of surprises? I think you and I are going to have a very interesting conversation in a few hours."

She gestured toward the pinnace. "Load him up. As soon as they recover Annette, we're getting out of here."

The corporal grimaced. "There's some trouble. Some of the aliens just attacked the other aliens. Captain Vitter isn't responding to communication attempts from the other pinnace. They're not picking up her implants at all."

"Crap," she said. "Everyone in. We're going in hard and fast. Again, stun only, if possible."

By the time they were loaded into the pinnace, she was already strapping on a set of unpowered armor. Everyone might think she was dangerously impulsive, but it was only when she had no other choice.

They arrived over the ambush site about the same time the second pinnace landed near Annette's fighter.

As soon as the ramp came down, the marines charged out. Kelsey could hear metal-on-metal impacts in the dark woods, as well as people screaming and shouting. There was a battle taking place.

The first people Kelsey saw were two aliens swinging swords at one another. One of them quickly achieved the upper hand and stabbed the other through the torso. The second alien fell with a grunt.

She shot the victor with her stunner, and to her amazement, he shook it off. A second shot took him down, though.

"Be advised that the aliens have some resistance to stunners," she said over the combat link. "Shoot twice and be sure. Don't leave anyone awake behind you. They might stab you in the back."

With the pinnaces and drones scanning the forest, they took out the fighters inside half an hour. A number of the aliens were dead or grievously injured.

Kelsey ordered the dead and injured loaded onto one of the pinnaces. The prisoners went on the other. She sent both small craft back into orbit to *Persephone*. They'd come back for her in less than an hour.

The only thing they didn't find was Annette Vitter. The pilot was gone.

* * *

RAUL STEPPED in front of Veronica and smiled at the lieutenant.

"They asked if you could give them a hand loading the crates," he said with a smile.

The man gave him a slightly confused look before nodding. "Sure. I was about to go do that anyway. Thanks."

The skin between Raul's shoulder blades itched as he kept walking. All it would take was for the man to ask the wrong person who they were and they'd sound the alarm.

But no cry came. The odds were good that the man had assumed they were legitimate. By the time anyone figured differently, he and Veronica would be long gone. Hopefully, they wouldn't realize their mistake at all.

"I thought we were toast there," Veronica said softly as they made their way into the ruined town. "That guy had us dead to rights."

"One thing I've learned in security is that people are inclined to believe what they see. Behave as if you belong, and you can get in almost anywhere.

"For example, the secure area on the Dresden orbital. One of the enemy officers waltzed right in and attended a classified briefing. No one realized they'd made a mistake and escorted the wrong person inside."

Veronica looked impressed. "Somebody had some serious balls."

He nodded. "Yes, she did. Let's hope we don't run into her again before we make our exit."

By the time they'd made their way across the ruined town and back into the forest, it was almost dawn.

They waited until there was enough light to continue on their way. They were especially careful when they climbed the slopes of the volcano, so it was almost noon by the time they'd safely arrived at the abandoned base.

He couldn't believe they'd gotten away with it. That almost made him laugh. Compared to the crime they were contemplating, this was petty theft.

The destroyer's engineer had gotten the water system in the base back online, so he showered while the attached unit cleaned his uniform. He still had to make do with survival rations but perhaps not for much longer.

Once he was clean and full, he went in search of Veronica. He found her on the stolen cutter with her engineering officer. It looked as though they were installing the stolen transponder.

"Refresh my brain how this works," he said to them. "Does this transmit our identity at all times or only when specifically queried?"

"Only when someone sends a signal requesting our identity," the engineering lieutenant said.

"It's standard procedure in our version of Fleet to query a vessel when we first detect it," Veronica said. "The ship then tags the identity of the vessel and assumes it is legitimate if the transponder is good. There's no reason to continually request an identity."

"So as long as they haven't realized we've stolen the transponder, they shouldn't give us another glance?"

"Probably not, though if they're expecting the cutter to come back to the carrier and then we head for the recovery ship, that may raise some alarms."

"Well, we can't very well go on board the carrier," Raul said reasonably. "Otherwise, we might just as well have surrendered down below and saved ourselves the trouble."

The destroyer commander smiled. "True enough. Even if they ask us where we're going, a decent lie might get us through. Like you said, people are inclined to believe stories that make sense."

"And what story might we have for bypassing the carrier and heading for the recovery ship?"

"Damned if I know," she said. "I'm going to be thinking about that before we take off. When do you plan on going?"

He considered the time. "We need to leave as soon as it gets dark again. We don't want the people below seeing us lift off from the volcano, but we have to get out of here."

"What about our prisoners?"

There was something odd in her tone. He wondered if she suspected he'd executed the Dresden senior staff.

If she did, she had to realize why he'd done it. He couldn't allow the enemy to have access to the manufacturing equipment. The ability to produce Marine Raider implants or re-create the lords would be a disaster.

Yet he didn't expect her to accept that without some misgivings. She was a Fleet officer, not a security officer. Summary executions to protect the Empire were outside her normal duties.

"We'll take them with us," he said in his best reassuring voice. "The intelligence they can provide is worth the risk."

"Having someone guard them while we hijack the recovery ship is going to be awkward. We don't have enough bodies as it is."

He smiled widely. "As much as it pains me, I suppose we'll have to stun them again. Justine will be most put out with me."

Raul imagined the noblewoman would be quite angry. Yet, he had to confess it would give him great pleasure to take her down. Her shrill voice was getting on his very last nerve.

"Everyone needs to get as much rest as they can," he said. "Get a good meal, take a nap, whatever it takes to relax. Once we start moving, things are going to be tense and stay that way for quite some time.

"With any luck, we'll be out of the system before they realize we've left the planet. By the time they grasp that there's another flip point, we might even be several systems away. Once they lose us, we'll be able to make our way back home eventually."

Then the war would begin in earnest. With his help, the Empire would crush the last remnants of the old dictatorship and the ghosts.

The lords were quite generous to those who pleased them. He could only imagine the rewards he'd earn for his part in this. He could retire a wealthy man. One raised to the higher orders by their decree.

Oh, yes. The days ahead were going to be very nice indeed.

31

Annette woke slowly. She remembered almost immediately that she'd been stunned, but her groan ruined any chance of pretending she was still out.

She opened her eyes and tried to ignore the stabbing headache. She was still outdoors, but the landscape had changed. Instead of being in a small clearing in the forest, she was on a mostly open hillside covered with large rocks.

Some were big enough to block the wind, and a large overhang of stone provided a break for a cheery little fire. The flames bathed her with warmth.

An alien—presumably the same one she'd been fighting—sat nearby. His hands were busy with a small knife and piece of wood, possibly carving something, but his eyes never left her.

"I see that you're awake," he said levelly. "Good. We have some talking to do, you and I."

He'd bound her hands in front of her and tied her ankles together. Her captor was taking no chances.

"What makes you think I'm going to cooperate with you in that conversation?" she asked as she sat up slowly.

"I could make some grand statement about how I have you completely in my control, but I'm not certain that's the best course of action," he admitted. "You seem to be a woman of action. One in possession of unusual and unique equipment."

The alien gestured to his right where she saw her weapons. Since he'd had a stunner of his own, he probably knew what the flechette pistol was too.

Her night-vision goggles were missing. He must've overlooked them in the dark when he'd kidnapped her. Pity. She'd loved those things.

"There are a finite number of these weapons in existence," the alien continued, his tone almost lecturing. "While it is not unheard of for one to turn up in an unusual location or in the possession of someone who should never have had it in the first place, it is never functional.

"You see, it takes power to charge the magazines. Yet, I must assume you know that. Both these weapons are fully charged. I confess to a great curiosity in how you managed that."

He smiled, his expression almost human. "Perhaps we should begin by introducing ourselves. My name is—as you might expect—not a comfortable one in the human tongue. You may refer to me as Derek. That is similar enough to be useful in interspecies communication."

"Annette," she said. "My people are going to find me. When they do, I suggest you surrender peacefully or risk getting seriously injured."

The alien's smile widened. "I *do* like your confidence, but we've traveled quite some distance. The likelihood of your friends finding us is very small.

"While I am a civilized man, it would behoove you to remember that my people do not take well to threats or intimidation. Even if only implied."

Annette laughed. "I have no idea what you're talking about. Frankly, you're the first person of your species that I've ever met. Based on what I knew, I never expected you to be able to speak Standard as well as you do."

He frowned slightly. "I find that aspect of your story… unlikely. Humans might be standoffish, but none of them live in such isolation that they wouldn't have ever met one of my kind."

"That's where the problem comes in. I'm not part of the population on this world."

The alien considered her for a long moment. His smile slowly faded until his face was expressionless.

"That is a serious and frightening statement."

She raised an eyebrow. "Serious? Yes. Frightening? It doesn't have to be."

When he didn't respond, Annette continued. "It's obvious that I've stumbled into something that I didn't expect. Frankly, that isn't too surprising considering how very little we know of your people. All we were trying to do was have a quiet word with the human traveling on the road."

"Allow me to make certain that I understand you correctly," the alien said slowly. "You are claiming that other humans have now found us?"

"That's right, and my compatriots won't stop looking for me."

"And *that* is why you frighten me. If what you say is true, it might best serve my interests to shoot you in the head right now and walk away."

That shocked her. "Why in the world would you kill me out of hand just because I'm not from this planet?"

"Because humans are dangerous, unpredictable, and dogmatic on the very best of days. Without access to the technology that was once theirs, your kind is relatively safe. If more of your kind has arrived, war is at hand."

Her mind raced as she tried to figure out what the hell he was talking about. Why would the ghosts be such dangerous people?

"Do I appear unpredictable and dogmatic? I'll agree that I'm dangerous, just on general principles, though."

The alien's smile returned. "I like you. That isn't to say that I might not have to kill you before the night is through. I suggest you tell me enough of your story to convince me that you should live."

"Since I have absolutely no idea why being human would be inordinately dangerous, I'm not certain what I can say to reassure you. Perhaps if you told me why you feared my people so much, I could explain why that's not true."

He considered her for a long moment. "Very well, I'll play your game for a little while. If you want to pretend that you don't know your history on this world, I will explain it in greater detail.

"Rest assured, however, that I do not actually believe you come from somewhere else. I'm uncertain what game you're really playing, but it's not going to work out in the way you hope."

The alien took a deep breath and launched into a short story. "This story begins just over six human decades ago. That's when Clan Dauntless arrived on my world. We knew nothing of your people or the war you wage with one another before a great burning streak filled the sky.

"*Dauntless* itself came down with a great clap like thunder heard across the kingdoms. None knew if the gods had decided to smite us or if some other great calamity was at hand. Then our people began finding humans."

He reached over to his side and grabbed a small pack. He opened it and pulled out what looked like beef jerky. He used his knife to cut part of it off the chunk and handed it to Annette.

She held it in both hands and tore a strip off. It tasted good.

"These humans came from escape pods, or so we eventually learned. Your clan chief ordered *Dauntless* abandoned when it came crashing down. A wise decision, as none survived the crash. All who remained on board perished.

"Over the next several months, my people gathered the surviving humans in our territory. We did not speak Standard, of course. Some humans chose to fight. They died. Others surrendered. They lived.

"That turned out to be natural selection. Survival of the fittest. Those who could not set aside their warlike natures culled themselves from your gene pool. Only those who could be reasonable remained."

He smiled a bit coolly. "Which isn't to say that humans are not wily and capable of fighting. No. Only now the unthinkingly violent are gone."

The alien extended his hand toward her. "You do not seem to be the type who is prone to lashing out at anything or anyone that opposes you. That disinclines me to believe your story, because if you are not of Clan Dauntless, then you are either from a different clan or from the great enemy. Both of those possibilities seem unlikely to me."

"That's an interesting story," she admitted, "but there are a few holes in it. You see, it turns out that there are other humans in the galaxy. Some that are neither associated with the humans on this world or their enemies.

"Which brings me back to why I came in the first place. We're trying to find the associates of the people who crashed that large ship. I'll assume that the battlecruiser in question was *Dauntless*. I'm not certain how clans come into this, but I'm hoping that becomes clear in time.

"My name is Annette Vitter. I am a Fleet Captain belonging to the Terran Empire. Not the Empire these people would have been fighting. My people also escaped the great civil war that we call the Fall. We're only just now beginning to struggle against the AIs."

She smiled widely. "If you don't mind taking a little trip, I can prove my story. And, my commanding officer would no doubt make it worth your while to listen to what she has to say."

The alien leaned forward. "It sounds mad to me," he said softly. "One of my closest friends belongs to Clan Dauntless. It was him that you tracked along the road.

"Which, allow me to assure you, would not have turned out the way you hope. He is one of the smartest men I have ever met. Confronting him would not have turned out the way you'd planned."

He sat silent for a long minute. "I find myself uncertain what I should believe. If you want me to go back toward where the ambush happened, that isn't going to happen. I left my men to eliminate our enemies. They will rejoin us here tomorrow. That will be soon enough to find out the truth of what you're saying."

The alien added some wood to the fire. "I suggest you get some sleep while you can. Once they arrive, we'll be traveling quickly and not back the direction we came from."

* * *

Talbot stared at the cutter. "Is it normal for a grav drive to just fail like that? I thought these things were pretty robust."

The marine crew chief shrugged. "Me too, Major. We still haven't tracked down what's wrong, but I suspect we'll be able to fix it relatively easily when we do. I've never seen anything like this, frankly. It has to be some bizarre combination of factors we've never seen before. The drive is probably fine."

The marine officer had barely made it back to the island before the crew of the cutter reported the problem. Luckily, this wasn't a critical mission. One of the other cutters would be able to take care of business until they got this one fixed.

"I suppose asking you how long it's going to take to fix this would be an exercise in futility," Talbot said. "Do the best you can and let me know as soon as it's functional again."

The crew chief nodded. "Will do, sir. Any word when we'll be done down here? The insects are starting to bug the hell out of me."

Talbot laughed. "Insects. Bug. Nice. I'll bet you've been waiting all day to use it on me."

The marine-enlisted man shrugged. "I was bored."

"They shuttled the last of the prisoners down about an hour ago. I figure they'll have moved the last of the cargo in about four or five hours. Then we can focus on searching this blasted planet."

The other man considered him for a moment. "I'm not sure we're going to find the escapees, sir. Now that they've managed to evade discovery for this long, the odds of them just turning up have to be falling dramatically."

"You'd think so, but that's not really true," Talbot said. "They've got a limited amount of oxygen on board. They can't just hide at the bottom of the ocean forever.

"At this point, we're pretty certain they're not on any of the landmasses along the equator. We've got cutters and pinnaces searching the frozen north and south, but they're even less likely to be able to hide there for a long period of time."

"Why's that, sir?"

Talbot gave him a chilly smile. "They've got survival gear but nothing that will allow them to live in the frozen tundra for very long. No. They might manage to continue hiding for another two or three weeks, but they're going to have to come out and get some food or air. When they do, we'll get them."

The other man excused himself to head back inside the cutter and get back to work.

Talbot stared off into the forest. It was maddening. Patience was going to win the day, but he wanted to do something now.

Well, he should just focus on doing his damned job. Sooner or later, the rebel officers were going to make a mistake. When they did, he'd have them.

The key was going to be getting ready ahead of time. Opportunities were fleeting. When the other guy made the wrong choice, you had to be ready to capitalize on it. He'd be ready.

32

Kelsey watched her human prisoner as he began to shrug off the effects of the stunner. She'd relocated him to the cabin her mother had used when she'd been on board *Persephone*. It would provide a more relaxed setting in which to question him.

Now that he was unarmed, he was no longer a threat to her. She suspected he was a very resourceful man. Not only had he carried a flechette pistol and a stunner, but he'd also had a worn marine knife.

She'd thought the metal immune to scratching, but the blade he'd possessed had obviously seen hard use. The surface of the blade had actual nicks. Maybe he'd carved his way through a bulkhead, as she'd once hypothesized such a blade would allow her to do.

The young man blinked and sat up. His transition from unconsciousness to wary wakefulness was immediate. He took her in and then scanned the rest of the compartment.

"It seems my confidence in myself was ill-placed," he said. "You're much quicker than you look."

"That sounds about as insulting as saying I'm smarter than I look."

The man grunted softly in apparent agreement. "No insult intended. Or perhaps I should say no further insult intended. Would this be the appropriate time to say I regret trying to kill you?"

"I think that's a great place to start," Kelsey said. "Why did you feel the need to attack me?"

"Shouldn't you be concerned that I'll do so again? I rather expected to wake up in chains."

Kelsey had a stunner at her waist, but it was the concealable one. She undoubtedly looked unarmed.

"I'm not nearly as defenseless as I appear. If you feel the need to get up and take a swing, please, be my guest."

The man smiled wanly. "Perhaps they treat guests differently where you're from. It's generally considered poor form to attack one's host."

"Yet it would be very instructive for you," she said. "I'm not going to call a guard in. I'm not going to pull some hidden weapon and disable you. If you want to determine that I'm telling you the truth, let's settle this right now. I am not the defenseless woman I appear to be."

Kelsey stood and advanced to stand in front of the couch where he sat. "Here I am, right within your grasp. You tried to kill me. Don't tell me that you'd shy away from hitting me."

He remained seated. "Under the circumstances under which we met, I felt justified. That justification does not hold true now."

She sighed. "You just had to ruin my dramatic moment, didn't you? Well, I feel justified in making my point."

"If striking me atones for some of my actions, then feel free," he said calmly.

"Thank you."

She grabbed him by the front of his shirt, hauled him to his feet, and raised him as close to the ceiling as she could. His feet dangled just above the floor.

He stared down at her smiling face, his mouth agape. The moment drew on, and she held him there effortlessly with one arm.

"I feel confident in expressing that you have my full attention," he said in a quiet voice.

Kelsey set him back onto his feet and pushed him back onto the couch. When she was certain he'd stay seated, she walked back to her chair and sat.

"When I say that I'm not from around here, that means I am not from your planet."

"I fully accept that, at this point," the man said. "No one can possibly be that strong. Not without technology beyond anything in the legends. Even my father's stories from *Dauntless* don't mention anything like that."

"As I said last night, my name is Kelsey Bandar. I don't know who you are or who your people are. At this moment, we are on board my ship in orbit. We've been observing your planet for several days and noted the crashed vessel on the surface.

"The aliens have obviously been extracting technology from it for quite some time. The fact that you had a stunner and flechette pistol indicate that you have not lost the technological acumen of your people.

"The thing is, I know nothing about where you came from. My computer indicates that's probably a crashed battlecruiser on the surface. I assume your people escaped the rebel forces during the civil war inside the Terran Empire.

"So did my people. We're just now beginning to fight what has sprung up in its place. I've heard rumors from prisoners about something they called the ghosts. Ships that attack from nowhere and then vanish again. If I had to make a guess, your ship was one of those. Am I close?"

He stared at her silently for a long moment. "My father would be very angry if I assisted you in any way. That being the case, I feel almost obligated to do so.

"My name is Jacob Howell. I've heard my people called ghosts before. We don't call ourselves that, of course. So I think it does no harm to tell you that we are indeed the people you believe us to be.

"That said, I don't believe you're going to find very many people willing to trust your story. My people are significantly easier to deal with than the other clans, I suspect, but none of them will willingly assist you in any way."

That's not what Kelsey wanted to hear. Especially not when she still had a missing officer to find.

"That situation can be dealt with in time. I have a more pressing matter to discuss with you. Someone set up an ambush for you. A number of aliens were lying in wait at a campground. I'm not certain what precipitated it, but they began fighting amongst themselves.

"Somewhere in the melee, one of my officers has vanished. Undoubtedly, some of the people involved in the fighting got away. They've taken her with them. You're going to help me get her back."

He raised an eyebrow. "If she's as strong as you, then I cannot imagine how that occurred."

"Don't play games with me. I'm a civilized woman, but I'm not going to let someone blather inanely at me when one of my people is in danger. If you ever expect to get back to where you came from, then you'd best start making me happy. What was going on down there and where might those survivors have gone?"

They stared at one another silently for several long moments before he spoke again. "If, as I suspect, your officer is in the custody of one of my friends, I'm not going to tell you a thing."

Perfect, she thought sourly. Any other time she'd be pleased to find somebody with integrity. Now it was just a big pain in the ass.

"We're continuing to search the area. We'll find whoever has my officer. If anyone has harmed her in any way, I'm going to hurt them. Do us all a favor and start talking."

"No."

This was going to be as tiresome as she'd expected. Well, it wasn't as if she had anything else to do while the drones scoured the area around the ambush looking for Annette and the people holding her.

* * *

VERONICA STEPPED into the cutter just after dark. Castille had already moved the prisoners inside. The men were sullen, but the ex-empress was incandescent. Castille had bound and gagged her.

"It certainly seems that you have a happy camper on your hands," Veronica said cheerfully.

The security officer grinned. "You could say that. You'd be wrong, but you could still say it. What's our plan going to be?"

She headed for the cockpit, trusting that he would follow. She began strapping herself in and waited for Graham to get the power back on. The engineering officer had gone over the cutter with a fine-tooth comb. He'd declared himself certain there was nothing that would give them away or allow the enemy to control them remotely.

Veronica turned in her seat while she waited. "As soon as it's fully dark, we'll come out of the volcano along the open side and put the mountain between us and the landing field. We'll go out to sea and then head for orbit at a leisurely rate.

"Once we get high enough to determine the distribution of the ships in orbit, we'll start for the orbital. If we have any luck at all, no one will even question our presence. They'll assume that the people on the ground got the damaged cutter functioning again.

"If no one pays any attention to us, we can adjust our course and go straight to the recovery ship. If they direct us to land at the orbital, we're going to have to do that.

"If that happens, you're going to have to come up with a plan to get us from the landing bay to somewhere else that will get us onto the recovery ship."

Castille sat at the flight engineer's console. "Let's hope that doesn't happen. It would make our lives so much simpler if we could go straight to the recovery ship."

He sighed. "Which almost guarantees they're going to direct us to land at the orbital, doesn't it?"

Veronica still thought that wasn't the worst outcome. The enemy might order them to land on the carrier. They'd be completely screwed if that happened. Best to plan on something that at least allowed the mission to go forward.

"If they send us to the orbital, what are you going to do about the prisoners?" she asked. "We can't parade them around in front of anyone."

Castille frowned thoughtfully. "Perhaps we should preemptively stun them. There are some crates inside the base I can pack them inside. If we have to move, we could unload the crate and carry it deeper into the orbital.

"I'll have to improvise if somebody asks us what we're doing, but if that happens, we're going to be in trouble anyway."

At that moment, the consoles came to life. Veronica began performing a quick preflight to make sure that all the systems were showing green. The last thing they needed was to have something go out on the flight. Having to declare an emergency would be embarrassing.

All systems looked operational, so she returned her attention to Castille.

"If you're going to get a crate, you should get it loaded now. By my calculations, we have about twenty-five more minutes before we can leave, but I'd rather not waste a single moment. We really have no idea what their schedule of operations is."

He nodded and stood. "Yes, arriving on station an hour after they depart would be awkward."

Once he'd left the cockpit, Veronica devoted her time to a more in-depth preflight. She ran a more detailed diagnostic of every major system while she waited for Castille to pack the prisoners away.

Even through the closed hatch, she heard the female prisoner screeching something and then the blast of the stunner. It made her smile. That woman *really* got on her nerves.

Candace joined her in the cockpit, taking the copilot seat. "I finished going over the exterior of the cutter, ma'am. Everything looks good."

"What's the status on the rest of the crew?"

"They're aboard and secure. We just sealed up the ramp. Commander Castille should have the prisoners in the crate in about five minutes."

Almost to the second, Castille stepped into the cockpit and resumed his seat at the flight engineer's console.

"We're ready to go, Commander," he said as he strapped himself in.

Veronica took a deep breath. This was a high-risk gamble. If they won, the payoff was huge. If they lost, they'd be in the carrier's brig.

She brought the cutter to a hover and eased out over the water inside the volcano. She wasn't going to miss that old base. Even a cell would be preferable.

Veronica could see some lights down by the abandoned town as she came over the volcano's collapsed side but knew that they would not be able to locate her visually. The risk was they'd be scanning, but she wasn't detecting anything.

Deftly, she eased the cutter around the volcano until the massive slabs of rock blocked any possibility of detection. At that point, she was able to open it up and head out over the water.

At about the twenty-kilometer mark, she began a gentle rise toward space. There was always a risk that someone was going to note their passage and wonder where they were coming from.

Considering how intensely they had to be searching for the missing cutter, that was a very real possibility.

She felt herself tensing as they exited the atmosphere. Her passive scanners had located the Dresden orbital. It was just coming around the curve of the planet.

That was a relief. It hadn't yet departed.

The huge carrier followed along behind it, partially shielded by the orbital's bulk. That really didn't mean anything, but it made her feel better than having to pass directly by the massive warship.

There were two cutters rising from different areas of the planet's surface ahead of her. She'd know very quickly if the carrier's flight control was directing each one.

Her heart jumped into her throat when the com system came to life. The carrier was signaling her directly.

"Gamma three two six this is *Audacious* flight control. I don't have you on my schedule. Where are you going, and what are you carrying?"

This was it. Either the enemy would believe the lies she was going to tell them or all hell was about to break loose.

33

Annette slept poorly, tossing and turning on the rocky ground. So far as she could tell, her captor hadn't slept at all. Perhaps that was normal for the aliens. She had no idea.

In any case, he was still sitting where he'd been when she'd gone to sleep.

Her understanding of alien expressions might be flawed, but he looked worried to her. Since he'd said he expected his compatriots to arrive by dawn, the fact they were still alone was probably the cause.

She sat up, stretched, and stared at him pointedly. "I have to take care of business, if you know what I mean. Are you going to be reasonable or are we going to have a problem?"

He shook his head and handed her a small pouch with some kind of primitive wipes.

"There's no need for difficulty," he said. "You can go over behind that large rock and take care of it. Just rest assured that I'll see you if you attempt to escape. I'm much more agile in this environment than you are. If I have to chase you down, you're going to regret it."

"I'm not going to run. Be right back."

Annette went around behind the large rock and took care of business as well as she could. The wipes were adequate.

She didn't like the idea of littering, but she certainly wasn't going to carry them around with her once she was done. She found a nice rock to bury them under. She pocketed a stone that might make a handy weapon.

Once she'd finished, she headed back around to the fire. There hadn't been anything cooking, but she hoped breakfast was on the agenda. She was starving.

He gestured toward a handy rock. "Sit. I think we have much to discuss."

"If we're going to talk, then I want something to eat. It's been a long time since lunch."

The alien grunted. "In case you've forgotten, you may call me Derek. I have some travel rations, but you may not find them very agreeable. My compatriots should have been along with our supplies by now. They are overdue."

Annette allowed herself to smile as he pulled a leather pouch from his backpack. "I'm not surprised to hear it. My friends are probably very annoyed with them right now. They'll get our location from somebody fairly quickly, so feel free to take your time."

The alien's expression turned decidedly sour. It was astonishing how familiar many of his characteristics were.

There had to be something wrong with that. Aliens were supposed to be… alien.

She took the hunk of what looked like cheese that he handed her and nibbled at the corner. It was extremely hard but not too bad in flavor. He followed that up with what looked like some kind of bread. It was like chewing rock.

"I'm not ready to believe you've captured my men," Derek said bluntly as he ate his own share of the meal. "My men are most capable. They've been with me for years. I seriously doubt anyone could capture or kill them all."

Annette smiled coolly. "You have no idea. When I said that I believe they're expanding the search and will find us, what I really mean is I'm astonished that they haven't already done so.

"As I told you, we have significantly more technology available to us than you're used to. Those weapons you have don't even begin to cover it."

"I've heard the same stories. We can all talk a good game about what humans used to be able to accomplish. That hasn't been true since before I was born. Give up this fantasy you're trying to sell me. Just tell me the truth."

"I can prove my story. All we have to do is go to where I parked my ship."

Derek gave her a bark of laughter. "As if I would take you back to where you might rejoin with your companions. The goal is to escape."

"Your goal, maybe. Mine is more complex. I'm trying to get information. I have no objection to going along with you. I have complete confidence that things are going to turn out in my favor before too long."

"I've never met anyone like you. Most humans are clannish, unsurprisingly. They stick to themselves and don't mingle with our folk. My friend Jacob is an exception to that rule, however.

"He and I grew up together at my father's court. I feel confident in saying I understand humans better than virtually any of my people. Jacob tells me that I've mastered your expressions and many of your attitudes, but I still can't claim to completely understand you."

He considered her more closely. "Even with that understanding, you baffle me. I could have killed you last night. Yet here you sit, coolly and calmly bantering with me. That's the kind of behavior I would expect from a warrior."

Annette tilted her head. "Of course it is. I *am* a warrior."

Derek shook his head. "Humans don't have female warriors. Not one. That isn't how your society works. Even if you were not from here, as you claim."

"Seriously? I thought humans were far past that kind of sexism. I'm just as much a warrior as you are. If you hadn't surprised me last night, I could've taken you."

"You might carry weapons, but that does not make you a warrior," he disagreed. "And before you ask, no. I have no desire to prove it to you."

She finished her meal, such as it was. "Then what is your plan? Do you have any water? That stuff made me thirsty."

He handed her a pouch made of animal skin that sloshed with liquid inside.

Annette stared at it and then gave him a flat look. "You carry water inside of animal skins? That's disgusting."

Derek laughed. "Don't be so prissy, warrior. What do you carry water in?"

"Sterile flasks." Putting aside her revulsion, she forced herself to drink. The water had kind of a metallic taste to it. She took the minimum she needed to slake her thirst and handed the pouch back to the man with a shudder.

"So if we're not going back to look for your men, where are we going?" she asked.

"We'll wait here for a few more hours. If no one comes, I'll take you back to the city."

She felt herself frowning. "If you mean that little spot up the road, I don't think I'd call it a city."

"Nor would I. No. I'm speaking of the capital."

"You say that as if it's supposed to mean something to me. Is that some type of political affiliation?"

"You take this game too far. I am of course referring to the Kingdom of Raden." He gestured in the direction from which the sun was rising. "It will take us about a week to get there."

Annette brought up an overlay map from her implants. There was a rather large city in that general direction, but she doubted they'd be making it there in a week on foot. The forest was far too thick for that.

"Is that some kind of joke?" she asked. "If it's the place I think you mean, we can't possibly go that far through this kind of terrain in so short a period of time."

He laughed. "And you call yourself a warrior. We'll make it there in a week, Annette Vitter. You may not enjoy the process, though."

She really hoped it didn't come to that. If they actually managed to elude the searchers that were undoubtedly scouring the countryside for her, Princess Kelsey might have to leave her behind. That would truly suck.

* * *

Raul tried not to clutch the chair he was sitting in as Veronica responded to the query. This was the moment of truth. All their plans hinged on this conversation.

"The ground crew managed to find the fault and get us going again, Control," Veronica said calmly. "We still have a little bit of cargo that they decided to put on the orbital, so we're headed there."

Control was silent so long that Raul feared they were checking her story, but they finally spoke again. "Copy that. You are cleared to proceed."

Once he was certain the communication had ended, he let out the breath he had been holding all at once. "Well done. Very well done."

She glanced back at him. "That's just one step of many we're going to have to get right for this to work. Since we know they're watching us, we're going to have to land at the orbital.

"I can get you out so you can make your way to the recovery ship, but they're going to expect this cutter to undock again before they let the orbital go. That means I'm going to have to stay with it at least long enough to complete the undocking maneuver."

He frowned. "How is that supposed to work? I'd rather not leave you behind."

"Don't be ridiculous. While we're docked, I'm going to find a vacuum suit. Once I take the cutter back out into space, I can program it to head back to the surface. I'll jump off and land somewhere on the orbital and make my way to the recovery ship. You'll just have to let me in once you've secured the ship."

"Can a cutter successfully land without anyone aboard?"

She smiled slyly. "Probably not, but that's not a negative in this particular case. They'll expend resources searching for injured and dead at the crash site. That should conceal where we've actually gone long enough to get away, I hope."

Raul wasn't at all certain about that, but he had to trust her to do her job. He nodded his agreement.

"We'll make it work. The next task is going to be getting out of the cutter without anyone asking awkward questions. Finish docking, and I'll brief your officers.

"You're doing one hell of a job, Veronica. Don't think that I'm going to forget this. When we get home, everyone is going to know how crucial you were to the success of this operation."

The woman's smile turned wry. "After I surrendered my ship and the others under my temporary command, I'm not at all certain that's going to be enough to make a difference."

"Don't undervalue what we're bringing back with us. No one could have done any better than you did at Erorsi. They ambushed you with overwhelming force, and your commanders have already paid in full for their errors. The lords will understand that."

"I wish I felt as certain as you do," she said, sighing. "Forgive me, but you really have no idea what they'll do."

"I think I know them well enough." He left her in the cockpit after gesturing for the copilot to accompany him. Once he had all the officers gathered in the rear of the cutter, he laid out his plan.

"Once Commander Giguere lands, we'll unload the crate. We're not going to leave it in the docking area. We'll take it to the security zone. We can lock the unconscious prisoners into one of the cells and make our way to the recovery ship.

"Commander Giguere is going to take the cutter back toward the surface of the planet. She's going to exit before it leaves the area around the orbital and join us at the recovery ship. Commander Bakersfield will find her a vacuum suit."

He waited for them to nod before he continued. "We don't know their schedule of departure, so we're going to need to improvise as we go along. Does anyone have any questions?"

The officers glanced at one another and shook their heads.

"Excellent. Follow my lead if anyone tries to stop us."

He strapped himself in to one of the seats and waited. It seemed to take forever for the cutter to dock, but he finally felt it landing.

The ramp began lowering as he unstrapped himself.

They'd barely started getting the large crate with the prisoners unloaded when they ran into trouble.

A lieutenant with a clipboard intercepted them. He was staring at the crate.

"Excuse me, Lieutenant. We're done here. What's that?"

Since the number of commanders on even a large ship was extremely small, he'd pilfered the rank tabs from one of the prisoners. So had Veronica. They were both junior-grade lieutenants now. A rank that had numerous holders on a ship the size of the carrier.

"Something that was inadvertently left in one of the cutters," Raul said smoothly. "They don't want to leave it down where the prisoners can get their hands on it."

"I'll need to mark down the contents," the other man said. "Have your people set it down and open it up."

Raul eyed the officer and surreptitiously looked to see how many people would see if he had to do anything drastic to the man.

Unfortunately, four marines had just come into the cargo bay and were watching them curiously.

"Lieutenant?" the man asked. "Did you hear me? I need you to open up that crate right now."

34

Kelsey was extremely annoyed with Jacob Howell. Even though it was apparent he'd accepted the basic outline of her story, he'd refused to help her find Annette Vitter. She'd argued with him until she was blue in the face, but he hadn't budged.

She admired his loyalty, but this was costing her precious time and putting her officer at needless risk.

By now, the sun had risen, and Jacob's friend was probably carrying Annette even farther from the search area. The marines had scoured the forest with drones and turned up nothing. It was as though the two had vanished.

Kelsey had gotten a few hours of sleep and allowed the man to stew in his makeshift cell. To her annoyance, he probably hadn't been bored. It was obvious he was absolutely delighted to be on an operational ship.

He'd demanded to know the ship's name. Once she'd told him, he'd insisted that she was chief of Clan Persephone. Great. That did absolutely nothing useful to her way of thinking.

Angela was hard at work questioning the alien prisoners. Kelsey suspected she'd probably get something useful before the stubborn human cooperated.

When Kelsey had reviewed the latest reports from the searchers and eaten breakfast, she headed for Jacob's cabin. The marine guards let her in, and she found the man examining the inside of the kitchen cabinets.

"What is this material?" he asked. "I've seen it before, but never in this condition. The salvaged pieces were exposed to the elements for decades."

"It's a form of what we call plastic. I'm not sure of its precise makeup, and that probably doesn't matter. I couldn't make it if my life depended on it."

She sat on the edge of the couch. "This has to stop. You're needlessly putting my officer in danger. I couldn't care less about the two of you or what's going on below. By all means, continue working whatever Machiavellian scheme you're involved in without us."

He came out of the kitchen and sat down beside her. "What does that mean?"

"Devious. Convoluted. Subtle. You can pick any of those words to describe the man the word refers to. He lived on Terra before spaceflight.

"What I mean is that I'm not trying to interfere in anything that you're doing. All I wanted to do was talk with you. I'm doing that. My goals are satisfied. I'll be happy to release you once we're done without any conditions."

His look took on a slightly amused air. "That seems rather plain spoken. You've come a very long way for information that was out of date decades before I was born. Whatever information I have about the clans won't be very useful."

"Considering that I know nothing about them, I disagree. All we've ever heard them referred to as are ghosts. We suspect they are Imperial forces that escaped the civil war, but that's just a guess. Beyond that, even old information would be useful.

"We don't want to fight them. It's very likely that we're fighting the same enemy."

His expression turned sad. "Then you are in for disappointment. The clans won't work with you, I suspect. They'll see you as just another part of the corrupt Empire.

"I suppose giving you some information won't hurt. Your guess is correct. The clans were formed by ships that escaped during the great war. They persevered in the system on the other side of the defective flip point. If I remember the old stories correctly, they called it Icebox.

"It kept them prisoner for decades until they devised an escape into other systems. In the time since, they've grown strong. Much stronger than any raiding you've heard about would have indicated."

She leaned back in the couch and gave him a curious expression. "How do you mean?"

"First, you need to understand my background and that of my clan. Clan Dauntless was one of the founding units in the Council of Clans. Our chief supported the goals of the Council to take the war back to the corrupt Empire. To bring it down and restore what had existed before.

"When the Others came, we were skeptical. We did not believe that they had the best interests of the people at their heart. Over time, the Others swayed the Council and turned them against us. That's why we fled."

Kelsey frowned. "Others?"

He opened his mouth to say something, but closed it again. Moments later, he started again. "My apologies. I've heard the story so many times that I forgot you don't have the background to know that.

"The Others are human, but not of the Empire. They represent a political entity known as The Singularity. Their leaders favor tattoos on their faces, as I recall."

"I've heard of them," Kelsey said. "Something about their leadership being genetically engineered."

Jacob raised an eyebrow. "I'm not certain I understand what that means. In any case, my father said that these people were exceptionally cunning. They spent many long years helping the Council build the kind of infrastructure needed to fight the corrupt Empire. Fleets of powerful ships.

"The leadership of Clan Dauntless never believed that they wished us well, though. I'm told they believed The Singularity was manipulating the Council. Suborning it.

"That is what convinced the clan to flee through the Icebox system and try to find a new home elsewhere. The Council allowed us to depart, but Singularity warships trailed closely behind and attacked us.

"We had no intention of going into the Icebox system, as I understand it. It was a dead end. Superior numbers forced our hand. There was a great battle. One in which *Dauntless* emerged victorious, but was crippled.

"Our leaders took a great chance and tried to take it through the defective flip point. Something our engineers did allowed us to make our way through, but not to the system we thought existed on the other side. We found this one instead."

"Your ship must've been in very bad shape if it crashed," she said after a moment. "My missing officer believes that someone almost brought that ship down to the surface. Was that their intention?"

He shook his head. "The story is that our leaders remained aboard the ship when her engines failed during orbital insertion. They chose to crash with the ship to allow the clan time to escape. No officer above the rank of lieutenant survived.

"Unfortunately, the prisoners that the clan had collected after the battle also escaped. The Others. They now work with the repressive regime in the Empire of Kalor. I'd wager they're suborning it in much the same way they did the Council of Clans. Unless I miss my guess, it was Kalorian soldiers who made up the ambush you mentioned.

"That is why my friend and his soldiers came to assist me. We were trying to flush them out and eliminate them. They've been causing the kingdom trouble for many years. They wanted me as their prisoner."

She considered him for a long moment. "Why did they consider you so important? What are you to them that you would make a good hostage?"

Jacob grinned. "Me? I'm nothing. It's my father they would like to control. He is the chief of Clan Dauntless. The Others still hope to escape this world."

"And you don't?"

"I hadn't, not until I learned of your ship. Now the impossible seems possible."

"It's possible," Kelsey said, "but only if you start cooperating. I'm more than willing to take you back down to the surface myself, along with all of the men we captured. We'll turn you all over to your friend in exchange for my officer. All you have to do is tell me where he is."

"At this point, I'm almost willing to give it a chance," Jacob said. "I can't honestly say I know where he would go, though. There are several possible destinations. He's a very canny woodsman. The chances of you tracking him are slim."

"They wouldn't have been if you'd talked to me last night," Kelsey said acerbically. "Why didn't you just cooperate then?"

He shrugged. "I couldn't take the chance. I believe you now, but I was uncertain then. My friend's name in Standard is Derek. His father rules the Kingdom of Raden. I couldn't risk giving you the opportunity to take him hostage."

Kelsey sighed. "Just another piece of political maneuvering that I have no interest in. Come on. I think it's time to give you a tour of the ship, and then we can go talk to your friend's men."

She rose to her feet and led him toward the door. "I don't have time to play games. Events are unfolding, and our time is limited. If I have to waste days hunting for your friend, no one is going to be happy when I find him."

* * *

Veronica heard the raised voices from inside the cutter and made the decision to head down the ramp to see if she could settle whatever the problem was. She found Castille arguing with a lieutenant holding a clipboard.

That was never a good thing. The general rule of thumb was to worry if you found a lieutenant with a clipboard or a map.

She sauntered down the ramp as casually as she could and walked up to the group. "Is there a problem, sir?" she asked the man with the clipboard.

"Yes. We finished tallying the remaining cargo, so I need to see the contents of the crate to add it to our list."

"Ah," she said. "I understand. I'm afraid we're not going to be able to do that, sir."

He blinked at her. "Excuse me?"

"It's classified. Why do you think we're moving it onto the orbital at the last moment? The orders for this came from the very highest level. Princess Kelsey. You can contact her for confirmation, of course."

Veronica really hoped it didn't come to that, but she doubted it would. The odds of a lieutenant disturbing somebody of that exalted social position with something like this were slim. It was still taking a chance, but what part of this escape wasn't?

"But she hasn't been in the system for a week."

That surprised her, but she kept her face bland. She hoped it didn't mean they'd discovered the distant flip point. That would complicate matters.

"That's outside my control, and it still doesn't change my orders,"

Veronica said. "Look, it's only one crate. We're going to secure it inside the orbital like she told us. It's not as if it will somehow cause a problem. Do you really want to raise a stink over this and deal with the consequences, sir?"

No officer in her right mind wanted to deal with angry superiors by questioning their orders. It was much simpler just to go with the flow.

"I don't recognize you people. Are you based on *Persephone*?"

"That's right."

"Figures." After a long moment, he sighed. "I suppose you're right. It's only one crate. I'll make a note that it was delivered and stored as per Princess Kelsey's orders. If there's a problem, you can explain it."

The man moved off and drew some nearby marines with him. As soon as they stopped paying attention to her, Veronica gestured for Graham to go get a vacuum suit for her.

It only took him a few moments to get one out of an emergency locker and carry it into the cutter. The lieutenant and his companions were no longer in sight, so she casually followed him in. He set it on a chair, grinned at her, and headed back out to rejoin Castille.

Once she'd sealed the cutter, Veronica put the vacuum suit on. This next part was going to be tricky, and she didn't want to waste any time.

She lifted the cutter off the deck and took it slowly out of the landing bay. After she was in vacuum, she bled the air out of the cutter and opened the ramp.

It wasn't difficult to lay in a course that took the cutter past the recovery ship. She wasn't going to be exceptionally close to it, but she had some experience in maneuvering a vacuum suit. She'd be able to get onto the hull without too much trouble.

Once she was there, she'd wait for Castille and her people to join her.

The cutter would maintain its slow speed until it was clear of the orbital and then accelerate toward the planet at a normal velocity.

The damned computers on board weren't too smart, so it was probably going to mess up during reentry. That should make a nice splashy problem for their enemies to sort out.

She carefully made her way down the ramp and braced herself against the cutter's hull as it slid past the recovery ship. Taking a deep breath, she aimed at a good landing place and launched herself into the void.

The kick off hadn't been precisely even, so she began rotating almost at once. That didn't overly concern her. She'd be able to use the suit's built-in thrusters to steady herself and then slow down before landing.

Veronica brought up the thruster controls and blanched. The suit had no reaction mass. She was stuck with the momentum she'd gained from jumping off the cutter.

The heavens spun around her as she coasted toward the recovery ship. It was hard to tell, but she thought she was going to come close. Of course, close didn't really matter if she still missed. Or if she hit hard enough to bounce off.

She cursed herself for not checking the reservoir levels. That little bit of stupidity was probably going to kill her. She'd only have one chance at this.

To her relief, her initial jump had been true. She collided roughly with the hull of the recovery ship.

That didn't mean that everything came up roses. She hit at an awkward angle, something snapped in her left forearm, and her helmet bounced off the hull.

Veronica scrambled to grab anything and caught something mounted to the hall with her right hand. The rebound almost yanked her shoulder out of its socket, but she managed to hang on.

She ended up bruised and bloodied, but secure on her destination. She was happy with the result until she saw that the corner of her faceplate was cracked.

A quick check of the interior instruments confirmed she was slowly losing air. Probably not through the crack itself or it would have blown out already. She'd probably torn her suit when she rammed the ship.

She wasn't going to have time to wait for the rest to join her. She had to find a way into the recovery ship right now, no matter the risk.

So, of course, the nearest personnel hatch was locked up tight.

35

They'd only been marching through the forest for about three hours when Annette saw her chance to turn the tables on her captor. The hills they were moving through were relatively steep, so he kept her close in front of him to prevent her from either falling or trying to get away.

Unfortunately for him, that meant he was also in range for her to take action.

The rocks on the slope were relatively stable, but there were a few that didn't seem as deeply embedded in the ground. She kept her eyes peeled for those. Up until this point, it was so she could avoid taking a nasty tumble. Now she was deliberately going to use one of them.

She just hoped her wild plan didn't end up with her tumbling down the side of the hill and breaking every bone in her body.

Annette tried not to tense when she stepped on the loose stone, but that proved impossible when it skidded out from under her feet and she flew backwards. She just hoped Derek interpreted her premature stiffening in a different manner or missed it entirely.

The reason she'd chosen this particular stone was that they'd just passed a fairly loose bit of ground. When she fell back into her captor, his feet slid out from under him as he struggled to hold her weight and maintain his footing.

She had to give him credit. He made a Herculean effort to both stay on his feet and keep her from falling down the hill. One that fell short of absolute success, but not by as much as she'd hoped.

Derek's feet stayed mostly under him as she slammed her upper body into his, right up until a rock shot out from under one of his feet and he went down hard.

Her hands were already in motion as they fell, and she came up with the pistol he had strapped to his waist.

That didn't stop her from sliding half a dozen feet down the hill and fetching up hard against a boulder. Thankfully, she'd been able to use her artificial arm to stop her fall. She didn't feel like anything was broken, but she imagined her back was covered with bruises.

Belatedly, she realized she could've used her arm as proof of her story. A cut with a knife would have revealed the machinery within. The damned thing felt so real that she'd forgotten about it.

That was usually a plus, as she had no desire to recall the horrific crash that had amputated the original. Oh well.

Derek slid to a halt about a dozen feet away. He started to reach under his jacket but stopped when he realized she had a weapon aimed at him.

"I'd really rather not have to shoot you," Annette said casually. "I'd hoped to get your stunner, but I'll use this flechette pistol if I have to. Don't make me kill you."

The alien shook his head slowly. "That was stupid of me. I allowed you to lull me into a false sense of security and then use the terrain against me. Clever. So what do we do now? Go back and search for your Kalorian allies?"

"Seriously? You didn't hear a single thing I told you?"

"I heard you. I just don't believe you."

She smiled coolly. "Then let's see if I can make you a believer. Toss your weapons over here. Where are mine?"

"I have yours stored in my pack," he said as he gingerly levered himself to his feet.

He made a show of slowly removing his stunner from a holster on the other side of his body and tossing it halfway between them. She wasn't going to fall for the bait and come into his range.

She gestured up the hill with her free hand. "Up you go. Don't try to get fancy with any rocks. I'll be watching."

Once he'd climbed far enough ahead of her, she squatted and picked up the stunner he'd tossed. She relaxed a little bit as she stuffed the flechette pistol into her jacket. She didn't really want to kill the alien.

Annette half expected him to try something before she made it back up to his level, but he only stood there watching her expectantly.

"What do we do now?" he asked.

"I prove I was telling you the truth. We head back the way we came."

He raised an eyebrow. "You could very well be leading me back to be captured by your companions."

"You're already captured. I have even less reason to lie now. I think the fact that none of your friends came away from the ambush should tell you something too. Do you think the people you were attacking were numerous enough to take you all out, even with surprise on your side?"

"No. Still, it's a more likely turn of events than the story you've been trying to sell me."

"I suppose we'll both find out what happened, won't we? I suggest you take it slow and stick to areas where no one will see us. I'd rather not be captured by the people setting up the ambush, either."

Considering the tangles and dense foliage he led her through on the way back toward the campsite, Derek was taking every precaution to avoid discovery. Annette stayed far enough back that he would not be able to surprise her.

She supposed that meant he was far enough ahead to escape, if he really wanted to. She'd already decided to let him go if he tried. Well, if the stunner didn't bring him down anyway. She wasn't going to chase after him, and she wasn't going to kill him.

They didn't run into anyone as they came back into the area near her fighter. Annette halfway expected to find it gone, but it sat in the clearing just as she'd left it.

Derek stopped short as soon as he saw the small craft. He stared at it, not moving.

After a long, long moment, he turned his head and stared at her. "I must confess that I thought you were lying. My apologies."

She stepped into the clearing and into range of the fighter with her implants. The computer inside immediately forwarded her a message.

An image of Princess Kelsey appeared. She seemed to be staring straight at Annette.

"If you're seeing this, you made it back to your fighter before we found you. We've already cleaned up the area around the campsite and are searching for you. Let us know, and we'll have a marine pinnace on your location in five minutes, if you need it. We picked up the guy on the road too."

Annette dismissed the message.

She smiled at Derek. "Apology accepted. According to a message my friends left for me, they have your friend and your men in custody. Would you like me to take you to them or trust that I'm going to see them returned?"

His eyes narrowed. "Precisely where are you holding them? Better yet, how did you get that message?"

She tapped the side of her head. "Implants. At short range, I can link with the computers in my fighter."

To prove her point, she instructed the canopies to open.

"I've never seen or heard of such a thing," Derek said quietly, watching the fighter open up with wide eyes. "I don't believe I've ever seen a piece of recovered equipment this functional, either. Except for the handheld weapons, of course. I believe I'd like to see where you're keeping my friends."

Annette gestured toward the front of the fighter. "You get in up front. Once you're inside, I'll see that you're secured and off we go."

Getting close enough to strap him in was a risk, but one she was willing to take at this point. She didn't think he'd attack her until he'd seen everything she had to show him.

He stared curiously at the cockpit as she secured his restraints. "Even after having seen what was left of *Dauntless*, I confess that I never expected to actually fly anywhere. It still seems mythical."

"Well then, you're in for a treat."

Annette sealed up the front canopy and climbed into her seat. She'd contact *Persephone* as soon as she lifted off. She wanted to get off the ground before anything else went wrong.

* * *

Raul felt mildly ridiculous stashing the unconscious prisoners into the high-security cells. The power was on, and they'd have plenty of food and water once they woke up, so it was the best call. Still, literally anyone could come in and find them.

He took the opportunity to drop into his office. Someone had ransacked it and opened his safe. The armored door was actually half melted. He certainly hoped they had fun with the encrypted chips it had contained and the false data stored on them.

Raul reached under his desk and touched a hidden button. He then made his way into the attached washroom and opened a previously hidden safe built into the tiled walls.

This was his *actual* safe. He pocketed the data chips containing his actual files and then began pulling out his weapons. The extra stunner went into his pocket, the heavy-duty flechette pistol went onto his belt, and the plasma grenade stayed in the pouch it came in.

Out of habit, he closed and locked the safe when he was done. He then went out to rejoin the destroyer's crew. He handed his spare stunner to one of them. That meant all of them were armed now.

With the weapons they'd seized from the marines and the cutter pilot, that provided a stunner for each of the officers. Veronica had chosen not to take one with her, because she wasn't going to need any firepower for her part of this operation.

He hoped none of them had to use their weapons. If they did, someone would realize something was wrong. As it was, they were running a risk that the nosy lieutenant would, if they were still aboard the orbital when he left.

The man would probably check the interior scanners to verify that no one was moving around. He'd make a call across the interior communications systems too. The people in the cells wouldn't be able to respond, and the man wouldn't see them.

He consulted a map of the orbital and made a guess at the closest airlock to where the recovery ship was attached. It took them another fifteen minutes to get there, and they quickly donned vacuum suits.

Once they were ready, he led them into the airlock and bled off the pressure. The exterior hatch slid open, and he was pleased to see that the recovery ship was virtually on top of them.

Raul didn't have much experience working in zero gravity, but he had enough to avoid making a fool of himself. He led the others onto one of the arms where it connected nearby and then onto the hull of the recovery ship.

"I see Commander Giguere ahead," Graham Bakersfield said. "She's up near one of the airlocks that we had designated as a potential entry point."

It took a moment, but Raul spotted her. She had her arm wrapped around something to hold on to. He supposed that made sense, but something looked wrong.

They didn't dare risk anything more powerful than short-range communication. They wouldn't be able to talk with her until they were less than a dozen meters away.

Bakersfield took the lead and closed the distance to his commanding officer. The man glanced down before straightening abruptly and gesturing for them to hurry.

The man dug into a satchel he'd acquired somewhere and began scanning the surface of Veronica's suit.

Something *was* wrong.

"What's the matter?" he asked as soon as he arrived beside them.

"Her suit integrity is compromised, and she's lost a lot of air. Too much. I don't think she's breathing. She used an emergency cable to secure herself. We need to get her out of that suit now."

"Get the hatch open," he ordered. "It must be locked down if she couldn't get inside. We'll have to hope we can resuscitate her once we get inside."

The engineer pulled out a hammer, braced himself, and shattered the controls. Once he had the parts of them separated, he reached inside with his gloved hands and did something. The hatch slid open.

They managed to get Veronica's body inside the airlock, and Raul hit the control to seal it. Air began rushing in.

As soon as the pressure was high enough, they got Veronica's helmet off. She still wasn't breathing. The helm and tactical officers began working on resuscitating her.

Raul hoped their efforts were successful, but he had other work to do. He gestured for the other two officers to join him and headed into the ship.

"It's possible someone noticed the airlock cycling," he said quietly. "If they did, we're going to have trouble in very short order. If they didn't, we need to secure the ship before anyone finds out we're here.

"Lieutenant Bakersfield, go to engineering. Stun anyone you find. Search carefully to be sure no one is hiding there. Lock it down so no one can come in once we begin the assault on the bridge."

He looked at the executive officer next. "Commander Fuller, I want you to hit the crew quarters. I'll take the bridge."

The three split up and went their separate ways.

Raul almost made it to the bridge before he encountered anyone. The man wore blue coveralls that were nothing like those Fleet used. He was also warier than a Fleet officer would've been.

The man barely laid eyes on Raul before he turned and sprinted toward the bridge. Raul had his stunner in hand and took him out just short of the bend in the corridor.

He raced to the bridge and found it fully manned. One of the occupants was already heading toward the hatch. He must've heard something.

Raul set the stunner to wide angle and took them all down. All told, he'd stunned seven people.

He dragged the man in from the corridor and locked the hatch behind him.

Once he'd shot each one again with a full stunner blast, he sat down at the command console and tried to make sense of what he was seeing.

It looked as though someone had been laying in a course to the outer system. Perhaps they were getting ready to depart orbit.

Five minutes later, there was a rap on the hatch. Raul rose from his seat and walked over to the intercom. "Yes?"

If it was someone he didn't know, they were about to get the surprise of their life.

"It's Fuller. I think we got everybody."

Raul opened the hatch and gestured for the officer to come in. "Find a compartment with a hatch you can lock and drag everyone into it. Search them closely. Leave them no tools or weapons. Strip them naked. That will make sure.

"By the time they wake up, I'll have the computer system secured against intrusion. Leave Graham guarding the hatch and search the ship again. We can't chance that anyone is still hiding."

He stopped the man before he could exit the bridge. "Is there any word on Commander Giguere?"

The other officer shook his head. "Not that I've heard. Even if they save her, there may be permanent damage."

Raul grimaced. He certainly hoped that wasn't the case. Veronica was an amazing officer. Her loss would be an incredible blow to the Empire.

A chime from the command console drew his attention. They had an incoming call.

He gestured for Fuller to go. "I'll take care this. When you pass the airlock, send Lieutenant Wells to join me."

Without turning on the video, he accepted the call. "Go ahead."

"We've accounted for everyone aboard the orbital," a voice said. It certainly sounded like the lieutenant Raul had been dealing with earlier. "Is there some reason you're not using video?"

"We're doing maintenance on that system," Raul said coolly.

There was a long pause before the man continued. "Copy that. No one is showing up on internal scans, so you're clear to depart."

"Roger that. We'll see you once we drop this thing off and get back."

He killed the com. Raul had no idea how to actually move the ship, so he wasn't even going to try. He'd have to wait for the helm officer to arrive. Then he'd find out whether their resuscitation efforts had proven fruitful.

36

Kelsey was intensely relieved when word came that Annette was on her way back up in her fighter. The marines searching for her had hastily loaded up in the pinnaces and caught up with her just before she was ready to dock.

The shroud the engineers had cobbled together that allowed the fighters to pull next to a standard dock and open their canopies while still inside an atmosphere was something like Frankenstein's monster. It basically provided a large, inflatable seal leading into a standard dock.

There was no way to secure the fighter to the dock, so they used the short-range remote controls to relocate it to the slot on the hull reserved for it once the pilots were clear. A work party then had to secure it manually.

At some point, they'd have to come up with a better way of doing this. Thankfully, this had worked out so far.

She'd been on the bridge with Jacob Howell. As she'd expected, he couldn't tear his eyes away from the people sitting at their positions and flying the ship. The view of the planet below on the main screen had mesmerized him.

"This is both exactly as I envisioned it and entirely different," he confided as she led him into the corridor leading to the docking area.

She gave him a smile. "That can mean anything."

He shrugged. "I don't have the words. I wish my father could see this."

"Maybe some other time. Once we have your friend on board, we can start loading all of you onto one of the pinnaces. We'll take you down wherever you'd like to go. As I said earlier, I have no need to keep you prisoner.

"I'm overdue back in the other system. There are important matters there that I have to keep abreast of. Some tasks that I hope they've successfully completed. Once I check in with them, I intend to come back and have a much longer discussion with you about the clans and the Others."

He grinned. "My schedule seems to have miraculously cleared. If you have no objection, I would take it as a great personal favor if you'd allow me to accompany you. I suspect that Derek will be of a similar mind, once he's assured that his men are safely sent below."

By this point they'd arrived at the docking area. Four marines stood by, ready for any trouble.

The hatch was just opening to admit Annette and a Pandoran. Kelsey made a mental note to inquire what they referred to themselves as.

The alien and Jacob clasped forearms. "I feared I'd seen the last of you, my friend," the Pandoran said.

Jacob gestured toward Kelsey. "I met a new friend. Allow me to introduce you to the chief of Clan Persephone. Kelsey Bandar, this is my friend Derek.

"By the way, she has all of your people here. Some of them were injured attacking the ambushers, but none died. I've spoken with them all. They're in as good a condition as possible. Better than I'd expected, honestly. The medical facilities on the ship are astounding."

The alien turned toward Kelsey and bowed his head. "I appreciate the care you have shown my people. I regret capturing Annette Vitter. I didn't believe her story."

Kelsey extended her hand. She wasn't sure the alien would take it, but he did. His grip was firm, and he made no attempt to overpower her.

"As Jacob said, my name is Kelsey Bandar, and this is my ship, *Persephone*. Jacob and I have been getting to know one another."

The alien raised an eyebrow. "Indeed? The closest human pronunciation of my name is Derek. It would please me if you would call me such."

"Kelsey is not only chief of Clan Persephone," Jacob told his friend, "but she is also a senior leader in their council. Her father is high clan chief of the New Terran Empire, and she stands to inherit his position."

Derek seemed suitably impressed. He bowed again, this time more deeply and with more of a flourish.

"I'd rather not get tangled up in that right now," Kelsey said. "As I told Jacob, I'm on a rather tight schedule. I want to continue the discussion we're having, but I have to visit the system next door. I've prepared your men for transport. You're more than welcome to accompany them down."

"I've offered to go with her on this journey," Jacob said. "I think you should come with me. Think of what you could learn for your father."

Derek seemed to consider that. "Once I have seen my men to safety, if you have no objection, I would like to accompany you. I have wronged Annette Vitter by disbelieving her story. I want to learn as much as possible before I speak with my father about you."

That would certainly make getting more information about the clans possible, Kelsey mused. "We should have your people loaded for transport in about twenty minutes. You can tell the pilot where you'd like to land and go down with them. Once you get back to the ship, we'll depart."

While the circumstances were looking up, she still hoped that Talbot had good news about her mother. As long as that situation remained unresolved, she'd be on pins and needles.

* * *

Talbot was starting to get annoyed with the mechanics working on the damaged cutter. How hard could it be? Find whatever was causing the fault and swap it out.

No matter what the technicians checked, the solution always seemed to elude them. It had taken almost two days now. If they didn't solve the problem soon, he was going to have an aneurysm.

That's when *Audacious* called down with an alert. A cutter decelerating from orbit had come in for an emergency landing.

Marines from every quarter of the planet headed for its location and began searching. They'd found the cutter in rough terrain. It looked as though the pilot had put it down hard. Talbot set out to join them.

As he examined the crash site from the air, Talbot wondered why the pilot hadn't tried for an area a few kilometers to the south. The terrain was much more conducive to a safe landing there.

In any case, it looked as though it had survived well enough that someone probably had walked away.

Mysteriously, they found the cutter empty. The ramp was still up, but no one was aboard. Maybe they'd closed it after they'd gotten clear. Yet, where had they gone?

He immediately instituted a search of the area. The survivors would turn up in short order.

Half a day later, he'd had to reevaluate that assessment. They'd gone over every centimeter of the forest around the crash site without finding survivors, bodies, or even a trace that anyone had ever lived there.

Talbot was still trying to figure out what that meant when Commodore Anderson signaled him from orbit. "What's the word, Talbot? Give me some good news."

He scowled at her image. "I'm getting a big pile of nothing down here. It's as if the cutter was empty. Who the hell was flying this thing? What the hell were they doing?"

"I'll get that information for you by the time you get up here. *Persephone* just flipped back into the system. Princess Kelsey is on her way here now. I think you should come up and brief her in person."

Talbot sighed. "Great. Now I have to give her bad news on top of everything else. I feel like I haven't accomplished a damned thing on this planet."

"Then come on up and meet her. Leave your subordinates to continue the search. We'll figure this out."

He made his way back to the cutter he'd arrived in and instructed the pilot to take them up. Their scanners were able to detect the approaching Marine Raider ship while it was still a few hours out.

Since they were headed toward one another, it only took them about an hour to rendezvous. One of the pinnaces detached so he could board.

Kelsey was waiting for him. She wasn't alone. An unknown man in odd-looking clothing stood beside her. What floored him though, was the alien biped standing nearby.

He had seen images of the aliens Kelsey had discovered, but he didn't expect to find one on *Persephone*.

His wife pulled him into a hug. "It's so good to see you. A week away is far too long."

She turned toward the human man. "Allow me to introduce Jacob Howell. Jacob, my husband, Russel Talbot. He's also a major in the Imperial Marines."

The man reached out, and Talbot raised his hand automatically. It wasn't the type of handshake he was used to—the man grasped his forearm rather than his palm—but he recovered well, he thought.

Kelsey gestured toward the alien. "This is his friend Derek. I'm given to understand that that's not the actual pronunciation of his name, but that's the accepted version for humans."

The alien repeated the same strange handshake.

Talbot had intended to launch into an update about her mother, but the strange visitors threw him off. He wasn't certain he should speak about her at all. There was no telling what Kelsey had told them or, more to the point, what she hadn't told them.

He opened his mouth to inquire what she wanted to do, but an incoming communication stopped him. It was a priority message from Commodore Anderson. He accepted it at once.

"Talbot, we have a problem," the commodore said. "We've identified the cutter pilot. Unfortunately, he's still on the island that you came from. He's waiting for them to fix his cutter."

Talbot frowned and held up a hand to stop Kelsey from interrupting. She couldn't hear the communication, so he shunted what he'd already received to her and linked her in.

"Why do you think that pilot was the one flying the downed cutter?" he asked.

"Because we have transponder confirmation. Flight control registered it coming up from the island and docking with the orbital. It was after that it returned to the surface and crashed."

Kelsey gave him an odd look. "What are we talking about? There was a cutter crash?"

His mind raced ahead, and the obvious conclusion about floored him. "Oh crap. Commodore, you need to contact the recovery ship at once. They've got stowaways on the orbital."

"We've already called them," the commodore said grimly. "They're not responding."

"Where are they at?" Kelsey asked.

"They're probably out of the system. They've been too far out for us to detect for a while."

Kelsey smiled. "They've got nowhere to run. We'll change course immediately and pursue them."

Once Talbot was satisfied that the conversation was over, he terminated the link. He waited until Kelsey had explained the situation to their visitors.

She ended her recitation of facts with a wolfish grin. "But now they've made a terrible mistake. We'll be able to find them no matter where they go."

The man named Jacob glanced at his friend. His expression seemed troubled.

"That may not be true," he said slowly. "According to the stories I've heard, the flip point leading to the Clan systems lies that way. At least it exists in the outer system."

"What?" Kelsey demanded. "I thought the Council worlds were on the other side of what you called the defective flip point."

The man shook his head. "No. So far as I know, no ship other than *Dauntless* has ever managed to use one successfully. At least to go anywhere other than here.

"My father told me that there was a previously unknown type of flip point in this system. One that existed far outside the normal orbital radius."

After a moment, the man shrugged. "I must admit I'm not certain I completely understand the concept of flip points at all, so it's possible I'm making some kind of mistake. The story might be wrong.

"The Council of Clans revealed the existence of the distant flip points to the Others, but not the defective one. They still hoped to devise a means of using it, I believe. In all likelihood, they have found more over the centuries.

"Only the fact that we destroyed the ships that pursued us and took all the prisoners allowed us to escape through the defective flip point. Otherwise, I am certain that the Others would never have rested until they tracked us down. They wouldn't want our knowledge to ever return to the clans."

Talbot stared at his wife in horror. No. This wasn't a mistake. If the prisoners had gone to the trouble of stealing a transponder—which was what he thought they'd done—and then hijacked the recovery ship to head for the outer system, they knew *exactly* where they were going.

He had no idea how they could've known. Maybe they'd found something inside the town that he'd missed. Hell, he didn't even know how they'd managed to go undetected on the island for a week. His people had searched every inch of it.

"What's on the other side of this flip point?" he asked.

The other man shrugged. "Based on the battle stories my father told me as a child, the system on the other side has a clan world. It wasn't heavily invested, as I understand it, but that could have changed in the years since then."

Kelsey overrode Talbot before he could ask what the hell that meant. "We've got to get after them right now. We can't allow them to escape this system. Take command of the marines on board this ship and get ready. We're going to have to board the recovery ship and stop them."

His wife smiled coldly. "I've been itching to do something ever since they escaped. Now I can finally drive the events. Let's wrap them up in a bow before they even realize we're coming."

37

Veronica swam slowly back to consciousness. She had a blinding headache and felt as if someone had turned her inside out.

"How are you feeling?"

She looked over and saw Brent Kowalski standing beside her. Her tactical officer's brow was furrowed with worry.

"Like crap," she said, astonished at how weak her voice was. "Though I suppose that's better than the alternative. I didn't expect to wake up at all."

He helped her sit up. "I'll confess to having my doubts too. You were in bad shape when we found you. What happened?"

She waved a hand at him. "That isn't important right now. What's our status?"

He stopped her from standing up. "You still look pretty unsteady to me, Captain. I think you should take it easy. We're not in any immediate danger, so there's no need to rush."

She wanted to argue, but he was right. A few minutes wasn't going to make any difference one way or the other. She was alive, and they'd escaped. That was all that mattered. At least she assumed they'd escaped.

"Are we still in orbit around Icebox?"

"No. The ship got orders to move out within half an hour of us taking it. We've been slowly boosting for the outer system for almost a full shift. There's no sign of pursuit, so Commander Castille believes we've gotten away."

She'd been out far longer than she'd suspected. That worried her, but she'd deal with it when she had time.

"When has anything gone that easily for us?" she asked rhetorically. "Sooner or later, they're going to figure out what we did and come after us.

When we get on the other side of the flip point, we're going to have to run for it.

"The downside is going to be that we don't have any information about flip points in that next system. The odds are very good that they'll follow us before we locate an exit from the system. So, we're going to have to find an excellent hiding place to wait them out."

Veronica decided that she was feeling as good as she was going to be. With Brent's help, she slowly stood. It would have to do.

She'd been in a very rudimentary medical center. It was barely large enough for two beds and some cabinets. She hoped they never actually needed to treat someone in it.

Veronica would have liked to say she didn't need his help getting to the bridge, but that would've been a lie. She was significantly weaker than she'd ever remembered being.

Castille and Candace were flying the ship. Well, Candace was. Castille was sitting in the commander's chair looking pretty.

He rose as soon as she came in to the bridge. "Veronica! It's *so* good to see you back on your feet. We were all very worried."

She thought he actually sounded sincere. Her feelings about him had become more complicated as they discovered the truth about the revolution. She suspected he'd be willing to do anything to further the AIs' cause. Still, he sounded pleased that she hadn't died, so that was something.

"I think I'm only provisionally back on my feet. Do you mind if I take your seat?"

He stepped away from the commander's chair and gestured for her to sit. "Please do. All I'm doing is occupying space. I don't really know what I should be doing to command a vessel in space. Candace has actually been running things."

"And running them well, I'm sure," Veronica said. "She's an extremely talented and competent officer. What's our status?"

Castille sat at one of the spare consoles against the bulkhead. "We captured the ship without any incident. Commander Fuller is guarding the prisoners. They all seem exceedingly competent, so I don't trust leaving them out of our sight. Even without tools, they almost managed to escape from a sealed compartment."

She nodded, impressed. "That does sounds remarkably competent. Are they Fleet officers?"

He shook his head. "They don't appear to be. My guess is that they're civilian specialists. I'm sure their story is fascinating, but at this point, I'm only interested in keeping them locked away until we can complete our escape."

"How far are we away from the flip point?"

He shrugged and gestured toward Candace.

"As near as I can tell, we're about two hours away from the flip point," the woman said. "We're far outside the normal area where one would exist, so there's no danger the ships in orbit around Icebox will detect it.

"At this point, I don't believe they can detect us, either. We're not moving very quickly, so our grav signature is low. We actually changed course several hours ago, so even if they come looking for us, they're not going to find us in the area they'd expect."

"They'll search the outer system when we don't come back," Veronica said. "They're eventually going to find the flip point. When they do, they're going to come after us. We need to have a plan for when that happens."

"I've been thinking about that," Castille said. "As soon as we cross into the next system, we'll get as far away from the flip point as we can and hide in the outer system. We can go out into deep space and wait. We have plenty of food and water, so all we're worrying about is time."

That was about what she'd expected. All things considered, it was the best plan. "What about our original prisoners? Did you put them in with the crew from the ship?"

"I didn't want the two groups discussing things between themselves. We brought them on board, but Justine and her military associates are in a separate cabin. As you might imagine, she's frothing at the mouth over her treatment. I can totally understand why her daughter locked her up."

Veronica chuckled. "Families are complicated. If you don't mind, I think I'll rest before we flip. I think I need to be at my best."

Castille rose to his feet. "I'll see you back to a cabin. Lieutenant Kowalski can remain here to assist Candace. We'll wake you twenty minutes before we flip."

The cabin was exceptionally plain, but it looked to have a comfortable bunk. That's all she really cared about.

Once Castille had departed, she laid down and closed her eyes. They'd caught more good luck than anyone could justify. She couldn't help feeling that it would run out at the worst possible moment. Then she was asleep.

* * *

Annette cursed the escaped prisoners again. Where the hell had they gone? She'd taken her fighters out along the course they'd held when *Audacious* had lost sight of them, but they were gone. Had they already flipped out of the system?

She sure as hell hoped not. Her fighters didn't have the capability to detect a flip point, even if they weren't relying solely on passive scanners. They might fly right past it.

"I think I have something, Captain," one of her wingmen said. "Just a hint of a signal. I think it's a grav drive."

She linked her fighter to his and examined what he was seeing. That certainly did look like a grav drive signature. It was way off the projected course, so they'd have to alter their trajectory if they hoped to get a better reading.

"Everyone, follow my lead." Annette curved her fighter around and boosted her speed a little.

She was still going slowly enough that she wasn't worried about the recovery ship spotting her. To say their scanner suite was rudimentary was a profound understatement.

Five minutes later, she was certain they'd found the recovery ship and the Dresden orbital. They were making fairly good time considering the mass of the vessel and its cargo. She was close enough to detect the short-ranged scanning pulses they must be using to search for the flip point.

Annette opened a directional channel at where *Persephone* would be and sent a message detailing where they'd spotted the recovery ship, its course, and speed. Princess Kelsey would adjust her approach to match.

The Marine Raider strike ship was the very epitome of stealthy. Given enough time, they could sneak up on the recovery ship before the enemy detected them.

If, of course, they had the time to do it. If there really was a flip point out here, the recovery ship might be almost on top of it.

* * *

KELSEY FELT like a caged animal sitting in her command chair. She wanted to pace the bridge, but that wouldn't project the right image.

The damned ship was right there in front of her, but she couldn't rush the job. This had to be done exactly right or her mother would die.

Talbot laid a hand on her arm. "She's going to be okay. I'll do my absolute best to make certain of that."

She sighed and tried to relax a little. "I know you will, but I can't stop worrying. If any part of this goes wrong, we're so screwed.

"I think it's about time you headed down to get your marines suited up. We'll launch the pinnaces in fifteen minutes. You should be able to sneak up on them with all the stealth materials built into the pinnaces' hulls."

"The marines are already loaded," he said. "All I have to do is go down and get into my armor. Just keep breathing. We'll save her."

"Then you'd best be on your way. I'll let you know as soon as we're ready to launch and give you a final update on the situation."

Talbot gave her arm another squeeze before heading for the hatch.

"Not to be a wet blanket, but you know it's not going to be that easy, don't you?" Angela asked.

Kelsey sighed and slowly nodded. "Nothing ever is. Especially around us, it seems. How long until we're within range to launch the pinnaces?"

The marine checked her console. "We could launch in ten minutes, but I think we can probably slip in a little closer. That fifteen-minute time frame you mentioned is probably just about right."

"Any sign of the flip point?"

"We're not going to see it on passive scanners. We'll just have to hope that we're nowhere close to the damned thing. We can start scanning once we secure the recovery ship and make sure the prisoners are safe."

"I'm worried," Kelsey said. "Not just about this operation, but about what we're going to find on the other side of that flip point. I have to be honest, these ghosts aren't sounding like quality allies, if you know what I mean."

She'd learned a little bit more from Jacob about the history of the clans. In one respect, they were just like the New Terran Empire. They were determined to overthrow the Rebel Empire and restore civilization. They meant to crush the AIs.

The problem was that they'd known for five hundred years that they were going to have to do this. There was a hardness to them. A grim resoluteness where the ends justified the means. At least that's how it had sounded to her. She hoped she was wrong.

These people sounded fanatical. She wasn't certain that they'd see much difference between the New Terran Empire and the Rebel Empire. They intended to rule and would fight to make that happen.

With any luck, she'd stop the recovery ship before it came anywhere close to the flip point. The clans would figure out something was up here when they came to collect their crops, but that was at least eight months away.

And it wasn't as if the new prisoners really knew what had happened to them or how they'd gotten here. All Kelsey and her people needed to do was slip away undiscovered and make it home. They could come back and make contact with the clans in a more organized manner before things went to hell.

"The recovery ship is changing course," Jack Thompson said. "They might have detected something."

The course change was relatively minor, but since it was the first time the recovery ship had deviated, Kelsey was certain it meant something. If the recovery ship was close enough to the flip point to detect it with their crappy scanners, time was exceptionally short.

She checked the timer on her implants. Talbot had left the bridge twelve minutes ago. She opened a channel to him.

"You're on. It looks as if they might've detected the flip point. Launch the pinnaces. Remember, I want everyone alive. Stunners only."

"I'll do the best I can, but no promises. If one of them does something epically stupid, like threaten the prisoners, I'm going to blow them away."

She felt a slight jar as the pinnaces undocked from *Persephone*. They glided ahead of the strike ship and arrowed toward the target. By her best estimate, they'd be there in another fifteen minutes.

Kelsey prayed that was soon enough.

38

Raul was so focused on the flip point that the helm officer had to repeat herself before he grasped what he was hearing.

"Sir? I'm detecting a scanner anomaly behind us. It's almost as if there's a shadow of some kind."

He pulled up the readings on his console and cursed. "I think you're right. There's a ship back there. It's almost undetectable, but I think some of the gravitic waves coming off the flip point are screwing with their stealth."

Raul wanted to redirect the scanners to the rear and boost their power, but he didn't dare. That would give them away.

"We can only hope those are small craft," he said after a moment. "If they can't flip, we'll still get away."

"We're only about five minutes from the flip point at this speed," Wells said. "I'll call the captain."

"No. If that *is* an enemy ship coming to collect us, there's nothing she can do. We'll flip to the other system and see what we find. If a ship comes through after us, I suppose we'll have to surrender."

Of course, it wouldn't be that simple. He couldn't allow them to take him again. It was always conceivable they could break him and get the codes to access the manufacturing equipment. He couldn't allow that, no matter what.

Time flowed like molasses. He expected the shadowy ship to attack at any moment. Yet, they didn't.

"We're inside the outer boundaries of the flip point," Wells said.

"Are you certain that if we attempt to flip, we'll succeed? Let me stress that if we fail, that ship—if it is one—will certainly attack."

"As certain as I can be without trying, sir. I've given it a large margin of error since we haven't thoroughly charted it yet."

"Initiate the flip."

He held his breath and then relaxed as they flipped into the new system. They'd made it!

"Possible hostile vessel detected," the helm officer said. "It's a big one, sitting just off the flip point."

That was not what Raul wanted to hear. "Call Commander Giguere. What can you tell me about the ship?"

Wells stared at her console. "I'm not certain it's a ship now that I'm getting a better look. It might be some kind of station. Like the guard fortresses at Dresden."

Raul certainly hoped not. The recovery ship was completely unarmed. His options if they challenged him were to flee or surrender.

"We're also picking up vessels moving inside the system," Wells said. "Quite a few of them. It seems we've stumbled into an occupied area."

"One controlled by the ghosts, or so it seems," Raul said. "Have we gotten any reaction from that station?"

Wells shook her head. "Not yet. Perhaps it's unmanned or abandoned."

No one was that lucky. Raul was certain that they'd surprised the people on the station, but they'd respond shortly.

"Incoming signal from the station," the junior officer said. "A demand for our identity and surrender in the name of something called the Clan Council. What should I do, sir?"

If only there was something they could do. These were the ghosts. The jig was up.

Then a plan of action occurred to him. They might not survive doing it, but it would certainly screw things up for the New Terran Empire.

"Maximum acceleration directly toward the station," he snapped. "Prepare to jettison the arms holding the Dresden orbital on my command. And open a response channel."

When she nodded, he continued. "This is Commander Raul Castille of the New Terran Empire. We've found you now, and we're going to exterminate you."

He made a gesture to kill the channel. "Cut the Dresden orbital loose as soon as it's on a collision course with that station."

"Jettisoning arms in three… two… one… mark!" Wells said.

The ship jarred abruptly as it ejected its cargo arms. The helm officer must've begun slowing them down because the orbital was quickly receding ahead of them.

Commander Giguere came into the compartment. "What's going on? What's our status?"

Raul ignored her. "Are we still inside the flip point, Lieutenant Wells?"

"Barely, sir. The flip capacitors are still charging but should be online in less than thirty seconds."

"Take us back as soon as you can."

Raul turned to Veronica with a sad smile. "We found the ghosts. Or perhaps it would be better to say that they found us."

"The station's firing missiles," Wells said. "They're going to shred the orbital, but that's not going to save them. The debris field is going to hit them like a shotgun blast."

Veronica stared at him in horror. "What the hell have you done?"

"The best thing I could under the circumstances," he said. "Made our enemies' lives much more difficult."

"Flipping in five seconds," Wells said.

A fierce burst of light announced the destruction of the Dresden orbital. Nothing came close to the raw power of a failing fusion plant.

As Wells had said, the debris from the explosion would still slam into the station. There was no way to stop it.

He smiled coldly. He certainly hoped Princess Kelsey enjoyed the havoc he just unleashed upon her. With any luck at all, he'd ruined any chance she had of making allies of the Empire's enemies.

* * *

Kelsey was still cursing the bastards' timing when they reappeared. Talbot had been just about to board them when they'd vanished. Now they had another chance.

"Go fully active," she ordered. "Open a channel to that ship."

As soon as she was certain the transmission was going out, she began speaking. "This is Princess Kelsey Bandar. Surrender your ship at once."

That's when she noticed something was wrong with the recovery ship. Its arms were gone, and so was the Dresden orbital. Why the hell had they cut it loose?

The other ship failed to respond but began accelerating into the system.

"The pinnaces are going to latch on in about twenty seconds," Angela said.

That would put an end to that fight. The escaped prisoners were no match for marines in combat armor. They'd be able to secure the ship in very short order.

Right then, the recovery ship cut acceleration.

Angela gestured toward the screen. "Incoming transmission."

An image of the escaped destroyer commander appeared on the main monitor. The woman looked haggard.

"We surrender."

That had to gall her, Kelsey suspected. The woman had done far too much surrendering to the New Terran Empire for her to be comfortable.

"My marines will be boarding you in moments," Kelsey said sternly. "You will not resist them. Have any of the people you took hostage been harmed?"

"I'll quibble terms with you, Princess Kelsey. We don't have hostages. That implies that we we're holding them in exchange for something from you. Those people were prisoners. And no, none of them have been harmed."

Kelsey forced herself not to relax as relief flooded through her. Her mother was okay.

"Quibble as much as you like, Commander Giguere, so long as you don't resist us."

"I don't see much point in resisting. The damage is already done. We found the ghosts on the other side of this flip point. Commander Castille made certain that they're not going to be well disposed toward you."

Kelsey had no idea what that meant, but she could figure it out later. "Where is he?"

"I believe he's returned to the cabin he was using. No doubt he wants to surrender in his own way. Or maybe resist. I have no idea."

Ice flooded through Kelsey. "You need to secure him right now. When he escaped from us, he killed almost all of his fellow prisoners. If he harms any of the people on your ship, I'm going to hold *you* personally responsible."

The woman's expression became stricken. "I'll make sure he doesn't."

The screen went blank.

Angela turned toward her. "The pinnaces just locked onto the recovery ship's hull. They'll be inside very shortly. They'll stop any shenanigans."

Kelsey certainly hoped that was true. "If they ran into the clans on the other side of that flip point, there could be a hostile response coming back through that we can't deal with. From what I've been able to gather, they sound like the kind of people that shoot first and don't bother asking questions later.

"Launch an FTL probe through the flip point and signal *Audacious* to gather every one of our people. It's very possible that we're going to have a fight on our hands before too long."

"Should they come out to join us?"

"No," Kelsey said. "Have them start for the multiflip point with the freighter. If we can conceal its existence, or at least the fact that it has multiple destinations, we might be able to slip away. I'd rather not get into a shooting war with the clans."

"I thought the multiflip point was too constrained to allow *Audacious* to pass through."

"It is. Carl is going to have to jury-rig some kind of frequency modulator for the carrier's flip drive. Otherwise, the clans are going to be able to bring enough ships to overwhelm us. Thankfully, his calculations indicate the freighter should be able to make the flip. Signal Commodore Anderson to get moving.

"As soon as we have the recovery ship secure, we need to get everyone off it and get moving too. *Audacious* will be able to beat us there as it is. We can't afford to waste a single moment."

39

Veronica raced out of the bridge as soon as she cut the com channel. If Castille did anything to the prisoners, they were screwed.

She found Armand Fuller guarding the corridor where they were holding the prisoners. He raised an eyebrow as she ran up.

"We've flipped twice," he said. "Is something wrong?"

"You could say that. Where's Castille?"

Her executive officer frowned. "On the bridge, I assume. Why?"

"I don't have time to explain. Release the prisoners. We're about to be boarded, and we're surrendering. Make sure none of our people put up a fight."

She ran toward the rear of the ship without waiting for a response. He was a solid officer. He'd do what she'd ordered him to.

Where else could Castille have gone? She didn't believe for a moment that he'd gone back to his quarters. Still, she checked them all. Empty, as expected.

That really left only one place that he could've gone. Engineering.

Her blood ran cold as soon as she arrived in the engineering compartment. Graham was slumped over the console just inside the hatch. It looked as though he'd been stunned.

Moments later, she found Castille beside the fusion plant. Not the controls. The plant itself.

"What are you doing?" she asked.

He glanced at her and smiled. "What duty demands of me. I figured your engineer wouldn't understand. You know what I'm talking about, though. I can't allow them to capture me."

She wished she'd picked up a weapon. He was bigger than she was and armed. "That doesn't mean you have to kill everyone."

Castille straightened. "I'm afraid it does. Trust me. It's cleaner this way."

Veronica nodded slowly. "I suppose you're right."

She took two steps toward him, making certain to move slowly so as not to alarm him.

It didn't work. He raised the flechette pistol he'd held behind his back. "You can stop right there. You're an exceptionally resourceful woman, so I can't allow you to come any closer."

Right at that moment, the sound of metal on metal echoed throughout the hull. Someone had just docked, and they hadn't been gentle about it. The enemy was here.

"Well, I suppose we'll have guests just in time to—"

Not waiting for him to finish what he was saying, Veronica snatched up a wrench that Graham must've left sitting next to the grav drive and hurled it at Castille.

He ducked, raised the flechette pistol, and opened fire.

Veronica was already moving, throwing herself against the fusion plant. A glance where he'd been standing showed a jury-rigged bomb composed of a plasma grenade.

She yanked it free just as he shot her leg. Intense pain lanced through her as it gave way. She landed hard, and the bomb tumbled from her grasp.

The plasma grenade shed the tape holding its activator spoon down as it rolled across the compartment and stopped at Castille's feet. The pinging noise of the light metal hitting something in the engineering compartment when it flew free was ridiculously high pitched.

Castille cursed and dove for the grenade. He snatched it up and drew back to throw it toward her.

Veronica barely had time to cover her eyes before it went off in his hand.

The blast picked her up and hurled her across the engineering compartment. She slammed into the bulkhead and felt bones breaking.

Since she was still in agony, Veronica assumed the fusion plant had somehow survived the explosion. The tears in her eyes clouded her view of the engineering compartment, but it certainly looked as if the grav drives were wrecked and the flip drive was a smoking ruin.

The fusion plant wasn't undamaged, either. The overhead lights flickered and went out as it shut down. Emergency lights sprang up, but they only dimly lit the interior of the engineering compartment.

The arrival of armored marines with their weapons out was almost hilariously anticlimactic.

They fanned throughout the compartment searching for hostiles. Two of them aimed their rifles at her, so she didn't move. Someone searched her for weapons and then bound her hands behind her. That brought on an entirely new level of pain.

She looked up at the closest marine. "I need to speak with someone in charge. You're in terrible danger. Commander Castille destroyed a battle station controlled by the ghosts. They'll be coming."

He didn't look as if he believed her, but another marine arrived in engineering a few minutes later. He squatted down beside her and took his helmet off.

"Commander Giguere? My name is Major Russel Talbot, and you are my prisoner. Again. What's this I hear about ghosts?"

She filled him in on what Castille had done in as few words as possible.

He cursed and turned to the man standing beside him. "Get everyone aboard the pinnaces. We're headed back to *Persephone* in ten minutes."

* * *

Kelsey already knew they were in trouble before Talbot called her. The FTL drone had seen the disaster.

The battle station just off the flip point was completely destroyed, but there were ships inbound. Two of them from fairly close to the flip point and others from deeper in the system.

Kelsey cut Talbot off as he tried to warn her about the danger. "You can't leave the computers on board the recovery ship intact. We have to be absolutely certain that no data about us is left for the clans to capture."

"I can destroy the computer," he said, "but if there's a tablet or data chip that has something I don't know about, I can't control that."

"Can you destroy the ship by overloading the fusion plant?"

He shook his head. "It's trashed. It looks like Castille tried to blow the ship up, but Commander Giguere stopped him. The resulting explosion still disabled everything in the engineering compartment."

Kelsey turned to Angela. "We're going to have to blow the ship up ourselves."

"I don't think that's the best idea," her executive officer said. "If it's already destroyed when the enemy arrives, they're going to suspect something. They have to see it blow up when they attack, or they'll come looking for us. The closest ships are about forty-five minutes out."

"I want the scanner records," Kelsey told Talbot. "You have fifteen minutes to get that data and anything else of interest. Then I want you off that ship and on your way back over here. If we're going to fight, I don't want to have to worry about any pinnaces being undocked."

"On it." The com channel died.

"The closest two ships could be any size," Angela said. "Even if we're lucky and it's only two destroyers, we're still going to get chewed up."

"We'll bracket the ships between Annette's fighters and *Persephone*. We'll try to reason with them. If they shoot first, they can take out one of the hostiles. We'll take out the other."

Angela looked uncertain. "If we're talking about a pair of cruisers, we're in big trouble."

Ten minutes later, Talbot sent the scanner data across. The recovery ship's scanners were crap, but the reading of the battle station would still be useful.

The FTL drone was sending them data about the approaching ships. She still couldn't be certain about the classes. There was a squadron of vessels about seven hours behind the lead pair.

"Talbot is undocking," Angela said. "He'll be back aboard in five minutes. The other pinnace just finished unloading the crew from the recovery ship. Talbot has our escapees, your mother, and the people captured with her."

The oncoming ships were about twenty minutes away from the flip point. One was a destroyer, but the other was a light cruiser.

This was going to be more dangerous than she'd expected.

The other grouping of ships was still too far away for any kind of identification, but there were two dozen grav drives in operation. That meant there was going to be a higher percentage of capital ships. There was no way *Audacious* could take on that kind of firepower.

"Signal *Audacious*," Kelsey said. "Carl has to come up with something to get the ship through to Pandora."

"I'm sure he'll do his best, but that might not be good enough," Angela said. "He's a genius, but there's not a lot of time."

"He's got all those other research scientists. They have about six hours to get to the other flip point, modify their flip drive, and get the hell out of here. Tell them we'll meet them there and hope for the best."

It was one hell of a risk. If the carrier's flip drive burned out like the cruise liner, they'd be stuck in this system. If the clans got prisoners, they'd eventually drag the truth out of them. Castille had left them in one hell of a spot.

"Five minutes until transition," Angela said.

"Arm all missiles. We'll give them one chance to talk. If they start shooting, we'll take them down. If we have to fight, have Annette fire on the light cruiser. They actually have a stronger first-strike capability than us."

Persephone wasn't built to fight another ship head to head. They'd be lucky to take out the destroyer. The antiship missiles the fighters carried would be deadly at this range. Five fighters were a small group to take on a light cruiser, but that was the situation they found themselves in.

The clan ships paused long enough to make a pass through where the battle station had been located. The wreckage of the Dresden orbital had smashed it into pieces. That was sure to piss them off.

The two warships maneuvered into the flip point. Kelsey hoped they managed to avoid exchanging fire, but knew that was a long shot.

* * *

ANNETTE TENSED as the ships appeared in the flip point. *Persephone* transmitted a plea to stand down, but the warships opened fire anyway.

Their missiles completely shredded the unarmed recovery ship, but *Persephone* used electronic countermeasures to spoof the first salvo aimed at her. That wouldn't work twice at this range.

That gave Annette's people an opportunity. It put her and her wing mates in terrible danger, but she had to count on Princess Kelsey to protect them.

At this range, the antiship missiles on her fighters would tear a ship apart if they got through its defenses. She just had to hope the counter fire didn't blow her fighters to pieces.

Without saying a word, she launched both her antiship missiles at the light cruiser. Her board lit up as the other fighters did the same. Ten small sparks closed the distance between them and the larger ship at a rapid pace.

Whoever was in charge over there had been ready for trouble. Antimissile railguns immediately swatted four of the missiles. The survivors dove in, but the defensive gunners still took out another two in short order.

The ship fired a swarm of missiles toward her fighters. That was gross overkill. If even one of them detonated in their midst, it would take them all out.

"Scatter!" she shouted over the short-range com.

Her fighters flew away from each other, and the light cruiser blew up. One of their antiship missiles must've gotten through.

Annette noted that one of the missiles had picked her as its prom date. Fantastic.

She designated it for her antimissile defenses and tried to dodge as they strove to take the missile down. Explosions behind her told her that not all of her friends were going to come home at the end of the day.

As focused as she was, she still managed to note the destruction of the destroyer. *Persephone* had killed him cleanly. No matter what happened to her, the princess was going to escape.

The decoys meant to distract the missile didn't put off the one chasing her. Luckily for her, her other defenses managed to disable it while she was still outside destruction range.

Annette brought her small ship around to help her wing mates, but the fight was already over. Her fighter was the only one left.

40

Talbot knew the clock was ticking. If they were going to make it back to the multiflip point before the next wave of Clan warships arrived, he needed to finish recovering the survivors of the battle in the next half hour.

With only two marine pinnaces, that was challenging. Not only did they need to recover the people alive, they had to destroy the life pods. A bunch of empty pods would certainly make the enemy suspicious.

Thankfully—and he used that word advisedly—there hadn't been that many survivors.

Honestly, he was surprised anyone had ejected at all. There couldn't have been time to order anyone to abandon ship. Not that fast. The battle had lasted about fifteen seconds from the arrival of the Clan warships and their destruction.

The four pods he was tracking must've launched without any orders at all. No doubt the ship's captain would have been quite angry, if he'd survived.

Persephone's pinnaces had already caught up with two of the pods and were shepherding them back toward the ship. They'd use the jury-rigged docking envelopes to get the people out.

While the marines aboard the Marine Raider strike ship took the prisoners aboard from the first set, he'd led the effort to retrieve the second set of escape pods.

That task done, he docked and allowed the other pinnace to destroy the pods as they were ejected from *Persephone.*

Once aboard the ship, he made his way to where they were detaining the prisoners. There weren't many of them. The pods were designed to hold dozens of people, but the makeshift prison compartment only had a dozen men and women inside.

His guards had them covered with stunners while the ship's medical officer examined them. To his untrained eye, most of them looked a little rattled but relatively healthy.

Senior Sergeant Coulter—the most senior noncommissioned officer aboard the ship—pulled him aside.

"We've got something of a problem with the last pod, Major."

Talbot stepped into the corridor so that the prisoners couldn't hear what they were saying. "What's up?"

"The guy inside the pod is weird. I mean seriously weird. First of all, he was in there by himself. Second, he's dressed funny and has tattoos on his face."

Talbot started to say something but changed his mind. "Put him in a separate compartment. Come get me when he's secure."

As soon as Coulter had moved away, Talbot called Kelsey.

"We picked up a surprise," he said by way of greeting. "Based on the description, it sounds like we have somebody from The Singularity."

"Seriously?" Kelsey asked. "Does this person have the same kind of tattoos as the woman in Emperor Marcus's last broadcast?"

"That's what Coulter says. The prisoner is male, though. How do you want me to handle him?"

His wife said nothing for a moment. "Make sure to have him medically screened and keep him in isolation. I want to handle him with kid gloves for the moment."

"Are we going to question him once medical clears him?"

"We'll let him stew for a while. Make sure that he has whatever food he requires, but don't answer any questions. I'll deal with him once the rest of the situation is taken care of. In fact, I think I'll wait until we're out of the system entirely."

About that time, he heard the second pinnace dock. "It sounds like we've just finished up our work here. What's the plan now?"

"We join *Audacious* and the freighter at the multiflip point. I haven't been bugging him, but I hope Carl has some type of frequency-modulation unit designed for the carrier. If not, I'm not sure what we'll do."

He nodded. "Or what we'll do if the flip drive burns out when we try to use it."

"You are just a ray of sunshine. *Audacious* will beat us to the multiflip point by about an hour. By the time we get there, the second wave of ships will be less than half an hour from transit. We have an exceptionally small window to make our escape."

"Do you think we'll make it?"

Kelsey shrugged. "Damned if I know. I suppose we'll have to surrender if we can't escape. I feel very confident that we won't be treated with kid gloves if that happens.

"What about the other prisoners? Are they in good shape? Does it look like we got any officers?"

It was his turn to shrug. "I've only glanced in, but everyone I saw was in civilian clothes. I didn't see a Fleet uniform or anything like that. We're going to have to question each of the prisoners separately and see what they have to say. There's not very many of them. Only twelve."

"I wish we hadn't had to fight them," Kelsey said. "Based on everything that Jacob had told me, these aren't the kind of people we want to align ourselves with, but they didn't have to be our enemies. At least not this quickly.

"Damn Castille and his idiotic stunt. It's really screwed things up for us. We had to defend ourselves, but we pretty much assured that the clans are going to be our enemies."

"You did everything you could to try to avoid this," he said. "Sometimes you just have to accept that the situation worked out badly and do the best you can with the hand you're dealt."

"I'll get over this," she said. "Take care of your prisoners. I'm headed down to the medical center to see Commander Giguere."

* * *

Veronica was finally settling into the tiny medical center. Thankfully, the place wasn't swamped with injured. She'd heard the ship going to battle stations and launching missiles.

Probably against ships that were pursuing her after what Castille had done.

She felt badly about that. There'd been no need. She and her people had already lost. Getting the ghosts riled up was only going to cause them all a major headache in the future.

The doctor that had treated her stepped over to her bed.

"Good news, Commander. It doesn't look as though you're going to need a trip into the regenerator. We've been able to stabilize the broken bones, and you're already on the mend.

"That's not to say that your recovery is going to be easy. I'm afraid you're not going to be walking around until your legs are in better shape. You certainly won't be doing anything athletic until after your ribs heal."

The shots he'd given her earlier had blissfully numbed the pain. "I'm done resisting, doctor. I'm just happy none of my people were killed."

He nodded. "From what I understand, Princess Kelsey found a compartment to lock them up in. They're under heavy guard—as are you—so they won't be escaping again. You've given everyone quite a bit of heartburn over the last week."

"One does what one can."

The man laughed softly. "I suppose so. I stopped by to tell you that you have a visitor."

Someone had come to ask her questions. Well, she supposed that was only natural. She'd cooperate. The time for resistance had ended.

The person who'd come to interrogate her was a surprise, though. Princess Kelsey Bandar stepped through the hatch. The short blonde woman wasn't smiling, but she wasn't snarling, either. Veronica supposed that was the best she could hope for.

"Commander Giguere, that was quite the stunt. I had an entire battalion of marines when I stole the Dresden orbital. You took it back with half a dozen people. My compliments on a brilliant plan."

"I think it's only brilliant if it succeeds," Veronica said dryly. "Harebrained might be more appropriate for what happened. For what it's worth, I'm very sorry that your mother was caught up in this. That was not part of our plans. Just her bad luck."

"I'd guessed that from the timing," the other woman said. "You had no way of knowing she was arriving as you were trying to sneak out of *Audacious*. I don't blame you for that. In your shoes, I'd have done the same thing.

"That doesn't mean that I'm happy with it, however. You and your people have proven yourselves to be entirely too resourceful. For the time being, I'm keeping you all securely under lock and key."

Veronica chuckled. "I don't think I'll complain. We've already abused your hospitality once. I'm not certain when your doctor is going to let me out of this place, though."

"When he does, you'll join your compatriots. Let's spend a moment talking about how you were injured. I'm given to understand that you got into a fight with Commander Castille in the engineering compartment on the recovery ship. One that resulted in his death, as well as your injuries.

"I get that you were fighting for your life and the lives of your people, but I'm grateful that your actions spared my mother and the other prisoners under your care. When the time comes, you can rest assured that I will take that into account."

The short woman put her hands on her hips and stared at Veronica. "I wish we'd been able to convince you of our honesty. You would've made one hell of an ally."

Veronica laughed a little until the sudden pain in her ribs stopped her. "Surprisingly, I was mostly convinced that you were telling the truth. Then the facility we found down on the planet proved it."

Princess Kelsey frowned. "What facility? The town? Is that where you were hiding? I thought we'd searched it completely."

Veronica explained about the hidden facility inside the volcano. Then she detailed everything they'd found inside it, including the journal and all the classified files.

"I transferred everything to a data chip," Veronica concluded. "It was in my pocket when you captured me. It's not encrypted. I hope it proves as educational for you as it was for me.

"All I can say at this point is that I know the AIs lied to us. I didn't know that before, but now I'm certain of it. They're enslaving us just like you said. I'm not certain how I can convince you of my sincerity, but I'll try."

Princess Kelsey nodded. "We'll have plenty of time to discuss that once you're feeling better. Focus on your healing while we see if we can get ourselves out of the mess that Commander Castille got us into."

The noblewoman left without another word.

Veronica lay back in her bed and considered the events that had gotten her here. It had been one hell of a journey, both physically and intellectually. She felt adrift. Everything she'd worked so hard to achieve was gone.

Even once her body had healed, she had no idea what she'd do now. Even if she could, she'd never go home. She had no doubt the AIs would find out what she'd learned. They couldn't allow that kind of information to spread into the Empire.

Worse, she knew she could no longer deny the truth. Her people were slaves. Even a gilded cage was still a cage. She had a lot of thinking to do, but she had to do something about that.

41

Kelsey stopped outside the compartment where her mother was waiting. Part of her really didn't want to have this conversation, but they had to settle this business. Their relationship wasn't healthy. That had to change.

As much as it galled her, her mother wasn't going to be the one making alterations. Trying to change other people was a recipe for going crazy. If they were going to settle this, Kelsey would have to do the settling.

She pressed the admittance chime and waited. A few moments later, the hatch slid open.

Her mother stood on the other side. She'd obviously used the time to clean up from her imprisonment.

Kelsey smiled a little. "I'm glad to see that you're—"

Justine Bandar yanked her daughter into a tight hug. "Enough. I can't stand what's come between us. I don't know that I can ever change what I've done or who I am, but I love you with all of my heart, and I'm sorry I've hurt you."

That was more than enough to get Kelsey to crying. The two of them stood there, arms around one another. Finally, her mother stepped back.

"I've got some tissues beside the couch," her mother said as she wiped at her own damp eyes. "Come in and let's talk."

Kelsey sat down beside her mother and did what she could to dry her eyes. It wouldn't last, she knew. This was going to be that kind of conversation.

She took her mother's hands in hers. "I've been so worried about you. Ever since they took you, I thought I'd never see you again. I don't want what I said to be the tombstone of our relationship. Yes, I'm hurt, but that doesn't matter. We'll find a way around this."

"It *does* matter," Justine said. "You're absolutely right that I've been selfish. I always have been. I've just gotten worse at hiding it.

"I can't change the past. I cheated on your father, and I certainly should've told you that Karl wasn't your father. I just never expected to be called on it."

Kelsey shook her head. "He might not have been the man who sired me, but he is assuredly my father. And, as much as you cannot stand the idea of it, Jared is my brother."

Justine sighed. "I think that's going to be the hardest thing for me. I've hated that boy since the moment I heard about him."

"Why?"

"It doesn't make any sense," her mother said with a shrug. "It's all emotion. I've never bothered to consider why I can't stand the outcome of my ex-husband's infidelity when you and your brother came from mine.

"I'll find a way. Somehow. Just as I'm going to have to accept the fact you're married to a commoner who isn't afraid to tell me unpleasant truths."

Kelsey raised an eyebrow. "You've met Talbot?"

Her mother shuddered. "The good major came to visit me before I was kidnapped. I can't see what you like about the man. He's probably covered with hair."

Indeed, he was. Thankfully, that was something that technology could deal with.

"He's very good at everything he does. You'll need to upgrade the rank if you talk down to him again, though. We're going to be stuck with a large number of marines for the foreseeable future, and we have too many majors.

"I want Talbot in overall command of all the marines, so I'm promoting him to lieutenant colonel. That's appropriate for a brigade-level assignment. I'll get around to telling him eventually."

The corner of her mother's mouth quirked upward. "It's good to see that nepotism runs in the family. That seems oddly appropriate.

"Again, I have to accept that it doesn't matter what I think about him. He's your husband. If I want to improve my relationship with you, a good first step would be accepting that he's part of the package. I can't promise that I can change, but I'll try. I really will."

Her mother took a tissue and dried her eyes again. "I understand you captured the people that took me prisoner. I thought you were making all that up.

"I was wrong. The man who led that other group is dangerous. He's smart and ruthless. Keep an eye on him."

Kelsey smiled a little. "One good thing to come out of this is that you don't have to worry about him anymore. He didn't precisely want to come peacefully. I'm afraid that he died resisting."

That wasn't precisely the truth, but it was close enough for this conversation.

"I don't have time to go into the details of what happened to them or what's happening now. Events are in progress that give us a very narrow window to escape some very unfortunate consequences.

"Hopefully, we'll be able to get clear of the situation in about five hours. If things work out, we'll have plenty of time to talk. Mother, no matter what happens, I love you. That will never change."

Of course, Kelsey wasn't actually certain that she liked her mother. That was a stretch. Also, there was an all-too-real chance that her mother would revert to her old behavior.

Well, if that happened, it happened. She'd deal with it.

Kelsey rose to her feet. "I've got to go. There's still a marine outside your hatch, but it's not because you're under arrest. If you need to go anywhere, he'll make sure you get there safely. There are a lot of dangerous areas aboard a warship. I don't want you walking into something you're not prepared for."

Justine rose to her feet and pulled her daughter into another hug. "This isn't going to be easy. Not for me and not for you. I'm absolutely certain that I'm going to fall short. People don't change in a day. Or a week.

"But no matter what happens, I don't want us to ever stop talking. I don't want to ever see you hate me."

"I'll never hate you, Mother. I'm sorry, but I've got to get going."

Kelsey kissed her mother on the cheek, let herself out, and headed back toward her quarters. If she was going to get any sleep before they arrived at the multiflip point, she had to get it now.

She'd been awake long enough that she was starting to feel the effects of exhaustion. Her mind needed to be sharp when she made the final throw of the dice.

Besides, it had been over a week since she'd seen her husband. When he finally finished with the prisoners, she had no doubt that he had a very special welcome in mind for her.

* * *

Four hours later, Kelsey was back on the bridge, and *Persephone* was approaching the multiflip point. She felt better than she had since they'd kidnapped her mother. Things might still go to hell, but she was going to pray they didn't.

Her new friends Jacob and Derek sat in spare chairs against the bulkhead. They watched everything with wide eyes. She was certain that they'd wanted to be on the bridge during the battle, but she couldn't afford to take that risk.

The readings from the FTL probe in the Clan system indicated the enemy task force was a little more than an hour away from the flip point. The readings were still sketchy, but she felt confident that there were at least half a dozen capital warships. Possibly more.

She'd dropped a second FTL probe on this side of the flip point to watch their emergence. Once she was ready to take *Persephone* through the multiflip point, she'd send the destruct signal to the one in the Clan system. She couldn't take the chance that they'd find it later.

True, it supposedly had a self-destruct package that would take it out if an unauthorized ship came close, but she wasn't in the mood to risk it. They'd never tested that feature, and all it would take was one failure for someone else to get the FTL technology.

Angela turned. "Incoming signal from *Audacious*. It's Commodore Anderson."

"On screen."

The display of deep space cleared to show the flag bridge of the carrier. Zia Anderson sat in the center seat.

"We're about as ready as we're going to be, Highness. We've already sent the freighter through. Carl and his team have installed some type of modulator for us, but he won't give me any kind of odds about how it's going to work out. He says he just doesn't know enough to guess."

"What happens if it doesn't work? Is it going to burn out the flip drive?"

The commodore shrugged. "Probably. It's not as if we have a choice."

Kelsey nodded. "We're coming up on you right now. Cross your fingers and press the button."

"One roll of the dice coming up. No snake eyes."

The com channel closed, and Kelsey watched the image of the carrier floating in the darkness. The longer it sat there, the more worried she became that the flip drive had failed. Then, with a flicker, it vanished.

"Did you see that?" she asked.

Angela grinned. "I sure as hell did! They made it!"

Kelsey held up her hand. "No, not that. They didn't just vanish. They kind of flickered before they were gone."

Angela brought up the playback and watched it again. Then she slowed it down a great deal and played it for a third time.

The carrier had definitely disappeared and then reappeared before disappearing again. Not just once, but three or four times in the space of a fraction of a second.

"I've never seen anything like that," the marine said quietly. "I've never even heard of anything like it."

"Drop an FTL probe and let's get to Pandora," Kelsey said. "We need to make sure they made it. They could have gone to any of the potential branches. If they went to Archibald, we're totally screwed."

The helm officer touched his console. "Probe away. We're ready to flip at your order, Colonel."

"Take us across."

A moment later, they flipped into the Pandora system. To her relief, *Audacious* sat just ahead of them, and the freighter was a ways off to the side. They'd all made it.

"Incoming signal," Angela said. She threw it up onto the screen.

Zia appeared, frowning. "I've got good news and bad news. Obviously, we made it. The problem is that the flip drive burned out. It's completely nonresponsive. We're trapped here."

Kelsey sighed. "Well, that beats being trapped on the *other* side of the flip point or going to Archibald. Maybe you'll be able to repair it."

"I suppose anything is possible," Zia said. "I wouldn't hold my breath, though. What do we do now?"

Kelsey looked toward Jacob and Derek. "I believe we have some visitors to take home. It seems we'll be staying longer than we'd anticipated, so we might as well make as many friends as we can while we're doing it.

"Continue monitoring the FTL probes we left in the other system. We need to know what the Clan task force does. From what I understand, even if they suspect we've gone through the multiflip point, the default destination isn't this system. We should be safe here."

"What do we do if the drive is beyond repair?" Zia asked.

"That's a little more complicated. We know the multiflip point can get us to Archibald. If push comes to shove, we may have to insert a team into that system and acquire the parts we need."

The commodore didn't seem convinced. "We don't have a lot of experience dealing with the Rebel Empire. Even if we did, those kinds of parts are going to be difficult to obtain. Perhaps impossible."

Kelsey smiled. "We always seem to find a way. Don't count us out of the fight."

"Whatever you say, Highness. If you'll excuse me, I'm going to get us headed toward Pandora."

"Pandora?" Jacob asked. "What's that?"

"The name we decided to use for your planet. We had no idea what you called it, so we had to have a name. What name do you use?"

He shrugged and deferred to Derek.

The alien shook his head. "We have no name for ourselves or our planet that would make sense when referred to by someone not from here. Pandora will suffice. Does that make me a Pandoran? You'll have to explain what that means at some point when we have more time."

Kelsey nodded and sat back in her seat. No matter how good a face she put on this situation, they were in a real bind. One that might be impossible to solve.

She didn't know what she was going to do if that were the case, but she had the best people in the universe to work the problem. They'd find an answer. Or die trying.

The hatch slid open and Lieutenant Commander Clark Malone came onto the bridge. The medical officer gave Jacob and Derek an odd look before walking over to her chair.

"Might I have a few minutes of your time, Colonel? Outside?"

That was unusual, but she assumed he wouldn't have asked if it wasn't important. She excused herself and stepped into the corridor.

Once the hatch had slid shut, she raised an eyebrow. "What is it?"

The doctor licked his lips. "I was examining some of the medical waste left over from treating the aliens. I didn't have much of a chance to look them over while they were aboard. Things were a bit tense, as you recall."

She nodded. "That they were. I understand the injured only had relatively minor cuts."

"That's right. I didn't want to look the dead over very closely at the time. Their living comrades were already on edge. I finally had a chance to test some of the tissue and blood samples, though. I found something bizarre."

"They're aliens. That isn't shocking."

He shook his head emphatically. "What's shocking is how recognizable their DNA is. And I use that term with the specific meaning for deoxyribonucleic acid. Colonel, they might look alien, but their genetic markers are not only the exact same material that organisms from Terra have, but they are more than ninety-six percent identical to human DNA."

Kelsey frowned. "What? That's impossible."

"I thought so too. I checked the results a dozen times. Pandoran DNA is derived from human DNA. There is no mistake. It's obviously been modified at some point in the past, but the roots are crystal clear."

She opened her mouth to argue but stopped herself.

"I see," Kelsey said after a moment. "That's unexpected. Can you tell how long ago the modification took place?"

The medical officer shrugged. "A long time ago. Tens of thousands of years, probably. Perhaps even longer than that."

That really was impossible. That almost certainly meant the modification had happened before the formation of the Terran Empire. Hell, before humans had ventured into space at all. Definitely before they'd had that kind of skill with genetic manipulation.

"Find out everything you can," she finally said. "Take the samples over to *Audacious* for further testing with Doctor Zoboroski. Keep this quiet. Only tell Commodore Anderson."

He nodded. "Will do, Colonel. I'll let you know if we make any headway on figuring this out."

Kelsey rubbed her face as the officer left. What did this mean? Was there some other player they didn't know about? It would have to be another alien race.

Considering that the Old Empire had never found any evidence of nonterrestrial sentient life, this was getting ridiculous. Worse, how did she and her people keep stumbling across them? What would happen when they found a more advanced species?

She had no idea, and ignorance might kill them.

THE TERRA GAMBIT

BOOK EIGHT

Sent on a mission critical to the survival of the New Terran Empire, Jared Mertz must travel deep into the AI-dominated Rebel Empire on an operation of deception.

Only there are games afoot that no one could foresee and players at the table that no one could expect. The stakes couldn't be higher.

When unexpected enemies deal themselves in, Jared must bet everything on a single hand. Bluffing might get him killed but folding isn't an option.

1

"I left her there," Jared Mertz said. "This is my fault."

"Have you met my daughter?" Emperor Karl Bandar of the New Terran Empire asked his son. "Kelsey has a streak of what we'll generously call impulsiveness. If she thinks she has a better plan than you, she's likely to execute it and then beg forgiveness while you pick up the pieces."

Jared stared at his father for a few seconds and then laughed softly. "I suppose you're right. Still, I should've seen this coming. I let her talk me into leading the attack on the Dresden orbital to recover the data on manufacturing the Marine Raider implants. I figured they'd be in and gone before trouble came looking for them, but I was wrong. Again."

The two of them were sitting in the Emperor's private quarters at the Imperial Palace, sipping on aged whiskey. Jared had left his task force at the sealed Erorsi flip point a day ago and come home alone to report.

Based on the FTL probes they'd deployed as they'd fled the Rebel Empire, the enemy had only been about twelve hours behind them when they'd transitioned to Erorsi and put the flip-point jammer there back into service.

Even though he'd destroyed the FTL probes as his fleet had fled, he'd decided to leave the ones in the system just past Erorsi intact. He positioned them far enough out to avoid any chance of detection and could always send the self-destruct signal if anyone seemed to have detected them.

Jared had waited in the Erorsi system with his fleet in case the Rebel Empire made a concerted attempt to force their way through, but they hadn't. The FTL probes didn't have the best view of the enemy using passive scans at extremely long range, but he could tell that most of the Rebel Empire ships were setting up around the Erorsi flip point.

Based on the amount of debris that had come through, they'd sent several waves of probes to test his defenses. No ships had attempted to flip, so the complete lack of response had spooked them. That wouldn't last.

The flip-point jammer set up a gravitational resonance in the wormholes that allowed travel between star systems up to hundreds of light years apart. Nothing had survived the transit. Eventually, they'd figure out what he was doing, and then the real fun would start.

His people would have to take the flip-point jammer down for maintenance, but that day was over a month away. He'd worry about that when he had no other choice.

"We'll just have to hope she finds another way home," the emperor said. "I have every confidence in Kelsey's resourcefulness. Besides, she has Commodore Anderson and *Audacious* to help her get the technology home.

"The Raider implants might be the most useful militarily, but learning how to build AIs could help win this war. That would make all the trouble worthwhile."

The fact that the Dresden Orbital had held facilities to build sentient AIs had been a game-changing surprise, one they couldn't pass up. Kelsey had stolen the entire orbital with a ship used to transport large vessels that couldn't move themselves and fled in the only direction open to her.

The Fleet carrier and swarms of fighters in her belly would make for a very stout defense as well as an improbably strong arm of attack. Jared knew the Rebel Empire didn't use fighters. It would be a very unpleasant surprise for anyone that chanced across his sister.

"For the time being, Erorsi is secure," Jared said. "The downside is that they know exactly where to find us now. They're going to build up quite a Fleet element on the other side of the Erorsi flip point, and they'll keep probing it.

"Sooner or later, they're going to catch us while we're performing maintenance on the flip-point jammer. Then they're going to come through and try to swamp us."

His father nodded. "We'll keep your entire task force there. In fact, we'll transfer as many ships and fixed defenses as we can from Harrison's World to back them up. That's going to leave Commodore Meyer shorthanded, but such is life."

Sean Meyer had once been an executive officer for one of the worst Fleet commanders Jared had ever met. Meyer could be arrogant and condescending. To his pleasure, Jared had discovered the commodore was also an exceptionally capable man.

"He'll manage. I'll make certain that Erorsi stays secure."

"Actually, you won't. I have a different mission in mind for you."

Jared raised an eyebrow and sipped his drink. "What might that be, Majesty?"

"I thought I told you not to use titles when we're alone."

"When you start giving orders, this isn't a social call anymore."

Karl Bandar laughed. "You're an interesting mix of contradictions,

Jared. While I certainly believe we need to keep Erorsi secure, we also have another very important mission that requires the most capable commander possible."

"You mean sending a destroyer from Harrison's World to give an annual status report to the AIs?"

Jared and his original makeshift force had managed to ambush and defeat the artificial intelligence controlling the Harrison's World system. He'd very much like to keep the other Rebel Empire AIs in the dark about the change in management.

The AI had been housed inside an old Fleet sector base called Boxer Station. After the civil war that had destroyed the Old Empire, the triumphant AIs had brought all the wrecked ships that had survived the fighting to orbit the station and created a gigantic graveyard.

He and his people had worked with the leadership on Harrison's World to bring the repair bays at the station back online. That allowed them to begin recovering and restoring the ships that were least damaged. Even the first of those had provided a very powerful fighting force for the New Terran Empire and their allies, the Pentagarans.

The crown princess of Pentagar—Elise Orison—was Jared's wife, and he wished he'd had the opportunity to spend more time with her after his return from the Rebel Empire, but he'd had to make do with just one night of her coming to visit him in Erorsi. She wouldn't be pleased to learn the emperor was sending him away again so soon.

"Understood," Jared said. "As far as I know, the automated destroyer the Harrison's World AI sent to report every year goes to a specific system and transmits a very basic report of all the events that occurred since the last report.

"We have records of everything sent since the AIs suppressed Harrison's World a decade ago. It should be a simple matter to send a captured ship to deliver a forged report."

Harrison—the newly formatted AI on Boxer Station—would be able to create a report that raised no electronic eyebrows. The friendly AI had none of the murderous core rules that its predecessor had. He was firmly allied with the New Terran Empire.

And allied was the appropriate word because the Imperial Senate had recognized AIs as individuals worthy of all the rights and responsibilities of citizenship. Boy, had that caused a ruckus. Jared just wished they had more of the sentient computers to help them.

"Exactly how often have plans proceeded precisely as we wished?" the emperor asked. "No, I think it might be best to send a team of our very best people to be sure this critical mission goes off without a hitch. And you, my boy, are the right man to lead it." The older man grinned. "I realize that command of a destroyer is a big step down for an admiral, but I think you'll remember what needs to be done."

Jared laughed. "Considering I was commanding a destroyer just a couple of years ago, I think it'll all come back pretty fast. When do you want me to depart? I need to get back and brief Charlie Graves about taking command of the defenses at Erorsi."

"Immediately," his father said. "The fast courier will take you straight to Boxer Station. Then she will deliver new orders for Commodore Graves to assume permanent command at Erorsi. The mission is scheduled to depart any day now, so you need to get familiarized with this new ship and assemble your crew at once.

"And with the Rebel Empire now aware of our presence, the chances that you will need to improvise are even greater than normal. I think we need to plan on things working out differently than we imagine." The older man leaned back in his chair. "I said immediately, but I suppose we can have dinner first. I wouldn't want to send you out on an empty stomach."

* * *

COMMODORE SEAN MEYER considered Coordinator Olivia West across her dining table for several moments. "I don't think so."

"Don't be ridiculous," Olivia said then took a sip of her wine. "Of course I'm going."

Sean and she were supposedly having a *working* dinner at her residence on Harrison's World. He suspected no one was fooled by their charade, but he had to keep up appearances. The two of them had discovered a spark while they worked hand-in-hand to restore Harrison's World to its former glory. He hadn't been involved in a serious relationship for many years.

She had lost her fiancé years ago. Fleet Captain Brian Drake had taken his own life on the flag bridge of the superdreadnought *Invincible* when the System Lord suppressed Harrison's World a decade ago, making it impossible for their rebellion to succeed.

The man had held on as long as his supplies had allowed inside the superdreadnought that they'd secretly restored. Then, once he and his people had no other option, they'd taken the painless way out.

The fact that Olivia and he were lovers now didn't change anything, he told himself. Her presence on board the ship wasn't necessary. He didn't need to risk their strongest ally in the region. Even he had to admit that sounded like a lame excuse.

He gave the ruler of Harrison's World a quelling stare. It bounced off her smug expression ineffectively.

Sean sighed. "Why in the world would I send you on a mission involving a Fleet ship? You wouldn't know the first thing about what to do in a crisis."

"Wrong. I know exactly what to do first in a crisis. Stay calm."

"Let me rephrase," he said repressively. "What would you contribute to the mission? We're sending a destroyer to send an automatic message and then come back. It's not going to interact with anyone."

She pointed her fork at him. "Are you certain of that? Just because it hasn't happened before doesn't mean it won't happen this time. What will you do if you're required to have inside knowledge of how the Rebel Empire operates? You need someone who knows."

"We already have someone like that. Lieutenant Commander Michael Richards, the computer specialist we captured at Erorsi. If they need specialized information, he'll have it."

"That assumes the emperor will allow him to accompany you," she said. "That's doubtful. In any case, meaning no offense to the good commander, he's only of the middle orders. If your ship has to deal with someone from the higher orders, it's a completely different—what's that term you use?—kettle of fish.

"Perhaps sometime you can explain why anyone would keep a kettle of fish around and exactly how they differ from one another. No, you need to have someone on hand who can explain what the rulers of the Rebel Empire are actually thinking. That means me."

He wished he could argue, but she was probably right. In any case, he knew by now that he was going to lose this fight.

"Admiral Mertz arrives tomorrow," he said. "The Emperor appointed him to command the expedition ship. I just got word of that a few hours ago. If you're going, then I'm going, too. It should be a short trip, so my absence here won't make any difference."

She raised an eyebrow. "And you think that Admiral Mertz is going to just allow the station commander to go along on this mission?"

He grinned. "You're not the only one who can be persuasive. We need to have the very best selection of people aboard. I feel confident that I can wiggle my way into the executive officer's position. I have quite a bit of experience in the role, you know."

"Weren't you fired the last time you were an executive officer?" she asked archly. "I seem to remember hearing a story about you being thrown into a cell. Well, two cells, if you count when I did it."

Sean grunted sourly. That had certainly been true. He'd rescued Princess Kelsey and Jared Mertz from his previous commander, Captain Wallace Breckenridge, and been thrown into the brig for mutiny.

Then the AI had captured *Spear* and many of the crew had been sent to Harrison's World. Olivia had locked them all up in a prison camp. One he'd escaped from, but he didn't think he needed to mention that little detail right now.

"I do hope you realize bringing that up is going to cost you," he said with a grin.

Olivia set her wineglass down and smiled back at him. "And what is the price that I shall have to pay? Does it, perhaps, involve some late-night entertainment?"

"Considering this might be the last evening we'll have to ourselves, you're damned right it does."

2

Crown Princess Elise Orison wasn't a happy woman. Her sources inside the Imperial Palace at Avalon in the New Terran Empire had told her that Jared's father was sending him off on another mission.

Not exactly the news a newly wedded woman wanted to hear when it involved her husband of only a few weeks, particularly when they'd only had stolen moments to celebrate alone. Well, they'd had one night after the wedding, but it was so rushed that it barely counted. It had been divine but far too brief.

The night she'd come to visit him at Erorsi was even worse. The threat of imminent attack had hung over them, distracting him when she wanted his undivided attention.

Jared was a serving Fleet officer, one critical to the defense of both the New Terran Empire and her own Kingdom of Pentagar. His focus had to be on the war with the Rebel Empire, but that didn't mean she couldn't arrange for a little more time at his side.

By all accounts, the journey to deliver the message would take six days, and then they'd spend the same amount of time coming back. Two weeks sharing their marital bed, even with his attention focused on the mission, would just about satisfy her. For now.

That was how she found herself waiting for him in the Nova system aboard His Majesty's fast courier *Lance*. The quarters were cramped, but such was the nature of a ship designed to get from one place to another at the fastest possible speed. The little vessel was mostly drives. That meant her closet back at the palace was bigger than her current accommodations.

Not that she cared. She was focused on work. A princess's duties were never done.

A rap at the hatch drew her attention from the report she was reading. She rose to her feet, crossed over, and opened it.

Lieutenant Commander Gerald Parker, the ship's commanding officer, stood outside. "My apologies, Highness, but we have a priority message for you."

"You could have just sent me a message through your implants," she reminded him.

He grimaced. "I'm still trying to get used to the idea, and it's only a few steps from the bridge to your door. Just contacting you seems rude when it took scarcely ten seconds to come in person."

She smiled and shook her head. "I suppose it makes no difference. What's the message? Admiral Sanders needs something? My father? Maybe even Jared?"

The young officer shook his head. "It's from Omega, actually. He indicated that he needs to speak with you in person as soon as practical. His words."

"Truly? And he asked for me?"

"He did, Highness."

"Then I suppose I'd best go see him straight away. I assume you have a suit I can use?"

He nodded. "All ships are now equipped with hard suits that can survive in the radiation here for just such a contingency. We have three. Shall I accompany you?"

Elise shook her head. "Not inside, no. You can fly me over, though."

An hour later, she stood on the hull of the alien space station, looking at the bright gas circling the black hole where the sun in this system once gave its worlds life. Never in her wildest dreams had she ever imagined seeing such a thing.

"Welcome to my station, Highness," a male voice said through her suit's com system. "The journey through my hull is disconcerting, but safe. Are you prepared?"

She waved at Commander Parker. He stood in his ship's sole cutter watching her.

"I'm ready, Omega. And it's a pleasure to finally meet you."

"As it is for me. Here we go."

The hull deformed under her, sinking in to deposit her into a corridor filled with liquid. Water, so she was told. Omega had come from an aquatic species before he'd volunteered to physically become part of the station.

"You're right," she said. "That *was* disturbing. What did you need to speak with me about?"

"That is something of a complex issue. There is a chamber around the ring where an environment suitable for humans is maintained. It would be much simpler if you were there. Turn right, and it is only a few minutes away."

Moving through the liquid in the heavy suit taxed her skills, but she managed to slowly make her way around the alien ring. That gave her plenty of time to think about where she was going.

The story of the chamber she was heading for was gruesome. Omega's station had been designed to capture the power of his race's star and create bridges to other realities. That was how his people had escaped the death of their world. They hadn't had flip drives.

Her people were slowly adopting the term "flip point" in place of "space-time bridges" simply because it was less formal. Before the arrival of the New Terran Empire destroyer *Athena*, the Pentagarans hadn't had interstellar drives and had been trapped in their own system, so not many people needed to use any term to describe them at all.

In any case, after the explosion of the sun in the Nova system, the station seemed to have been somehow linked to all others of its kind across the multiverse. In effect, they became a single station with Omega as the being in control.

Something about the bizarre situation made the skin of the station impenetrable and indestructible. It also meant that people from any universe where the station existed could make the trip inside it, if they solved the riddle of opening its skin.

In those days, Omega had been unable to communicate with humans. He had no basis for establishing a dialogue with the humans trapped inside his station, people that were variants of others Elise knew. People that had died building that chamber she was heading for while they waited for rescue that never came.

Carl Owlet—Sir Carl, she corrected herself—had managed to crack that secret, just like so many others the brilliant young man had solved. He'd also found the dead bodies of a number of people he knew in the chamber, including several versions of himself. That had to be eerie. And macabre.

Elise arrived at the hand-built airlock leading into the compartment and started cycling herself in.

"Once you get inside, I think it best you know that you aren't alone," Omega said as the water began draining from the lock.

"What?" Elise straightened in surprise. "Who else is here? Our ship was the only one in the system."

"True, but there is a visitor from another reality."

Elise started to ask again who was waiting on the other side of the hatch but stopped herself. It was already swinging open. She might as well find out the old-fashioned way.

She also made a mental note to explain the difference between pleasant and unpleasant surprises to the alien when she had the opportunity.

* * *

To Olivia's mind, her original tour of the destroyer had been a tad underwhelming. Of course, it had been converted to computer control and no longer had the fittings for human habitation at that point.

The Fleet personnel of Boxer Station were rapidly correcting that deficiency, and she wanted to see her new quarters. Lieutenant Logan Butters, one of the base's engineering officers, was escorting her.

They exited the cutter that had delivered her to the destroyer in its repair slip. The inside of the ship seemed much the same as she remembered, but men and women were bustling about and getting everything prepared for the human crew.

"How long until the ship is ready to depart?" she asked her guide.

"It could leave tomorrow, Coordinator, but the refurbishment will be complete the day after that. Call it forty-eight hours. They've reserved one of the senior officers' cabins for you."

"I do hope that no one was displaced to make room for me."

He shook his head. "No. They're running with a reduced crew, so they didn't need all of them. The automated systems will allow them to get by with roughly two-thirds of a normal crew."

They stepped into the lift, and he sent them up. Moments later, the lift doors slid open, and they continued down the corridor.

He went a little farther and then gestured at one of the hatches. "This is it. I've taken the liberty of linking the controls to your implants."

Olivia sent a signal to the hatch, and it slid open. She walked inside and schooled her expression. It was even smaller than she'd imagined. Well, she'd make do.

They'd moved standard Fleet furnishings in, so she had a bed, a desk, and all the other aspects of life she would need for the next two weeks. Everything had probably come from ships in the graveyard. Including the bed.

Sleeping on something belonging to a long-dead Fleet officer was a little ghoulish. That might take some getting used to.

"I took the additional liberty of providing all the consumables you'll need," the lieutenant continued. "They're stashed in compartments in the bathroom and in here. Let me show you."

Over the next half hour, he gave her a detailed tour of her accommodations and demonstrated everything. Much of it was already familiar to her, but some was new and strange. It would take a little getting used to.

Once she was satisfied she had everything committed to memory, she turned to face him. "Could we see the bridge?"

The officer nodded. "Of course. This way."

It was on the same level and just down the corridor. She imagined that the designers had wanted to put the senior officers right at hand in case of an emergency.

The hatch leading in was open. Unlike other parts of the ship, the bridge work was finished. All the modifications for human control were in place.

Olivia marveled at how much smaller it was than the flag bridge on *Invincible*. Cramped didn't begin to describe the difference.

She took a great liberty and sat in the commander's seat. Everything was so intimate. She could almost read the screens on the other control consoles.

The main screen showed the interior of the semi-open repair slip on Boxer Station. A man on a small sled zipped by, probably delivering something to the massive ship just visible behind him in the next slip.

That was the superdreadnought *Implacable.* The battle damage that had killed her was still all-too visible down her flanks. The crew had committed suicide by dumping their air when the AI-controlled ships had brought her to heel.

The idea of so many people still floating unrecovered in the ships of the graveyard turned her stomach. She knew how their friends and family must have felt. Intimately.

Fleet Captain Brian Drake, her lover a decade ago. The memory of his suicide still tore at her heart, even though Sean Meyer had brought her feelings back to life.

She'd seen Brian and his comrades buried with every bit of pomp and circumstance. The same was true with the dead from *Implacable.* The ship was going to be the nucleus of the new fleet based here at Harrison's World. It seemed only right.

That left the millions of bodies still entombed on tens of thousands of derelicts. Recovering them and seeing them laid to rest would take decades. Well, they'd been waiting five hundred years already. What were a few more?

At one time, Fleet in the New Terran Empire had buried their dead at a monument called the Spire. There was no way that could continue, so she had overseen the dedication of an identical monument here on Harrison's World. Located in the area around one of the cities destroyed by the AI during the suppression of her world, it had space for all of the dead they might find.

"I'm surprised to find you here," a voice said from behind her.

She turned in her seat and found Sean standing beside the hatch. Lieutenant Butters was nowhere to be seen.

"I must've gotten lost in thought," she said as she rose to her feet. "This little ship isn't much to look at."

He smiled. "Yet she'll fight hard if she needs to. The mettle of a ship isn't in her hull; it's in her crew. Have you had lunch? We can drop in on the mess hall and see if the cook is any good."

"Can we replace him if he isn't?"

Sean laughed and held a hand out to her. "I'll see what I can do. Come on. We'll eat, and then I'll give you the grand tour."

3

Jared frowned as he examined the display over the captain's shoulder. The bridge of the fast courier *Javelin* was small, and he already missed his spacious flag bridge. Even *Athena*'s control center had been bigger.

"What are they doing?" he asked, more to himself than anyone else.

"Looks like they're waiting for us," Lieutenant Calvin Fassbinder said.

"Well, I suppose I'd best find out what this is about," Jared said. "Might I borrow your seat?"

The young man rose and took one step away. That put him almost against the bulkhead. The bridge was that small.

Jared sat and switched the view to the communications controls. The Pentagaran ship sat near the flip point linking to Avalon, where there was zero chance they'd miss Jared's transit and they were close enough that the incredible radiation density wouldn't overwhelm his signal.

Even with the suddenness of his orders, they'd known he was coming. Jared knew that because they'd asked for him by name. They hadn't said so, but he suspected they either had orders to lure him to Pentagar, which he would have to reluctantly decline, or they'd brought his wife out to see him. That would make refusing her entreaties even harder.

Well, that was why they paid him his exorbitant salary. He opened a com channel. "*Lance*, this is *Javelin*. What can we do for you?"

The image of the ship vanished, replaced by Lieutenant Commander Parker's face. The man smiled. "Lord Admiral Mertz. A pleasure to see you as always, Highness. Your lady wife requires some of your time on a matter of urgency. And delicacy."

That caused the corners of Jared's mouth to twitch upward. "I see. Well,

I do have *some* time to spare, though not nearly as much as I might like. I'll be over in a few minutes."

The other man's expression became more serious. "Bring your guards, Lord Admiral. All of them."

Parker killed the channel before Jared could ask why.

With a shake of his head, he relinquished the console. "I'll need your cutter, Lieutenant. Let me go collect my guards. My wife must be more annoyed than usual."

The other man gave him a look. "That's why I'm staying single, sir."

"You say that now, but you'll find the right person eventually. Never say never."

The trip back to his quarters was quick. On a ship this small, getting anywhere fast was never a problem.

As they were going directly from Avalon to Harrison's World, only needing to transit the Nova system, he didn't have to worry about actually spending the night in the cramped cabin. His father had sent him out first thing in the morning after their dinner, so he was good to go.

His staff was holed up in the small compartment. His guard complement consisted of a mixture of Imperial Guards and marines. There were situations where one or the other group might be more appropriate.

Lieutenant Colonel Adrian Branson was in overall command of the mixed unit. He sat on the bed beside Major Karalee Smith, the marine detachment leader.

The two of them were more co-leaders than superior and subordinate, so Jared had wisely decided to keep his mouth shut about their budding relationship.

Frankly, he was surprised he'd figured it out on his own. Elise was much better at that sort of thing than he was. He hadn't even noticed Kelsey and Talbot were a couple until someone pointed it out to him.

The third person sitting on the bed wasn't a guard. In fact, he wasn't even an Imperial citizen or in any branch of the military at all.

Alexander Alexander—Double Alex to his friends—was Jared's Pentagaran manservant. There'd been discussion about giving him both a Fleet steward and a Royal manservant, but he'd drawn the line at one person.

Hell, one was too many, but he'd seen himself losing that fight. A good officer knew when to perform a fighting retreat.

Alex could be a little obsequious when he chose, but in private, he'd shown himself able to unwind a little. There was a spine in there somewhere. Out of all the choices presented to him, Jared thought their personalities might mesh the best.

This trip on the destroyer was sort of a test. If Alex didn't drive Jared insane in two weeks, they'd probably be able to do this. If not, he'd send the man packing and find someone else that his wife approved of.

"I'm headed over to the Pentagaran fast courier *Lance*," Jared said as he opened his closet. "I was told I needed to bring my guard."

Branson heroically managed to avoid rolling his eyes. "Of course you need to bring your guard, Admiral."

The two of them had had a long discussion on the use of titles. The Imperial Guard officer preferred "Highness" since Jared was technically a prince of the blood and the Prince Consort of Pentagar, but he'd accepted Jared's decree to only use that during unambiguously social affairs.

So, the man had acquiesced to using his rank in all other circumstances. That defaulted to almost every situation, which pleased Jared to no end.

"I see what you did there, but I mean he made a *point* of telling me to bring you. That's weird."

The Imperial guard's eyes narrowed. "Then we'll go over in force. I'll summon the ready squad." His eyes flicked to Major Smith. "You get everyone else ready to come over if we need them."

The slender woman shook her head. "Won't work. We only have a single cutter. You need to have it there at all times in case you have to retreat in a hurry. We don't have suits to make the jump in this hellish environment, either."

The man in Imperial whites scowled but nodded. "Then we pack everyone into the cutter. Everyone. Get them there."

The marine rose without a word and strode out of the compartment.

While they'd been speaking, Jared had pulled out his gun belt. He didn't go armed as a matter of course—unlike Kelsey—so he'd left it in his closet. He certainly didn't think he'd need a weapon now, but it was prudent to bring it.

A few minutes later, the entire security detail was crowded into the cutter. It was an exceptionally tight fit.

All told, he had over four dozen people in his security detail, so they could handle multiple shifts and situations. A cutter was designed to comfortably seat three dozen people in the passenger compartment. It turned out one could hold everyone on his security staff. Barely.

Double Alex took one look at the sardine can and headed for the cockpit, declaring he would ride at the flight engineer's station. A wise man.

Jared evicted the co-pilot and took over control of the flight. "Remind me to make sure we have a pinnace as our small craft going forward," he told the Pentagaran. "It has a lot more internal space. It has to, to deliver seventy marines in powered armor."

The man nodded. "I've already done so, Highness. One suitably modified for dual use, as I doubt you'll be needing marines every trip."

Jared exchanged words with *Javelin*'s bridge and detached the cutter. The trip to *Lance* would only take a few minutes. That still gave him plenty of time to worry.

What the hell was going on over there?

* * *

Work was continuing on preparing the destroyer for human habitation and control, but Sean was satisfied that she was far enough along for a test flip to be certain everything was functioning correctly.

He'd consulted with Fleet command about renaming the ship. *R-4587* just didn't have snap to it. With their concurrence, he'd secretly rechristened the ship.

Sean suspected Admiral Mertz would approve of her new name: *Athena*. The original would finally be sent to the breakers at Harrison's World and remade.

"We're at the weak flip point, Commodore," Commander Janice Hall, their helm officer, said.

The position was a big step down for a woman who'd recently commanded a light cruiser, but she didn't seem to mind. And since the ship's captain would be an admiral, well, it wasn't too big a downgrade in comparison.

"Take us over as soon as we get the green light from our escort."

Sean had chosen to have one of the fully operational ships flip with them, in case there was a serious failure. Not that he expected any trouble, but the Nova system was not the place to have a breakdown.

The light cruiser *Brazil* had recently finished her trials and was heading for Avalon. He figured the two ships could travel together to the artificial flip point that Omega had created. By then, he'd be sure of *Athena*'s stability.

"My compliments to Commander Meissner, Wanda. Tell her we flip in sixty seconds."

"Aye, sir," Commander Wanda Dieter, their com officer, said. "She reports that they'll be ready."

"Battle screens up, Commodore," Commander Evan Brodie said. Their tactical officer was grinning.

"Excellent," Sean replied with an indulgent smile. Something about the man excused his occasionally excessive exuberance.

Sean tapped his console and opened a link to engineering. "Are we there yet?"

"Obviously not, sir," Commander Katheryn Pence said. The chief engineer's tone was mildly acerbic, but neither of them were overly bothered by their antics. She'd served aboard *Spear* with him for years. "We are, however, ready to flip at your command."

"We flip in… fifty seconds."

"Copy that. Engineering out."

The hatch to the bridge slid open, and Olivia West walked in, accompanied by the ship's doctor, Commander Emmett Dishmon.

"Am I in time?" she asked.

"Barely," he said with a nod. "Have a seat. Forty seconds to flip."

The new arrivals secured themselves at the observation consoles just in time.

"Flipping the ship," Hall said.

The familiar twisting tore at his guts. It lasted only an instant but still made him grimace.

The view from the main screen had changed. Instead of a star field, everything was a haze. The radiation and stellar matter thrown off in the titanic explosion that collapsed this system's sun into a black hole had flooded the outer system with this crap. It only cleared up once one reached the inner system.

"*Brazil* reports a good flip," Dieter said. "They're ready to proceed."

"Set course for the inner system and take us in," he ordered.

He turned to face Olivia. "How was your first flip?"

She stuck out her tongue sourly. "I'm glad I took Doctor Dishmon up on the shot. I can't believe you do that all the time."

"Fleet implants make it more tolerable. The civilian modules you have might not be up to the task. Before we had any implants at all, this was a real pain in the ass. First timers usually lost their lunches."

Her face took on a look of revulsion. "Heaven protect me from that. How humiliating."

"It was like a rite of passage," he mused. "We'll have to come up with new ones now."

"You know that's hazing, right? Can you do that?"

"Within certain limits, a little. You should hear what the fighter pilots do to their new recruits." He shuddered theatrically. "Trust me. This is nothing."

Doctor Dishmon was rubbing his chin. "I think I have everything on hand to update most of her implant components to Fleet standards. Maybe all of them. If not, I can get the missing equipment before we depart Harrison's World. Would you like an upgrade, Coordinator?"

"I'd never considered it before," Olivia said. "Should I?"

"The nanite package is worth it all on its own," Sean said. "I say you should do it. After all, you're normally so busy that you couldn't block out the time. Why waste the opportunity?"

She considered that and then nodded. "Then I will. What does the procedure entail?"

"I'd go in and swap out the implant processors, but the cranial wiring is the same for both Fleet and civilian," Dishmon said. "You'd get some upgrades in processing capability and only half a day of light duty to make sure everything is calibrated.

"During that time, the new nanites will propagate. Once I insert the new population, they'll override the civilian units and take over. That means I need to swap out the nanite fabricator, but that's hardly worth mentioning.

"It would be different if you were getting Raider implants. Not that we could do them, mind you. Those would keep you down for a while and take multiple sessions over six weeks."

He saw Olivia shudder. Knowing what he did of how the heir had gotten her implants, he understood.

"No," she said. "I think Fleet-level implants are quite enough, thank you. Perhaps we can get them done now? Then I'll be fully back to normal by the time we get home. I'll have a last flurry of things to take care of before we head into the Empire. Excuse me, the Rebel Empire."

Dishmon glanced at Sean, so he nodded his approval.

"Absolutely," the doctor said as he stood. "We can start right now, Commodore."

She stepped over and kissed Sean. "Don't worry. I'll be fine."

It amused him how the bridge crew were studiously working on their consoles after Olivia left. The woman really knew how to push his boundaries. He wasn't the kind of man that appreciated public displays of affection, so she'd made absolutely certain everyone now knew they were an item.

Well, that would be obvious as soon as they started visiting each other at night. A destroyer was a small community, far too small for secrets like that.

Knowing her, she also wanted to get the word out back on Harrison's World. Olivia West did nothing by accident. Everything was always planned and considered.

Sean smiled. He'd have to take the chance to turn the tables on her with some surprising behavior. Fair was fair.

"Yes," he said dryly. "Coordinator West and I are seeing each other. Carry on."

"We're not the ones carrying on, sir," Evan said in a sotto voice.

Everyone laughed, including Sean. "Touché. Now, how about we get this ship on the move? I'd like to get things wrapped up before the admiral gets to Harrison's World. Make it happen, people."

4

Olivia thought the procedure to update her implant hardware to Fleet standards took very little time and seemed to be a simple process.

At first glance, everything felt the same. She supposed that the differences in performance speed and capability were subtler than she'd imagined. As long as they made the flips more tolerable, she could live with that.

Doctor Dishmon ran a set of diagnostics on her after the procedure. "Everything looks good. Remember to take it easy for the next twelve hours. Your new nanites are settling in, but I'd like to get them established before you need them."

"I'm not seeing much difference between them and the ones I had before," she said as she sat up. "Am I missing something?"

"The Fleet version has significantly more redundancy and will perform better when you have a lot going on. In general use, both are fast. I'd wager you see the difference after you really get to put them through their paces."

She nodded. "That sounds good. I suppose I should let you get back to business."

He laughed and gestured at the mostly empty medical center. "I don't have a lot of customers right now, but that's how I like it. I'm sure I can find some paperwork to handle. Fleet loves paperwork."

Olivia started to make a joke about the nonexistent paperless society, but an incoming call preempted her attention. It was Sean.

"We have a situation developing," he said tersely when she accepted the call. "Can you meet me at the docking level?"

"I'm on my way," she said, waving to the doctor as she strode into the corridor. "What's wrong?"

"I'm not sure. Admiral Mertz is already here and is meeting Crown Princess Elise on her ship at Omega."

That sounded innocuous. "They're married. I think he's safe enough."

"Then why did they make sure he brought all his guards with him? All of them."

"You're right. That does sound odd. Why don't you ask him?"

"I did. He's heading over via cutter and has no idea. I tried to get the details out of the Pentagaran commander, but he said it was best not to say. I think we need to head over and see for ourselves."

Olivia stepped into a lift, and it whisked her down to the docking level. "Did you tell Admiral Mertz you were coming? Is he concerned? Might there be something wrong with the princess? What if we need a medical team?"

"Commander Parker told me no one was injured but to have a medical team on standby. Nothing urgent, but it sounds damned odd."

The lift opened, and she stepped out to find Sean waiting for her. Together, they headed for the nearest cutter.

"They're being very mysterious," she said as they entered the cutter.

An ensign was waiting to see them strapped in. He gave Sean a nod and stepped into the cockpit. Moments later, the cutter detached from *Athena*.

"We should arrive a few minutes after the admiral, but I asked him to wait for us," Sean said. "This makes me nervous."

They spent the next few minutes pondering what could be going on but arrived at the Pentagaran ship as clueless as when they started.

"Admiral Mertz's cutter is undocking to make room for us," he said. "We'll find out pretty quick, I suppose."

The docking seemed to take forever, but they were actually standing in just a few minutes. When the lock opened, she found Admiral Mertz on the other side. He had his guards with him. Dozens of them.

"Don't you think this is overkill?" she asked as she stepped out.

"Coordinator," he said with a nod. "I suppose so, but Commander Parker said Elise had instructed him to tell me to bring them all. I'm not sure what's wrong."

The lift doors opened, and Commander Parker stepped out. "My timing is good. Welcome aboard, Highness, Coordinator. I'm sorry to have been so mysterious, but Her Highness was very specific that I not say what the situation is."

"Are we in danger?" Jared asked.

The man shrugged. "I'm not precisely sure I'd call this situation immediately dangerous, though it might have elements that I haven't grasped yet. If you'll accompany me to the main deck, I'll give you a rundown of the basic elements I know."

"Why isn't Elise here?" Olivia asked. "Is she okay?"

"I saw her not ten minutes ago, Coordinator. She is fine."

Jared turned to his guards. "Follow me up."

"I think not," a man in New Terran Empire Imperial Whites said. "We send a team up first, and I go with you."

"Is all this really necessary?" Sean asked Parker.

"I believe so, Commodore," the other man said gravely. "Basically, we arrived here a few hours ago, and Omega summoned Princess Elise. She didn't come back alone. It seems we have a visitor."

Olivia frowned. "A visitor? From Omega?"

Jared's face showed he'd grasped the situation. "From another universe. Oh, crap."

The lift returned from taking the first set of guards up. Parker, Jared, the guard commander, and she went into the lift with a few more guards. The trip up took only a few seconds. They rejoined the other guards.

"I see you've grasped the basic situation," Parker said. "Her Highness is waiting in our wardroom with our guest. She is concerned that this meeting might go… badly."

"Who is it?" Jared demanded.

The hatch slid aside, and Olivia looked inside the room. What she saw sent a cold chill through her. Crown Princess Elise of Pentagar waited there, with a very familiar figure beside her.

The short woman in black armor had her helmet off, and Olivia recognized Princess Kelsey Bandar. Only, this woman was not *their* Kelsey. This woman had a deep scar on the left side of her face and some kind of artificial eye under a metal plate.

What Olivia could see of the woman's natural face didn't hold the cheerful expression she would've expected. No, this woman glared at them all with a look of mixed anger and revulsion.

"Just my luck," the new Kelsey said in a low growl. "The Bastard."

* * *

Jared stood there in shock for a moment before he roused himself. "Kelsey. I suspected we'd get visitors from other realities, but I hadn't considered you might be the first."

She tensed. "Don't be familiar, Mertz. You don't get to use my first name. Only my friends do. I am your crown princess."

The sense that he was caught in some strange nightmare washed over him. He opened his mouth to tell her that wasn't how it was but stopped himself. This might have been how they'd turned out if things had gone differently.

Obviously, it was exactly how they'd turned out in her universe. He'd best keep in mind that this was *not* his sister. This was Crown Princess Kelsey Bandar, a woman who obviously loathed him.

"Forgive me, Highness," he said with a small bow. "I will, of course, respect your wishes. Might we come in?"

The woman glared at him before stepping back.

Elise stood there, a stricken look in her eyes, one she masked almost as soon as he'd seen it.

He wanted to take his wife into a hug, but he needed to keep his eyes on the unpredictable threat in the room. This Kelsey obviously hated him and, based on her armor, had Marine Raider implants. She could kill him anytime she chose.

Interestingly, she showed no sign of recognizing Olivia West. Yet, unless things were very different in the other universe, she'd come through Harrison's World to get to the Nova system.

He started to step into the compartment, but his guards moved in first. By some unspoken cue, the Imperial Guards moved to the side of the compartment that Kelsey stood on, and the marines backed him up. Their hands were close to their weapons, and the tension in the air went up.

"Stand down," Kelsey told the guards in white. "Call off your dogs, Mertz."

Jared made a gesture, and they all relaxed just a hair. Interestingly, she only seemed to associate the marines with him. He decided not to correct her misapprehension and communicated his intent over his implants to the guards.

Keep things low key. She's not associating the Imperial Guard with me, so let's keep it that way for now.

Colonel Branson looked unconvinced but nodded almost imperceptibly. His implant response was very direct, however. *We'll play it your way, Highness, but she's not our princess. If she makes a move on you, we'll come down on her.*

Let's hope it doesn't come to that. He stepped cautiously into the wardroom and gestured to his companions. "You've already met Elise. This is Commodore Sean Meyer and Coordinator Olivia West."

Kelsey's natural eye narrowed again. "Mind your manners, Bastard. That's Crown Princess Elise to the likes of you."

The absurdity was almost too much, but this wasn't the time or place to educate her.

"Of course. Forgive me, Highness," he said to Elise.

Anger flashed in her eyes but also horror and sadness. His wife swallowed and nodded. "Of course, Admiral. Shall we all sit? This might take a while."

Kelsey ignored her and walked over to Sean. For him, she had a smile. "This is a well-deserved promotion, Commodore. It's good to see you again, Sean. Even if you aren't precisely the same man I know."

If her reaction shocked him, he hid it well. "It's good to see you, too, Highness."

She shook her head. "We're long past that, my friend. It's been Kelsey for years now. In my universe, we're the very closest of allies. I certainly hope that's true here, too."

"It is," he said with a smile. "I'm just trying to make sure I don't make a mistake because of what I know about you here."

"For you, I'll forgive any lapse," Kelsey said, momentarily taking his hands into hers in an obviously intimate gesture.

Olivia narrowed her eyes, but Kelsey was turned so she couldn't see it. The expression had vanished by the time the princess turned to face her.

"Coordinator West, I'm sorry to say that I don't know you. Is that a title in the empire here?"

"In a manner of speaking," Olivia said evenly. "I rule Harrison's World as part of the New Terran Empire."

Kelsey opened her mouth to say something but stopped herself. When she finally spoke, it was with great sadness. "I see now why I don't know you. In my universe, the AIs sterilized your world. By the time my people and I arrived, there was no one left to meet. I'm very sorry to have to tell you that."

Olivia wilted. "I see. I wonder if we managed to ambush the AI there and that caused it to go even farther than in this universe."

"We couldn't tell," Kelsey said with a shrug. "If it's any consolation, we destroyed it along with the old Fleet station it was using as a base."

Princess Kelsey sighed, turned to the table, and sat at its head. "So many things didn't work out as we'd hoped."

Jared considered sitting at the other end of the table, but he suspected that would cause more instinctive hostility from his sister. Instead, he chose to sit in the middle of the table. "You came to visit us for a reason, Highness. What can we do for you?"

She pinned him with a cold stare. "You can help me save the empire. I realize that might not be your first instinct, but I urge you to try it as a change of pace."

This had gone far enough. If he didn't draw a line in the sand, she'd walk all over him.

"First, with all due respect, you don't know me. The Jared Mertz in your universe is not who I am. If he's anything like me, he loves the empire and would give his life for it. You demand respect from me, so remember that it is *you* who are the guest here, not me." How he managed to say that without an edge to his tone, he had no idea.

It still didn't stop her from sneering. "Please. You're still the same toad here, I'll wager. A man who wants to steal the empire from the rightful emperor, the man you tried to kill. Did you succeed here? I can't imagine how else you'd style yourself an admiral."

Rather than react with the anger he felt, he simply shook his head. "I can't speak for your universe, but I never tried to kill anyone here. I simply protected myself when your brother tried to have me murdered. I serve the emperor with all my loyalty."

Kelsey laughed. "How can you say something so absurd? In my universe, you're a damned regicide and traitor."

"You're no longer *in* your universe, Highness. As hard as it is to believe, we're close friends and allies here."

She leaned forward with a palpable rage. "Never. How could that be when you killed my… her father?"

Sean cleared his throat. "That's probably easier here since your father is still alive and on the throne."

Kelsey's head whipped around and she stared at him. "What did you say?"

"Your father still rules here," Sean said in an even tone. "What Admiral Mertz says is true. In our universe, you and he are close friends and family. Together, you fight against the AIs."

"Is that true, Elise?" Kelsey asked slowly.

"Very true. Are we friends in your universe?"

Kelsey nodded. "Friends and allies, yes." Her expression darkened. "I only hope you're still okay there."

"Then listen closely when I tell you that Jared Mertz is not your enemy here."

"How could you know? He made a career of fooling everyone around him before he betrayed everything he supposedly held dear."

Elise smiled. "I know him better than anyone. He's my husband."

The silence was profound.

"I've obviously fallen through the looking glass," Kelsey said. "The world is turned upside down."

"I'm sorry that our history in your universe is so bad, Highness," Jared said slowly. "But we're the people you have to work with. Why did you come?"

Kelsey jutted her chin out defiantly. "As much as it galls me, I need your help to save the empire. I have to go to Terra, and *you* have to help me get there."

5

Elise's eyes were on Jared as Kelsey asked for their help. This had to be surreal for him. This was his sister that hated him. She longed to intervene, to tell Kelsey that all the things she'd said about him were wrong, but this was not the time or place.

Hell, she might even be wrong. The Jared in Kelsey's universe might be the bad apple she said. Or this Kelsey could be as paranoid as her brother had been here.

If her father was dead there, that probably meant Ethan Bandar ruled the New Terran Empire. She certainly hoped he wasn't the same kind of man he'd been here. That would've been an unmitigated disaster.

Which, on reflection, certainly sounded like Kelsey's situation, based on the few hints she'd picked up. Really, they needed to get to know one another before these preconceptions ruined any chance they had of working together.

Elise cleared her throat. "We really should get to know one another better before we continue. Everyone seems to think they know everyone else, but it's obvious that nothing is what it seems.

"Before we make any errors that cannot be easily forgotten or forgiven, I think we should take a step back and give Kelsey time to accept this is not her universe."

Kelsey opened her mouth to argue—Elise could see it in her eyes—but looked at her more closely before she spoke. "Perhaps that would be for the best. I wish I could speak to the emperor, but that would take far too long."

There was a longing in her eyes. The man was dead in her universe. How could she not want to see him again?

"Would you like to speak with him?" Elise asked. "We can make that happen in a few hours."

The comment left Kelsey thunderstruck. "What?"

"We have our ways," Jared said, rising to his feet. "I think it best we do exactly that. If you'd care to speak with my wife, I'll make arrangements to get you face-to-face with your father on Avalon."

Elise stood. "Jared, make that happen. Kelsey and I will talk. Everyone else, out."

Everyone except Kelsey and Elise filed out of the room. While they did so, Elise gave orders to Commander Parker over her implants to coordinate their travel with Jared. The flip point to Avalon was only a few hours away. That might be enough time to figure out the strange woman who looked so much like her friend.

Or maybe not.

Once the hatch closed, Kelsey leaned forward and focused her attention on Elise. "Is it true? You married the Bastard?"

Elise have her a stern look as she resumed her seat. "It's true, and I would take it as a great personal favor if you stopped calling him that."

The other woman's expression was a wild mixture of disbelief, revulsion, and anger. "They can't be that different. That just isn't possible."

"You told us who Jared Mertz is in your universe, or at least who you *think* he is. Let me tell you who he is here. He's the man who saved Pentagar. You did, too, but that's beside the point.

"He also performed miracles in keeping the New Terran Empire safe and whole. He's not a traitor here. Exactly the opposite. He's a national hero. Did you see the Imperial Guards? Why do you think they were here?"

The woman's good eye narrowed. "I thought they were here because the… Admiral Mertz assumed some kind of Imperial power."

Elise shook her head. "Assumed, no. Was granted, yes. By your father. And before you say it, he wasn't under any compulsion. Your father pushed these awards on my husband over his strong resistance."

"I *can't* believe that," Kelsey said slowly. "The man is as power hungry as they get. What precisely did my father supposedly push on him?"

After a long, steady stare, Elise spoke. "A number of things. A knighthood, a duchy, and he inducted him into the Imperial Family as a prince of the blood. The guards are his by right. I should make him take some of mine, honestly. He's the Prince Consort of Pentagar, too."

Kelsey rubbed her face. "This can't be *real.* My scientists told me that Omega could bring me to a universe not so different from my own, but that was obviously a mistake. This is a land where everything is backward.

"How could I be friendly with the likes of him? He murdered my father and tried to kill my brother. He abandoned the New Terran Empire in its moment of need. *Abandoned?* Hell, he stuck a knife in its back."

"I can prove how close you two are here with one video," Elise said quietly. "Would you like to see my wedding? It was yours, too. We had a double wedding just a few weeks ago."

The news seemed to stun the other woman. "Married? Who would I marry?"

"Talbot."

Kelsey blinked and frowned. "I don't even know anyone by that name. How could I marry someone I don't know?"

"Of course you know him. He was your strong right hand when you were learning to deal with the implants the Pale Ones forced on you. He was a senior sergeant on *Athena* back then."

The other woman shook her head almost violently. "No. That was Lieutenant Angela Ellis on *Ginnie Dare*. She's my rock."

"She still is, even here," Elise said with a nod. "In our universe, you're away on an important mission together. She's your executive officer on *Persephone*."

"*Persephone*?"

"The Marine Raider strike ship we recovered."

Kelsey sat bolt upright, her eyes wide. "You found a Marine Raider ship? Was the computer intact?"

"It is," Elise said with a wry smile. "It makes you crazy since it won't accept anyone other than you as its captain. And since you haven't found it in your universe, it did have complete specifications of your implants in its memory."

She considered mentioning the other memories waiting inside Ned Quincy's implants but rejected the idea. This wasn't the time to explain that taking in a dead man's memories would create a sentient AI in her friend's head.

"Things *are* different here," Kelsey said. "I think I'd best see this wedding."

Elise had the official video in her personal implant storage, as well as her personal recordings. She sent them all to Kelsey.

The other woman sat back and turned her focus inward. The look of incredulity that spread across her features would've been comical under other circumstances.

A minute later, Kelsey came out from under the spell and stared at Elise with a truly horrified expression. "I honestly don't know what to say right now."

"Perhaps its best if you say nothing," Elise said. "Instead, let me tell you what's happened here without asking questions or telling me how I can't be right. That can come later. For now, you need to hear it all."

"I suppose I have to," Kelsey said as she leaned back in her seat. "White is black, and right is wrong. This is bizarro world."

* * *

Sean escorted Admiral Mertz over to *Athena*. It would return to Avalon with the fast courier the admiral had come on, the Pentagaran fast courier *Lance*, and the light cruiser *Brazil*. He had no doubt everyone wanted to see how this would play out.

Once they were safely aboard, Olivia took charge. "To the captain's office. I think we need to talk this over while we have a stiff drink. Perhaps a *very* stiff drink."

Mertz snorted. "There isn't enough alcohol in the universe—any of them—to make this less crazy."

"You're telling me?" Olivia asked with a shake of her head. "She just told me that the plan I put so many years into working on *Invincible* got everyone on my world murdered. My view of the universe is a little shaky right now, too."

"I'd imagine," Mertz said as he headed for the bridge. "Who is in command, Sean?"

"Me, until you assume command. I'm hoping to wrangle the executive officer's slot before I'm done, though, so alcohol is to my advantage."

Mertz laughed softly. "I've always had a completely different idea of how being plied with drink worked. And you don't need to convince me. I suspect our mission might expand before this is all over. With your seemingly excellent relationship with… ah, the other Kelsey, you'd be an invaluable asset to have in my back pocket."

"Admit it," Sean encouraged. "You almost said 'Evil Kelsey,' didn't you?"

"I did," Mertz admitted with a shake of his head. "I can't ever do that. It's not accurate, no matter what all the movies of things like this portray. Worse, it makes it far too easy to make a serious mistake in judging her."

The lift they'd climbed into deposited them outside the bridge. Admiral Mertz was about to pass through it and go toward the office, but Sean stopped him and gestured at the plaque beside the hatch.

Mertz looked at it and did a double take. Then he smiled. "You're a sneaky man," the admiral said. "You got Fleet Command to rename her *Athena*. I appreciate both the sentiment and the fact that you recovered the original plaque. I'd know it anywhere."

"It seemed appropriate. I suspect there will always be a ship of this name on active duty and that it will be a plum posting. The people following in your footsteps will have a lot to live up to."

Sean gave the bridge crew a high sign and led Admiral Mertz into the office, where he closed the hatch behind them. Once they were alone, he opened the small bar.

"If you're like me, I suspect Kelsey's taste—our Kelsey, that is—in entertainment is coloring your perceptions. This isn't the Mirror, Mirror universe. At least I hope not."

"What happened to her face?" Olivia asked. "Why didn't she get her eye regenerated?"

"Maybe she couldn't," Mertz said as he accepted the drink Sean offered him. "We really don't know the first thing about her universe. Perhaps they didn't get access to all the Old Empire technology. Or something went wrong.

"Of more concern to me is what she wants us to do. There's only one reason to go to Terra. She knows about the key and the override."

Sean frowned. "What key and override?"

Admiral Mertz smiled. "It's a secret that I could get into a lot of trouble for revealing, but you both need to understand the importance of what we're talking about. Emperor Marcus sent the Imperial Scepter to Avalon with Lucien.

"It's not just a symbol of the emperor's power. It's an actual key to the Imperial Vaults under the original Imperial Palace on Terra. Inside that, there exists a physical override that can force the primary AI at Twilight River to submit to our commands."

Sean considered that as he sipped his whiskey. "That's incredible. If we get our hands on that, we could end this war once and for all."

"That's a big 'if,'" Olivia said, crossing her ankles as she leaned back. "Terra is a long way from Harrison's World, and Twilight River is almost on the other side of the Old Terran Empire. The current occupants might be loath to allow us free transit.

"Plus, Terra is locked down much more thoroughly than Harrison's World was. The AIs don't even allow humans into the system. Even supposing we found a way in, we'd still have to sneak onto the planet past numerous computer-controlled stations and into the ruined palace. What if they flooded the planet with something like the war machines?"

"We can't live our lives as if everything is impossible," Mertz said. "If we give up before we start, we'll all die for sure. Frankly, everything we've managed to accomplish so far was impossible when we started. Yet, here we are."

Sean had been considering the new situation while they spoke, and she turned the conversation back to Olivia. "How will this help the new Kelsey? Even if we get the override, what's to say it will work in her universe? If the device is even slightly different, it probably won't function the way she hopes."

Admiral Mertz shrugged. "I have no idea. If I know my father as well as I think I do, he'll order us to help her, if it doesn't put us in a bad place. Obviously, our universe has to come first. We can't let her take the key until we use it ourselves.

"That presents a whole new level of challenge. She's a Marine Raider. If she resorts to force, we're not going to be in any position to stop her without killing her."

"Her and a lot of other people," Olivia muttered. "This is a mess. Are you sure the emperor will side with her on this?"

"Pretty sure," Mertz said with a nod. "Come to it, I support her, too. Those are our people, and she's my sister. Even if she hates me. Even if I'm a cad or worse in her universe."

"Do you think the two of you can work together?" Sean asked delicately. "She *really* hates you. I'm talking Crown Prince Ethan levels of animosity."

"Somewhere under there is my sister," Mertz said with a shrug. "I have to believe that I can eventually convince her I'm not the man she thinks I am. That isn't to say that it will be easy.

"No, it'll be just as hard as convincing Ethan I had no designs on his throne. And we all know how well that worked out."

The three of them considered one another and downed their drinks.

6

Kelsey still couldn't get her mind around what these people were telling her. Of course, she'd known that *some* aspects of alternate realities would be different. Just not *this* different.

After speaking with Elise for more than an hour, she asked for a place she could think. Alone. They'd speedily provided her with a cabin and some quiet, if not peace.

She wanted to reject everything her friend had told her out of hand, but that would've been stupid. But she couldn't just accept it at face value either.

The biggest sticking point for her was, of course, the Bastard. He *couldn't* be the hero here. He'd killed her father and tried to kill her brother. Hell, he'd tried to kill her before he'd deserted with his followers. Even now he was off somewhere, plotting to seize the throne from Ethan.

So that begged the question, how could he have fooled everyone here so thoroughly? Elise was no idiot. For that matter, neither was Sean.

She'd always trusted the man's judgement, and he'd never ever been one of the toadies that coddled up to the Bastard. How could he be in the man's camp now?

Yet this was the reality she had to deal with, one where the Bastard had them all under his spell. One where she had to get the assistance that her people needed to survive over his inevitable sabotage and backstabbing.

On the plus side, her father was still alive here. She could warn him what a viper he'd taken to his breast before it was too late.

The thought of seeing him again made her cry, a weakness she couldn't afford to let anyone see. Not here. Not ever.

Her father's assassination had started the civil war no one had seen coming in the New Terran Empire. One it could ill afford. Sadly, it had also thrust her brother onto the throne before he'd been prepared to shoulder the burden.

Mistakes had been made. That was inevitable when fighting two powerful enemies at the same time. But that boat had sailed. There was no going back to do things over. Not in *her* home.

A rap at the hatch made her jump. "Give me a moment."

She rushed into the bathroom and washed her face. Once she was satisfied she looked as normal as possible, she opened the hatch. Sean Meyer stood outside.

He smiled at her. "We're in orbit around Avalon. The admiral has asked that I escort you to the Imperial Palace. He felt this wasn't the time for the two of you to work out your differences."

"As if the two of us will ever 'work out our differences,' except on a battlefield where I leave his smoldering corpse behind."

The vehemence she felt didn't surprise her, but it was more than she'd wanted to show. She had to at least *pretend* to get along with the Bastard until she got what she needed.

"I can see how that might seem to be a difficult task," Sean said with admirable aplomb. "I'm grateful we don't seem to have such baggage."

Kelsey sighed. "You've always been a good friend and wise advisor to me. I have to confess that I don't understand how things here are so *wrong*. My father is truly alive?"

He nodded. "And in excellent health. God willing, the Empire will have him at the helm for many long centuries."

She frowned. "Centuries?"

He raised an eyebrow. "We still have a lot to learn about each other. I can't see how you don't know why that is, but I can discuss it with you on the way down. I'm afraid I must insist that you leave your armor behind."

Kelsey had expected that. "I want your word that it will be returned to me once I have finished meeting with my father. It's irreplaceable."

"Done," he said at once. "And the same is true of your weapons. I realize that you're technically a weapon, too, but I have to trust that you don't intend your father any harm."

"Absolutely not," she said with a firm shake of her head. "I would die to protect him. I couldn't the first time, but I won't allow him to be hurt again. Ever."

He nodded. "I've taken the liberty of getting a uniform for you." He gestured for a crewman to bring it to him and then handed the folded garment to her. "You can leave your armor in marine country. It'll be safe there."

Kelsey seriously doubted the uniform would fit. She was far smaller than most women. Still, it would do until she could get something in her size.

She allowed him escort her to marine country. It was set up exactly like the one on *Ginnie Dare*. How she wished Angela were here with her now.

The strange sense of déjà vu lasted until she stepped into the changing room, and what she saw stopped her dead in her tracks. The bulkheads held rack after rack of powered armor. Dozens of suits.

"Is something wrong?" Sean asked, a slight frown on his face.

"Where did you get these?" she asked reverently. "Do they work?"

"They wouldn't be of much use if they didn't," he said dryly. "You act as if you'd never seen anything like them."

She ran a hand along the arm of one of the massive suits. "Only in video images."

Thank God there had been none aboard *Courageous* when the Bastard had stolen her. That would've been the end of the New Terran Empire.

After staring at the armor for a few seconds, she turned to face Sean. "Where did you find them?"

"The graveyard around Boxer Station. Didn't you say you'd been there?"

She felt herself frowning. "Graveyard? I don't understand."

He gave her an odd look. "The mass of wrecks left over from the Fall. The AIs brought everything that survived there and put them in wide orbits around Boxer Station. We think there are around fifty thousand derelicts."

"Fifty thousand—" She snapped her mouth closed as her eyes widened. "There were no ships there. Hell, there was barely a station even before we blew it up. Are you joking?"

He shook his head. "It's where this destroyer came from. The same for most of the new ships in Fleet. All this armor was recovered there and refurbished."

Her throat squeezed shut as if someone were choking her. She felt faint. "Nothing like that exists in my universe," she said softly. "This is an Old Empire ship? Like *Courageous*?"

"It is," he said with a nod. "We have the newly repaired light cruiser *Brazil* with us, and that isn't the only ship in orbit around Avalon, though most of Fleet is at Erorsi."

The absurdity of the situation made her laugh bitterly. "I doubt you'd be interested in my old, beat-up armor then. Look at these things. Oh, what we could do with something like this."

She was grateful the Bastard hadn't found a place to rearm the stolen Old Empire battlecruiser. With enough missiles, he'd have conquered the New Terran Empire by now.

"I suppose I'd best get changed," she said with the shake of her head. "I can't wait to see what other revelations you have for me."

"I can see we need to make a pass by *Gibraltar* before we head down. I'll let you change in peace."

He stepped out of the chamber and left her with several marines. Not all of them female.

She cleared her throat. "If you gentlemen would excuse us, I need to get out of this."

They shared what looked like confused glances, and the men departed.

The two women who remained would be barely enough to help her get the armor off, but she'd manage.

"Do you want to use the rack over here, Highness?" one of them asked.

"I've never had a rack. How does it work?"

They got her into the contraption, and it made getting out of her armor a damned breeze. She'd have to get her people busy making something like this.

The women's eyes widened when they saw her body, and both stepped back. Kelsey was sadly used to that kind of reaction, which was one of the reasons no one *ever* saw her naked.

Puckered scars crisscrossed her entire body, a never-ending reminder of when the Pale Ones had stolen her innocence.

She was eternally grateful the doctors on *Spear* had managed to get her face, skull, and hands regenerated. She missed her left eye, but the artificial one worked well enough, even if it was hideous.

The other blessing was that the scientists had restrained her wild rage until they'd scrubbed the corrupt code from her implants. The mere thought of being a slave to the AI's programming again made her quail.

She'd kill herself if that ever seemed likely. The damned things were still a threat but one that she hoped they beat before too much longer.

Ignoring the stares, Kelsey stripped off her underwear and dressed. She was astonished to discover that the bare uniform fit as if it had been made for her. As short as she was, that *never* happened.

Once she was dressed, she had the marines bring Sean back in. "I'm ready to see my father."

* * *

To say Jared's father was surprised to see him again was an understatement. They met in the same private room they'd dined in last night

The older man raised an eyebrow. "Did you forget something?"

"You might want to pour a drink and sit down before I tell you."

That sent the other eyebrow up to join its companion. "This doesn't sound promising."

The emperor sat—minus drink—and gestured for Jared to join him. "What's wrong?"

"Not so much wrong," Jared said as he sat, "more like sideways. Something that isn't inherently good or bad but wasn't planned for. We have a visitor from another reality via Omega. It's Kelsey."

Karl Bandar considered Jared for a bit without saying a word. When he did speak, his voice was soft. "I knew that was a possibility, but that hardly prepares one. Is she like our own Kelsey?"

Jared gave him a long stare and then shook his head. "I don't have time to get into the specifics because she can't be more than an hour behind me, but events didn't progress in her universe the same way they did here. Let's just say that her opinion of me tilts more toward how Ethan felt."

His father grimaced. "Oh, Jared. I'm so sorry. I know how close you've become and that has to hurt."

"More than you can imagine, but that's hardly the only difference. Things have not gone nearly as well in her universe as here. I can't speak to the specifics, but Elise was able to figure out a number of differences.

"We'll have to work out a timeline at some point, but I'm guessing they haven't actually met the Rebel Empire in direct combat just yet. They didn't get the ships at Boxer Station. The AI there sterilized Harrison's World, and there were no derelicts. No AI, either. Just rudimentary defenses.

"Honestly, I don't think *Courageous* was in as good a condition, either. Kelsey was hurt at some point and has an artificial eye. Their regeneration tech must be deficient, and her nanites need looking at.

"In any case, they don't have the battlecruiser now. Evil me stole it. Sometime around when I killed you and tried to kill Ethan, if the story is to be believed. Ethan is the current emperor there, by the way. I'm the one trying to steal the throne."

"Amazing," his father said sadly. "That's what Ethan said here, too, yet we both know he was unbalanced."

"I have no idea," Jared said with a shrug. "This Kelsey might not even know. In the end, it hardly matters. She believes what she believes, and she's come to ask us to do something. She knows about the key and the override."

"That *is* awkward," the emperor admitted. "We need them for ourselves. Yet, if I could help her, I would. In some sense, her people are my people, too. The very least I can do is hear her out. She's my daughter. If I can find a path that saves our people and helps hers too, I'll take it."

Jared nodded, but inside, he worried that they just didn't know enough about the enigmatic Kelsey to make a decision like that. Was she telling them the truth, or did she have ulterior motives of her own?

There was only one way to discover the truth. They had to let things play out. Meanwhile, he'd take what precautions he could.

"Before you meet with her, we need to think about security," Jared said. "She's got Kelsey's implants, and all our computers will recognize her as the heir to the Imperial Throne. We have to come up with a way to restrict her authority."

The emperor nodded. "An excellent point. Luckily, we have a solution to that. I'll speak with the Imperial physician and have him declare her medically unfit. I'll have to tell the senate and get their backing, but Breckenridge will understand. This isn't about my daughter here—and she isn't even in the same region of space—so I think the two of us can work something out."

"Send Elise to talk with him," Jared urged him. "She and Breckenridge have managed to develop a good working relationship. And she was waiting for me in the Nova system when the new Kelsey showed up on Omega. She's up in orbit now."

The emperor nodded decisively. "Talk to her while I deal with your sister. Your *sort of* sister? You and she have my full backing in bringing the senator around.

"And start planning for a more ambitious mission into the Rebel Empire. I think you might be taking a much longer trip than we'd first intended."

7

Olivia was waiting for Sean and Kelsey when they arrived at the docking level. She silently approved of seeing the smaller woman in something other than her armor. She wondered briefly why her armor was black rather than gray but decided that really didn't matter.

She stepped forward as they approached. "I've decided to join you, unless anyone objects. I've never seen Avalon in person and would like to."

"Of course," her lover wisely agreed. "If the two of you will board the cutter, we'll get started."

Sean sat on the other side of Kelsey from Olivia. "Once we undock, I've instructed the pilot to make a pass by Orbital One on the way down. I think you'll want to tap into the cutter's scanner feed."

The cutter bumped a little as it came loose from the destroyer and began moving under its own power. Olivia had tapped into scanners before, but it was still a new and interesting process for her.

Even though she'd been born to a social class that implanted their children at a fairly young age and she'd been so equipped for her entire adult life, she'd never had the opportunity to use a ship's scanners before the New Terran Empire came to visit.

The higher orders had the odd habit of working around their implants rather than with them. She'd begun wondering if that was an intentional change in the social structure made by the AIs. They needed the implants to control the leadership of the Rebel Empire but didn't want them actually becoming a threat.

She turned her attention to Kelsey. "You said that my world was dead in your universe. The AIs destroyed it. Could you tell how long ago?"

The smaller woman shrugged. "Recently. Decades, probably. There wasn't a whole lot left to put together. I'm sorry."

Olivia was still in shock about the events on her world in the other universe, but they felt like someone else's story.

"It's not your fault. If anything, it's mine. I was part of the resistance. We planned to rebel against the System Lord. Ah… the AI ruling the system from Boxer Station. I suspect it didn't work out nearly as well as we'd hoped."

"That sounds like something of an understatement," Kelsey agreed. "We found the weak flip point in Erorsi almost by accident and had to retreat through it later. A few flips more, and we came across your world, though we didn't know its name.

"The planet had three stations in orbit with orbital bombardment weapons. Someone had used them to exterminate the population. No area was left untouched, and we found no survivors. It was horrible."

Olivia nodded, feeling a bit faint. "We'd intended to restore a mostly intact ship from the graveyard in secret and depose the system Lord. In this universe, we never got a chance to try. Something or someone tipped off the AI, and it locked us down. I wonder if we managed to try in your universe, and that was our reward."

Kelsey shrugged. "The old Fleet base was mostly intact but had a lot of battle damage. The damage looked recent, too. It fought us, but we managed to sneak up on it, and a lucky shot set off one of its fusion reactors.

"There were no signs of other ships in the system. We blew up the orbital stations to be sure they couldn't hurt us. We found the weak flip point leading to that horrible system with the nova and figured out how to use the battle screens to get a ship over.

"Thankfully, that was one of the technologies we managed to keep when —" Kelsey clamped her lips shut. "Well, let's just say that it's hell when you have something like that snatched from your grasp."

It made Olivia sad to see how much pain this Kelsey had gone through. She'd thought what her friend had endured was bad. This only proved how lucky they'd all been.

"So," Olivia ventured, "how are you handling the Rebel Empire there?"

"I assume that's what you mean by what's left of the Old Empire," Kelsey said. "We worked with the Pentagarans to ambush the freighter bringing supplies to Erorsi. The destroyer was tough, but Captain Breckenridge used *Courageous* to turn the tide."

Kelsey raised her eyes and stared at Olivia. "To answer your question, not well. I was there in Erorsi when an overwhelming number of Old Empire ships—probably under control of something like the Pale Ones—came into the system and attacked everything in sight.

"My ships were out near the weak flip point, so we fled that way. The Pale Ones and those computers don't know about the weak flip points. Thank God."

Olivia had a decent idea of the timeline there. Something just didn't make sense. Well, a lot of things didn't make sense, but one thing in particular stuck out to her. "You and the expedition were trapped in Pentagar space. If Jared Mertz wasn't with you, how did he steal *Courageous*? I thought he staged an attempted coup on Avalon. He can't be in two places at once. Did you find another way home?"

Kelsey shook her head. "No. We're still looking for a way."

Olivia shared a glance with Sean. This Kelsey only thought she knew how bad things were. If the Rebel Empire had succeeded in taking Pentagar in her universe, they might find out about the weak flip points.

"I'm very much afraid the situation in your universe is significantly more dire than you imagine," she said. "The Pale Ones are an aberration. Something left over from the Fall almost by accident.

"The AIs that control what's left of the Old Empire are sentient. They subjugated the humans that survived and have brainwashed most of them into being blind servants. The forces that came to subjugate Pentagar were manned by Fleet personnel from the Rebel Empire, not Pale Ones."

She allowed a moment for that to sink in. "They will have eliminated all resistance on Pentagar, but they won't mindlessly obliterate everything. They'll almost certainly hear about your arrival and how you saved Pentagar from the Pale Ones."

Kelsey swallowed noisily. "I have to pray that Elise and her people manage to keep that secret to themselves. Otherwise, the cost is everything I love."

They sat in silence for a bit before Kelsey continued. "To answer your earlier question, Mertz rebelled while we were gone. He and a number of renegade Fleet officers tried to seize power. My father was assassinated. Mertz tried to kill Ethan, too, but my brother is smart.

"Mertz escaped with perhaps a third of Fleet and made his way to Pentagar. We didn't know he was there. He used another officer to claim to be a rescue force. We were damned glad to see them and never questioned things."

Sean nodded. "We sent reinforcements here, too. With different results, obviously."

"We never suspected a thing," Kelsey said bitterly. "They slipped more than enough people onto *Courageous* and took her. Captain Breckenridge died in the fighting. Mertz seized control and left through the Erorsi weak flip point with all his ships. We had nothing that could hope to stand against an Old Empire battlecruiser, even one in the condition we found her.

"Eventually, the attack on Erorsi drove us after him. I've got Captain Breckenridge's original task force. That's it. We had a single set of battle screens. That was enough to protect one of the destroyers. That's how I was able to explore the nova and find the alien space station."

The other woman shook her head. "Only my armor was strong enough to resist the radiation so I could visit the station. The alien there told me about you, as hard as it was to believe, so here I am, trying to find any solution I can to save my people."

Olivia's heart went out to Kelsey. Her universe had really, *really* drawn the short straw.

Sean cleared his throat. "I hope we can help. We're passing by Orbital One."

That reminded Olivia that she should've been watching the scanner feed. The massive space station was right there. In close orbit around it was the newly reformed Home Fleet commanded by Admiral Yeats. And his flagship.

"Holy God," Kelsey said softly. "What is that?"

"That is the superdreadnought *Gibraltar*," Sean said. "Admiral Yeats's flagship. We recovered her and the rest of the new ships at Harrison's World. We're still getting the force together, and this is only part of it. Most of our ships are at Erorsi holding off the Rebel Empire. Admiral Mertz was in command of that force until he came back to perform a special mission."

Kelsey turned to face Sean. "No wonder you were able to resist him. Look at the size of that thing. Is she fully operational?"

"She is," Sean said with a nod. "But, Kelsey, Admiral Mertz recovered that ship. It wasn't even repaired when he led a force of over a hundred Old Empire ships back here to Avalon."

Her lover focused his attention on the princess from another universe. "I can't speak to events in your universe, but in this one, Jared Mertz sat on the flag bridge of a ship just like that one—the superdreadnought *Invincible*—when he entered Avalon orbit.

"Let me lay this out so I'm being as clear as possible. He had more than a hundred Old Empire ships under his command, and Fleet had nothing that could stand against even *Invincible*."

Sean relentlessly continued. "His fleet consisted of a superdreadnought, a Fleet carrier, six battlecruisers, eight heavy cruisers, twelve light cruisers, two dozen destroyers, thirteen Fleet transports, ten colliers with extra missiles and supplies, six Marine troop transports, sixteen fast couriers, twelve scouts, a dedicated science vessel, two hospital ships, four factory ships, a liner to carry civilians, and a Marine Raider strike ship. All Old Empire tech and manned to fight."

The silence that statement produced was profound.

"Kelsey," he said softly, "if Admiral Mertz wanted to take over the New Terran Empire, he could have reached out his hand and done so. No one could have possibly resisted. He turned all those ships over to Admiral Yeats and submitted to the emperor's authority willingly. Jared Mertz—at least our version of him—has no designs on the Imperial Throne."

Kelsey stared off into space until the cutter began descending into Avalon's atmosphere. Only then did she sit back and slump. "*Courageous* was more than enough to take the New Terran Empire," she said softly. "I can't believe this is true."

"There must be plenty of records," Olivia offered. "And you're going to see the emperor. He'll tell you."

Kelsey rubbed her face. "My father never saw Mertz for what he is. He died still wanting a relationship with the Bastard. As much as I loved him, my father was a trusting fool."

Olivia shook her head slightly when Sean opened his mouth to respond. "In the end, you'll have to decide what to believe. Perhaps in your universe, that's the way things are.

"In this one, Kelsey Bandar has stood back to back with Jared Mertz. Together, they fought the enemies of the New Terran Empire. All we ask is that you entertain the possibility that things here are different, that people and events might have progressed in a different manner than you remember."

"I suppose I don't really have a choice," the short blonde said. "I won't promise that it'll change how I feel, but there seems to be enough evidence that things in this universe are not the same as in mine. People here *might* be different."

Olivia heard the slight emphasis on the word "might." It was probably the best anyone could hope for at this point.

8

Elise took a different cutter down to Avalon than Princess Kelsey, Sean Meyer, and Olivia West. They'd already left *Athena* by the time Jared had contacted her with this mission, and frankly, it was best the others didn't know what she was doing anyway.

Getting an appointment with Senator Nathaniel Breckenridge was as simple as calling ahead and asking if he had time to speak with her.

The same young woman who had met her on her first visit was standing beside the landing pad and smiling at her. "Crown Princess Elise, welcome back to Avalon. The senator is waiting for you."

Elise was thankful that her implant memory made remembering names and faces easy. She extended her hand to Jean Trouville, the aide to the Imperial Affairs Committee. "Miss Trouville, it's a pleasure to see you again."

The woman's smile brightened even more. "For me, too. I saw your wedding. It was *so* romantic. And your husband." She made a motion fanning herself with her hand.

That made Elise chuckle. "Jared is all that and more."

The aide led Elise into the Imperial Senate building. It was still a bit too modern for her taste, but her initial edge of dislike for the design had faded. Perhaps it had more to do with how she'd felt about Nathaniel Breckenridge at the time.

He was the powerful uncle of Captain Wallace Breckenridge, the man who'd betrayed them all at Erorsi, and she'd known him to be their enemy, someone so dedicated to power and wealth that he would work against them every step of the way.

And she'd been completely, *utterly* wrong.

Nathaniel Breckenridge had ending up working hard to help them meet their goals and been shot rescuing Emperor Karl Bandar. It wasn't often that Elise misjudged someone, but this had been one of those times. As Kelsey would have said, an epic fail.

The man was also Kelsey's biological father, something he hadn't known before the attempted coup. That was still something neither her friend nor the senator quite knew how to approach, but he would listen very closely to what Elise had to say.

Senator Breckenridge had also been the father to Crown Prince Ethan Bandar. He'd known that by the time he'd chosen to keep the mad prince off the Imperial Throne. While he hadn't directly had a hand in the man's death, she imagined it still kept him up at night.

This time, no one had any issues with her guards. The protocol had been established, and the Senatorial Guard knew the people in the Royal Guard. A number of guards from the elite Pentagaran unit lived on Avalon now, providing security for their embassy.

Miss Trouville led Elise to the same office she'd visited before and handed her off to the senator's assistant. He speedily passed her inside to the senator himself.

Breckenridge was already in front of his desk with his hand extended. "Crown Princess Elise, it's a pleasure and a surprise seeing you again so soon. Your wedding was magnificent. I hope you and Prince Jared find every happiness."

It felt as if everyone had seen the state wedding when she'd married Jared and Kelsey had married Talbot. The viewership numbers confirmed that. It was literally the most watched broadcast in both the Kingdom of Pentagar and the New Terran Empire. Only people living in caves had missed it.

She gave the senator a wide smile. "Thank you, and we both hope so, too. Also, thank you for agreeing to see me on such short notice."

"You said the matter was urgent. I've cleared my schedule, and I'm at your complete disposal."

Elise looked around his office. "I need to make certain the room is secure."

"It was swept for listening devices a few days ago, but I'll have my people come in and give it another look."

Once he'd tasked his assistant, she raised an eyebrow. "I'm curious. Do you find many listening devices? My people are absolutely paranoid about the things, but I've never asked what they found."

"Surprisingly, yes. In the last year, my people have found three. One was crude, and the perpetrator was quickly identified. The other two were of exceptionally high quality, and we still haven't proven who put them here, though I have my suspicions.

"The new technology makes finding them easier for now, but as it gets out to everyone, the bugs will become much more sophisticated. The senate has a room that's secure from eavesdropping. Eventually, we'll need more of them."

His eyes narrowed. "Do you think it best we use the room now?"

She nodded promptly. "Don't let me stop you from securing your office, but this matter couldn't be more important, and I don't want anyone to catch wind of it."

"How intriguing. Come this way then."

He led her down the hall to a room with a massive hatch. It looked like something she'd have expected to see on a ship protecting a sensitive compartment from destruction. Two members of the Senatorial Guard stood outside.

Breckenridge spoke softly with one of the guards. The woman signaled and stepped into the room once the hatch opened. A few minutes later, several men and women—Imperial Senators, she assumed—came out.

One of them jokingly accused Breckenridge of shooing them out to disrupt their plans to get some piece of legislation passed. He laughed and said he was actually inclined to support it, if they could come to agreement on a few details. They made an agreement to meet in a few days to discuss the matter.

"I'm sorry you had to disrupt their meeting," she told the senator as he led her into the room.

"Think nothing of it," he said dismissively as the Senatorial Guard searched the room for listening devices. "They'd already exceeded their reservation time. In case this is a surprise to you, politicians love the sound of their own voices."

Elise laughed. "I've noticed that. How long did you reserve it for us?"

"An hour. Is that sufficient?"

"You'd best make it two, just to be safe."

"Done."

Once the guards declared the room clear and departed, Breckenridge sealed the hatch and activated the antilistening equipment.

He gestured to the table. "I can get us refreshment from the small kitchen over there. If you need to take a break, there's a restroom beside it. We made sure that once a meeting started, no one would need to leave the room."

"I'm fine," she said as she sat at the table. She waited for him to sit next to her and then launched into events of the last day.

He listened closely and didn't interrupt, even though she could tell the news of a Kelsey from another universe shocked him.

"She's probably at the Imperial Palace now," Elise concluded. "She's going to want help, but that's not why I'm here. The problem is that every computer in the Empire recognizes her as the heir, and we *really* don't know her."

Breckenridge leaned back, his expression still reflecting his shock. "I can see where that would be a concern. There are no allowances made for people from other realities. At least people can be warned. Well, the ones who need to know."

He immediately shook his head. "No, that won't work either. The news would get out. Well, this is a complex problem. What can I do to assist?"

"The emperor has decided the simplest solution is to declare Kelsey medically unfit. That would allow him to restrict her authority. As the heir, that means such a decision requires the senate to approve the recommendation."

Breckenridge nodded slowly. "That might work, but it creates a different set of complications. As you said, politicians love to talk. That includes telling secrets to people that aren't cleared to hear them. Still, for something this important and delicate, it's possible we can keep word of the situation to a small group."

His eyes took on a haunted look. "On a personal level, I'm troubled by how badly this Kelsey has been hurt. It tears at my heart."

Elise nodded. "Mine, too. I don't think she knows about your role in her parentage, so you'll have to be very cautious when you interact with her."

That comment made his eyebrows rise. "You think I should meet her?"

"I do. The senate has to hear from one of their own. I think you should come with me to the Imperial Palace as soon as we finish here."

He chuckled ruefully. "I can't imagine she'll be pleased to see me, even if she doesn't know what I did with her mother."

"You might be surprised. From what I've been told of her story, she and Wallace were close allies."

"That's… troubling on a completely different level. My nephew was never the smartest Fleet officer. It brings her judgment into question."

With a shrug, he rose to his feet. "I suppose I'll find out. This can't wait. I should meet her and the emperor as soon as possible and get the ball rolling."

* * *

Kelsey was amazed at how intact the capital was. The images she'd seen from after the attempted coup had shown her a city partly in ruins. This place looked pretty much as she remembered it.

Oddly, there were some differences in the skyline. She was able to find half a dozen buildings that were changed in some way from what she remembered even without consulting her implants. That brought it home to her that this was not her universe in a way just being told couldn't manage.

She wondered again what the version of her from this reality was like, aside from having the worst judgment of people she'd ever heard of.

Yet, perhaps not in all things. The woman had fallen in love with a marine, someone who had filled the same role as Angela Ellis in her world.

That, she could understand. Angela was her strong right arm and firmest ally. If it were the same here with this Talbot, she could imagine how the relationship had developed.

She said nothing as the grav car left the city and headed for the Imperial Palace. The coup had left her home a smoking ruin. She longed to see it whole again. And to see her dead father once more. Even if he wasn't truly her father.

The thoughts threatened to make her good eye start tearing up, so she set that aside and looked at Sean. "What happened to my brother here?"

His expression became grim. "You did. Rather, our version of you. She allowed him to run to the system with the alien spaceship in it. Without battle screens."

That revelation made her suck in a deep breath. Her scientists had told her the radiation there was intense enough to kill everyone inside a ship in minutes. Hell, even the ship's systems would fail in an exceptionally short period of time.

She'd killed her own brother? That was unthinkable.

"Your universe might be different," Sean continued relentlessly, "but Crown Prince Ethan was paranoid here. Not in small measure, either. He believed *everyone* was out to get him and he poisoned your father. He then framed you for the crime."

"Perhaps that's what some people want you to believe," she responded, unconvinced. "I've known my brother my entire life. He is not a villain. He loves the Empire."

The Fleet officer shrugged. "Again, I can't speak to that. I wasn't on Avalon, but I saw the testimony before the Imperial Senate where they laid it all out. A number of people opposed your father naming you as the heir, and Ethan's actions had to be spelled out with hard evidence.

"There was a diary in his own image and voice, one he'd kept for years, documenting the various people he felt had wronged him. Of what he'd done to get even. Here, he killed people. Had them killed, anyway. Tell me, do you know Carlo Vega?"

She nodded. "He came with me on the expedition. He taught me everything I know about being a diplomat. I like to think he's a close friend."

"In our universe, your brother sent a gift from the palace to Jared Mertz in your father's name. Something, it happened, the admiral didn't care for, so he gave it to Mister Vega. One piece was poisoned. Carlo Vega died before you even found Pentagar.

"I watched the recording your brother made after the expedition left. I saw the hatred and glee at the likelihood Jared Mertz would die. In our universe at least, he was not the brother you know."

"I want to see it. All of it." She would see through the lies and deceptions. Of that, she had no doubt.

"I'll see to it," he said with a nod. "Along with the exhaustive verifications that prove none of it was doctored."

Since there was nothing left to say on that subject, they traveled in silence until the Imperial Palace came into view. It was miraculously intact, a sight she'd never expected to see again.

The grav car came down onto the main pad, and everyone exited. The

Imperial Guard was out in force, armed for trouble. It both saddened and amused her that she was the threat today.

Her Marine Raider implants made her a force to be reckoned with, but she wasn't a danger to her father. Not only did she love and miss him, but she desperately needed his assistance, particularly if Coordinator West's tales about the Rebel Empire were true.

She'd left her precious armor and weapons back on their ship. If they wanted to take her, they could. A number of guards had neural disruptors that could kill or stun her before she could take them all out.

Lisa Devonshire, her father's majordomo, stepped out and bowed as if meeting a new Kelsey was an everyday occurrence. "Highness, welcome to Avalon. The emperor is eager to meet you. If you and your escort will follow me."

Seeing the familiar corridors intact as she passed through them was surreal. She allowed the sights to distract her from the heavy contingent of guards surrounding them as they proceeded toward the official audience chamber.

That wasn't like the father she knew. He hated the place. Every meeting that could happen under more intimate circumstances was done that way.

Maybe it hadn't been his choice, she decided. If they wanted to keep her under the gun, they'd need a lot of room to assure the emperor's safety.

"Do you have restraints?" she asked. "Arm and leg shackles that I can't easily break?"

Sean frowned and opened his mouth to respond, but Devonshire interrupted him.

"We do," the majordomo said as she came to a halt, stopping everyone around her.

"Use them before you take me before my… the emperor. His safety is paramount. It's not going to offend me. If you wanted to take me prisoner, you could do so right now."

"That isn't necessary," Sean objected.

The majordomo seemed to disagree as she gestured for one of the Imperial Guardsmen to bring over a set of handy restraints.

Kelsey smiled wryly at Sean. "Don't take it personally. I'm not. Hell, I'm a dangerously unknown and unknowable threat. I'd lock me up, too."

"This is only until we get to know you well enough to dispense with them," Devonshire said.

She allowed the guards to pull her hands behind her and lock her wrists down. A belt around her waist provided an extra point of attachment for the arm and leg restraints that followed.

The chains looked flimsy, but she took the opportunity to throw her fully enhanced strength against them. Might as well. The restraints kept her arms securely locked behind her. She wasn't going anywhere or hurting anyone without them being able to take her out.

Walking was more difficult once they resumed moving forward. The chains between her ankles only allowed for short steps. It was kind of funny, seeing the large group around her creeping down the long corridor at her pace.

After what felt like forever, they arrived at the main doors to the audience chamber. At their approach, the doors swung back, and half the guards entered, no doubt to join others already waiting.

Kelsey held her head high and strained to catch sight of her father. When she did, a giant fist clamped down on her heart, and she found she could no longer see out of her natural eye because of the tears welling up.

He was alive. Oh, God, he was alive.

And he was angry.

Her father hadn't been on the throne but pacing in front of it. At the sight of her, his face contorted with rage, an expression she rarely remembered seeing on the gentle man.

He strode toward her with his lips tightly compressed. "What is the meaning of this? Get those things off her this very instant!"

Kelsey only barely suppressed the laughter that threatened to burst out of her. How very like him.

"I asked them to do it," she said, her voice rough. "I may look like your daughter, but to them, I'm a potential threat. This way, you can be certain of your safety."

He brushed her words aside just as quickly as he did the guards who tried to step between them. "Take those damned things off my daughter right now. Right. This. Second."

The majordomo looked at her liege for a few seconds before she gestured to the guards. They quickly removed the restraints.

Kelsey opened her mouth to say the words she'd settled on as the best greeting from another universe, but only managed to squeak when he yanked her into a tight hug.

"Oh, my poor darling. What happened to you? You're safe here. Always and forever."

Her planned speech died as emotion overwhelmed her, and she sobbed on her father's shoulder. A shoulder she'd never expected to see again this side of death's veil.

9

Sean stood with Olivia as the tearful meeting between the emperor and his daughter from another universe took place under the watchful eyes of every Imperial Guardsmen in existence. Or so it seemed. Not that any of them could do a damned thing if something went wrong.

Thankfully, it seemed as if this Kelsey had no evil intentions toward the emperor. She merely clutched him and cried. From what Sean could tell, she'd been through more than enough to need the comfort.

"It's nerve-racking," Olivia said quietly, "not knowing how she differs from our friend."

He nodded. "I'm glad I don't have to make the hard decisions this time."

She poked him a little. "You're a Fleet commodore. They pay you to make the difficult decisions."

"Not this difficult," he disagreed. "The people in her universe are so far behind that I'm not sure we can change their outcome. And that's even if we had help to give her this very second. "By the time we're in position to help her, the New Terran Empire might be under the Rebel Empire's heel there."

Olivia scowled at him. "You're a ray of sunshine on a dark day."

"I'm a realist," he countered. "Plan for the worst while hoping for the best."

"Have you considered who you are over there?" she asked.

He had but wasn't sure he could adequately put his feelings into words. He liked that he was someone Princess Kelsey considered a friend, but he'd seen how wrong about Captain Breckenridge he'd been here. His judgment was questionable.

Of course, she hated the one man who had saved the Empire here, so that Princess Kelsey was doing even worse.

"I hope I'm not much different. It sounds as if Captain Breckenridge died there, too. The circumstances were different, but I suspect I'm the senior Fleet officer in the ships with Kelsey. For her sake, I hope I do better this time around."

Someone behind them cleared their throat.

He turned and saw a man in a white lab coat. "Pardon the interruption. I'm Rueben Beecher, his majesty's personal physician. Might I have a few moments of your time?"

"Of course, Doctor," Sean said. "What can we do for you?"

"His majesty directed me to look into Princess Kelsey's medical condition. Ah… *this* Princess Kelsey. I see that she has some kind of prosthetic eye. Are you aware of any other health issues she might be suffering from?"

"I am," Sean said with a sigh. "I haven't personally seen them, but I'm told the regeneration of her original implantation procedure left most of the scars on her body. I'm guessing, based on that and some other things she said, but I don't believe her medical nanites are operational."

Olivia sucked in a deep breath, obviously horrified. "God," she whispered. "I've seen the video. Those are still there?"

He nodded grimly. "All over her body, with the exception of her head, hands, and arms. Several female marines saw them. Kelsey also had no idea what I meant when I told her that her father might rule for centuries."

His lover seemed to be thinking furiously. "That explains so many things," she said. "I'll wager without Jared there to come for her, the Pale Ones turned her into one of them. The good guys must've recaptured her and overwrote the corrupt code. We should've checked it before we came down."

"I suspect that is fine," the doctor said. "She has interacted with her own people and you without overt violence. Still, for the sake of everyone else's blood pressure, we'll verify that first."

Beecher narrowed his eyes and pursed his lips to one side as he considered Princess Kelsey. She was walking with her father toward a table he must've ordered brought in.

"I suspect they'll be talking for quite some time, so I'll have plenty of opportunity to prepare for an exam. If she'll allow it, I might be able to do something with her remaining injuries, though the amount of time that has passed will work against us.

"At the very least, I should be able to improve upon the ocular replacement. There's no reason it has to look so slapdash." The last word was said with a moue of distaste.

Sean wasn't sure how amenable the woman would be to allowing someone she didn't know to mess with her like that. If anything, this Kelsey might be even more averse to the idea than he was.

The Pale Ones had made her one of them and forced her to do things against her will. He only prayed they hadn't made her fight and kill her friends.

"Realistically, what do you imagine you can do, Doctor?" Olivia asked softly.

The man shrugged. "I can certainly get her nanites working. We have some of Princess Kelsey's on hand for study, and the fabricator is probably still inside this young woman. If we seed it correctly, the population should take hold.

"That said, it may be too late for them to repair all the damage done to her, even in conjunction with regeneration. Marine Raider nanites are incredibly capable, but even they have limits."

His eyes narrowed as he considered his potential patient. "I'd imagine the visible scarring can be dealt with, given time and repeated regeneration sessions. Those might not erase the damage at a cellular level, but we should be able to restore her physical appearance."

The man sighed. "And we can't forget the elephant in the room. She lost an eye. Even with Old Empire technology, that's probably more than we can undo. That said, I can create a lifelike replacement and regenerate the skin and muscle she lost around the injury. No one has to look like that."

Sean pondered the man's words and nodded slowly. "I can't speak for her, obviously, but I suspect she'll at least consent to an examination. I'll stretch that and wager she'll agree to have her nanites restored once she learns what they can do for her. She'll probably jump at the chance to get rid of her scars, too.

"As for the eye, I just can't say. I don't know how deeply she'll trust us. Not until she knows us far better than she does right now."

The man nodded, obviously already thinking ahead. "I can prepare for every aspect of care. If she rejects treatment, then I can try to sweet talk her. Or ask her father to do so."

He refocused his attention on them. "Thank you very much for your input. It has been quite helpful."

"Do you think she'll agree to all of that?" Olivia asked after the doctor had hurried off.

Sean shrugged. "Probably not, but all she can do is say no. Anything we can do to give her comfort is worth the effort."

The emperor and Kelsey were deep in conversation at the table. He had her hand in his and was saying something with an earnest look on his face.

Her expression was just what Sean imagined a daughter would look like if a beloved parent had come back to life and she wanted to remember everything.

He understood that, too. Even if everything worked out here, she'd one day return home and likely never see him again. He'd be dead once more. Lost to her forever.

Sean vowed to do everything within his power to help her.

* * *

Jared rose to his feet when his father came into the room. "How did it go?"

Emperor Karl rubbed his face tiredly and poured himself a very stiff drink at the small bar. He didn't speak until he'd downed half the glass. Only then did he turn to his son and sag a little.

"As well as could be expected, I suppose," the older man said. "God, she's so like my girl, yet hurt in ways Kelsey managed to avoid with your help. She's a wounded bird, and it breaks my heart."

His father sat in one of the chairs and slumped back. "After meeting her, I'm convinced she isn't a threat to the Empire or to me personally. You, on the other hand, had best keep your distance. I think she hates you more than Ethan ever did."

Jared took the liberty of pouring a drink for himself and joined his father. "I'd gathered that. Without unbiased data, she might have every right to those feelings. Other me might be a traitor and backstabber. I can see how my life might have gone in that direction if I'd developed different attitudes."

"I can't see that, but I'm glad things worked out the way they have. Your mother wanted to see Kelsey, but I convinced her that it might be counterproductive."

Jared snorted. "Considering how Kelsey feels about me, I can only imagine how she sees the woman you had an affair with. No, I think we should avoid unnecessary provocations. We have enough landmines already."

He resisted the urge to ask his father what help they intended to give. That the man would help was a given, but the specifics would come out in time and without his prompting.

"I'm told that Senator Breckenridge is on his way," the emperor said. "He's going to assess Kelsey and then take my recommendation to the Senate Imperial Affairs Committee. They'll fill in the rest of the Senate and hope that no one leaks the details."

"They won't," Jared said. "It's tied into Omega and the existence of alternate realities. They've kept that information under wraps. It's an Imperial secret, and they know we'll use one of the AIs to find the leaker. None of them is going to risk their careers over this."

"I love how certain you are," his father said dryly. "I'm usually the optimist. I hope you're right."

"If I'm not and the secret gets out, what does that really change? It won't hurt our defensive posture. Hell, most people won't believe it anyway. It sounds like science fiction."

His father considered that and nodded. "I suppose so. In any case, it's not as if we have a lot of choices about how we respond to her arrival."

Jared felt his lips twitch. Here came the compassionate response.

"The needs of the Empire—our Empire—come first, of course," the emperor said, "but we'll try to help her and this other Empire. We can best do so by getting our own house in order, stopping the AIs we have to deal with, and then turning our attention to her situation.

"I'm expanding your mission. We need to get to Terra and retrieve the override. Depending on the circumstances, we can then decide the best way of getting to Twilight River. Perhaps sneaking will work. Or it might require brute force. One way or another, we need the tools to defeat the AIs."

He nodded. "Did she tell you what they know about the key and the override?"

"We spoke briefly about them. She's aware the Imperial Scepter is the key to get into the Imperial Vaults on Terra. She also knows that it requires DNA from the Imperial Family. DNA she was shocked to discover she didn't have when Ethan tried to access their Scepter.

"Just like in our universe, neither of them are direct descendants of the Imperial House. Unlike in ours, there are no surviving cadet branches of the family. The only man who fits the bill there is at war with them, so they need other options."

"Based on her reaction to me, she didn't come looking for my help," Jared said. "She was hoping other members of the Imperial Family were still alive here. She's grasping at straws."

"No," his father disagreed. "She'd clutch at anything that will keep her head above water. Drowning people do that. Hope is fading there.

"Once we end the reign of the AIs, we won't need the override. We can certainly hope it works for them. I'll cheerfully give it to her then."

"What if it doesn't?" he asked. "What if the override is somehow different? They might fight their way to Twilight River and then it fails to work."

His father nodded glumly. "I'm hoping that during the process of acquiring the override here, she'll get all the data they need to do so in their own universe. The key isn't required to open the vaults. We have the complete plans. It would be difficult but not impossible."

"You're not suggesting that I—"

His father shook his head. "Absolutely not. Based on her reactions, you wouldn't be a welcome sight to anyone there. Under no circumstances do I believe you should go there. In fact, as much as I hate to say this, you need to take precautions.

"Desperate people do desperate things. I can foresee circumstances where she might be very tempted to kidnap you and force you to help her. Do not allow that temptation to bloom. She's an honest woman. I'd prefer we help her stay that way."

Jared had been thinking along the same lines. It wouldn't have been easy for this Kelsey to get him away from his ships and into Omega. Then she'd need to convince the alien to open a way back to her own universe.

Daunting obstacles, but as his father said, desperate people would take terrible risks. He should know.

"I think the safest way to scotch that plan is to lay it out for her," Jared said after he took a sip of his whiskey. "If she knows we're on the lookout for her to try something, then she won't. We need to give her hope, though. Despair is a terrible thing."

"That's why I'm sending her into the Rebel Empire with you," his father said as he set his drink down on the table between them. "She must be part of the success. I want you to take her back to Omega with you and assist her in gathering some of her people to join you. A trusted cadre but not a group that's a threat to you or your people.

"Limit the number of people on your mission that are duplicated. They won't have implants, so identifying them should be simple enough, as long as your crews are diligent and the computers keep track.

"If you send anyone to her side, be certain you have passwords and code phrases. And make sure Kelsey understands that. Once again, we'll keep the honest people honest."

Jared nodded his understanding. If she had her own people along, they'd learn what obstacles they had to overcome when they went for a repeat back in their own universe.

"Then you will complete phase one of your mission," his father continued. "Send the report the Rebel Empire expects from Harrison's World. That buys us critical time. After that, you'll probe toward Terra. That means you'll need the Imperial Scepter.

"I'll also send the small transport ring with you. Sadly, a situation may arise where you are forced to send the override back to your ships in a hurry."

Jared understood his father's meaning at once. It might become necessary to send the override back because they were trapped by the AI's forces. A suicide mission, in other words.

"Finally, I've changed my mind about how much force to send with you," the emperor said. "You're going to need *Invincible* and a strong escort in case the way is blocked or you have to provide a rear guard while someone sprints for home with the override."

That would be the worst-case scenario, if they got the override and had to make a stand while others got it safely away. It would be worth it, though.

His father leaned forward. "The best result is for you to slip onto Terra like you did Dresden. Then you could do the same while moving toward Twilight River. Use weak flip points to get into unexpected locations, if it seems safe. Use stealth to bypass enemy strong points when it doesn't. In any case, your orders are to retrieve the override and take the fight to the master AI."

"I'll do my best," Jared said, inclining his head. "Let me urge you one more time to allow Commander Richards to accompany us. His assistance could be critical."

The emperor shook his head. "No. You may trust him, but I'm not quite there yet. Coordinator West will be a better source than the good commander in any case, and she's already on the mission."

Jared sighed. He really wished he could change his father's mind, but he'd just have to make do.

This mission was his most daunting one yet. So many things could go wrong. The way might be blocked. The Imperial Palace might be destroyed. The AI might be too heavily protected.

No matter how he went about this, the mission would be a long, difficult one. One fraught with risk. One he had to make happen.

10

Kelsey stared at her father's personal physician—her other father, that was—with some confusion. "What are medical nanites?"

"Extremely small machines programmed to perform repairs on a continuous basis," he explained in what she assumed he meant to be a reassuring tone. "They come from a reservoir inside your body that continually refreshes them. Or that would if they were operational."

The thought of little machines running through her made her skin crawl, particularly ones installed by the damned Pale Ones.

"And everyone has that kind of thing here?" Judging from his expression, she hadn't entirely kept the horror she felt out of her voice.

"Yes and no," he said patiently. "Everyone with implants has them. That was true in the Old Empire, too, by the way. These are not harmful in any way. Far from it.

"That said, the Marine Raider implants come with nanites of greater capability. We're still studying them, but once again, there is *no* danger. Your doppelgänger in this universe provided the samples I have on hand and has been living with them for years now without any ill effect whatsoever. Quite the opposite, really."

"How can you trust anything done by the Pale Ones?" she asked. "If I could undo everything they did to me, I'd jump at the chance. The idea of these things sends a shiver up my spine."

"Princess Kelsey didn't complete the procedure you went through," he said slowly. "I'm very sorry for bringing these traumatic memories back to you, but you need to hear this and consider it with as clear a mind as you can."

He took a deep breath and continued. "Princess Kelsey was scanned by the Pale Ones for implants and had them forcibly implanted. Admiral Mertz and his people rescued her before they altered the programming in her implants.

"I'm told that's the reason your nanites are dead, by the way. The computer controlling the Pale Ones didn't allow its slaves to have any healing capability other than what their bodies normally provided. We surmise the nanites might have had some negative effect in allowing it to maintain control."

He held up a hand when she tried to speak. "Let me finish before you reject the idea out of hand. The code I pulled from your implants is very similar to what our people worked out, but not identical. We'd need to overwrite what you have now to allow the nanites to function, which would also prevent them from overwriting it themselves, so we're not talking about anything that could even be done immediately.

"Yet you need to know the differences between your history and your doppelgänger's. I have implant recordings and marine helmet cam video. It will be extremely upsetting to watch, but I can't think of any other way to bring this home for you."

He sent her a set of files through her implants. She was shocked. She'd had no idea that was even possible between people. She'd only used them to work her armor and weapons. Nothing else her people had would interface with the dammed things.

With more trepidation than she cared to admit, she opened the first file. To her horror, it was the same implant recordings she'd made automatically when the Pale Ones butchered her. She paused it almost at once and examined the still image.

The marines trapped with her were different. One of them was even familiar, that Talbot guy she'd married. No, that her doppelgänger had married. It was best to get into the habit of thinking that way.

In her world, none of the marines captured with her had made it. Some had died in the fighting when Commander Roche came for her, sadly fighting for the Pale Ones against their comrades. Others had died during the implantation process. Those were memories she wished she could get rid of.

She'd had to fight her own people, too. They'd used neural disruptors to stun her. She was deeply grateful she hadn't killed or seriously injured anyone.

Struggling to keep from hyperventilating, she restarted the playback. The events deviated from what had happened to her almost immediately. The marines managed to distract one of the Pale Ones, and this Talbot fought one by himself to give her time to do something.

In the end, this Kelsey managed to kill the Pale One, and the marines ended the other one. She never went into the final machine. This other her was so blessed.

The next major deviation was when the rescuers arrived. They came much more quickly than in her world. There, she'd spent several days as a

Pale One being brutalized in every way imaginable by the savages and the AI.

In this universe, only minutes passed. To her shock, the Bastard was there. How could he have come for her? That made no sense.

More amazingly, he seemed relieved to find her safe. He'd actually risked his life for her, something she would've considered impossible.

Unlike in her universe, she was awake to hear what happened as they fled the orbital and arrived on the destroyer. It couldn't have been *Ginnie Dare*. It was another ship.

The video ended there, so she opened the second one. It was a marine helmet cam. It showed the damage to her body just as she remembered it. The scarring had been there too long for the regenerators to deal with in her case.

She opened the final video and immediately knew why the marines with Mertz had recoiled. This Kelsey didn't have the scars anymore.

Kelsey refocused her attention on the doctor. "I see. Your Kelsey was very lucky. I think I hate her for that."

The man nodded sadly. "I suspected as much. Still, in conjunction with multiple targeted regeneration sessions, the nanites could probably eliminate the visible scarring that remains. There would likely be some internal damage left at a cellular level, but the amount of pain you suffer from it would be greatly reduced."

She allowed one corner of her mouth to rise. "I'm not in pain, Doctor. The drugs inside my implants keep it under control."

"That probably isn't healthy over the long term," he cautioned, mirroring what Doctor Guzman on *Spear* had said. "You really should take what I'm saying as sound medical advice."

"I will, Doctor. Forgive me, but I have to think about this for a while before I make a final decision."

The doctor stood right away. "That's all I can ask. Let me leave you to consider it and thank you for coming down."

She sat there after he'd gone, considering what she'd seen. The Bastard had actually come for her. Not to kill her, but to rescue her from the worst days of her life.

The mere idea boggled her mind. It was, quite literally, inconceivable.

Worse, it meant she needed to make a real effort to determine what the truth here was. This Mertz was obviously not the same man as in her universe. And that might be the hardest thing of all to accept.

* * *

ELISE INSISTED on accompanying Breckenridge to see Kelsey once she'd finished her consultation with the emperor's personal physician. If there was going to be trouble, she wanted to be right there to stop it. She'd arranged to use an intimate little seating room for the get-together.

She needn't have worried. Kelsey smiled widely when she saw Breckenridge and came over to hug the flummoxed man.

"Nathaniel, it is *so* good to see you," she told the senator warmly. "I can't tell you how long I've waited for this moment."

Elise had trouble imagining the senator at a loss for words, but all he could do was stare over Kelsey's shoulder at her in shock, his mouth moving but no words coming out.

"I take it you know one another," Elise said wryly.

Kelsey turned to her and seemed mildly scandalized. "Of course we do. His nephew saved my life. He sent me many messages and helped the Empire organize its response after the expedition. I still haven't made it home in my universe, but I feel as if we're family."

"Me too, Highness," he said in a strangled voice. "I'm just not used to you being so friendly to me. We work well together here, but there's… tension."

She stepped back from the senator and frowned. "Why? Is my doppelgänger an idiot?"

He chuckled and shook his head. "Far from it. Might we sit? We've got a lot of ground to cover."

Kelsey sat and seemed relaxed. Perhaps that was because both Elise and Breckenridge were her close allies in the other universe and she felt at ease. Whatever the cause, Elise was happy there was no tension.

Breckenridge took control of the meeting. "I regret that we're meeting in a situation where I have to discuss business, but events are marching on, and we need to get in front of them. There is some concern that you represent a threat to the Empire. Our Empire."

The other princess considered that and nodded. "I'm an unknown outsider with a familiar face. You have no idea what I'm capable of. I get it. I can't do anything, though. You know who I am. It's not as if I've secretly replaced your Kelsey."

"That's where the problem comes in," he said. "With implants becoming more commonplace, so are the computers that interface with them. Computers that know you as the heir to the Imperial Throne."

Kelsey frowned. "I'm not following."

"Consider *Gibraltar*, the superdreadnought you saw in orbit," Elise said softly. "Its computer would recognize you as the heir. There's quite a bit of havoc you could cause. Computers aren't like people. They wouldn't know you're not *our* Kelsey."

That made Kelsey sit back and frown. "What the hell would they let me do?"

"I haven't the slightest idea, and no one else really does either."

"I'll grant you that is a problem," the other woman admitted. "What do you have in mind?"

"His Majesty has come up with a solution that shouldn't inconvenience you too much," Breckenridge said, crossing his legs. "He's going to have the senate declare Kelsey Bandar medically unfit to serve as heir for the time being. Since our Kelsey isn't here, that won't cause anyone any problems."

"Okay," she said. "It makes perfect sense, though I don't understand why you're consulting me about it."

"I needed to meet you so I can answer any questions my colleagues have. And I wanted to see you for myself."

Kelsey nodded. "I felt you tense up, so my friendliness wasn't what you expected. Are we enemies here in bizarro world?"

"Our relationship is… complicated. Our Kelsey didn't have the best rapport with my nephew. He tried to imprison her and supported the coup attempt. Sadly, he was responsible for a lot of needless damage and loss of Fleet lives."

The other woman laughed a little bitterly. "Of course he was. Why is nothing the same between my universe and yours? So if we have a complicated relationship, does that mean we get along on some level?"

The senator gave her a lopsided smile. "We do, though not in the way you imagine. I'm probably about to cause other me some serious problems, but it sounds as if his life is going more smoothly than mine has. He probably deserves this.

"Elise tells me that you know the emperor isn't your father by blood. Due to some youthful indiscretions, I'm actually your biological sire."

Kelsey's eyes bugged out. "You're my *what*?"

No, she hadn't known. Elise reached out and took the other woman's hand in hers.

"It ended before you were born," Breckenridge said. "Neither of us knew this until the attempted coup, so we're still trying to figure out how we feel about it. Needless to say, our version of you is still angry with me."

"Then she *is* an idiot," Kelsey declared, rising to her feet and pulling the man up and into an embrace. "That's the first thing I've learned that actually makes my life better. I already respect you. While I miss my father every day, I couldn't be happier to have you be even closer to me."

It was hard for Elise to keep a straight face at Breckenridge's expression. Flummoxed no longer seemed adequate. Flabbergasted was better. Then Elise stopped trying and just laughed.

Kelsey gave her an odd look and then saw the expression on Breckenridge's face. That made her laugh, too.

"I've stunned you, haven't I? I'm sorry." The grin on the woman's face told a different tale.

"I may never understand you," he said in a bemused tone. "But no matter what universe you come from, I am and shall remain your friend and steadfast advisor, if you'll have me."

After one more hug, Kelsey resumed her seat. "I trust what you two say more than so many other people here. Let me ask you about medical nanites."

With growing horror, Elise listened as Kelsey told them of her current condition and what the emperor's personal physician wanted to do to address it. Elise pulled her into an embrace when she finished.

"Oh God, Kelsey. I've lived my life fearing exactly that fate. I'm so sorry."

"It's done," the other woman said sadly. "I'm going to have to live with it for the rest of my life. I'm ruined. A travesty of a human being."

"Don't believe it," Elise said. "Don't fall into the trap that this ends your life. It doesn't."

"Have you seen the horror they left behind on my body?" Kelsey asked with a shake of her head. "I've often wondered whether I'd be better off dead."

Elise stared into the other woman's eyes and held her hands tightly. "Listen to me very carefully, Kelsey. Let them put the nanites inside you. They'll heal your body. Maybe even more than the doctors expect. It's the right thing to do."

"Allow me to second Princess Elise," Breckenridge said as he too leaned forward with an expression of sympathy. "Our Kelsey has recovered mentally and physically. I know it seems impossible to imagine, but you are far stronger than you give yourself credit for. You can triumph over this adversity. Let us help you."

Kelsey looked at them both in turn and slowly nodded. "If you say to trust this doctor, I will. Would it be possible to have a someone I trust do this, if he's available? Doctor Guzman might not know me here, but I know him. I trust him."

Elise nodded. "He knows you and has examined our version of you. He's at Erorsi, but I can get him, I'm sure of it. Take one more piece of advice from me and allow Doctor Lily Stone to do the work. She was with you every step of the way here. She knows your implants almost as well as you do. If anyone can fix your body, she can."

The other princess seemed to shrink into herself. "Will you stay with me?"

"Every step of the way," Elise promised fiercely.

Kelsey wiped her natural eye. "Then I'll do it."

11

Olivia stepped off the cutter and into the landing bay on the hospital ship *Caduceus*, currently in Erorsi orbit. It was set up to have small craft come directly inside the hull to expedite patient care. It had a veritable fleet of specialized ambulance cutters to make that happen during emergencies.

Her trauma bays were clustered close to the landing bay to receive the most critical cases immediately. Thankfully, there was no current need for those services.

She'd been the obvious person to brief Commodore Lily Stone, the ship's commanding officer. Well, not precisely her commanding officer. She had a flag captain that actually commanded the ship, but Stone called the shots.

Doctor Stone stepped forward with a smile. "It's good to see you again, Coordinator. Welcome aboard *Caduceus*. I believe you know Justin."

"Doctor Stone, Doctor Guzman, it's a pleasure to see you both again. Can we go somewhere private? Time is short."

Stone gestured for her to accompany them as they retired to a briefing room.

Olivia made certain the hatch was locked behind them. The room probably wasn't as carefully screened as her offices, but no one should expect critical secrets to be under discussion on a hospital ship. Secrets like the ones she was about to spill.

Once everyone was seated, she started. "Sean is delivering orders from the emperor to Commodore Graves as we speak. They've decided to pull most of Jared's fleet back to Avalon and send them to Terra. You're coming along."

Stone seemed surprised but nodded. "Terra? We can certainly make that happen, but why brief us personally? We're doctors, not combatants."

"Because you're going to be working on a patient that has what I'll kindly call serious issues while the mission proceeds. One who it's critical we keep quiet about until the mission is under way. Perhaps even then. I'm not completely sure of how they'll want to play it."

The two physicians glanced at one another in obvious confusion.

Guzman took the lead in following up. "Why us? Are the doctors on Avalon not up to the task? The word I'm getting is that they're catching up with the new technology pretty fast."

"I suppose," Olivia said with a shrug. "The key here is your experience. Particularly Doctor Stone's. We have a woman who was forcibly implanted with Marine Raider implants several years ago and is now suffering from the complications it brought on as well as subsequent injuries."

Stone leaned forward. "I thought we'd taken care of the Pale Ones. The teams on Erorsi forced them to come to them and overwrote their implant code with the clean version. They treated the injuries they could and didn't find any recent converts, only the savages. Did they miss one?"

Olivia shook her head. "No. The patient is Princess Kelsey Bandar. Not ours, but one from an alternate universe. She came through Omega looking for help."

The news made both doctors sit up straight in shock. Stone recovered first. "That's astounding. Of course we'll help. Did you bring her records? I assume she's been examined by someone."

"The emperor's personal physician looked her over and recommended treatment," Olivia said with a nod. "Her history is somewhat different there than what we experienced. To the point, she wasn't rescued until several days after the Pale Ones implanted her.

"She was savaged by the monsters. Her nanites are inactive, she lost an eye and has some kind of crude replacement, and the surgical scarring was not regenerated except for her head, hands, and arms."

Stone's jaw hardened, and her eyes narrowed. "Leaving aside the emotional damage she has to have suffered, that will create a very challenging path to physical recovery. Why didn't she get a full regeneration treatment on *Courageous*?"

"Let's just say the expedition there was not the same one we went on. A lot of her personal history is different. Jared wasn't in command of the mission. Commander Roche and *Ginnie Dare* went with *Best Deal.* Things played out much differently."

"Obviously," Guzman said. "I can't wait to hear more about it, but I get why we're keeping this quiet. Someone from an alternate reality has come to see us. Amazing."

"We need to review her medical files and start developing a treatment plan," Stone said. "Activating her nanites has to be step one. We'll make sure her implant code is up to spec, insert some of our Kelsey's stored nanites, and get the new Kelsey's body to repairing what damage it can. Let me have the files."

It only took a moment for Olivia to send them. Stone threw them onto the wall screen.

"It looks so much like her, except for that eye," Stone said with a frown. "We can't regenerate something like that, but I can put in a replacement that will be lifelike. Oh, my heart is breaking. The horrors she must've gone through.

"*Caduceus*, secure all discussion in this room under the file KB2 and lock it to only myself and Doctor Guzman. Then connect me with Captain Kemp."

"File secured, Commodore," the computer said through the overhead speakers. "Connection open."

"Yes, Commodore?" a woman's voice asked.

"Prep the ship for movement, Deloris," Stone said. "We'll be getting movement orders shortly, and I don't want to wait a minute longer than we have to. In fact, contact Commodore Graves and inform him that we're deploying. Gather the chicks and get us all moving for Avalon at best speed."

"Aye, ma'am. Bridge out."

"Chicks?" Olivia asked.

"Hospital ships aren't supposed to fight, but we do have escorts to keep trouble off our backs. Two heavy cruisers, four light cruisers, and eight destroyers. They're supposed to shield us while we run like good little noncombatants.

"What else can you tell me about this Kelsey? You've met her. What challenges are we going to face?"

Olivia grimaced. "Her universe has it tougher than ours. She's not Jared Mertz's friend there. There was an attempted coup there, too, and her father was killed. Ethan Bandar is on the Throne.

"I have no idea if that's because the man actually pulled off a coup or if that Jared Mertz is a cad. Honestly, I don't think Kelsey knows either. She hasn't made it to her version of Avalon yet.

"In any case, Jared stole *Courageous* and fled. Harrison's World is a sterilized husk, there's no graveyard, and they're in an awful bind. The bottom line is that they have very little access to recovered Old Empire technology."

Stone shook her head. "This is going to be complicated. I assume she doesn't know me."

"No, but she knows and trusts Doctor Guzman. Elise has convinced her to let you lead the treatment, but she needs to have a face she trusts standing beside you. That's why she needs you both."

"This might not have a perfect outcome," Guzman said with a sigh. "Her recovery is probably going to be difficult and incomplete."

"That's why we're bringing in the best the Empire has," Olivia said. "With the technology on this ship and your combined experience, you'll make as much magic happen as you can. The emperor considers this Kelsey his daughter, too. He's counting on you. She's also counting on you, even if she doesn't know it yet."

Stone's expression firmed with resolve. "We'll figure something out. We always do. If you'll excuse us, we have a lot of preparatory work to get started."

* * *

SEAN WATCHED Charlie Graves as he paced around the office just off *Courageous*'s bridge. He understood some of the feelings the other man must be feeling. The new orders put him into something of a bind.

"We're not exactly full strength here," Graves muttered. "I don't know how many Rebel Empire ships we're going to accumulate on the other side of the flip-point jammer as things progress."

"I hear you," Sean said. "The Pentagarans have moved their ships here to back you up, so the overall strength won't drop that much, other than the fact they made a great reserve force that you no longer have."

Graves grimaced and stopped pacing. "Exactly what I was thinking. What's the schedule on refurbished units at Harrison's World?"

"We've built up a fairly sizable force," Sean admitted. "We're short on trained personnel, though. I discussed the issue with Admiral Yeats before he finalized everything. Most of that reserve will be on its way to Avalon to pick up crew within the next week.

"It can be here before the jammer needs maintenance. It won't completely replace what Admiral Mertz is taking, but it'll give you a credible force.

"It'll have a new command for you, too. Much to his annoyance, Admiral Yeats has decided he has to pass *Gibraltar* on to you, so you have the most powerful fleet command unit possible. I wouldn't be surprised if you got a bump to admiral along with it. Congratulations."

"That's not as shocking as it would've been a few months ago," Graves said, rubbing his face. "I'm basically doing the job now. It'll be nice having the extra firepower. I'll miss this ship, though.

"With as many admirals as we're going to have running around, I'll need a chart to know who outranks who."

"I wouldn't worry about that. I gather His Majesty intends to create a new position for overall command. In the next few days, you'll get notice that Grand Admiral Yeats is in charge."

"That makes sense and far better him than me." The other man walked to the screen mounted on his wall. It displayed a tactical representation of the Erorsi system.

"I'm not sure why the emperor wants to make a push to Terra, but that's his call to make. I think based on the requirements you've given me, the best plan is to send *Invincible* and her escort back with you.

"They're used to working as a team now. I'd rather Kelsey had them with her, but she doesn't. A superdreadnought, two battlecruisers, four heavy cruisers, six light cruisers, and a dozen destroyers should provide him a good screen.

"Combine that with four marine transports, six colliers to rearm everyone, eight fast couriers, six Fleet transports, and all twelve scouts, and he should have a pretty potent force at his command."

Sean nodded. "He'll also inherit a light carrier that just came out of the docks. So will you. We have all the files that Commodore Anderson put together on fighter doctrine. These ships are based on battlecruiser hulls, so they only have one squadron of fighters to deploy, unfortunately."

"A force of Thirty-six fighters is nothing to sneer at," Graves said. "I'll take them. Will the ships come with escorts?"

"Sure will. Two heavy cruisers, four light cruisers, and eight destroyers. They should have more, but we're light on repaired hulls and even lighter on crew.

"These ships will come close to tapping the last of Fleet's trained people. The plan is to implement heavy training on boosting skills in our current crews while new people are recruited.

"As repaired ships come online, the experienced crews will split to form the nucleuses of two ships and start over. We're going to keep going as long as we can, but that's going to require a lot of hard work on everyone's part."

"That's going to be rough on morale, but I get it," Graves said. "I'll manage with the people we have left, I suppose. If we can catch a break when we take the jammer down for maintenance, we'll have even longer to get new ships into play."

The flip-point jammer was the weak link here at Erorsi, Sean knew. While it was up, the wormhole was impassible. When it was down, the enemy could send probing ships through and attack in force.

"How long is the maintenance cycle?" he asked.

"Based on the few times we've done it, anywhere from four to eight hours. That's assuming there isn't a major problem."

"Mind some advice?"

The other man shook his head and came back to sit beside Sean. "Not a bit. Lay it on me."

"You're playing defense. Switch your mindset around into an attack strategy."

Graves frowned. "I'm playing defense because I have to keep them out of this system. What am I missing?"

"My suggestion for when it comes time to perform maintenance is to mass every ship you have here at the flip point. Not to defend it, but to attack while the flip point is open. If they send a probe through at an inopportune moment, go after them with everything you have.

"The Rebel Empire ships will back off and play defense. You set them on their heels long enough to perform the maintenance and then race back to Erorsi. Played right, they won't even be in a position to rush you."

Graves smiled. "Because we'll have rushed them first. That's brilliant. Thank you."

"My pleasure. I wish I could take credit for the idea, but one of my tactical officers on *Spear* came up with it in a simulation. She really deserves the credit."

"Send me the simulation details along with her name, and I'll do exactly that," Graves promised. "I just got word *Caduceus* and her escorts are pulling out. We need to get you to *Invincible* before she gets too big a lead on you. Speaking of that, why do you need a hospital ship?"

"Can't say," Sean said as he rose to his feet. "Not specifically for the mission to Terra, though. Emperor's orders."

"Can't say or won't?" Graves asked shrewdly. "I suspect there's something else afoot."

Sean smiled blandly and shook the other man's hand. "Give them hell, Commodore."

"I will," the other man assured him. "And good luck on your secret mission. Keep the admiral safe."

"He'll get everything I have. You have my word on that."

12

Jared stood outside the room where Princess Kelsey was meeting with her doctors via FTL com. He would rather not interrupt them, but he needed the other woman's attention. She didn't know it yet, but they'd be leaving to meet the hospital ship and all the other vessels at Harrison's World shortly.

The Empire had gotten lucky with the relay between Avalon and Pentagar. Though the distance was considerable—even individually over the two artificially created flip points—the repeater was able to connect to both worlds.

Maybe that was because both flip points were new, because the termini in the Nova system were adjacent to one another, or perhaps it was just a fluke. Only about half the repeaters worked in connecting systems more than one flip away from one another.

That meant half didn't. For example, the repeater to Harrison's World hadn't. Luckily, they both had single flip connections to the Nova system, and Omega didn't mind repeating the transmissions. He'd have done the same with Pentagar, but this was better.

Why the alien could do it and the automatic repeaters couldn't was a mystery.

Carl Owlet had suspected he'd misunderstood part of the new theory on FTL and believed he'd eventually solve the problem. Only he wasn't here. Ironically, he was far beyond FTL range inside the Rebel Empire with Jared's Kelsey.

Jared rapped his knuckles lightly on the hatch and waited for it to open. He wasn't nearly as tense as his guards. By now, he suspected that this version of Kelsey was reevaluating him. He felt relatively safe that she wouldn't attack him.

The hatch slid aside, and Kelsey gave him a hard look. "I'm rather busy," she said brusquely.

Elise stepped up and put a calming hand on the other woman's shoulder. "I'm sure he knows that. Perhaps you should hear what he has to say before dismissing him."

Kelsey grunted a little and stepped back. She smiled when her gaze shifted to where Jared's guards were eyeing her worriedly.

"I'm not going to hurt him. You have my word of honor."

The half dozen guards at his back seemed unconvinced, but Jared motioned them back. "Her word is good enough for me. Wait out here."

He stepped through the hatch and closed it in Colonel Bronson's face as he tried to slip inside. Jared turned to fully face Princess Kelsey. The wall screen was on, he saw.

Lily Stone smiled at him. "Jared, it's good to see you again. I wish I were there in person."

"Me, too, but I'm going to have to end this consultation a bit early. The emperor is sending us to meet you and wants to see Princess Kelsey before she leaves. We'll meet you at Omega. Sorry."

The other woman shrugged. "We've accomplished about all I could honestly expect without being in the same place. This is as good a time to wrap up the consultation as any. Just give me a few more minutes."

Lily turned her gaze to Kelsey. "I understand that you have no reason to trust me, but I know your implant hardware inside and out. Hell, I know your body inside and out, right down to the cellular level.

"I also know this sounds daunting. That's because it is. I'm not going to sugarcoat this. We won't get you back to the same level of recovery that our Kelsey managed. There's been too much injury, and it's had time to set in.

"What I can promise you is that we'll do everything within our power to repair as much as we can. That's going to be huge. No matter what universe you come from, I will always do everything I can to keep you in the best health possible. I only ask that you trust me as much as you can."

The corner of Kelsey's mouth quirked up. "Believe it or not, I actually do trust you. Maybe it's the doctor vibe, but I honestly believe you're in my corner and will do everything you can. I'm deeply appreciative, Doctor Stone. Lily.

"You and Justin have my complete confidence. Whatever you recommend, I'll do. I only wish that I could take you home with me when this is all over."

Lily smiled warmly. "I don't want to steal His Majesty's thunder, but we *have* spoken about that. You're probably going to bring some of your people over to join you on this mission. I hope you can bring a full medical team or two to take a crash course with me and my staff.

"We've got plenty of spare equipment to send back with them. I wish we could send ships, but that isn't realistic. What we can do is transship cargo containers full of medical gear and the know-how to use it. Once you have the data and knowledge to manufacture your own equipment, the sky is the limit."

The expression on Kelsey's face was profoundly grateful. "Thank you. It will mean uncounted lives saved, and you will have my eternal gratitude. All of you."

"It's my deepest pleasure. I realize that you and Admiral Mertz don't precisely get along, but you need to know that he urged me to make this proposal to the emperor. He's been a strong advocate on your behalf and that of your people."

Kelsey's eyes slid over to him. "Has he now? I'm starting to worry that my feelings toward this version of him might be misplaced. Maybe."

She returned her gaze to Lily. "I make no promises about how I feel toward him, but recent events have given me food for thought. Your loyalty to him tells me something about his character, too.

"I'm nervous but ready to get this process started. I will never forget the kindness you do me and my people. Neither will the emperor. My emperor. Until we meet, farewell."

The call ended, and Kelsey turned to face him. "I can't make the same promise for you, but I do appreciate the assistance."

He bowed slightly. "Believe it or not, it's my pleasure. If you and Elise would accompany me, His Majesty would like to see you one more time before we leave for Harrison's World."

"I'm going to cry," Kelsey said sadly. "Seeing my father again was an unlooked-for blessing. Returning to a world where he's dead is going to open those wounds all over again." She strode to the hatch without giving him a chance to say anything.

Jared fell in behind her with his wife at his side. Together, they all headed to the final audience with Karl Bandar before they left for Terra.

* * *

Kelsey entered the Imperial apartments with a heavy heart. As much as she wanted to see her father again, she knew he was dead. This version of him wasn't the man who had raised her, no matter how alike they seemed. Her father was dead and buried.

Not that her traitorous emotions cared. They knew he was her father in every way that mattered.

Karl Bandar rose to his feet as they entered. He smiled at her and gestured to the three chairs he had set up. "Kelsey, please join me. Jared, you too. Everyone else, wait outside."

She didn't like the idea of sitting down for a casual chat with the Bastard, but this wasn't her show. If she were going to get the tools her people needed to survive, she'd have to hold her nose and do it. At least he wasn't insisting they have dinner.

Once they'd all sat, her father considered her. "How did your consultation with Doctor Stone go?"

Kelsey shrugged. "As well as it could. The damage to my body has set in, and the prospects of a complete recovery seem unrealistic. Still, any improvement will be a welcome change."

"That grieves me deeply. When I first heard what had happened to you in this universe, I was heartbroken at the pain and suffering you'd endured. I now realize that my version of you got off lucky.

"Another thing the two of you share is that you're both stronger than you think. You stand up to adversity and force it to your will. You will overcome this."

"I appreciate that you think so, but you really don't know what my home is like."

She flicked her gaze toward the Bastard. "And I'm not convinced you know the people around you as well as you think, even if it's becoming apparent that this Jared Mertz isn't the same as mine. At least not openly."

Her father digested that before he shook his head. "I refuse to believe that. While I can certainly misjudge people, I saw how Ethan became at the end. I pray he isn't mad in your universe, but he drove the coup here. Even my Kelsey agreed."

"I really don't know how much weight to give things here," she said with a sigh. "The differences at Harrison's World illustrate that things are not identical between our universes, but so many things seem similar."

Mertz cleared his throat. "I can't speak to the other me. Honestly, I know with all the prejudice I dealt with in Fleet because of my parentage, I could've become bitter. I might be the bad guy there.

"What I can say for certain is that I'm not one here. I love the Empire and have zero desire to run it. Kelsey has become my sister in reality, and I love her. My father is a bit more intimidating, but I'm trying."

He turned to face her squarely. "What I can promise unequivocally is that I will do everything within my power to help you and your people, with the understanding that my Empire comes first."

"Perhaps it would be helpful to know precisely what you want us to do," her father said. "You came here with a plan in mind. Based on your earlier comments, I believe you're looking for the key and the override. Is that right?"

Kelsey nodded. "I was able to send information through the weak flip point and back to the Empire, just like you. We also found the information that allowed us to deduce that the Imperial Scepter was the key to the Imperial Vault on Terra and what that vault probably contained. Unfortunately, that's when the coup took place."

She gave Mertz a hard look. "You staged a coup. My father died in my universe. So did everyone with any hint of Imperial blood, except for you. The damage to Fleet and Avalon was significant.

"You took the Imperial Scepter and fled when you couldn't kill Ethan. Your ships guarded the weak flip point while you came through. You managed to convince Captain Breckenridge to let you onto *Courageous*, and then you and your traitorous cohorts killed him, stole the ship, and fled through the flip point leading to what I now know is the Rebel Empire."

She sighed. "I hope to eventually kill that version of you, but the key is lost. Even if I had it, I can't use it. When I found Omega and learned of your universe, I knew I had to beg your help. I need your key and someone with the right genes to unlock the Vault."

Her father leaned forward and took her hand. "I feel terrible for the pain you've suffered, both physically and mentally. It rends my heart. Yet I must look out for my people first.

"I cannot send the key with you until we have the override. Even so, it might be that our key is different. It might not work."

"Worse, you don't have the ships to get to the Master AI at Twilight River," Mertz said. "It will be heavily guarded, as will Terra. Without the graveyard, you'll need to use stealth, and that might not be enough to bypass the defenses."

"It's all I have," she said. "I refuse to just give up."

Her father nodded. "I've authorized the transfer of knowledge and hardware from our universe to yours. You can bring people over to receive training in using the equipment. That will make a difference.

"Once we get that started, you and some of your people may accompany Jared to Terra. The knowledge of what you have to face there may make the difference between success and failure back in your universe.

"Finally, once we have the override, you're welcome to our Imperial Scepter with my blessing."

"The key is useless without someone to use it," she said. "Doctor Stone told me that my DNA is identical to her Kelsey. That gives me hope that the Imperial DNA in my universe is the same, too."

"I'll wager we can figure out a way to short-circuit that lock," Mertz said. "My friends are very talented."

Kelsey very much doubted that, but saying so wouldn't help her cause any. She'd take what help she could get. "Thank you."

Her father rose to his feet. "Time is short, but I'd appreciate it if you dined with me. Just the two of us. Sorry, Jared."

"I understand," Mertz said as he stood. "I'll go to Orbital One and get *Athena* ready to move out." He inclined his head toward her. "I know this is hard, but I'm not your enemy, Kelsey. I'll do everything I can to help you."

She only wished she could believe the lying bastard.

13

Elise was waiting for Kelsey when she finished the meal with her father. The other woman's expression was closed, but she knew her Kelsey well enough to see the turmoil roiling under the doppelgänger's calm expression.

It wasn't too hard to imagine any number of things getting to the woman, but odds were good that her father was high on the woman's list of deep thoughts.

Rather than intrude, Elise simply walked Kelsey out to the landing pad where a sleek grav car was waiting for them. In moments, they were flying toward the city and the spaceport.

Kelsey didn't say anything for the first few minutes but finally turned toward her. "You married Mertz. Why? Political survival? Because your people needed the Empire?"

Rather than being offended, Elise was glad for the opportunity to talk about Jared directly. Kelsey needed to understand who he was, or they'd never accomplish anything long lasting.

"No. Our version of you made a treaty that gave us a fighting chance. I married Jared because I really do love him."

Under other circumstances, the look of incomprehension would've been amusing. Okay, it still was.

"I just can't force myself to understand that," Kelsey said, disbelief clear in her tone. "I hear everyone talk about what a great guy he is, but my Mertz is a total dick."

Elise smiled. "That leads to a discussion of nature verses nurture. Is someone's personality determined in the womb? Or do the circumstances of our lives make us who we are? I'm inclined to believe the latter. Life is what we make it, and it in turn shapes us."

She turned in her seat to face Kelsey directly. "I've learned a lot about Jared since we met at Pentagar two years ago. That includes the circumstances of his birth and some of the ways it worked against him. Not only with the hatred you and Ethan gave him, but the slights his fellow Fleet officers perpetrated against him.

"Admiral Yeats admitted to me that, at the time of the exploratory mission, Jared would've been a senior captain rather than a commander if he'd been fathered by anyone else. Frankly, I'm amazed Jared isn't bitter."

"How do you know he isn't?" the other woman asked intently. "Perhaps he's a simmering pot of resentment inside with great acting skills."

Elise shook her head. "I have implants. I might not be able to read his thoughts, but I can certainly sense his moods. I was good at that even before I got implants, but linking with him allows me to be absolutely sure.

"In your universe, you're the only person who has implants. You have no idea what it means to interact with someone else who also has them. Particularly someone close to you. Allow me to demonstrate."

She initiated a call to Kelsey's implants. Previously, Kelsey had only received files. This should be a real education for the other woman.

Once Kelsey accepted the call, Elise spoke only with her mind.

This is what it feels like to communicate through the implants. It's almost like just talking. Do you feel anything about me?

Kelsey shook her head. "No. It's like you're whispering in my ear."

Elise nodded. "That's right. Even with implants, this is how most people communicate, but there is another layer for those who are *really* close. Frankly, it's asking a lot to even make this offer, but you need to understand precisely how sure I am.

"Implants allow extra depth for those in a relationship. Intimate mode. It's designed to sense emotions and even the physical body of one's lover.

"Not even close friends use this with one another because it's intensely personal, invasive even, when the two aren't actually intimate. Yet I need you to understand the true depth of my certainty. Are you willing to do this for a minute?"

Kelsey stared at her before nodding wordlessly. "We're close friends in my universe. I trust you."

"I apologize in advance. You can terminate the contact at any time you choose. You're always in control."

Elise offered her friend a connection in intimate mode. Moments later, Kelsey accepted.

The mental link expanded to include brushing up against Kelsey's emotions. She felt the other woman's uncertainty and doubt on a level that was beyond question.

She also had an uncomfortable awareness of her friend's body. In intimate mode, she was deeply connected in a way meant to enhance a lover's touch and to feel their reactions as if they were her own.

With Jared, that meant she could truly feel his physical reaction to her touch. Making love was like sharing his body. The intensity of the connection in those moments was an almost spiritual experience.

Kelsey reached out hesitantly and ran her finger down Elise's arm. The gesture was nonsexual, but the resonance between them in intimate mode caused Elise's body to tremble a bit and sent a jolt down her spine.

The other woman snatched her hand back as if the contact had burned her.

"I felt that," Kelsey said, her voice shocked. "I felt myself touch you and your reaction to it. How it made you uncomfortable. How it made you—" She clamped her mouth shut.

Elise ended the connection, relieved to once more be alone inside her own skin. "That's how I know how Jared feels. He's my husband, and I've been in intimate mode when he's spoken about any number of things. He's not your enemy or the Empire's in this universe. I'll stake my soul on it."

The other woman rubbed her face. "This is impossible. How can people live with that kind of intimacy? You… ah, make love with that turned on?"

Even the thought of that made Elise react physically, and she was deeply glad to have ended the contact with Kelsey. She didn't want to have the other woman experience the rush of arousal the very idea sent through her.

"Oh yes. I'd never imagined how it would be to not only feel one's own pleasure, but to feel someone else's at the same time… it's indescribable. I instantly know how he feels, even how my body feels to him. When we make love, it's almost as if we're one being, body and soul."

She shook the thought away. "But that's too personal to think about right now. Can you see why I'm so sure?"

"I suppose," Kelsey said with a slow nod. "I'm not sure how I can accept it deep inside. And no, I am not doing that with him. No way. I might throw up."

Laughter bubbled up in Elise's throat. She tried to stifle it but failed miserably as she started giggling.

Kelsey smiled and chuckled. "That was pretty funny, I suppose. You've given me a lot to think about. Thank you."

"That's what friends are for. We're almost to the spaceport, so let's get ready for the trip up."

* * *

Sean made the transition to the Nova system from Pentagar on *Invincible*'s flag bridge. The amazing ship and her control center made him so jealous. He'd be planning some upgrades at Boxer Station on this trip.

"Transition complete, Commodore," Marcus said over the overhead speaker. "All ships have checked in. It doesn't look as if Admiral Mertz has made it yet. Shall we wait here for him?"

He considered that, and then shook his head. "No. Let's get into orbit around Omega. The admiral will bring Kelsey there so she can pass word back to her people. Now that we can give them some suits, she'll get an escort. What steps can we take to get them set up here while maintaining security?"

"The emperor has already ordered there be only limited duplication with our current personnel, but I foresee problems. This Kelsey likely trusts a number of the same people we have along. We need to come up with a way to allow for that."

"None of the doppelgängers have implants, or so I am led to believe," Sean said slowly. "Only Princess Kelsey has them, and the senate has already declared her temporarily unfit to be heir, so none of our automated systems will allow her to use her implants to do anything to override the command officers."

"Good news, but I'm less certain about Harrison and myself."

That made Sean sit up a bit straighter. "I'm not following."

"When I was created, Carl Owlet altered the original Imperial core imperatives. To be specific, he removed the prohibition preventing me from using weapons and mandated my obedience to Jared Mertz and Kelsey Bandar.

"He used their implant serial codes for that. Obedience to those directives is nondiscretionary. If our visitor ordered me to open fire on the rest of the fleet, I would be compelled to do so."

"What happens if Jared orders you not to?" Sean asked.

"Carl Owlet put some logic in place for that. As I was intended to manage this ship—he apparently never considered the possibility that I would move on, for which I shall need to chastise him—he put a rule in place that Admiral Mertz had senior authority.

"I understand that she isn't the Kelsey I was meant to obey. Carl Owlet obviously intended to have our Kelsey have authority, not the one from another universe. Yet they share an implant serial code. To my core rules, they are the same person."

Sean nodded unwillingly. "I get you. How do we work around your core rules?"

"It sounds like cheating when you phrase it that way," Marcus said with a chuckle. "To honor the spirit as well as the intent of my rules, Admiral Mertz needs to give me very specific and defined orders about precise things.

"For example, he could order me to disallow her control of the antiboarding weapons until he specifically removes the exception or a year has passed. I could do that because it is limited and I know it is intended to reserve the command authority for the designated individual with an expiration date."

"Why does it need to be limited? Isn't a rule absolute? Like two is always bigger than one."

"That edges into one of the differences between a computer program and a sentient AI. Think of my core rules like a moral compass. My version of right and wrong, if you will. A computer will see things in black and white. I have shades of gray.

"If Admiral Mertz were to give me an open-ended order, I would feel compelled to disregard it as a violation of the spirit of my core rules. A more circumspect set of instructions tailored to the specific circumstance we find ourselves in would make me willing to shade the letter of the law to suit the situation."

Sean nodded and sat quiet while absorbing that. It was a lot more nuanced than he'd expected. "And Harrison is the same?" he asked after a minute. "He can fire weapons, too?"

"Indeed he can. I'm surprised he hasn't already mentioned that to you."

"Believe it or not, he tends to stay quiet and runs mostly in the background. Perhaps I'd even call him shy. Introverted."

"Interesting," Marcus said slowly. "I need to spend more time talking to my sibling. He and I have so much in common, yet we also have so many subtle differences."

Moments later, Marcus spoke again. "Orbital One indicates that *Athena* has left for the flip point. Admiral Mertz and Princess Kelsey will be here in a little over two hours."

"Then we'd best get those rules you spoke of worked out. I'd like to be able to pass them on to the admiral for his consideration once he arrives. Let's try to restrict her without being obvious about it. If she doesn't realize we've locked her out, she can't be offended by it."

14

Olivia made the trip from *Caduceus* to pick up Kelsey and Elise. The Crown Princess sat in the back and almost immediately fell into a light doze.

Kelsey's reaction to the fleet of ships in orbit around Omega as their cutter undocked from *Athena* almost made Olivia smirk. Stunned didn't seem adequate. Dumbfounded, perhaps.

Kelsey was using her implants to access the ship's scanners. The ships were too far away to pick up by eye, even with the woman's Marine Raider implants.

After a minute of staring into space, Kelsey refocused her eyes on Olivia. "This has to be some kind of trick."

"Why?" she asked.

Kelsey pinched the bridge of her nose. "Because I need those ships. My people need them. Yet, in our universe, they aren't where we can get to them or repair them. And I can't believe that Mertz had all this firepower at his command and didn't do something."

Olivia shook her head. "Oh, he did something. Just not what you think he would've done if he were the kind of man you believe him to be."

"Maybe he couldn't convince enough people to go along with him," the short woman said with a frown. "Though he had no trouble getting almost half of Fleet to rebel in my universe."

"That's not the man I've come to know. He literally risked everything to save my people. The AI came very close to killing him and everyone with him."

"I see plenty of reasons he would risk everything," Kelsey said with a gesture at the bulkhead. "This fleet gives him a base of power to do whatever he wants."

"Yet he hasn't skulked about doing any of the dastardly deeds you seem certain he really wants to commit. Once he defeated the AI, he could've ordered the few ships he had left to stay at Harrison's World and taken *Invincible* home once she was repaired. Fleet wouldn't have been able to stand against him."

She raised a finger to stop the retort she saw coming. "And before you object that his crew wouldn't follow his orders to subdue the Empire, let me tell you about the computer on his superdreadnought.

"It's not a standard Old Empire unit. It's a sentient AI like the ones running the Rebel Empire, only it has a core imperative to obey Jared. It can also fire the weapons. He could order it to stun everyone aboard with the antiboarding weapons. None could have stood against him at Avalon."

Olivia shook her head before the other woman could respond. "This conversation is getting old. Let me give you a pro tip from someone who has actually ruled a world. If the facts don't match the results you're seeing, you've miscalculated."

Olivia knew she shouldn't be angry, but she was. Not at how Kelsey felt. Not really. It was more because of how unfair the woman's attitude was to Jared Mertz. The man was a damned saint as far as Olivia was concerned. Hearing this duplicate of her friend slander him stung in unexpected ways. She needed to get a grip on herself.

Kelsey sat slumped into her seat for half the trip and then spoke softly without looking at Olivia. "I can't put what I feel aside. He killed my father. Perhaps your version isn't the same kind of man, but that doesn't change the rage and loathing I feel for him."

Olivia turned to Kelsey, making sure to keep her expression neutral. "And I could say that having seen your brother Ethan in action over here, I can't get past that. The man was a mad dog that tried to kill your father and plunge the Empire into civil war.

"Is he that way in your universe? I hope not. He managed to hide his condition from everyone here. By your logic, I'd be doing your universe a favor by shooting him. Is that fair to him? No."

She sighed and put her hand on Kelsey's arm. "This is complicated in ways that no one else can understand. The people around you look like the ones at home, but they've lived different lives. You have to be able to see past appearances. Discover the truth without your prejudices."

"I don't know if I can," Kelsey said in a whisper.

Olivia squeezed the other woman's arm. "You can. Kelsey Bandar is the strongest person I know. She can quite literally do anything. Remind me someday to tell you the story about how she saved tens of thousands of people on my world by doing something absolutely mad. Just say 'fist of god' and I'll know exactly what you mean."

"I wish I was her. I really do," Kelsey said as she slumped farther in her seat. "I've failed at so many things. It's as if she got all the good luck and I got the bad. Is that how karma really works? Am I destined to be the Kelsey that failed?"

"Destiny is wrapped around what other people think. It says nothing of the conflict we feel or the struggles to succeed. Kelsey has her doubts, too. She puts them aside and does what needs doing. You can do it, too. I'm sure you already do."

The cutter docked with the hospital ship. That woke Elise, and the three of them made their way out. Doctors Stone and Guzman were waiting outside the lock.

Lily extended her hand to Princess Kelsey. "Welcome aboard, Highness. I believe you already know Justin."

"I do, though everything here is so strange and unexpectedly different in ways I'm having trouble adjusting." Kelsey shook Lily's hand and then Justin's.

"No matter the differences, we'll do everything in our power to heal you," Guzman said softly. "We take our oaths very seriously. Lily risked getting shot to save the emperor during the coup. Elise *was* shot."

Kelsey tilted her head and looked more closely at the Crown Princess of Pentagar. "I hadn't heard. Thank you both."

"I didn't do that much," Lily said, waving a hand as if dispersing smoke. "Just took a blood sample and found a compound that I could combine with nanites to give him a chance. It was a damned close thing. Elise did the dangerous part."

Guzman shook his head. "Lily was with him in the Imperial infirmary during the coup. Getting that sample would've been worth her life if… well, if the wrong people saw her taking it."

The princess from another universe didn't say anything about the man's delicate pause, but Olivia interpreted her sour expression for comprehension about what he'd not said.

"In any case," Lily said. "Let's get you to the medical center and do a complete scan."

"The Imperial physician did one," Kelsey said with a scowl. That was a trait the two Kelseys shared.

"He's not me. I want to use my own equipment and make my own decisions about what's possible and what's not. He's a good man, but I have a lot more experience with Old Empire technology. The goal isn't to do a good job fixing you. It's to do the absolute best job possible."

Elise put her hand on Kelsey's shoulder. "I understand you don't like being poked and prodded, but I'll be with you the entire time."

The short woman sighed. "If I must."

"On that cheerful note, I'll take my leave," Olivia said. "I'll be on *Invincible* if you need me."

As she headed back into the cutter, Olivia sighed. This was going to get worse before it got better. Once Kelsey had people from her universe reinforcing her view of Jared, it would set in stone again. That would be an unwelcome addition to an already stressful mission.

* * *

KELSEY FELT OVERWHELMED as they made their way into the largest and most advanced-looking medical center she'd ever seen. Men and women in white lab coats bustled about.

"How many people are you expecting to treat?" she asked Doctor Stone. "Capital Hospital on Pentagar was nothing like this. No offense, Elise."

Her friend smiled. "None taken. We're doing everything in our power to rectify that. Doctor Plant, the man who first treated you there on my version of Pentagar, is very enthusiastic."

The memory of the jovial man in a white smock lightened Kelsey's mood. "He treated me, too. I'm glad. I hope I can at least jump-start something like that in my universe."

She put her uncertainty behind her. Time to get this over with. "What next?"

Next turned out to be several hours of intensive scans followed by dinner with Elise while the doctors wrangled over the new data.

Once she'd sated her never-ending hunger, they returned to Stone's office. The two doctors were already seated at a small table and gestured for the women to join them.

Kelsey sat across from Stone. "Did you discover anything else I need to know about?"

"We managed to get some higher resolution readings of potentially problematic areas," Stone said. "That improves your potential outcome.

"Another factor that the Imperial physician couldn't account for was something he doesn't really understand: Marine Raider nanites. While I gave the emperor a shot of them with the cure, that was just a stopgap measure. He has the standard Fleet version now."

Kelsey felt herself frowning. "Since I don't have them at all, I really have no grasp of what that means. Is there a difference? Why not give him the better set?"

"Unfortunately, we couldn't at the time, though we're now in a position to change that," Stone said. "You'll have to ask Admiral Mertz about the specifics of that, as it's classified.

"The difference is that Marine Raider nanites are significantly superior. While the standard Fleet version can't repair the deep scarring in your body, I believe that a combination of Marine Raider nanites and a targeted series of regeneration sessions might eliminate virtually all of the pain you have to be feeling."

Kelsey shrugged. "I'm not in pain. I haven't felt much since the Pale Ones did this."

Stone's expression told her that the woman didn't consider that a positive thing.

"Your pharmacology unit contains some powerful painkillers. They only mask the damage. It would be better to eliminate the scarring. If you agree, we can seed your nanites now and start regeneration sessions tomorrow."

"I've already agreed," she told the doctor. "I have to trust your knowledge, even if the idea of machines inside me makes me a little sick."

Stone smiled. "For what it's worth, Kelsey felt exactly the same way. She warmed to the idea when she started getting hurt. These nanites are very powerful. They were cutting-edge Imperial tech before the Fall.

"Not even the Old Empire knew precisely how powerful an effect they would have on a person over the long term. Someone with Fleet nanites can live past three hundred years. What's possible with Marine Raider nanites boggles the mind."

"What?" Kelsey said with a frown. "Hundreds of years? That can't be right."

"You'd be surprised," Stone said. "What did you find on Erorsi?"

The nonsequitur made Kelsey blink. "Uh… a planet full of raging monsters? We managed to eliminate the orbitals but had no reason to look closer. Why?"

"Believe it or not, there's an old defense bunker hidden there. At least there is in our universe. The residents are descended from the people who tried to hold out. They had a man with them who was kept alive through a combination of Fleet nanites and a stasis chamber. He's ancient, but still alive."

The idea didn't register for a moment. "Wait. Are you saying someone down there was alive before the Fall? That's impossible."

Stone shook her head. "It's true. Ensign Reginald Bell was dropped off there by *Courageous* to assist in the original defense of Erorsi. I hope you get a chance to meet him. He actually saw Imperial City on Terra with his own eyes. Imagine growing up in the Empire at its height."

Kelsey felt her stomach do a slow roll. "God. To live through that and still be alive all this time later. How sad he must be."

Maybe her life didn't suck as badly as some. She made a mental note to find out about the refuge on Erorsi. It was too late to hold on to *Courageous* now, but if these people still had access to Old Empire tech and skills, their help would be critical to the survival of the Empire.

But that was a task for later. Right now, she needed to get this damned procedure done.

"We might as well get this over with," she said, resigned to yet another medical procedure. "Will it hurt?"

"Not at all," Justin said. "We'll use some of the nanite samples we retained from our Kelsey to create a template in your nanite fabricator. Once we have it reactivated, it'll begin getting them into your system. It should only take ten minutes, and you won't feel a thing."

"That may not be completely true," Stone said with a shake of her head. "Once your pharmacology unit senses the damage being repaired, it will begin reducing the dosage of the pain killers. In a day or so, you might feel a low-level ache or worse. Nothing sharp. That will last until we finish the series of regeneration procedures."

Oddly, the fact that it would hurt made her feel better.

"What about the elephant in the room?" Kelsey gestured toward her artificial eye.

She'd lost the original during the terrifying weeks she'd spent as a Pale One. Her version of Justin Guzman had figured out the medical equipment on *Courageous* well enough to put her eye together, but it didn't look pretty.

It also didn't work correctly all the time. Every once in a while, it glitched and reset. Or switched modes to infrared at inopportune moments.

Looking in the mirror every morning was a reminder of what she'd lost. If they could do anything about this, she'd kiss their feet.

"We can replace that with a version that looks normal," Stone said. "I wish we could regenerate it completely, but there are limits to Imperial technology. That said, it will look exactly like your original eye. No one will be able to tell it isn't natural.

"We can also regenerate the area around it. The scars will take a while to fully disappear, but I anticipate a complete success with the procedure. I recommend that we save that for a few days from now, however. Let's get the nanites active and start the targeted regeneration first."

Justin smiled. "That'll give me time to refresh myself on the literature and work with our technical people to create an eye with the same capabilities as your Marine Raider implants grant your natural one."

That hardly seemed important, since she never used any of the ridiculously powerful features in her ocular implants. Why anyone needed to be able to see telescopically or microscopically, she had no idea.

Still, that made better sense than some of the other Raider modifications. Her sense of smell could now do a chemical analysis of things around her, and she could eavesdrop on conversations in the next compartment.

As a child, she'd read some comic books about people with super powers. She'd thought it would be amazing to be able to do those things. Now she knew that it would be a huge pain in the ass for the poor bastards.

Well, time to make the magic happen.

She rose to her feet. "Let's do this."

15

Jared sat in his private dining room aboard *Invincible* with Sean and Olivia. They'd just finished a quiet meal. Alex had outdone himself. Jared was warming to the idea of having a manservant with this kind of talent.

"It's time to work out the plan going forward," he said after taking a sip of his drink. "It's not going to be as simple as I'd imagined. Not only do we need to deal with Kelsey's doppelgänger and her friends, but we also have a large number of ships we'll need to conceal. I think direct command of the destroyer will need to be in a different set of capable hands."

"You mean mine," Sean said. "At least I hope you do. I've been preparing various little pitches to be your executive officer."

Jared started to say something, but Olivia interrupted him.

"And I'm going along." Her tone left no doubt that she considered the matter settled.

Amused, he nodded. "Permission granted. Your unique insight into the Rebel Empire will be a huge plus."

The woman shot Sean a smug look.

"Okay, I'm beaten," Sean said. "Be gracious in your victory."

"We'll allow Kelsey to return to her universe and gather some people to bring back for training," Jared continued. "That means they'll need suits capable of withstanding the radiation."

"I have a hundred suits prepared," Sean said. "If they insist on more people—and you allow it—we'll have to make multiple trips."

"A hundred sounds like a nice round number," Jared said after a few seconds. "If she pushes the issue, I'll authorize up to two hundred. I'd prefer most of them not be people already on our ships, but I know there'll be some overlap. Keep it below ten percent. We need to be sure of who we're dealing with."

Sean grunted. "I've consulted with Doctor Stone about that. If Kelsey was honest about her people not having implants, we can make sure the serial numbers are different should we decide to give them any. We can also tweak their implants so we get a notification when we're dealing with people not from our universe."

"Are we going to do that?" Olivia asked. "Give them implants?"

Jared nodded. "Of course. We have more than enough Fleet implants to share at this point. They'll need them to absorb all the material.

"I like that idea, particularly if we can introduce a system like Sean is proposing. Something like an identify friend-or-foe check."

Their combat forces used IFF systems to recognize friendly units. It should be possible to do the same as soon as everyone got the longer-range com systems Carl Owlet had designed. Lily had finished her checks, and they were almost ready to start replacing the standard units in all Fleet personnel.

The new implant coms would have better range than the headsets the Old Empire had used. She'd verified Carl's declaration that they were stable and consistent at ten kilometers. In fact, she'd had no failures until just a bit more than thirteen kilometers and had had successes out to sixteen. They'd publish ten as the listed maximum just to be conservative.

As part of the implant procedure, the units could be given the codes specific to their own universe. This might not work if they ever had visitors from a universe that had implants and upgraded coms, but they'd deal with that when the time came. This solved their current problem.

Sean nodded. "Good idea. If it's implemented correctly, we should be able to update things seamlessly in the future, if we have to. Luckily, Omega will have insight if anyone else from other universes arrive."

The commodore smiled a bit more widely. "I had Doctor Stone and her people make a modification to the basic package Carl developed. His original setup didn't allow us to turn the implant signals off. One of the captured officers at Erorsi spotted the marines as implanted and flipped out.

"With the new implants, we can activate what I'm calling stealth mode. The implants stay active but don't interact with anyone else. No external signals."

"That's a great addition," Jared said. "Well done. Contact Lily and work out the details for rolling out the upgrade. I want priority for everyone on *Invincible* and *Athena*. Make sure Grand Admiral Yeats has the most recent specs for all the other units."

"Aye, sir."

"Who's going to accompany her?" Olivia asked. "It needs to be someone with implants. You can't be sure you get back the same person otherwise."

He gave her a considering look. "You've made a good impression with her and seemingly don't have a doppelgänger. Would you consider going?"

She nodded at once. "Of course."

Based on his scowl, Sean disagreed, but he didn't say so out loud. "Getting everyone over will take a while if they're as suspicious as she was. Are we going to do the tech transfer, too?"

"No," Jared said with a shake of his head. "That'll take too long, and they need training for it. This is a dangerous mission, so she'll need to bring two sets of people, I suppose. One to go to Boxer Station and one to come with us.

"I know this is important, but we need to get *Athena* on her way. The messages have always been perfunctory, but we know how things change. If we assume this is going to be an easy mission, it'll go to hell."

Sean snorted. "Isn't that the damned truth. I'll start ferrying the suits over to Omega in anticipation of the transfer. Olivia can speak with Kelsey and make sure she knows the rules.

"The visitors will have escorts outside their quarters, and we'll make sure the duplicates are monitored even more closely. Marcus can keep a close eye on everyone aboard *Invincible*. We'll have to take extra precautions and be diligent when anyone leaves the ship."

"That works. Are you going to be able to manage that, Marcus?"

"Yes, Admiral. If you mandate that they be monitored for potentially hostile activity, my subroutines will make certain they don't plan anything out of the ordinary, even in their private quarters. None of the data is retained or made available to my primary personality unless it meets very stringent criteria."

"Do exactly that," Jared ordered. "I'll make sure that Kelsey knows in general what I've ordered. We'll keep the specifics to ourselves unless she directly asks. We won't lie. We just won't volunteer unnecessary detail. Understood?"

The other two nodded.

"Excellent." He focused his attention on Olivia. "We'll need a verification code to be sure you're you when you come back. How about a quote from one of the old Terran movies? 'I'm here to kick ass and chew bubblegum.' They shouldn't know that."

"Not many people would," the woman said with a sly smile. "'And I'm all out of bubblegum?' You have as odd a sense of humor as your sister. So be it. When are you sending her?"

"As soon as she finishes on *Caduceus*."

"Then your timing is good," Marcus said. "Her cutter just detached."

Jared stood. "Then let's be about our business."

* * *

IT WAS ACTUALLY the next day before Olivia stood inside Omega with Kelsey. She'd seen how worn the other woman was and put her foot down. Jared might want to move on, but eight more hours wouldn't hurt them.

The princess seemed refreshed the next morning, so it had been the right call.

"You look better," Olivia ventured as they waited for Sean to clear the area.

Kelsey had been delighted when the marines had shown her how to activate the holographic projector. That meant Olivia could see her face rather than a blank expanse of metal.

On the other hand, she was grateful they hadn't told her about the demon heads that her Kelsey favored during battle. She'd seen the one that the princess had worn while attacking the island on Harrison's World. The loyalists had tried to use a nuke to get Calder and King freed. Talbot had called the attack the Fist of God.

"That's part of it," the other Kelsey said. "Mostly I think the nanites are doing something. And the regeneration session I had right before we left might have contributed. I woke up after six hours of sleep and pestered *Invincible*'s doctor to do it. Stone sent him the details last night."

After a moment, she continued. "I can't believe that ship. She's a monster. I wonder where the derelict ships ended up in my universe? I want her."

Olivia smiled sadly. "I suspect you won't find her. She probably died ten years ago, trying to beat the AI in my system. They moved all the ships in the decade that followed, so they might have dropped them into the sun. I can't imagine why they didn't do that in the first place."

Kelsey blanched a little. "I'm sorry. I forgot for a second that was your system."

"As sad as it is, that really wasn't me. I have to accept the world as I find it. In your universe, I'm dead. In return, I know for a fact you have some people there that are dead here. It's complicated."

"Isn't that the damned truth?"

"Ladies, are you ready?" Omega asked over their com. Once they said they were, he gave them a countdown and then opened the hull of the station. The way it came in and plucked them out into space was disconcerting.

"That is very disorienting," Kelsey said. "It's like he's some kind of space monster devouring us and spitting us back out."

"You realize I can hear you, right?"

Olivia laughed at Omega's dry tone. "You're getting quite good with human humor."

"Thank you. The ship you arrived in the system is too far away to see, Princess Kelsey, but I've signaled them to come pick you up. The cutter will be in range for com in a few minutes. Should I bring the suits out now?"

"I think so," Kelsey said. "Can you do it a little bit away from us?"

"I can do it on the other side of the station, if you like. The surface of my station doesn't need to correspond to a specific point inside."

"That makes no sense. Then again, none of this makes much sense. Bring them out just a little bit away from us."

Olivia watched the hull deform about a hundred meters away, sinking down for a second and then rising with antiradiation suits standing like a cluster of statues. They began floating slowly away from the surface but stopped within a meter.

Like the suit Olivia wore, they were designed to keep station above Omega's hull. The strange metal surface wasn't ferrous, so magnetic boots didn't work. Small grav units in the suits used the built-in scanners to stay near the surface.

Then two of the suits moved, coming closer. They weren't empty. Once they got closer, Olivia saw Sean and Elise inside.

"What are you doing?" Olivia asked.

"It's my fault," Elise said. "I decided to come with you, and Sean wouldn't let me come alone. It took me a while to convince Jared to let me. Sorry."

Kelsey smiled. "Don't worry about it. You're always welcome."

Olivia gave Sean a hard look. "You were just looking for an opportunity to come keep an eye on me, weren't you?"

"I'm only making sure Elise is safe," he said with an obviously false smile of innocence. "Admiral Mertz would be very upset if I lost his wife."

"She's in no danger here," Kelsey said with a grimace. "No matter what we feel about him, she is beloved among my people."

A flicker of movement off to the side resolved itself into a cutter approaching slowly.

"I think our ride is here," Olivia said. "Kelsey?"

The other woman watched the cutter come to rest on the surface, not sticking to it, but floating much like the suits. The ramp lowered.

"Let's grab a dozen suits to take with us," Kelsey said. "We'll put them in the back of the cutter."

Getting them inside was simple. They just detached the line from the suit and tugged it along. The built-in grav unit did all the hard work.

Fifteen minutes later, they were flying away from Omega. The cutter pilot spoke briefly with Kelsey but was locked into the flight control area. They rode mostly in silence.

Olivia wondered what meeting these people was going to be like. Kelsey had been difficult at first. Would they present other problems? She hoped not. There was too much to do.

Five minutes later, the cutter docked with a thump.

"Welcome to *Ginnie Dare*," Kelsey said.

Kelsey took off her helmet and was first onto the ship. She met the armed and armored marines waiting for them. A Fleet officer stood in front of armed men and women, smiling.

Olivia recognized Commander Scott Roche. He was dead in their universe but alive here.

"Princess Kelsey," he said with a smile. "Welcome home. You brought guests?"

"I did. We brought along some radiation resistant suits. You'll need to send a team out to recover the rest of them from the alien station while I get out of this armor."

"I'll take care of it."

They all followed Kelsey into marine country. Unlike in Olivia's universe, there was a separate area for women.

The suits were designed for easy removal and entry, so Olivia and Elise speedily extracted themselves. Kelsey took longer, but they were able to help her get out.

The visitors had taken the precaution of bringing clothes and Kelsey retrieved a Fleet uniform without any insignia from a handy locker.

Once they were ready, Olivia came out and rejoined Sean, who was deep in conversation with Commander Roche. She remembered that he'd served with the other man for a long time. His death had deeply saddened her lover.

"Well, what do we do now?" she asked Kelsey.

Before the other woman could answer, Roche cleared his throat. "As much as it pains me, I need to verify who I'm dealing with. Princess Kelsey, until I can be sure you're the same person who left, I'm going to have to take you into custody."

He looked at the rest of them. "And the rest of you will be joining her in detention until I have a better grasp of what we're dealing with. You'll note that the marines have neural disruptors. Please don't make them stun you."

16

Sean was a little surprised that Scott Roche had waited as long as he had to take them into custody. He'd been expecting the move as soon as they boarded the destroyer. Perhaps Scott was concerned that the suits were like Kelsey's armor. Or that they had weapons stashed inside the suits. Or both.

Whatever the case, he wasn't going to resist. Far from it. While there were obvious differences, he felt certain he could bring the Fleet officers around more quickly than Olivia would have been able to. She might be a great politician, but a familiar and trusted face carried a lot of weight.

His assumptions were proven correct when the marines separated him from the three women. Apparently, they'd be staying in a locked compartment in marine country for now, which made sense. A commander wouldn't let someone he wasn't sure he could trust wander around his ship, even under guard.

Four marines escorted Sean into the marine briefing room where Scott sat waiting. Two stayed close at hand. They were burly but unarmed. The trailing pair had neural disruptors. If Sean put up a fight, they'd almost certainly stun everyone and sort it out at their leisure.

"Have a seat," Scott said. "We need to talk."

Once Sean was seated at the other end of the table, Scott eyed his rank tabs. "A commodore? Congratulations. You were a captain the last time I saw you."

Sean smiled wryly at this version of his dead friend. "I was a commander in my universe when the promotion came. It was a bit of a shock, let me tell you."

The other man nodded. "I'll bet. We're going to sort out the situation with Princess Kelsey in short order, but I wanted to take the time to ask you a few pointed questions.

"She came back from the alien station and told us that she was going to a different universe. I confess I didn't believe her. Not until you came aboard, you and Crown Princess Elise. I know for a fact that you're at Harrison's World and Princess Elise is back on Pentagar."

"It was hard for us to accept, too," Sean said softly, "even with the proof we found on the station. Dead bodies of others trapped there. Including multiple versions of a number of people.

"After talking with your Princess Kelsey for a while, I think I have a fair grasp of events here in this universe. Some came out better for you, but most didn't. Believe it or not, we're here to help as much as we can."

Scott leaned back in his seat and considered him. "Perhaps. That's actually above my pay grade. Oddly enough, you'll be making the final decision on what to do about… well, you.

"This is such an odd situation that I just wanted to see if it was really was you. I'm going to send you to the medical center for a checkup. It's not optional, so please don't resist."

"I wouldn't dream of doing so," Sean said. "I want to convince you that we're for real and that there are things we can do to help you fight the AIs."

"I'm sure you'll explain that in more detail, but first, my questions. When did we meet?"

"That's not a good question," Sean said. "If you're the man I think you are, I can do much better than that. We met when we were lieutenants serving on Orbital One in my universe. A lot of people might know that. I bet they don't know about Commander O'Neil."

The other man's face paled a little. "God, I hope not. What a disaster that was. I learned the lesson about dating superior officers, even if they weren't in my chain of command, the hard way with her. I never told anyone about her except you."

"It went bad fast," Sean agreed. "Let me add that you absolutely shouldn't get caught two-timing a lieutenant commander before the second date."

"I wasn't, and you damned well know it," Scott groused. "Lieutenant Arnold made the pass, not me. I turned her down, but O'Neil came in at the wrong time. Man, I had no idea she was so jealous."

The other officer shook his head. "I'm convinced. You're Sean Meyer. Now, since you're here to help us, why don't you give me the digest version of your plan?"

"In a nutshell, we had better luck retaining Old Empire technology in my universe. The suit that I came over in is an example. We have hardware and know-how that we'll be happy to share.

"Your Princess Kelsey also wants us to help her get to Terra and recover something to stop the AIs. We're going to do that, though I have my doubts about the keys being the same in both universes.

"Honestly, if we can show you how to get inside the Imperial Vault and get your own version, that would be the best outcome."

"I have difficulty imagining how that's even possible," Scott said with a shake of his head. "Terra is a long way from Pentagar or Harrison's World. We're not going to be able to just slip over there without them seeing us. We have no idea what lies between us."

The other man sighed. "Maybe if the Bastard hadn't stolen *Courageous*. Losing it hurt us badly, and I'll wager you don't have a way of getting us anything like that."

"Maybe," Sean said. "There are a couple of options that might see that outcome."

That caused Scott to sit up straight. "Really? How?"

"The first way is the alien space station. It was designed to open portals to other universes. It's going to take a while to store the energy to do so, but Omega knows where this universe is now. He can create a bridge between your universe and mine big enough to send ships through."

Sean had never discussed that potential plan with Admiral Mertz, but he wasn't giving much away. Anyone with three working brain cells could guess what the station was built to do, particularly since it already provided a way into other realities.

"That's quite a helping hand," Scott said softly. "I have difficulty believing you're so generous. You have a powerful enemy to fight, too. The same one we do."

"We have a lot of ships but not enough to stop them if they come for us. A few less won't make much of a difference if it comes to that kind of fight. Still, that's beyond the purview of what I can negotiate anyway. The second option really depends on what's in the Harrison's World system."

Scott stared at him. "A dead world, a blown-up space station, and a lot of nothing."

"Sometimes there's more than meets the eye. I assume you're taking us there."

"The fleet is waiting for us," Scott said. "We'll get you all into Captain Meyer's hands so he can decide what we need to do."

"Then it'll be easy to see if I'm right. If so, I think we'll be giving you a serious boost at no cost to ourselves."

The second idea was also not one he'd run past Admiral Mertz. That could be bad, but it would build a hell of a lot of good will. He'd just have to take the chance.

It put out some risks for the Jared Mertz in this universe, too. Yet after speaking with Princess Kelsey, Sean had the feeling that this other Mertz was more like what Sean had thought of the admiral before he met him.

It was a hell of a risk that might have terrible consequences, but these people were already fighting a civil war. The only winner if they didn't end it would be the AIs.

* * *

Elise sat on a bed in the small bunk room that her compatriots had turned into a prison cell for them. "What did you think they would do? Welcome us with open arms?"

"I didn't expect Scott Roche to lock me up," the short woman growled as she paced. "We worked out a code so that he would know it was really me."

"One we could have gotten from you," Elise said reasonably. "This probably isn't some dark plot, just a sensible precaution. He'll be along soon enough to verify who you are."

"What is he doing?" Kelsey snarled, stopping to glare at Elise with her fists on her hips. "Why make me wait? Why interrogate Sean first?"

Olivia chuckled from where she sat across from Elise. "Because he knows Sean better than he knows you, I'd wager."

"Explain that. He's been with me for over a year."

The coordinator from Harrison's World shrugged. "I don't know the specifics, but they're both Fleet. They served in the same task force for a long while. Odds are they knew each other earlier in their careers. This isn't a difficult jump to make since he *did* start with Sean."

Kelsey collapsed onto another of the tautly made bunks and draped her arm across her eyes. "This is maddening. We have so much to do already. This is going to set the timetable back even further."

"I'm pretty sure that Jared didn't expect us back right away," Elise confided. "He said he didn't, anyway. He told me that he'd allowed time in the schedule for you to convince your people we were making an honest effort and for you to select those you're bringing back."

That didn't really satisfy the other woman, but what could they do other than wait?

In the end, it was almost an hour before Commander Roche showed up in the company of Sean Meyer. The Fleet officer watched Sean and Olivia embrace with an odd look but kept most of his attention focused on his princess.

She climbed to her feet and gave him a stony look that didn't bode well for him in the short term.

"My apologies for the delay, Highness," he said deferentially. "I needed to ask Commodore Meyer a few detailed questions. Let's get your identity out of the way, shall we?"

"Space is big, but the Empire will one day fill it again," she intoned.

"That's not the passphrase," Scott said with a scowl. "You're an imposter."

Kelsey frowned. "What? Yes it is!"

The man smiled. "It is. Just checking to be sure."

"And because you want to see me squirm!" the blonde said in an accusatory voice.

"That, too. We're on our way to Harrison's World at flank speed. We'll make the flip in about two hours. Perhaps you should take the opportunity to have dinner.

"I'm assigning marines to watch over you all, so please don't get any ideas. They have orders to stun everyone if need be. Including Princess Kelsey."

The Crown Princess of the Terran Empire nodded. "I'm starved. Let's go."

Sean and Olivia followed her out. Scott Roche fell in beside Elise as she brought up the rear. Marines trailed them.

"Princess Elise," the man said cordially, "I apologize for needing to take such precautions, but we can't be too careful."

"I can't argue," she said with more than a bit of amusement. "We're likely to do exactly the same once we return with your people to our universe. None of us really knows one another, even if we've known our counterparts for years."

"So I discovered when I got into some of the more recent events in Commodore Meyer's life. Might I ask a question about your universe?"

When she nodded, he continued. "I'm dead there, aren't I? He never said so, and it seemed strange to ask the question of someone I've known so long, but I'm getting a bad vibe."

"You died at Harrison's World," she said sadly. "You and your ship. Very few of your crew survived."

"I thought as much," he said with a sigh. "Tell me then, what is Jared Mertz in your universe?"

"Did Sean say something?"

"No, which only makes me more curious."

Elise imagined Sean hadn't wanted to fall down that particular rabbit hole. "It's not as if we haven't told Kelsey. He's not the man you think he is. Not in our universe, anyway. He's a hero there. He didn't cause the civil war you suffered under, but he did his part to stop it."

Roche shook his head as if it were filled with cobwebs. "That's going to be hard to accept for all of us. I might never believe it."

"Another difference between here and my own universe is that I married him."

Roche stopped dead in his tracks. "You what?"

She tugged him back into motion with a smile. "You heard me. I married him. He's really a good man. Honestly, that's the reason I talked him into letting me come along on this trip.

"He needs an advocate. Your Kelsey has accepted that the facts in our universe aren't the same as in yours, but she's never going to be his champion. Not like our Kelsey."

"And you kept your Princess Kelsey over there so as to avoid confusion?"

"Actually, she's off on a mission. Both Jared and I wish she were here. It would make this so much easier."

The marines split them into two groups at the lift. Roche stared at her as if he couldn't believe anything she was saying. He probably couldn't.

"I think I'd like to hear more," he eventually said. "Captain Meyer is going to get as much of the story as he can, but if our peoples are going to work together, you'll need to convince many more of us about the… about Jared Mertz."

"Certainly. If it helps, I brought a ton of data and recordings with me. More than enough to convince anyone with an open mind that our Jared isn't a villain."

"That's going to be a tough sell, but I'm willing to let you make the pitch."

The lift returned, they walked in, and it whisked them away. She knew just how hard convincing them would be. The time she'd spent with their Kelsey had convinced her of that.

Still, Roche wasn't related to Jared like her blonde friend. He hadn't grown up with his prejudices. It might be possible to create enough doubt to give this a chance. If she could do that, he might set the tone for others.

Well, nothing worthwhile was ever easy.

17

In the end, Kelsey was annoyed at how easily Captain Sean Meyer accepted what his counterpart from the other universe said. One hardly seemed to need to even finish sentences before the other was nodding.

She, on the other hand, got questioned for five hours after they returned to the Harrison's World system. Kelsey finally called Sean on it inside his office on *Spear*.

"Why are you picking my story apart and accepting what other you says at face value?" she demanded. "Exactly whose side are you on, anyway?"

The corners of his mouth twitched upward, and he rose from behind his desk. "Yours, of course. I'm sorry I gave you that impression. Drink?"

"Whatever you're having. Just not beer." She shuddered. Everyone in the other universe seemed to think she loved the stuff. She couldn't understand it.

He gave her an odd look but said nothing as he poured her a glass of wine. He handed it to her and resumed his seat.

"I distrust everything that man says," Sean said. "I'm just very good at understanding him while he makes his pitch. Whereas I trust everything you say while still finding it hard to believe."

"That's convoluted," she said then took a sip of her wine. The red had good body. Pentagaran wines were the best.

"This entire situation is convoluted," he said. "I'm giving him the chance to prove at least some of what he says while Scott takes the other ladies to the corpse of Harrison's World.

"He asked me to take him to one of the gas giants. I have no idea why, but I suppose we'll find out shortly. What I really want to know is what *you* believe."

"That's not an easy question to answer," she said after thinking about it. "A lot of what I've heard is difficult to believe. Impossible, in some cases.

"Yet I've seen an Old Empire superdreadnought. I've talked with what I'm assured is a sentient AI. I've even seen mountains of evidence that Jared Mertz in that universe isn't an unmitigated bastard and traitor."

"Seeing evidence is not the same thing as being convinced by it," he observed. "Knowing the Bastard as you do, is this other man the same person?"

She sighed and sipped her wine. "I honestly don't know. Other you believes in him. The Senate testimony I saw had the other me give a him a ringing endorsement on video. My father, the man he murdered in our universe, blames Ethan for the coup in his, and he trusts Mertz implicitly. So does Elise."

Kelsey threw up her hands in frustration. "Hell, it might all be true. There, at least. I still do not believe our emperor is insane or a murderer. There are so many details that differ between the two universes, that's even believable, if you hold your nose."

The com on his desk sounded, and he answered it. "Meyer."

"Bridge, sir. We're in orbit around the gas giant."

"We'll be right out."

He rose to his feet. "Let's go see if there's anything more than gas to my doppelgänger's story, shall we?"

Kelsey followed Sean onto the bridge and stood beside the command chair when he took it over from his executive officer.

"Anything on scanners?" he asked the tactical officer.

"Nothing, sir. All clear."

Sean raised an eyebrow at Kelsey.

"I'll see what he has to say," she said as she headed for the lift.

Twenty minutes later, she was back in marine country. For the life of her, she couldn't figure out what the other Sean Meyer was playing at. There was nothing in the gaseous clouds below them.

The only saving grace to going along with his odd requests was that she couldn't imagine this as an assassination plot. It was far too strange.

The pinnace detached from the heavy cruiser but stayed in orbit near it.

"What now?" Kelsey asked the other Sean.

"I need to send a com signal. This will either work brilliantly or I'll look like an idiot."

"I'm voting for option two at the moment. Go ahead."

He sat at the marine commander's console and worked silently for a few minutes. Then he looked up at her. "Here goes nothing."

A second after he touched the control, she saw a response over his shoulder. A shoulder that relaxed just a bit when it came in, she noted.

"What the hell is that?" she asked, leaning forward. "Where did that come from, and who sent it?"

"That's the big surprise," he said with a relieved grin. "There's a hidden station down below the clouds in a clear band of atmosphere. We found the one in our universe, and I have control codes that allow us safe passage. I was hoping they were the same here, and I got lucky. So did you."

She felt her eyes narrow. "A hidden station on a gas giant? What's in it?"

"Why don't we go take a look? Let me start a homing beacon, and you can have the pinnace take us down."

Kelsey gave the pilot orders to take them down and watched the console over Sean's shoulder. The clouds were opaque to the visible spectrum, and nothing was showing on regular scanner returns. She had no idea if that was normal or not.

As the pinnace settled into the atmosphere, the scanners started picking up something below. The gas giant made a good hiding place. But why put a station deep into an out of the way place like this? It made no sense.

While she still couldn't see it, the scanners finally got a good reading on the station. It was small and wholly unimpressive.

"That's it?" she asked. "That little thing?"

He grinned at her. "That's the defensive station above the main one. See all the missile tubes along the top? It protects the prize."

"Which you're not going to tell me about," she said with a sigh. "Fine."

The Fleet officer killed the scanner readout and left only the visual display up. As they were inside the clouds, there was nothing to see.

"Wouldn't want to spoil the surprise," he said smugly.

Not for the first time, she wished this was an Old Empire pinnace that she could link her implants with. That would've made life so much easier. The things the people in the other universe had taught her to do had highlighted the limitations of her ignorance.

With no warning, the pinnace came out into a clear zone. Layers of colorful clouds above and below bracketed an incredible sight, a massive space station with some kind of odd projections on four sides.

Projections that supported massive grav cradles holding…

Kelsey sucked in a shocked breath. "Are those battlecruisers like *Courageous*?"

Sean smiled widely. "Indeed they are. And unlike *Courageous*, those four are in perfect working order. The AIs stashed them here as a reserve force. You'll need people with implants to effectively run them, but I can turn the keys over to you today as a gesture of goodwill between our universes.

"They're currently set up for automated use, so the living accommodations are extraordinarily underwhelming, but that can be remedied. You'll want to disable the AI controls as soon as practical, too.

"You won't need to scrub the computers. It's all separate hardware. In fact, the AIs left the original systems intact. All that data we gave you about the Old Empire will be inside them. You can verify it all. Hopefully, there won't be a lot of differences in the historical record."

She stared at him in shock. "You're just giving them to us?"

He shook his head. "Absolutely not. They were never ours in the first place. This is your universe. Those have always been yours. You just needed a little help finding them.

"Let's go down and take a tour. You'll want a lot of video to take back to other me. He's a suspicious sort. He doesn't trust me and will want proof. And while we're there, I'll tell you the story about how you captured that station from Rebel Empire loyalists in our universe. You'll like it."

Kelsey's brain didn't want to work. All she could do was stare at the huge space station and the four Old Empire warships in shocked awe. This was the break they needed. Now the Empire stood a fighting chance.

"Well," she said, "I'd say this settles matters for me. I'm going to urge Captain Meyer to trust you. We'll get the people selected to go back over with us as soon as we get back to *Spear*.

"Once Elise and Olivia are done at Harrison's World, we can head back to your universe. I know your boss is champing at the bit to head for Terra. Now, so am I."

* * *

Elise stood beside Commander Roche's command console as *Ginny Dare* neared Harrison's World. "You say you found no one alive on the surface? Did they use a biological weapon of some kind?"

He shook his head. "Mobile weapons platforms with Old Empire weapons, Highness. The surface is swarming with them. We didn't dare send people down."

She'd seen those damned weapons after Jared had captured this system in their own universe. They'd been manufactured on Boxer Station by the humans under the control of the System Lord. Nasty things.

"How many are we talking about?" she asked

The man shrugged. "Hundreds of thousands? Millions? More than enough to exterminate every living person on the surface over a decade."

Just the idea of such a slaughter made her want to throw up.

"We're in orbit, Captain," the helm officer said.

"Are we over the target coordinates?"

"Yes, sir."

Roche turned his attention to the tactical officer. "I want a detailed scan of the zone. Locate as many weapons platforms as possible and tag them for the team."

The woman turned from her console. "We'll have to get drones into the area to get detailed readings, but I don't see much aerial activity. Maybe a dozen are moving fast enough for me to detect from orbit."

Roche rubbed his chin. "I wonder how well they communicate with one another. If we eradicate them, will more come looking to see what happened?"

"In our universe, they were remotely controlled with only certain responses programmed in for very limited situations," Elise said. "You could try jamming them to see if that gets the other platforms excited."

"That's an interesting idea," he admitted. "Paula, get the marines ready to depart. We'll use their drones to disrupt communications down there while we examine the target coordinates."

"Aye, sir," Paula Danvers, his executive officer, said. "Lieutenant Ellis says she's ready to go."

"Excellent. Get them in motion."

After he returned his attention to the main screen, Elise cleared her throat a bit. "Has your Princess Kelsey ever met Angela Ellis?"

Roche considered that and shrugged. "I don't think so."

"You should introduce them. In our universe, Angela has become her strong right arm. Really strong, considering her size."

He smiled. "That would be kind of disconcerting. Her Highness is so short, and Angela is damned tall. There must be half a meter difference between them."

"Pretty much. Of course, she's not much like her boyfriend, either."

Roche raised an eyebrow. "Angela has a boyfriend? She's always been so focused on her duty that I've never heard a whisper about her dating anyone. Who is he? A marine?"

"Not even close," Elise said with a smile and a shake of her head. "I somehow suspect you've never met him. Carl Owlet."

"The name isn't familiar." He turned to his console and entered the data. "No record of him in Fleet service either. He's a civilian?"

"More so than just about anyone you could imagine. Do you have records for the science folks on the exploratory mission?"

"I do. He isn't listed. Who is he?"

"A computer genius from Imperial University, a graduate student who isn't old enough to drink."

Roche's eyes narrowed. "You're having fun with me, aren't you? That's a good one."

She raised her hands. "I promise, this is all real. I wish there was an interface so I could show you pictures."

"Would a tablet work? Princess Kelsey brought one back from your universe and left it for us to examine in the lab."

"Have them bring it up."

Ten minutes later, an orderly delivered the tablet, and Elise examined it. It wasn't locked.

"This will work," she said. "Let me transfer a picture."

He took the tablet when she handed it over and laughed. "Now I know you're joking! He's not even shaving regularly."

"No, but he developed the faster-than-light communications theory and hardware Kelsey told you about. That and a lot more. He saved Angela's life in a firefight, too."

Roche didn't seem convinced, so she added a video of the dinner party the emperor had thrown the night before they'd all left for the reconnaissance in force. She had a short segment of the two dancing and laughing.

He stared at the tablet as the video played. "I wouldn't believe it if I hadn't seen it with my own eyes. We'll just keep this to ourselves right now. Did everyone hear that?" he asked in a raised voice.

A chorus of "yes, sirs" came from the bridge crew.

"A genius, you say?" Roche asked quietly. "One not afraid to fight? I can't see it."

Elise considered the situation. "I'm going to play something. It's classified in my universe, and I think it should be here, too. He built Princess Kelsey a weapon, one she forbade him from recreating. It hit a few rough patches during development."

She played the recording from the Grant Research Facility where Carl used Mjölnir to destroy the weapons lab.

Roche watched it through several times before looking at her with wide eyes. "What was that? What happened in there? It looked as if it went through a plascrete wall and vaporized an Old Empire suit of combat armor."

"That's exactly what happened. The weapon has a few high-tech features. A partially collapsed matter shell, a grav-fusion power pack, a battle screen, and FTL com capability. It left his hand, broke the sound barrier on the way to the target, smashed through the wall, reversed course, and came safely back."

"I wouldn't call that safe. It really messed him up."

"He did a little more work on it. I hear it carried him and Angela to safety one night at about Mach fifteen. And that hammer was a side project he worked on for the princess after hours when he wasn't working on what he called 'the important stuff.'"

He stared at her. "Paula, make a note to have someone find Carl Owlet on Avalon and get him into protective custody. The man is obviously an Imperial treasure, even if no one knows about him."

"Will do, sir. It looks like Lieutenant Ellis is arriving in the landing zone."

Roche handed the tablet back to Elise. "Let's hope they find something useful."

18

Olivia stood behind Lieutenant Angela Ellis, trying not to throw up at the sight of her ravaged home world. The images as they'd descended to the surface showed a world scrubbed clean of life, her once proud cities now empty and rotting.

The marine gave her a look of sympathy. "I know words are entirely inadequate, but I'm sorry."

"I killed all these people," Olivia said, her voice thick with horror. "Not in this universe, but my plans are the ones that failed here, too."

She closed her eyes, more distraught than she'd expected to be. "If this world was like mine, it had a population of twelve billion people. That's a lot of blood to have on my hands."

"You did not do this," Angela said firmly. "Not even my universe's version of you. The AIs did. Never fall for that logical fallacy."

"That's cold comfort," Olivia said with a shake of her head. "In fact, it's no comfort at all. I was a fool."

"Maybe, but that won't change a thing. What's done is done. You need to find a way to get some payback. I've deployed our drones, and we're jamming the frequencies you told us to block. No reaction from the machines here or in the nearest large city. What next?"

"We need to land in the small town long enough to get out. There's a diner. Go directly in front of it.

"If we can clear the area of autonomous weapons platforms, that should make future operations safer. You're going to need to do it anyway. The cities are filled with technology that might help you."

"We're a little short of people for that kind of thing," the marine said with a shrug. "The Pentagarans can help, I'm sure. I'll signal the pilot to take us down."

After she did that, the officer turned toward her marines. "We're going in hot. Be ready to take out any of these things if it gets interesting. And if Coordinator West gives you an order to stand down or to shoot something, do it without waiting for me to confirm."

The pinnace jolted slightly, and Olivia expected the ramp to begin lowering, but it didn't.

"What was that?" she asked.

"Our gunner just took out one of the platforms. No reaction from the others at this point. They probably have assigned areas of responsibility. Whoever programmed them was an idiot."

"How so?"

The marine smiled coldly. "Because they should've mandated they come looking for units that fall out of communication rather than relying on them to report an enemy sighting. If these things don't react to losses, we'll just clear an area and slowly expand, taking them out as we go. It'll take a long time, but we can do that."

The pinnace jolted a little harder, and the ramp started down. The marines rushed out and set up a defensive perimeter before Angela allowed Olivia to start down onto the soil of the dead world.

The little town was a wreck. Most buildings were intact but had been shot to hell. A few had burned down. Even a decade after the event, she could smell a hint of ash in the air.

More unsettling were the bones scattered in the street, the remains of people who'd died when the AI unleashed the autonomous weapons platforms.

"Incoming!" Angela said. "Take cover."

Olivia wasted no time scurrying into the diner as the pinnace lifted off. A roar assaulted her ears as the marine officer and her people followed her in.

"Must've been another unit on patrol," Angela said. "The pinnace took it out with a missile. I wish we had some of those Old Empire pinnaces. Ours are pretty primitive in comparison. I'd love to have flechettes.

"Still no reaction from the other units in the area. That one must've been in a building. We didn't detect it until it came out."

"There might be more," Olivia said. "Let's get out of sight."

She led them to a freezer in the back. The smell, even after all this time, made her gag. Rotted meat filled the sealed room. Now Olivia *really* envied the marines their sealed armor.

Without pausing, she rushed to the back of the freezer, lifted the lid of a container marked "malthar bites," and scrambled down the concealed ladder. Only when she was fifty meters away did she try to breathe. Through her mouth.

"That was horrible," she gasped at the marine officer. "Let's never do that again."

"Unless there's another way out, we'll have to do it one more time. What next?"

"This tunnel ends at a grav rail terminal. If the car isn't here, we'll call it. Then four of us go on a little trip."

The rail tube stop did have a sleek car waiting for them. Dust covered it, but it looked operational. Olivia hoped it still had power and that the tunnel was clear all the way down.

"Flanders and Ulysses, you're with us," Angela said. "Everyone else spread out and keep an eye for trouble. Talk first with people. Shoot no one unless they start shooting first."

The rail car still had power and responded to her codes. The track showed as clear, but they wouldn't know for sure until they made the trip.

Ten minutes after she sent them on their way, they pulled up at a station very similar to the one they'd left behind. This one had a massive vault door where the exit tunnel had been in the first one. Dust and debris covered the platform. It didn't look as if anyone had used it in years.

Olivia really hoped the people inside were still safe. So many of her friends had been here. Not all of the resistance, of course, but the Grant Research Facility had been their main base.

"Time to see if anyone is home," Olivia said softly. "Keep your weapons down. These people will probably be nervous, and I'd rather not have a shooting match at fifteen meters."

She wondered if her codes would open the hatch but decided it would be safer just to signal for admittance. With a deep inhalation, she tapped the grimy pad beside the door. The green light came on, but no one spoke.

"I know this is going to be hard to believe, but I'm Olivia West, and I need to talk with someone. Lord Hawthorne, Captain Black, or anyone at all."

For a few seconds, she didn't think there would be a response. Then the light went out, and the hatch began opening slowly.

"Weapons down," Angela ordered. "Hands out in a nonthreatening manner."

Armed men in Old Empire powered armor rushed out and covered them. Olivia kept her hands out at her sides.

Once several of the defenders had relieved the marines of their weapons and searched Olivia thoroughly, Lord William Hawthorne and Fleet Captain Aaron Black came out.

To Olivia's deep shock, her dead fiancé, Fleet Captain Brian Drake, was with them. The sight of him was like a punch to the gut. From his poleaxed expression, the feeling was mutual.

Olivia steadied her nerves and smiled at the suspicious group. "I'm probably the very last person any of you expected to see, particularly if there's a version of me in there.

"I can prove my identity, but the short version is that I'm from an alternate universe and I've brought some people that can help you retake Harrison's World. They could also use your help."

William stepped forward and examined her. "If this is surgery, I'm quite impressed. You even have the same implant serial numbers as Olivia, something I'd always thought was impossible."

He turned to his companions and raised an eyebrow. "I can't see the harm in talking at this point. They obviously know we're here. Objections?"

The others shook their heads wordlessly, and William returned his attention to her with a wide smile. "I've always enjoyed a good story. If you can somehow convince me that you're telling the truth, I expect we'll have a lot to discuss."

Olivia allowed herself a sad smile and glanced at Brian. "Indeed. I'm looking forward to hearing what you have to say, too. Shall we find a more comfortable place to talk? Say the conference room on level seventy?"

"You intrigue me with your knowledge of the base layout," her old mentor admitted. "What else do you know?"

"This is the Grant Research Facility, and you're Lord William Hawthorne. The officers are Aaron Black and Brian Drake. Drake and I were engaged in my universe, before his untimely death."

Brian swallowed. "Olivia is dead. Those damned weapons burned her down a decade ago. I don't know who you really are, but this had better be really convincing."

Nothing was ever easy, she decided.

"Then we should sit down and have a long talk. This is Lieutenant Angela Ellis of the New Terran Empire, by the way."

"This should be fascinating," William said. "By all means, do come in."

* * *

"Incoming signal from Omega," Marcus said.

Jared looked up from the reports on his desk screen. It had been three days, and he'd started worrying after two.

"Put him on audio. Hello, Omega."

"Hello to you as well, Admiral Mertz. Your compatriots have returned and await your transport."

The relief that flooded through him was like a splash of ice water.

"Excellent. Are they alone?"

"No. It seems they've brought back all the suits you sent filled with people."

"We'll get some pinnaces on the way for them right away. Thank you for helping us."

"Oh, it's my pleasure. Life is so much more interesting with your people in it. I hadn't realized how truly bored I was before."

The connection ended, and Marcus spoke. "I have a call from Elise for you, as well. I had her holding."

"Put her on."

The screen on the desk switched from a boring report to the camera inside his wife's helmet. She'd see his face via her implants.

"Hey!" he said. "I'm glad to see you back. Really glad. Did everything go okay?"

"Nope. We were kidnapped and replaced by exact duplicates. By the way, I'm now a dominatrix."

"That isn't funny," he said repressively. "Well, except for the last part."

She grinned. "I have a different opinion. And I had to work my code word in there somewhere."

"Tell me again why you picked 'dominatrix' as a code word?"

"Because I can't imagine any version of me using the word in normal conversation. Why? Do we need to do some role-playing?"

He laughed. "I think I'll pass. How'd it go?"

"It took a little work to convince Captain Meyer to trust his doppelgänger, but our Sean did very well. You might not approve of his methods, though.

"Olivia made contact with people in the Grant Research Facility, too. They had a hard time with her story, but they sent a representative along as well. Sean isn't pleased, but that's a different kind of problem."

As much as he wanted to ask what that meant, Jared restrained himself. "I assume you have the people coming for training with you."

"We do but only half the load. Kelsey wants to have a total of two hundred. We'll have to send the suits back, but everyone is ready. It shouldn't take more than a few hours."

Jared nodded. "Was Sean able to keep duplication down to a minimum?"

"Far more easily than I'd expected, actually. The vast majority of the people coming our way are from *Ginnie Dare*. Commander Roche will be in charge of them."

Now he understood. Almost none of the crew from that ship had survived in his universe. There wouldn't be many people to mix up.

"I barely had a chance to get to know the man, but I liked him," Jared said softly. "This will be unexpectedly hard."

"Just be glad we're only dealing with other universes," Elise said with a chuckle. "Imagine if time travel were possible. I'm reminded of one of those old shows Kelsey favors. Two versions of the same grumpy man standing next to one another saying, 'I hate temporal mechanics,' at the same time."

Thankfully, that wasn't possible. At least Jared fervently hoped it wasn't possible. What a nightmare that would be.

"We'll have pinnaces to Omega in a few minutes," he said. "How did Sean convince them he was one of the good guys?"

"You know the hidden station at the gas giant near Harrison's World? He led them to it and helped Kelsey recover the four battlecruisers there."

Jared opened his mouth to object about not being consulted on something that important but paused. Would he have done anything differently? Probably not. It wasn't as if he was going to get the ships over here anyway. Or that he had any right to them.

Sean had made the right choice. It would make things difficult for Jared's doppelgänger, but he wasn't even sure the man was a good guy.

"That's fine," he said. "Most of the people here for training need to go to Boxer Station. Those ships will need crew with implants and training to be effective. Captain Cooley will probably have to rotate them back to their universe and do multiple sets.

"Thankfully, we're doing exactly that with so many Fleet personnel already that adding a few hundred more won't even make the instructors blink."

"That's what Sean said," Elise agreed. "He helped them get the ships into orbit around Harrison's World before we left, so they're already using the manual controls to start the familiarization process.

"Kelsey did some checking in the computers and verified a lot of the data we gave her about the Old Empire. She's sent a ship back to Pentagar to meet with the people on Erorsi and bring back help from Pentagar. Since the Rebel Empire didn't send a fleet like they did in our universe, they have a little more time to get ready."

Jared had been considering that problem. If the Rebel Empire invaded the other New Terran Empire, there would be nothing there that could stop them and Pentagar would fall first.

He could pass along the technology to build flip-point jammers, even without the people at the Grant Research Station, but it would take a long while before the others could use it. That was cutting-edge stuff.

The scientists at his Grant Research Facility were a few months away from having the ability to mass produce flip-point jammers—if creating three or four every month counted as mass production. Still, they'd have a few they could pass on to their friends in the other universe while their Grant people got busy playing catch up.

"Well, I should let you go," he said. "I'll be there to greet you all when you come aboard."

"Excellent. Plan for dinner and some alone time tonight. Talk to you soon."

Jared leaned back in his chair after the call ended. This side show was over. It was about time. He needed to get back to the real mission, or they'd never get to Terra at all.

19

Sean tried not to scowl at Fleet Captain Brian Drake as they stepped into *Invincible*'s marine country after stripping off their hard suits. The other man had no control over this awkward situation. It wasn't his fault he'd lived in the other universe and that his Olivia hadn't.

Now the two of them were talking like long-lost lovers. Which, of course, they were, ones who had been engaged before their respective untimely deaths.

Since the other man wasn't shooting looks at him, Sean was willing to bet Olivia hadn't told Drake about him yet. That didn't necessarily mean anything, but he was concerned.

"Is something wrong, Commodore?" Scott Roche asked quietly.

"Just a personal matter," he said. "Nothing to worry about."

The other man's eyes narrowed. "You and Coordinator West?"

He allowed himself a snort. "I forgot how perceptive you were, Scott. Yes. And of course, her dead fiancé. Who is now in our universe and alive again."

Scott winced. "Ouch. I can see where that might make for a few awkward moments. You need to get that settled before those old feelings get a chance to rekindle."

"I don't think she'd appreciate me puffing out my chest and strutting around. Or peeing on her leg."

"Probably not," the other man conceded. "But you'd better put him on notice. Or would you prefer someone else pass him the word? That might lower the tensions once it comes out."

He considered that possibility. "Are you volunteering?"

"I suppose I am. I've known you a long time, and I owe you. Well, some version of you. We're friends, and that's what friends do."

"I'll have to pass, but thanks. This is the kind of thing that I need to do in person. So, what do you think of *Invincible*?" he asked, changing the subject firmly.

"I had no idea anything this powerful was even possible. Did the Old Empire make anything bigger?"

"No. This was the most powerful mobile unit in sheer firepower, though I'd argue the carriers are more dominant once you add their fighters in. Boxer Station is a lot more dangerous in a stand-up fight, but it can't move. We'd never have beaten it if we hadn't ambushed the AI from point blank range."

Scott pursed his lips. "Really? I didn't think it was that tough."

"They'd probably moved the AI. A regular computer doesn't compare. Not even close. You'll find out soon enough."

The hatch to the main corridor slid open, and Admiral Mertz stepped inside. Sean sensed Scott tensing beside him.

"Relax," he said softly. "This is not the same man from your universe."

His friend gave him a somewhat incredulous look. "Are you honestly telling me you don't believe this guy is a power-hungry usurper? Well, potential usurper over here, I suppose."

"Without even a trace of doubt," Sean said firmly. "I was wrong about him in this universe, and so was Captain Breckenridge. This man had every opportunity to take the Imperial Throne and didn't. Our Princess Kelsey trusts him for good reason."

Scott sent him a sidelong glance of uncertainty. "If you say so. I guess it's your universe."

"He might really be the Bastard in yours," he said with a slight smile. "Circumstances are different. You'll have to figure that out on your own."

Mertz cleared his throat. "If I could have your attention? My name is Jared Mertz, and I want to ask you all to give me a little benefit of the doubt as we get to know one another. I understand that I don't have the best reputation in your universe. Give me a chance to prove I am not that man."

"Well, Princess Elise married him," Scott said softly. "She always seemed like a sharp operator to me. If everyone here tells me things are different, I'll give him a chance."

The Fleet officer from another universe stepped forward. "Commander Scott Roche, Admiral. Might my senior officers meet with you for a few minutes, so we can settle what we're going to be doing?"

"Absolutely, Commander," Mertz said with a nod. "We'll use the marine conference room right here. Commodore Meyer, if you'd get everyone else settled, we'll be pulling out for Boxer Station as soon as the pinnaces get back with the second load."

"Aye, sir."

The admiral escorted Scott, Princess Kelsey, Captain Drake, Lieutenant Commander Paula Danvers, and the other Doctor Guzman into the briefing room. Elise and Olivia joined them. He'd be willing to wager he could guess at the seating diagram.

He sighed inwardly and tagged Marcus to ask about the arrangements.

It turned out that Marcus had set aside temporary quarters for the people going to Boxer Station and wrangled a block of cabins for those staying on the superdreadnought for the mission. It would be easier to keep an eye on them if they were clustered together.

Unable to get his mind off the odd fix he was in, Sean made his way to the observation lounge. The compartment didn't really have a window stretching from bulkhead to bulkhead, but the holo emitters certainly made it appear as if it did.

There wasn't much to see as the ship powered through the cloud of radioactive particles surrounding the black hole at the center of the Nova system. That was fine by him since it meant he was alone and that gave him privacy to think.

The best outcome was if Drake stayed on Harrison's World while Olivia went with the mission as planned. He wasn't holding his breath on that.

The worst-case scenario was both of them staying. The odds of that were higher than Sean liked. Perhaps he should encourage them both to come on the mission. Was he likely to get push back from Olivia?

On reflection, he didn't think so. She was in a relationship with him, and he didn't see her stepping out, even with a formerly dead lover.

Yet people were complicated. Did he talk with her about it or trust that she'd do the right thing?

He slumped into a chair and stared sightlessly toward the screen. No matter what he did, there was a chance this would all blow up in his face. God, he'd rather fight a desperate space battle than contemplate losing her.

* * *

Kelsey stared out at the veritable sea of derelict ships floating around Boxer Station. With her implants, the superdreadnought's scanners were more than capable of seeing the scope of the scene.

"There are tens of thousands of ships here," she murmured. "When I learned about the Old Empire, I had no idea they had so many. Why?"

"And these are only the ones that weren't destroyed outright during the Fall," Mertz agreed. "They had several reasons. The biggest one was that they weren't the only human civilization out there. True, they were the biggest, but the others were a threat, particularly if they ever banded together. And many of them were not very friendly.

"Take the Singularity. They left the Old Empire in the early days, going deep into the void to set up a society more to their taste. The two societies eventually found one another again and they fought a constant low-level battle along their entire border for thousands of years. To the point that it became like ritual and tradition."

"Over what?" she asked, giving Mertz her full attention.

"Mostly over implants and genetic engineering. The Old Empire went the route of cranial implants, which the Singularity saw as an abomination that endangered Humanity. Rightly, as it turned out.

"On the other hand, the Singularity chose to edit the human genome to create a class system that the Old Empire saw as monstrous. As you might imagine, each was eager to do the other harm, and they raided across their common border for something like twelve centuries.

"Each side built a massive fleet to make certain they could defend themselves if need be. Or to crush their enemies if the opportunity presented itself."

She considered that situation. "I wonder what happened to them after the Fall. The Singularity, I mean. Did the AIs conquer them, too?"

Mertz shrugged. "No one knows. The Singularity was on the far side of the Rebel Empire. Since the AIs don't exactly share information, they could have crushed them, too. Or they might have stopped at the border. I suppose we'll find out one day."

She gestured around them, not at the ship but at the derelicts floating all around *Invincible*. "How many of these do you think are salvageable? God, I wish there were still some in my universe. They would be an incredible boon."

"If even one percent is reparable, I'll be astonished," he said sadly. "These are mostly just huge coffins filled with millions of dead Fleet personnel."

"What do you do with them?" That was a morbid question, but she wanted to know.

"We take them to Harrison's World for burial. The Spire on Avalon isn't capable of holding the number of people we're talking about, so Coordinator West built one there in an area that was large enough to hold such a memorial.

"The process of getting the poor bastards there is slow and time-consuming, but it has to be done. We have entire crews of people recovering the bodies, identifying them if they can, and seeing they get to Avalon before the wrecks are sent to the breakers to salvage what they can."

"Can you really afford to use resources like that? You need to put every person toward getting ready for the enemy and the fight that has to be coming. Why not just bury the dead in space? Drop them into the sun?"

He seemed to consider her for a long time. "It comes down to respect. They died defending the empire and never knew that to an extent they succeeded. We owe our brothers and sisters in Fleet the rest that our ancestors promised. Sometimes the right thing isn't easy. You do it anyway."

That certainly wasn't the answer she'd expected to hear from the Bastard. Since they hadn't found all these ships in her universe, she had no idea what the man there would have thought.

This wasn't going to be easy, she decided. Not only was this man challenging her assumptions, the records she'd reviewed certainly supported the general consensus that he could've used this ship to put his boot on the throats of everyone in the New Terran Empire. And he'd chosen to do nothing of the sort.

Instead, he'd fought beside another version of herself to stop a coup and keep her father on the throne. And alive.

The recordings she'd seen of Ethan in the Imperial Throne room getting ready to sentence this man to death spoke volumes about both. Her brother here had been mad. She was convinced of it now.

Oh, the implant recordings that Mertz had put into the record could have been forged, she supposed, but they matched the statements of the Imperial Guard present at the time. Added to so many other clues and evidence, she was sure Ethan had been mad here. Paranoia and megalomania, at the very least.

That didn't mean he was mad in her universe. Not even close. Her brother was as sane as she was. She'd spent countless hours going over everything she could remember about their interactions and how he differed from the man in this universe.

She'd stake her life on her brother. And that probably meant the Mertz there was just the kind of man she'd always believed, but a worm of doubt still existed deep inside her mind.

Well, that wasn't a problem she was going to solve today. She needed to put her distaste aside and give this Jared Mertz a chance, as difficult as that was. She needed his help to get to Terra and to recover the override.

Potentially, she needed his help repeating the entire mission in her universe. Only he had the DNA to use the key and open the Imperial Vault. What if the override required his DNA, too?

The Bastard had taken the Imperial Scepter when he'd killed her father. He hadn't had implants at the time, so he probably hadn't had a clue what it really represented. Well, unless his sources inside the Imperial Palace were a lot better than they all suspected.

With the resources aboard *Courageous*, it was likely he'd found a way to get implants. Could he have worked out the secret? It was always possible the man would try for the override himself with the goal of making the AIs answer to him.

As horrifying as that idea was, that was also a problem for another day.

Kelsey forced herself to smile. It felt unnatural in this man's presence, but the two of them were going to be working closely together for the foreseeable future.

"When do we leave for Terra?"

"We'll head out to make the yearly report for the AI as soon as we get your people settled on Boxer Station and Olivia gets back from our Harrison's World. The target system isn't too far away, so we can probably leave from there and make our way toward Terra."

"Do you think we can get to Terra? From what you've said, the Rebel Empire has the entire system isolated."

"We have to," Mertz said with a shrug. "The Empire is depending on us."

Indeed, difficult times truly did show a person's character.

20

Olivia watched Brian as the cutter descended toward the newly constructed spaceport on her home world. The System Lord had vaporized the original spaceport a decade ago when it locked the planet down.

This time, they'd taken the precaution of moving it far away from any city and would not allow it to become heavily populated. If war came again, millions need not die because of where they lived.

The people working there had to deal with the imposition of a long commute by hypersonic grav rail from the closest population center several hundred kilometers away. Only people on duty or in transit were at risk, and they'd have a lot of warning if the enemy came.

Of course, any enemy would have to deal with the flip-point jammers and the heavy Fleet presence in the system. Sean's command was growing to be almost as powerful as the one Jared commanded, if one included the repaired ships being worked up and the Fleet personnel here for training. The Rebel Empire would not crack this nut easily.

"This is unreal," Brian murmured as they came over the landing pad and settled on the plascrete. "We haven't dared send out more than a few stealthed drones, but it was more than enough to know our world was dead. Now it lives again."

"It made me want to vomit," she said as she unstrapped. "Knowing that I came up with the plan that killed everyone. Twelve billion people, dead because of me."

He stopped and turned toward her. "You and the entire leadership council. None of us knew how powerful the System Lord was. What I'd like to know is why it didn't kill everyone in this universe."

She didn't answer as they exited the cutter. Honestly, she wasn't even sure what the answer was.

"What was *Invincible*'s status when the System Lord attacked?" she asked as they went down the ramp.

A sleek black grav car sat waiting for them. Overhead, several others circled. Her guards. She'd ordered them to keep their distance today. Farther out, far beyond sight, Fleet fighters kept overwatch. That last was more a training exercise than a need.

"It was almost operational," he responded as they climbed into the car. "I'd only just arrived back at Grant when all hell broke loose. We never did figure out what set the Lord off, but it started using the orbital bombardment platforms to blow the hell out of everything. The most likely thing was that it had somehow detected *Invincible*."

His eyes grew shadowed. "You were at the government center when it destroyed the capital. I've always comforted myself with the idea that you never really knew what was happening before you died. You didn't have time to be afraid."

Olivia closed the door behind her, strapped in, and patted his hand. "I'm sorry you had to live with that."

He nodded, but his gaze was penetrating. "I died here. How?"

"You were trapped with the crew on *Invincible* when the Lord locked the system down. Something different triggered it here, which might explain the difference in its response.

"Without the computer, there was no way you could fight, so you and your people waited until supplies ran out and then ended things on the flag bridge. I was only able to bring you home and bury you a few months ago."

"It sounds as if you had it harder."

She shook her head. "No. You had to live in a hole while the AI murdered our people. Still, we don't have to make this a comparison of who had it worse."

"I suppose not. Did you ever find someone else?"

His expression told her that he probably hadn't.

"Only recently. You were a hard man to get over. You've met him. Commodore Meyer."

The corners of Drake's mouth edged up. "Ah. That explains the odd looks of semi-hostility he kept shooting me. I wasn't sure what to make of it. Now I know."

"He's actually a very good man. You're very much alike, I think, which, on reflection, might not be the best thing."

She faced Brian squarely. "I'm committed to my relationship and my work is here, just as yours is back on *your* home. As much as this might seem like a second chance for us, I don't want you to build unreasonable expectations."

He shook his head sadly. "I'll admit I've allowed myself the fantasy. Who wouldn't? I'll try not to make an ass of myself, but I'm putting you on notice. If your relationship doesn't work out, I intend to try again."

Olivia rubbed her face. "Why does everything have to be so complicated? You need to find a woman in your universe. One that can make you happy. Our time is done."

"I disagree. In fact, I resoundingly reject your premise. Aaron and Lord Hawthorne have everything there well in hand. Since I'm not alive here, we decided I would make the perfect emissary from our universe to yours.

"If the two Grants can work together, imagine what they can do. We could potentially double our capacity for research at the very edge of Imperial technology. And part of that mission means bringing our peoples closer.

"Though I'm not staying here after I make the introductions and start the process by sending some of your people back to my Grant. Lord Hawthorne ordered me to accompany this Admiral Mertz on this mission to learn what I could. So I'll still be with you for a while."

That was just about the worst thing for them both, she imagined. Could she order him to remain here? Ask Jared to block him from the mission?

Probably not and develop the kind of relationship the two Grants needed. One more complication. Sean would be thrilled. Well, more thrilled than if she were staying here on Harrison's World with Drake, in any case.

She stared out of the grav car. They were passing over the farmlands surrounding the Grant Research Facility. It was closer to the spaceport than the city, only in the opposite direction.

That was by design. They'd wanted covert access to the flight patterns to insert their own traffic. No one knew it, but the flight controllers at the port were all members of the resistance. Anyone with insight into the traffic around the port went through intense scrutiny.

They were almost to the small town nearest Grant when she looked back at Brian. "I *can* imagine what is possible, but I don't want you to have the unreasonable fantasy that Sean and I will break up. That isn't going to happen.

"In fact, I've been expecting him to propose at any time. Meeting you will almost certainly speed things along on his end. In fact, if he doesn't mention it before we leave on this mission, I will. He and I cannot and will not have you dividing us. I'm sorry."

He grunted as if someone had punched him in the gut. "That's hard, but you were always the kind of person that squarely faced her problems. I'll bet you make one hell of a coordinator."

"You're damned right I do." After a moment, she sighed. "Don't take this rejection personally, Brian. I loved you so deeply that I couldn't imagine life without you. Now, when I've finally found a way through the pain, you can't expect me to come running back into it."

"What a difference a few months could have made." He sighed. "It's going to take me a while to get over you again, but seeing you happy will help. Hurt, but help, if you know what I mean. Maybe that's what I need to move on."

The grav car started descending. He smiled as he looked down at the town. "I want to get some malthar bites. I can't tell you how badly I've missed them. In fact, I've been authorized to negotiate a shipment for my Grant."

She laughed, more than happy to move past the awkward conversation they'd absolutely had to have. "I'll see that we send some back. I'd imagine there are plenty of wild malthar back there. I can probably manage some processing equipment to help you get the plant back up and running after you clear enough of the autonomous weapons platforms."

"It's going to take years to clear them out," he said glumly.

"Maybe not. I've been thinking about that. Harrison has the original data cores from the System Lord here. I'll wager the override codes are buried in the data somewhere. If we can send them back, you might be able to order the platforms to shut down all at once."

He frowned. "Who is Harrison?"

Olivia smiled widely. "That's an even longer conversation. I'll tell you on the way back to *Invincible*. Right now, you need to focus your attention on making a good impression."

"That didn't work so well with you," he grumbled.

"Let it go."

He nodded, but she wasn't convinced he was ready to release all hope of a reconciliation from beyond the grave. That would cause them problems going forward if she didn't scotch it early.

Well, she had time once they got back to the ship to deal with it. Maybe she should ask Jared to marry them. That would end this particular issue. She hoped.

* * *

IT WAS LATE when Elise finally got Jared alone for dinner. Getting their visitors moved to Boxer Station had taken more effort than she'd imagined, but it was done.

And now that Olivia had returned from Harrison's World, the fleet was —finally!—on its way to the meeting place to give the Rebel Empire their false report.

The defenders at Harrison's World had turned off the flip-point jammer long enough to send a stealthed probe through. No ships were detected, so the Rebel Empire was still unaware of the change in management.

With safety assured, the destroyer *Athena* had led the way through. Sean Meyer was in command of her for now. This part of the Rebel Empire was basically empty of inhabited worlds, so they had a week or so until they needed to get some real distance from the fleet.

It would take them a bit more than a week and a half to get to the destination. They'd join Sean on *Athena* once they needed the separation from the fleet.

But enough of that for now. Her days in this luxuriously large stateroom

—relatively speaking—were limited, so she planned on savoring them, not worrying about the future.

"Has Olivia spoken with you?" she asked once they'd finished their meal and were relaxing on the couch with wine.

"About what?" Jared asked.

"I'll take that as a no. Sean."

He frowned a little. "Why would she talk with me about Sean? Is there a problem?"

"You could say that," she said as she put her glass down on the end table. "Its name is Brian Drake."

That caused her husband's frown to deepen. "He's a problem? I thought they used to be close friends."

"And he'd like to make that true again."

His expression cleared. "Ah. Ouch. That *is* a complication. How can I assist her with that particular problem, though? It seems as if the chance for that is gone. I could've made sure he stayed at Harrison's World if you'd told me. You being anyone, actually."

"No, you couldn't," she said firmly. "Think about it. How would that have affected his people's relationship with us?"

Jared opened his mouth to respond but paused, obviously reconsidering his first thought. "Maybe not in the best way," he admitted, "but those were waves we could have managed. What can I do now?"

"Marry Sean and Olivia as soon as they ask. And they will. Do not delay."

"You sound so sure. Of course, I've never met anyone as canny as you at predicting this kind of thing."

"That's very kind and most diplomatic," she said dryly, "but Olivia is much more shrewd, and I know it. Believe me, the education I'm getting on this trip will be well worth my time.

"If they wait a full day, I'll be shocked. My advice is for you to prepare to hold the ceremony within an hour's notice. Get all your ducks in a row and be ready to execute the ambush."

His eyebrows crept up. "Ambush, is it? How much warning do you think Sean is going to get?"

"Virtually none. Are they scheduled to come to *Invincible* tomorrow?"

"We're having a briefing, but I'd assumed he was doing it remotely."

"Mark my words," she said with a smile. "He'll attend in person. Olivia will be having that discussion with him tonight. Or if she's feeling particularly subtle, tomorrow morning."

"An ambush, indeed. I'm not betting against you. I'll review the details in the morning. It's a good thing I have recent familiarity with the marriage ceremony."

She tipped her glass back and finished her wine. "I'm certain there are significant differences between the Pentagaran ceremony and what Fleet does. Have you ever performed one?"

"I've never had that privilege," he said as he finished his own drink and set the glass down.

"There you go," she said as she stood. "It will be a pleasure, I'm sure."

His smile widened as he stood. "That word brings something completely different to mind for me. Are you ready for bed?"

"Yes," she said as she extended her hand toward him. "But I'm not at all tired."

"Me, either."

21

Kelsey stared uncertainly at Doctor Stone and the pair of Doctor Guzmans. They were kind of spooky standing together like that.

"Are you sure this is the *right* first step?" she asked. "It seems as if replacing my eye would fall later in the process. Isn't that kind of a big thing?"

"It is," Lily Stone confirmed. "It's also the largest impediment to the regeneration process. Forgive me, Highness, but that's a far larger—and uglier—prosthetic than you need. The Old Empire had the technology to make them look lifelike. Yours is anything but."

As if she needed to hear the woman say that. Kelsey knew how hideous she was, inside and out. The Pale Ones had turned her into a beast, and she'd fought like one.

She was really getting tired of hearing how well her doppelgänger had done in comparison, though. Even when she wasn't explicitly mentioned.

That woman had caught all the breaks. Everywhere Kelsey had bad luck, the other woman had good. It was almost as if she'd been stealing luck across universal boundaries.

Well, it hardly mattered where she started the healing process started, did it?

"What's involved?" she asked the Guzman twins.

Having them both there was an odd experience and really pressed home that she was in another universe. The two men were identical, other than some purely cosmetic differences in appearance like hair length and different rank tabs on their uniforms.

That reminded her that she needed to tear a page from her doppelgänger's playbook and promote some of her people when she got back.

"It's not as complex as it sounds, Highness," the Justin Guzman from this universe said. "And it's absolutely necessary to give us access to the tissue on your face. The plate has undoubtedly scarred the flesh beneath it.

"With the assistance of your nanites, we can regenerate that to a great degree. Perhaps even completely with a number of sessions, though I hesitate at tempting you with an outcome that may prove elusive."

"What are the risks?" she asked. "I've become a bit risk averse in the last few years."

"None, really," Stone said. "The optic nerve is sound, so the hardware replacement is straightforward. The new prosthetic eye will fit into the socket more easily and look completely natural.

"From the conversations I've had with the techs who built the eye, they've worked hard to duplicate all the Raider enhancements your natural eye has now and added even more capability.

"They were a bit cagey with the specifics, but they were trained by Carl Owlet, so that's not at all surprising. He loved surprises. And geekdom."

"I've heard his name before in passing," Kelsey said as she tried to get into the right mental space to agree to this surgery. "I didn't know him in my universe. You speak of him as if he were dead. Did you lose him?"

"More like we've misplaced him. He's away on the same mission the other you is on. We're hopeful they can get home with the data and equipment they stole from the Rebel Empire soon, but we do worry."

"What kind of data and equipment?"

"The manufacturing specifications and equipment to make Raider implants and sentient AIs."

A cold chill washed over Kelsey, and her throat threatened to swell shut. "I've spoken with Marcus, but the idea of making more of those things fill me with dread. What could *possibly* go wrong?"

"Why don't you lie back so we can get started," Stone said. "As for AIs, we're behind the Rebel Empire and really don't have a choice if we want to beat the bastards.

"Trust me, our allies are a lot more like people than the Lords. Marcus and Harrison are firmly on our side. Harrison is really the driving force behind the repair ships in the graveyard. Without him running everything, I can't imagine we'd be nearly as far along."

Kelsey lay back on the operating table. "Is this going to hurt?"

"There will be some pain once the procedure is complete, even with regeneration," her Guzman said. "We're going to be reworking the tissue under the current prosthetic plate. With your pharmacology unit, that should be more than manageable and will abate over the course of the next several days."

"Let's get it over with, then."

"The somatic unit will put you out without transition, and you'll wake up the same way," Stone said. "Basically, you'll blink, and it'll be over."

"And I'll feel like you punched me in the face. Got it."

Stone laughed. "Nothing like that. The pain will be more of a dull ache."

"Like the rest of the dull aches I have? Wonderful. What's the plan on addressing my other damage?"

"You're stalling," Stone said accusingly. "Goodnight, Highness."

Kelsey opened her mouth to object and blinked when Stone suddenly was on the other side of her. Neither Guzman was in evidence. They'd vanished.

"That was very disconcerting," she informed the Fleet physician. "You might want to make note of where people are when you put someone under just so you can make the return a little less jarring."

Stone nodded. "I hadn't considered that, but it's a good idea. We could put the primary surgeon as the only visible person and make sure that things are the same once the surgery is complete. I'm still getting used to the Old Empire technology, even after a few years."

"I take it everything went okay?" Kelsey asked. "My vision seems about the same. The new eye works to that extent."

The doctor put a hand on her shoulder when Kelsey made to sit up. "Let's give your body a few minutes to adjust. Here's a mirror."

Kelsey took the small mirror the other woman offered and examined her face. To her pleased astonishment, the metal plate was gone, and her left eye looked just like its natural counterpart.

The flesh around it where the plate had been was red and rough, but it was there. And the nasty scar that was the testament to the wound that had taken her natural eye was much reduced.

"Wow. I never expected to look like a human being again," she said, her throat threatening to close up with unexpected emotion. "I was always going to be that cyborg woman."

"You will look completely normal once the tissue has a few more regeneration sessions," Stone assured her. "And to answer your other question, I expect we'll be able to remove the visible scars all across your body now that we can use the full-body regenerator.

"The micro scars inside your body may or may not completely heal even with a combination of regeneration and your new Raider nanites. Only time will truly tell. At the very least, the pain your pharmacology unit is suppressing should disappear."

Her face ached a little, but nothing like Kelsey had expected. Perhaps this was going to work out. "How many regeneration sessions are you anticipating and over what space of time?"

Stone's expression took on a calculating air. "Let's plan on five initial sessions, one per day. It will take more, but I need to see how they progress before I can make an educated guess at the overall duration.

"No more than ten sessions, I'd imagine. By the time you need to depart for the destroyer, we'll almost certainly be done."

Kelsey sighed. She would look like a regular person again. That alone made this trip so worthwhile. "What about the eye? Did your tech friends tell you about their special sauce?"

"They did not," Stone said, somewhat peevishly. "They insist on going over it themselves with you later today. Let's sit you up and start checking basic things like your balance. You should be fine, but I want to be sure there is no subtle difference in the combined input to your brain."

"Can we do lunch afterward? I'm starving."

"Why don't I have something delivered?" Stone countered. "We're going to be busy for the next few hours."

"I suppose," Kelsey grumbled. "I hope I get used to my metabolism one day."

* * *

Sean was shocked at the speed at which his life was changing but still thrilled. He hadn't expected a matter-of-fact proposal over breakfast, but that's what he'd gotten.

Much more surprising was her proposed timetable. He'd hoped to marry her soon, but he had expected a little more than two hours' notice.

She was obviously as concerned about Brian Drake as he was, if for somewhat different reasons.

While she made sure that he understood she wanted this because she loved him, there was also a somewhat cold-blooded element of political expediency behind her desire to make it happen quickly.

He wanted to seal the deal so the other man would back off. She felt the same but also had to make sure there was no damage to the political relationship between the two Grant facilities.

Sean admired the way politics flowed in her blood, but it was sometimes a trifle annoying.

And then she'd dropped it on him that she intended to ask Admiral Mertz to marry them as soon as their planning meeting was done this morning. His objection that they needed time to prepare was met with amused derision.

Olivia had been busy last night before she'd come to bed. She'd enlisted people to make sure her dress was ready, his dress uniform was perfect, and that her friends received more notice than he did.

Honestly, it felt a little like an ambush, and he'd probably feel differently if he hadn't planned to speed the process along himself.

Now he was aboard *Invincible* and immersed in the planning session with the captains and executive officers of each ship in the fleet. They'd come into this mission with a rough idea of what would happen, but now they were gaming out the things that might go wrong.

"As I see it, the two worst possibilities are that they see through our ruse or a random ship happens to chance across us on the way there," Admiral Mertz summed up. "What can we do to further mitigate those possibilities?"

"If the status delivery takes place like all those over the last ten years,"

Marcus said, "there's only a very small chance of them finding anything in the message or the destroyer to cause them to look deeper.

"And by small, I mean inseparable from zero. The reports are virtually copied and pasted from one year to the next, and Athena is programmed with all appropriate responses the robotic destroyers have had."

"And if they do get frisky, we have a fleet of ships that has significantly more firepower than we anticipate finding in that system," Sean added. "That doesn't guarantee anything, but we should keep the odds in mind. Frankly, I think a random ship is a much bigger threat."

Mertz nodded. "I agree. We have FTL probes out in all directions, as well as positioned in the flip points ahead of us and behind, in this system and the ones beyond. What else can we do?"

They batted various options around, but nothing seemed more effective than staying slow to not show up on a ship's scanners. Before they transitioned to the next system, they'd send scouts and use a spread of FTL probes to make sure the area was clear.

There was always going to be a risk that they missed a ship, but these actions made it far less likely they would be seen.

After an hour of exploring the possibilities, Mertz seemed satisfied. "Okay, we'll maintain that posture until we're one system away from the target system. None of the intervening systems is occupied, so that won't be a worry.

"Now, while this meeting is adjourned, I'd like to ask you all to remain for a little longer."

He turned a wide smile toward Sean. "It so happens that Commodore Sean Meyer and Coordinator Olivia West have asked me to wed them today, and I think this is the perfect time and audience. All of the other guests have been impatiently waiting for us to finish talking, and the time has arrived."

Sean's stomach did a little flip, but it wasn't fear. No, never that. Just a little nervousness.

The sour expression on Captain Drake's face pleased Sean, but the man couldn't know that was why Sean was grinning. Well, okay, he probably did.

"I'll need a few minutes to change into my dress uniform, Admiral," Sean said.

"They've taken the liberty of setting up the next cabin over as a dressing room," Mertz said. "The ladies are done, and it's all yours. While you change, we'll get the decorations up. No rush. I hear the coordinator has scheduled you an entire twenty minutes to get ready."

That caused a wave of laughter among the officers present. Even Drake smiled a little. His Olivia must've had many of the same traits.

"Well, I suppose I'd best go get ready," Sean said as he stood. "I don't suppose there's a honeymoon suite on *Athena* that I missed."

Mertz grinned. "And you'd be wrong. I've had the officers and men under your command rearranging the schedules so you have the next few days off and setting up what amounts to a lavish hotel suite for your honeymoon. The manservants that my wife insisted guide my new steward are making sure nothing is forgotten.

"Now, if it were me, I'd plan on taking a trip somewhere very nice once we return to the Empire, but this will do for now, I hope."

The admiral made a show of looking at the door. "Your bride is impatiently waiting for you to get into the changing room so she can get here unseen, Commodore. You are dismissed."

Another laugh filled the room as Sean headed for the hatch. Knowing his bride to be, that wasn't too far off the mark. He'd make sure to dress quickly and ping the admiral through his implants to be sure they were ready before he returned.

Anticipation of being married to his love overrode the anxiety about the ceremony itself as he strode down the corridor and into the waiting arms of four stewards. He gave Drake's discomfiture one last pleasant thought and then put the man out of his mind.

This was the first day of his new life. He wanted to focus on his bride. His wife. After all, if things went badly, he might be leaving her a widow in a week and a half. Best to live each day as if it were their last.

22

Ten days later, Jared Mertz sat on the bridge of the destroyer *Athena* as she prepared to make the flip into the target system. He'd done everything he could to prepare, but he realized this was going to be make-or-break for the New Terran Empire.

Sean Meyer stood beside his chair, obviously just as nervous as he was. "What do you think we're going to find?"

"The same thing that every destroyer from Harrison's World has found for the last ten years," Jared said. "There's no reason to expect anything different. If something has changed, there has to be a reason for it, and that means trouble.

"Unfortunately, we don't know a lot about what's here or what the procedures are. The records merely report the destroyer made the trip and transmitted the report on command. The specifics are unknown."

The helm officer, Commander Janice Hall, turned in her seat. "We're ready to flip, Admiral."

"Take us across," he said firmly, suppressing his worry.

Unlike with previous systems, he didn't dare risk sending an FTL probe into this one. He knew it was occupied. Potentially, there were ships watching the flip point, even if there were none in the current system. If a strange probe popped out, that would set off alarms.

That didn't mean he couldn't leave some on this side, which he had.

The rest of the fleet he'd brought with him was located back at the flip point they'd used to enter this system, far out of normal scanner range but getting data from the probes *Athena* had deployed for them. That also put them well within the range to receive any FTL communication from *Athena* from the target system.

The Rebel Empire did not have FTL communications, so they wouldn't be expecting this capability. That didn't mean it was undetectable, however. So unless he had to, Jared would remain silent. The rest of the fleet knew that he'd only call if they ran into trouble. Otherwise, he'd send the report he was required to send and return.

At that point, they'd have to go around the target system via another set of flip points to get to Terra, taking at least a week longer to get there and arriving at a different entry point to the home system. That couldn't be helped. The lay of flip points was what it was. He would just hope that didn't come to pass.

"Flipping the ship," Hall said.

A brief queasiness accompanied the destroyer flipping into the target system. Everyone had implants, so the nausea that used to accompany every flip was no longer a major issue. Thank God.

"Ships detected," Commander Johan Berman, their tactical officer, said. "Weapons platforms detected. Significant numbers of both surrounding this flip point."

Jared tapped into *Athena*'s scanner feed using his implants. Berman was right. This was a lot of ships and battle stations in a globe around the flip point they'd just come through.

The robotic destroyers that the System Lord sent to make the yearly reports from Harrison's world did not bring back scanner records from this system. Jared couldn't be certain if this was new or standard procedure. They'd have to proceed under the assumption that it was standard.

"We're being challenged," Hall said. "The computer has responded as programmed. We've been instructed to proceed into the system."

Jared frowned. "We're sending a report. Shouldn't we be doing it from here?"

The helm officer shrugged. "I have no idea. That wasn't in the records."

"Well, if nothing else, this is going to give us a good opportunity to see what else is in the system," Jared said with a sigh. "We might be coming back with a fleet someday. Without going active, get as good a reading as you can of the platforms and ships. That'll be useful in analyzing their force strength."

The computer took the destroyer into the system at about eighty percent of her maximum speed. That was Rebel Fleet standard for nonemergency situations. His Fleet's standard, too.

"Where exactly are they having us go?" he asked.

"The primary world in this system. Imperial records have it labeled as El Capitan, the same name as the system itself."

"Do we have any indications that it's inhabited? All of these ships could be under AI control."

"I'm picking up a lot of signals," Hall said. "It's inhabited, and these people are not restricted to the primary world. They're scattered all across the system."

So these people hadn't done anything to earn the wrath of the System

Lord ruling them. Of course, they probably didn't have an old fleet base in the graveyard of ships that the AIs were worried about either.

He signaled Olivia through his implants.

I need you on the bridge. We're going deeper into the system, and I'd like your read on exactly what we're seeing.

I'll be right there. Should I bring Elise?

The more, the merrier. If she's around, bring Princess Kelsey and Commander Roche. They need to see this, too.

That can't be good.

I'll leave it to you to decide about that. See you in a few minutes.

At this rate, it would take them approximately nine hours to reach their destination. They'd have plenty of time to analyze everything they were seeing. Most importantly, he suspected the transmissions they were picking up from around the system would provide them with critical intelligence data.

The only other Rebel Empire system they'd spent any time in had been the one adjacent to Dresden. It hadn't been that large and neither had Dresden, even though the latter held the critical research base that Kelsey had stolen.

Unlike Harrison's World, this system seemed to be in a relatively unfettered state. Sort of like watching people in their natural habitat. By the time they were done here, they should have a treasure trove of information about how everyday people lived under the AIs' rule.

"If going into this system isn't standard operating procedure, what do you think this means?" Sean asked.

"Probably nothing good. Worst case, they want to send something back to the AI at Harrison's World. That might get complicated very fast."

"Are you going to call the fleet via FTL and let them know?"

After weighing the benefits against the risks, Jared nodded. "Janice, pack all the data we've gathered so far into as tight a file as you can manage, along with our status and where we're going, and send it back to *Invincible* via burst FTL."

"Aye, sir."

Fifteen seconds later, she nodded toward him. "Transmission sent. We received a brief acknowledgment from Captain Marcus that he has received the data and will disseminate it."

"Any indication the transmission was detected?"

"Nothing so far, sir. I'll continue monitoring everything I can and look for changes in behavior on any of the ships or signals that seem out of place. If I detect anything, I'll let you know immediately."

Jared hoped the Rebel Empire didn't become aware of their use of the FTL. Even if they didn't realize it was a method of communication, detecting the transmission would clue them in that something strange was occurring. He'd rather not give them even that little bit of information.

He glanced over at Sean. "Start rotating the crew so they can get meals and rest. It looks like we're going to be here longer than we expected. Make sure the marines are prepared to receive any unexpected visitors on short notice."

* * *

Olivia's brain felt like mush. She'd been reviewing the passively collected data for eight hours without a break. Mind-numbing work, but extremely educational. And unexpectedly productive.

She'd left the bridge, choosing to do her work in the room she shared with Sean. It was tiny when compared to what she would normally expect for the coordinator of Harrison's World, but her implants made space a luxury rather than a requirement.

It took very little time to step over to her husband's office, which was directly next door to their quarters. She savored the thought of their new status once again with deep satisfaction.

Even better, in the wake of their nuptials, someone had convinced Brian Drake to return to Harrison's World. One less stress in their lives. Of course, the man would be underfoot once Sean and she returned home, but the cooling off period would allow the other man to put her firmly in his past.

Jared had banished Sean from the bridge once it became clear that the Rebel Empire wasn't taking any notice of them. The two officers were splitting the intervening hours with four on and four off.

Her husband was preparing to return to the bridge when she came into his office. "I found something important. Take a look at this."

She sent him a transcript of routine radio traffic between the world of El Capitan and one of the moons of the first gas giant in the system.

With his implants, he would be able to scan it quickly, but he wouldn't notice what she had seen.

"Before you go through that in detail, allow me to point out what I'm looking at. There is a sequence of communications between several sources on both El Capitan and the largest moon. They look routine. However, appearances can be deceptive.

"In each of the communications that I've highlighted, either the sender or receiver has used a code phrase known to the resistance."

Sean sat up a bit straighter. "As in the same resistance that you're a member of?"

"Exactly so. Everything is context driven, so depending on a number of factors, the recognition phrases will change. Before we were cut off by the System Lord, we were in communication with other branches of the resistance, though not this system.

"These organizations have existed since the Fall. Each system is separate from every other. We don't know anything about the other organizations so that if we're compromised, we don't endanger anyone else.

"However, we do know enough to recognize these call signs. Rather, I should say, the leader of the resistance and their top-level assistants are made aware of them in case there's ever a need to contact another cell."

Sean considered her. "That seems kind of dangerous. If the leadership of any cell is compromised, they could recognize the presence of the resistance inside any other system."

"True," she said. "We take precautions, but they boil down to making certain that none of the senior leadership is allowed to be captured alive. If need be, we'll make certain of that ourselves."

"You'd kill yourself?" From his tone, he wasn't exactly thrilled to hear this.

"Of course I would. And so would you, if the Rebel Empire had the means to get information dangerous to the New Terran Empire. Tell me you wouldn't destroy your ship to avoid capture under the circumstances."

He sighed. "You know I can't say that. Okay, so either one of us would take our own lives before we endangered the people we protect. Got it.

"So you've recognized these call signs. What practical effect does that have? It's not as if we can contact them without raising suspicion from anyone that happens to notice. As far as I can see, there's no reason for a completely robotic destroyer, which is what they think this is, to contact anyone."

"Ordinarily, I'd agree, and I'm not certain of the circumstances where we could arrange contact, but if we can do so in a manner that doesn't generate undue attention, the resistance in this system could give us a lot of data."

He leaned back in his chair. "Like what?"

"If they're anything like the resistance on Harrison's World, they've had plenty of time to gather detailed information on the military presence here and potentially other systems nearby. It's even conceivable that they know something about Terra that we don't."

That last made him frown. "You make a good point. We're about an hour away from El Capitan. Let's go to the bridge and see what the admiral has to say. If he agrees that there's a need to contact the resistance, he can drag everyone else in to brainstorm the best way to do so.

"For the life of me, I still don't understand why the Rebel Empire has summoned this destroyer to El Capitan. If, as Admiral Mertz suspects, they intend to place a cargo aboard for the AI at Harrison's world, things could get very ugly.

"Yet that may present an opportunity to contact the resistance on the planet itself, if we can work out a subtle method of doing so."

"Do you really think they're going to put people aboard the ship?" she asked. "It seems unlikely that they would go any farther away from the docking and cargo areas.

"If we evacuate all of our personnel and keep track of anyone who comes aboard so that we can move around them, odds are good that they won't see anything out of place."

"That meshes pretty well with what the admiral is thinking," he said. "Over the last eight hours, he's had people scrubbing the most obvious locations where anyone could go of any sign of human habitation. Basically, everyone's belongings are being piled in maintenance tubes far away from the docking area.

"If no one has come to strip our quarters, it's only because they haven't gotten to us yet. We're leaving nothing to chance."

"And what happens if they still see something out of place? If something that we never considered triggers them into a wider search and they find us? There are a lot of warships between us and the flip point."

He smiled without the least hint of humor. "I believe we discussed this earlier in the conversation. The team in engineering will compromise the fusion plant. The entire ship will go up, and we'll never know that we're dead."

"Let's hope it doesn't come to that," she said. "Now, let's head for the bridge so that we can get a team working on this problem. We have to plan for success while we pray against disaster."

23

Kelsey leaned back in her seat, rubbing her eyes. The feel of her face without the plate she'd worn for years still felt wrong. Not that she was complaining, of course. Not about looking like a human being again in other ways, either.

The regeneration sessions she'd completed before she left *Caduceus* had eliminated the visible scarring all across her body. Doctor Stone was very pleased at the reduction in the microscopic damage, too. She had expressed cautious optimism that Kelsey's new nanites would be able to completely eliminate even that in time.

A full recovery had never been laid out as an option when they started, so Kelsey still didn't know what to think about it. She was pleased that her pharmacology unit no longer had to dispense drugs to cover the pain. She hadn't realized she'd had a subtle cloud over her senses before it had stopped.

She'd thought that had been a shock, but getting a good look at this Rebel Empire system had been an even bigger one. A close examination of Harrison's World had not shown the potential threat her empire faced as clearly as she saw it now.

On this robotic destroyer, she could interface her implants with the ship's scanners. They were locked into passive mode, but there was so much data to process. The number of enemy warships in this system was staggering.

Just a cursory look had tagged dozens of them. Potentially, there could be as many as a hundred war craft. Even if they were only destroyers, that was more than sufficient to conquer the New Terran Empire, at least in her universe.

The chime that indicated she had a visitor sounded. A check of her implants revealed Scott Roche standing in the corridor. She signaled the hatch to open, and he came in.

"Highness."

She gestured toward a chair. "I understand they're going to be here in a few minutes to move all the furniture, so enjoy a seat while you can. What can I do for you?"

"I've been examining the scanner readings," he said as he settled into his seat. "I'm worried."

"Ironically, I've been doing the same thing. The fact that I can interface with their scanners using my implants probably drives home the fact that things are worse than you think."

"Great," he said with a shake of his head. "I can't imagine how the Empire possibly survives. Our universe doesn't have all of these repairable ships lying around. When the Rebel Empire finds us, they're going to conquer us."

"I can't get around that gloomy assessment, either," she said with a sigh. "And unless they get very lucky here, the same is true. Yes, they have all these wonderful ships: superdreadnoughts, carriers, and swarms of smaller ships. None of that makes one bit of difference.

"Once the Rebel Empire learns of their existence, which from everything I've heard is already true, it's only a matter of time until they send an overwhelming force to destroy the New Terran Empire here."

The Fleet officer rubbed his eyes. "What do we do? Give up? Surrender and accept slavery? Or do we fight and die?"

"Why can't there be some kind of middle ground?" she asked. "These people at Harrison's World had developed technology to block flip points. They call them flip-point jammers. When one of them is running, the flip point is impassable.

"Surely they could surround their systems with these flip-point jammers and keep the Rebel Empire at bay."

Scott looked skeptical. "Let's say that works. They're free from direct oppression, but they're trapped. They'll never be able to leave their systems, not even to take the fight to the enemy. You can rest assured the Rebel Empire will invest those border systems with overwhelming force, too.

"And that assumes that what man builds, man cannot overcome. Suppose that the Rebel Empire comes up with technology that neutralizes these jammers. Then they'd just pour through. Or perhaps they'd find one of these weak flip points and send ships straight through into an unexpected area."

Kelsey sighed. "Or play the really long game. Their ships can be computer controlled. They could build a massive fleet and get it close in normal space before sending it across the gulf between systems. I have no idea how close their nearest system would be, but even if it took centuries or millennia, these computers could still win.

"The New Terran Empire, both in this universe and ours, has to actually win this fight. We're in far worse condition than Admiral Mertz's forces.

This mission to Terra is our best chance. The data we gather now makes a long-shot mission in our universe a possibility."

The two of them sat in gloomy silence for several minutes before Scott spoke. "We don't even have a destroyer that could fool the Rebel Empire in our universe. The only person with an Old Empire ship is the Bastard. And he has the Imperial Scepter.

"Do you think he knows what he has? That it leads to Terra and the vaults underneath the Imperial Palace? Does he know about the override?"

She considered that for a few seconds before shaking her head. "I don't think so. I've been over the roster of those who defected to his side. He just doesn't have the scientific support to probe the scepter.

"Even if he figures out that it has an Imperial computer inside it, which isn't certain since the designers made sure it never signals its presence, the memory sector that holds the message from Emperor Marcus is fiendishly well concealed.

"While I'm as far from a scientist as you can get, I've looked over what this Carl Owlet discovered and believe that only someone of his intellectual caliber could've found it. The man is probably the greatest mind the Empire has produced in our lifetime."

Scott smiled a little. "I sent a message back home to locate and sequester him. Once they start sending data and hardware back to our universe, I expect he's going to prove very useful indeed. If only we could come up with a way to get him implants."

That wasn't very likely, at least not in the short term. While there were potential paths between the New Terran Empire and Pentagar, they were not short. Sending anyone out to make the trip to this universe and be implanted would take roughly six months. Then they'd have to get home.

A better option was taking implantation hardware back into her universe and sending an expedition home. That would still take six months, but it gave them much greater flexibility in preparing their homeland for this conflict.

She intended to have a discussion with the alien on the space station inside the Nova system. It had created artificial flip points between its system and both Pentagar and Avalon in this universe.

Kelsey understood the rather large power requirements in doing so limited its ability to do so again in the short term, but the shortened travel time between it and the occupied systems fighting the Rebel Empire might provide at least a slim chance for them to survive.

The chime at the hatch sounded again. This time a group of Fleet crewmen stood in the corridor. It was time to head for the bridge. Very soon, she'd see what the possibilities were, if they made it out of this system alive.

* * *

Elise had decided to be on the bridge when the destroyer achieved orbit.

Just like Olivia, she'd been going over all the data she could get her hands on. While she didn't have the same experience of being part of the Rebel Empire that her friend had, she'd found a few interesting things.

It seemed that the Rebel Empire was very restrictive in what it allowed its citizens to talk about. That didn't mean that they no longer discussed those other things, only that they'd became much more circumspect about how they did it.

There were a series of fascinating discussions that she tapped into where the participants used subtext to get around any number of potential roadblocks to whatever it was they were discussing.

True, that didn't provide her with a lot of useful information for their current task, but it did confirm something she'd suspected for a long time. Something Olivia had become blind to.

The citizens of the Rebel Empire were not as cowed as one could be led to expect. And since the sentient AIs that ruled it were not complete idiots, they obviously tolerated a certain level of subversion.

Oh, not in any serious manner. For example, if someone were to discuss planting a bomb or committing some act of terrorism, no matter what language they use to talk around it, she was certain that the System Lord would detect it, if it were in a channel the AI was monitoring.

But if it were two brothers discussing how they could safely skirt certain regulations about proscribed technology as it related to manufacturing in space, that might be allowed to pass. At least, it wasn't stopping the two brothers she'd found.

Elise was relatively certain they wouldn't be discussing such matters or even mentioning that the technology was technically disallowed unless they expected to have some level of safety in doing so. The brothers in question were not members of the higher orders. They might not even be members of the middle orders. She still wasn't quite certain she grasped how everything fit together in the Rebel Empire on a societal level.

"We've entered orbit," the helm officer told her husband. "We're about a thousand kilometers away from what has to be the biggest orbital I've ever seen. The thing is a monster."

Jared nodded. "Easily three times the size of the Dresden orbital. I can only imagine how long it took to build. Any idea of what they want with us? Have we received a signal to transmit our report?"

"Not yet. Again, the System Lord back at Harrison's World didn't retain that level of detail about any previous report, so this might be perfectly normal. Or something could be seriously wrong."

Olivia cleared her throat from where she sat beside Elise. "Is there any possibility of piggybacking a communication onto something here in orbit? Of getting a signal down to the surface of the planet?"

The helm officer shook her head. "I'd have to be desperate to try, ma'am. There are so many ships in orbit that the chances of detection are absurdly high."

"I think you'd best give up your idea of contacting the resistance," Jared told the other woman. "While it was a wonderful thought, we can't do anything to endanger our mission. That means we have to be the most cautious individuals you have ever met."

"Fine," Olivia grumbled. "I just hate missing the opportunity to steal a march on those rebel bastards."

The helm officer sat up a little straighter. "We just received instructions to transmit the report. The computer sent it just as planned. We've received a confirmation that the orbital has it."

"Now what?" Princess Kelsey asked. "Do we head back?"

Kelsey had been more quiet than usual since the surgery on her face, Elise noted. She'd offered to talk to the woman from another universe about what she was going through, but Kelsey had declined.

It had to be traumatic. Kelsey had been living with her disfigurement for years. She'd seen how everyone recoiled at her appearance. That kind of thing left a mark on one's psyche.

Jared shook his head. "We wait. If it were as simple as heading back immediately, they'd never have brought us in. Something will happen."

He turned his attention to the ship's tactical officer. "I want everything in our area watched. If any ship or small craft heads toward us, I want to know as soon as possible."

"There's a ton of traffic around the orbital," the man said, "but we're outside the regular pattern. If anyone is interested in us, I'll see it as soon as they start toward us."

"I've got everyone who can be spared in the maintenance passages," Sean said. "Only critical people in engineering and here are out. We've looked over every area they might come into, and there are no traces we were ever here."

"Good," Jared said. "I hope all they intend to do is send something back. There's no indication they've ever sent people before. If they do, this is going to be very, very tricky.

"We'd have to let them take control of the ship and wait until we flipped out of the system to subdue them. Nine hours during which we'd be the ears in the walls and didn't dare reveal ourselves."

Elise suppressed a shudder. The maintenance passages were cramped under optimal conditions. Now that they were filled with people and furnishings, she'd be sitting in someone's lap the entire time.

"I have a cargo shuttle inbound," the tactical officer said. "ETA twenty minutes."

"Any signals?" Jared asked.

The man shook his head. "It looks as if they expect to dock without warning the computer they're coming."

"Everyone to their assigned hiding places," Jared said grimly. "We're going to have guests for dinner."

24

Sean monitored the intruders from the safety of a nearby maintenance tube. It was cramped, dark, and packed with heavily-armed marines. Thankfully, he was able to use his implants and the ship's own cameras to monitor their unwelcome visitors.

They'd taken every precaution to make certain the Rebel Empire personnel wouldn't detect *Athena*'s rightful crew's use of the ship's systems. Hopefully, the people exiting the cargo shuttles would unload whatever they'd brought, pack it away, and depart quickly.

Worst case, some of them would stay aboard. If that happened, everyone would remain in hiding in the maintenance tubes. They'd only reveal themselves once *Athena* had exited El Capitan.

Things were looking pretty good. Fleet crewmen, under the watchful eyes of their superiors, were unloading crates and securing them in the cargo section nearest the destroyer's docks. There was no way to know what was in those crates, but that hardly mattered at this point. There would be plenty of time to look into their contents once they were safely away.

It took them almost two hours to unload the cargo shuttles. As they got closer to finishing, Sean's tension rose. Not that any of the personnel had come near any of his hiding people. In fact, they hadn't left the cargo area.

His heart soared when the officers ordered the enlisted men back aboard the cargo shuttles and they undocked. It looked as if *Athena* wouldn't be having long-term company after all.

He was about to order his men out of the maintenance tubes to inspect the crates when Admiral Mertz sent a general message through everyone's implants.

We have a cutter inbound, people. Maintain positions.

Sean cursed under his breath. This wasn't good. With the cargo secured, the only reason another vessel would be coming their way was to drop off passengers or do some kind of inspection. Neither of those options was promising.

He tapped into the ship's passive scanners and watched the cutter approach. It was alone, so there wouldn't be very many people to deal with. The Rebel Empire used the same design as the New Terran Empire, now that they had upgraded to using Old Empire tech, so he knew the capacity of their cutters.

They could hold thirty-five people plus a flight crew of three in comfort, twice that if they were stacked like logs. He doubted the incoming cutter was running heavy, so they were looking at a maximum of three dozen people. Troublesome, but not beyond handling if need be.

The cutter docked without incident and disgorged three dozen men and women. Unlike the previous individuals, these immediately left the docking area and headed for the critical sections of the ship: the bridge, engineering, and the computer control room.

Not good.

Admiral Mertz could handle the people going to the bridge. He and his team were actually in the bulkheads directly surrounding the bridge. They could gain entrance through concealed hatches that weren't on any schematic. The same was true of engineering and computer central.

Sean had made certain *Athena*'s crew had places to hide as he was overseeing the refurbishing of the destroyer. Having done so before, he'd known there was a possibility they'd have to attack intruders in critical areas of the ship, so he figured they might as well make it easy on themselves.

The incoming personnel settled at the control consoles in the three areas and immediately took control of the ship away from the computer. They used specific key phrases and implant codes to do so.

Of course, the ship's computer wasn't the standard version that they would have expected. It reported itself at their disposal, but it was still under the New Terran Empire crew's control. And now they had an interesting set of codes they might be able to use again at some future point.

The woman in the center seat opened a communications channel to someone on the planet below. Based on the way the man she called was dressed, he was a member of the higher orders.

The woman on *Athena*'s bridge smiled. "We're ready to depart. I don't anticipate any trouble. We should be back in a couple of months."

"Excellent. You know how important this mission is, so I won't tell you to do everything you can to make it a success. I trust you'll do that as a matter of course. Safe journey, Jaleesa."

The man terminated the connection without waiting for a response. Sean supposed that firmly established who was the superior in that relationship.

He wondered what the woman and her people intended to do back at Harrison's World. Were they going to install some kind of equipment? Until they really dug into what was down in the cargo area, they weren't going to be able to determine what the Rebel Empire's goal really was.

He was about to close down his connection to the bridge when he noticed that the com signal to the planet below hadn't terminated. Even though the woman in the command chair was no longer in communication with the man she'd called, *Athena* was still talking with someone.

More interestingly, the com signal wasn't being logged the way it should be. Electronically, there was no indication it was happening at all. If he hadn't been directly tapped into the outgoing signal, he wouldn't have noticed it.

Before he could dig into the contents of the call, the additional signal terminated. Perhaps they had been adding some raw information to the end of the verbal communication. Still, why hadn't it been logged by the computer?

Sean used his concealed access to *Athena*'s systems and began searching. He quickly found a small program that had been inserted into the computer to hide communications on a certain frequency.

He sent an implant signal to Admiral Mertz.

Sir, we might have a problem. He explained about the concealed transmission.

The admiral sent a mental grunt back to him. *I feel pretty confident I know who to blame for that: your wife.*

Sean blinked. *My wife?*

I'd be willing to bet a month's pay that she signaled the resistance on the main world even though we told her not to.

Now that Sean thought about it, that did sound like his wife. When Olivia decided on a course of action, she'd execute it over every objection. She was stubborn that way. Of course, in his new circle of friends, that was a common trait.

What do we do about it?

The admiral sent a mental shrug. *We wait. Hopefully, the wrong people don't become aware of our presence.*

* * *

JARED CROUCHED in the maintenance passage encircling the bridge and considered their situation. It was obvious the intruders were preparing to leave El Capitan. They'd spent a decent amount of time going through the systems and disengaging computer control.

At this point, they really did have full control of *Athena*, though his people could take it back far faster than the enemy would've dreamed possible.

They only had control of the critical systems. There were only three dozen people on their team, barely enough to run a destroyer. They'd focused on propulsion and power. They'd left the automated systems controlling the weapons in place but inserted themselves as the initiators of action rather than the ship's computer.

He really wondered what was in the crates they'd brought aboard. Harrison's World was completely suppressed according to all the information they had. The population was under the heel of the System Lord. What could they bring that would assist in that, or how did they intend to change it?

Well, he'd find out as soon as they left this system. Unknown to them, Jared still had complete control of the antiboarding weapons via altered control interfaces. Once they made that first flip, he'd stun every single one of the intruders and resume control of *Athena*.

Janice Hall edged past some of the others in the maintenance tube until she was beside him. "Sir, we have a problem."

"What's wrong?"

"We just left orbit, and we're heading for the wrong flip point."

He pulled data from the passive sensors and double-checked their course. They were indeed making way for the other flip point in the El Capitan system. ETA five hours at this speed.

While it was certainly possible to work around to Harrison's World from the new target system, it would make for a much longer trip. No, these people had another end destination in mind.

"Pass the word that we might have to kick this party off early," he said. "We'll have to work out a new rendezvous with the fleet."

"Aye, sir."

They really didn't have a choice now. If this supposedly automated destroyer suddenly changed course, the powers that be at El Capitan would have a conniption. They'd quickly dispatch ships to catch up with *Athena* and find out what had gone wrong.

And then there was the force surrounding the flip point leading to Harrison's World, one they'd never be able to slip past if the System Lord figured out something was wrong. No, they were stuck taking a side trip.

"I want you to start looking into potential destinations," he continued. "Once we have something workable, send it to me for verification. Then we'll use the FTL com to send a burst packet to *Invincible*.

"This has to have something to do with the cargo these people brought aboard. We'll find out what that is once we flip to the next system and take them out. If, of course, it's safe to do so. What exactly do we know about the system we're headed toward?"

The woman shrugged. "We have information from the Old Empire databases but nothing recent. In the old days, the next system over was used for heavy mining. Asteroid belts and moons primarily. Lots of heavy metals and even some rare elements. Now? We won't know until we get there."

"Go get me what you can."

Once the woman was gone, Jared sighed. What had once been populous and productive systems in the Old Empire were abandoned under the control of the AIs. Hopefully, that was what they'd find when they flipped.

Then again, it might be possible to find out before *Athena* left El Capitan.

He opened an implant channel to Olivia West. They'd relocated her to a maintenance tube just off engineering.

Got a minute?

Her response was immediate. *Of course. What can I do for you, Admiral?*

Aren't we being formal today? Tell me, did you just signal the resistance on El Capitan? Or more pertinently, did they respond?

That was a moment of silence over the implant link. *How did you know?*

Surely you expected me to monitor all communications. A good commander is always aware of what's going on aboard his ship.

Her tone held a hint of chagrin when she responded. *As it turns out, I did send a message to the resistance. I'm sorry, but the opportunity was too good to let pass by. Our visitors were sending a message of their own, so it was very easy to piggyback on their signal.*

I haven't received a response yet. Frankly, I'm not certain that I will. Nevertheless, it was worth taking a chance. Other than identifying myself as a visitor from another resistance cell, I asked for basic information that they would be willing to share with any resistance group. Both about El Capitan and this area of the Rebel Empire.

Which they call El Cap in most of the local communications, by the way. I'm not sure why.

He considered what she'd done. It was far too late to do anything about it except hope for the best.

If the situation was reversed, would you respond, Olivia?

It would probably take several hours before I made up my mind, but I'd answer. Any chance to help overthrow the AIs is worth taking. It's not going to put them in any danger, sending a response. Not really.

They have communication cutouts. Even if the AIs became aware that they sent a signal, it would never be able to trace the response back.

Jared considered that before responding. *That makes sense. Do you expect them to send a general signal that we'll be able to pick up? Or will it be something directed specifically at us? Do they even know where your signal came from?*

I never said, but they'd have to be fools not to guess. Athena *just arrived in their system. I'd wager they're fairly certain at this point where we are.*

He wasn't exactly happy with the risk that she'd taken. Frankly, if the resistance had a mole in their organization, someone could make sure the System Lord found out.

Jared made certain to insert a strong note of disapproval into his mental tone. *I had very good reasons to turn down your request to initiate contact, Coordinator. I like you very much, but rest assured that there will be serious consequences for violating my orders.*

If the resistance responds, I expect you to pass that information to me immediately. And, Olivia, this had better never *happen again. Right or wrong, this is my mission, and I set the rules. Cross me at your peril.*

Her tone became conciliatory. *I swear that I'll follow your orders going forward. Next time I'll just argue more strenuously.*

Wasn't that going to be fun? Well, since the die was cast, perhaps their response could shed some light on one of the things that confused him.

When they answer, if *they answer, maybe they'll tell us why the AI decided to use this ship. It had to be planned long in advance and I don't get it. There are a lot of ships already here. Why us?*

Oh, I can tell you that now, Admiral. If they used a local ship, they'd have to displace the entire crew for security. Word would get around. This way, no one has a clue what Athena *is being used for.*

That made sense to him.

Well, I'll leave you to what you're doing. Contact me the second you receive a response of any kind.

I'll do that, Admiral.

Perhaps in the end, it'll turn out that you're right. I guess we'll find out.

25

Through concealed video pickups the New Terran Empire crew had left scattered around, Elise watched the Rebel Empire personnel working in engineering. The tiny units were far too small to be noticed unless someone was specifically looking for them, so she wasn't concerned the enemy would spot them.

She was no military expert, but it was apparent these were not Fleet personnel. They wore no uniforms, and their demeanor was not what one would expect from someone in a military organization. These were civilians. High-ranking civilians, certainly. Undoubtedly members of the higher orders.

Not a single person lacked an implant. The Rebel Empire didn't give implants to anyone unless they were either a member of the higher orders or a Fleet officer.

That raised some interesting questions. Why were members of the nobility running a warship? Better yet, how did they know how to do so in the first place? These people were obviously very familiar with the systems on this ship.

From what she'd seen of the higher orders, Elise didn't believe they'd had a burning desire to learn how to fly spaceships. That meant that these people had been specifically trained for this mission.

Their conversation thus far had been obscure, at least to her. They obviously knew one another very well and limited their conversation to the duties at hand. That would probably change once people started going off shift, but thus far, everyone was proving remarkably uncommunicative.

The pickups had very sensitive audio receptors, so she was able to hear every word uttered in the large compartment. With her implant processing power, she managed to keep track of all the individual conversations at the same time.

"Jocelyn, could you take a look at this?" one of the men standing beside the main engineering console asked.

"What is it?" an older woman asked as she stepped over to him.

"Look at this maintenance log. Does it look off to you?"

The woman leaned forward and examined the screen. "Off in what way?"

"It's too clean. There should be more errors listed."

Elise felt her stomach sinking. This was the kind of thing that Jared had worried about. That they had *all* worried about.

The woman raised an eyebrow. "So let me see if I understand you correctly, Austin. You're concerned because the equipment is operating too well. You think it should be more problematic?"

The man smiled a little. "Not precisely. I'd expect an autonomous destroyer to have more minor system errors. Particularly in life support. After all, the system should have been shut down until we ordered it brought online.

"And speaking of that, look at the reserves. The oxygen levels are particularly low, considering how they haven't been used. I would've expected the tanks to be virtually full. They're actually down by about ten percent."

The woman frowned. "It's conceivable that some of the reserve has bled off through small breaches in the system over time. I don't think we should read too much into this, but you're right to bring it to my attention.

"Begin a systematic review of all engineering systems and provide me with a status on them by the time we reached the flip point. Not that I think there's something wrong, but we're going to be on this ship for a while. I'd like to know for certain that everything is in order."

"I'll start that at once," the man said with a nod. "I should have a preliminary report ready by then. It's going to take significantly longer, on the order of several days, for us to do a complete systems analysis."

"That's good enough. Thank you."

The woman walked back over to stand beside the flip drive. The older man she'd been speaking to before raised an eyebrow.

"Is something wrong?"

"Austin believes he's found something of concern. He seems to think that the maintenance logs are too clean. Unusually so."

The man studied her. "Are *you* concerned?"

"Not overly so," she said with a slight shrug. "This destroyer came from Harrison's World in an unoccupied state. The System Lord there has likely been using it for any number of purposes. The fact that the maintenance logs are not as we would've expected doesn't necessarily mean anything.

"It's entirely possible that the Lord keeps these vessels in a higher state of readiness and in better condition for peripheral systems then we'd believed. It's also possible that it felt no need to fully top off the oxygen reserves. Honestly, we have no way of knowing."

The man looked away from her for a few seconds. "I assume you told Austin to research it further."

"Indeed I did. He should have a preliminary report by the time we make flip out of El Capitan. A detailed analysis will take several days more. One of the downsides of having a small crew."

"Stay on top of it. If there's something unusual happening, I want to know about it before we leave the system. See if you can pry any other personnel away from their normal duties to assist in checking the critical systems."

The woman nodded. "I'll take care of it."

Elise immediately passed word to Jared that the intruders had spotted something that concerned them. She really hoped they didn't find anything else that raised their suspicions even further.

If they did, Jared had positioned the marines so they could flood the critical compartments in short order. Hell, he could just trigger the antiboarding weapons and drop them all in their tracks.

The trouble would come if someone was expecting these people to send a final communication before they flipped out of the system. If that were the case, there was more than enough force present at El Capitan to chase *Athena* down.

She would just have to hope that they managed to keep these people in the dark for just a little bit longer.

* * *

Olivia had made the conscious decision not to watch the Rebel Empire personnel inside *Athena*. Rather, she focused her attention on gathering as much data through the ship's passive scanners as she could.

They weren't going to have another opportunity to visit El Capitan, so it behooved her to make the data collection as complete as possible. The ships here might very well make the journey to Harrison's World and visit war upon them.

Also, she kept hoping that they'd receive information from the resistance cell here. If her message had been convincing enough, the locals could provide them with far more data than she'd be able to collect on her own.

With her attention focused outward, she was able to catch the message she'd been hoping for as soon as it arrived.

Her respect for the resistance cell on El Capitan notched higher as she reviewed what they'd sent. This was clever. The message header indicated the transmission was a data set for a mining ship out in the belt. It "only happened" to pass close enough to *Athena* for the ship's receivers to pick it up.

The data was encrypted, but the audio message attached to it gave her clues as to the key. Yet another of the code phrases the resistance used in communicating between systems.

She applied the decryption key and was dismayed when it failed. Had she done something wrong?

Olivia considered potential variants to the code phrase. With decryption, every single letter was important. Thankfully with her implants, she was able to try multiple different passes, and one of them unlocked the data.

She let out a slow breath and opened the file.

The contents were more than she'd hoped for. Not only did the data set contain observations of the Fleet vessels stationed at El Capitan, it also held data about the surrounding systems, including the one *Athena* was currently headed toward.

Olivia skimmed the data and quickly determined the system was occupied but not heavily so. Seemingly, it was heavily stocked with rare elements useful in constructing flip drives and other complex equipment. So there was a mining presence but not much more.

The flip point was guarded, though only on the El Capitan side. Perhaps even more heavily so than the one leading toward Harrison's World. She wondered what they were worried about.

Maybe the ghosts—the strange raiders that Kelsey had learned about at the Dresden system—were the reason. The New Terran Empire's working hypothesis was that those people were remnants of loyal fleet units still hiding inside the Rebel Empire.

With as much force as the rebels had at their fingertips, Olivia wasn't certain why they hadn't crushed the ghosts already. They'd had over five hundred years to hunt them down. Still, if the loyalists were still able to fight, she wasn't going to worry about how they'd managed it. The important thing was that they were still fighting.

As one of the leaders of the resistance on Harrison's World, she was somewhat surprised that she'd never heard about the ghosts. That was the kind of juicy rumor she'd have expected to at least have some clue about.

It seemed that the rebel Empire had gone out of their way to make certain that talk about the ghosts was minimized. It was also possible that the other resistant cells deeper in the Empire didn't consider rumors worthwhile enough to pass on.

She raised an eyebrow at the thought and skimmed the data, looking for any mention of the ghosts. Nothing. Yet one more mystery.

While she didn't consider herself as knowledgeable as a Fleet officer, she knew enough to categorize the firepower present at El Capitan. There were enough ships here, though none larger than a heavy cruiser, to give Admiral Mertz's fleet a run for its money.

There was also a Fleet base here. Based on the information in the data set, it was about a hundred fifty years old. So something not built under the Old Empire.

That meant she didn't have any idea of how it was laid out, though the resistance had given them some generalities about its capabilities. Just like Harrison's World, it was the home of the System Lord.

That alone made the fortress immensely powerful. With the firepower that modern technology could bring to bear, the sentient AI magnified its lethality by orders of magnitude.

El Capitan was going to prove a tough nut to crack when the time came to invade. Of course, any system with this level of firepower was going to prove challenging.

She was about to route the data she'd received to Admiral Mertz when she had another idea. What do they know about Terra?

As it turned out, a little bit more than she did. They had never been to the capital of the Old Empire, but the resistance here had gotten word from another cell closer to the center of the Empire.

According to the resistance sources, each of the three standard flip points was heavily invested with defensive stations, both in the Terra system and on the other side of the flip point.

Interesting. Even an important system like El Capitan only kept its forces on the defending side. She'd assumed that the Lords had decided to protect systems like that, regardless if it made sense or not.

What exactly were the AIs protecting against? Were they worried about people accessing Terra or were they more concerned about the people imprisoned on the capital eventually making their way out? Perhaps that was why it was defended on both sides of the flip points.

Terra had a System Lord. That wasn't a surprise, though it was going to make the mission more challenging.

It maintained control of the defensive systems on the far side of each of the flip point via targeted rules of engagement. Only ships with the correct passcodes could even approach the flip points without being fired upon.

Not that she imagined very many ships wanted to transit to Terra in any case. From everything she'd heard, the capital was a smoking ruin.

The resistance data had no information about whether that was true or not. They'd find out when they got there.

The last thing she found in the data set was a list of important people on El Capitan, mostly members of the higher orders that ruled the planet. Those would be the most loyal members of the Rebel Empire present in the system.

Unless, of course, there were leaders of the resistance sprinkled among them. That last brought a smile to her face, since that was exactly what she'd been on Harrison's World.

It was very possible that a similar situation existed here on El Capitan. If so, she wouldn't find that information in the data sent by the resistance. They would go to great lengths to conceal their identities.

The data did provide some information about the people aboard *Athena*. A brief check of the records gave her matching faces for several of the people on the ship right now.

Interestingly, each of them was a member of the higher order. And not just minor members of the nobility either. These were people with influence and authority.

The highest ranking of the individuals was on the bridge. Her name was Jaleesa Keaton. She was a sitting member of the system's ruling council. That was the equivalent of the group of leaders Olivia had chaired as coordinator of Harrison's World. Two dozen of the most powerful people on the planet.

She verified that the numbers on El Capitan were about the same. The woman at the command console was far too important to be commanding a mission away from the planet, yet here she was.

The next most senior was Bertram Gust. He was a junior member of the ruling council. Apparently, he was closely aligned with Keaton.

The third in command, as far as Olivia could see, was a woman named Jocelyn Oldfield. The records the resistance had sent indicated she was Gust's assistant.

What were such powerful and influential people doing on board a supposedly automated Rebel Empire destroyer?

Well, they'd find out soon enough.

Olivia sent the information from the resistance to Admiral Mertz. He would undoubtedly use it to help formulate their plans going forward.

26

Kelsey sat in the near darkness of the maintenance tube and tried not to fidget. The close confines were making her antsy. The claustrophobia reminded her too much of being trapped inside the machine that had forcibly implanted her.

She didn't use to feel this way about tight spaces. She'd spoken with Justin Guzman about the change at length over the last few years. Therapy, he'd called those sessions. Reliving torture was how she thought of them.

Still, those conversations had helped give her some distance from the trauma. Now, sitting here unable to do anything, she felt the fear and anger flowing back into her. The raw terror at not being able to control her own fate.

Another check of her internal chrono revealed that only five minutes had passed since the last time she'd checked. Five minutes. It felt as if five hours had gone by.

Ironically, five hours was exactly how long they still had to wait until *Athena* flipped out of the El Capitan system. Hopefully, these hours would be quiet ones.

"Highness, we have a problem," Commander Roche said softly in her ear.

"Of course we do," she said, resigned. "What is it?"

"Some of the enemy personnel have begun doing systems checks. Right now, they're only working on accessing everything remotely, but if they're going to be thorough, they'll need to do some checks in person.

"Unfortunately, the maintenance tube we're sitting in runs behind the computer center. If they intend to verify the computer's functionality, they'll need to send someone here."

"Where can we relocate to? Are we even going to be *able* to relocate?"

He shook his head slightly. "I don't think so. We have a lot of equipment stashed in the back end of this maintenance tube. While it's conceivable that the intruders will miss seeing it, that's not something we can bank on.

"Also, it would be reckless to try to move the equipment. We're sitting in the middle of a heavy-traffic area. The odds of someone seeing us approach certainty."

"Perfect," she said with a sigh. "What can we do? Wait for someone to stick their head into the maintenance tube and punch them out?"

That brought a slight smile to the Fleet officer's face. "That's not such a bad plan, all things considered. The only problem I see with it is that they'll miss whoever they send fairly quickly.

"I know Admiral Mertz wants to avoid any interaction at all until this vessel has left El Capitan. That's the smart move. If the intruders become concerned, they could warn someone back on the planet. That might spark a mission to Harrison's World once we make a break for it."

Thereby voiding everything the New Terran Empire in this universe had accomplished so far and leaving them in a terrible position. That couldn't be allowed to happen.

She drew in a deep breath and let it out slowly. "I'm not sure we can do anything to change what happens next. If they come looking into this maintenance tube, we can't just wave at them and let things pass. We'll have to take out whoever comes through that hatch."

"And bluff our way through any last-minute communication once we reached the flip point," Scott agreed. "Let's hope they have enough things to look over without coming into this maintenance tube for the next five hours."

If Kelsey had thought that time was passing slowly before, it crawled now. Every second was like a drop of syrup preparing to fall onto a pancake.

And of course, thinking about pancakes made her hungry. Kelsey had taken the precaution of stuffing her jacket with survival rations. They fed the gnawing hunger in her gut, but they were hardly pancakes.

She started using her implants to access the feeds from engineering and the corridors around the computer center. Her anxiety level rose, but things were quiet for now.

At the one-hour mark, she started to think that they'd made it. Of course, shortly after that, disaster struck.

One of the men in engineering walked over to the woman in charge of the compartment and told her that he was going to check the computer center. She told him to hurry up because she wanted him back at his station by the time they flipped.

"Scott," Kelsey said softly, "we've got trouble." It amused her darkly to use the same warning he had earlier. This wasn't the time for levity, but she couldn't help herself.

"Tell me."

"One of the people in engineering is coming to the computer center to do some systems checks. I hope that means he's just going to be in the center itself and not going to stick his head into this maintenance tube, but we can't plan on that. We need to be ready."

He glanced at his wrist unit. "We have about fifty minutes until we can flip. Whatever happens, it's going to take place while *Athena* is in the middle of all those battle stations and ships around the flip point. Even if we make a run for it, the mobile units stationed there will chase us down.

"Destroyers are fast, but they'll be right on top of us. They'll be able to fire missiles immediately after they flip into the next system.

"Also, we really don't know what's on the other side of this flip point, other than the unverified information Olivia got from the local resistance. They say it's empty, but they might not know everything.

"We can't take chances, so we'll be as prepared as we can get. Whatever happens, we need to assume the consequences are going to be drastic if anyone learns of our presence."

Kelsey nodded. "I'll keep an eye on this guy's progress and keep you updated. If I even think he's headed toward us, I'll let you know."

As she was positioned right next to the hatch, she'd be the one dealing with the problem. There were marines in the tube with her, but she had those vaunted Marine Raider implants. If the guy caused any trouble, she could shut him up the fastest.

The stunner at her hip would be the safest means of dealing with him. She'd rather not kill a man simply for being in the wrong place at the wrong time.

Also, she couldn't be certain that his death wouldn't register on some piece of equipment or in his superiors' implants. Simply stunning him stretched out the time that those people might wonder what had happened to him but not be overly alarmed.

To her relief, the man went directly to the central computer core and began a detailed inspection of the consoles and control runs inside the room. Using the concealed video pickups Mertz had planted there, Kelsey scrutinized his every move.

It was almost as if she were looking over his shoulder. She could read what he was typing into the various consoles, and she could make uneducated guesses about what the parts he was examining were.

With about fifteen minutes to go until the ship arrived in the flip point, he began closing up the consoles and access panels. He didn't interact with the other people in the room, so Kelsey wasn't certain what his next course of action would be. She hoped he'd return directly to engineering.

He dashed that hope when he came directly toward the maintenance tube where she was hiding.

Oh crap.

"Everyone get ready," she said. "We've got someone coming to look in the maintenance tube. I've got him."

Considering the deadline the man was operating under, he shouldn't be wasting his time like this. With only a dozen minutes left before he had to report back to his station, she wasn't certain what he thought he'd see.

No matter what his motivation, this introduced some serious complications into their plan.

Kelsey opened an implant communication channel to Mertz. It was still difficult not to think of him as the Bastard. She was trying, but it was hard.

As soon as he answered, she got straight to the point.

We've got a situation. One of the people from engineering is about to look into the maintenance tube behind computer central. I'm going to take him out.

Make it quick, Mertz sent back. *We don't know if they have some kind of automated monitoring, but we can't let him scream for help.*

I've got it covered, but he's expected in engineering in ten minutes. What do we do if they delay the flip because he's not there?

I'll worry about that. Just shut him down fast. If you don't, we're all screwed.

No pressure.

Kelsey positioned herself near the hatch, drew her stunner, and readied herself. She heard marines moving into position behind her, ready to back her up if things went wrong. She hoped she wouldn't need them.

A minute later, the hatch slid open. She aimed her weapon at the opening and waited. And waited. *And waited.*

Where was he?

She took a deep breath and leaned forward just enough to peer into the corridor. The man was standing half a dozen meters away, frowning at an open access panel.

He was half turned away from the hatch, but that didn't stop him from seeing her, curse the luck. His eyes widened, and he opened his mouth to shout something.

Kelsey shot him before he could make a sound. He dropped quietly into a loose heap.

Had he gotten off an implant warning? No way to know for sure unless things went completely into the crapper.

Looking in both directions to make certain no one else was present, Kelsey stepped into the corridor, closed the panel the man had been peering into, slung him into a fireman's carry, and ducked back into the maintenance tube.

A touch on the controls sealed the hatch behind her. It was all up to Mertz now. Her fate—all their fates—were in his hands.

* * *

JARED CONSIDERED the situation as soon as he disconnected from Kelsey. If things were going to go wrong, the worst possible time would be right now.

They were a little more than eight minutes away from the flip point at their current speed. The destroyer was virtually on top of the defensive fortifications. If the people on his bridge sent any kind of distress signal, it was all over.

Just to be certain that something like that didn't happen, he initiated a lockdown of outgoing communications. If things seemed normal when they reached the flip point, he could enable their ability to communicate with their comrades with only a moment's notice.

One of the side benefits of allowing these Rebel Empire jerks aboard *Athena* was that *they* had no problem running the scanners at full power. What would've seemed incongruous from an automated vessel wouldn't be questioned from a live crew of people known to be loyal.

That meant they were getting priceless data that they could use against the Rebel Empire at some future point. The detailed information from the fortifications would be very valuable when they had to assault this system or one like it in the future.

Jared sent a message to Commander Hall. It was time to send a final data packet to *Invincible* through the FTL com. *Athena* might transit with little to no warning, so he wanted to be sure he got all the critical information to the fleet.

She quickly had the data compressed and burst transmitted it to the superdreadnought. Marcus had confirmed receipt of the transmission and returned the path they would take to meet him at Terra.

It would take the fleet a bit more than a week longer to get there, but he'd already known that. They would arrive at a different flip point linking to Terra. Also unavoidable. He'd have to improvise to get them in. Somehow.

The Rebel Empire personnel on *Athena*'s bridge were focused on their tasks. Jared hoped the upcoming flip would consume their attention. With any luck at all, no one would notice the missing man had not returned to his post.

He knew better than to assume that was going to happen, though. No. Far better to prepare for the worst-case scenario.

Though the control systems aboard the destroyer wouldn't show anything, he still had the ability to trigger the antiboarding weapons. That meant Jared could drop every single intruder aboard his ship with a thought. If it seemed as though they were about to discover his people, he'd stop them in their tracks.

He also kept an eye on the team in engineering. Since they had dispatched the missing man, if anyone was going to notice his absence, it would be them. Their actions or lack thereof would dictate how he responded.

In a perfect world, he'd let them make the flip and deal with them on the other side. He fervently hoped the next system was empty of human presence. That would allow them to deal with the Rebel Empire crew immediately.

Because he was monitoring the situation in *Athena*'s engineering compartment, he saw one of the senior people glancing at the main hatch more frequently. And he also saw the deep frown that suddenly appeared on the woman's face.

She walked over to the unnamed man Jared assumed was the senior officer in engineering. "Austin isn't back. He's not responding when I call him, either."

That caused the man to frown as well. "Perhaps he's inside a section of the ship that's interfering with our implants."

"I suppose that's possible," the woman allowed. "But I was *very* clear that I wanted him back here before we flipped. According to my timer, that's only three minutes away. He should have at least started back."

The man laughed. "As if Austin is the most punctual individual we know. If you let him bury himself inside some piece of machinery, he'll completely forget what time it is. The man is an unrepentant gearhead."

The woman didn't seem convinced, but she nodded. "I suppose his presence here isn't really required. I don't want to send anyone to search for him until we've flipped. Should we notify the bridge?"

Jared tensed. This was the kind of problem that might cause the woman occupying his chair on the bridge to abort the flip.

The man shook his head. "I don't think we need to bother Jaleesa. I'll just make a notification over the ship's internal speakers in the area where Austin is working. It should only take a second for him to step out and give us a call."

Moments later, the man spoke again. "Austin. Aren't you forgetting you need to be somewhere? Contact me at once."

Jared knew the man's voice was echoing throughout the area around computer central. The monitors they'd placed throughout the ship told him the transmission was localized to that area.

Meanwhile, on the bridge, the woman called Jaleesa was getting an update from her helm officer.

"Two minutes until we're in the prime flip zone."

"Understood," she said. "Bring us to a halt as soon as we arrive."

Two minutes was such a short amount of time. Jared knew that would drag along slow second by slow second.

The woman was stopping rather than just flipping. That implied she was going to open communications with someone at the defensive perimeter. Or she might just be a stickler for the rules.

Ships were technically supposed to come to a halt inside a flip point. Traveling at any real speed exacerbated the stress of transiting the wormhole. In practice, experienced Fleet officers knew that only high speeds were a danger to a ship's integrity.

In an extreme case—like the original *Athena*—going at very high speed could cause the ship's spine to warp. He'd wrecked his original command by transiting the flip point at Erorsi at maximum military speed with the Pale Ones in hot pursuit.

That was not something he could risk repeating.

The man in engineering seemed to become more concerned as the silence from his compatriot dragged out. With thirty seconds left before the flip, he shook his head.

"Something's wrong. I'd best notify Jaleesa."

Time to pull the plug, Jared decided. He sent the order to trigger the antiboarding weapons in every compartment except for the maintenance tubes.

And nothing happened.

27

Sean was keyed up. The sand in the hourglass had run out, and they were either going to flip or all hell was going to break loose.

He'd watched the Rebel Empire's people in engineering react to the missing man with growing concern, but there wasn't anything he could do to change the situation. Admiral Mertz had the keys to the antiboarding weapons and would use them when the time was right.

And that really seemed like right now. The unnamed man in command of the engineering compartment was about to call the bridge with a missing man report. That would trigger all kinds of bad things.

"Get ready to deploy," he ordered Commander Pence, *Athena*'s rightful chief engineer. "We move as soon as the admiral takes them out. I want positive control of the drives first. We flip on his order."

"Aye, sir," she said calmly. "My people are ready."

He turned in the other direction and focused his attention on Major Adrian Scala, the senior marine on the destroyer. "We need to account for every single enemy as fast as we can. I don't want anyone slipping through the cracks."

"I've already briefed my people," the large black man said. "We're ready as soon as things go down."

We've got a problem, Admiral Mertz said through Sean's implants. *My connection to the ship's systems isn't working. No antiboarding weapons. Take them out.*

Shit.

On it.

"Major Scala, the admiral can't control the ship's internal weapons. Take the enemy out."

He heard the marine officer's command go out over the marine command net.

All marines, this is Damocles Actual. Execute Hotel. Execute! Execute! Execute!

Engineering had more than a few maintenance tubes attached to it. All of their hatches slid open more or less at the same time, and the marines came flooding out, stunners already in play.

Scala was the first out of their tube, but Sean was on his heels, his stunner tracking on the enemy commander. His first shot took the dumbfounded man down with a blue flash.

He tried to take out the woman he'd pegged as the second in command, but she dove behind a console. Hell.

Internal alarms began blaring, and the virtually impervious main engineering hatch slid closed. Too bad for them that Sean and his people were already among them.

"Disable the external coms before they start screaming for help," he shouted, ducking as someone fired in his direction. The beam from the weapon shaded red, showing it was set in the lethal range. He hoped no one had been hit.

"That control run over there," Pence said, pointing at a thick conduit on the wall. "We need to disable the transfer station beside it, too. Cover me."

Scala instead pulled something from his belt and hurled it across the compartment at the transfer station. "Fire in the hole!"

Sean barely had time to clap his hands over his ears and turn away from the danger zone before the grenade went off. It wasn't a plasma grenade, but it still sounded like the end of the world and half stunned him.

The transfer station was a smoking wreck, and the conduit was on fire. New alarms began blaring, just in case anyone had missed the explosion.

"I'd have liked to have been able to use that again sometime soon," Pence growled loudly. "The ship is just crossing into the flip point. What do we do?"

"Flip the ship," Sean ordered. "Do it manually."

"Shit."

The engineer bolted across the compartment toward the nearest console. A red bolt took her in the back, and she dropped, dead before she hit the deck.

Sean didn't hesitate. He ducked lower and raced across his friend's still-twitching corpse. He dropped behind the console a beat before several red beams flashed through where he'd been a second before.

Raising his head high enough to see the controls was quite literally the most dangerous thing he'd ever done.

He was no engineer, but he was a command officer, so he knew what needed to be done. It took an interminable three heartbeats to bring up the right screen.

His command overrides disabled the control interlocks, and he firmly pressed the button, activating the flip drive.

His gut told him they'd transited the wormhole, and the risk of the Rebel Empire crew warning anyone at El Capitan was over. That didn't mean he and his people were any safer.

Scala dropped in beside him. "I see four holdouts. They're behind the gravitic drive, so our options are limited."

"I guess we have to do this the hard way," Sean said, gripping his stunner more tightly. "This is going to suck."

"Welcome to the marines," Scala said with a dark grin. "We're always on the lookout for ways to make any given situation suck more."

The two men came up at the same time as the rest of the marines, and everyone charged the holdouts.

* * *

KELSEY WAS nearest the hatch when the call to attack came. Rather than do the smart thing and let the trained fighters lead the way, she left the maintenance tube at a run, sprinting for the computer center.

It had a hatch that could hold them off if the crew got a chance to close it. They could wreck the computer if they had time. She had to get there first.

She felt the world start to slow down around her and knew she'd somehow managed to trigger her pharmacology unit into dispensing Panther into her system.

Having a name for the drug and Doctor Stone's detailed explanation of what it did to her made the experience far less terrifying this time. That was something, she supposed.

Intellectually, she knew the drug itself didn't really make her much faster, but it felt as if she had all the time in the world to act. That only went so far, though.

Alarms blared from the overheads as she raced around the final corner and pushed herself as hard as she could toward the hatch that was already closing. It was going to be close. If she committed and was wrong, the massive hatch would kill her.

Kelsey bounced off the door frame and made it inside the computer center just as the hatch closed behind her.

Three men and a woman were at the consoles. All were drawing weapons with deceptive slowness.

The odds against her were dire, so Kelsey did the only thing she thought would make a difference. She ordered her Raider implants to eliminate the threats even though the idea of the cold computer controlling her body was her very worst nightmare.

Her implants threw her to the right while shooting the closest man with her stunner. A bolt of red missed her by centimeters as her body twisted. Someone was playing for keeps.

That changed the automated responses she knew. Oh God.

As soon as her body was stable, the powerful artificial muscles in her legs sent her completely over the console. Her left arm swung back, and her fist smashed into the head of one of the remaining men with a sound like dropping a melon, killing him instantly.

Two down. Two to go.

The remaining man was out of reach, but the woman was right beside her. The combat computer in Kelsey's head fired her stunner at the man even as her free hand clamped around the woman's throat.

The sound of her hand crushing the woman's windpipe and snapping her spine was far worse than when she'd killed the man.

Her implants released the dying woman and assessed the threats as contained. It released control of her body back to her. She hadn't really believed it would.

Kelsey promptly threw up even as her body began to shake violently.

Scott Roche and the others were frantically calling over her implant com, but she couldn't stop the blind terror that smothered her mind and froze her limbs.

Being a prisoner in one's body but unable to do anything except scream as it killed was *exactly* like being a Pale One. And it brought back all the horror she'd suffered.

Kelsey, open the door. Please let us help you.

It was Scott.

She retched again but managed to crawl toward the hatch. With what felt like the last of her strength, she hit the manual control.

The hatch slid open, and marines rushed in, weapons up. Scott came in right behind them.

Her friend took one look at her, dropped to his knees, and took her into his arms as she started sobbing.

* * *

Not being privy to the enemy's implant communications, Jared didn't know exactly what had triggered the Rebel Empire commander to hit the alarms, but he didn't let that slow him down.

At his order, marines blew the micro charges on the three concealed hatches along the periphery of the bridge and charged into the midst of their shocked foes. Blue stunner bolts took everyone down before they could do more than scream in shock.

Jared raced to his command console, dumped the unconscious woman out of his seat, and sat just as *Athena* flipped out of the El Capitan system. His implants were still locked out of the ship's controls, but he had decades of experience working without them.

This side of the flip point was blissfully empty. He let out a sigh and waited for his team to get into their seats. The marines were securing the prisoners and setting up a defensive position inside the main hatch in case of counterattack.

"Commander Hall," Jared said, "as I recall, this system only has one other flip point. Set course for it at maximum military power."

"Aye, sir," she said, her hands dancing over the controls. "Maximum military power. All propulsion systems nominal. ETA fourteen hours, ten minutes. Shall I launch probes to verify the system is clear?"

"Do so. Let me know if you find anything interesting."

Jared turned his attention to his ship. There was fighting in engineering. His people had the upper hand, though. Computer central was in loyal hands, though it looked as if Princess Kelsey had been hurt.

The balance of forces in engineering dictated his people would come out on top, though he saw people on the deck, either unconscious or dead That meant he needed to focus on the rest of the ship.

Athena's internal scanners located sixteen intruders scattered across the ship, mostly alone or in very small groups. None of them seemed to have a clue what was happening. He planned on keeping it that way.

"Lieutenant Laird, take a team and apprehend the intruders. Hit them in whatever order you see fit and coordinate with Major Scala. I want my ship back without anyone else being hurt or causing a ruckus."

"Aye, sir," the red-headed marine said as she gestured toward two-thirds of her people. "We'll take care of them for you."

By the time her team had departed the bridge, the fight in engineering was over. Jared called Sean over the ship's internal com. The other officer appeared on his console seconds later.

"Status?"

"We have control of engineering, but we encountered some problems," the other officer said tiredly. "These bastards went right to lethal weapons.

"Commander Pence and half a dozen others are dead. And we blew up the power transfer unit feeding the ship's external com system. I hope you don't need to talk to anyone for a while."

The news about his lost personnel was a gut punch.

"Dammit," Jared said bitterly. "Send Major Scala to assist the rest of the marines in rousting any other holdouts. Use lethal force if they show any sign of resistance."

"No argument from me. I vote we space these bastards as soon as we get what we need from them. The indiscriminate use of lethal force is a violation of Imperial Law and Fleet regulations. Both Fleets."

Jared shook his head. "As much as I'd love to let you handle that little detail, these people are intelligence sources. Important ones, I suspect.

"That doesn't mean you can't lock them down tight. Arm and leg restraints. Two marines each when they wake up. Very restricted movement and isolation from one another. No information about us at all."

"Are we clear?" Meyer asked. "Did we escape El Capitan clean?"

"So far, but that could be because we surprised them by leaving so quickly. They might dispatch a ship to find out what made us so standoffish at any time. Get that com system back up in case we need it."

"Will do. Do you want me to take the lead on questioning the prisoners? I really want to know why they were so trigger-happy."

Jared considered that before shaking his head. "Let Olivia take the lead.

Have her make up whatever story she likes. She knows these kind of people far better than we do. Let's use that familiarity."

He really hoped she could get to the bottom of this without setting the prisoners off. If they triggered someone, they wouldn't be able to undo the damage.

Whatever the reason, these people had started out shooting to kill. He needed to know why as soon as possible. Their lives might depend on it.

28

Elise rushed to Kelsey's side as soon as Jared sounded the all clear. Doctor Stone had the princess from another universe in the medical center, but the marines had flatly refused to let her out of the maintenance tube until the ship was cleared of intruders.

She passed one group of marines carrying the unconscious or dead bodies of some of those intruders on the way to the medical center, but she didn't stop to ask questions.

Commander Scott Roche was waiting for her outside the medical center.

"How is she?" Elise asked, a little short of breath.

"Bad, but nothing physical," the Fleet officer said softly. "She used her combat mode function. Having her implants control her body was too much like being a Pale One, and it hit her hard."

Elise felt herself blanch. Her people had dealt with the savage Pale Ones for five centuries. She knew far too well what the other princess had to be feeling.

"I'll see if I can help."

"Thank you."

She strode into the medical center and found Kelsey sitting in a chair, wrapped in a blanket. Lily Stone was hovering a few steps away.

Elise rushed over and dropped to her knees beside the chair. She took Kelsey's hand in hers. "I hear you had a little trouble at the computer center."

The other woman's damp, haunted eyes came up. "You could say that. I killed two people."

"But that's not what's bothering you, is it? Not really."

"I had to let my implants control my body. I had a panic attack when it was all over."

"You did what you had to do," Elise said soothingly. "Your people had already overwritten the corrupted code, and we upgraded your implant hardware. No one will *ever* do that to you again. You were ultimately in control."

The blonde woman wiped her wet eyes. "I understand that, intellectually, but I was one of those monsters for weeks. I have nightmares about spending the rest of my life like that, and I couldn't breathe when it was over."

"Our Kelsey has nightmares, too. I realize she didn't suffer the way you did, but it will get better. I've seen you do it before."

Kelsey shook her head and stared at the bulkhead. "I can't imagine how I will ever get past this. Your Kelsey sounds like a hero from an old story. I'm not like that. I can barely stay sane."

"You're stronger than you think."

The other woman's eyes shot up, filled with sudden heat. "I am *not* her. You all insist I am, but she didn't break like I did. She had all the good luck, and I got the bad. I *hate* her."

The bitterness in her friend's voice was heartbreaking.

Elise squeezed Kelsey's hand tighter. "My father once told me that you get through the tough times by focusing on small steps. One after the other, they will take you through the flames and to safety."

Kelsey snorted. "Forgive me, but what does he know about flames? You grew up a lot like I did, I bet. A life of privilege and being shielded from danger."

That offhand, dismissive tone ignited a burn in Elise's belly, but she kept her expression compassionate. "Perhaps, but we always knew we were one attack away from the horror that found you. And not just weeks of it, but for the rest of our lives.

"Princess or pauper, each of us lived every day knowing exactly how horrible an end awaited us. Did you know I carried a small knife in a necklace since I was a girl? Useless little thing.

"Unless you needed to slit your wrist. Let me tell you, having the royal physician give me a lecture at ten years old on the best way to kill myself is a memory I will carry to my grave."

Kelsey sagged as the fire went out of her. "I didn't know that. I'm sorry for being a selfish bitch."

Elise smiled sadly. "I'm not trying to equate our situations or make you feel better toward our Kelsey. She caught some breaks that you didn't. And she had Jared. Believe me, that makes a difference. At least in this universe."

"I hate him, too," Kelsey said bluntly. "But I get it. He's not the same man as in my universe. Everyone here gives him so much respect that he must've earned it. It's difficult to believe my eyes over my heart, but I'm getting there."

The other woman rubbed her face. "Are all the prisoners under lock and key? By the way, they tried to kill me right off. Is everyone else okay?"

A glance at Lily told Elise that not everyone had made it.

"We lost nine people taking the ship," Lily said. "That included Doctor Dishmon and Commander Pence in engineering. It sure looks as if they started with the lethal option."

"From the first shot," Kelsey agreed. "We had total surprise. They had no idea whatsoever that we were here. I don't get how they could go right for the kill."

"That's a great question," Elise said with a nod. "Olivia is going to handle the questioning. She was one of their class her entire life. The rest of us might slip up and let them realize we aren't from their society. She won't."

Kelsey stared at her with unblinking eyes. "I'm still sorry I killed those two but not because they didn't deserve it. I'm sorry because I have to live with the memory of killing them.

"Still, it's far from the most terrible thing I've ever done. If she needs someone to make an example of one of them, I can hardly have fewer nightmares."

The idea of having someone do something like that, knowingly inflicting harm on themselves in the process, sickened Elise. This Kelsey really was a different person than her friend. One with different moral standards, it seemed. A bit more brutal and deeply hurt inside.

"That won't be necessary," Elise said firmly. "If Olivia needs to get answers from someone that doesn't feel like sharing, I'm sure Lily can come up with a drug to help."

"Don't worry about making them pay for what they did," Lily said, stepping closer. "They will pay for the lives they took."

The doctor frowned. "Now that I think about it, why were they all armed in the first place? Surely, they didn't expect trouble here in their own system."

Elise couldn't begin to guess the answer to that. She'd be watching over Olivia's shoulder with interest via her implants when the interrogations started.

Of course, that wasn't without risk either. Olivia West had been the coordinator of Harrison's World, a powerful leader in the Rebel Empire's higher orders, even if she'd secretly been an Imperial loyalist.

She was like this Kelsey in a lot of ways. Ruthless. She might not need someone to be the bad guy in the questioning. Maybe watching that wasn't such a good idea after all.

* * *

Athena didn't have a real brig, Olivia discovered, much less an area capable of holding dozens of prisoners. Jared Mertz had put them into individual compartments with marine guards.

The guards were out of uniform to maintain the ruse that they weren't military, even though that was a tad threadbare. The men and women looked exactly like marines out of uniform.

So she'd concocted a ruse to explain why they had implants: they were *former* marine officers. Still odd, but not so dangerous.

They couldn't afford to trip any of the buried subroutines in these peoples' corrupted implant code. Keeping someone like that locked up would be a nightmare.

The New Terran Empire destroyer had been racing across the next system over from El Capitan for almost four hours. No one had come after them. It appeared as though they'd gotten away.

Jared had sent people to look at the crates and found them sealed with what certainly looked like explosives. In this case, plasma grenades or the equivalent.

Since he now had control of the computer again, he locked the prisoners out of the com net. They had original Old Empire implants, so without a headset, their top range was ten meters. Enough to communicate with those close to them, but nothing more.

She would have preferred keeping them from communicating at all, but that was impossible. A destroyer just wasn't big enough to spread the prisoners out far enough for that.

So she decided to pick the prisoner most likely to talk and ensconced him far away from the others. He would crack eventually, she suspected. He didn't seem as hard as the others.

He hadn't even been armed. He was the only one of the intruders not carrying a neural disruptor set to kill. That marked him as special and perhaps not as dedicated to their cause as the rest.

These people had fought hard from the very first moment. They'd expected trouble and hadn't believed themselves safe even in their own system.

Discovering why was her first order of business.

The man Kelsey had captured at the maintenance tube seemed more of a technician than the rest. Of course, he was a member of the higher orders. It wouldn't do to underestimate him.

Olivia had him tied to a chair with actual cord rather than plastic restraints. She made certain his legs were tied to the chair legs and that his hands were very secure. She bound his wrists behind the chair and tied his upper arms together behind his back. Then she secured them to the chair.

It wasn't that she feared he would get loose. The marines would keep her safe. She wanted him to feel powerless. It was purely psychological.

That theme could've been taken further. She could've blindfolded him. She decided not to because she'd wanted an unobstructed view of his reactions.

He'd already proven that consideration valid. The prisoner—his first name was Austin—had actually been awake for the last few minutes, but he gave no sign of it. Only the medical monitor she put on his wrist let her know when he'd awoken.

All of the other prisoners had been included in the database the resistance had sent Olivia. Not him. A curious omission. She wondered if that was because the man wasn't considered important or if they'd excluded him for some other reason.

In any case, it was time to get started.

"I know you've been awake for the last few minutes," Olivia said, leaning a little forward in her own seat placed a few meters in front of him. "You might as well open your eyes."

The man's eyes popped open, and his head came up. So she could surprise him. Good.

His eyes narrowed. "Who are you? Why have you attacked us?"

"I'm the woman in charge now. You can call me Olivia. Now that we have that settled, I'd like you to state your full name for the record."

Austin's eyes narrowed. "For what record?"

She almost smiled. "You're full of questions. You don't have the need to know. Let's just say that not every part of the Empire is behind your mission, and I was sent to ask a few questions."

"We have orders from the Imperial Lord. You wouldn't dare to defy him."

Now she did smile. "And yet, here I am. Every single one of you is my prisoner. Your name, please."

"Austin Darrah. I found your command tap, by the way. You were just a few seconds too late to stop me from disconnecting it."

It took her a second to figure out what he meant. It was probably what had allowed Jared to command *Athena* remotely. Until it had stopped working.

"Do you feel proud?" she asked, allowing a hint of sadness to seep into her tone. "You'd still be our prisoner if you'd left it in place, but we wouldn't have had to kill any of your companions. Or lose our own people."

He swallowed but put on a brave face. "I did what I had to do. I'd do it again, too." His eyes flicked over to the marines leaning against the bulkhead. "They're military. Officers of some kind. Marines?"

"Ex-marine officers, yes. What's in the crates you brought aboard, and why were your friends so quick to jump to lethal force?"

"If you don't know, I can't tell you."

"You'll talk," she assured him. "It can be voluntarily or with assistance, but you will tell me everything I want to know."

Some part of her conviction must've gotten through to him, because he swallowed again. "You're mistaken. I literally can't. The System Lord implanted explosive devices in our heads and amended the code in our implants. We can't tell you *anything* about this mission, or we'll quite literally lose our heads."

A low alarm began sounding. Not ear-splittingly loud like the call to battle. This was lower key. An implant call from Jared came a moment later.

Olivia, there's been a situation. The prisoners have some kind of suicide charge in their skulls. They all just blew up. Are you okay?

She eyed the man, wondering if he was going to explode. Probably not, if someone else had to send the signal. He'd been too far from the rest to get the signal.

I'm fine, and so is my prisoner. He'd just told me about the devices when the alarm went off. He says he can't talk about his mission because the device will kill him.

Jared was silent for a second before he continued. *Break off questioning. Get him to the medical center, and let's see what Lily can tell us about the device. If we can disarm it, then you can pick up right where you left off.*

He's the last surviving member of this Rebel Empire crew, and we can't risk losing the chance to find out what they were up to.

29

Cleaning up the compartments they'd used for holding the now dead Rebel Empire nobles was a grisly task, Sean decided. Whoever had put those bombs in their heads had used far more explosive than was necessary to kill them.

The blasts had painted the compartments with blood and brains while causing significant damage to their torsos.

It had also gotten the unfortunate marines keeping watch over them, too. Perhaps it was meant to make a lasting impression on anyone around the unfortunate bastards.

It wasn't hard discerning the order of events. The prisoners had awakened and discovered their new circumstances. The woman who had been in Jared's seat on the bridge had taken a good look around her just before the suicide charges went off.

She had to be the trigger woman. She'd sent the destruct order, killing herself and her crew.

Not everyone was in range of her implants, but they'd been close enough to their friends. The signal traveled out in a relay from person to person, each retransmitting the destruct code before it blew up.

The only person out of range had been the young man Olivia had been questioning. Since he hadn't blown himself up, he either didn't have the codes or wasn't interested in killing himself just yet.

Sean wondered if the self-destruct command had been meant to blow up the cargo, too. He'd have done it that way. Thankfully, the prisoners hadn't been close enough to the cargo bay to trigger the plasma charges.

Equally good was the fact that Admiral Mertz had locked the prisoners out of the ship's systems. The computer could've relayed the woman's command all over the ship.

As a precaution, Sean had ordered the engineering team—now working under Lieutenant Commander Anthony O'Halloran—to look over the destroyer's systems closely. He'd been afraid of a larger self-destruct option, like setting off one of the fusion plants.

To his relief, it seemed as if they hadn't felt the need to go that far. Or they'd believed they would have time to set one off manually.

"Commodore?" one of the engineers asked. "I've found something you might be interested in."

Sean pulled himself together and looked up from the engineering console he'd been staring uselessly at. "Talk to me, Tony."

"The computer had logs of the activity on all the consoles, including the bridge. I found some calculations from Admiral Mertz's position. The Rebel Empire commander was plotting potential courses."

He smiled. That was useful. "Where was she going?"

"Terra. She had a single course laid in, and she marked each system with a very narrow window of dates. Some also had long codes next to them. Possibly passcodes. Sir, she was in something of a hurry. She has them arriving in three weeks."

Based on his research, Sean thought that was a bit aggressive for a realistic timetable.

"They must've been on a pretty tight schedule. I wonder if their little bombs were on a timer, too. Show up on time or not at all."

"It's possible," the engineer said with a shrug. "There's not enough left of the bombs to be sure."

"Not in the dead ones," Sean agreed. "I'll go see what Doctor Stone can tell us about the survivor."

He rose to his feet and headed for the lift. Too bad the people Princess Kelsey had killed had been close enough to pick up the destruct command. That would've made discovering the particulars of the explosion easier.

Sean walked into the medical center to find everyone clustered around the heavily guarded prisoner. The ludicrously over-guarded prisoner, in his opinion.

There were six marines present, two in unpowered armor. The man himself was secured to an exam table, and his wrists and ankles were bound in flex cuffs.

Olivia was standing off to the side, observing Doctor Stone scanning her patient.

Sean stepped over to his wife. "He looks dangerous. You want someone in powered armor, just to be sure?"

The look she gave him indicated that she thought he needed to work on his delivery. "Funny. Also, not my call. Jared said he wanted to make sure our young friend didn't even consider getting froggy."

He felt the corner of his mouth quirk upward. "Froggy? Is this something Kelsey taught you?"

"Obviously. A frog on Terra has long, powerful legs and can jump quite a distance. So the meaning is that we don't want the prisoner to try anything."

"You heard what happened to the rest. Any concerns that he might blow his own head off?"

Olivia shrugged. "Not really. It seems as if he'd already have done it if he were so inclined. And he warned us that he couldn't talk about what they were doing before the others popped their corks. He mentioned the explosives, and it's no likely he'd have told us about it if he intended to use it."

He chuckled. "Popped their corks? You've picked up quite an arsenal of sayings."

Lily Stone murmured something to the prisoner and stepped back from the exam table. Once she turned and saw Sean, she headed over.

"I've done an initial scan," the physician said. "He definitely has some kind of explosive charge in his skull. I'll have to actually open his scalp and take a closer look before I decide if it can be safely removed."

"I didn't realize bomb disposal was among your list of talents," Sean said with a slight frown. "If that thing goes off, it could kill you at that range."

"I'm a Fleet officer," she retorted. "I could die any number of terrible ways. If I started letting that drive my decision making, I'd need to retire."

She looked back toward the prisoner. "My initial scans don't indicate any antitampering mechanism. It's probably linked into his implants. If they think he's being messed with, they could set it off. If so, I may be able to take them offline and remove the explosive charge."

"I don't want you doing something overly risky," Sean said firmly.

"I agree," Olivia added, "but I want him to answer questions, too. We need to know what's in the cargo area. He needs to tell us what they planned to do."

Sean couldn't really argue with that. He was about to reluctantly agree when the hatch slid open and Kelsey walked in.

The petite woman stopped when she saw the prisoner. Then she eyed the enhanced guard detail before going over to them. "Should I get into my powered armor and make sure he doesn't try anything?"

Sean laughed. "I said something very much like that, Highness. How are you feeling?"

"A little better," the woman admitted. "Oddly, them killing themselves made it clear to me that the people in the computer center would have done something terrible if I hadn't stopped them. They were fanatics.

"People willing to kill at the drop of a hat, whether themselves or someone else, are too dangerous to be allowed to walk around freely."

"I'm going to see if I can remove the risk for this gentleman," Lily told Kelsey. "Would you care to observe the process?"

Kelsey's eyes narrowed. "That sounds like a trick question. Is it going to be gross?"

"I'll have to make an incision on his skull, but it shouldn't be terrible. Unless he explodes on the operating table, that is."

The princess sighed. "The way my luck has gone recently, you might be better off without me. Still, this could be something we need to do in my universe. If he explodes in my face, I'm making you pay for my therapy."

"If he explodes in our faces, we can attend sessions together. Come on."

* * *

KELSEY CHANGED into a white smock before joining Doctor Stone at the exam table. The prisoner looked up at her, a disgruntled expression on his face.

"You really screwed me."

"Did I?" she asked. "You seem to be breathing."

"I won't be when Lady Keaton gets ahold of me," the man muttered.

She flicked her gaze over to Lily and caught the slight shake of the other woman's head. They hadn't told him that his friends had killed themselves. Good to know. Kelsey wished they'd mentioned that up front.

It took her an instant to remember how to initiate a com call through her implants.

Any other subjects off limits for him, Doctor?

We're not telling him anything at all about the other prisoners or who we are. We also aren't asking him any questions. Who knows what might set him off? If he asks any questions, don't answer them. If he states something, let it stand even if it's not accurate.

"I'm going to fit a high-resolution scanner on your head," Stone told the man out loud. "It will allow me to get a more detailed reading of the device in your head."

"It won't help," the man said, resigned. "I tell you, the bomb is linked to my implants. It won't go off unless they decide that I need to die because I'm going to talk or if you attempt to remove it. There isn't anything you can do to change that."

Stone didn't answer him. Instead, she put a device over the man's skull and tapped the control pad on it. The man's eyes closed abruptly, as if he'd gone to sleep.

"Interesting," Kelsey said. "I didn't know scanners could do that."

"I lied," the physician said with a smile. "This is a somatic stimulator. It basically forced his brain to go into a deep sleep.

"The Old Empire used them in place of drugs when they wanted someone to be unconscious, say for a medical procedure. He won't respond to anything, not even when I make the incision."

"Won't his implants still monitor what you're doing?"

The Fleet doctor picked up an instrument. "They shouldn't care as long as I'm not messing with the bomb, which I won't be. Instead, I'm going to access his implants directly and overwrite his implant code."

"I didn't have an incision for that. You only knocked me out for the hardware upgrade."

"And so it is here. I spoke with Admiral Mertz, and he agreed that anyone we captured in the future needed to be made safe from being enslaved again."

Kelsey considered that and slowly shook her head. "That's not a good idea. If they escape and run home to Mommy, the AIs will know you can lock them out."

"They'll know if they ever capture any of us, too. It is a risk, but we believe it's the right balance of protection for everyone."

She was certain the doctor was wrong, but it wasn't her place to argue. They'd made their decision.

"Why don't you educate me about this new hardware?"

"The mechanism that allows for updating the implant code is in one of the sub-cores surrounding the central implant. I'll use a manipulator to remove the compromised core entirely and replaced it with one that's more secure. It takes less than half an hour from incision to regeneration."

"What prevents the AI from removing the new hardware and replacing it with compromised hardware?"

"Without the appropriate codes or the patient's explicit prior permission, any attempt to remove the hardware will fry the implants themselves. It won't harm the person, but the original wiring in the brain will be compromised. Replacing it is significantly more complex than the original installation. Perhaps even impossible."

So anyone captured by the AIs might never have implants again. Kelsey considered that a small price to pay for not becoming a Pale One.

Stone shaved a spot the size of a fingertip on the man's skull and made a small incision. She staunched the blood and held the wound open with a small hand tool.

Once that was done, she inserted a device into the cut and spent about ten minutes removing a very small metal object and replacing it with another one. Then she reversed the procedure and closed the incision.

She used a handheld regenerator to quickly heal the minor wound. The only remaining trace of the procedure was a small bald spot.

"Shouldn't you have updated his implant code before you did that?" she asked as the doctor started cleaning up. "Now you can't, right?"

"Future updates now will require his permission, but I did it before I removed the old hardware. The process used to take hours, but we figured out we weren't doing it correctly.

"The details are far too technical to get into, but Carl Owlet discovered a much more efficient method. Five minutes, and it's done. I overwrote his corrupted code while getting everything set up to make the hardware swap."

This Carl Owlet was a most resourceful fellow. She knew that Scott Roche had already arranged to have him contacted, and she couldn't wait to meet him.

She spent a few seconds examining the unconscious man. "So you could've saved his companions."

"I could have. If I'd known about the bombs, I wouldn't have waited for them to wake up. Lesson learned."

"Are you going to remove his explosives?"

Stone shook her head. "I'll have to take those deeper scans I mentioned and let the tech people consider the options. If there is an antitampering device, we may have to leave it there.

"If so, a localized jammer implanted beside it might protect him, but it might also affect him in other ways. Frankly, it's just too soon to tell."

Stone set another device on the man's head and frowned at it. "This is my deep scanner. You can tap into its feed if you like."

Kelsey found the data stream and drew it in. The core it was focused on was linked directly to the man's implants. The details of the device were beginning to become clear as the scanner went across it again and again.

"We won't be able to access the internal code," Stone said. "I'm more concerned with the hardware. If it detects separation from his implants, it might detonate."

She focused in on the diagram and tried to make sense of it. She wasn't a tech, but her implants occasionally provided insight on things she didn't directly understand.

A small window popped up in her vision, and her implants started tracing the circuitry. This was something she'd asked Elise about days earlier. Apparently, this was not something everyone could do. It was an enhancement provided by her Raider implants.

Almost as soon as it began, the window closed, and another one opened. This one had data on the Raider implants themselves. This same circuitry was in her own head, though thankfully not attached to a bomb.

It *was* a kind of antitampering circuit but, in her case, one that would wipe the classified intelligence stored in her implants if an unauthorized person attempted to access them.

She didn't actually *have* any classified intelligence, but the design was there. A Raider was supposed to store secret stuff in a specific segment of internal memory for safety. Good to know.

Kelsey accessed the manual these people had provided for her and read everything about the antitampering circuit. There was a way to get around it, but it was very technical and seemed to require specialized equipment she didn't have.

Maybe the New Terran Empire did.

In any case, the circuit was to prevent access to the hardware. Not to stop anyone from removing it. The man's implants would probably have been monitoring for removal and triggered the explosives under those circumstances.

With the compromised code gone, it should be perfectly safe to remove it. Of course, it wasn't her head she was talking about. The unconscious man would likely object. Strenuously.

Thankfully, she didn't have to make that decision. She'd tell Doctor Stone and let her make the decision. And stand farther away for that procedure.

30

Jared walked into the prisoner's room without knocking. That was rude, but he needed to set the tone for this meeting. He held all the cards, and the prisoner needed to understand that on a visceral level.

The man wasn't bound, though he was guarded. Two marines stood on either side of the hatch, just inside the compartment. Two more stood in the corridor beyond. What's more, they'd made certain the prisoner was aware of how thoroughly they were watching him.

Every angle inside his make-do prison cell was under conspicuous observation at all times. Also, the man was never allowed to be alone. Even the bathroom. The marines inside the compartment kept him in their sight at all times.

That might seem like overkill, but Jared couldn't take the risk that the man would find another way to kill himself now that Lily had disabled the bomb from his head. The information he possessed was far too valuable to take chances.

The man sat on a small couch, reading something on a handheld viewer. He set it aside as soon as Jared entered, but he didn't stand.

Jared wondered what status this man had on El Capitan. As he had implants, he was a member of the higher orders. That was a certainty because there was no way he was a Fleet officer and those were the only other people allowed to have implants.

Well, there were nobles, and then there were *nobles*, he supposed. Austin Darrah was obviously very low in the hierarchy.

"Mister Darrah," Jared said with a slight nod. "I regret having to keep you under close guard. I wish things could be different, but until you answer some questions, I need to be certain that you're safe, even from yourself."

The other man shook his head slightly. "We have different definitions of the word 'safe.' You know who I am, sir. Might I ask your name and position?"

"Of course. My name is Jared Mertz, and I command this ship."

"Well, you certainly do now. What did you do before? Where are you from? What do you want with me?"

Without asking for permission, Jared sat across the coffee table from the man. He crossed his legs and tried to exude an air of confidence. It helped that he actually was confident.

"While this might be difficult to believe, I was in command of this vessel when it entered the El Capitan system. If you're wondering, we didn't sneak on board the ship while it was orbiting your planet. We were already here."

The man looked bemused. "I can't figure out what that's even supposed to mean. This is an automated destroyer. Even these furnishings shouldn't be here. At least I don't think they should be.

"Why would you go to the trouble of sneaking aboard a vessel like this to get into El Capitan? You couldn't possibly have known about our mission. What were you really doing?"

"Well, that's quite a story. I might even tell it to you once we're done finding out about you and what you were doing aboard my ship.

"Let me lay out a few salient facts for you. You brought aboard a number of cargo containers protected by plasma-based explosives. You and all your compatriots had bombs planted inside your heads. And let's not forget how you opened fire on my people with your weapons set to lethal force the moment you saw us."

Jared leaned back in his seat and crossed his legs.

"I can't tell you," the man said in an exasperated tone. "Remember the bomb in my head that you mentioned? If I try to tell you anything, it will go off. But I will point out that I wasn't armed."

"True enough," Jared said with a smile. "The bomb would be a factor if we hadn't disabled it during your little nap in our medical center."

The man's mouth dropped open. "Have you lost your mind? How could you possibly have thought it was a good idea to mess around with the *explosives in my head*? If you actually did."

"Come now, Mister Darrah. Give me a little credit. I have a lot of questions for you, so it doesn't serve my purpose to have your head explode before you answer them.

"I realize that requires taking a lot on faith when your life hangs in the balance, but run through the possibilities. Under what circumstances would I intentionally have you do something that so drastically curtailed my options going forward?"

The man gave a sharp laugh. "I have no idea. All I know for certain is that I can't trust anything you say. You could be *anyone*. Maybe you just want to record me exploding so that you can use the video to intimidate my companions. Frankly, I'm the most expendable of our crew, so that makes sense."

"You're hardly expendable," Jared disagreed. "Here's where I give you a little bit more information to operate from.

"The lady who was questioning you earlier had you segregated from the other prisoners. So, to your good fortune, you weren't anywhere near them when your leader ordered everyone's bombs to explode.

"You are my *only* prisoner. If you like, I can provide you some video of what happened to them. Allow me to warn you that it's not pretty."

Darrah considered Jared carefully. "No, I imagine it isn't. Let's say for the moment that you're telling me the truth. If I'm your only source of information about what we're doing here, why in the world would I help you?"

"Do you really enjoy having these marines watching your every move? Observing you going to the bathroom? Watching you take a shower? Would you like to sleep in a room by yourself?"

The other man grunted. "There is something to that. Still, you're obviously a man who's up to no good. I want to know who I'm dealing with before I start dropping secrets. The System Lord was very adamant about keeping our mouths shut."

"That's certainly true," Jared agreed "Anyone that puts bombs in people's heads really does intend for them to stay silent. Did it occur to you that once you were finished with your task, it would set off the bombs to make sure that none of you never spoke of this?"

"You don't know that," Darrah said. His tone indicated he wasn't completely certain he believed his own words.

"Let's try something simple, shall we? You were going to Terra, correct?"

The man clamped his lips shut for a few seconds before sighing. "One way or the other, I'm going to regret this. Yes, we were supposed to deliver the special cargo to the System Lord at Terra."

His expression said that he was waiting for his head to explode. When it didn't, he sagged a little.

"See?" Jared asked. "Safe as houses."

Darrah gave him a confused look. "What's that supposed to mean?"

"Forgive my obscurity. I meant that there was no danger."

"Ah. How odd. Before we see how far I'm willing to go, I need to understand what's in it for me. I'm a dead man if the Lords find out about this. How can you protect me and still make it worth my while to be cooperative?

"And don't tell me I should be glad I'm alive at all. Be realistic. You need what I know in a very short window of time if it's going to do you any good at all."

Jared didn't disagree. "And this is where I bring the woman you met before, Olivia West, back in to negotiate. She's much better at this than I am."

* * *

Olivia made a point of rapping her knuckles against the hatch when she arrived for her second interview with Austin Darrah. One of the marines inside the compartment opened the hatch for her. It wasn't as if the prisoner had the option of refusing her entry. Still, it paid to be courteous.

Unlike the last time she'd seen him, the man wasn't tied to a chair. Now he sat tensely on a small couch. He rose when she entered the room, but it seemed like an unwilling gesture.

"Mister Darrah," she said with a genuine smile. "I'm pleased to see that you survived the recent unpleasantness. As you might perhaps recall, my name is Olivia West. Shall we sit? Perhaps you'd like me to order us something to eat?"

The man sat and gestured for her to take the place across from him. "Your food is one thing I have no complaints about. Whoever does your cooking is quite excellent. None of my former companions had the talent. Meals were something of a chore during our hurried training."

She nodded as she sat. "I'm not much of a cook myself, but I've picked up a few tricks along the way. We do have a few people with real gifts for the culinary arts, though.

"Jared tells me that you're willing to discuss working with us. What would you expect in return for your cooperation?"

While he was considering how to answer her question, she used her implants to send out an order for sandwiches, tea, and coffee. The crew manning the galley had been warned to expect her call. They'd be along shortly.

After almost thirty seconds of silence, Darrah grimaced. "While I have some leverage, I'll confess that I've never been good at this sort of thing. You're probably going to take advantage of me."

"Allow me to let you in on a little secret about negotiation," she said conspiratorially. "The best deals are the ones where everyone feels as though they've gotten something they want. If I take undue advantage, your cooperation will be grudging.

"We don't want you feeling as if we have you over a barrel. We want you to cooperate willingly. So rather than worrying that I'm going to use some lapse or lawyerly clause against you, why don't you tell me in very basic language what you see as the best outcome for you."

He shrugged. "The bridges behind me are merrily burning, so I doubt I can salvage the life I had. It's gone. I'll have to focus on what comes next.

"I don't know which planetary system you people come from, but you can hide me. You can make it so the System Lords don't know that I'm there. You can give me a good life where I'm not scrambling to survive. One that keeps me out of the public eye but lets me indulge in the things that I love."

"That's a reasonable request," she agreed with a nod. "But I think we can do better. I can't go into the details at this point, but I can assure you that once we have completed our mission, we can put you into a society where you don't have to fear the System Lords, one where you can walk around and have as open a life as you choose."

His expression turned skeptical. "The System Lords have eyes everywhere. All it takes is for my face to come to their attention, and I'm a dead man."

Olivia nodded. "As I said, I can't get into the specific details of the situation, but let me raise the bar to where I think it should be. You have information that I suspect is critical to our survival and our mission.

"That's worth quite a bit to me and my associates. In exchange for your full and complete cooperation, we can arrange for a life that might be considered luxurious in comparison to the one you've lived until this point. I say so even with the understanding that your background lies in the higher orders. Does that interest you?"

He watched her suspiciously for a long while before he asked, "How do I know that you aren't lying? You could promise me anything and then take it all away once you have the information you want."

"You can't know for sure," she admitted. "I could promise you the moon and stars without meaning a single word. I could also simply mention the kind of pressure we could deliver to make you talk, but that's not the kind of people we are.

"I think you realize how difficult a spot you're in. There's no need to emphasize the potentially bad outcome. I'd much rather craft a realistic agreement we can both live with that takes our unfortunate situations into account. Wouldn't you?"

The man sighed. "I suppose so. No matter what happens to me now, the Lords will have no choice but to silence me. When I was part of a group with members as important as the other people in my party, there was at least some chance for me. Now I'm a dead man if they get ahold of me.

"I suppose I should be bitter, but the odds of me coming out of this excursion in one piece were never that good. Once the System Lord selected me, I suspected my days were numbered. Particularly with this thing in my head."

She allowed him to stew a little longer, and he sighed again. "I'll just have to take you at your word. What do you want to know first?"

"The cargo. What's in it? Why is it boobytrapped?"

"I don't officially know since no one felt the need to brief me. I was selected for this mission because of my technical knowledge. Imperial Fleet technology is something I've researched all my life. I know it as well as anyone else in the higher orders. Probably better.

"The Lord pulled me out of a life of relative quiet and gave me no choice in the matter. I was here to assist the crew in making all the systems function as designed. They've had intensive training in their specific areas of responsibility, but that only goes so far. I was here to bridge their gaps in experience."

"But you have your suspicions," Olivia pressed. "The cargo is outfitted with antitampering systems and plasma charges. That's pretty serious."

He shrugged. "I did overhear some people talking about them. Based on a few vague comments, I think they contain a bio weapon."

Olivia felt a chill run down her spine. "Obviously you're not sure, but can you be more specific?"

"Something that's going to Terra. I think the Lords have grown tired of the resistance there and intend to eliminate it once and for all. Probably along with the entire remaining population."

31

Elise listened closely as Olivia recounted what she'd learned from their now cooperative prisoner. His tale was horrifying on both a personal level and in the scope of the task that the Lords had set for these people.

Jared leaned forward as Olivia wrapped up. "To summarize, these people were on their way to Terra to exterminate an unknown number of people. The cargo we're carrying is probably the most dangerous and shocking thing I've ever heard of.

"The next thing we need to work out is how to get rid of it safely. Considering the paranoia displayed so far, it will probably explode if we attempt to move it."

"And if we don't," Olivia added. "These people were on a strict schedule. They're supposed to meet some people a few systems over to assist them in their mission. They have to be there in five days maximum."

"That sounds ominous," Elise said. "I hear an 'or else' in there."

"Very astute," Olivia granted. "The cargo does have a self-destruct timer, and it gives them no more than six days to get there. If the people they were meeting fail to enter the appropriate code, the cargo will explode."

"And what happens if it does get the code?" Jared asked. "And who are these people? What skills do they bring to the party?"

"Our guest doesn't know. He wasn't part of the cabal in charge of this mission. More like the unwilling labor. The senior people on this ship were part of the Lord's inner circle. True believers.

"They had all the critical information in their heads. He only knew what he needed to know to keep everything working. They kept him in the dark as much as possible.

"Personally, I think they intended to try to protect him when everything was over. Otherwise, why not tell him? They could kill him anytime they chose."

"These people sound like assholes," Kelsey said from her chair in the corner behind Sean. "I've met more than my fair share of that kind of people over the last few years. No offense, Elise."

"Pentagar does have a few," she admitted. "Are you speaking of Lord Admiral Shrike?"

Kelsey's eyebrows rose. "No. He always seemed a bit stuffy to me, but he was polite enough. Why?"

Elise shook her head. "When you get back to your universe, you might want to tell your version of me about him. He led a coup here that almost overturned the monarchy. His people left the other you to the Pale Ones."

The blonde woman's expression hardened. "I have a very special place in my heart for traitors. Trust me when I say that I'll see that you take care of him expeditiously. Make a note, Scott."

The Fleet commander beside her nodded. "I'll add it to my action items. This visit is showing all kinds of people in a new light. Does anyone mind if I ask a question?"

When no one objected, he continued. "Our options going forward seem somewhat constrained. If we don't meet with these unknown hostiles, our ship explodes with us in it. If we do, we have to bluff our way past a group of people that might find out that we're imposters the moment they see us, if they're expecting people they know.

"On the other side, if they're meeting this ship with no prior knowledge of the crew, there will be recognition codes. In either case, we'll probably be exposed as soon as we meet them. Lastly, does anyone want to place a bet that these new people have a destruct code for the cargo if they don't like that they find?"

He looked around the table with that last question. No one took his wager.

"What are our options?" Jared asked. "The kind of information that we need won't just be lying around. The only place I envision it being is inside the heads of the expedition leader and perhaps her second. Heads that blew up in a rather permanent manner."

Elise sighed. "Is none of the implant hardware recoverable? If we can pull data off the hardware, we can sidestep this issue."

Sean shook his head. "Trust me when I say that the charge was implanted in such a way and with sufficient power to make certain nothing was recoverable. The System Lord didn't intend for any record of this mission to survive."

"It wasn't the System Lord that killed these people," she objected. "Their own leader did. Why? What would make someone commit suicide to protect something like this?"

"Fanatical devotion," Olivia said grimly. "The Lord picked someone to lead the mission that it knew would have no objection to ending it under the appropriate circumstances. I'd wager there was some major payout to the leaderships' families.

"Let's not delude ourselves. These people knew what they were doing and that they wouldn't survive this mission. The System Lord at Terra would have eliminated them as soon as it confirmed their mission objectives had been met."

"Heartless monsters," Elise muttered to herself.

Jared leaned back in his seat. "It might be possible to bluff our way through this, but I'd rather not have to. If there are any mission briefing chips, they might have data on the contacts and their codes. Hell, they might even have the codes to deactivate the bombs."

"I doubt that," Kelsey said firmly. "These AIs don't seem the type to allow their minions the ability to turn off the things driving them. Contact protocols are possible, maybe even a mission brief. Nothing more.

"With implants, the chances of even that are almost nil. Why leave sensitive data just lying around when it could be locked up in your head?"

Olivia smiled. "Here is where one of the quirks of the higher orders comes into play. We have implants but go out of our way to not use them efficiently. Perhaps that is some kind of innate stubbornness on our part, or a facet of the System Lords' control, but it's real.

"I'm not saying this means there *is* a data chip with incriminating evidence stashed somewhere. Even if there is, it'll be heavily encrypted. We might not be able to get inside it. Still, it's the best chance we have."

"We know every place the woman in command of the mission went," Jared said. "If she had a chip on her, we'll find it. We'll need to do the same for every single intruder. We can't make the assumption that anyone was ignorant of this critical information.

"We have five days until we meet our new associates. I want everyone searching for any bit of data they can find. This has priority. We all need to be looking for as many hours a day as we can. Dismissed."

* * *

Kelsey did her part in searching for any concealed data chips but came up dry. So did everyone else. After twelve hours of intense effort, it became clear that there were no hidden data chips waiting for easy discovery.

There was a lull in the search as most people got some well-deserved rest, but her Raider implants left Kelsey with a need for what only amounted to catnaps. So in the middle of the ship's night, she found herself wandering the corridors lost in thought.

She should probably try to sleep more hours than she did, but the incessant nightmares tormented her. Memories of those few days as a Pale One, subject to whims and drives implanted by the mad computer on Erorsi.

It angered her when these people told her that their Kelsey had nightmares, too. As if the two women shared the same horrors. As if their situations were the same.

She tried to keep her animosity toward the other Kelsey to a minimum, but it was hard. That woman had gotten off so easy. That woman's trials hadn't even come close to what she'd endured. It was going to be an effort not to punch other her in the face when they finally met. If they met at all.

With her mind wandering, she was mildly surprised when she ended up at the computer center. Not exactly the place she'd hoped to see. Not the memories of the people she'd killed there clamoring for her attention in the dark of night.

True, they'd have died in any case, and they'd been trying their best to kill her, but their blood was on her hands. Any other interpretation was sophistry.

The main hatch was open, so she stepped inside. The man at the main console looked up and smiled.

"Highness. Can I help you?"

"I doubt it. I'm not even sure why I'm here."

"Couldn't sleep?" he asked sympathetically. "Feel free to commandeer a console. I don't mind the company. No need to talk, even."

That was better than meandering aimlessly through the corridors with only her own thoughts for company.

"Thanks."

She sat at the console farthest away from where she'd killed the intruders. It came to life at her touch.

What should she look at? The computer had lots of old files from before the AIs had captured the ship. The ones that had come later were probably not very interesting.

If she'd been the other Kelsey, she could've looked at some old entertainment vids. She had no idea why those interested the woman. They made little sense, and the special effects were juvenile at best.

Lacking enthusiasm, she limited her search to files that had been modified or uploaded since their arrival in the El Capitan system. Others had already checked and found nothing, but it wasn't as though another check could hurt anything.

Most of the files seemed to be related to ship's operation. That made sense, too. These people had jumped right into running the ship. None of them had even taken time to select quarters.

The two they'd identified as the leaders had been located on the bridge and in engineering. Those locations generated a lot of files, so she started excluding those created by normal operations. That reduced the tsunami to something manageable, if one stretched the term far enough.

She then sorted the remaining files by who had generated them. The number left for the two leaders was only in the hundreds. Plenty of time to glance at each one personally.

A few minutes later, she came across one that puzzled her. The file was supposedly text only, but the contents were gibberish. Random letters, numbers, and special symbols. Not even a space to denote a break in the flow.

She cleared her throat and waved the Fleet man over. "I've found something that I don't understand. Can you tell me what this is?"

He stepped over to her console and looked at the file. "Huh. Maybe it's corrupt. Let me give it a closer look."

The man shifted one of the chairs over and began doing incomprehensible things to the file via the console's interface.

Knowing she wouldn't be much help, Kelsey slid a little farther aside and copied the strange file into her internal memory. Her implants scanned it as soon as she selected it and ordered them to report on its contents.

Moments later, they reported that the file was encrypted and asked if she wanted to run any decryption programs.

Kelsey sat bolt upright. Encrypted? Shouldn't the computer scans have reported this earlier?

"Excuse me," Kelsey said. "I don't think I asked your name."

The man smiled at her. "No worries. I'm Commander Ralph Adonis. I'm the resident computer expert."

"Ralph, I'm Kelsey. Tell me, did you scan the computer for suspicious files related to the newcomers?"

"Of course," he said with a nod. "I finished that hours ago with nothing to show for my efforts. No encrypted files."

"Hmmm. That's odd. My implants tell me this file isn't corrupt. It's encrypted."

The man frowned and focused his attention on the console while his hands flashed over the interface. "No encryption shown on the file. It's plain text."

"I don't know much about my implants, but I doubt they'd get this wrong. They're cutting-edge Old Empire technology. I'm inclined to trust them on this."

The two of them stared at one another for a bit before he spoke again. "What kind of encryption do they think this is?"

A quick check told her that it was some kind of text cypher. She had to look that up to get the gist of the meaning. Plain text was run through some kind of filter and turned into gibberish.

With an appropriate key, anyone could reverse the process and get the original text. Lacking that, the file would remain unreadable.

She passed the information on to Ralph.

He scowled at the screen. "That's crazy. You swap letters out until it makes sense? The ship's computer could unlock something like that in a few seconds."

"It only sounds simple," she said. "Without the correct key, there are probably places in the file where the substitution logic changes. The key tells it where to look for that."

"Hmmm. Let me see if I can do something about that. Are you really sure it's a code?"

"No, but my implants are."

"I should report this, then. Let the admiral know."

If she was wrong, she would look like an idiot. Well, better to be thought a fool than to do something stupid and prove it.

"Do it."

While he was working on the file, she instructed her implants to decrypt the file contents. Her implants seemed more knowledgeable with codes like this than the ship's computer, but they had far less processing power. It was anyone's guess who, if anyone, would manage to get to the secret contents first.

32

Sean had the late shift, so he got the call from the computer center about the potentially encrypted file. He briefly considered waking Admiral Mertz but decided against it. At this point, it might turn out to be nothing.

The last few hours had been filled with false alarms. They couldn't afford to miss a single thing, so they'd instructed everyone to pass along even the most minor oddities. None had panned out, and this latest one would likely be the same.

But he wouldn't know for sure unless he actually went down and looked for himself.

He gave the helm officer the conn and headed down to the computer center. When he got there, he found Princess Kelsey and Commander Adonis hunched over a console examining something.

"What have you found?" he asked as he stepped behind them.

The Fleet officer glanced back at him and shrugged. "I'm not sure, sir. Maybe nothing. Maybe something."

"A plain text file filled with strange characters," Kelsey added. "It looks like gibberish, but my implants insist it's an encrypted file."

That made him lean forward to look at the console more closely. "Your implants are a lot more specialized than the programs we have. If it says this is a code, it probably is. Can you unravel the thing?"

She shrugged. "I'm running quite a few decryption programs, but it's slow going. The programs might be amazing, but this is proving a bit more troublesome than I'd hoped."

He sent an alert to Admiral Mertz. If her implants insisted this was a coded file, it wasn't a dead end. The admiral signaled receipt of the message and that he'd be there in a few minutes.

"Is there any way we can offload some of the processing to the ship's computer?" he asked Adonis.

"Possibly. That's something that people used to do. They'd set the computer to doing intensive work and have it forward the results back to the user.

"Unfortunately, the princess's program code is considered classified under her specific Raider protocols. It doesn't want to move the program code off her implants."

"Could we cede part of the computer to her as a classified virtual machine? If her implants can verify the area is secure, it might allow the transfer."

Kelsey's eyes lost focus. "My implants inform me that they will allow me to copy the programs to a dedicated virtual machine that only I have access to. It can be isolated from the rest of the computer, so you don't need to worry that I have access I shouldn't have."

"Work with her, Adonis," Sean ordered. "Give her what she needs while maintaining operational security. No offense, Highness. I have my orders on that."

She snorted delicately. "I get it. I'm from another universe, and you don't know me all that well. If the situation was reversed, I'd do the same."

It took Commander Adonis five minutes to work out an acceptable compromise with the Raider implants. Once he dedicated and restricted the partition on the ship, Kelsey's implants formatted and encrypted it.

"I've offloaded the process," Kelsey reported. "Wow. That's much faster."

"Any idea how long it might take?" he asked.

"No clue. Maybe forever if this is unbreakable."

"Nothing is unbreakable," Sean said with a laugh. "It just takes unrealistic amounts of time for the impossible stuff."

Admiral Mertz walked into the computer center, his hair slightly mussed and his eyes red with interrupted sleep.

"What have you got?"

Sean summarized the situation, and his commanding officer grasped the significance as quickly as he had.

"This is the real deal," Mertz declared. "Excellent work."

"I haven't done anything," Kelsey objected. "We can't read it."

"We certainly couldn't have read it if you hadn't found it," Mertz disagreed. "Now we have a few days to let your programs crack the code. We still might not manage it, but life is often the art of the possible. I'll take it."

Kelsey blinked. "The program just cracked the code." She sounded shocked.

"Even better," Sean said. "Can you pass the plain text to us?"

His implants received the file a second later. He brought it up and began reading.

The file was a diary with all the attendant meandering. The man who'd wrote it had been the mission's second in command, Bertram Gust. He also seemed to be a gossip, filling the pages with details about everyone around him. He made numerous complaints about the hyper secrecy they were under and how that negatively impacted his social life.

His chatter wasn't restricted to this mission, either. The date stamps went back several decades. Sean guessed the man had started this while at university. If he allowed himself to go all the way to the beginning, this would take a while.

Sean limited his search to six months before his arrival in the El Capitan system. One entry led to another, and he found several sections of the diary that seemed to be in a different code. At least they didn't make any sense as they were currently decoded.

"Can you bury code inside of code?" he asked. "I found something that looks odd."

He passed a link to the sections back to Princess Kelsey.

Almost half an hour passed before she grinned triumphantly. "Cracked it! This sure looks like the brief for this mission."

Sean accepted the freshly decrypted text and smiled. It was exactly that.

He skimmed the details until he found the most critical part: the data on who they were meeting and the codes to establish their bona fides.

Well, they might just have a chance after all.

* * *

Jared went over the information they'd gleaned from the dead man's diary. It wasn't much, but it included the information they most desperately needed: the contact codes to both verify the crew of this ship to the people they were to meet and the codes that verified the identities of those people.

No names were mentioned, so he nursed the hope that the people he had to fool wouldn't know precisely who they were meeting. After all, they really couldn't expect that they needed to watch out for ringers. What kind of idiots would come walking in, pretending to be part of some dastardly plot?

The one thing that wasn't included in the dead man's ramblings was what these new people would be doing to advance the AIs' plans. If they already had a deadly virus in their hold, what else did they need?

Well, he'd find out soon enough.

He'd focused on getting the ship ready for visitors. They'd cleaned up every sign of battle and got the external com systems back online. At the same time, Olivia coached everyone on how to behave around their expected guests. Hopefully, the visit would be brief.

Now that Jared knew what to expect, he could mitigate the potential damage these new people could inflict. Discreet jammers scattered throughout the ship would blanket all implant communications on his command. A second set would make certain that the deadly cargo received no orders to explode.

Of course, they couldn't do that straight off. They needed the new people to extend the detonation time of the plasma explosives. Otherwise, this would be a very short trip.

The next five days simultaneously flew by and dragged interminably. As they transitioned to the destination system, he sat tensely on *Athena*'s bridge. Just like at El Capitan, the defenses were internal to the system.

That didn't mean that there weren't recon drones on station, watching for approaching ships. During the approach to the first Rebel Empire system, he'd been cautious enough to keep his active scanners offline.

Now he behaved more boldly, scanning the supposedly empty flip point leading to the new system, Jaidon, with every tool he had available. The Rebel Empire probes scattered around the wormhole weren't easy to see, but they *were* there.

That was actually something of a relief. He'd had trouble believing the enemy was comprised of idiots. This made their actions comprehensible, if lazy.

In their shoes, he'd have stationed ships in the systems leading up to their population centers: probes in all the flip points leading into the buffer systems, destroyers to monitor them and intercept any intruders, and ships positioned directly in the flip points leading to the population centers that were ready to run and scream for help as soon as trouble came calling.

In fact, that was pretty much what Admiral Yeats had done on the border systems of the New Terran Empire and in critical systems deeper in their interior. Not that it would help them if the Rebel Empire came calling in force.

Thankfully, the time required to get information across something as vast as the Old Terran Empire was significant. The people in this section of the Rebel Empire would get the word of the raid on Dresden in three or four weeks. Then their defense patterns might change. Until then, it was business as usual.

Jared worried about how the AI leadership of the Rebel Empire would respond. They wouldn't take the loss of the Dresden research facility lightly. Or that of the equipment used to manufacture Marine Raider implants or sentient AIs.

To put it lightly, they would lose their digital minds. They wouldn't rest until they got to the bottom of the raid.

The reaction force from Dresden had already pursued Jared and his fleet to Erorsi. They'd run headlong into the flip-point jammer.

They had no frame of reference about that kind of technology or the faster-than-light communications his people had with the drones he'd left monitoring the buffer system.

Jared was shocked at how quickly the enemy commander had grasped the threat. He hadn't poured ships into the flip point when none of his probes returned.

He'd sent probes. When none of them had returned, he'd settled into a siege. Smart.

The AIs would heavily reinforce that system as soon as they caught up with events. They wouldn't hesitate to keep probing Erorsi. The jammer had to be given regular maintenance. That would allow the enemy a window of time to take advantage of.

Jared really hoped Admiral Yeats took a risk and moved one of the jammers from Harrison's World to Erorsi to minimize the danger. That left that system vulnerable, but the enemy had no reason to probe it. Yet.

He shook himself out of his thoughts. No amount of worry would help that situation now. He'd best focus on the problems at hand.

Commander Hall turned away from the helm console. "We're almost ready to transition, Admiral. Five minutes."

They'd switched to civilian clothes. None of the intruders had been Fleet officers, so his people needed to fit the new profile.

Olivia had gone over each outfit and made changes that she declared necessary. She hadn't shied away from robbing the bags of the dead Rebel Empire nobles to make up for anything she thought lacking.

Jared felt faintly ridiculous in his new outfit, but he'd manage. He rose to his feet and stepped away from his console. As they'd already discussed, Olivia took his seat, looking a little uncomfortable.

"I'm still not very happy with this change," she said softly. "I'm not a Fleet officer. What if something goes wrong?"

"I'll be right here," he reassured her. "If they call, I want you already settled in. Trust me. They'll notice you fidgeting if you wait until the last second."

The remaining few minutes passed in silence until Hall announced that they were ready to flip.

"Take us across," he ordered.

This was it. Rather than fighting or hiding, now they had to fool knowledgeable and canny enemies in their own territory.

Any slip would doom them and potentially the people of Terra, too. It would certainly stop the AI in charge of the Terra system from inviting them in with open arms.

In a word, everything had to go right from here on.

33

Olivia felt a bit overwhelmed. That hadn't happened to her in a long time. She was used to being in charge of any situation.

Seated at the command console of a warship sneaking into the very heart of the enemy was something outside her range of experience, though. Fooling people into thinking she was their ally in serving the Rebel Empire and the Lords… that, she could do. She'd done it her entire life.

"Flip complete," Commander Hall said calmly. "Enemy warships and fortifications detected. Transmitting our ID code."

That had been something different from the secret recognition codes they'd found in the diary. These had been left on the command console by the woman sent by the System Lord of El Capitan to command the ship. Basic recognition and authorization codes allowing for the ship to transit the Rebel Empire in pursuit of its goals.

The System Lord at Harrison's World had provided similar codes for their use. Rather, the data it had stored away before they'd beaten it had provided them.

"How do the defenses stack up against what we saw at El Capitan," Jared asked.

"Somewhat heavier," Hall said. "Perhaps fifteen percent more firepower and a greater allocation of heavy cruisers. The battle stations are about the same size. They've accepted our codes and have allowed us passage."

"How long until we reach the main planet in the system?" Olivia asked.

"We're not going there," Hall said. "We've been directed to a station orbiting a gas giant in the outer system. ETA six hours."

Olivia supposed that made sense. Better not to allow a biological weapon near an inhabited world. She'd thought the System Lord at El

Capitan had been taking a terrible risk. If something went wrong, it would've killed billions. Not that she suspected it cared.

"Once we're an hour away from the flip point," Jared said, "I want to start rotating people off station for food and rest. Everyone but you, Olivia. If they call, we need you right here. Welcome to the joys of a space command."

"You can keep it," she said tartly. "I'll stick to planetary leadership. The sleeping quarters and perks are better."

"No doubt," he agreed.

His caution proved warranted when someone called for them two hours out from the station.

"Incoming priority communication," Hall said. "They're using the recognition code."

"We're on," Jared said, straightening. "Take it away, Olivia."

She took a deep breath and nodded toward Hall. "Accept the call and put it on the main screen."

The image of the star field faded and was replaced by what appeared to be opulent quarters. A man with the eyes of someone used to being obeyed sat at a desk made of dark wood.

"Greetings and welcome to Jaidon," he said in a low, melodious voice. "My name is Oscar Fielding. You've received my code. I'll have yours now."

This was the moment of truth. If they'd misinterpreted the significance of the data in the encrypted file, it was all over.

She sent him the code and sat there with an artificially calm expression as he reviewed something on his console.

He smiled. "All in order, just as I expected. If I might be so bold, who are you?"

"Jaleesa Keaton," Olivia lied with a smile of her own.

"Welcome, Jaleesa. I only have a list of your people, so I had your name but not your picture. We need to discuss the next steps we must take to meet the operational requirements for the Lords. I will come to your ship and examine your equipment.

"That will also allow me to extend the timer on the security system as well. Hopefully enough for us to meet our obligations without worrying about any unexpected delays," she said dryly.

He frowned. "What makes you worry about delays?"

"Nothing specific, but life has a way of dealing you an bad hand when you can least afford it."

Fielding grunted. "True enough. I'll want Jocelyn Oldfield on hand to assist me with the examination of the equipment. She oversaw its assembly, so she knows it better than all of us."

"Of course," Olivia assured him. "She'll be standing by when you come aboard."

"Excellent," he said with a superior smile. "I'll see you as soon as you reach orbit. I'll send out a pair of system defense patrol craft out to meet you, so don't be alarmed. They'll ensure safety for us both."

The transmission terminated without another word.

Olivia turned to Jared. "What now?"

"We meet in him in orbit," the Fleet officer said. "Good work, by the way. You got us past the chanciest part."

"Did I?" she asked, raising an eyebrow. "It seems as if the in-person meeting is far riskier."

"At least we understand what's happening, to a degree," Jared said. "He might have known what the person he was meeting looked like, or we could have had the wrong code. Damned perilous, if you ask me.

"Not to say the next stage of this game is without its dangers. We can still screw up. Who shall we use for Jocelyn Oldfield? Elise?"

Olivia shook her head. "She has the coolness, but her accent would give her away. It sounds pleasant to the ear, but her delivery is distinctly different from any I've ever heard in the Rebel Empire. It needs to be Kelsey."

Jared didn't seem convinced. "She's not used to playing that kind of game."

"She's stronger than you give her credit for," Olivia disagreed. "She can pull this off."

After a second, he shrugged. "If you say so. I guess we'd best brief her together. At least we can monitor the situation when she meets with this guy and give her pointers over her implant coms."

Olivia wasn't certain that was necessary. Kelsey, even the one from another universe, was more resourceful than her brother gave her credit for.

* * *

"You've lost your mind," Kelsey told Mertz firmly. "What makes you think I can fool someone like that? He'll see right through me."

"Necessity is the mother of invention," he responded coolly. "We don't have much choice in the matter."

"Surely you have someone else. Anyone would be better than me."

Olivia shook her head. "We've considered everyone else aboard. Maybe Doctor Stone, but I still think you're the right choice. You grew up in a position of power. Even though you never acted as the emperor of the Terran Empire, you had a lifetime to observe your father and brother. You know how to behave."

"This is insane," Kelsey muttered. "What do you need me to do?"

"Honestly, we have no idea. You'll be meeting with the senior man in this system as far as this project goes. He wants to inspect our cargo, and you're supposed to know all about it."

"What could possibly go wrong? I have no idea what the cargo is or how to inspect it. If this really is a biological weapon, Doctor Stone is a *far* better choice. What if he expects me to open the cargo?"

"We're not expecting that," Mertz said. "He has the codes for the antitampering charges, so he'll have the codes to get it open."

This sounded like a huge gamble to her, but what choice did she have?

"If we all die, it's your fault," she said darkly. "There's something more to this. Stone would be a far superior choice for this. Why me?"

Mertz and Olivia shared a glance.

The other woman smiled sadly. "We know you have what it takes to pull this off. We've both seen it. You can do this."

"I'm not your Kelsey," she disagreed. "She has skills and confidence that I just don't have. If you put me in there, I might blow this entire mission sky high."

"And you might save it from some unexpected occurrence," Mertz said. "Our Kelsey felt exactly the same way in the beginning. She found a way forward to success. You will, too. We'll help you."

Kelsey covered her face with her hands. "This is madness. I've screwed up so many things. Find someone else."

Mertz's eyes lost focus. "The cutter with our guest is about to dock. The system defense craft are escorting him in. You're up, Kelsey. I know you can do this. I believe in you."

"Then you're an idiot." She took a deep breath. "Let's go."

The three of them made their way to the docking level and arrived just as a cutter docked, sending a loud clang of metal on metal through the area. Moments later, the hatch slid open with a puff of super chilled gas.

A tall man with a hooked nose and an arrogant expression walked through the hatch with two men and two women in black tunics at his back.

Kelsey's Raider scanners identified weapons on all four of the followers. Guards, she wagered.

The man didn't offer his hand to any of them. Instead, he smiled coldly. "Lady Keaton. A pleasure to meet you in person." He turned to Mertz. "Lord Gust, I presume?"

"Bertram Gust," Mertz confirmed. "And this is Jocelyn Oldfield."

Apparently, that was her new name.

The man smiled at Kelsey. "Lady Oldfield, I've read your reports with interest. Well done."

She extended her hand, even though the others hadn't. "The pleasure is mine. I'm looking forward to moving to the next stage of this project. Shall we?"

His grip was light and dry. "Indeed. Lady Keaton, Lord Gust, I believe it best if Lady Oldfield and I proceed alone."

Olivia bowed slightly. "Of course. We'll be a call away if you need us."

As the other two abandoned Kelsey to the intruder, her internal com received an incoming call from Olivia.

Kelsey, I'll be your handler for this. Keep sending me everything that's happening and be ready for me to give you quick instructions if something awkward happens.

Too late for that, she responded grumpily.

Lord Fielding gestured toward the lift. "Shall we?"

Kelsey was grateful the cargo area wasn't very far away and that she had instant access to the deck plans of the destroyer. Getting lost now would be bad.

The large crates sat where the original intruders had secured them in the center of the large bay. The six crates were each taller than she was. All were locked down tight with codes that she didn't have and protected by bombs she couldn't turn off.

Fielding stared at them before he turned to her. "Amazing, isn't it? So much misery in a single location. Does it ever give you nightmares?"

Kelsey nodded. "Terrible ones. I wish this wasn't necessary."

That might be laying it on a bit thick.

She ignored Olivia and focused on the Rebel Empire noble. "What about you?"

He sighed. "I hadn't thought it would when the Lord instructed me to develop my part of this project, but it *has* given me pause. Killing traitors should be a pleasure as well as a duty, but this weapon isn't clean. They'll suffer a lingering, painful death.

"Not everyone will get sick immediately. Some portion of the target population will become symptomless carriers, spreading the plague far and wide before succumbing.

"This is a terrible thing we've been tasked with. The extermination of an entire planetary population. No one will ever be able to even approach Terra once we start. Even if they used space suits or remote devices, they could never be certain they hadn't picked up the Omega Plague."

So it had a name. Ironic that it had the same name as the alien that had brought her to this universe.

This was going to be a serious problem. If they allowed this weapon to be deployed, she'd never get her hands on the override. She had to make sure they stopped the Lords' dastardly plans. And to do that, she had to make this man believe she was part of his team.

"I confess that the technical aspects of my work were delightfully challenging while the implications were horrifying. If something goes wrong, we could exterminate all human life in the galaxy."

His shoulders relaxed a little. "That's understandable, I suppose. Well, we should open up the crates and verify the contents."

"Agreed," she said hurriedly. "If you'd be so kind."

This was a potential sticking point. If he didn't have the codes to the crates, she'd have to take him and his guards out. That would blow the plan, and they'd die here in very short order.

Thankfully, he sent a coded signal to the crates, and they all began opening. Her enhanced Raider gear picked up the code, so she forwarded it to Mertz. If they had to get into these crates later, that might prove very useful.

Her gaze swept over the contents. Hundreds of drones in racks. She'd expected large vessels or small vials containing the biological agent, but this was the delivery equipment.

She spotted the antitampering charges. No one had been tasteless enough to put timers on them, so she had no visible way to determine how much of the countdown remained.

"All seem to be in order, but I'll need to verify them as we proceed," Fielding said. "I'll increment the antitampering charges another seven days now. You only had ten hours left. Good thing you didn't dawdle on your way here."

No, she supposed. That would've been bad.

He was more careful with his second signal. This time she didn't get the code for the bombs as he went from crate to crate updating the explosives. Pity.

"What comes next?" she asked.

"I just signaled for the cargo shuttle to deliver the agent. We'll load it in here while we isolate the rest of the ship. If there is some kind of accident, your compatriots can escape before the protective fortifications destroy this ship.

"As you no doubt already understand, the Lords are very serious that no word of this mission or even any components of it become known to the public. That's why they segregated the labs developing the agent and your part in creating the delivery drones."

Kelsey sighed internally. The virus had never been on board. Damned paranoid AIs.

Well, they hadn't had any choice about coming here. The real question was what they did next.

If she was supposed to help load the deadly cargo, she needed to know something about the drones. She really hoped the woman she was masquerading as had put detailed plans into the devices.

A quick check got her complete schematics for them. They were quite simple, really. Made to avoid detection and search for people. If it found them, it released a minute quantity of the virus upwind of them. They would never even know they'd been infected.

Fortunately, the plans had the loading instructions appended. They seemed quite basic, but she forwarded the data to Mertz. His people would go over it with a fine-toothed comb and guide her when the time came.

She hoped that kept her safe, but a nagging uncertainty roiled her stomach. This could still go very badly.

34

Elise wasn't going to interact with the intruders, and that annoyed her. She understood that her accent and Pentagar's linguistic drift would make her stand out, so she tried to keep things in perspective. That didn't make her any less grumpy, though.

The bastards were carefully loading the deadly virus into the drones. The engineering team and Lily Stone were helping Kelsey with any data she might need to fulfill her role as the resident expert on the dispersal equipment.

Everyone in the hold was dressed in specialized suits in case there was a breach. Not that Elise expected them to allow anyone exposed to leave the ship.

She sat in a maintenance tube with their prisoner and two beefy marine guards. They'd moved a few spartan pieces of furniture in to allow a minimum of comfort. Perhaps that would make up for the survival rations and water they had to live on until their guests departed.

The guards might not have been required. Austin Darrah had just as much to lose as they did now. More, really. The Lords would torture the man to make sure they got every bit of data he'd passed on to the New Terran Empire if they suspected anything.

"Did you know this was what you were doing?" she asked. "Exterminating the entire population on Terra."

He shrugged. "I had my suspicions. Like I said, I wasn't given a briefing. I had to eavesdrop to find out anything of substance.

"If what you really meant to ask was if I approved, hell no. I don't want to kill a single person, much less a planet full of people. But I didn't have a choice in the matter. It was comply or die. The Lord needed someone who could fix anything on this ship, and it didn't trust Fleet not to have an attack of conscience."

She raised an eyebrow. "It didn't believe you'd be prone to the same desire to spare lives?"

"More like it didn't believe that I would have an opportunity to make good on any impulses. A Fleet officer could potentially use violence to sabotage the mission. Me? I'm as harmless as they come and have no training in weapons or fighting.

"No access to armaments, either. The Lord knew damned well that I would have no choice but to do what I was told, even if I strenuously objected." The last came out bitterly.

Elise nodded, thinking he might even be telling the truth. "How did you get interested in Fleet technology?"

"Oddly enough, I can lay blame for that at the feet of my family's choice in guards. We have estates near the spaceport, and my grandfather chose several marines led by a retired marine officer to secure them back in the day.

"Those original people have long retired, but they had influence over who came onto the scene afterward. My mother never approved of my sneaking off to hear stories from them. She said they were a bad influence, teaching me how to be a member of the middle orders."

His expression turned ironic. "If only she could see me now. She'd be so proud."

"She doesn't know where you are?"

He shook his head. "All she knows is that the Lord specifically selected me for this mission. I'm sure my extensive knowledge of Fleet technology being the driving factor in my selection scandalized her. A very backhanded compliment, my mission."

"So you heard stories about Fleet," Elise said, nudging him out of his introspective silence. "That doesn't necessarily lead to technical knowledge."

"No, but it did give me enough know-how to start acquiring books about it. Well, the unclassified portions, anyway. My relationship with one Fleet officer led to getting to know others who had contacts that could get me anything I wanted shy of a flip drive or a fusion plant.

"I gained experience with those advanced systems once I became an adult. One of my uncles owns a shipping consortium. He helped me out by allowing me to work on one of his ships for a year, primarily just to annoy my mother.

"It was a spectacularly successful ploy, I might add. She was furious." He grinned at that last bit.

"It gave me hands-on experience with the same kind of equipment Fleet uses, short of the weapons and defense systems. I'd planned to look them over very carefully during this mission." He sounded wistfully disappointed that he wouldn't get the chance.

"If we can keep a handle on the situation, that isn't out of the question."

Austin perked up. "Really? You would trust me that far?"

"It's not as if you could fire a missile while the system was locked down or make it detonate in the tube."

He gave her a mildly guilty look. "Actually, I might be able to figure something like that out, given a little time."

She laughed. "You remind me of someone I know. Carl Owlet. He's a scientist with a penchant for pulling off the impossible. I suspect the two of you would get along like a house on fire."

Austin squinted. "Why would you want to lock us in a burning house?"

"It's an old saying. It means that you'd really like one another."

"You people have some very odd phrases in your vocabulary. And you have a funny accent. Where are you from?"

She shook her head. "A planet cut off from contact with the Empire a long time ago. The name is unimportant. Our situation did lead to some linguistic drift."

He smiled wryly. "Is it irony when you really mean the name is so critical that you don't dare tell someone you can't fully trust? Really, I do understand, but it's darkly funny.

"Can't you tell me anything about what's happening? Being locked out of the ship's systems is really boring. Surely an update on what the others are doing, if kept general, wouldn't be harmful. My life hangs in the balance, too."

Elise knew the opposite was true if he intended them harm, but she had those marines to keep him manageable. "They're loading the virus into drones kept in the cargo containers. Six crates total, and they've finished four. I'd imagine we'll be on our way in a few hours, once Lord Fielding finishes."

He perked up. "Oscar Fielding? Are we at Jaidon?"

Shocked, she nodded. "You know him?"

"You could say that. He's the uncle I told you about."

* * *

Sean listened to Elise's report grimly. This was not good. Their prisoner was related to the main bad guy. There was no way the man wouldn't demand to see him at some point, even though it looked as if the man had thrown his own kin under the bus, so to speak.

She concluded her description of the situation with a question.

What do we do?

Great question. He wished he had an equally great answer.

We play it by ear. You say the boy doesn't seem like a mass murderer. Keep playing that angle with him. When the inevitable happens, we'll just have to hope for the best when we trot him out.

That could go wrong in so many ways, but it wasn't as if they had a choice. Not making him available upon demand would trip all kinds of alarms for the Rebel Empire noble. They'd never get out of this system alive.

He considered the potential options as soon as he signed off from the call. Each one of them involved trusting the prisoner to an uncomfortable degree. One word from him, and the gig was assuredly up.

If Lord Fielding was the man's uncle, he would undoubtedly insist on some privacy in meeting his nephew. Depending on how paranoid the man was, he might even insist it happen away from the destroyer.

How could they assure that they at least knew if their cover was blown? Could he plant a listening device on Austin Darrah? One that couldn't be detected?

Possibly, though not in the strictest sense of the word. Princess Kelsey had Marine Raider implants, including enhanced hearing that could pick up a surprising amount of information from an amazing distance. Almost as good as a parabolic microphone.

She was also a known element to the Rebel Empire Lord. He would probably understand if the mission leader insisted one of their own keep an eye on their junior player.

That was a lot more like playing spies than Kelsey would be ready for. He dearly hoped she was as good as her counterpart at improvisation. Well, perhaps with fewer explosions.

Sean sighed and focused his attention back on the loading process. Kelsey and Fielding had loaded the drones in the fifth crate and were servicing the final ones now. Based on their previous speed, they would finish in roughly half an hour.

As a betting man, he wagered that would be when Fielding made his play. Time to try to stack the deck.

Keeping a mental eye on the loading via his implants, Sean headed for the maintenance tube where they'd concealed Elise and Darrah. Both rose to their feet as the marine guards tensed. He waved them back down.

"It's okay. I'm just dropping in to have a word with Mister Darrah."

Elise rose from her seat again. "Then sit. Looming over people doesn't make for an easy conversation."

It flew in the face of his upbringing, but he took the offered seat. This conversation was going to be difficult enough without adding elements of intimidation.

Once he'd settled in, he leaned toward Darrah. "I assume you've seen images of the man who might be your uncle. Is it him?"

Darrah nodded. "Damned if I understand what he's doing here. As I said to Miss Orison, he's not part of the mission."

Hearing the man not use Elise's title rankled a bit, but he hadn't been told. That was one of the secrets they'd decided not to share as it gave him too much background. The other was the fact she was married to Admiral Mertz.

"The facts prove otherwise," Sean said in a low tone. "He knows everything, and he's probably the head man on this end of the mission. What you should be wondering is how much he likes you."

"I don't understand," Darrah said with a frown.

"This might come as a shock to you, but I've wondered how expendable you were once the mission was complete. Unlike the others, you weren't an enthusiastic conspirator. Once they finished, they might've dropped you out the nearest airlock.

"But with your uncle being high in their plans, I wonder if that's so. Or at least if he has the intent to change the plans in your favor. He did train you, after all."

"Trained me," the prisoner repeated. "You think his assistance in learning all the systems on a ship was to enhance this mission? That was years ago."

"One doesn't hatch a conspiracy of this scale the day before one executes it," Elise said reasonably. "The leaders and other conspirators didn't have the luxury of vanishing from the public sphere with no warning. People would talk.

"In fact, now that everyone has left, people are undoubtedly trying to figure out where they vanished to so abruptly and why."

"The Lords planned for that," Darrah said. "Everyone is part of a supposed trade mission. We'll be gone for six months and then return. My assumption was that the deal was already done or that we would proceed there as soon as we finished at Terra."

Sean agreed with that assessment, only he suspected the entire ship would vanish with all hands. Done in by the fanatical leader or even the AI at Terra. In no case would the ship be allowed to leave that system.

The System Lords couldn't risk allowing the contagion to escape stellar containment. That probably meant the System Lord there had some kind of escape plan.

"In any case," Sean continued, "your uncle will be done loading the bioweapon in perhaps ten minutes. As soon as he finishes, nothing will be holding this ship here. I expect him to call for you.

"We either have to produce you or start shooting. One way or the other, you can stop us. We want to save the lives of everyone on Terra. Are you truly willing to murder millions or billions of people?"

Darrah deflated a bit. "No. Since the Lord press-ganged me, I've been powerless to change the outcome of this mission. Honestly, does helping you do more than put it off for a few more months? How long before the Lords send a second mission?"

"That depends on how long we can make them believe the mission was a success. If we can, of course. But that's dodging the question.

"If you help them, you're a murderer. If you put them off, the people might still die, but you did everything in your power to save them. Which kind of person are you?"

The man smiled a little. "I'll keep my mouth shut and help you, but I have my own price for that cooperation. When we leave this system and head for Terra, you have to tell me everything.

"I know there's a big secret you all keep talking around. You're on an important mission of your own. You didn't come to stop the attack on

Terra. I want to know what it is and see if it's something worth helping you with."

Sean considered the man's counter proposal and then nodded. "I don't control when you'll be told, but it will be sometime after we leave here and no later than when we reach Terra. You have my word."

"As a Fleet officer?"

That made Sean blink. They'd been so careful to keep that under wraps.

"What makes you think that I'm a Fleet officer?"

"My eyes and my experience interfacing with men like you. Just like I know these two fellows guarding me are marine officers. Do you deny it?"

Sean shook his head. The men were simple marines, but that was close enough as guesses went.

"No," Sean said slowly. "I don't suppose you need my confirmation, but you have it."

He blinked as Jared called him through his implants.

Fielding just asked to speak to our prisoner.

Sean checked the vid feed and saw the crates were all closed now. Kelsey and Fielding were stripping out of their suits. It was showtime.

We'll be there in a few minutes.

Sean rose to his feet. "He's called for you. I guess we'll find out what kind of man you really are now."

35

Kelsey hadn't known what to expect when the dreadful task of loading the bioweapon was done, but she'd been praying for the rapid departure of Lord Fielding and his people so that she could get the hell out of here.

The sight of Sean and the prisoner they'd captured shot that down. What in the hell was the man thinking? They were so screwed.

Lord Fielding smiled at the prisoner. "Austin, I'm sure this is quite the shock, but I'm pleased to see you."

"Shocking indeed, Uncle Oscar. I didn't know that we were coming to Jaidon, much less that we'd meet you here. You obviously know far more about all this than I ever expected."

"Life is a great circle, nephew. It turns, and past becomes future."

The man turned to Sean. "I'll want some time with my nephew. No need to displace anyone. I'll take him back to my cutter."

"I'm afraid that we have an obligation to keep an eye on him. Lady Jocelyn can accompany you while staying out of earshot."

The Rebel Empire noble considered him coolly for a few seconds. "I suppose we all have to make compromises. Lady Jocelyn, if you would please escort us to my cutter."

She shot Sean a sharp look. *What's happening?*

We're making lemonade. Keep an ear on them and let me know if our little mouse betrays us. If so, take them down, and we'll try to make a run for it.

Kelsey had seen the scanner readings, so she had no illusions how that would turn out. If the man betrayed them, they'd die here.

No pressure.

She nodded to Sean and fell in beside Lord Fielding. The prisoner—Austin, she corrected herself—might be his nephew, but she was masquerading as someone higher up the societal food chain, so she got the more prominent position in the parade.

The trip to Fielding's cutter was short, and he walked in silence. He'd already told her more than enough about the damned weapon as they'd loaded it. She'd definitely have even more nightmares now.

She was grateful that she'd managed to do what she needed to do in assisting him with the grisly task. The engineering people and Lily Stone had given her what she needed via her implants, and she hadn't screwed up.

That was a refreshing change of pace.

Lord Fielding's cutter was different from the Fleet models Kelsey was used to, not larger on the outside, but significantly more luxurious on the inside. Rather than allowing for as many people, it could hold a far smaller number in absolute comfort. Gold finishes, dark woods, and expensive-looking cloth abounded.

The sight didn't seem to surprise Austin. This must be more common in his sphere than Kelsey had thought.

Fielding turned to her. "I'm going to step into my private compartment with my nephew. I'll leave the hatch open so that you can carry out your observational duties. Feel free to sample something from my bar. You've more than earned it."

Kelsey inclined her head and watched them go through the unobtrusive door at the rear of the compartment. This was it. If the prisoner was going to betray them, it would be now.

As she might be under observation, she did pour a glass of something. The dark liquid burned smoothly as she sipped it. Not bad.

When Lord Fielding spoke, even though he kept his voice low, Kelsey could clearly hear him.

"Austin, I'm sorry. I truly am."

"Are you really, Uncle Oscar? It seems to me that my presence here is your doing. Far from being accidental, you've put me in a situation I probably won't survive. There are two major paths in front of me, and neither seem to have a very good chance of me getting back home."

The older man grunted softly. "Contrary to what you think, I didn't take this step lightly. Like you, I have to balance the demands of the Lords against my family. I made the best choice I could."

"Against your family or against your own interests? It seems as though you've abandoned me to enrich yourself."

"Don't be more of a fool than you have to be, boy," the older man grumbled. "Life isn't simple. We have to navigate the shoals and whirlpools that are determined to sink us. I did what I had to."

There was a short pause before Darrah answered him. "I see. Well, let me tell you what I know. They put a bomb in my head, and I have little doubt they'll dispose of me as soon as this mission is done. You'll forgive me if I don't see how you've done what you could for *family*."

"You think you were the only one the Lords forced into their plans against their will? Do you think I wanted to concoct this devil's brew? Bah.

"The Lords ordered me to do what I've done, and I did it. Here's a little surprise for you. I have a bomb in my head, too. Don't think I'm unaware of how this might turn out."

Kelsey relaxed a little. Maybe the boy wasn't going to betray them after all. She sipped the drink again.

"I think you've missed the point," Austin said. "You personally betrayed me. I didn't have to be part of this. I'm sorry the Lords came after you for this terrible task, but why give them my name? Why train me for a task that will kill your sister's son? Do you hate us that much?"

Fielding sighed. "I don't hate you, and you know it. I love you both. In fact, I have a gift for you. The code for disarming the bomb in your head."

Kelsey perked up. They'd wiped the code that could trigger the device. What would happen if the older man tried to disarm the bomb and it failed to respond?

"Even that won't save me," Austin said. "They can shoot me down at any time or shove me out a handy airlock. Don't think they won't, either. That said, I'll take the code and hold it in reserve. They might know if I turned it off."

"Here you go. I doubt they'll know if the device is deactivated, but keep it to yourself."

"How did you get it, and do you have your own code?"

"Let's just say that I have ears in many places, and I'm not worried about my head exploding. I have a plan to keep you safe once the mission is completed, too. I'll need to speak to Lady Keaton, but it should more than serve to protect you."

"You sound very confident," Austin said cautiously. "What will you do?"

"Something that will more than prove I love you, boy. Come on. Your watcher is probably growing concerned. You can watch me work my magic in person."

* * *

Jared sat in *Athena*'s small conference room with Olivia and nervously waited for Lord Fielding to arrive.

Sean walked in a few seconds later. "We're ready to break orbit as soon as you give the green light. All of the workers have departed in the cargo shuttle that brought the bio agent. Only Fielding and his guards are still on board. Once they leave, we can get the hell out of here."

"Kelsey said Fielding has some kind of plan to protect his nephew. I hope it doesn't screw us up. They're in the lift now. Park it, and we'll find out what curve ball he's going to toss at us."

The hatch slid open a few minutes later and let Lord Fielding, Kelsey, and Austin Darrah into the briefing room. Olivia stood, so he and Sean joined her.

"Please sit," Fielding said. "We have just a few more items to discuss before you embark on the final stage of your mission. Allow me to compliment you on how well you've done so far. Excellent work, particularly from Lady Oldfield."

Kelsey silently inclined her head as she took a seat next to Austin. The young prisoner eyed everyone at the table with what Jared suspected was secret amusement glinting in his eyes.

Once everyone was comfortable, Fielding continued. "First, I need to warn you just how dangerous the agent is. While it's locked away in the drones, it should be safe enough, but due care *must* be taken.

"The Lords tasked me to use my labs to bring this ancient weapon back to life. Gods only know why the dictator felt the need to kill every human being on a world and render it uninhabitable forever. Let me tell you, creating this organism from scratch was no easy task and had more than its share of setbacks. Lethal ones."

Olivia studied the noble for a long while before she added her thoughts. "While I've seen a summary of what to expect, why don't you fill me in on the details. We have to get this right the first time. What kind of setbacks are you speaking of?"

The man grimaced. "We used all due caution. This mining orbital oversees extraction of rare gases on the giant below us, so it's isolated. Perfect to maintain the secrecy the Lords demanded.

"In addition, there are smaller stations used for specialized refining. One of them became the primary laboratory. After several months of work, they recreated the correct genomic sequence. That was a tremendous achievement for them. The accidental release of the agent inside the station was equally tremendous but in a very negative manner.

"We all got to see the terrible progression of the disease up close and personal. The System Lord insisted we allow the scientists to perish so that we could record the data rather than ending their lives quickly. It was just as horrible as you might imagine.

"Once the last person was dead, we deorbited the station and allowed it to burn up in the gas giant's atmosphere. That was more than sufficient to sterilize everything."

"That's awful," Jared agreed. "But as you say, we have the agent in the drones now. What risk is there?"

Fielding fixed him with a cool smile. "I suggest you keep the cargo hold hermetically sealed and bleed off the atmosphere. The little beast is pernicious. It can cross any air gap you'd care to place around it. Only hard vacuum will keep it at bay.

"I don't think it will leak, but you dare not take chances. Given one moment's inattention, you won't be allowed to survive, and you won't want to. Diving this ship into the nearest stellar body will be the only way to be sure you've cleansed it."

That sounded pretty dire to Jared. They'd be ultra-careful.

"We could detonate the plasma charges to eliminate the threat," he suggested. Getting the codes for the antitampering devices would be a huge relief, if he could manage it.

"Sadly, the Lord has forbidden dispensing them," Fielding said with a small smile that seemed faked. "Still, what you say has some merit. The damage to the ship would be severe, but if the agent was limited to the cargo holds, the plasma would cleanse it.

"Your thoughts parallel something I've been pondering. The trip to Terra will take two weeks. Secrecy and safety are paramount. I've come up with a way to expedite your journey while increasing your odds of arriving at Terra safely."

Jared felt himself tensing.

"How would that be?" Olivia asked in the guise of their leader. "If we don't have the codes to the plasma charges, we can't very well use them to protect the Lords' secret."

This time Fielding's smile was large and genuine. "The original plan calls for you to meet another ship a week out from Terra so they can extend the timer on the charges. An encouragement for you to be speedy and remain on task.

"After discussion with the System Lord, he has allowed that there is another way to accomplish the same thing while increasing the overall odds of success on this mission."

"How is that?" Jared asked, a sensation of dread settling in his stomach like a lead ball.

"It's quite simple, really," Fielding said with a grin. "I'm coming with you."

"Well," Austin said into the deafening silence with a wry smile, "this is promising to be a much more exciting journey than I'd expected."

That was the understatement of the year.

36

Nine hours later, Elise snuck out of the maintenance tube where she'd been hiding and made her way to the cramped storage room just off the enlisted crew's mess.

By *Athena*'s clock, it was the middle of the night. Their unwanted guest was safely tucked away in the quarters he'd appropriated from Sean earlier, much to the commodore's annoyance.

The destroyer had just flipped out from Jaidon, and she had no trouble admitting to the relief she felt. They were no longer under the guns of all the ships and fortresses.

Now, if push came to shove, they could deal with the intruding Rebel Empire noble should he discover their deception.

That wouldn't save *Athena*, though. The man was the only person aboard who had the codes to reset the timer on the plasma charges that would gut her. All he needed to do to destroy the ship was sit idly by. In seven days, the destroyer would be wrecked, and they'd be screwed.

Elise was the last to arrive in the storage room. Jared, Sean, Olivia, Lily, Princess Kelsey, and Commander Roche were already seated on portable chairs around a makeshift table.

Her husband gestured for her to sit beside him. "I'll bet you're happy to get out of that tube."

"I'd be much happier if I could sneak into my husband's quarters for the night," she said grumpily. "And before you tell me that's much too risky, that doesn't change how I feel. Has there been any change? How are we going to deal with Fielding and his guards?"

Jared shrugged. "Anytime he is outside his quarters, we keep a close eye on where he goes and what he sees. We're doing what we can to make certain that he only interfaces with our senior officers. They've got the best chance of maintaining the charade.

"I don't see that situation changing. The odds of us being able to get the codes for the plasma charges is almost nonexistent. That's the only trump card he has to play, and he'll never just hand them over."

"I think it's much more serious than that," Olivia said, shaking her head. "He's playing some kind of game. There's very little reason for him to come along on this mission. Oh, I know he says he's doing it to save his nephew's life, but that's bull. If we were truly the Rebel Empire nobles in command of this mission, his presence would only assure his own death in the end."

"So we've got a new player," Sean said slowly. "If his end goal isn't to save his nephew, then what does he hope to accomplish? He's one man against a ship full of people. Even with his guards, we wouldn't have any trouble suppressing him.

"Just look at how everyone was armed when we left El Capitan. With the exception of our techie, everyone was armed at all times, and their neural disruptors were set to kill. Whatever plan Fielding intends to set in motion, he can't reasonably expect to overpower us."

"I've discovered that when a bastard is smiling, he knows something that you don't," Kelsey said with a grunt. "Are we absolutely certain that he doesn't have access to the computer systems? Is it possible that he could set off the antiboarding weapons? If he stuns all of us, then he has control of this ship."

"Not happening," Sean quickly responded. "While we were removing the lockout that our new ally put in place, we checked the entire system to make certain that we had total and absolute control. There's no way that Fielding can subvert the system, not even by digging through the manual controls."

"You'll forgive me if I remain unconvinced. It seems that things haven't quite gone as planned on this mission. At this point, I keep wondering when the next disaster is going to happen and if it'll be our last."

"I understand how you feel, Kelsey," Elise said, clasping her hand around the other woman's. "This has been a very chaotic experience. We came into this mission with a certain expectation of how it was going to work that didn't work out. We're improvising."

"The Rebel Empire has never done anything like this before," Jared said. "We had no reason to expect this side mission when we delivered the report. All we can do now is try to accommodate the unexpected and turn the situation to our advantage.

"Look at it this way, so long as we play along with the Lords' plan, they'll welcome us into the Terra system with open arms. We don't have to fight our way in. We don't have to trick the System Lord stationed there. It will be expecting us."

"Lord Fielding might not have known the people he was meeting, but the System Lord will," Kelsey said. "As soon as it sees what you look like, it will know that something has gone wrong. What do we do then?"

"The best we can," Jared said bluntly. "I've got some people working on a filter in the com system that will swap out Olivia's appearance with that of the dead Rebel Empire noble who was supposed to be running this mission.

"I don't know how effective that'll be, but at this point we don't have a choice. We're committed to making this run."

He turned to Lily. "Is there any chance of getting a sample of that virus and concocting a vaccine or an antidote that could be administered after infection?"

The doctor nodded. "Kelsey was able to capture the code that opened the crates. The drones themselves don't have specific antitampering functions. I should be able to get into one of them and extract a sample safely.

"That said, the laboratories aboard the ship are not exactly cutting edge. I can't guarantee I'll be able to discover a vaccine in the short amount of time we still have available. Or at all, for that matter. Not without the labs aboard *Caduceus*."

From what little Elise had seen of the massive hospital ship, she could well believe the capabilities on the destroyer might be a little short of what they needed.

"Is there any possibility that we'll be able to rendezvous with the fleet as it makes its way around toward Terra?" Elise asked. "If so, we might be able to use those labs to make this happen."

Jared shook his head. "The flip-point layout makes that impossible. We're going by the most direct method, and the fleet is taking the long way around. At flank speed, they're still going to arrive at Terra at least a week after we do, and they won't be at the same flip point."

He looked gravely around the table at all of them. "Whatever happens on this mission, we're only going to have the resources we have with us now. It's going to be up to us to make lemonade with the lemons we've been given.

"Once we arrive at Terra, we're going to look the situation over as we make our way to the home world. It's possible we could gain access to the System Lord and, through it, all the defensive fortifications that protect the system. If that happens, we can let the fleet in when it arrives."

"And if there is no reasonable way to access the System Lord?" Kelsey asked. "What do we do then? It's going to have access to offensive weaponry that could turn this ship into scattered molecules. Not only that, if we deviate from the mission parameters, Lord Fielding is going to know.

"Just how far do we go to maintain our cover? Just how close to an occupied planet do you intend to take this virus?"

Jared grimaced. "If we can't get access to the System Lord, our options are extremely limited. To answer your basic question, we'll most likely die, but I have no intention of allowing this virus to get anywhere near Terra."

"We've been in more difficult situations," Elise said firmly, keeping a resolute expression on her face. "The odds might be stacked against us, but the Rebel Empire isn't going to win this fight. The AIs will not triumph in the end."

She sat back, hoping that her bold words actually foreshadowed success. Despite what she'd just said, she knew the odds stacked against them were damned high.

Jared began laying out potential courses of action. Since they didn't know precisely what they would find at Terra, everything was suitably vague.

Elise consulted her implants and made note of the time. They had about four hours before Lord Fielding would join the rest for breakfast.

She set an internal alarm for two hours. If the meeting hadn't concluded by then, she'd bring it to a close herself. An hour alone with Jared in their quarters would be painfully short, but she was determined not to waste what might be their last days together.

* * *

KELSEY LEFT the meeting in a fairly depressed state of mind. They were probably screwed. She honestly couldn't figure out any possible way they'd come out alive and in possession of the one thing her people absolutely needed to survive: the AI override from the vaults underneath the Imperial Palace.

When she made to turn toward her quarters and catch a few hours of sleep before she had to be up, Scott turned with her. "If you've got a few minutes, Highness, I'd like to go over a couple of items with you. Nothing too big, but I'd rather not risk any of our unwelcome visitors overhearing them."

"Sure."

When she'd let them both into her quarters, he raised an eyebrow at her. "Do you suppose our associates are monitoring you?"

"No," she said with a shake of her head. "I used the information in my Raider implants to build a handheld scanner with a lot more resolution than the ones generally available even to the New Terran Empire in this universe.

"Frankly, it was just to test out my capability to use the data. Something to pass the time. I used it to scan my quarters because I was curious about how far they trusted me, too. No bugs."

"Could you show me how it works?" he asked politely.

She shrugged, retrieved the scanner from her nightstand, and ran it around the room. The process took less than sixty seconds and came back clean.

"All secure," she said. "It doesn't sound like you want to discuss mundane issues. What's going on, Scott?"

He took a second to verify the hatch was locked before sitting at the small desk built into the bulkhead. He waited until she'd sat on the edge of her bunk before he continued.

"Highness, I'm more than a little concerned that you've thrown your lot in with the Bastard and his associates. Granted, it doesn't appear that he's the same man here as he is in our universe, but his primary goal on this mission is the salvation of his own people. If anyone is going to look out for ours, it needs to be us."

Kelsey frowned, crossing her legs. "I'm not quite sure where you're taking this. If it seems as if I've thrown my lot in with them, it's because they have the only viable plan to get what we need. There's only one override. If I want to take it home, I've got to help them defeat the AIs in this universe."

"That's not true, Highness," he said deferentially. "We can follow their plan up to a point and still get what we need. Our agreement to assist them wasn't meant to be a suicide pact. In case you haven't noticed, these people take unbelievable risks. How long before they overestimate their own capability and take us down with them?

"And you can't forget that no matter how reasonable he seems now, he's still the Bastard. How far can we really trust him? Don't let him pull the wool over your eyes. Don't be his willing accomplice in this at the cost of our people's lives just because he puts on a good front."

"I don't appreciate even the implication that I would ever cooperate with someone like the Bastard," she said coldly. "You'd best retract that insinuation right now."

The Fleet officer bowed his head slightly. "My apologies, Highness. I didn't mean to suggest that. Let me try to phrase my thought a different way. As decent as these people appear to be, they aren't *our* people. We have an obligation to do whatever is necessary to save *our* Terran Empire, even if that harms the people in this one."

A cold chill washed through her. "You're suggesting we betray them. That we help them along until an opportune moment and then seize the override for ourselves."

Scott scrunched his face up slightly. "Nothing so blatant. While I have a mustache suitable for twirling, I'm not a villain. All I'm saying is that we should keep our options open. As distasteful as it might be, saving our Empire is worth any price we might have to pay.

"Jared Mertz and his associates are raving lunatics if they think they can dupe the AI in control of Terra. One misstep, and we'll be praying for death. You met the Pale Ones the hard way. Do you really want to experience something like that again?"

Kelsey couldn't repress the shudder before it took her. No, she absolutely didn't want to give anyone control of her body again. She'd kill herself first.

She considered him and then sighed. "Even if I stick a handy knife into Jared Mertz's back, we'd still be stuck in the Terra system. We have no way to escape.

"You heard them. The AI controls all the defensive stations at every flip point and all the mobile platforms. We can't control this destroyer by ourselves. Hell, we can't take it away from them either. I'm tough, but I'm not *that* tough. Like it or not, all our fates are intertwined."

"For the moment," Scott agreed. "Yet we don't know what the future might bring. Let's say that something happens that allows us to bypass the System Lord and gets us to Terra. What are we going to find there?

"That's all I'm asking you to keep in mind, Highness. These people have made great promises to assist us in our universe, but if it comes down to their survival or ours, I know what they'll do, and so do you."

She shook her head sharply. "They gave us four intact *battlecruisers*. Fully operational warships that are individually a match for the one the Bastard stole. They've transferred an immense amount of information to us. They're training our people to utilize implants that they are giving us. That is huge.

"And before you suggest they've tampered with the implant designs, I found other references to them in places they can't have gotten to. Not to all of them. They're being upfront with us. They're helping us when they didn't have to."

Scott shrugged. "Let's say that you're right. Let's say that they're generously helping us. In fact, I'll even concede that's likely the truth. If push comes to shove, are you going to allow these benevolent folks to triumph if it condemns us to death and slavery as the price for victory?"

He let his words hang in the air before he continued.

"I just want you to keep our options open, Highness. Keep considering what's best for the Empire. If you decide that's continuing to assist these people, so be it. If you see that the situation is spiraling out of control and the choice is either to join them in death or act in our own self-interest, I hope you'll be ready to move when the time comes."

Kelsey felt numb. She knew these people were honestly helping her and her people, but Scott was right. This wasn't her universe. She had to keep in mind that their interests might not always coincide.

She prayed it never came to that, but if these people got themselves into an irretrievable situation she had to have other options in mind.

"As much as I want to disagree, I understand," she said slowly. "I refuse to see betraying these people as an unavoidable event, and I pray that we can come up with a plan that saves everyone. But if the crisis comes and I see no other choice, I'll do what I have to."

That broke her heart, but she had to stand for the Empire. *Her* Empire.

She prayed that Jared Mertz found a path to success, because if it came to a choice between her honor and the safety of the Empire, she'd do what had to be done for her people.

HIDDEN ENEMIES

BOOK NINE

Trapped between murderous xenophobes and calculating artificial intelligences, an interstellar war threatens to wash Princess Kelsey Bandar away in a tide of blood.

With her most powerful ship crippled, only a desperate mission to steal what she needs right out from under the noses of her enemies offers a way to get her people safely home.

As if that wasn't hard enough, success requires her foes never learn of her existence and therein lies the problem. Few have ever accused Kelsey Bandar of subtlety.

1

Kelsey Bandar stood at the edge of the bazaar and tried to take everything in. People everywhere were shouting and calling to one another, likely hawking their wares. She didn't speak Pandoran, so that was just an educated guess on her part, however.

The similarities to places she'd seen in old Terran movies was striking. Particularly since everyone was dressed for the hot, dry climate in flowing clothes, mostly light colored with bright sashes and wraps around their heads. They looked like blue alien Bedouins.

Her guide had provided her with the same kind of clothes so she didn't stand out. They felt strange to her, the cloth both heavier than she was used to and somewhat coarser against her skin. She'd chosen to go with a bright-red sash and head wrap to hide her blonde hair.

Unfamiliar scents filled the air around her. Most were aromas from spices in open bowls at a few tables nearby, but some came from vendors cooking delicacies for the hungry crowd.

Well, perhaps delicacy was the wrong word. That made it sound as if the food was prepared for discerning diners at a fancy restaurant. As the daughter of the Terran emperor, she'd eaten at such places many times. Good food but not nearly as satisfying as nachos and a beer at a flea market.

Which, she realized, was exactly what she was looking at. Just like the ones at home, even though it was laid out differently and had a desert feel.

Aside from the aliens. While there were humans in the crowd, they were few and far between. One in a hundred at most. Probably fewer.

Every other being present was a Pandoran. That was the name she'd given them when her people had discovered their preindustrial society on the far side of an unexplored multiflip point.

The Pandorans were so close to being human that it beggared the imagination. They averaged a little taller and had arms and limbs that were of the same proportions and in the same places. Their eyes were a little larger, their teeth a little more pointed, and their noses somewhat more slender.

The similarity was amazing until one got to their bluish skin tones. The youngest of them were a pale blue that shaded duskier as they aged until the elderly were almost midnight in color. Their hair was dark without exception. No greying for them.

Her medical people had discovered just how such an unexpected parallel development had occurred, but the information had raised far more questions than it had answered. In the distant past, someone had manipulated human DNA and relocated these people here.

While her doctors were still wrestling with the time scale involved, it had to be much farther into the past than humans had had space travel. Aliens had done this. Real aliens, like Omega. Not him or his people, of course. They'd left this universe for an alternate dimension and never known about flip points.

She hadn't told them yet and that was, thankfully, a problem she could put off until later.

They'd only just made contact with the Pandorans and knew virtually nothing about their society. That was the reason she was here. Well, one of the reasons.

Kelsey couldn't imagine how she was going to get a handle on everything that needed doing. There was just so much needing her attention. Yet this initial contact had to be from her.

She could solve one problem by getting something to eat. The heavenly scent of the roasting meat was making her mouth water.

Kelsey turned to Derek. Her guide was the son of the ruler here in the Kingdom of Raden. A warrior, he towered over his fellow Pandorans, which meant he was close to two-thirds of a meter taller than she was.

At first, she'd wondered if the Pandorans watching them thought she was a child. At a meter and a half, Kelsey was far more petite than most women. In the presence of such a large man, she probably didn't strike most people as more than a teen.

Derek's name was longer and significantly harder to pronounce in the Pandoran tongue—she'd had him recite it for her, and he'd laughed when she'd tried to repeat it—so the tradition was for them to use a simpler name when dealing with humans.

"Could we get something to eat?" she asked. "I'm starving."

With her Marine Raider enhancements, Kelsey was always hungry. Thankfully, after several years of being in this condition, she was no longer embarrassed by her gargantuan appetite.

There was a spicy scent coming from a haunch of meat cooking over a fire nearby. She gestured toward it as her preference.

"Of course," he said, his Standard unaccented.

He and his people had learned to speak the language when the survivors of the Clan battlecruiser *Dauntless* arrived on their planet sixty years ago. They were one more complication she wasn't sure how she was going to handle.

"Roasted varl is a tender meat with an aftertaste that both our peoples find pleasant," he said. "I suggest you find another vendor though. The scent you are probably smelling is a spice called Jedawa. Most find it quite hot."

Kelsey felt the corners of her mouth quirk up. "Now I have to know what it tastes like."

"Don't say that I didn't warn you."

The Pandoran noble stepped over to the vendor and exchanged some coins for two hunks of roasted meat on sticks and two crude flagons of what looked like beer.

She helped him carry the purchase to a rickety wooden table set on the smoothed flagstones. Other diners were seated around them, sampling various kinds of foods.

With Derek's warning in mind, she took a tentative bite of the meat. It *was* spicy but not so hot that it ruined the taste of the food.

Kelsey closed her eyes and tried to fit the meal into her previous dining experiences. The varl tasted like venison, she decided. It was tender and rich. She could easily envision adding something like this to her diet going forward.

Considering that none of them knew how long they'd be orbiting Pandora, getting some trade going for food was yet another task she had to see to, but she wasn't going to let worrying about it ruin her lunch.

The spice was a bit much for general consumption, she decided. Maybe half as much would be a better fit. Or something else entirely. Though she vowed to make sure Talbot got the full experience first. She wanted to watch her husband squirm.

She turned her attention to the beer. It was good and tasted very much like some she'd sampled on Avalon. It was a pale ale of some kind and the aftertaste was quite pleasant.

"This is good," she said after taking another bite of the meat. "A bit spicy, but I can deal with that. I'll want another stick before I'm done. The beer is great too. A local brew, I assume?"

Derek chuckled. "In our society, almost all food and drink are locally produced. I couldn't tell you who brewed this, but I agree it is one of the better ones I've had over the years."

"Did you have beer before *Dauntless* crashed on Pandora?"

His smile widened. "We did have a society before humans came. Beer has been a staple of our people for as long as we've kept records. Though I will admit that humans have brought innovation even to that. They ferment some powerful liquors with new and interesting flavors."

Kelsey nodded. "Humans do like their booze. I'm going to have to talk with someone about food and such for my ships at some point. We're outfitted for long journeys, but with *Audacious* damaged, we might be here for a while."

In fact, the carrier might be there forever if they couldn't repair her flip drive.

Derek nodded seriously. "Once you've revealed yourself to my father, I'm certain that trade can be quickly and easily established. You undoubtedly have much worthy of trade."

That was the reason she was here in the capital city of the Kingdom of Raden. She wished there'd been a secure way for Derek to get word to his father, but the man hadn't trusted anything other than speaking in person for knowledge of the new humans on their world.

A pinnace had dropped them off within walking distance of the city before dawn, and they'd made their way in on foot. Now they were waiting for Derek's human partner, Jacob Howell, to get back from the palace.

Jacob was something of a spy for Clan Dauntless, but he worked hand in hand with the Kingdom of Raden. He knew how to get into the palace without raising any eyebrows.

As if conjured by her thought, Jacob stepped out of the crowd beside their table. His expression hinted at bad news.

"We need to get you out of here," he said to her in a low voice. "Someone knows you're here."

"Who?" she asked as she stood, her excellent meal forgotten.

Two human males entered the square to her right and almost immediately spotted Kelsey and party. They started through the crowd with determined and displeased expressions.

Derek stood. "Take her. I'll distract them."

Jacob took Kelsey by the elbow and guided her away from the oncoming men. "We can get out of the square and lose them in the side streets."

"Why are they after us?" she asked as she allowed herself to be taken away.

She knew she wasn't in serious danger. With her Marine Raider enhancements and the concealed weapons under her loose clothes, she could handle ten times that many people without being in any trouble at all.

He opened his mouth to respond but stopped dead in his tracks when two men blocked their escape route. They were armed with swords, though those were still sheathed, and seemed as displeased as their fellows.

One stepped forward. "Stand fast, Jacob Howell. I summon you and your companion in the name of Clan Dauntless."

Kelsey moved her hand closer to her stunner, but Jacob didn't look as if he intended to resist.

"Damn the luck," he muttered.

"What did you do?" Kelsey asked.

"Nothing this time. They're here for you."

She swiveled her head toward him. "Excuse me?"

"My name is Isidro Poston," the man in front of them said to her. "In the name of Clan Dauntless, I instruct you to accompany me to the clan chapter house at once to explain yourself."

"That's going to be something of a challenge," Jacob said. "But one we cannot avoid at this point. I suggest we accompany them, and I'll try to make this less painful for everyone."

Kelsey considered raising hell but decided that might make enemies she could ill afford at a time like this. Instead, she forced herself to relax.

The two men from the other side of the square were now standing behind Jacob with Derek off to the side. The alien man shrugged.

"This had better be entertaining," she warned Jacob. "This hasn't been a very fun week."

"It will undoubtedly be entertaining," he said with a small smile. "The question will be who laughs loudest."

* * *

COMMODORE ZIA ANDERSON surveyed the parts spread out on the battered wooden table in front of her. There was a disassembled coolant transfer conduit and what looked like the electronics from a life-support substation. All of the pieces were heavily corroded.

Efrain, the Pandoran that Derek had assigned to watch over her before he took Kelsey to the capital, stood passively behind her, but he noted her glance back at him.

"They are sorting the recovered debris, cleaning it, and attempting to determine what use it might currently serve," he said in a diffident tone.

That made sense. There was a lot of similar activity going on around them. Hundreds of Pandoran workers were processing debris on the covered tables surrounding the wrecked hulk of the battlecruiser *Dauntless*.

On her other side, Carl Owlet shook his head. "Won't do them any good. Those circuits are fried."

The young scientist was accompanying her to find out if by some miracle the battlecruiser's flip drive was salvageable. The odds against that were long, but it never paid to ignore the obvious first play.

Carl had declared in advance that the flip drive was toast, even if it had survived the crash. He was certain that it had burned out in the same way as her ship's had on the transit from the Clan system called Icebox through the multiflip point.

She prayed he was wrong, or they were going to be here a *very* long time.

"The conduit itself might be used to transport any number of things," she told the young man somewhat repressively. "The circuits might yield rare elements, and the alloys might prove useful. Don't think that getting them back into service is the only use for something like that."

Carl grunted a little but nodded. "I see what you mean, but I stand by my original impression."

Zia gestured for Efrain to lead them on. As interesting as this was, it wasn't getting the survey of the wreck done any faster.

The stealthed drones she'd deployed to watch the crash site had already revealed that the engineering section was somewhat intact. As the flip drive was a large piece of equipment, that might mean it was still in there. Getting something like that out without having access to the massive hatch on the ship's underside would be almost impossible.

No one down here could tell her for sure if they'd taken it apart. They'd never bothered keeping records of what had been removed and repurposed over the last six decades.

The three of them walked between a series of buildings and came out in the vast area at the center of the artificial town. The wooden sheds and buildings had been built around the crash site and conformed to how the debris had ended up, so its layout was somewhat arbitrary.

Zia had seen battlecruisers before, obviously. That said, she'd never seen one sitting on the *ground*. That made a huge difference in scale. Comparing a ship with another ship, station, or distant planet didn't make it seem monstrously huge.

Dauntless was monstrously huge.

Even with a broken back and terrible tears in her hull, the wreck was still mostly intact. It towered above their heads, rising into the sky like some kind of alien skyscraper. A skyscraper covered with scaffolding so that the Pandorans could remove and access various things.

In addition to going up a tremendous distance, it was also quite long and wide. Zia and her companions had stepped out of the surrounding buildings near the engineering section. It seemed as if the ship stretched as far as she could see going forward, though she knew that wasn't true.

If she was going to compare it to something of a similar size, the wrecked ship covered three or four blocks going forward. Maybe five. It was two blocks wide.

"That really puts things in scale, doesn't it?" she asked in a hushed voice.

Carl took two steps forward and craned his neck to look upward. "I didn't realize these things were so tall. Intellectually, I know exactly how many decks they have and roughly how much space a deck takes up but that's not the same thing as seeing in front of me like a building."

Zia turned to their guide. "Can we go inside? What are the protocols? I assume someone owns this and we need to get permission to come in to look at things."

The Pandoran nodded. "The wreck is owned by the Kingdom of Raden. Clan Dauntless was paid both in money and land, among other things. Technically, my Lord Derek has sufficient authority to grant you access to *Dauntless*.

"That said, he does not have the authority to give you anything inside the wreckage. There is a company formed by the government that you would have to negotiate with to exchange anything from inside the wreckage for something they value."

She nodded. "So we're window shopping. How do we get in? This is the section of the ship that we're interested in."

The Pandoran man pointed at a wooden arch next to the ship. "Entrances like that have been set up at ground level. While the metals are tough, those splits are large enough to allow equipment in and out. Go wherever you like, and I shall explain our presence if anyone asks."

The wooden archway wasn't just to keep the weather out, Zia saw. Several metal beams were set up behind the wood to make certain the torn hull of the ship didn't shift.

"Just how stable is the interior?" she asked. She didn't aim the question directly at Carl, but she was interested in what both the Pandoran man and her young friend had to say.

Their guide spoke first. "With the understanding that this is a wreck, it's stable. There's no large-scale movement these days. That stopped in the first couple of decades.

"That doesn't mean things are completely safe. Things occasionally fall down, and new weaknesses in walls, ceilings, and floors are occasionally detected. When we become aware of such things, we reinforce them or restrict the area to prevent injury.

"I can't be more specific without knowing precisely where you're going to visit. If it's somewhere outside the zones we've cordoned off, I'll need to get one of the overseers to accompany us."

Carl gave the man a long look but finally nodded. "I can't exactly argue with their experiences over the last half century. If it were me, however, I'd be very careful. Ships like this were designed to be very tough, but when parts fail, they can fail catastrophically.

"Even though it might have been safe for the last sixty years, it wouldn't be fun to be in a location that has metal fatigue that suddenly decided to give way."

"We just want to go to the main engineering compartment right now," Zia said. "If something there convinces us we need to see another section of the ship, we'll let you know."

The journey through the wrecked battlecruiser was surreal. It reminded her very much of her time spent aboard *Courageous*. Except the air hung around them, still and dead. The smell of rust and mechanical decay was strong.

The interior lighting was a lot dimmer than Zia would've preferred, but at least it was powered by electricity. While the illumination was low by human standards, it was probably more than sufficient for Pandorans with their much better night vision.

She could only imagine how torches would behave inside such a confined environment. The smell would be awful, and the fumes from the burning matter would probably sting the eyes.

Zia gestured toward the haphazard lighting. "What's powering your lighting?"

"Residual energy from one of this vessel's power plants," the man said.

Carl stopped in his tracks and slowly turned toward the Pandoran. "Are you telling me that one of the fusion plants is still operational? We didn't detect anything like that from orbit, but I'll confess that I wasn't looking for that kind of activity."

The Pandoran shrugged. "You'll have to ask one of the overseers. All I can tell you is that these lights were rigged up during the time following the crash."

"That's not good," Carl said. "While it's certainly possible that some surviving engineering personnel verified the safety of that unit after the crash, it's been sixty years. I think we might need to look at that before we examine the flip drive."

Zia had personally seen what happened to ships when a fusion plant failed. She had no intention of being anywhere near a damaged unit that had been operational for decades.

"Let's go," she said, increasing her pace.

2

Lieutenant Colonel Russell Talbot watched the prisoners through the vid feed in his implant. To be certain they didn't concoct some kind of common story to tell him, he'd ordered all the prisoners be housed separately. *Audacious* was a large ship with plenty of space for thirteen prisoners.

Of course, they'd said almost the same thing about Commander Veronica Giguere and her officers. They'd thought they'd allowed plenty of space to securely restrain them, but they'd still managed to escape.

Commander Raul Castille, the Dresden orbital's security officer, had orchestrated the murder of most of his comrades, escaped the ship with Commander Giguere and her officers, and no one on Talbot's side had been the wiser until they were long gone.

Their plan had been something worthy of Kelsey, though his wife was loath to admit it. She thought she had a monopoly on making crazy plans work.

Admittedly, they'd upped the stakes for the princess when they'd kidnapped her mother at the same time. And, as mothers-in-law went, the woman was a real piece of work.

The situation had reminded him of a joke he'd heard in one of the old vids his wife favored. A man watching his mother-in-law drive off a cliff in his new ground vehicle—an expensive one—might be a bit torn about how to feel. He'd thought it was hilarious until recently.

After Castille had used the stolen orbital as a weapon to provoke the Clans, Princess Kelsey had tried unsuccessfully to talk the strangers down. She'd had no choice other than to fight when they'd opened fire, though. She'd destroyed both Clan ships.

Talbot wished Castille had survived the fight so he could punch the man in the face. He'd really screwed things up.

Now they had Commander Giguere under secure watch in the medical center, her crew locked down under heavy guard in their original quarters, the few prisoners they'd kept from the Dresden orbital in the brig, and the new prisoners isolated so that they couldn't concoct some common story before Talbot started asking questions.

A dozen of the newcomers were human enough, though none of them had been in uniform when his people had picked them up. They were undoubtedly Clan officers of one kind or another. Considering that the New Terran Empire knew nothing about the Clans or their worlds, he was going to approach them with kid gloves.

Basically, all they knew thus far was that a task force had escaped the Fall of the Old Terran Empire, settled these worlds, and now called themselves the Clans. The leaders of those clans—based around the original vessels—worked together to make broader policy.

From what the Pandorans had indicated of their interaction with the survivors from Clan Dauntless, these were the kind of people that shot first and didn't really bother asking questions when they were done. The aliens thought humans in general were violent, though they admitted that after the most virulent of the crash survivors had fought to the death, the remaining humans seemed peaceful enough. Natural selection at work.

Kelsey's contact with Jacob Howell, the son of the current head of Clan Dauntless, had indicated that no one above the rank of lieutenant had survived the initial crash. The man had suspected higher ranking officers would've been even more resistant to integration into Pandoran society than those that had had to be put down.

It seemed that the people of the Clans were, well, clannish.

That was certainly going to make dealing with the people Castille had provoked difficult. Particularly since the man had blown up one of their battle stations and forced Kelsey to destroy two of their warships. They'd be out for blood, and no amount of talking was going to help.

He pulled his mind back to the task in front of him. Yes, questioning the dozen Clan prisoners was going to be interesting. But it was the thirteenth prisoner that had his attention now.

Unlike the others, this one was very different than anyone Talbot had ever seen before. The man was isolated in a small stateroom under the guard of three marines in unpowered armor. They were armed with stunners and had strict instructions not to harm the man even if he attacked them.

He was human, or so appearances would lead one to believe, but he sported tattoos on his cheeks and forehead and was dressed in flowing robes of pale green. The tattoos were stylized but definitely portrayed some type of predator bird.

"So how do you want to play this?" Major Angela Ellis asked him.

She was the executive officer of Kelsey's ship, the Marine Raider strike ship *Persephone*. She'd come over to give him a hand with the prisoners and consult with Commodore Anderson before the flag officer had headed down to the surface earlier.

Oh, and see her husband, of course.

Talbot still couldn't quite see what the powerfully built woman saw in Carl Owlet. Not that the marine had anything against his young friend, but the boy—and boy was the appropriate word—was very much a nerd. One not even old enough to drink. He'd come aboard the original mission as a graduate student, far ahead of his schoolmates back home his own age.

Angela, on the other hand, was just over two meters tall and was built to scale. Tough, strong, and combative, the marine officer didn't seem the type to be deeply in love with a scientist. No matter how much raw destruction said scientist had managed to wreak over the years Talbot had known him.

"I'm not quite sure," Talbot said, putting his previous thoughts aside. "He's not going to know about the New Terran Empire, of course. He'll suspect that we're from the Rebel Empire. I might not disabuse him of that notion either.

"We're eventually going to have to face up to explaining who we really are and why it wasn't us that attacked the Clans, but that can wait. Stuck here the way we are, we've got plenty of time to figure out precisely who we're dealing with."

She raised an eyebrow. "Aren't you a little concerned they're going to be coming through the flip point after us?"

He shook his head. "No. While they know the multiflip point exists, they've never been successful in utilizing it in the past. There's no reason to believe they're suddenly going to develop the technology necessary to get one of their ships through to this side."

Score one for Carl.

"Only his modifications to *Audacious*'s flip drive made it possible for her to make the jump," he said. "The same goes for the freighter we brought with us. While big, the freighter managed to come through with its flip drive intact. The carrier burned hers out.

"*Persephone* seems to be the largest ship capable of going through from the Icebox side unmodified. And it's the smallest flip-capable ship I've ever seen. No, I'm not worried."

Angela didn't seem convinced. "It's not as if the Icebox system has any other location we could've gone. The multiflip point is the only place we could've come through. They'll be asking themselves how we managed to get back, and they'll start working on it."

"I'm not sure that's true, at least not right away. They're going to tear that system apart looking for where some Rebel Empire warships might be hiding. In fact, that's *exactly* what our FTL drones are showing them doing.

"While they've stationed a pair of warships at the multiflip point, I don't think they really believe anybody went back through it. They're more worried other ships are going to come through from the Rebel Empire."

"They've got people at the planet itself, and we can be sure they're going to talk to the people marooned there," Angela objected. "That includes the roughly ten thousand people we captured with the Dresden orbital."

Talbot smiled. "Who are just as in the dark about who we are as everyone else on the surface of the planet. The only people in the Rebel Empire who know about the New Terran Empire are either dead, safely in the New Terran Empire, or on board this ship.

"While finding so many new people is going to be a shock to their systems, it's not really going to tell the Clans anything about us. I'm more than happy to let them jump to the conclusion it was the Rebel Empire behind the attack on them. After all, that's *exactly* what happened.

"The only indication they're going to find of the phrase 'New Terran Empire' is going to be that one transmission that Castille made before he blew up their station. For once, mistaken identity is going to work in our favor, I think."

"I never took you for an optimist." The inflection she put on the last word made it sound like a curse. "I'm going to put some money down that it doesn't work out the way you expect."

"Hardly anything ever does," he grumbled.

"Are we ready?" she asked.

"Not yet. I want one more opinion before we confront our unexpected guest."

* * *

Commander Veronica Giguere, late of the Rebel Empire Fleet—very late, as it turned out—sat in a small room just off the medical center. It offered a bit of privacy, but she knew that was an illusion. The New Terran Empire had her under very close surveillance.

Which in and of itself was hilarious. The fight with Raul Castille in the engineering compartment aboard the transport ship had ended with an explosion strong enough to render her incapable of more than resting.

The doctor had set her broken legs and made her broken ribs safe, but that didn't mean she could walk. No, she wasn't going anywhere for a while. Regeneration was good for a lot of things. Knitting broken bones? Not so much. It took time and multiple sessions for that.

The hatch chimed and she used her implants to see who was calling. Commander Zac Zoboroski—*Audacious*'s chief medical officer—stood outside with a floating contraption. It looked like a chair.

Oh, and the four marines making sure she didn't crawl away when no one was looking were out there too. That seemed like overkill to her, but she'd already snuck out of their custody once. Talbot had muttered something about barns and horses, but the comment made no sense to her.

She opened the door with her implants and watched the Fleet medical officer come in with the floating chair.

"Doctor," she said, inclining her head. "What's that?"

"A grav chair," he said in his pleasant voice. "Believe it or not, this is the same one Princess Kelsey used after she got her Marine Raider enhancements. The doctor on *Persephone* had it in storage, and I realized it would be perfect for you."

Veronica studied the chair closely. It was crude but seemed functional enough. Definitely not up to Imperial standards.

"You made that?"

"The Pentagarans did. They were also cut off from the Empire during the Fall. Their grav tech was better than ours back then. I really need to have someone put together a better model, but we haven't exactly needed one until now."

"And why do I need this? Am I supposed to go somewhere?"

"Lieutenant Colonel Talbot requested your presence. It seems he wants your opinion on something. If, of course, you have time."

She chuckled a trifle bitterly. "My schedule happens to be wide open. Though I will admit that I'm not sure why he wants *my* opinion. I'm not exactly the most popular person on this ship right now."

"Don't sell yourself short," the man said, moving the chair around beside her bed. "Kelsey's mother is still aboard. Besides, getting out and about will be good for you. There's nothing forcing you to go, but I'd recommend it. Boredom slows recovery time."

He was right about the boredom, so she allowed him to help her into the chair. The controls were straightforward, and they were soon on their way. The marine guards fell in around them.

The trip through the massive carrier took a bit. She still marveled at the sheer size of the warship. The Empire no longer had anything like it. The AI Lords had seen to that.

Eventually, the doctor guided her chair through a hatch into what was obviously an observation room. The far wall had a viewscreen showing another compartment. There was a very strange man standing in the displayed compartment.

Remembering her manners, she noted that Colonel Talbot was not alone in this one. A tall, well-built woman stood beside him. She wore the uniform of a marine major.

"Thanks for bringing her down, Doc," Talbot said to Zoboroski. "We've got it from here."

The doctor departed, but the marine guards stayed. Yeah, they weren't trusting her very far at all.

"Colonel Talbot," Veronica said. "The doctor said you needed my opinion. I can't imagine why, but I seem to have some time on my hands. What can I do for you?"

"Commander Veronica Giguere," he said. "Allow me to introduce Major Angela Ellis, *Persephone*'s executive officer."

Interesting. Why a marine rank rather than a Fleet one?

The woman stepped over and extended her hand. While it was very subtle, Veronica noticed the other woman stumbled just a little bit as she walked.

"Are you okay?" Veronica asked as she shook the woman's hand.

The tall marine nodded. "I had some work done on my legs, and I'm still getting used to moving around. I'm told that in a couple of days no one will even be able to tell. Other than me."

"What kind of work?"

The tall woman glanced at Talbot, and he nodded.

"I've gone through the initial procedure to become a Marine Raider. They've fully enhanced my legs and put the pharmacology unit in. Once I recover from that, I'll get my upper torso done and get the more subtle add-ons. I'll be a fully functioning Marine Raider in a week or two. Until then, I'm still getting used to walking again."

Veronica nodded, impressed in spite of herself. She'd seen what Princess Kelsey could do. Not only her physical prowess, but they'd showed her a couple of recordings of the woman in combat. If an untrained woman of that stature, raised in the higher orders of her society, could cause such destruction, Veronica could hardly imagine what a trained marine of Ellis's size could accomplish.

"I'm impressed," she admitted. "I didn't believe your people would be able to begin the process so quickly after seizing the equipment on the Dresden orbital."

Ellis shrugged. "We already had the implant equipment. We didn't have any hardware. We got some of that before we even got to Dresden. It'll be a while before we can set up manufacturing for something like that, but we can handle all the marines we have on this mission, if we decide its safe."

That was frightening. *Audacious* carried a lot of marines. More than a ship her size should have. From what Veronica had heard, the New Terran Empire had stuffed a battalion of marines onto the carrier to seize the Dresden orbital.

"In any case," Talbot said, cutting off her thoughts. "That's not why I asked you down here. I'm much more interested in hearing what you think about the gentleman on the screen."

Veronica edged her chair closer to the display. The man seemed normal enough, if one discounted his clothing and those outrageous tattoos. Who put tattoos on their *faces*?

"He can't see us, can he?" she asked.

"No," Talbot said. "He can see the camera, however. He's been watching it for the last half hour. Frankly, I'm not certain what he finds so entrancing."

After considering the man for a full minute, Veronica shrugged. "I have to confess that I've never seen anyone quite like him. Admittedly, I didn't interface with the prisoners down on that planet when we escaped. Is that where he's from?"

The marine officer smiled. "He's from much farther away than that. Unless I'm very much mistaken, that gentleman is from a political entity called the Singularity. Have you ever heard of them?"

She shook her head. "Not that I recall. Of course, the Lords aren't exactly forthcoming when it comes to talking about people outside the Empire. Do I need to know something about them to give you my opinion?"

"I think it would be more useful to get your opinion without tainting it beforehand. I'm going to step inside and question him. You'll pick up some of his history from the questions I ask, but I'd like to get your take once we're done. Unless I miss my guess, this is going to be an educational meeting for you."

"For us too," Ellis said sourly. "And probably not in a good way."

3

Kelsey examined the city as their new companions escorted Jacob Howell and her to what they'd declared as the Clan Dauntless chapter house. She assumed that it was something like an embassy but didn't know enough to be sure.

They searched Jacob for weapons and confiscated what he'd been carrying: a sword, two knives, and that flechette pistol he'd tried to use on her when they'd first met. To her amusement, they didn't check her at all.

Boy, that was going to embarrass someone.

Derek had excused himself, indicating he was going to go speak with his father. The four men that had come for Jacob and Kelsey didn't attempt to stop him. Whether that meant they had no authority over the Pandoran or they just figured it wasn't worth their time, she didn't know.

The chapter house was a low building on the outskirts of the city. Only two stories tall, it covered a fairly large area. It was the equivalent of an entire city block, she guessed.

Made of a mixture of stone and wood, it blended in seamlessly with the buildings around it. There was nothing to indicate that it housed humans as opposed to Pandorans.

Just inside the open front door, two men stood guard. Based on their relaxed stances, they weren't expecting any trouble.

One of them grinned at Jacob and extended his hand to him. "I knew it was only a matter of time before they brought you in. What did you do this time?"

Jacob laughed. "Not what they think. Arturo, allow me to introduce Kelsey Bandar."

The man turned his attention to Kelsey, raising a hand to stop the escort leader when he opened his mouth to object, based on his expression. "I'll hear what you have to say in just a moment, Isidro. Don't you know it's impolite to speak over a woman? Behave yourself."

The man examined Kelsey with eyes that seemed far more discerning than her escort's. "There's more to you than meets the eye, Kelsey Bandar. I must confess unfamiliarity with your name.

"At first glance, one might take you for a child or a very young woman. That does you a great disservice, I think. After all, not very many women of any age wear swords underneath their robes."

"What?" the escort leader demanded, rounding to stare at Kelsey.

She'd arranged things so that the hilts of her swords rode low, but they were still high enough that she could control them if need be. Since they weren't all that long, concealing them hadn't been too difficult so long as she used the over-the-shoulder harness that had come with Ned Quincy's old weapons.

Kelsey saw the moment when the escort leader spotted the weapons riding over her shoulders. She raised a hand as soon as he reached toward her.

"Let's just get this out in the open. I don't answer to you, and I will not accept anyone attempting to put their hands on me. Rather than see you get hurt or deeply embarrassed, I suggest you stop right there and allow cooler heads to discuss this matter."

If anything, her words seemed to inflame the man's anger. Too damned bad.

"I will *not* be spoken to in that manner, least of all by a woman." He batted her hand aside and reached for the hilt of one of her swords.

Rather, he *attempted* to bat her hand away. What happened instead was her stopping his hand cold, twisting his arm behind his back, and forcing him to his knees as he cried out in anguish.

The man's three companions began drawing their swords but stopped when Arturo laughed and held his hand up.

"Hold!" the man called. "There will be no fighting inside this chapter house. Rash actions serve no one. Am I clear on that?"

When the three men hastily removed their hands from their weapons, Arturo gestured for Kelsey to release the man she was holding.

She complied, taking a step back and reaching up to flip her cloak away from the hilts of her swords. If someone else drew a weapon, she'd make a much more dramatic demonstration of why that was an exceptionally bad idea.

The man they'd called Isidro leapt to his feet and whirled toward her with a snarl on his face. "You will pay for your insolence!"

"Get in line, pal," she advised. "I've got far more dangerous people eager to make me pay for various things. You're not even in the top ten."

The man called Arturo grabbed Isidro's wrist as it darted toward his weapon. "Now, now, let's not be hasty. Tempers are up, and people are likely to say things that get under our skins. Walk it off, Isidro. Now."

Isidro tried to jerk his hand out of the other man's grip and failed. Only when that was readily apparent to everyone did Arturo release him. The offended man stalked deeper into the building.

"I'll be wanting my weapons back very shortly," Jacob called out after him, earning him a finger shot up over the departing man's shoulder in the universal sign of offended negation.

Arturo stood there with his arms crossed giving Kelsey a deeper examination. "I can't recall ever having seen a woman under arms. And, in any case, I'm unfamiliar with the material used in your hilts, and I thought of myself as very educated when it comes to weaponry.

"We've come to something of an impasse. You've been summoned to account for yourself, but I cannot allow anyone to bear arms before a tribunal of the clan. Yet here you stand, armed and defiant, completely unknown to me. How shall we solve this conundrum?"

Kelsey gave him a flat look. "How you solve this situation isn't my problem. I was going about my business when your people insisted that I come along whether I wanted to or not. Well, here I am. How are *you* going to solve this problem?"

The man threw his head back and laughed again. "You do have spunk! I cannot wait to find out what the true story behind your presence—and weapons—is. Yet I must insist that you disarm. I give you my word as a lesser chief of the clan that I will hold them safe and return them to you as soon as the tribunal dismisses you."

She shook her head. "Nope. I'm not here willingly, and I will stay only as long as I decide to. You don't get my weapons. Try again."

Jacob cleared his throat. "The situation is… complex, Arturo. I'd rather not explain it standing here in the foyer. Can we perhaps speak alone on this matter before you escort us to see the tribunal?"

The big man snorted. "That's rich, you saying something is complex. Everything you touch is complex. Very well. We'll make a stop along the way, and you can explain to me in private why this young woman needs to have a pair of swords riding on her shoulders and likely other weapons scattered about her person.

"You can also explain to me how she has the training—or the strength for that matter—to put a trained warrior's hand behind his back. And I confess that I cannot wait to hear you try to sweet-talk this situation with the tribunal."

He gestured for them to follow him deeper into the building.

The situation did have its amusing elements, Kelsey decided as she went in the indicated direction. Jacob had been right about that. With any luck, she'd still be laughing in a few minutes.

* * *

Zia led Carl and Efrain deeper into the ruined battlecruiser. She'd thought she'd known the fastest way to the main engineering compartment, but collapsed corridors and gutted areas made her circle around to take less direct paths.

Rather than taking ten minutes to get there, it took almost twenty. The low level of lighting meant that virtually all of the large compartment was lost to the darkness, but she could see areas where people were working in pools of dim illumination. None of the Pandorans even looked over at them.

"Which fusion plant is running?" she asked Carl.

"I'm not sure. The computer and support systems are either locked down or offline. Not even the engineering systems are available to my implants. I suggest we follow the power lines."

He pulled a powerful portable light from the bag over his shoulder and started tracing the lines of lights.

The brighter light drew some attention at last. Everyone turned to stare at them as the scientist led Zia and their guide deeper into the cavernous compartment. By the time Carl had stopped beside a fusion plant, a delegation of Pandorans was at their side.

Zia left the scientist to his work and smiled at the men. "Good morning. I'm Zia Anderson."

The leading Pandoran, an older man based on his darker skin tone, pointed at Carl. "Where did he find that, why is he using it, and what do you think you're doing?"

Efrain cleared his throat. "Commodore Anderson, allow me to introduce Overseer Halbreth. He is in charge of this site. Overseer, the commodore is here with Derek's approval. She has his full confidence."

The interruption only seemed to irritate the older man, so Zia wished the alien hadn't bothered.

"Overseer, my associate brought the light with him," Zia said. "He didn't find it here. That is true for everything in his bag."

The alien's eyes narrowed. "That isn't an acceptable answer. What is a 'commodore?'"

"A military rank. My associate and I are from… ahem, elsewhere."

Efrain didn't look pleased at her just saying that, but it wasn't as if she had a lot of choice. The aliens would know the truth as soon as Carl started trying to access the ship's systems.

Halbreth blinked. "Elsewhere? What does *that* mean?"

"We're from another star system," she said matter-of-factly. "We're not of the Clans or even the places they came from before they crashed."

The older Pandoran barked out a harsh laugh. "Impossible. How would one even prove something like that? What kind of game are you really playing?"

Before she could answer, Carl opened the access panel he'd been working on and peered inside.

Halbreth took a step forward. "Get away from that! You'll break it or kill yourself. I can live with the latter but not the former."

Carl looked back at the man and shook his head. "I'm fully conversant with the safety procedures for this piece of equipment."

He turned his attention to Zia. "The implant access is manually switched off. I need to turn it on. That should be safe enough to allow me to assess the plant's condition."

"Do it," she said.

Before the overseer could do anything, Carl reached into the fusion plant and touched a button. It changed from amber to green.

"The equipment is accessible," Carl said, stepping back and raising his hands. "Its status is remarkably good, but someone ramped it down below the rated minimum output and shut off the safeties. It was never designed to work that way, and the logs show a downward trend in safety margin over the last few years.

"It really needs to be taken offline and serviced, but it can probably keep going for a while if I bump the output up to minimum. There are risks of systems overloading, but if I don't, this plant will fail sometime in the next year or so. At that point, getting it online again will take significantly more effort on our part."

She turned to the Pandoran overseer. "You heard my associate. He can make this system provide more power for your lights and other uses and make it safer in the long run. Would that prove anything to you?"

The man snorted. "It would prove your insanity. Even the crash survivors knew little of this power generator. No one can change anything about it, and I refuse to allow anyone to touch it."

"He doesn't need to touch it. Carl, bump it to a safe minimum output."

That was a pretty substantial risk. If something went wrong, they'd be in trouble. Hell, they'd be in hot water even if it went perfectly.

The scientist didn't move, but the lights around them started coming on. The makeshift lights brightened too.

Halbreth stared up with a shocked expression as the overhead lighting came up to about sixty percent of normal and revealed the full extent of damage to the compartment.

Of course, along with the success came some failure. One of the consoles near the front of the compartment started smoking and abruptly shorted out in a cloud of smoke.

"Stop what you're doing," the overseer shouted. "Stop it! Guards!"

His cry drew several men into the compartment at a run with their swords drawn.

Zia hadn't anticipated this level of confrontation, so she raised her hands as she headed for the fire suppression unit nearest the smoldering console. "I'll put this out, if you don't mind."

She half expected the now suspicious aliens to stop her, but they allowed her to pull the fire suppression unit off the wall. It was as simple and uncomplicated as possible, so it was still good. She knew it would be because of the recovery efforts on *Courageous*.

Frankly, the console would stop burning on its own, but she wanted to be seen doing something that "corrected" the damage she'd caused.

It only took a moment to slap the console release, causing the top to spring up. She unleashed a spread of retardant powder on the smoking boards and then hit the kill switch to cut power to the console.

Zia noted the guards closing in as she set the fire suppression unit down and kept her hands where they could see them.

Overseer Halbreth walked over to her and scowled deeply. "You have created a safety concern by toying with things you had no business touching. I don't care who your sponsor is. You're expelled from this site and will not be allowed to return."

4

Talbot stepped into the compartment they were using to hold the man from the Singularity. It was a comfortable single occupancy cabin that had been stripped of anything that might serve as a weapon.

Two marines stood guard in the corridor and two more stood just inside the compartment. The outer pair were armed with stunners. The inner pair had their muscles.

The man with the tattoos, who was already standing, turned to face Talbot without saying anything. His expression seemed a bit superior. It reminded Talbot of how Commander Raul Castille had looked down his nose at the people from the New Terran Empire. Only more so.

Talbot stopped just inside the compartment and examined the man closely, allowing the silence to draw out. He wanted to see if the other man was the nervous type.

Under the tattoos that formed some kind of predatory bird, his features were average. Bland even. A nose neither large nor small, a mouth on the wide side with thin lips, and eyes of pale blue.

His eyes were his best features by far, in Talbot's opinion. Alive and intelligent, they studied him. The man still didn't speak.

The man's body seemed on the thin side under his loose garments. His arms—what Talbot could see of them—seemed somewhat scrawny. Not a warrior, most likely.

When it became clear that the prisoner wasn't going to initiate the conversation, Talbot smiled a little more widely. "A man with patience, I see. I'm Lieutenant Colonel Russell Talbot, Imperial Marines. Who are you?"

The other man's lips curled up just a little. "I'm your prisoner, though I expect that situation to change in the near future. The arrogance of Terrans is legendary among my people, but you picked a fight with the wrong people this time."

The man's Standard was excellent. It sounded like his native language, though what they'd learned led Talbot to suspect it wasn't.

"When you say your people, you mean the Singularity?" Talbot asked.

That caused the man's eyebrows to rise. "That isn't a name I expected you to know. Your Lords seem determined to eradicate all mention of the People from your records."

Talbot hadn't been aware they called themselves that. "We're full of surprises. What are the People doing with the Clans?"

The man's smile widened further. "You're shockingly well informed, Lieutenant Colonel. You may call me Theo."

"Shouldn't there be a number with that?"

This time the man's smile seemed genuine. "You astound me again, Lieutenant Colonel Talbot. I'm the only Theo here, but if you simply must know, I am Theo 309. Might this one inquire why you attacked the Clan warships? From what I saw, and to my stark amazement, they weren't the aggressors."

"We'll get to that," Talbot said. "First, allow me to compliment you on your Standard. It's excellent. And useful since I don't speak the tongue."

"You even know what we call our own language? I'm seriously impressed. No outsiders have spoken the tongue since the great sundering of the Terran Empire and the enslavement of the people living there. Your people."

"Since this is ancient history for you, how did your people fare when the AIs rebelled against the Terran Empire? Did the fighting spill across your border?"

The man who called himself Theo sat down on the edge of the couch and crossed his legs with an easy grace. "For someone who's surprisingly knowledgeable about my people, I'm amazed you don't already know the answer to your own question. Why is that?"

"Being educated about a historical entity doesn't mean knowing what's going on with them in modern times," Talbot said. "I've read documents and reports talking about the Singularity but, as you said, my people and yours have not interacted directly in quite some time.

"Unless of course you count the Clans as my people, which is only tangentially true. We sprang from the same source, but they seem to have developed their own personality."

Theo laughed at that last comment. "That's something of an understatement. A rather vast one. The ships that formed the Clans left the Terran Empire during the great sundering. Since then, they have developed some very peculiar societal quirks, I agree.

"One of those being that they are extremely xenophobic. They barely trust one another, much less anyone outside their circle of 'family.' By destroying one of their stations and several of their ships, you've assured that they won't rest until they've found a way to strike back at you."

That was very much what Talbot was afraid of. Castille had certainly done his level best to spoil any chance of a decent relationship between the New Terran Empire and the Clans.

"You're an outsider," Talbot pointed out. "If they're so xenophobic, how is it that you were aboard one of their ships? You certainly don't appear to have been a prisoner."

The man smiled. "Oh, I wasn't. I act as an envoy between my people and the Clans. We reached an accommodation quite some time ago, you see. It suits my people to grow the forces that may one day retake the Terran Empire.

"I'm not quite certain how thorough your knowledge of the People is. We have our own societal quirks too. Ones that caused us to leave the Terran Empire many thousands of years ago. We don't believe in implanting devices into our bodies, and we don't allow machines to control our lives. Perfection takes a different turn than the perversion your people created to enslave yourselves.

"It's an endless source of irony to me that the war caused by your sins have meant that the Clans are no longer able to follow that horrific process. One bright light in the sea of darkness that is the rest of their society.

"So, it serves my people's interests to strengthen the Clans into a force capable of once again ruling the Terran Empire. And it certainly doesn't hurt that we've made ourselves indispensable for when that day comes. Which, because of you, will likely be sooner than either of us thinks possible."

That certainly sounded ominous.

"Considering the shape these people were in when they escaped the Terran Empire and AIs, they certainly wouldn't have been in shape to fight without a lot of help," Talbot said. "What benefit does it serve the Singularity to build them up so much? Surely, they become a threat at that point.

"After all, you've probably done your part to make certain the Clans are xenophobic. Let's just say that the people from the Singularity have a reputation for being somewhat manipulative."

The man's smile deepened. "Oh, you *are* perceptive. I deny what you've said, of course, but appreciate the compliment. Your insight seems as keen as your imagination. My congratulations.

"Now, as a neutral survivor from the battle, I'm afraid I must request that you release me. My people took no part in this combat and have not raised arms against yours. While I doubt very seriously that your people will respect my diplomatic immunity with the Clans, if you wish to avoid making the situation worse, you'll let me go."

Talbot made an expression of doubt. "Didn't you just sit here and tell me that you were helping the Clans build a force capable of overthrowing the Terran Empire? That seems fairly hostile to me.

"No, I think we'll be holding on to you for now. If you decide to be cooperative, I'm certain that additional amenities can be provided to enhance your comfort. On the other hand, if you prove problematic, we have a nice cell in the brig waiting for you. Far less comfortable than this cabin."

Talbot stepped toward the hatch. "I suggest you consider very carefully how we're going to work together going forward, Theo 309. We'll speak again."

He stepped out into the corridor before the man could respond and allowed the hatch to close behind him.

Well, that hadn't gone as badly as he'd feared, but the man certainly wasn't a pushover. Getting real information from him was going to be difficult. Perhaps impossible. Time would tell.

Until then, there were a few other threads he could pull on.

* * *

VERONICA WATCHED the interview with interest. The strange man was very smooth. It seemed as if nothing Colonel Talbot said had fazed him. There was a lot going on under the surface and she doubted the man was going to give any information to his captors willingly.

The hatch behind her slid open, and Talbot stepped inside. "That didn't go nearly as well as I'd hoped. He's really good at this. Commander Giguere, what did you think?"

"I can't add anything to what you just said," she said with a shrug. "I've seen smooth characters like that before. Mostly diplomats and used grav-car salesmen. The kind of people that could lie to your face with a bland expression of mild interest. You're not going to get him to talk."

Talbot grunted. "I certainly hope you're wrong, but that pretty much matches my expectations too. We've got time to deal with him, I suppose. It isn't as if we're going to see Clan warships rushing through the flip point at any moment."

Veronica raised an eyebrow. "Perhaps I'm a bit biased, but what makes you think that you're so much better than them? Why can't they figure it out too?"

"Because they don't have Carl Owlet," Talbot said smugly. "The man is a freaking genius. Plus, they don't even know what a multiflip point is. Their understanding is basically what we knew back when we first discovered one.

"We were certain that whatever it was, it was a one-way trip. Nothing we could do managed to get a ship back through the flip point. No amount of toying around with power levels and so forth made any difference whatsoever.

"It took a ton of research to figure out what we were really looking at, and then Carl had to come up with a theory covering how we might exploit what he thought was there. Then he had to develop the hardware. That's not going to happen overnight."

Veronica shifted herself in her chair and shook her head. "That's being arrogant. They aren't going to find any of your ships back in that other system. They know there's enough force floating around somewhere to destroy two of their ships. Not to mention the fact that they almost certainly obtained some kind of scanner readings of the Dresden orbital before it rammed their station.

"By now, they have to realize that a significant force came through the Icebox flip point. When they don't find it, they'll know it had to have gone back through. Once someone knows something is possible, it's only a matter of time before they figure out how to do it."

Talbot grimaced. "I certainly hope you're wrong, but we've never managed to get out of any problem the easy way. It isn't as if we have a lot of choices at the moment. *Audacious* is trapped in this system. If they come for us, we're not going to be able to run."

"That's… unfortunate. From what that man said, the Clans don't seem like the forgiving types. Do you have any plans for repairing this ship? Is it even possible to repair it outside of dry dock?"

"That question is above my pay grade. We've got people down on the planet right now looking to see if the flip drive on the crashed battlecruiser is salvageable."

Veronica felt one of her eyebrows rise. "Crashed battlecruiser? I don't think I've heard this particular story."

"That's more because you were in the medical center rather than because nobody was going to tell you," Angela Ellis said, speaking up for the first time in a while. "There's a lot that we haven't told you, some because they haven't come up, and others because… well, you *are* the enemy."

Veronica slumped a little bit in her chair. "That's not particularly true anymore. I get that the AIs actually conquered humanity and the history I learned as a child was a lie.

"The problem is that I have no way to convince you of that. I want to help you. Really, I do. I've given up. Everything you've told us has been right. Still, you'll never trust me. You'll never trust any of us."

She could hear the bitterness in her voice. It annoyed her. One more thing she couldn't do anything about.

Talbot smiled. "Actually, that might not be true. I got a little piece of information last night that changes that particular set of circumstances."

He turned to Ellis. "Remember the freighter we captured at Dresden? Turns out it had a little secret cargo in a locked compartment. A brand-new AI."

His words sent shivers down Veronica's spine. "I hardly see how that's good news. Those things are monsters."

"Not if you utilize clean code from the very beginning," he said with a grin. "In this case, they didn't send any operating software with it at all. Just the hardware.

"Thankfully, we have a clean set of code in our database. The commodore was busy, so I ordered the AI brought over to *Persephone*. She has less room but is mobile. If trouble comes knocking, we'll want the AI leaving with us. It's too valuable to let someone take with the carrier.

"Once we have it put together, we can boot it from clean code, and it will be able to determine if you're telling the truth or not."

"How could it possibly do that?"

"That's going to take a little faith," he said seriously. "You have to allow it access to your implants to monitor your brain while you tell us how you've seen the light. It will be able to determine if you're being truthful."

"You want me to allow one of the Lords access to my *brain*?"

"It's not as if it's able to change anything in your memory. As they say, it's read-only access. Of course, you have to trust that I'm telling you the truth. That, I'm afraid, is the price of admittance. If you want us to trust you, you're going to have to trust us first."

None of that made Veronica happy, but she nodded slowly. "When are we going to be able to do it?"

The marine officer shrugged. "Maybe today, maybe tomorrow. I haven't been keeping a close eye on the progress. We'll have you on hand when we bring it online. I want you to see the difference between a free AI and one of your System Lords first hand."

"I'd say that I can't wait, but that would be a lie. Should I just go back to the medical center?"

He shook his head. "No. I'm going to stick my neck out a little and give you a chance to see what we're doing. Angela and I are about to have a little chat with Commander Renner. Would you like to come along?"

Violet Renner had been the incoming security officer about to replace Raul Castille on the Dresden orbital when Princess Kelsey had stolen it.

"I wouldn't hold my breath if I were you. She's going to be even less cooperative than Theo 309."

"Let's go find out," Talbot suggested. "It's not as if you have anything more pressing on your plate."

5

Kelsey followed Jacob and Arturo into a room just off to the side of the main entrance. It looked as if it were normally used for intimate private meetings.

The exterior wall used wood and stone as its primary building materials while the interior divisions were made solely of wood. The furniture was made of roughly hewn wood with padded seats covered in coarse leather.

Two columns formed from whole tree trunks supported the ceiling above. Someone had taken the time to carve images of a battlecruiser onto its surface. The art was relatively crude and in places inaccurate, but the general shape was unmistakable.

Once Arturo had closed the stout door, he turned to Kelsey and Jacob, planting his hands on his hips. "Jacob, who is this young woman, and why is she armed? And how is it possible for her to subdue a warrior like Isidro?"

Rather than answering, Jacob walked over to a small bar set into the wall, picked up a pitcher of what sounded like ice water from the rough plank, and poured himself a mug. "Does anyone else want water? This might take a while."

"I'll take one," Kelsey said.

Then she turned to fully face Arturo. "We were going to have this discussion with the king of Raden first, but I suppose I don't have a choice in telling you. The problem is that I'd prefer to do this as few times as possible."

The warrior considered her for a moment. "While I want to know the complete story, at this particular moment I'll settle for why you're armed and what the nature of your arms are. If you can convince me that you should retain those arms, I will let you speak to the tribunal while retaining them.

"This is something of a first for me. I've never heard of an armed woman. Well, nothing more than a knife used for self-defense anyway. Yet you carry swords, and those do not look like wooden hilts to my experienced eye. They're not even wrapped in leather. Explain this portion of the mystery to me."

"I'd do it if I were you," Jacob said as he handed a mug to her. "Arturo is much more reasonable than Isidro. Your story will be more than sufficient to make him an ally. And against slime like Isidro, one needs as many allies as possible. You can rest assured that idiot is going to speak against you at the tribunal."

Kelsey considered Arturo for a few seconds and then shrugged. This moment had been coming since she'd arrived. She'd reviewed the questioning of the prisoners they'd found on Icebox while they were there. The Clans took women from among the prisoners to other locations.

From what Jacob said, the Clans put women into secondary roles: homemakers and raising children. The men were responsible for protecting them.

She wasn't certain how willingly the women of the Clans submitted to this but didn't know enough to say they were treated as second-class citizens. Yet.

If she found that was true, she and Jacob would be having an unpleasant conversation. Kelsey wasn't the type to stand by and allow slavery, no matter how prettily it was dressed up.

"You want to know why I'm armed and what my sword hilt is made of?" she asked. "Easily solved."

She drank her water, tossed the empty mug to Jacob, and drew one of her swords. The short blades had originally belonged to Ned Quincy back when he'd been alive.

Even though his intelligence lived on as some kind of odd AI program, asleep for the moment while Carl Owlet searched for a way to relocate him to a new body or machine, he'd trained Kelsey in the use of these weapons until they'd become extensions of her body in combat.

In conjunction with her artificial muscles and combat enhancements, they made her exceptionally lethal in hand-to-hand combat. If those men at the entrance had attacked her, her blades would've gone right through both their weapons and their bodies. They were made of hull metal, just like regular marine knives, and the edges were measured in molecules of width.

Flipping the sword around, she extended it to the man on her palms. "I'd be very careful with that if I were you. It's much sharper than you can possibly imagine. Testing the edge will cost you a thumb."

Arturo hefted the sword, smiling indulgently at Kelsey. "I've spent my life around swords. Trust me when I say that I know what a sharp weapon can do."

With that, he lazily swung the sword at a handy chair that had obviously seen similar attention in the past. There were small nicks and cuts in the thick legs where people had banged their weapons against it in the past.

The blade of her short sword cut completely through not only that leg, but the leg on the other side. The chair immediately collapsed under its own weight with a clatter.

Arturo stood frozen, his attention riveted on the chair he'd just destroyed with a casual stroke of her weapon. After several heartbeats had passed, he turned his attention back to the sword and examined much more seriously.

"I'm grateful that I didn't chop at one of the supports," he confided to them in a quiet voice. "It would've been quite embarrassing to have the ceiling come down and kill me for my hubris.

"This weapon is very much like the knives our people could once make. Precious heirlooms from when the Clans fled the Terran Empire. Sharp as a demon's claw and indestructible."

Jacob nodded. "I have one, as does my father. The legends say they were once quite common in the Clans, but they've been hidden away until only a few are publicly acknowledged now. On this world, they are even rarer."

Arturo turned his attention to Kelsey. "I have never heard of swords formed in that same fashion. Where did you get these, and why are you carrying them?"

"They were given to me by my mentor," she said with a smile. "His name isn't known here so it wouldn't mean anything to you. He was once a Marine Raider in the service of the original Terran Empire."

The big man's smile turned a little cynical. "The Terran Empire died long before either of us was born. And while I'm quite familiar with how machines once kept people alive for miraculous periods of time, even those people did not live five centuries. You are pulling my leg."

Kelsey shrugged and held her hand out. "The story is true but complicated by technology I can't adequately explain. I have other forms of proof, but I'd rather not have to tell this story more than once. Your tribunal is going to doubt everything I say just as much as you do.

"Our little gathering here was solely so that I could convince you I was worthy to wield these weapons. Have I done so? If not, I believe I can put on a somewhat more… impactful demonstration."

He considered her words for a moment, shrugged, and returned her weapon to her in exactly the same manner she'd given it to him, only with a slight bow accompanying it.

"I certainly hope your demonstration is less destructive than my bumbling efforts. I'm certain we'd like to continue using this room, so demolishing it would be less than optimal."

"Oh, I can make my demonstration without destroying a single thing," Kelsey said with a smirk.

She sheathed her sword with practiced ease and walked over to the table. Smiling sweetly at Arturo, she reached out and picked up one end with just the tips of her fingers, being careful to watch her balance. Even with her incredible strength, she had very little mass when compared with something like the massive table.

Even with her strength and graphene-enhanced bones, that put an incredible stress on her digits. Nevertheless, the heavy table rose two feet into the air with very little visual evidence of the strain she was placing on herself.

The two men stood there, thunderstruck. Jacob had never seen her exercise her strength in a manner like this. Arturo had undoubtedly never even considered this possible.

"If you boys would pick up the other end of the table, we'll move it out of the way so I have room to work."

As if sleepwalking, the two men picked up the other end of the table. From the strained expression on their faces, it wasn't nearly as light as they wished it were. Together, the three of them moved the table to the far side of the room. They quickly had the chairs sitting on top of it.

Except for the destroyed one. That went under it.

As soon as the floor was cleared and she'd gestured for two men to step aside, Kelsey drew her weapons and dumped Panther into her system. The world seemed to slow as the combat drug took hold, but she knew that her observers would see her movements as something faster than humanly possible.

As soon as the drug had sped up her thinking and nerve pathways, she launched into a fairly aggressive kata.

Much like a training dance, it was almost ritualized. Her slashes and strikes were inhumanly precise as she allowed her Raider implants to guide the angle and speed of her blades. She knew from watching recordings of herself in action that it seemed as if she were cutting her way across the room filled with opponents at lightning speed.

And the actions didn't just include blade work. Her powerful legs allowed her to run and jump to heights that a normal person couldn't dream possible. She made certain to run toward one of the walls and literally take several steps along it just below the ceiling before launching herself out in a move that any gymnast would be thrilled to be able to execute, landing lightly on her feet.

With her incredible physical prowess and agility, she leapt and flipped in midair, dropping behind imaginary enemies and dicing them. She continued at a pace that would have run a normal person into the ground after mere seconds.

At the end of the three minutes set, she sheathed her weapons and stood quietly before the two warriors, not even breathing hard.

"So tell me," she said with a deep smile. "Does that prove I've earned the right to carry these weapons?"

Jacob bowed low, an elaborate gesture filled with sweeping arms. "I was already convinced, but now understand how far short of reality my feeble comprehension was. You are not just a warrior or even a master, you are a demigod of battle."

Arturo's bow was far less flowery but similarly deep. "I have no objections to you bearing arms before the tribunal. In fact, I urge you to come speedily before them so that they may question you. I cannot imagine how what my eyes have seen is even possible, and I hunger to know the full truth about you, Kelsey Bandar."

She held up a hand. "Honesty compels me to admit that I'm armed with weapons far more deadly than these blades. These swords aren't even close to the most powerful weapons on my person.

"If someone like your friend wants to fight me, it will not turn out well for them. I realize that I don't look like much of a threat, but I'm the most dangerous person you've ever met."

The large warrior bowed again with a grin. "Then let's see if we can't avoid Isidro. The man is an ass at the best of times, but I'd rather not see his guts spilled all over the floor."

With that, Arturo led them from the small room and deeper into the Clan chapter house. They passed several sets of guards, all of whom bowed diffidently to the large warrior and allowed them past without delay.

At the rear of the chapter house were a pair of thick wooden doors. They were unadorned and covered with steel strips and studs, obviously made to resist being forced. Even with her strength, it might take a while to open them by hand. She had great personal strength but very little mass.

Maybe if she could get a grip under the door and plant her feet, she could pull one free. Part of her longed to try, but that wasn't very neighborly.

Another pair of guards opened the doors and allowed the three of them into what was probably a communal dining hall as well as a location for ceremonies. The far side of the room had a raised dais with a long table set perpendicular to the entryway.

Three men sat at the table, all scowling toward Kelsey. Beside them stood a sneering Isidro. Based on his body language and the smirk on his face, he'd filled their heads with nonsense, and they didn't look nearly as receptive as Arturo had been.

Wonderful.

The center man cleared his throat. "How dare you defame our chapter house by bearing weapons and assaulting one of our warriors, woman! Identify yourself and submit to the will of this tribunal, or we will use every force necessary to subdue you."

Yep. It was going to be that kind of day.

6

Veronica thought she'd be going directly to meet the Rebel Empire security officer, but Doctor Zoboroski was waiting for her outside the small compartment where she'd met with Colonel Talbot and Major Ellis.

"Time for your next regeneration session," the man said cheerfully.

She'd already gone through three sessions and her ribs and broken bones were well set. That reduced the pain to almost nothing but didn't give her any additional mobility.

"Exactly how many sessions am I going to have to have before I can move around on my own?" she asked tiredly.

"I think we'll need an additional two sessions beyond this one, but you should be able to get around without that chair this afternoon. We can run a second one tonight and another in the morning. After that, I'll pronounce you healed and send you on your merry way."

She sighed a little bit at that, relieved. "I like you well enough, Commander, but I think I'll be happy to have a little bit more privacy. Even if it is under watchful eyes."

"That doesn't hurt my feelings. I'll give you another checkup after three or four days to make sure everything looks good, but so far you've been a model patient."

"As opposed to a model prisoner," Talbot muttered.

Veronica laughed. "If your Fleet is anything like mine, you'd have had an obligation to escape too. Besides, after some the stories I've heard about your Princess Kelsey, you should be used to this by now."

"Why is it that the women in my life have this drive to complicate things?" he asked, his eyes rolling toward the ceiling.

"Am I a woman in your life?" she asked, raising an eyebrow. "I hardly know you, and your wife is quite possibly the worst person to make jealous in the history of humanity."

"So true," he said with a sigh. "I'm going to set up things so we can see Commander Renner. Angela will go along to make certain you find your way back to the next interview room."

His expression grew serious. "This next session is going to be intense. If you want to sit it out while I go in and question her, I'll understand, but I'd rather have you beside me. You know far more about the Rebel Empire than I ever will, but I'll understand any reticence."

Veronica felt her eyebrows drawn together. "I haven't gone through this trustworthiness test of yours yet. Why would you let me sit in on an interrogation where I could ruin things?"

"Because I consider myself a pretty good judge of character. The AI will be able to confirm you're telling the truth, but I'm willing to give you the chance even though I might be wrong."

She wasn't sure how that made her feel. Part of her felt guilty at betraying the Empire. Another part felt elated that she was going to be able to help these people fight against the System Lords. A third part just felt lost and confused.

Doctor Zoboroski guided her chair out of the compartment and back to the medical center. It only took a few minutes to get her loaded into the regenerator and start the session.

She lay there with her eyes closed, thinking about everything that had happened and those things she knew were about to happen. She had no doubt she'd made the right decision. It might be years before she fully accepted her choices, but that would come in time.

Half an hour later, the regenerator opened up and Doctor Zoboroski slid out the table she lay on. "Let's get you on your feet. I want to see you walking around before I trust your stability."

The pain she felt was subdued, but it would definitely keep her from exerting herself. It seemed the regeneration had made her bones ache more than before the session. No running for a while.

That said, her mobility was pretty good. She was able to walk around the medical center without any assistance. So long as she kept herself from getting carried away, she thought she'd be able to do whatever needed to be done.

"How does that feel?" he asked solicitously.

"Good," she said firmly. "I can't wait until I'm finished with the procedures, but I feel confident I can at least walk safely."

He raised a warning finger. "You're still going to tire easily. That will go away, but for right now you need to bear in mind that you can't just walk for an unlimited distance and running is completely out of the question.

"You're still an invalid. Don't forget that, or you can end up back in the regenerator. No breaking out of confinement until tomorrow at the earliest."

"Yes, Mother," she said with a sigh and a grin. "I promise to be good. Relatively speaking."

Major Ellis cleared her throat. "If you're done horsing around, Talbot is probably ready for us."

The two women headed off for the interrogation room at a slow walk. Her frailty annoyed Veronica, but it wasn't the other woman's fault.

"Did I hear correctly that you're married to a scientist?" Veronica asked to get her mind off her condition. "I think I must've gotten something turned around in my head because there was this kid in the group of scientists talking to me after the fight. Someone mentioned he was married to a marine named Ellis. He didn't look old enough for that kind of thing."

Major Ellis smiled indulgently. "Trust me when I say that there's more than meets the eye when you look at Carl. He seems like a little science nerd, but he's got a backbone of steel when it comes to fighting for those he cares about. And he's freaking brilliant.

"I never saw the two of us as a couple, but now that it's happened, I wouldn't have it any other way. He completes me."

"This might sound rude but is he even old enough to drink?" Veronica asked. "Don't you feel like you might be robbing the cradle there?"

The marine grinned. "He is a lot younger than I am, but trust me when I say he's not in any way childlike. He's a kind, considerate partner. And an exceptionally attentive lover.

"Yes, I can pretty much carry him wherever I like, but when it comes to intellect, he towers over me and everyone else around him. Don't let his exterior fool you. He's not the senior scientist on this mission for nothing."

That stopped Veronica in her tracks, gaping. "He's the *senior* scientist you brought with you? How did that happen?"

Ellis shrugged. "My man has muscles in his brain. Those recent scientific breakthroughs that we've been making, many of those are directly related to his research."

"Including making that strange flip point work?"

"That and so much more," Ellis said emphatically. "I've heard some really smart people say he's probably the most brilliant mind of our generation and that with the addition of our enhanced technology and the expanded lifespan that medical nanites give him, the impact of what he does is going to profoundly change the New Terran Empire."

"Holy crap," Veronica muttered, impressed in spite of herself.

"Indeed," Ellis said with a smile. "Come on. Talbot gets grouchy waiting."

The room that Major Ellis led Veronica to was pretty much identical to the one they'd been in before but on a different deck. This time the viewscreen showed a woman in a Fleet uniform with commander's tabs.

She wasn't much to look at. Somewhat short, a little dumpy, and plain. If Veronica had passed her in the corridor, she wouldn't have given her a second look. On reflection, that was probably a plus for a security officer.

Raul Castille had been an exception to that rule. Handsome,

charismatic, and charming when he wanted to be. He'd also been a cold-blooded murderer when it was convenient. Veronica had no doubt that Commander Violet Renner was cut from the same cloth.

Talbot nodded at Veronica as she walked in. "It's good to see you up and about, Commander. You're just in time too. I was about to walk in and see what our good security officer has to say for herself. Care to join me?"

"If we go in together, she's going to assume that I'm in command," Veronica warned him. "Fleet trumps the marines every time in the Empire. If I were lieutenant commander, she'd still assume I was the senior officer. Hell, she might do that even if I was a lieutenant.

"Is that really how you want to play this? You can feed me questions, and I can ask her, but my presence is going to take her focus away from you."

He smiled. "I think that's actually to my advantage. If she dismisses me as just the muscle, she's not going to give weight to the questions I ask. And I *will* ask my own questions. I suggest you focus on the things that strike your curiosity. Trust me when I say that anything you want to know will probably be interesting to me too."

Veronica nodded. "I can do that. I'm confident that she's going to assume we're traitors and renegades. From what I've seen of your attack on the Dresden orbital, you took everyone out quickly and then kept the important people isolated. Her more than most?"

"She's been in total isolation," he confirmed. "She has no insight into who attacked the orbital, and no one has answered any of her questions. She hasn't had a chance to interact with any of the other prisoners either."

He gestured toward the hatch. "Consider this your interview to join the New Terran Empire. Take charge and let's see how this goes."

Veronica took a deep breath and quelled the butterflies in her stomach. This was the first concrete step down a path she could never turn away from. When Commander Renner got around to calling her a traitor, it would be completely true.

"Perhaps you could give me a clue as to what you're hoping to gain from this woman. She's a security officer, so she's never going to cooperate with us. From what I understand, you already have complete access to the research taking place at the Dresden orbital. Is that right?"

He nodded. "We don't need her for the specific information that Commander Castille could have provided. I'd rather know more about the Rebel Empire and how the System Lords operate. Yes, I know you grew up there and that you have knowledge about them. We need to know even more than that going forward.

"If we're going to take the fight to them, we need to have some kind of idea of what they really want. They crushed the Terran Empire from the inside and enslaved every human in sight. Simply based on the fact that we now have someone from the Singularity on the loose, we know that the AIs stopped at the border.

"If they wanted to expand out to cover the entirety of known space and all the polities of humanity, they could've done so. There's no doubt whatsoever in my mind that they stopped on purpose.

"Why is that? Does the AI at Twilight River have some kind of restriction that prevents it from operating outside the bounds of the Old Terran Empire? What does the Rebel Empire's security apparatus know? The insight that woman can provide into how the AIs operate would be invaluable."

Veronica snorted. "I stand by my earlier statement. She's *never* going to cooperate with us. Nothing you can do to her can force her to tell you anything, and no amount of cajoling is going to bring her over to our side, even if she tries to make you think that's possible."

"Maybe you're more persuasive than you know," he said with a smile. "Even given that the odds are against us, it only costs us time. She's not going anywhere. She can either sit in that compartment alone or engage with us. Any amount of contact is going to give us the opportunity to pick up something."

"Or allow her to lie her ass off," Veronica said in a cynical tone. "Well, I suppose it can't hurt to try. If nothing else, it's better than sitting in my little compartment too. Your ship's library is big, but talking to people is much more to my taste."

"I'll let you two handle this," Major Ellis said. "I've got to get back over to *Persephone*. Have fun."

Veronica stepped over to the hatch after the other woman had departed. "Shall we?"

7

To her annoyance, Zia wasn't able to talk her way out of being expelled from the wrecked battlecruiser. The warriors herded her, Carl, and their Pandoran escort politely but firmly out into the sunlight and stood watching them to make certain they kept moving.

"Well, that could've gone better," Carl muttered. "We only just got in, and now we're banned for life."

She poked the scientist in the shoulder. "Don't start that nonsense with me! You know as well as I do that a defective fusion plant is nothing to screw around with. If you'd left it operating below the minimum threshold, sooner or later it would have failed, probably with a significant explosion."

"It's still going to fail if they keep using it without shutting it down for maintenance. It's a miracle the damn thing kept working all this time anyway. I did what I could while I was linked with it and adjusted the safety parameters to make certain that if it starts acting the least bit unstable, it will go into a graceful shutdown.

"In other words, I implemented the most stringent safety protocols. The time to be generous with its operation protocols has long passed. A rogue fusion plant is nothing to toy with."

Zia glanced at Efrain. The Pandoran warrior shrugged, apparently unconcerned with the revelation.

"By any chance did you get a look at the flip drive while you were in the system?" she asked.

"No," Carl said with a shake of his head. "It was disconnected from the ship's systems or was completely burned out and inaccessible. To be absolutely certain what condition it's in, I'd need to access it directly, and I'll wager that's not going to be easy now."

No, probably not.

"I hope Kelsey made a good impression on the king," she said. "If he says we get access, that overseer is going to have to let us back in. Meanwhile, we need to look at other avenues to getting our ship repaired.

"The freighter is almost three-quarters the size of *Audacious*. Is it possible to use its flip drive on the carrier?"

From Carl's expression, she knew he didn't hold out much hope on that front.

"I'm going to give that a qualified 'no' and beg you not to try. Trust me when I say that *very* bad things could happen."

She sighed. That was about the answer she expected.

"So, if the freighter isn't an option and the drive on this battlecruiser is defective, what do we do? Hell, even if it was fully functional, the drive on *Dauntless* wouldn't be able to move a carrier, would it?"

Carl shook his head. "Probably not. This was always a long shot but not one I thought would bear fruit. There are other options, but I wouldn't call them *good* options. We can get to a system that almost certainly has the parts we need. It's just not very friendly, if you know what I mean."

She did indeed know what he meant: the Archibald system.

They'd explored the multiflip point enough to find five destinations from the Icebox system. One of the potential destinations was the Archibald system. It had been a major world in the Old Empire and was still bustling under the management of the AIs. There was almost certainly a shipyard there where they could theoretically get parts.

The other destinations from Icebox were Pandora and three uninhabited systems. One of the latter was in the Rebel Empire and not far from Dresden.

Those destinations weren't very useful at the moment as there were a number of hostile Clan warships sitting right at the flip point. Any strange ship would be promptly attacked and likely destroyed.

From the Pandora side, they could access four systems. One, thankfully, was Archibald. The other three included Icebox and two different uninhabited systems.

"Somehow I don't expect the Rebel Empire is going to be very cooperative," Zia said dryly.

"Probably not," Carl agreed. "That doesn't change the fact that that's the most likely location to get what we need."

Zia hadn't discussed this with Princess Kelsey yet, but she'd already decided getting everyone home wasn't actually what constituted mission success in this case. Everything of serious value that they'd captured on the Dresden orbital could fit aboard *Persephone* and the freighter.

If push came to shove, the Marine Raider strike ship could go through the multiflip point to one of the empty systems and search for linkages to new systems that might give them a path clear of danger and get them home.

Hell, one of these other systems might have one of those new flip points they'd discovered. Ones that sat far distant from the solar masses they were linked to. That's where the Clans had gone when they'd escaped Icebox. Through an unknown kind of flip point sitting in the outer system.

That course of action was chancy at best, but it beat being trapped here with the crippled carrier. Eventually, the Clans would find a way to use the multiflip point and find them. That wasn't going to be fun.

She suspected the heir to the Imperial throne had already thought of that. The woman was bright, and she wouldn't have missed that option. Not that she'd be easily convinced. It was going to take either a disaster or all other options failing before Princess Kelsey abandoned the carrier and its crew.

And that's what it came down to. There was no room to fit everyone from *Audacious* aboard the freighter and have enough life support to get them very far. No matter how the situation was juggled, someone was going to have to stay behind if the forces from the New Terran Empire left Pandora without repairing the carrier.

So, that meant Zia needed to explore every potential option if she was going to get Princess Kelsey safely home.

"Let's get back to *Audacious*," she said at last. "We're not going to solve our problems standing around down here. Maybe Colonel Talbot has dug up a few new leads for us to examine."

Carl grinned at her. "Oh, I think you could reasonably say that he has. I just got a message from him when I linked up to the cutter via the drone keeping an eye on us. I'll wager you've got one waiting for you too."

Zia checked her implants and found a message waiting for her. It was from Colonel Talbot and was marked urgent. She opened it and started the video playing.

A ghostly image of Talbot's head and torso appeared in front of her in the form of a translucent overlay hovering over the ground ahead of her. He was grinning.

"Commodore, the people I had searching the freighter just hit pay dirt. They found the hardware for a new AI. I had it moved to *Persephone*. I'll wager all that additional computing power and a sentient AI will help Carl figure out a way to get us home."

Well, that certainly did change things a little. Having met Marcus and Harrison, the two AIs the New Terran Empire had working with them, Zia felt confident that the presence of a sentient AI would be a real boon to them, under the right circumstances.

"Let's get going," she said with a grin. "We might just have gotten the break we needed."

* * *

Talbot followed Veronica Giguere into the compartment holding their prisoner. The woman didn't look all that dangerous, but appearances could be very deceptive. Having met Raul Castille, Talbot knew how resourceful security officers in the Rebel Empire could be.

The woman had sat down on the edge of the couch. She didn't rise as they entered.

As in the case of the Singularity prisoner, two marines were inside the compartment with her. Neither was armed, and they had compatriots in the corridor that could rush in with stunners if need be.

"So," the woman said in a slow drawl. "You've decided it's time to ask me a few questions. I'd wondered why it was taking so long?"

"Each thing in its time," Veronica said coolly. "As your hosts, I'm afraid we're going to have to assert a monopoly on asking questions. Perhaps if you're cooperative that situation may change."

Commander Renner smiled just a little bit. "You, I know. Commander Veronica Giguere, commanding officer of the destroyer *R-7322*. Somehow, I don't think that small a ship has such expansive accommodations, and I don't believe that I'm still aboard the Dresden orbital. That raises some interesting possibilities."

The woman shifted her gaze to Talbot. "You, I don't know. Based on your uniform, you're a senior marine officer. Would you care to introduce yourself? I figure I have perhaps a sixty percent chance of you providing your name. The lieutenants you have guarding me have proven uncooperative, though, so I might be wrong."

In fact, the men guarding her were noncommissioned marines. They wore the uniforms of officers to explain away the fact that they had implants. Inside the Rebel Empire, only officers had implants.

"Lieutenant Colonel Russell Talbot," he said easily. "I'm directly in charge of maintaining your… accommodations."

"I'm afraid that you're not going to get a very positive review from me," Renner said oppressively. "Guest services could use a lot of work."

The woman proceeded to ignore Talbot and focused her attention back on Commander Giguere. "Since I know you left with the fleet sent to eliminate that crazy computer, that leads me to wonder why you've come back and how you're connected to the people that attacked the Dresden orbital.

"I can't imagine you seized anything worthwhile. Raul Castille has a well-deserved reputation. So what is this all about?"

"Which part of 'we'll ask the questions' did you fail to understand?" Commander Giguere asked rhetorically. "As an Imperial security officer, you probably know the System Lords far better than anyone else. How do you think they're going to react to this attack on one of their classified research and manufacturing facilities?"

Renner laughed. "They'll hunt you down and exterminate you with what they call extreme prejudice. Though the odds of you learning much about the classified research is low, they cannot allow even the possibility of it being under the control of unauthorized human beings.

"Whatever system is responsible for financing you will be suppressed. Every ship that participated in this atrocity, and every person on board those ships, will be destroyed."

"That's an interesting word to choose," Talbot said. "The computer intelligences you work for exterminated trillions of human beings. That's the very definition of atrocity."

"You're a fool," Renner said. "You're also rebels and traitors. It's a tragedy that so many people died in throwing off the yoke of the old dictatorship, but one does not make an omelet without breaking eggs."

"I once thought the same as you," Giguere said. "Then I had my eyes opened. I saw proof that our history was a lie. I suspect you already know that. Commander Castille did. He said so before I killed him."

Talbot was impressed. Veronica Giguere was going hard-core. There wasn't any stepping back from that kind of admission.

Finally, Renner reacted. Her eyes narrowed as she stared at Giguere. "Did you, now? I'm going to take *exceptional* pleasure in killing you back."

With that, the woman launched herself off the couch and at Commander Giguere, her bladed hand slashing at the injured woman's throat.

Talbot moved to block the security officer, but he was slow. He knew he wouldn't be fast enough to stop that unexpected attack and that might just mean watching Veronica Giguere strangle to death with a crushed larynx before medical help arrived.

8

Kelsey felt her eyes narrowing. Having seen Isidro's personality, she should've expected the ambush. Well, at least Talbot had taught her what soldiers did during an ambush: they didn't run, they fought their way out.

She stalked forward until she stood just in front of the battered wooden table, planted her hands on her hips, and glared back at the man who had demanded her surrender.

"My name is Kelsey Bandar, and this tribunal has no authority over me. The sooner you accept that, the sooner we can both move forward."

"Preposterous," Isidro sneered from his position to the side. "Clan Dauntless has authority over all humans on this world. You don't get to just declare your independence."

From what she'd heard, that wasn't completely true. There were some few humans living inside the Empire of Kalor and Kelsey doubted they acknowledged the authority of Clan Dauntless. Not that she intended to mention that since it might imply she was one of them.

From the glance the man at the center shot the warrior, Isidro was speaking out of turn. The warrior didn't see it since he was too busy staring daggers at Kelsey.

With a sigh, the man at the center of the table returned his attention to Kelsey. "Young Isidro is correct. You are of Clan Dauntless, and you will submit to this tribunal's will. Explain yourself."

Kelsey laughed. "As I explained to Arturo, your first mistake is assuming that I'm of this world. I'm not. I only just arrived a few days ago, and I come from beyond. I am Kelsey Bandar, chief of Clan Persephone."

Now it was the man's turn to stare at her agog. He shifted his gaze to

Jacob and Arturo. "What madness is this? There is no Clan Persephone, even in the world we came from. The histories have no mention of anything like that."

Jacob offered the man a slight smile. "I have personally stood on the decks of her ship as it orbits our world. Her people were never part of the Clans. They are also not part of the Empire from which we fled. Let's just say their story is more complicated than we can get into right now.

"I was bringing her to meet the king of Raden. She needs to explain her situation to him. He will make the final decision on whether she speaks the truth or not, though I already know how he will decide. My blood brother, Derek, has also seen her ship. Even as we speak, he is no doubt briefing his father."

"Speaking of fathers, yours won't be pleased to be left out," the man warned Jacob.

"He rarely is," Jacob replied curtly. "Once the king is satisfied, we can journey to my father and tell him her story."

Isidro took two steps forward and snarled. "Lies! I don't know what kind of game you are playing at but you will not get away with lying to us."

"Isidro!" the man at the center of the table barked. "You overstep yourself. I lead here, and you will follow."

"If you were leading, you'd already have these two in chains for defying the Clan. This woman attacked me. She violates the laws of Clan Dauntless, bearing weapons and acting outside the prescribed behavior for women. For this, she must pay."

Kelsey laughed at him. "If Clan Dauntless wants to enforce its will upon me, it's welcome to try. In my world, women have exactly the same rights and responsibilities as men. No one can tell them that they must behave in some fashion or other, and I won't tolerate that kind of sexism."

Jacob cleared his throat. "Isidro overstates our ways. The Clans have never had a large female population. Elsewhere, the Clans forbid them from dangerous occupations and curtail their rights.

"Not here. We don't repress our women. We cherish them. Custom dictates they are not warriors on this world, but there *have* been exceptions to that rule. Trust me when I say that they are the very soul of Clan Dauntless and they wield as much political power as any man, though often from behind the scenes."

She considered Jacob for almost ten seconds. "I'm willing to give you the benefit of the doubt until I get more information, but I'm not a wilting flower to be protected. I've killed more men in combat than your most seasoned warriors, I suspect. I will not shy away from protecting my person with arms."

"Then I demand satisfaction," Isidro said with a sneer. "Meet me blade to blade, and we shall see who is a warrior and who is not."

"Isidro, you have no idea what you're getting yourself into," Arturo said sternly. "Following your own logic, challenging a woman would be murder and so not allowed. The fact that she's a far better warrior than you merely means injury and humiliation for you. Assuming, of course, that she doesn't cut your head off. Idiot."

The man at the center of the table surged to his feet. "I forbid this! There will be no fighting in this hall."

Isidro gave the man a dismissive glance and glared at Arturo. "Neither of you have the power to stop me. The law is clear. She assaulted me, and I demand satisfaction here and now. She claims to be a warrior, so I am within my rights. I will see her blood."

"Accepted," Kelsey snapped before any of the other men could respond. "But I will not fight to the death over something so trivial. First blood only."

"If you mean the initial spilling of blood, then I accept," Isidro said with a wolfish smile. "Whosoever shall lose the first drop loses this challenge."

Jacob held up a hand. "As the son of the chief, I feel it necessary to warn you what a terrible mistake you are about to make, Isidro. Did you learn nothing from when she subdued you the first time? Step back from this madness."

"You think your father shields you from all the consequences of life," Isidro sneered. "He doesn't have the fire of our ancestors. Perhaps one day, someone with true spirit will challenge him during the yearly festival and take leadership of the Clan back to revive our greatness."

Jacob laughed. "Do not mistake benevolence for weakness. My father is strong. The reason no one challenges him for leadership is that they know he's a wise ruler, even if he can be an ass. The people you speak of would take the Clan back to what they were before the crash—mad dogs fighting over bones."

Isidro's face reddened. "That mouth of yours will get you dead one day. You think over much of yourself. Gallivanting across the kingdom playing at being a spy. Your day will come too. Perhaps much sooner than your father's."

The man stepped forward into the center of the hall, walking outward until Kelsey was between him and the tribunal's table. "Face me with a blade in your hand, woman. I promise I won't take more than a finger or two for your insolence."

Jacob held up his hands in surrender. "I tried to spare your honor, but you're too willful to see good advice for what it is. I hope this loss will be relatively painless. Actually, that's a lie. I hope it hurts like hell."

He turned his attention to the tribunal. "I also hope this will be educational. Watch closely and you'll see that this woman is a powerful warrior who is not to be trifled with. Perhaps then you will hear her with an open mind."

Once Jacob had stepped to the side of the room, Kelsey drew her swords. The true challenge of this fight wouldn't be winning. It would be winning without grievously injuring her opponent.

Isidro drew his sword and stalked forward, a grin on his face. He began circling to the left of her, feinting with his weapon.

She didn't fall for his probing attacks. She had absolutely no doubt that she would spot the true strike when it came. And, on due consideration, she didn't have to actually use her sword to get that blood.

The next time the warrior feinted at her, Kelsey slashed at his blade with the sword in her right hand. Her edge struck his blade just above the hilt and cut cleanly through, sending the dangerous part of his weapon clanging to the floor.

He stood there, his mouth agape.

Rather than waiting for him to recover, Kelsey darted forward and knocked the hilt out of his grip with the back of her hand, sending it spinning into the corner of the room. She then slammed her forehead into his nose, sending him staggering back.

She'd very carefully pulled the strike as much as possible. She had no desire to kill the ass. With the graphene reinforcement to her skull, the impact hardly bothered her. In fact, it didn't even make her blink.

Not so for the arrogant warrior. He clapped both hands over his blood-gushing, broken nose and staggered back, howling in agony.

Kelsey sheathed her swords and turned back toward the tribunal. "Are we done here? Is there any lingering doubt that I'm a warrior?"

"Look out!" Jacob shouted.

Based upon the horrified expressions of the tribunal, Isidro had decided to go beyond first blood after all. Her enhanced hearing confirmed that he was racing up behind her, and her implants calculated his approach velocity and probable location.

He wouldn't be attacking with his bare hands, and his sword was ruined, so he probably had a short blade of some kind in his dominant right hand. Timing was going to be everything. She had no doubt that she could disarm and subdue him, but she wanted to do it with style.

When she believed he was in the appropriate position, she spun on one foot and lashed out with the other. He was indeed at just about the right spot with a dagger in his right hand and murder written on his face.

Her spinning back kick took the blade from his hand, snapping bones in the process since she hadn't held back on her strength. After all, there was a lesson to be taught here.

Even before his face began registering the terrible agony of his shattered hand, she'd planted the spinning foot and was lashing out at him with the foot she'd spun on. Strength was key here. She had to restrain herself to a very carefully calculated strike, or she might kill the man.

Kelsey's snap kick was just about perfect. Her foot rose and landed directly between his legs with just enough force to completely double him over.

He collapsed, gagging and retching. This fight was over.

Once again, she turned toward the tribunal. "I am Kelsey Bandar, chief of Clan Persephone. I am a warrior and will not be trifled with. I'm willing to explain how I came to be here and what I intend, but realize now that you have no authority over me."

The head of the tribunal's expression hardened a little. "Your ability to fight is shocking, but this matter is far from settled. Rest assured that Isidro will answer for his actions, but we will still judge you on your violations of Clan etiquette.

"And we will fully evaluate your claims that you do not belong to our clan at all. Trust me when I say that should that statement prove true you will have some explaining to do."

Kelsey started to answer, but a commotion outside the main doors interrupted her response. She turned toward the entryway just in time to see the doors open and a dozen Pandorans stride into the hall.

"All will stand fast," the tall Pandoran warrior in the lead said sternly. "I speak in the name of King Estevan of Raden. I call upon you through the treaty you have with our kingdom to assist me."

The tribunal, which had seated itself, once again rose to its feet. The man in charge bowed slightly. "Clan Dauntless will honor our treaty. What assistance do you require?"

"I seek Kelsey Bandar, chief of Clan Persephone. Is she present?"

Since he was staring directly at her, Kelsey was quite certain he knew who she was. She stepped forward and bowed.

"I am Kelsey Bandar."

The man nodded, obviously expecting her answer. "In the name of the Kingdom of Raden, I detain you. You will be taken immediately to an audience with the king. There you will explain yourself, and he will sit in judgment. If you resist, my warriors will use all necessary force to subdue or slay you. I command you to stand fast and surrender your weapons peacefully."

Well, that certainly sounded ominous.

Still, she didn't exactly have a lot of options at this point. "I will comply, but only with the understanding that my weapons will be returned to me when I am released."

The Pandoran smiled slightly. "That assumes that you will be released. You are not of the humans that were granted permission to be on this world. It is within my liege's rights to deal with you as he pleases. If he believes you to be a danger to the kingdom, you may be imprisoned or even slain. He will not allow mad dogs to roam this world."

Interesting. That was the second time that phrase had been used.

The Pandoran glanced at Isidro, who was still curled up in a fetal position on the floor, bleeding.

Not the best visual for a first impression, Kelsey had to admit. The idiot's timing had put her in an awkward light. Still, if push came to shove, the marines would get her out. It was far better to try to solve this peacefully than to fight.

Kelsey began removing her sword harness. "You'll want to leave the blades in their sheaths. They're very, very sharp. My other weapons are technological. I believe that Jacob is familiar with their use and can provide guidance in their safe handling."

The Pandorans surrounded her as she finished disarming herself. Some of them collected her weapons, and the rest began herding her toward the doorway. One way or the other, she had to make her meeting with the king of Raden work. Her people's survival depended on it.

9

Veronica hurled herself backwards, ducking to the side to avoid the madwoman's blow. She held no illusions about who'd win if they became fully engaged.

As quickly as she'd acted, Veronica only barely managed to avoid the lethal strike. Rather than hitting her in the throat, Renner's attack struck the side of her head with blinding force. Sparks of light shot across Veronica's vision as she fell out of the chair and sprawled on the floor.

Renner landed on top of Veronica and clamped her hands around her throat like steel bands.

"Die, murdering bitch," the security officer said, her eyes alight with murderous rage.

Moments later, Colonel Talbot clamped his arm around the other woman's throat and dragged her back. The two marines from beside the hatch pulled Renner's hands off Veronica's neck with great difficulty.

She sat there on the floor, gasping for breath as she watched the three marines struggle with the ferocious woman. The hatch opened, and extra marines rushed in to aid their companions, finally subduing the fierce, primal force that Renner had become.

All the while, Renner shouted at Veronica, promising her a horrible death that she couldn't escape from. It was surreal. What in the world had triggered the woman?

Once the marines had secured Renner's wrists, Talbot stepped back and helped Veronica to her feet. "Are you okay?"

"I'm fine," she said, surprised at how much her throat hurt. Her voice sounded a bit rough to her own ears.

Talbot gestured to his men. "Take Commander Renner to the brig. Lock her up and keep her in isolation. Put her into a restraint belt too. If she gets froggy again, I'd like to be able to take her down easy."

None of that slowed the invective that Renner was hurling at Veronica. Even after the hatch closed, she thought she could still hear the woman shouting.

Rubbing her throat, she stared at Talbot. "What the hell was that about?"

"Call it a hunch, but I think she had some kind of relationship with Castille. A serious one, I think, at least on her end. She went off as soon as you said you'd killed him."

"I'd imagine we're not going to get anything out of her at this point."

"Probably not," Talbot admitted. "We'll just put her on ice for a while and see if she cools down. Do we need to stop by the medical center and have Doc Zoboroski check you out?"

Veronica shook her head. "No, I'm fine. Seriously. She didn't have enough time to hurt me."

"If that first strike had landed clean, you'd be in a lot worse shape. I think I'm going to have to reassess our security protocols when questioning prisoners. I think we need somebody with a stunner in the room."

That wasn't a bad idea. Of course, most of the prisoners wouldn't be *that* aggressive. Veronica hoped not, anyway.

"So, what do we do now?" she asked. "I think I've had about enough interrogating for today."

"I'll bet," he said with a chuckle. "Let's go do something less interactive. I want to show you the new hardware we picked up. Have you ever actually seen a System Lord?"

"No. As you might imagine, they're picky about who they allow into their presence. Still, it's just computer hardware, isn't it?"

"Pretty much. Just a lot more of it than one might expect. Back when we installed one on a superdreadnought, it took up the entirety of the computer center and only just barely fit.

"Over on *Persephone*, the engineers had to gut and jury-rig several compartments adjacent to the computer center. I'm not sure how they managed to get the work done so quickly, but I suppose they have their ways."

Veronica gestured at the ship around them. "Not to criticize, but shouldn't you install it here?"

He headed toward the hatch, and she followed. "This ship is trapped here for the foreseeable future. That AI must get out and back to the New Terran Empire, even if *Audacious* doesn't. The commodore and my wife will understand that."

They stepped into the corridor and headed for the lift. She considered what he'd said for a moment before asking another question.

"Are you going to make it the ship's computer too? That seems dangerous. System Lords are ruthless. I shudder to think of what one in control of a ship could do."

"It's not as bad as all that," he assured her as they stepped into the lift and he sent it heading up. "We're using the *original* system code with a couple of tweaks made by Carl Owlet. This computer will not become a System Lord."

She considered him for a moment. "I've heard a lot about this Carl Owlet. I still can't believe that he's married to Major Ellis?"

Talbot nodded. "Yep. Those two are total opposites. She is an unstoppable physical machine and he is a brain without comparison. Together, they make a *formidable* couple."

Veronica thought about that on the ride over to *Persephone*. Building a System Lord still sounded reckless to her, but she had exactly zero say in what happened here. She could only pray for the best.

She monitored the approach to the Marine Raider strike ship through the cutter's scanners via her implants. The Empire had nothing like that ship and she wanted to know as much about it as she could.

Crews were working outside, apparently installing access hatches near where fighters were docked on the hull in makeshift cradles. This was probably something being done because the carrier couldn't leave this system and *Persephone* could.

The cutter docked in one of the ship's original cradles, and they boarded the ship. Major Ellis was standing there. Veronica wondered if the other woman knew things had gone a bit awry after she'd left.

"Welcome aboard *Persephone*," she said with a smile. "The commodore and my husband are already aboard. I have to get back to the bridge, but I wanted to take the time to officially greet you."

"She looks like an interesting ship," Veronica said. "I look forward to talking with you about her."

"Perhaps over dinner? I've got to run."

While Major Ellis headed off down a corridor, Colonel Talbot led Veronica to a lift. The trip was short. They stepped out near what Veronica knew would be the computer center on the small ship. Coming from the opposite direction were Commodore Anderson and the person she suspected was Carl Owlet.

Anderson smiled at them. "Colonel, Commander. I hope you're both well."

"Well enough," Veronica said. "We had a little bit of excitement, but it all worked out in the end. The colonel tells me you found an artificial intelligence. I have to confess that's scary."

"There's nothing to be afraid of," the young man assured her. "We've been through the code many, many times. These aren't the artificial intelligences you're familiar with."

"I'm certain the people that developed the System Lords thought pretty much the same thing," she said dryly. "Right before the computer killed or enslaved them."

"Hmmm. You might have a point there. Still, we do the best we can. The code that made the System Lords do what they did isn't in these iterations and we've had two of them for quite some time without any kind of problem."

The young man turned to Talbot. "We really need to consider where this one ends up once we get home. We have two, so it should probably go to the Pentagarans."

"We'll have plenty of time to figure that out," Talbot said as he gestured toward the hatch down from the computer center. "They should be just about finished setting up. Commander Giguere has offered to have the new AI verify her honesty when she says that she wants to work with us."

"Excellent news," Anderson said. "I'd much rather have you and your people as allies than enemies, Commander. You're far too resourceful for me to sleep easily at night, even with you locked up and under guard."

Veronica laughed and gestured at the marines trailing her. "I think you've pretty well got me covered. Even though I have no desire to fight you, I completely understand and endorse the caution you're taking. I have to confess, though, that hooking myself up to an AI is a frightening prospect."

"Then allow me to assure you that it's nothing to be worried about," Owlet said. "I've administered this procedure many times, and there's no pain or risk. It's read-only. The AI will have no access to directly affect you in anyway."

She sighed. "How long until it's operational?"

The scientist shrugged. "We were just heading in to find out. Based on the general information that I have, probably no more than half an hour. Explaining the situation to our new friend might take a little bit of time after that. I'd say if you allow for another hour, that will easily cover everything we have planned."

"Then let's get this over with. I'm tired of being your prisoner and I'm certain my people would like to confirm their loyalty and get out of that cabin as well."

* * *

ZIA STEPPED into the new annex beside the computer center aboard the small ship. It looked to have once been several compartments that had been made into one. The bulkheads seemed to have been reinforced too.

It was filled with computer hardware in solid-looking racks. Those were shielded too. Someone had taken steps to protect their new resource.

"Can we give the new AI complete control of this ship like we did on *Invincible*?" she asked Carl.

He shook his head. "No. The computer on *Persephone* is wired into every system, and it has encoded directives to direct and protect the ship that a normal computer doesn't have. While it might be possible to merge the two systems, I'd have to give that a lot of thought first.

"As far as bringing it online, it looks as though it's ready to load and boot right now. Call it fifteen minutes. I have to stream the base code over from *Audacious*."

Zia rubbed her nose as she considered what Carl had said. "In the end, what happens on this ship is Princess Kelsey's call, not mine. Load the software."

Carl moved over to the main console and began working rapidly, shifting from screen to screen and doing things that Zia wasn't certain she could ever really understand. His attention was immediately focused on his task and he seemed to forget everyone else around him.

"He's pretty intense," Commander Giguere said from beside her. "I can kind of see what Major Ellis sees in him."

"More power to them," Zia agreed.

Finally, the young scientist turned toward the trio. "The software is loaded, and I'm ready to boot on your command."

"Do it," Zia ordered.

Carl touched a control, and lights began coming on across the equipment as the system booted up. The screen on the wall went through a test pattern and then shifted to a view of what appeared to be a tall woman with dark skin dressed in a Fleet uniform with no insignia.

The image of the woman—who had to be the AI—smiled, her white teeth contrasting sharply with the ebony shade of her skin. "I have you in my database, Commodore Anderson. My name is Fiona. How may I assist you?"

Carl turned to Zia. "The baseline software has all the information that Marcus and Harrison have put together for new AIs. Except for our current mission, she should be up-to-date. She can scan everything we've collected thus far in just a few seconds."

"Play catch-up if you would, Fiona," Zia ordered. "You need to know everything we've encountered so that you'll be ready to help us figure a way out of the mess we've gotten ourselves into."

She turned her attention to Veronica Giguere. "And in just a moment you'll be able to pledge your loyalty to the New Terran Empire. Are you ready?"

The other woman took in a deep breath. "As ready as I'll ever be."

Zia thought she heard a note of uncertainty, but the other woman seemed determined enough. In just a minute they'd find out if the woman was being honest and then the real fun started.

10

While the commodore spoke with Veronica Giguere, Talbot pulled Carl aside. That didn't amount to much in the already cramped compartment, but it would have to do.

"You said these two computers might be merged." Talbot said in a low voice. "How would something like that work? The Marine Raider computer is aggressively protective of access to the ship's critical systems."

Carl shrugged slightly. "Both the AI and *Persephone*'s computer are designed to run stand-alone. Neither can work directly with the other system in a merger. What I'm envisioning would have to be more a matter of working hand in hand rather than being some kind of mixture of the two."

Talbot scratched his chin. "That really doesn't sound all that helpful."

"It might not be, and perhaps we shouldn't even try. This ship wasn't designed to operate in conjunction with a sentient AI. It was made to operate solo under the command of a human Marine Raider.

"The AIs were never designed to command ships either. Marcus is doing a fine job, but that wasn't what his creators envisioned. Based on the initial code, they were intended to work hand in hand with humans on things like research projects and helping to control complex systems like orbitals or manufacturing centers—perhaps even to do tasks for Fleet like war-gaming various scenarios or managing logistics. At this point, we may never know the full scope of what the designers intended."

Carl clapped his hand onto Talbot's shoulder. "What I'm saying is you shouldn't be thinking so narrowly. Let *Persephone* control itself while Fiona helps us with more important tasks. She can pull data together in ways we can't begin to imagine."

Talbot nodded and thought as Carl moved forward to the main console again. The young scientist was going to be occupied explaining things to either Zia, Fiona, or Commander Giguere for the next few minutes. That gave him an opportunity to consider what the best options were going forward.

In the end, this wasn't going to be his decision. Either Kelsey or Zia would be the one deciding how best to use the AI. That didn't mean that he couldn't game out the potential options so that he could argue for the ones he thought best served their interests.

As powerful as *Audacious* was, until she was fixed, she was a liability. She couldn't go anywhere, and she could only defend herself. If the Clans came calling, they'd undoubtedly wear down the massive warship and destroy her.

That was the reason he'd placed the AI on the Marine Raider strike ship. Mobility was going to be the key to their overall success. Even if his wife didn't want to hear that.

While it was possible the crashed battlecruiser held the key to repairing the carrier's flip drive, that seemed like a long shot. The fact that Zia hadn't even mentioned anything about it only told him that the mission to *Dauntless* had failed.

No, if there was to be any hope of repairing *Audacious*, it was going to come from outside the system. Probably from a place that manufactured flip drives. To his mind, that meant Archibald.

Marine Raider strike ships were exceptionally stealthy. While he wouldn't want to try to slip *Persephone* into orbit around Archibald, the small ship could certainly get into the Rebel Empire system without being detected. Once in place, she could begin scouting.

Such a task would be dangerous, and his wife would insist on leading the way. And to be fair, her participation would increase the chances of success significantly.

He sighed. Why did all the smart choices end up putting Kelsey into danger?

At least, if Veronica Giguere were being honest with them, they would have someone at hand that could provide keen insight into the Rebel Empire. The same was true for all her officers.

Talbot doubted that any of them had ever been to Archibald, but they'd traveled through their section of the Rebel Empire and knew how society worked there. That kind of insider knowledge would be key to the success of their mission.

His people also had access to technology that the Rebel Empire couldn't match or anticipate. FTL communication, teleportation through the transport rings, and the help of a sentient AI who could process data far more quickly than anything other than another sentient AI.

Speaking of which, Archibald was large enough of a system to have one. Somewhere on the other side of that flip point resided a Rebel Empire AI just as powerful as Fiona. Only with hardwired instructions to enslave humanity and destroy any threat to the rule of its kind.

Based on what they'd found at Harrison's World, there might also be a hidden station at one of the gas giants with four battlecruisers that the thing could use if it wanted to. Possibly even orbital bombardment platforms too.

They couldn't allow the AI to realize they were there. If it mobilized the resources in the Archibald system to find them, it would. Their only chance at success was staying off its scanners.

Sadly, Kelsey was not well known for lying low. In life, there was the easy way, the hard way, and Kelsey's way. Which normally involve blowing things up and killing bad guys.

He hadn't heard anything from her since she'd left on her mission to meet with the king of Raden, so he hoped that meant things were going well. She'd insisted on going alone so as to keep things quiet. A rare exception to her unspoken rule.

He really should ask her for an update. Assuming that everything was going well just because she was quiet wasn't the safest option. As Lieutenant Timothy Reese, his former commander, had discovered the hard way, Kelsey was obstinate. She'd occasionally keep doing things that were counterproductive simply because she didn't feel like giving in to outside pressure.

Talbot connected to *Persephone*'s com system. There was a drone flying over the city below that would act as an intermediary between Kelsey and the ship. It wasn't always in direct communication with his wife, but if it wasn't, he could instruct it to move closer.

The drone connected immediately and moments later she accepted the com request.

I'm a little busy right now, she said through her implants. *Can this wait?*

I just wanted to make sure you're okay. Is everything going smoothly down there?

As they were married, he often had deeper insight with his wife when connected by implants. He could sense emotions and physical sensations. It worked much better when the two were together, but it didn't go away just because they were separated by greater distances.

He felt a mixture of amusement, irony, and a dash of worry. Not exactly reassuring.

It's going about like I expected. I'm on my way to meet the king right now. I had to stop off and explain my presence to some representatives from Clan Dauntless. There was a little bit of hostility there, but nothing I couldn't handle. Now, seriously, I really need to focus on what I'm doing.

Talbot parsed her words for hidden meanings. Honestly, she could mean exactly what she'd said or she could've gotten into a gunfight with somebody. It was really hard to tell.

He'd just have to hope she'd yell for help if she needed it. There was a squad of marines in a pinnace not too far away. She could call them in for immediate support if things spun out of control, if she'd just do it.

Keep safe, he said. *There have been some developments up here that might make things easier over the next few days, but I can explain them when you come back up. Love you.*

I love you too. See you in a while.

Somewhat reassured, he headed over toward the others. It was time to see if Veronica Giguere was being honest with them or not.

* * *

KELSEY PUT the conversation she'd just had with her husband out of her mind as the guards escorted her into a squat building that looked more like a fortress than a palace. It was built from large blocks of rough stone that had been closely fitted together, leaving no gaps of significance.

She didn't know that much about masonry, but it seemed as if that meant someone had gone to a lot of trouble to fit them all together. Raymond Orison, the king of Pentagar, had learned the work when he was a young man. She'd have to ask him when next they met.

The guards let her up to a massive pair of doors that were easily twice the size of those protecting Clan Dauntless's hall. These were coated with metal plates and guarded by armed and armored Pandorans.

The interior of the keep—that's what she'd decided to call it—was put together much the same as the clan chapter house. If she had to guess, the Clan had designed their building to be consistent with how the Pandorans did things. She wondered how far into the human society that sort of thinking carried.

After a few minutes of navigating large halls and even larger chambers, the group finally came to an interior set of doors similar to the ones at the front of the building. These were already open and her escort walked through without pause.

The layout of the massive chamber was one she immediately recognized. This was an audience hall, the place where a ruler sat before his people to hear grievances and make judgments. A formal sort of thing at the best of times, so not that promising.

The hall stretched about seventy meters in front of her and was about forty across. The only place to sit in the entire room was on the raised dais at the other end. It held what could only be called a throne made of some type of bluish stone carved into fantastical shapes.

A number of guards stood along the perimeter of the room and all watched her closely. Another pair stood behind the throne.

Kelsey doubted these men were limited to medieval weapons. Surely some of the weapons salvaged from the crashed battlecruiser would be brought to bear on her if she proved to be threatening to their monarch.

Her escort spread out and cleared the way for Kelsey to go forward. The unnamed escort leader stayed at her side as she walked forward until she was twenty meters in front of the ruler. He stopped her there.

A door to the side of the room opened, and Derek entered the audience chamber. He smiled at Kelsey as he walked to stand beside his father.

"Kelsey Bandar," Derek said gravely. "You stand in the presence of my father, King Estevan of Raden. Father, allow me to present Chief Kelsey Bandar of Clan Persephone."

The older Pandoran considered Kelsey for a few seconds. She was no expert at reading Pandoran expressions, but the man didn't seem entirely pleased. When he finally spoke, his voice was deeper than she expected and somewhat gravelly. It held a lot of gravitas.

"I'm uncertain what type of welcome to give you, Chief Bandar," the man said. "My father told me of the time after *Dauntless* crashed. Many humans were like wild animals and had to be put down for the safety of those around them. Violent doesn't begin to describe the most severe cases of xenophobia."

She was surprised to hear a word like that come from his mouth. Then she was ashamed of the thought. The king was obviously well educated and she'd best keep that firmly in mind. Low tech didn't mean ignorant.

"I'm not the one that gave me the title of chief nor is Clan Persephone an actual thing," she said. "My people do not come from the Clans. We don't have that kind of negative reaction to those unlike ourselves.

"As I told your son, my title is actually crown princess. My father rules the New Terran Empire, a grouping of dozens of worlds like this one. We survived the Fall of the original Terran Empire by fleeing much like the Clans, but the similarities end there."

King Estevan considered Kelsey and slowly nodded. "I'm willing to accept the possibility for the purposes of this discussion. The name *Persephone* belongs to the ship you came in. Is that correct?"

"It's one of three ships," she agreed. "Not the strongest nor the weakest. I command her, but I also have political authority over all of my people. It's complicated.

"My intent was to announce myself to you quietly. I understand that my people aren't covered by the treaty you have with Clan Dauntless, but we would like to forge a way forward in friendship."

"And if I'm not willing to grant you leave to stay on my world?"

"We don't have to land on your world, but I understand there are other political entities that might welcome us. I've already met your people, so I can be confident of the kind of relationship we might have. Others are less certain. In the end, the final decision is yours."

The king gestured for his son to bend forward and whispered in his ear. They held a brief conversation back and forth before the ruler nodded.

"My son counsels me that I should have a longer discussion with you and learn more about you before I make a final decision. I'm willing to grant you leave to stay in my kingdom—at least some of you—while we hold those talks."

Kelsey relaxed just the slightest bit. "I know we can help one another once you're more certain of what kind of people we are. Unlike the people of Clan Dauntless, we have fully functioning ships and understand the technology completely. We're willing to share that information with you in exchange for your assistance."

The Pandoran ruler nodded. "Such knowledge could be quite useful, considering the tense relations between my kingdom and the Empire of

Kalor. Anything that can bring that conflict to an end without further bloodshed is worth discussing."

She was about to open her mouth to respond when one of the guards behind the dais moved. His hand slipped inside his tunic and pulled out a flechette pistol. It was a subtle movement, and even the man standing five meters to his left failed to notice it. His eyes told Kelsey that his target was the king of Raden.

Kelsey couldn't possibly reach the man before he fired and there was no way the king could get out of the field of fire in time. The smart thing for her to do would be to dive for cover until the shooting stopped.

So, being her, she shouted a warning and leapt toward the assassin.

Unarmed and too far from the assassin to stop him from opening fire, Kelsey hurled herself toward the monarch and his son. She was in a race to move them out of harm's way before the assassin launched a deadly hail of flechettes into their backs.

Of course, now that she was committed to the act, she realized her own chances of survival weren't terrific. It was her own fault. She shouldn't have turned over *every* weapon she'd had, even when they demanded she do so. One more thing for Talbot to yell at her about if she survived.

Even as she started moving, she was dumping Panther into her system. Her perception sped up, slowing the world around her as she raced forward. Derek and his father were just beginning to react to her sudden movement, but she'd surprised them as much as the assassin had surprised her.

The younger Pandoran wasn't an idiot, it seemed. Rather than treating her as a threat, he was already turning to face the rear wall, his hand dipping inside his tunic for a weapon, she was sure. He wouldn't get it out in time to do any good.

The assassin's weapon was almost in line with the king when Kelsey reached him. Using far more force than was probably necessary, she shoved the older man to the side.

Kelsey considered pushing Derek away, but he and his weapon were probably what was going to stop the assassin from following up with the king once he'd dealt with Kelsey.

She hunched lower and jammed her shoulder into the ornate throne that the king had been standing in front of. The angle was bad, and she ended up losing her footing, but coming from the floor below the dais gave her just enough angle to send the throne toward the assassin.

The stone was a façade. It shattered as she struck it, revealing the wood beneath. The lighter weight meant it moved far easier than she'd expected.

It didn't have enough momentum to actually reach the assassin, but it drew his fire at the last moment, spoiling his aim. His flechettes tore huge chunks out of the throne before he stopped his impulsive burst.

The tableau was over, and all of the guards were reacting to the man. Some were racing toward him while others seemed to be hurrying to get between him and their king.

Derek opened fire at last, but she didn't have a chance to see the results of his shots before one of the assassin's flechettes shattered the top of the throne and sent a chunk into the side of her head with great force. Pain lashed through her, and the world went abruptly black.

11

Veronica nervously sat in the chair Carl indicated for her. He'd told her there was no risk with this procedure, and she could accept intellectually that that was probably true. That didn't keep her from being completely and utterly terrified at the idea of allowing a System Lord access to her thoughts.

As if sensing her fear, the young man smiled reassuringly. "I promise there's absolutely no danger here. No pain, not even any uncomfortable sensations. You won't feel a single thing."

"How is this going to work?" she asked, relaxing in spite of herself.

The young scientist sat down across from her. "When I ask her to, Fiona will request access to your implants. She doesn't have the codes to write anything. Those are closely guarded secrets and when we upgraded you, we installed new hardware that mandates your informed approval to any access or changes. We did this to keep the AIs like the System Lords from being able to overwrite the clean code now running in your implants."

She gave him a skeptical look. "What someone can install, someone else can remove. You realize that as soon the System Lords figure out your trick, they'll be able to reverse it."

Owlet shook his head. "The package includes a very effective anti-tampering protocol and some other unadvertised surprises for them. It can even tell if someone is under duress. Without the correct codes, the implant will fry itself and all the wiring in the brain.

"Now before you start panicking, an outcome like that isn't harmful to the person. Sadly, it means that they can never have implants again because the process of removing the damaged wires and attempting to install new ones would be much more destructive than the initial implant procedure itself."

Veronica ran the options she could think of through her mind. In the end, she decided he was right. Being forever stripped of implants was a small price to pay to avoid mental slavery. Particularly when the new medical nanites they'd given her would allow her to live for centuries.

No one now living in the Rebel Empire had a clue medical nanites ever existed. All references to them had been suppressed. Modern scientists had said they were too complex to build, obviously at the insistence of the Lords. Veronica didn't know why the AIs didn't like the things, but they obviously didn't want to allow them back into existence.

"And how are you going to prevent the AIs from getting these codes?" she asked. "If they get them, it's game over all over again."

"That's our little secret," he said somewhat smugly. "What I will say is that the number of people with that critical information is very small and widely spread across the New Terran Empire.

"They don't have to be located where anyone needs an update. The update itself can be signed so that the implants recognize it's an uncorrupted, verified update. Even so, the update is unpacked into a segregated part of implant memory. Then the implants go through the code line by line verifying there's nothing harmful.

"Only once that is accomplished will they ask the user if they would like to accept the update. And the user can say no. It's your head. If you don't want to risk a change, don't."

She still wasn't sure that the cocky young man had thought of all the angles, but there was only so much human beings could do to protect themselves. It was always easier to break than to build. So long as humans had implants in their heads, there was a risk that the AIs would be able to seize control of them.

Veronica took a deep breath. "I'm ready."

Carl looked over to the image of the AI. "Fiona, please link with Commander Giguere and verify the honesty of what she's saying. Let me know the moment she revokes her permission or tells an untruth."

"Yes, Carl," the deceptively authentic-looking woman said with a smile.

The AI turned her cybernetic gaze to Veronica. "As Carl said, I not only mean you no harm, but I am incapable of inflicting harm upon you in this manner. Permission to access your implants can be revoked with a thought. Do you grant me permission to access your implants in a read-only configuration?"

"I do," Veronica said before she could change her mind.

She struggled to determine if anything had changed. She still felt the same.

Do not be concerned. You are in no danger.

Veronica flinched in spite of herself. The voice in her head had been Fiona.

I revoke your permission to be in my head.

"Commander Giguere has revoked permission, Carl," Fiona said, seemingly unperturbed.

The young man scowled. "I haven't even asked you any questions yet."

Veronica smiled a little. "I just had to make sure that I could do it. I once again give permission for Fiona to access my implants in a read-only configuration."

She waited a beat to see if the AI would say anything else in her mind but heard nothing.

Commodore Anderson cleared her throat. "I feel the need to add that for the time being, even once you've proven your loyalty, I'm going to require that the ship's computer monitor you at all times. Whether that's here on *Persephone* or back on *Audacious*.

"I'm not talking about monitoring inside your head but monitoring your physical presence. We've done exactly the same thing with other prisoners that have come over to our side, and it's just a precaution to verify you aren't tempted to change your mind.

"None of the data the computer gathers will make it out of a subprogram to the main system unless it detects something about you that it thinks means you're going to betray us. So not even the computer itself will know what you're doing in private that way."

Carl Owlet, Zia Anderson, and Colonel Talbot began peppering her with questions. All of them were related to what she felt about the Rebel Empire, the System Lords, and the New Terran Empire.

Veronica answered them as honestly as she could. She had nothing to hide. After less than ten minutes, the questioning was over and she again revoked the AI's permission to monitor her thoughts, intensely pleased that the whole process was done. She felt exhausted.

Commodore Anderson extended her hand to Veronica. "Welcome to the New Terran Empire, Commander. I think you'll find we're much easier to work with than your former coworkers."

That made Veronica chuckle. "That wouldn't be hard. You wouldn't believe how cutthroat Fleet is in the Empire. So what do we do now?"

"The next step is to bring all of your people over and repeat this," Talbot said. "The research scientists from the Dresden orbital have already gone through this process. We've verified they really are on our side, just like you.

"The only people that I suspect we'll never be able to clear are Commander Renner and Commodore Murdoch. Renner for obvious reasons. Murdoch because even though she has a grudge against the Rebel Empire, she doesn't really disagree with what they're doing."

Commodore Emilia Murdoch was a tough case, Veronica agreed. The woman had commanded the Dresden orbital until its capture. She wasn't a traitor to the Empire. No, she was one of their ardent supporters.

From what Veronica had heard, the commodore had only supported the New Terran Empire in getting the access codes to the secret research and manufacturing computers because her security officer, Raul Castille, had tried to murder her. He'd ended up breaking her neck, leaving her paralyzed from the neck down for the rest of eternity, particularly since the woman had medical nanites and would live that way for hundreds of years.

That was a ghoulishly terrible fate and Veronica felt sorry for the woman, but she completely understood why her new compatriots could never trust Murdock.

"Understood. If we can get my crew vetted, I'm sure we can assist you in some way."

Commodore Anderson smiled. "I don't suppose any of your people are familiar with the Archibald system, are you?"

Veronica had complete access to her people's service records. A quick check verified that none of them had ever been to Archibald. Wherever Archibald was.

"Sadly, no. That said, the Empire is fairly consistent in how worlds are laid out and run. I can probably give you a lot of information about the Empire in general that might be useful."

Anderson sighed. "I suppose that was too much to hope for, but it didn't hurt to try. Let's get your people over here."

Veronica nodded and took a steadying breath. She was committed. This rebellion was hers now too. It was time to take the first steps at getting her countrymen out from under the heels of the AIs.

* * *

Zia took a cutter back to *Audacious* once the verification of Commander Giguere's crew was complete. She was grateful that they'd all passed. It would've been awkward if one of them had failed and split what was obviously a well-functioning team of friends.

In combination with the research scientists, those people presented serious danger to the AIs. Their collective knowledge would give the New Terran Empire so much to work with.

Yes, they already had Lieutenant Commander Michael Richards, the computer officer they'd captured earlier in the conflict. He was cooperating, but he wasn't *here*. She needed information at her fingertips. Fleet Command might not approve, but she'd risk it.

Captain Brandon Levy, her flag captain, rose to his feet from the center seat. "Welcome back, ma'am. Did everything go as planned?"

"Pretty much," she said as she took her chair back. "It looks as if we have some new allies. Unfortunately, none of them knows a thing about Archibald. I suppose it would've been too much to hope for."

The big man nodded. "The Rebel Empire is a big place. It seems as if they've kept their Fleet officers segregated. Maybe the computer from the Dresden orbital has something about Archibald."

All the computers they'd salvaged from the Dresden orbital were set up in stand-alone mode in one of the compartments close to Carl Owlet's lab. While he wasn't aboard, the research scientists from the Dresden orbital were, and they could check them.

Carl had granted the researchers relatively high access levels to all the systems in the lab, and they were continuing their work. Well, some of them were continuing their work while others were struggling to understand the new hardware and science breakthroughs Carl had made in the last couple of years.

"That's a good idea," Zia said. She used the large command console in front of her to bring up a com channel with the lab. Moments later, Doctor Jacqueline Parker appeared on the screen.

The lead research scientist was a middle-aged woman with dark skin and curly hair. She hadn't been smiling much when they'd rescued her, but that had certainly changed over the last week.

Now the woman smiled widely when she saw Zia. "Commodore, what a pleasure. What can I do for you?"

"It's a pleasure for me, too, Doctor. I was wondering if you could access the Dresden computers for me. I'm trying to determine if we have any information on the Archibald system. It seems as if that's the closest location where we might be able to get what we need to fix our flip drive.

"Unfortunately, none of the people we have aboard from the Rebel Empire know anything about the place. I'm assuming that none of your people have been there, but I'm sure you'll correct me if I'm wrong."

The woman laughed and shook her head. "We lived on the Dresden orbital from the time we were children. I can assure you that none of us have been anywhere interesting. Let me check the computer and see what I can find. Hold on just a second."

It seemed that the Rebel Empire had been taking children that were offered by the mad computer on Erorsi and making them into research scientists at Dresden. Of course, it wasn't a very friendly sort of thing to do. They'd implanted explosives in the scientists' heads in what was almost certainly the worst retirement plan ever.

Leave it to the Rebel Empire to figure out how to ruin something that was actually humanitarian. She'd seen what the mad computer had done to the human survivors of the Fall. It had forcibly implanted them with Marine Raider implants and used them as fodder to attack the system next door. They were monstrous savages.

Thankfully, Pentagar had managed to rebuff all the attacks over the intervening five hundred years before Admiral Mertz and Princess Kelsey had destroyed the computer. Their stout defense hadn't stopped the computer from sending a tithe of children to the Rebel Empire every year in exchange for Marine Raider hardware and other supplies it couldn't build for itself, though.

To their credit, the Rebel Empire had finally decided to end the computer's rule on Erorsi. They'd also planned to conquer Pentagar, but Admiral Mertz and his fleet had been there to stop them cold. Which was where they'd captured Veronica Giguere and a lot of other Rebel Empire forces.

Most of the Rebel Empire survivors had gone to the New Terran

Empire for processing, but Brandon Levy had decided to make Veronica Giguere and her command crew his personal project.

The Rebel Empire didn't know that they'd lost so many ships and people. Not yet. And if she and Princess Kelsey could get the data they'd captured at Dresden home, that delay might just give the New Terran Empire a chance for victory.

Doctor Parker's eyes widened little bit. "It looks like I have something for you. There's only basic information about Archibald in the system, but I think I hit pay dirt in the Fleet section. It seems that one of the officers you've captured was stationed there when she was younger. Commodore Murdoch."

Zia felt her expression souring. The woman had given them the keys to open the research computers and manufacturing hardware to their use, but the woman's continuing despair at her medical condition made her unreliable at best. She'd done what she'd done to get revenge, pure and simple. Everything she said was suspect because they couldn't really trust her.

"I suppose that's better than a kick in the head," Zia said with a sigh. "I'll see if she's willing to cooperate. Otherwise, how are you doing down there? Are you getting settled in? Finding lots of interesting things to look at?"

The older woman nodded. "I must confess that I didn't understand how someone as young as Carl Owlet could be in charge of the science division when you brought me on board. Now I get it. I cannot imagine how he made the jumps in intuition to create some of these new scientific theories that he's working from.

"Take the FTL communications for example. It's brilliant. Point to point communication from one system to another through flip point. Potentially also to nearby systems not connected by flip points at all. Impossible to intercept and devilishly hard to detect.

"Though I will say that I think his theory is incomplete. It may be possible to communicate longer distances with some modifications to the hardware. The theory says that the range should be unlimited. I think that's right. It's just going to require a lot more experimentation to work out the bugs. That's where experience comes into play."

Zia felt the corner of her mouth quirk upward. "I'm sure Carl will be the first to tell you that he's feeling his way through a dark room trying to figure this out. He's a smart guy, but he's running on intuition. I hope you're right. That would certainly make things a little easier for us."

Parker nodded. "Every major breakthrough that humanity has made has come from someone trying something they didn't know was 'impossible' or making a fortuitous error that granted them insight into something they hadn't planned. I really think if you dig deep down, that's what you'll find.

"I've got my people working with the FTL coms right now trying out various general modifications to the hardware. Obviously, we won't be able to test anything outside the Pandora system. I'm just trying to get a general feel for how this works. We're dealing with some ghosts in the system right now, but I'm pretty confident that we can improve on Carl's design."

Zia frowned. "Ghosts in the system? Like what?"

The woman shrugged. "Sometimes, when we engage the modified hardware, the throughput drops to almost nothing. It's really strange."

"Keep me in the loop. I want to know what you find with that. Thanks again, Doctor."

"My pleasure. Good day, Commodore."

Zia sat back into her chair, thinking about the strange behavior of the FTL com. What could that possibly mean? And how might it help or harm them going forward?

12

Kelsey woke to find Derek hovering above her, his expression worried. Based on all the shouting going on, not very much time had passed. Probably no more than a couple of seconds. Her implants confirmed that.

"I need a doctor!" the man shouted, his voice loud in her ears.

She winced. "Did you have to do that right in my face? I've got a terrible headache."

And she did. Her head literally felt as if someone had clubbed her. Obviously.

A quick check got a basic physical condition report out of her medical nanites. Individually, the little things weren't very sophisticated, but each sent information back to her implants, and they put everything together. That gave her a fairly decent idea of how bad any damage was.

The good news was that her skull was intact. Her brain was also in good shape, though the impact of the throne fragment had jarred her pretty badly. The nanites were busy repairing the damage she had, and their prognosis for her was good.

Her scalp was bleeding profusely, of course. Head wounds always looked worse than they were. She knew all about that.

It was kind of embarrassing that such a small injury had taken her out, even if only for a couple of seconds. She decided she'd just leave this little part out when she filled Talbot in on what had happened while she was off making contact with the locals.

Kelsey sat up, wincing again when her head throbbed. "I don't need a doctor. Is your father okay? Did you get the shooter?"

"The assassin? Yes. My father is bruised but alive, thanks to you. At this moment, I'm much more concerned about your health. You took a nasty blow to the head and risked a terrible death on our behalf."

"Annette Vitter told you about the machines we have in our bodies, yes?" At his nod, she continued. "Mine are more advanced than what she has. I have a coating on my bones that makes them very tough. That includes my skull. I'll be fine."

He seemed unconvinced. "I think I'd rather have one of our physicians look at you in any case."

Looking around the room, Kelsey saw that his description of things was correct. The guard that had tried to kill the king of Raden was dead in a bloody heap with several other guards searching his body.

Derek's father was walking back from the man who tried to kill him, now with two hulking guards staring at everyone with enhanced paranoia. He stopped several steps away from her and examined her closely.

He turned toward the man nearest him. "Send for the royal physician. Tell him to make haste."

"It looks worse than it is, Your Majesty," she said. "I'm a lot harder to kill than I look."

"You're a lot faster than you look too," he admitted wryly. "I barely had time to wonder what was happening before you'd thrown me off the dais and saved my life. I suppose at this point, I'm going to have to accept my son's wild story as true.

"No one should be able to move so quickly. Certainly no one from the Clans. While their distant ancestors once had machines in their bodies capable of doing miraculous things, none still living have them. And none should have been able to do what you did, in any case."

An older Pandoran man rushed in clutching a dark bag. He raced up to the king and began circling him. He demanded something in the Pandoran language.

"Speak Standard," the king said. "Our guest is the one I wish you to examine. She saved my life. Make certain that she does not lose hers."

Once again, Kelsey considered arguing but decided that it wouldn't do any good. Doctors seemed to be the same from one end of the universe to the other. She'd bet the same drive extended to different species as well. She was just going to have to put up with it.

The man's poking and prodding were painful, but the powerful drugs her pharmacology unit had dumped into her system muted that somewhat. Eventually, he opened his bag and pulled out something to clean the wound.

That stung. Why is it that any liquid made to clean a wound had to sting like crazy? Even her painkillers seemed ineffective against the cleaning of wounds and always had. Weird.

Kelsey allowed the doctor to proceed until he pulled a needle and thread from his bag. That's where she held up her hand.

"My people have different healing techniques. If you can just put something over it, I'll see to it later. In fact, the machines in my body will make it close before very much longer in any case. There's no need for that."

More importantly, there was no need for her to go through the pain and discomfort of having him poke sharp objects through her skin.

Seeming somewhat disgruntled, the physician folded a cloth and placed it on the side of her head, using another cloth to secure it in place by wrapping it all the way around her head. He tugged the knot very tight, possibly because he was annoyed with her.

That, too, was par for the course when it came to physicians, whatever their species.

She rose to her feet, pleased that the world stayed steady. That allowed her to get a much better look at the throne. The assassin's flechettes had virtually destroyed the heavy chair. Its bulk had saved her life.

"Does that happen often around here?" she asked. "Should anyone with that kind of weapon be very trusted?"

"He was," the king said grimly. "That man diligently worked his way up in my service over the last three decades. Until today, I would've wagered any amount of money that he was perfectly loyal to me. I would do so for any of my personal guards."

"And now you'll be wondering if that man was only the first," Kelsey said softly. "Why now? What caused him to strike at you today?"

Derek inclined his head toward Kelsey. "It had to have been you. Nothing else makes sense. Your arrival changed something. Our enemies, who have obviously spent significant time placing knives close to our backs, felt it was necessary to discard their advantage because you arrived."

Kelsey wished she could argue with that idea, but she couldn't. It seemed her appearance had upset the applecart. Based on what she'd heard from Derek earlier, odds were very good that the assassin had worked for the Empire of Kalor.

That raised an interesting question for her, though. If they had someone close enough to execute the ruler of their enemies, why hadn't they used him before? Why allow the king of Raden to live one minute longer than necessary?

That was the question, wasn't it? And one she had no answer for.

"Perhaps we should speak somewhere a little bit more secluded," she said. "I suspect that you probably don't want word of what I have to say getting back to the Empire of Kalor."

The king grunted, waving the physician away. "That's probably a wise decision. Come. Let us retire to my private audience chamber to discuss matters of import to both our peoples."

As he led her toward one of the side doors, Kelsey wondered if she should call for backup. She knew that Talbot had marines on standby outside the city in case she needed them. If he found out that she'd gone through all of this and hadn't even summoned them to her side, he was going to be pissed.

But if she did, that might cause other issues. The king had no reason to trust her, really. She should start with small steps.

"Is it possible that I could get my weapons back?" she asked. "I'm feeling a little underprotected at the moment."

The king snapped his fingers, attracting the attention of every guard in the room. "Whoever has my honored guest's weapons, bring them to her immediately."

He smiled at her. "After all, if you wanted me dead, all you had to do was stand there."

"I'm not certain I could *ever* stand by and let something like that happen. That's not who I am."

The older man clapped his hand to her shoulder. "That's to your credit, young woman. Come. I want some closed doors around us, a hot drink in my hand, and your story in my ears."

As much as Kelsey wanted to leave it at that, she knew she had to do one more thing. If she didn't, Talbot would rightfully have her ass.

"Considering the unsettled situation, I need to send a message to someone. I hope you don't mind a few extra guests."

* * *

Talbot tried not to clench his teeth as the pinnace headed for the ground outside of the capital city of the Kingdom of Raden. He was sure that Kelsey hadn't told him the complete truth about the events she'd been through this afternoon, but what she had said had been bad enough.

He'd known sending her in by herself had been a mistake as soon as she'd suggested it. The woman was a trouble magnet. Wherever she went, chaos followed. And assassination attempts, absolutely. And likely large explosions, given enough time.

Because they were going to have to fly under the scanners, so to speak, all of the marines with him wore flowing cloaks and loose clothing over their armor and had their rifles hidden in rough bags that would barely slow their deployment.

He had absolutely no idea if their clothing would blend in with the locals, and he frankly didn't care. That was someone else's problem.

No matter what Kelsey had told him, there was no way he'd leave her here alone. How the hell had she even found any assassins? No one here even *knew* her.

The plan called for him and his men to make their way to a major road nearby. Kelsey assured him that there would be a party waiting for them there. He was curious whether it would be human or Pandoran or perhaps a mixture of the two.

His wife had insisted that she hadn't been seriously injured in the fighting. The way she'd stressed the word 'seriously' had him certain she was playing a word game with him, so he'd brought Doctor Zoboroski along.

To say the medical officer looked different would be something of an understatement. Talbot had only ever seen the man in uniform and now he looked like a desert raider. All he needed was some kind of turban and a decent war cry, and he'd be set.

"I've accessed her telemetry remotely," Zoboroski said. "It looks as if she took a knock to the head, but it doesn't seem serious. Her medical nanites are going to take care of the issue, I suspect. If not, I can pop her into the regenerator and have her back to baseline quickly enough once we get back into orbit."

Talbot raised an eyebrow. "You can access her nanites from here? I know that's built into the marine packages, but even though Kelsey is technically a marine officer, I didn't think she had that kind of remote access enabled."

The doctor smiled. "You're not the only one that knows our princess. Doctor Stone enabled the functionality and then passed word on to me when I became the senior medical officer in the task group."

"That's good to know," Talbot said. "Shunt me a copy of what you've got."

He examined what the doctor sent to him and nodded slowly. Looks like she'd taken some kind of blunt impact to the side of her head. Like someone clocked her with a club. Her pharmacology unit had registered a couple of seconds of unconsciousness but had labeled that only a minor concern.

Talbot wondered how the machine had made that determination. Anything strong enough to knock out a woman with a graphene-coated skull had to be pretty forceful.

He knew it was useless, but he was determined to get her back up to the ship as quickly as possible. She was their leader. She didn't need to be down here where people could take shots at her.

Of course she was going to resist. Tell him that this was diplomatic and that she had to be here.

It was complete and utter bullshit.

A chime sounded in his ear announcing their impending landing. Thirty seconds to touchdown.

He put away his misgivings and pulled the external scanner feed through his implants. They were coming down about a kilometer from the road. They'd already deployed a couple of drones in the area, so he knew there were no hostile forces waiting for him.

Unless, of course, the greeting party at the road were actually hostile. Low odds of that, but they'd be careful.

The pinnace settled into a small clearing that had been used at some point in the past as a campground. Not recently, though. The small firepit didn't appear to have been used in the last several months.

He let the team lead the way out as the ramp went down. Unlike some people, he knew when to let other people go in front.

Yeah, he was pissed. He'd need to get a handle on that before he bit Kelsey's head off in public. Or private, for that matter.

No, it was much better to be low-key and make her feel guilty. She'd be expecting a frontal assault, so he'd see about undermining her walls instead.

The marines spread out, and everyone began making their way toward the road. He heard the pinnace retracting its ramp and lifting off behind him. It would be waiting somewhere in the sky in case they needed fire support.

The other pinnace he'd put in the area was on the other side of the city, ready to drop reserve troops in if they needed them. He hoped to God he didn't, but one really never knew when Kelsey was involved.

About fifteen minutes later his people were within sight of the group waiting on the road. Talbot relaxed a little bit more. It was a mixture of Pandorans and humans, but he recognized one of them. Jacob Howell, one of the men they'd captured earlier and the son of the chief of Clan Dauntless, stood with the greeting party, obviously relaxed.

Talbot found himself smiling a little. If they felt the need to send out someone that important, he wasn't going to argue. Without a doubt, Jacob would know what had really happened. Better yet, he'd tell him everything. Then he'd know how to make Kelsey regret her impulsiveness.

13

Veronica stared around Carl Owlet's lab curiously. While she'd occasionally had cause to consult with specialists in what had passed for the lab aboard her old destroyer, she'd never been in such a *large* scientific facility with so *many* people working on various projects.

The young scientist had come back aboard the carrier with Veronica and her crew once they'd been cleared by Fiona. Apparently, now they were fully trusted. She didn't even have a guard.

That seemed a little shortsighted to her, but they apparently believed she couldn't fool the AI. Maybe they were right. She had absolutely no way of knowing because she really didn't plan on betraying them.

Just when she thought she was getting a handle on how large this man's lab was, he went to another compartment that was just as big and filled with even *more* people doing unexplainable things.

"Just how big is your lab?" she asked the scientist suspiciously.

He grinned at her. "There's another couple of compartments about this size. There were a lot of researchers on the Dresden orbital and they were working on a bunch of projects. We've rebuilt them here and the folks are getting back to work, only for the New Terran Empire now.

"I also have a private lab. We won't be going there. While we trust you guys, you're not cleared for everything that I'm working on. Some of it is *really* secret."

"That's fine by me. I understand need to know. What exactly are we doing?"

Owlet gestured toward a group of men and women huddled around a large bench with a couple of pieces of equipment strapped to its top. "My new associates have run into an unexpected glitch in their testing. We're going to see if we can figure it out. Commodore Anderson cleared you to see what we're working on."

As they approached the table, an older woman stepped away and greeted Carl warmly. She turned to Veronica with a gaze that seemed guarded.

"Commander Veronica Giguere, meet Doctor Jacqueline Parker. Jacqueline was the senior research scientist aboard the Dresden orbital."

Veronica immediately felt her interest level rise as she extended a hand to the woman. "It's a pleasure to meet you, Doctor Parker. Allow me to assure you that I've been completely vetted. I mean you no harm."

"So Carl said," the woman said. "You'll forgive me if I'm not completely convinced or enthused. People like you put a bomb in my head."

Unsure what to say—not sure that *anything* she said would ever be enough—Veronica only nodded. "I understand."

"What have you got?" Carl asked.

Doctor Parker never took her eyes off Veronica. "Concerns. A lot of concerns. I don't believe we should be sharing information like this with people like her. I don't care what your new pet AI says, neither she nor anyone else working for the Rebel Empire can be trusted."

The woman's words hung in the air for several long heartbeats before Veronica nodded. "I can understand where Doctor Parker is coming from. While I had nothing directly to do with what happened to her, people in similar positions to me enabled those who did that. And, to be fair, I've certainly done a number of things that I wish I hadn't done to comply with my orders.

"I think it might be best if I excuse myself. I don't need to know what you're doing down here, and I can help where everyone feels comfortable with my participation."

Carl shook his head. "I'm afraid you're both going to have to come to some kind of compromise. As we get allies inside the Rebel Empire, we can't be doubting them once the truth of their loyalty has been established.

"Jacqueline, I understand how you feel, even if I don't have all of your history to back it up. Commander Giguere isn't lying to us or concealing anything. She honestly intends to help us overthrow the AIs controlling the Rebel Empire. We *will* work with her. Commodore Anderson has made her will crystal clear. And now I'm doing the same."

Veronica was impressed. He hadn't seemed the type to be so firm, but his tone brooked no argument. He commanded here and left no doubt on that fact.

Parker didn't say anything for a moment but then nodded, her expression making clear her doubt. "If there's anything I understand, it's carrying out orders that I don't agree with. It's your show, Doctor Owlet. We'll do it your way."

Carl sighed as the older woman walked back over to the bench, her body stiff. "I was afraid of something like this. I'm sorry."

"You don't have anything to be sorry about," Veronica said. "The issues she has with me and everyone like me are things that *we* caused. Even though I didn't put that bomb in her head, I might as well have. You removed it, right?"

"No," he said with a shake of the head. "Its placement makes that too dangerous. We've completely disabled it though. Any external force strong enough to set it off would kill her, and nothing else can activate it now."

Well, that certainly sounded grim. Time to change the subject.

"So, what doesn't Doctor Parker want me to know about?"

"Faster-than-light communication."

Veronica laughed. "I can certainly understand how that would go wrong. It's impossible."

"Funny thing. We already have it working. Doctor Parker was just making a few modifications to an *already* functioning FTL com and got some anomalous results."

She stared at the young scientist, agog. "That's impossible."

"It's not only possible, but we have FTL coms installed on a number of ships and even on probes. We can send them through a flip point and get real-time communication from the other side. We have a number of them spread out across this system giving us real-time scanner information.

"The problem comes when we look at the theory. It says the range should be unlimited. Through testing, we've discovered it works through a single flip point. It won't go through a second. It also works through about three hundred light-years of normal space before the signal fails."

Veronica stood there, unable to speak for long seconds. When she finally managed to close her mouth, she grimaced.

"That's how you set up the trap that took out the task force I was part of. You were in communication all around us the entire time. You herded us into a trap because we couldn't see you, but you were busy talking about wherever we were going."

Even though she'd changed sides, she still felt bitterness at the realization. Her comrades and she had been herded together for the slaughter.

Carl shook his head. "That's not exactly what happened. The linkage comes in matched pairs of devices containing entangled particles, and it's possible to detect their use. They create small gravitic pulses that an eagle-eyed observer might spot. We didn't dare use them during the fight."

"Why are you telling me this?" she asked after a moment. "This kind of thing could change the balance of power between the Rebel Empire and the New Terran Empire enough to win the war. If you keep it a secret. Doctor Parker is absolutely right that I shouldn't be here."

Carl gestured for her to walk over to the table. "You're on our side now. Let's get you brought up to speed on this while I figure out exactly what's going on."

She took two steps before something else occurred to her. "If these are the secrets you're *willing* to show me, just what kind of things are you working on in private that you're not ready to share just yet?"

He grinned at her. "Things that would blow your mind. Come on."

Veronica couldn't begin to imagine what kind of scientific breakthrough would be even more astonishing than what he'd already told her. She'd known the boy was smart, but this was ridiculous. If he came up with this all on his own, he really *was* a genius.

* * *

KELSEY WAS PLEASED to see that her negotiations with King Estevan were going smoothly. Once they'd gotten past the little problem of him not trusting her, he'd listened to her entire story with an open mind and incisive questions.

Understanding the bind her people were in, he readily agreed to trade technological know-how for the assistance his people could provide in both food and other undiscussed terms. He seemed quite interested in forming a stronger bond with her people.

That probably had something to do with the assassination attempt. If the Empire of Kalor was as persistent a thorn in his side as she suspected, any advantage he could get over them might spell the difference between life and death for both him and his people.

The king leaned back in the chair he was sitting in. "I think I understand something that had been confusing me. One of the overseers down at the wreck of *Dauntless* sent me a complaint about someone there under the protection of my son.

"Apparently they broke something. Or set something on fire. I'm not precisely sure which. Was that someone you sent?"

Kelsey nodded. "Probably. A very important piece of equipment on board my largest ship was damaged. We're hoping to repair it, and I sent some people to quietly look at the inside of the wreck to see if something could be salvaged. I hope the damage wasn't significant."

The older man laughed. "To hear the overseer talk, your people just about burned the place to the ground. I suspect the actual impact was far less than that. The overseers tend to be doggedly protective of that ship. I'm sorry to say that he expelled your people. I'll send a message back instructing him to give anyone you designate his full cooperation and complete access."

A knock on the door interrupted her response. It cracked open to admit one of the king's guards. The man walked over and whispered in his monarch's ear. After listening for a moment, Derek's father nodded and gestured for the man to leave. Then he smiled at Kelsey.

"Jacob has arrived with your companions. They'll be here shortly."

That was fast. When Kelsey had set up the meeting between Jacob and Talbot, she'd expected it would take a little longer for her husband to get down here. It seemed he was in a hurry.

Yeah. He was probably pissed.

She smiled in spite of her sense of impending doom. "Then it's a good thing that we've finished working out our arrangement. Thank you for speaking with the overseer. I'll see that someone comes back down to finish looking at what we needed to look at. This time, hopefully without setting anything on fire."

Moments later, there was another knock on the door, and it opened before anyone inside responded. Jacob Howell stepped in and bowed to the king. "Majesty. I've brought guests from Clan Persephone."

The man stepped aside just in time to avoid Talbot running over him. Her husband shot her a look that promised he'd get around to dealing with her, but he focused his attention on the alien monarch and bowed low.

Kelsey stepped up beside him to perform the introduction. "King Estevan, allow me to introduce my husband, Lieutenant Colonel Russell Talbot. He is also my clan's senior ground warrior."

The Pandoran man raised his eyebrow. "If he is as good a fighter as you, he must be a terror on the field. Welcome to my kingdom, Russell Talbot. I would like to speak with you further, but I do understand that your wife was just in battle. You are undoubtedly concerned over her health.

"It might be best if we break our discussions for now, Princess Bandar. Send one of the guards when you're ready to speak again. I shall be just down the hall with my son and Jacob."

Talbot waited until the door had closed behind the Pandoran monarch before he rounded on Kelsey. Rather than yelling, he peeled back the cloth on the side of her head. He grunted when he saw what was under it.

"Exactly how do you manage to get into fights *everywhere* you go? I have Doc Zoboroski back with my men. I want him to look at this as soon as practical."

"I don't get into fights every single time I go off by myself!" she said, narrowing her eyes. "This wasn't my fault."

He didn't seem convinced. "While I'm willing to grant that you don't always go looking for trouble, every place you go seems more prone to having physical violence break out than if you weren't there. Obviously, you must be the common factor."

She stared at him for several long seconds before she saw the twinkle of humor in his eyes. She smacked his shoulder and scowled at him. "That's not funny."

"I think it is. Now, why don't you tell me what happened?"

Kelsey ran down the sequence of events and watched him wince when she described the fight at the chapter house. She knew she was going to get total crap because she'd gotten into two fights in one trip.

She held up a finger. "That one wasn't my fault either. That guy picked a fight with me that didn't need to happen."

"Uh-huh. It sounds like we need to take that guy back up to the ship and stuff him into a regenerator. We don't need to make additional enemies on this planet."

Kelsey wasn't exactly sure that even a full regeneration would make that ass any less angry and dismissive toward her. Still, it was a gesture of goodwill toward Clan Dauntless.

"I'll ask Jacob to make the arrangements. You can take him back up with you."

Talbot shook his head. "You mean that we can take him back up with us. We're going back up together shortly."

She crossed her arms over her chest. "You think that just because I've had these problems that you get to tell me I'm going back up into orbit? Think again."

He shook his head. "I'm not telling you that you *have* to go, but we both know that that wrecked battlecruiser isn't going to provide the solution we need. All of this exploration is a sideshow. There are others better suited to working out the details.

"We're going to have to conduct a mission to Archibald, and we both know it. The sooner we start planning and executing that mission, the better. Those Clan people are nuts. Eventually, they're going to start sending ships into the multiflip point hoping to get one to where we went.

"Even Carl doesn't know how successful they'll be. It wasn't as if the original ships could spare even a single flip drive. They had one failure and decided to call it quits. Now, they might throw ships at it until one gets through. And that might not take very many tries. We can't take the chance. We need to get moving."

Kelsey rubbed her face. "You're right. I want to explore here. I want to see what's going on with the first real alien society we've gotten to interact with. It feels like an adventure. This conflict between the Kingdom of Raden and the Empire of Kalor just begs for us to intervene. Or at least make sure that the other guys really are the bad guys."

"Are you worried that the people we're talking to are the bad guys?"

"No, but we don't exactly know enough to say that for sure. Still, you're right. I need to be back in orbit, and there are plenty of people I could send down here to finish settling the details.

"Let me explain that to King Estevan, and then we'll go by the chapter house and pick up our wounded butthole. There'd better be something interesting going on up there to make me feel better."

Talbot smiled wickedly. "Oh, I think there are a few things underway that'll capture your interest. Let's get this over with before you change your mind."

"Changing my mind is *my* prerogative," she huffed. "Fine. Let's do this."

14

Zia stopped outside Commodore Murdoch's compartment and took a deep breath. She hated visiting the woman. Hated seeing anyone in that condition. It sickened her.

When Commander Raul Castille had orchestrated his escape from *Audacious*, he'd killed the senior staff that had been captured on the Dresden orbital. People that were his supposed friends and allies. People he'd worked with for years.

He hadn't quite been successful with Murdoch. He'd snapped her neck, but she'd survived. Unfortunately, she was paralyzed from the neck down. No amount of regeneration could fix that kind of damage. Modern medical technology just wasn't that sophisticated.

Nevertheless, she needed to convince her enemy to help them again. Yes, Murdoch had given them her codes to the Dresden orbital research computers, but that had been an act of spite against the security apparatus that had betrayed her.

This was something more. No matter what she'd said earlier, the woman still believed in the Empire she served. One didn't become a flag officer with one's eyes closed.

Well, she might as well get this over with.

Zia pressed the admittance key, and the door slid open moments later. A medical aide was on duty, there to serve any need the commodore had and to socialize if the injured woman wanted it.

The compartment was relatively basic, but it wasn't as if Murdoch was able to enjoy very many amenities. Besides the bed and furnishings, one wall supported a large vid screen to provide entertainment.

It was interesting, Zia thought. People with implants could watch vids in their heads, but many preferred to watch them the old-fashioned way.

Commodore Murdoch was an older woman with lines across her face from scowling and various levels of displeasure throughout her life. It came as no surprise that she fixed Zia with a frown.

"What do you want now?" the woman demanded peevishly. "I've already given you the damned codes."

Zia gestured for the medical aide to leave them and took a seat by the bed. "We're about to take a trip into the Rebel Empire. Or, if you prefer, the Empire. A place you've been, I believe. Archibald. I was wondering what you could tell me about it."

The older woman's frown deepened as she processed what Zia had said. "That's impossible. We're nowhere near Archibald."

Zia allowed herself a small smile. "Without elaborating, I believe you already know we're fairly resourceful. You'll just have to take my word that we have a way to get to Archibald, and it won't take as long as you think.

"That said, we have specific things that we need to get there. This ship's flip drive burned out when we arrived in the system. We need to either get what we need to repair it or find something to steal to replace it. To make that happen, we need your help."

Murdoch laughed, her voice sounding dry and just a tad bitter. Of course, bitterness had colored everything the woman had said thus far since her attempted murder. And, to be honest, before that.

"I suppose if you were looking to get repair parts, that's one of the best places to look," she finally admitted. "It's a fool's errand though. There's no way you can actually get into a Fleet facility like that. It might not be guarded as well as the Dresden orbital, but you can be sure they don't allow just anyone to walk in."

"It seems like we did pretty good with the Dresden orbital, didn't we?" Zia asked. "In fact, we ended up stealing the entire thing. I'm not sure at this point what we can do at Archibald, but we have resources you're not aware of.

"Which brings us full circle. I can't go into the details of how we'll carry out this mission, simply because I have no idea what we're facing. I need you to tell me about Archibald and the Fleet facilities there."

The older woman considered Zia for almost twenty seconds, her expression calculating. "All right. I'll do it, but I want something in return."

"What?" Zia asked, waiting for the other shoe to drop.

The older woman smiled coldly. "The shipyard isn't the only thing Archibald has to offer. It's also the home of one of the Empire's top medical research facilities. Something like the Dresden orbital but with less security implications, if you know what I mean.

"I want you to work your magic at that facility too. If anyone has advanced regeneration equipment and techniques capable of repairing my spine, it's them."

That was actually a nightmare. They already had a difficult mission and didn't need to add a second intrusion to the first. That was just begging for trouble.

"Just because they *might* have the technology doesn't mean that they *will* have the technology," Zia objected.

"I want you to promise that you'll make a good faith effort to obtain the technology and know-how to heal me. That's my price."

Zia felt her teeth clenching. One more needless complication to a situation already fraught with danger. Unbelievable.

Part of her wanted to promise the old woman anything just to get the information she needed, but Zia wasn't going to lie and make knowingly false promises. If she agreed to this, they'd do their very best to make it happen.

Even if she *had* felt differently, Zia knew Princess Kelsey would take a promise like that and make it happen. She'd insist, and she'd be right to do so.

"I can't promise success," Zia said, feeling tired. "We'll make a good faith effort to get any technology that might see you healed and knowledge of the required techniques. That said, I'm not going to throw my people's lives away. If it looks impossible, we won't act."

Murdoch nodded, her expression somewhat glum. "Not exactly a ringing endorsement of our deal, but you're speaking with the voice of someone who actually intends to carry through. I really can't ask for more than that, can I?

"Very well. I was a junior officer when I was stationed at Archibald, but I was a flag lieutenant, and my commander occasionally dragged me into some interesting places, including the shipyard. I saw the area where they manufactured flip drives and other parts too."

The woman's smile grew cold. "The only way I see that you'll be able to get the parts you need is to plug the information directly into one of the manufacturing computers and have it make them on the spot.

"As one might expect, that's going to take some interesting timing and very likely require a diversion. Say, some kind of ruckus at the nearby medical research facility. And I haven't got the slightest idea how you can expect to get what you build out from under the eyes of the security officers on duty at the shipyard."

"I suppose I'll have to get all the information I can from you and figure that out, won't I?" Zia asked with a sigh. "I don't suppose you've ever been at the medical research facility, have you?"

"Sadly, no. There was no need. After all, I was young and immortal." That last bit came out with an exceptional amount of bitterness.

"At that age, aren't we all?" Zia asked rhetorically. "We'll run through the information you can give me now, and then I'll send a couple of officers to go over it again and get every little detail we can. We only get one chance at this, your mission and mine. If I can't make everything work, none of us is going to come away happy."

With a sigh, Zia began asking questions and getting specifics. She'd make another pass once she'd gone through the initial run looking for deeper details. Done right, the preparation for this mission would take days.

Knowing Princess Kelsey, they'd leave much sooner than Zia preferred, so it was best to get as much data as she could now. They'd probably need it all when the time came.

* * *

TALBOT TOLERATED Kelsey's bad mood until just before their pinnace docked with *Audacious*. Then he poked a finger in her side.

She twitched and fixed him with a flat stare. "Why are you poking me?"

"Because you're being an idiot. You couldn't find that guy that you messed up. So what? He didn't have to go scurrying off like a roach in the sunlight. He made a choice. Let it go. You can't fix everything."

Kelsey stared at him for a long moment before shaking her head. "Sometimes, you don't understand me at all. I'm not upset because I can't fix what happened. I'm upset because I'm dead sure that bugger is going to cause me problems later.

"It's a curse, I tell you. He's got bad guy written all over him, like a villain from the vids. He hated me to begin with, I totally trashed him and caused him a grievous injury, and now he's off somewhere licking his wounds. You can bet your ass he's going to come back looking for my blood."

"Seriously? He's a primitive. Let him get all freaked out. It won't do him any good or cause you any problems. Besides, Howell seems pretty competent. If he says he's going to find someone, I'd wager he's going to do exactly that. No matter how long it takes or how many rocks he has to turn over to find him."

She shook her head and sighed. "I agree that's what would happen under any normal circumstance, but tell me the last few years have worked out that way. Every time we cross someone, they come after us looking for a fight.

"At this point, I really hate leaving potential enemies behind. That's where our backs are, after all. You know those things that are really good at attracting knives? I'd much rather have healed the guy's injuries and maybe sidestepped this particular blood feud."

At that moment, the pinnace docked and the pressure changed slightly as the lock began cycling. Talbot undid his restraints and stood, holding out his hand for Kelsey.

"You did what you had to do to get through the crisis that guy created. If he pops up later looking to cause trouble, I'll be happy to give him some. Right now, we need to start planning our mission to Archibald. That has to be the priority. Until it's done, you're not going back down to the surface in any case. He can't exactly get to you up here."

They walked out into marine country. Major Gabe Collins, *Audacious*'s senior marine officer, stood waiting for them. Of normal height and somewhat abnormal width, the marine officer's hair seemed grayer than the last time Talbot had seen him.

That didn't seem likely, but Talbot wasn't going to rule it out. It had been that kind of month.

"You're not here to give me more problems to deal with, are you, Gabe?" Talbot asked.

The big man shook his head. "Not that I know of. I figured since you were just passing through my area, it would behoove me to at least greet my commanding officers. How was your visit below, Princess? Did you have any trouble? Maybe you need me to drop a detachment of marines to teach someone manners?"

Kelsey chuckled. "There were a few issues, but nothing I couldn't handle. What's your posture going to be like while we're conducting the raid on Archibald?"

The man shrugged. "It's not like you can stuff a battalion's worth of marines on board *Persephone.* If I did, Colonel Talbot would be in command in any case. I assume I'm going to be left here with the bulk of our marines because if you get caught, no amount of help I can give is going to save you.

"Whatever firepower you think is appropriate to go along for your heist, I'll send. You're going to have to tell me what you need, and I'll make it happen. Other than that, I figure I'll be providing security forces for any of the people that need to go down to Pandora's surface."

"As soon as I figure out what we're going to do, I'll let you know," Kelsey said. "It's really going to depend on what Commodore Anderson has to tell me. If the news is bad enough, then I won't go. There will be no suicide missions under my watch unless we have no choices left."

Talbot was proud of how much Kelsey had grown. A year ago, she would've flatly refused to consider any situation valid for a suicide mission. Now she accepted there might come a time where she had to call for volunteers that wouldn't come back.

"As soon as you know what you need, let me know. Good luck." With that, Gabe stepped back and returned to his office.

Talbot led Kelsey into the corridor outside marine country. "How soon is Zia going to brief us? Until we know what we're dealing with, we're at a standstill."

"Last I heard, she'd already finished talking with Commodore Murdoch. She's got people asking follow-up questions to nail down all the details they can, but she's back in her office. I'll go get the lay of the land.

"Meanwhile, I want you to go talk with Carl and find out what exactly we're going to need to fix the flip drive. If we need parts, that's probably a lot more doable than a full-size flip drive capable of moving a carrier through the flip point."

Talbot really hoped that they'd gotten good news from down at the wreck of the battlecruiser *Dauntless*, but that seemed unlikely. He also hoped that whatever they needed was going to be something they could easily sneak in to steal at Archibald. Based on their luck, he wasn't counting on things going that smoothly.

"I'm on it," he said, putting a good face over his worry. "Shall we meet for dinner? The VIP cabin Zia assigned us would provide some well-deserved rest and privacy."

She smiled widely. "Admit it. Rest is the last thing on your mind. Though privacy would be nice."

He grinned. "You know me. We marines like to live for today. Now go on. I'll let you know as soon as I find out what's going on with Carl."

She headed off in the other direction, and he kept a positive expression on his face until he was sure she couldn't see him anymore. Their situation was bad, and he didn't expect the news from Carl would make it any better.

They were in a tight corner this time. The odds against them being able to get the carrier out of this system were pretty steep. It might be trapped here forever. Then Kelsey would have to decide who they left behind when they took the ships they could and tried to get the tech they'd stolen back to the New Terran Empire.

That wasn't a choice he'd have liked to make. He didn't envy her position at all because that was almost certainly what would end up happening.

15

Veronica was relieved when Colonel Talbot arrived. Maybe he could explain some of what she'd been watching. Her own understanding of the science seemed… inadequate.

Stepping away from the lab bench didn't disturb the scientists fussing over the equipment in the slightest. In fact, they hadn't noticed Talbot arriving or her departing. They were completely immersed in a technical discussion that made Veronica's brain ache.

"Thank God you're here to save me," she murmured. "I think my head is about to explode."

The marine officer laughed. "You obviously haven't been demanding explanations in small words. Preferably those with three or fewer syllables. If you don't yank the science types up short, they'll run right over you. What are they doing?"

"It has something to do with interference and your faster-than-light communications system. Apparently, they were conducting some type of experiment with new hardware, and it's not working the way they expected."

"Good enough." He raised his voice. "Carl, what's going on? Take a break and explain it to me in small words. Princess Kelsey wants a briefing on this and other subjects, so be concise. Pretend you're explaining it to an idiot."

"That's like the opposite of concise," the young man said with a grin. "You know how much longer it takes to explain something to an idiot? If you've got the time, I can fill you in."

"Ha, ha. You're a very funny man. What's the problem?"

Owlet gestured toward a small table nearby. He and Doctor Parker sat on one side while Veronica took the other next to the marine officer.

"It's not exactly a problem," Carl said. "We're not experiencing any issues whatsoever with our operational equipment. What happened is that Jacqueline made some modifications to a testbed to explore the theory and the results didn't match what we expected to see."

"How so?"

The scientist compressed his lips. "We're seeing a reduction in data throughput between the testbed and the FTL probe we're using to send back data. It's positioned on the other side of the system so we can get information at FTL speeds. We send data to it, and it in turn sends it right back. Jacqueline thought that the changes she'd made to the hardware might increase the data throughput, but it seems to have had the opposite effect."

The older woman nodded. "While I'm still getting to the point where I fully understand the hardware, what I expected to happen was to have a slight but noticeable increase in data throughput. Instead, the data is moving at less than one percent of the normal speed.

"Worse, it's inconsistent. Sometimes the hardware is somewhat faster than normal and others it's being heavily throttled. The problem is that it's not behaving the same in every case. It either should work or not work the same way every time."

Veronica cleared her throat. "While I'm not a scientist, it seems to me that something is interfering with the test. We had something similar occur a few years ago when I was helping Fleet Design work on a new tactical simulator.

"Sometimes the thing performed brilliantly and other times it introduced stupid errors that none of us could explain. Worse, it did so on an unusual schedule. It took us weeks to locate the problem."

Carl crossed his arms over his chest and leaned forward, his expression curious. "If you don't mind my asking, what caused the issue?"

"An ensign," Veronica said dryly. "She was logging into the tactical simulator when it was supposed to be reserved and using the processors to work on simulations after hours. She figured since it was test equipment that no one else would be logged in and she'd be able to get a lot more processing time.

"It turns out that she was right. In fact, she managed to use so many processing cycles that it completely wrecked the testing protocols we were trying to run. And the fact that she logged in remotely and at odd times made it almost impossible for us to figure out."

The scientist laughed. "I can totally see that happening. Back when I was a graduate student, we'd steal processing time from any system we could get into. There were always too many people trying to use the regular systems."

Talbot nodded, his expression serious. "Is something like that possible here? Someone being on a system that they're not supposed to be or trying to tap into the same probe?"

Doctor Parker shook her head with a sigh. "If only it was something that easy. The way FTL communications work requires a dedicated pairing between devices because of the entangled particles. That means it's literally impossible for anyone else to be accessing that particular probe.

"And since we're standing next to the testbed and it's not linked to anything else, there's no way anyone is logged in to that machine and using it in some way. Even so, we've been through the logs. Nothing like that showed up."

They were all quiet for a short bit, probably trying to think of something they'd missed.

Talbot leaned back in his seat and shrugged. "I'm sure you'll figure it out. It's not really the most pressing matter on our plates right now, in any case.

"Princess Kelsey is with Commodore Anderson right now and they're discussing an operation in Archibald to get what we need to either repair or replace *Audacious*'s flip drive. We need to know if the drive can be fixed or if we need a new unit."

Carl grimaced. "The engineering people disassembled it as much as they could, and I've tested every part of the system. Usually a failure is in some system or subsystem that has to be swapped out. The basic framework of the unit isn't damaged during normal operations. Hell, even during abnormal operations.

"That's not the case here. When we came through the multiflip point, it set up a resonance deep inside the flip drive. That created power induction where no one ever anticipated anything like that. We'll either need to build structural parts that aren't to Rebel Empire specifications or we'll need an entirely new flip drive."

"Crap," Talbot muttered. "That's bad. That's real bad."

The scientist nodded his head in apparent agreement. "It's worse than that. *Audacious* is significantly larger than other military ships inside the Rebel Empire. Based on what I've seen and been told, the largest vessels they have in operation are heavy cruisers.

"The difference in size of flip drives used for heavy cruisers, or even a battlecruiser, is significant. I doubt very seriously that a flip drive constructed for use in a heavy cruiser would work more than once for a battlecruiser. It wouldn't work at all for this carrier."

Talbot turned to face Veronica. "Can you add anything to that?"

She briefly cast her thoughts back over her years of service for Fleet. Then she shook her head. "I'm afraid not. Doctor Owlet is absolutely correct. Until we ran into you folk, the concept of a battlecruiser was unknown to me. A superdreadnought or carrier? Unthinkable.

"But that doesn't mean we're out of options. What about a flip drive for a freighter of almost this ship's size? One designed for military service."

Carl's expression sharpened. "What do you mean 'designed for military service'? The freighter we have here isn't built to standards that would work for moving the carrier even once. There's a whole different level of quality control and precision necessary when making flip drives for warships. Even a freighter of the correct size wouldn't have a flip drive that would work more than a couple of times at best."

Veronica shrugged a little. "I honestly can't tell you much more than the fact that I've seen military transports that were only somewhat smaller than this ship. Huge freighters made to keep up with Fleet elements. Their grav drives were sufficient to move them at a decent speed, so I'm assuming they were military grade. It's entirely possible their flip drives are too."

Carl rubbed his chin thoughtfully. "That has possibilities. We need to see if any of the computer records we've captured have anything about those ships in them. Commander Giguere, would you feel comfortable working with us to try to locate any information we have?"

"Of course," she said with a nod.

"Excellent," Talbot said. "Be as quick as you can because we really need to get this operation moving. Every day we wait makes it more likely Clan warships are going to try to breach the multiflip point. That would be a disaster for us. It's already going to take far too long to repair this ship. Every minute we delay could spell the death of everyone aboard this ship."

* * *

KELSEY SURVEYED the map they'd put together from their single visit to the Archibald system. It wasn't much to work with considering how far out the multiflip point was, but it was all they had.

One thing it did provide was a rough idea of where the major hubs of communication were. Where people were talking, that's where they were living and working.

"What kind of information were we able to pull out of the various computers we've captured from the Rebel Empire?" Kelsey asked, tapping her lip thoughtfully. "As it sits, we'd be going in virtually blind."

Zia nodded her agreement. "I would love to have more information, but the Rebel Empire compartmentalizes itself. People from one area aren't likely to find much information on other places inside the Empire. That goes for Fleet too.

"The best source of information we have from inside the Rebel Empire is Commodore Murdoch. Before her transfer to Dresden, she actually worked inside this sector. She's been to Archibald and visited the shipyard."

Kelsey felt her face scrunch up. "Let me guess. She won't help us."

"Actually, she will, for a price. One I've already agreed to because I know you."

Kelsey leaned back and narrowed her eyes. "I'm not certain if I should be worried or annoyed. What does she want?"

Zia reached over the table and tapped the main source of communications in the Archibald system: the main planetary body. "Archibald Prime doesn't just have a shipyard, it also has an advanced medical research facility on the civilian station nearby. One that

Commodore Murdoch suspects might have regeneration equipment that could repair her spine."

The unexpected revelation made Kelsey sit back and think. "She wants us to get something to help her? How much complication is that going to add to our mission?"

The Fleet officer shrugged. "I haven't the slightest idea, but it's not going to make things easier. Still, knowing you as I do, I realized you were going to say yes so I agreed."

"And what was she able to give us in exchange? Something worth the hassle she's asking of us?"

"Probably not," Zia admitted. "Though we won't know until we get there. Her memory of the traffic patterns around the planet and some of the procedures will prove useful. I'm not so sure that the information she provided about the shipyard itself is going to help us.

"She was only there a couple of times and saw what they wanted her to see. She was acting as an aide to a flag officer, so she was taken on a grand tour and given explanations on how things worked. That's more than thirty years out-of-date, though."

Kelsey rubbed her face. "We're going to have to take a look for ourselves. The general information she provided, as well as what Commander Giguere can offer, might get us close. Until we can see it with our own eyes and make a judgment on the security, we're not going to be able to plan effectively."

"If the mission is too difficult, then you're going to have to take everything that we've captured back to the Empire and leave *Audacious* here," the Fleet officer said with a scowl. "The Empire needs that information and hardware."

"The Empire needs the information, yes, but I'm not just leaving you here. Castille stirred up the Clans. They'll figure out what they need to do to get through the multiflip point eventually. I'm not leaving you here for them to kill."

"They may never come," Zia insisted. "If they do, they do. Kelsey, you have to accept that you can't save everyone. Sometimes you've got to do what's best for the greatest number of people. Right now, that's the Empire.

"The loss of one carrier and everyone aboard would be a drop in the bucket compared to how many people would die if we don't get the Dresden information and that critical hardware for making the sentient AIs back to the Empire as soon as possible. You and I both know that. The smart thing to do is for you to accept that."

This was the kind of argument Kelsey was used to having with Talbot or Jared. God, how she wished her brother was here right now. He'd know *exactly* what to do. She worked off instinct while he was a planner. He could orchestrate this entire mission down to the smallest detail.

But he wasn't here, and she had no way to talk to him. She'd just have to do the best she could. And that meant not leaving any of her friends behind.

"Zia, have you met me? That's not how I work. And unfortunately for you, I have this thing called a title that lets me tell you what I want accomplished, and then we get to do it my way."

She smiled to take any sting out of what she was saying. She wanted to get across how inevitable this was, not just sound bossy.

The other woman sighed and rubbed her face. "What great sin have I committed against the universe to be strapped with such a stubborn friend?"

"Some of us just get lucky," Kelsey said with a grin. "Let's get the team together. We've got a mission to plan, and I want to be underway within twenty-four hours."

16

Zia wasted no time calling Angela Ellis and asking her to join her on *Audacious*. The woman was recovering from her final Marine Raider surgery, but she'd want to know what was going on. As expected, *Persephone*'s executive officer came right over.

This time, Angela was able to walk even though she'd had surgery today. This set of operations involved the work on her torso, upper body, and arms. It was going to take the woman some time to adjust to the artificial musculature, but this was it. The surgeries were complete. She was a now a Marine Raider.

Zia wondered if Kelsey understood that meant she might be ordered to turn the Marine Raider strike ship over to Angela once they got back to Avalon. That made the most sense. Kelsey was the crown princess and had more important things to do than commanding a specialized ship.

She grinned and stood at the tall woman as she came into her office. "So, what does it feel like to be the second Marine Raider in the New Terran Empire?"

"I'll let you know as soon as I stop crushing things with my hands," Angela said as she gingerly sat down in one of the chairs to the side of the desk. "Apologize to your maintenance teams for me. I accidentally ripped a support off a bulkhead when I was getting into the lift. My bad."

Zia chuckled and joined her friend. "I'll do that. Are you glad it's over?"

"I'm glad that I didn't have to do it all at one time. What Kelsey went through with the Pale Ones was a nightmare that I am thrilled I didn't have to repeat.

"It's still been painful and it's going to take a while before I'm fully recovered and can start getting up to speed at being a Marine Raider. My only consolation is that Talbot gets to be next. He's been an ass. A friendly, good old boy ass, but still an ass."

Zia shook her head. "I'm glad the two of you get along so well. Having Kelsey as your shared charge has got to be mentally draining. Even at one step removed, she exhausts me. At least now you'll have a chance at keeping up with her and maybe heading her off from doing dangerous things.

"Dangerous things like leading a mission into the Archibald system. And by leading, I mean personally taking the teams in to scout out a Rebel Empire system. That's what she just got finished telling me we needed to plan for. The mission launches in twenty-four hours."

Angela said something pithy that couldn't be repeated in polite company. "I knew this was coming. Really, it was the only way things could possibly go. You couldn't talk her out of it? Obviously not. So, what do we do?"

"We do the best we can to keep her alive and make this mission a success. We've got a lot of really talented people that we can put on board *Persephone* to help with this. I've called you over to start coordinating how we can use that talent to shield Princess Kelsey from herself."

The tall marine shifted in her chair resulting in a loud crack as she broke one of the hand rests off. Bemused, the marine held it up and stared at it.

"I hope you weren't attached to that chair. Sorry."

She carefully set the hand rest down on the small table and sighed. "We're going to have to approach this as cautiously as me sitting down. Kelsey isn't going to want to be protected. That has to be a side effect of what we're doing, not the goal or she'll get mulish.

"The best thing we can do is get all the main players together and start war-gaming on how we might approach this mission. Obviously, the goal is going to be getting in and out without revealing we were ever there. Or at least not having anyone connect us to what's going on while it matters."

"Agreed," Zia said. "We've got Cain Hopwood and his merry crew of recovery agents to start with. They'll blend in, I suspect, based on what I saw on Harrison's World. Fourteen heavily trained specialists skilled in breaking and entering will be very helpful.

"We can add Commander Giguere. She passed Fiona's inspection. The shipyard has a lot of Fleet officers moving through it, so she's going to be invaluable in that aspect of the mission."

Angela grimaced. "She might be able to help us get in, but she's not going to be able to work the equipment we need. For something like that, you're going to need Carl, aren't you?"

Zia smiled apologetically. "I'm afraid so. I already have the broad outlines of a plan in mind. The specifics are really going to depend on a couple of factors. If we can take a flip drive in whole, in parts that they've already manufactured, or if we have to get into their equipment and build something from scratch.

"That last option would be the worst, I suspect. Not only would we have to keep them from realizing we were there, we'd leave tracks that we built something unusual. I'd rather not give them any more information than we absolutely have to. Unfortunately, I really do suspect that's how things are going to go."

The marine settled back in her chair a little. "Could we even steal a flip drive? Those aren't small."

No, they weren't. The burned-out unit on board *Audacious* was about twenty meters in every direction. If they had to steal a completed unit, they couldn't exactly sneak it out in their pockets.

"I haven't got the slightest idea," Zia said with a shrug. "That's why we're going to consult with experts. The first stage of the mission has to come first, though. We have to know the landscape. We have to know exactly what we're dealing with as far as getting in and getting out.

"Once we have all the information we can get on the facility—or I should say facilities—then we'll start devising plans to cover every option we can: stealing a completed flip drive, stealing parts, co-opting the manufacturing equipment to build our own, etcetera."

Angela's eyes narrowed. "You said facilities plural. What does that mean?"

"That's the next complication," Zia said with a wry smile. She proceeded to explain Commodore Murdoch's requirements for her cooperation.

The marine huffed in irritation. "As if this wasn't going to be difficult enough. Do we really have to do it?"

"What would Princess Kelsey say?"

Angela slumped a little. "She'd say we're going to make it happen and then tell me to figure out how."

"So tell me how we're going to make it happen," Zia said with a smirk.

The marine laughed a little in spite of herself. "That's just cruel. I'd say we need to bring Doctor Parker and her researchers in on the discussions. While they may not be *medical* researchers, they probably can tell us a lot more about how to fit into a place like that than we would guess on our own.

"If we have Doctor Zoboroski helping them, they might be able to tell us how to probe the place and figure out what we're going to need to gain access. Then, what we need to do when we get inside.

"What a nightmare. How long did you say we had? An *entire* twenty-four hours? That's a different kind of joke all in itself."

"Look on the bright side," Zia said. "At least we're going to a civilized system and we can do some shopping."

"I hate shopping," Angela muttered. "Nothing ever fits me. I think I hate you."

The two women laughed, but Zia could hear an edge of tension in both their voices. They might make light of it, but there were so many ways this could go very wrong. If the Rebel Empire captured any of them, the New Terran Empire was screwed.

* * *

VERONICA HAD GIVEN up any hope of finding additional information that would be useful on the raid Princess Kelsey was planning when she chanced across something in the data from a previous mission.

Her new friends had captured the Rebel Empire destroyer *R-7386* during a previous supply mission to the Erorsi system. They'd captured the ship mostly intact but had only collared one officer. That man, Lieutenant Commander Michael Richards, had eventually decided to cooperate with the New Terran Empire in exactly the same way Veronica had.

He wasn't what had triggered her curiosity, though. It was his dead commanding officer.

According to the report, her name had been Commander Diane Delatorre. She'd apparently been a real piece of work. Just the kind of person Fleet liked to put in charge of a ship. A backbiting political animal determined to command a task force before she was fifty.

While there was some basic information about the woman in the reports, what caught Veronica's eye was her planet of birth: Archibald.

Much like Commodore Murdoch, the deceased commander started her career on the planet they were targeting. All well and good, though not exceptionally useful in and of itself.

What was useful was the fact the woman had blackmail material on various people that might well be on the planet they were interested in.

None of the juicy details were included in the reports she had access to, but Veronica hoped it would be able to put various people into compromising positions. That kind of clout might enable them to get into places that the Rebel Empire wouldn't want them to be.

But first she needed to know for a fact that they had the critical information.

She glanced over at where Carl Owlet and Doctor Parker were still busy working on the FTL com testbed, walked over, and cleared her throat.

"If the two of you would excuse me, I'm going to leave you to what you're doing and go talk to Colonel Talbot about someone interesting. It seems that one of the destroyer commanders you captured was born in the Archibald system. The one you captured at Erorsi."

Carl's eyebrows shot up. "You mean the one with a bedroom like a bordello? I couldn't believe it when I saw the place."

Now it was Veronica's turn to have her eyebrows rise. "You were there?"

The young scientist nodded. "I cracked her personal communications console while Princess Kelsey and Talbot searched the bedroom. Holy cow."

Doctor Parker shot Carl a sidelong glance. "Just exactly what was in her bedroom?"

Carl Owlet turned beet red, making both women laugh as he squirmed, trying to come up with some kind of answer.

"Let's not get sidetracked," Veronica said smoothly. "The file I accessed said the woman kept blackmail material. None of that is in what I have access to. Can you provide a bit more information about what and who the material covered?"

Obviously relieved to have a way out of answering the previous question, Carl nodded enthusiastically. "There were several encrypted data chips that I haven't taken the time to get into, but there were also a number of printouts in the safe.

"I have no idea who the people were, but since the data seemed… sensitive, I scanned them in and put them into a segregated drive space. I figured we could bring any portion of it we needed to into primary memory if it became important enough."

"Can you give me access to those files? Maybe find a little bit of time to take a look at those data chips?"

"I'll take the data chips," Doctor Parker said. "One of my people is an absolute whiz at breaking codes and data encryptions. One of the side effects of being a primary designer in systems that utilize them. Frankly, it's possible they're encrypted with one of the programs he created. If so, that might give him some unique insight into cracking them."

"I've got them in my office," Carl said. "I'll get them as soon I add Commander Giguere to the access list for the scanned documents."

Veronica smiled her thanks. "I'll just head back over to my console. Let me know when I can access them and where they are."

"You'll have access by the time you sit down. I'll send you the path to the data as well. Thank you."

The man was as good as his word and she already had a pop-up sitting on the screen waiting for her. She accepted the access, went to the files, and started reading.

She was impressed. The dead commander had certainly been building up enough dirt to get that command she wanted. There was evidence in these files of everything from infidelity to murder. And these were only the ones that she kept printed out. The really sensitive information was probably still locked up on the data chips.

Veronica turned the computer loose on the files and had it start searching for any matches in the data the New Terran Empire had collected.

Moments later, she had pay dirt. A number of the people and locations mentioned in the documents were at Archibald.

That made her grin widely. While it was true that some of them would be dead or have moved on, that still probably gave Princess Kelsey a handle to pull on, if she needed it. With any luck at all, the encrypted data chips would open to the researchers' skills and provide them a treasure trove of additional access.

Veronica scrolled back and looked at the image of Commander Diane Delatorre again. A small woman, with a cold face and hard eyes. A very small woman.

A woman with about the same build and size as Kelsey Bandar.

Well, that presented some interesting possibilities.

17

Talbot gave Veronica Giguere an uncertain look. "I remember Delatorre. The Rebel Fleet officer with that wild bedroom and even wilder closet. Are you sure she's from Archibald? If so, that seems like a negative point. People there will know that Kelsey isn't her."

"Maybe. Maybe not. It's been a long time since she left. I know her by reputation. She was working out of Dresden though I don't know that I ever met her in person. She did a lot of solo work for Fleet security. She had the personality for it, I understand.

"If her early career was anything like that, people will remember basic things about her: her height, her build, and her attitude. Minor changes can be written off as cosmetic face work or some such. Princess Kelsey has the perfect build to mimic her."

"But not the correct implant serial numbers," he said. "In a society like the Rebel Empire, that's going to give her away immediately."

Veronica gave him a smile. "You don't realize it, but you've already solved that problem. Carl tells me the latest updates in hardware he's developed allow for something he calls 'stealth mode.' The purpose of that being that people can pretend to be devoid of implants.

"Carl also informs me that he can put together some kind of interface that will present a false serial number to the world at large. From what he says, it would act as kind of a buffer between the real implants and any outside communications.

"If Princess Kelsey wants to interface with a piece of equipment or computer, the outgoing signal will go through the interface and it would leave her with the false serial number. Any communication to the false serial number would go through the interface and directly to her."

She paused for a few seconds. "That takes care of your other concern.

If someone sees her and doubts it's really her, they'll check her implants. People will see what they want to see."

"I understand where you're coming from," he said slowly. "But this is going to be a very risky venture, even if everything goes well. I'm not certain I want to trust her safety to unproven hardware. Carl is a genius, but he makes mistakes. Trust me, I've seen a couple of spectacular ones.

"Kelsey advanced the schedule and this mission kicks off shortly. Once we're committed, there's no going back. Did he tell you how long it would take to implant this false interface?"

The formerly Rebel Empire commander nodded. "He already has the hardware on hand. Doctor Zoboroski and his staff can put it in place in about twenty minutes. It's a very simple procedure. The princess already has the upgraded implants that would support stealth mode.

"Most people won't need a false serial number. However, if they get the false interfaces, they can program their own fake identities. Pick somebody off the street that has implants, clone their serial number, and suddenly you can pretend to be them. I'm actually shocked no one has tried to do this inside the Empire already."

That made Talbot grin. "Knowing criminals, they probably already have. Those guys are always on the cutting edge of identity theft. I'd wager the AIs come down on that kind of thing hard to dissuade the survivors from doing it anymore.

"What about the people she might meet from Fleet? They're going to know she's not assigned there. That her ship has been missing for a year. That makes for a lousy cover."

Giguere shook her head. "The differences between your Fleet and mine are tripping you up. The people here will have no insight into where she's been or what she's done since she left. The AIs makes certain that all data from different sections of the Empire is segregated.

"Trust me when I say that no one here is going to know that her ship has been missing. No one other than the System Lord. Our goal is to keep her off its scanners. That shouldn't be hard. We're not coming in with a warship. We're sneaking in on a freighter."

Talbot rose from behind his desk and began pacing. "That's another can of worms. That ship is going to be known to the System Lord. We stole it from Dresden, and you can be sure that word of that theft has gotten out by now."

Giguere shrugged. "From what I hear, there's still a lot of debris floating around Dresden. They might realize the orbital is gone, but maybe not the ship. In any case, we can give it fake papers and a new name. It, too, can be coming in from another sector."

"That seems chancy. While they won't have the information for a ship coming in from outside, it seems that would be a rare occurrence. Like you said, the System Lords don't exactly encourage immigration. Won't that attract the attention of the AI?"

She raised a finger. "I've come up with a solution for that. The freighter that was originally accompanying the dead commander's ship was of the same class. It was destroyed in the fighting, but your records have its codes. That's really all we need since there's no reason the AIs would be looking for that ship. Not here, anyway."

He wasn't completely sure about that, but it was a potential solution to their problem. At this point, he was ready to present the idea to Kelsey and see what she said. If anyone could make it work, it was his wife.

"Good work."

The Fleet officer nodded. "I've been talking with Commodore Murdoch and getting a feel for the place. That's a really conflicted woman, by the way. She hates your people but blames the Rebel Empire for her medical condition.

"If I were you, I'd double-check everything you possibly could that she's passing along. It wouldn't surprise me if she tries to betray you at some point. The woman has a reputation for being an asshole."

Talbot shook his head. "She wants to walk again. To make that happen, we have to get back with the right equipment. She's going to give us everything we need to succeed because her own future rides on it. Trust self-interest to trump everything else when it comes to Commodore Murdoch.

"That said, whenever possible we'll be very cautious with information we haven't verified. This mission isn't going to necessarily work if we rush it. One mistake could sink us. We'll be as careful as possible."

He rubbed his face. "I just can't help but worry about what we're doing. There's so much that could go wrong. Frankly, I can't imagine how we're going to pull this thing off."

Giguere rose to her feet. "It may seem impossible, but I've seen you and your friends work. If anyone can do it, it's you."

"Let's go present this crazy idea to Kelsey and see what she says," he said as he rose to his feet.

* * *

Zia sat tensely at what passed for a command console on the captured freighter, waiting for something to go wrong now that she'd taken it into the Archibald system.

Intellectually, she knew she didn't have much to worry about because *Persephone* had led the way. There was no enemy shipping close enough to detect them arriving.

That didn't keep her from clenching the armrests on her ratty chair anyway. This was a big step, and her new command was a lot less capable than her old one.

Unlike the magnificent bridge aboard *Audacious*, the freighter only had three console positions: helm and navigation, engineering, and cargo management. Since they'd unloaded the cargo before this mission, storing it inside the carrier, there was no need to man that last spot.

At least there hadn't been until Carl had made a few upgrades to the freighter's passive scanners and communications array. Nothing that would be visible from the outside, but ones that might make their lives a little easier.

That meant he was currently occupying the cargo management console, testing out the equipment to make sure everything was functional.

He turned his seat to face her. "The flip drive came through fine, but that's not a surprise. The segment of the multiflip point linking Pandora and Archibald has a fairly wide frequency band. Much bigger than the one between Icebox and Pandora."

Alan Barnes, the piloting specialist that came with the recovery team headed by Cain Hopwood, cleared his throat. "*Persephone* is headed in. Based on the pre-mission briefing, they're going to get into a decent overwatch position as we follow them. If we have to run, they're supposed to provide security for us, but you'll forgive me if I hope that isn't necessary."

She agreed with that assessment. If they had to flee, she didn't want to lead the Rebel Empire to the multiflip point. So long as they remained ignorant of these odd versions of the standard flip point, that meant that the New Terran Empire could continue sneaking around without being noticed.

They weren't going to be able to get all the way in before Princess Kelsey and the rest of the people selected for the mission took a cargo shuttle over to join her on the freighter. Zia had tried one more time to convince Kelsey not to put herself at risk. Once again, she'd been politely rebuffed. The small woman had a will of steel.

Thankfully, the multiflip point in the Archibald system was about as far off the beaten path as one could get and still be within a decent transit range with the main world. It sat above the plane of the ecliptic far away from anything interesting.

The trick was going to be inserting the freighter into the traffic pattern coming from the main flip point that sat on the other side of the sun from Archibald Prime. Any ships making their way into the system or back out again would note the freighter coming in at the odd angles necessary to join them. Her worry was that someone might talk.

Archibald had a second flip point, but while it was guarded, it didn't seem to get any use. That meant they could only use the main one in their ruse.

The probes that *Persephone* had sent earlier were keeping an eye out for any gap between ships that might give them the time to get close to position without being noticed by other vessels.

It wasn't as if freighters would be actively scanning for anything beyond debris avoidance. That would give them a window.

"What's our situation looking like for getting into the traffic pattern?" she asked Barnes.

He shook his head. "No openings large enough right now. We haven't been watching long enough to see if this is going to be constant or not. This is one of those things you can't rush, Commodore."

According to the plan, they'd edge as close to the traffic pattern as they could and wait for a suitable opening. When it came, they'd be able to make their way into the pattern and hopefully not draw any undue attention.

The main flip point had a battle station guarding it, but they didn't seem to be using it for traffic control. There was no sign of communication between the incoming ships and the battle station. The other side must be a trusted system.

Carl straightened abruptly at his console. "We might have a problem."

"What?" she said, a chill racing down her spine. They hadn't even been here long enough to settle in. What could possibly have gone wrong already?

"The probe at the main flip point just showed the arrival of half a dozen Rebel Empire Fleet warships. Two cruisers and four light cruisers. We have a second transit. Half a dozen destroyers. That makes a dozen enemy vessels."

That spelled trouble. Warships tended to be a little bit more observant. They might see something out of place when the freighter made its entrance. All it would take to ruin them was for someone to send over a boarding party to inspect their supposed cargo.

"What's their ETA to Archibald?" she asked.

The scientist shook his head, his face pale. "They're not headed for the planet. They've set course into the outer system. We need to reverse course, or we'll probably end up inside their detection range before they pass our location."

18

Kelsey examined the scanner intake through her implants as she sat down at the head of the small conference table aboard *Persephone*. The other senior members of her team began filing in moments later.

Talbot sat down beside her and took her hand. Not the most professional thing in the world, but she wasn't going to argue, squeezing back with a smile.

Carl Owlet, Commander Giguere, and Doctor Parker were next. Followed quickly by Zia Anderson and Cain Hopwood. The final two through the door were Doctor Zoboroski and Angela Ellis.

Well, she supposed that the final *person* wasn't actually there in the flesh. Fiona, the artificial sentience, was present in much the same way that Marcus was aboard *Invincible* for Jared.

Kelsey cleared her throat. "I'm sure by now that all of you are aware of why I've called you here. The Rebel Empire has invested the Archibald system with an additional dozen military vessels. We're not certain how many are already here, though we've detected some suspicious grav signatures.

"Two heavy cruisers, four light cruisers, and six destroyers entered through one of the two regular flip points a little bit more than an hour ago. That would be the flip point that has traffic. The other one is also guarded by a battle station but doesn't have ships coming through. The other side must not be occupied or along any major trade routes."

"Do we know what they're up to?" Angela asked. "The last I saw, it didn't look like they were headed toward Archibald Prime."

Kelsey shook her head. "They seem to be heading for the outer system."

"Is it possible they're searching for us?" Doctor Parker asked. "Could someone have detected our arrival?"

"It's always possible, but they don't seem to be looking for anyone. They're on a course that probably leads to the outermost gas giant. So far as we know, there are no facilities there, so I'm not sure what they're up to."

"Could it be the System Lord?" Veronica Giguere asked.

"Probably not," Carl said. "The AIs like being somewhat closer to the action than that. They like asteroid belts, if possible. The only known facility at a gas giant held reserve warships. Battlecruisers the AI could use in an emergency. It doesn't seem likely they are going to something like that, or it would ruin the secrecy."

"Is there any point in moving forward with the mission at this juncture?" Talbot asked. "If security is at a heightened state, it would be better to wait until things quiet down."

That left them all quiet for a few moments. Kelsey took advantage of that to lean forward and look around the table, capturing each of their gazes for a few seconds.

"I don't think slipping the freighter into place is going to be as much of a risk as you think. They're not going to be in range to detect us shortly. The one thing that we'll have to change is where we position *Persephone*. I don't believe that it's safe to leave my ship near the multiflip point now. We're going to have to take her deeper into the system."

Angela shook her head. "Anyone seeing a strange warship of a design they've never encountered before is going to sound the alarm. Once forces in the system get agitated, we're never going to escape. Or, if we do, we'll lead them right to the multiflip point, and that would be worse."

"I don't see that we have much of a choice." Kelsey rose to her feet and paced a little. "Also, the risk isn't nearly as significant as you might think. *Persephone* is designed to penetrate hostile systems without being detected.

"She's done similar things in the past, slipping up on Singularity warships without being noticed. Admittedly, that was before the Fall, but my people are up to the task. Ned Quincy saw to that."

Ned Quincy had been a Marine Raider before the Fall. In fact, he'd been the commanding officer aboard *Persephone* in those days. Fatally injured during one of the final fights, his crew had placed him in stasis. They hadn't survived the Fall, and neither had he.

Somehow—they still weren't quite sure how—Kelsey had brought many of the man's memories into her own implants and used software modified by Marcus to help sort through them. That had the unexpected side effect of creating an artificial intelligence inside her own implants.

Imperial theory said that wasn't possible. No one with any knowledge on the subject whatsoever could understand how it had happened, but it had. It wasn't the original Ned Quincy, but it had started life with many of his memories and experiences.

That gave Ned the ability and experience to train Kelsey's people in every aspect of what they needed to excel at operating a Marine Raider strike ship.

Before he'd gone to sleep and allowed Carl Owlet to extract him from Kelsey's implants, Ned had admitted to her that her crew was almost as good as his people had been. Almost, but not quite. They still needed to keep working hard if they wanted to be the best Marine Raider strike ship in Fleet.

And, of course, they needed to become Marine Raiders in truth. Angela had now been through the full conversion. The large woman still had weeks of workups and training before she was completely attuned with her new body, but she'd already proven she could take Kelsey in a full-on fight with no limitations one time out of three.

Give Angela a week, and she'd win every single fight. That annoyed Kelsey, but she'd known she wasn't a warrior. Angela had been fighting for the Empire her entire life, and she was so much *bigger* than Kelsey.

The only advantage Kelsey had in fighting the woman was her speed and experience. Sadly, that wouldn't be enough as Angela grew into her enhanced body.

That was one person. Talbot was next and then the rest of *Persephone*'s crew. There wasn't time to make it happen now. There wasn't even time to get it done over the next couple of months, not for the whole crew.

While she'd been reviewing her thoughts, the rest of them had been considering what she'd just said. No one seemed convinced, but in the end, that didn't really matter. She was in command, and she would make the final decision.

"Once the freighter is in orbit, the locals won't be paying it much attention so long as there is no unusual traffic to catch their eye. We should be able to get the people we need onto the orbital station without too much trouble. Once we have the lead team in place, we can get the rest of our folks aboard without taking that kind of risk."

Veronica Giguere frowned. "I'm not sure I follow. How will you get more people aboard without drawing attention?"

Kelsey smiled. "You haven't been completely briefed on some of the technological breakthroughs we have access to. Maybe we should take a couple of minutes to explain phase two of the plan. After all, Fiona has confirmed your loyalty. It's time to bring you all the way in."

* * *

VERONICA STARED at the massive ring they were assembling in the freighter's engineering compartment. Even after reviewing the recordings that Carl Owlet had made on board the alien station the New Terran Empire had discovered in the Nova system, she'd had difficulty believing this was even possible.

"I felt the same way," Doctor Parker said. The woman had been standing beside Veronica the last few minutes in silence.

She turned toward the research scientist. "This violates just about every concept I've ever had about how science works. Yes, flip points traverse great distances in the blink of an eye, but science can explain them. In general, anyway. Once you start getting into the specifics, only the experts really understand the science."

"Don't let them fool you. Even the experts really don't understand what's going on with them. Hence, the multiflip points and the far flip points. Imperial theory predicted neither of those two potentialities and no one noticed."

The older woman gestured toward the ring. "This is something completely different. Point-to-point matter transportation. Better yet, you can relocate the rings wherever you want within a short distance, and they still work. And yes, I'm calling five thousand kilometers a short distance. On the scale of flip points, that's nothing."

"How does it work?" Veronica asked. "How can it *possibly* work?"

Parker shrugged. "Not even Carl has managed to explain the science to me yet and he has all of the research that the Omega race compiled on the subject. There are a couple of barriers to understanding: first translating the original documents into Standard, then trying to get a grasp of both the science and manufacturing processes, and finally just getting a clue how they developed the science in the first place.

"This has to be connected in some way to their station in the Nova system. From what I understand, it's a transport ring taken to ludicrous extremes. One that doesn't need a matched pair which strongly implies the possibility that a ring this size could be used solo, though even the Omegans never cracked that mystery.

"The ring station originally tapped into the power of a star to create an opening into alternate realities. At least that's the story the alien tells. Somewhere in the theory for that lies the source of these transport rings."

Veronica could sort of see the connection. In a vague way.

"Do you think the transport rings came first?" she asked.

"Almost certainly. How an aquatic race ever developed this kind of manufacturing in the first place is beyond me. It seems extremely unlikely that they were able to work metal in an ocean. For the life of me, I don't understand how they became technological at all.

"Carl tells me that the alien gave him a set of disks made of some crystalline substance and a reader to pull the data off of them. Supposedly those discs contain the entirety of the knowledge of the alien race. That's a lot of data to parse.

"He's been working on some type of hybrid reader that could pull data off of the discs and put it directly into our computer mediums, but he hasn't quite gotten it worked out yet."

Veronica considered that for a long while in silence. "Those can't have been the only magnificent scientific breakthroughs that people made. Just to get to the point of creating a station that could use the power of a star to explore other realities would have to mean any number of tremendous breakthroughs that came before it.

"Hell, even the concept of alternate realities makes my brain spin. Are we talking about places where there are copies of you and me? Realities that one couldn't tell the difference between ours and theirs? Ones where humanity never developed? Universes inimical to all life?"

Parker nodded. "All of those and more besides. Considering the power requirements, I'd wager that no trans-universal gates will be created anytime soon, but the Omega station created a pair of brand-new flip points between the Nova system and two other systems: Pentagar and Avalon. Permanent flip points."

The thought of that kind of power frightened Veronica. The Omega race was so much further advanced than humanity that they could've crushed it, had the timelines matched up and they been so inclined. With enough time, the New Terran Empire could develop a level of technological power to bring the Rebel Empire to its knees.

If they had enough time to make it work.

Veronica considered Doctor Parker. "You're being friendlier than I would've expected, Doctor. I appreciate the courtesy."

The older woman smiled slightly. "I've had some time to think. While you might have served the Rebel Empire and the AIs, you've got the moral backbone to stand up to them. If you're going to leave your entire life behind to stand beside me, the least I can do is try to be civil."

"I appreciate that," Veronica said sincerely. "This is all so strange to me and my people, but we want to do the right thing. We need to correct the wrongs we've been allowing to occur through inaction. I believe there are plenty of others inside the Rebel Empire that would do the exact same if they only knew the truth."

Somewhat hesitantly, Doctor Parker reached up and put a hand on Veronica's shoulder. "The time is coming for an open conflict between the New Terran Empire and the Rebel Empire. You're going to have a chance to tell your story and be heard by millions."

Veronica frowned slightly. "What do you mean?"

"When the fighting starts, they're going to need people to tell the worlds that fall under the sway of the New Terran Empire exactly what's been going on. Who better to do that than someone from the Rebel Empire? Someone like you."

After staring at the scientist for a few seconds, Veronica felt her stomach give a slow roll. "I'm not much of a public speaker. I kind of have issues with that."

Parker grinned. "We all have our burdens to bear, Commander. I'm sure you'll do fine."

19

Talbot stood just behind Carl as his friend worked over the scanner console on *Persephone*'s bridge. Under Kelsey's direction, the Marine Raider strike ship had slipped farther into the Archibald system. The freighter trailed them at a safe distance, ready to retreat if an enemy ship came too close.

The Rebel Empire warships had continued on their way toward the outermost gas giant. To the best of their detection ability, the warships didn't even make contact with the station or shipyard orbiting Archibald.

In another stroke of good luck, once the warships had come through the main flip point, there was a gap of several hours before the next merchant ship had transited. With a little adroit maneuvering, it would be possible to insert their freighter into the traffic pattern with no one being the wiser.

The probes they'd seeded throughout the system had detected no transmissions from the battle station at the designated flip point, so there should be no record of which ships were expected to arrive at Archibald Prime. All the approvals had to have happened earlier in the journey.

Kelsey had launched a number of stealth probes to examine Archibald Prime from several vantage points. Her goal was to determine what assets were already in orbit and how they could be accessed, if need be.

The shipyard was the largest structure orbiting Archibald's moon and easily dwarfed the yards they'd seized in the Erorsi system when they'd captured it. It even topped the ones they were building back in the New Terran Empire by a good margin.

He wondered how many other yards like this existed inside the Rebel Empire. If there were similar ones in every major system, they could collectively produce a lot of ships in a relatively short period of time. That was bad news.

Still, there had been no yards at Harrison's World, so they couldn't be everywhere. Paranoia was only a good thing when taken so far.

The station in orbit around Archibald wasn't in the same league as the massive shipbuilding structure. It was comparable to Orbital One back home, so that was still saying something. He wondered why it was in planetary orbit but the shipyard was circling the moon. Wouldn't it make more sense to have them closer together?

Carl grunted and tapped his console, expanding a window. It looked like the passive scanner feed of the distant warships.

"What have you got, buddy?" he asked softly.

The other man turned in his seat and faced him. "All twelve of the enemy ships really are heading for the outermost gas giant. The question in my mind is, why? Are they heading to a secret station with battlecruisers like we found near Harrison's World? If so, what's driving them? They're supposed to be a deep, dark secret."

"I know we said that the AI would be closer in, but what if it's not?" Talbot asked. "Maybe they positioned this one way out there."

"That just doesn't make any sense. The communications lag would be big. Even with their normal positioning in an asteroid belt, that introduces a significant lag. This would be unworkable."

The young scientist turned his seat toward Talbot. "Whatever they're doing, it has to be something with the station holding the battlecruisers. That's going to impact our mission. The raid was risky before, but the odds of the Rebel Empire Fleet directly intervening had just gotten a whole lot worse."

Talbot considered that and then nodded slowly. "Agreed, but it doesn't change anything. Kelsey is still going forward with the plan. We both know that. Can you redirect an FTL probe to keep an eye on them?"

"Already done," Carl said with a nod. "I have several moving out that way slowly, so they won't reach the gas giant today. They'll arrive sometime tomorrow and start using their passive scanners to gather data. I programmed them to send their take every six hours with some randomization thrown in to keep any observers from detecting a pattern in the grav pulses."

"I know you keep saying the FTL coms are detectable, but realistically, how serious a risk is that?"

The scientist shrugged. "It's a low-order probability. The pulses are weak, and so long as they are kept brief, isolating exactly where they're coming from would be difficult. Just pulling them out of the background noise in a system this big would be a challenge.

"I'm taking extra precautions in having more than one probe watch the gas giant. Two will be in orbit around it and two others will be a long distance away. The close ones will use regular tight beams to get the data to the outer probes and only when the gas giant is between those and the targets will the distant probes use FTL coms."

"We should do something similar near the Archibald Station and the yard, just in case," Talbot said. "We could talk to *Persephone* and give Angela updates via tight beam. She wouldn't be able to return the favor, but something is better than nothing."

Carl nodded. "Already done. And if push comes to shove, we have a couple of FTL coms we can use to talk to her directly. Those are a last resort sort of thing, but if we don't have them, we might desperately need them."

"We'll need self-destructs on those. We can't let the Rebel Empire know about FTL."

"Already done. There's a plasma grenade in each that can be set on a timer, manually detonated instantly, or remotely set off just like the ones we've built into the rings. Princess Kelsey, you, and anyone you designate will have the codes to make it happen."

Talbot really hoped they didn't have to destroy the rings. They were priceless and irreplaceable.

Still, they'd gotten away with using them once already. The odds were against them this time and, if push came to shove, he'd destroy the rings to keep the Rebel Empire from getting their hands on the alien tech. Or even grasping what they could do, if he could.

"It would suck if we have to destroy the rings," he said after a moment. "I know we have the plans to build them, but that isn't likely to happen in the short term, is it?"

"No," Carl said with a shake of his head. "We're still designing the tools to build the machines that can start setting up other machines that can make the parts for the rings. They are easily a year or two out. Further if we run into problems, which is inevitable since we don't understand the theory completely."

"We'll plan as best we can and hope it doesn't come to that."

Carl laughed a tad bitterly. "We got lucky last time so I'm not holding my breath. Keep your options open and save the small ring, if you can."

"I'll try, buddy. I really will."

He knew that didn't mean much if things went bad, but he'd do his best to leave them with options when the time came.

* * *

Eighteen hours later, Zia was back at the command console on the freighter. Enough of a gap had developed in the flow of ships from the main flip point to Archibald Prime that they could slip into the pattern without raising any eyebrows.

Unfortunately, their time of anonymity was at an end. According to the data their probes had gathered, the freighter was just about at the range where traffic control would contact them.

If she said something wrong, there was no way the freighter could get back to the multiflip point without being intercepted. Worse, she couldn't even try, or they might find it. Everything had to go perfectly, or they were screwed.

"We have an incoming signal, Commodore," Alan Barnes said from the helm console. "It's traffic control."

"Call me Zia. One slip now and some very bad things will start happening."

The man nodded. "Got it. Sorry. You want this on the main screen?"

"Give it to me on my console."

Moments later, the image of a man in a Fleet uniform with lieutenant's tabs appeared. His expression seemed bored to her. Good.

"This is Archibald Control," he said, his voice monotone. "I need your port of origin, manifest, and the names of any shipping companies you're doing business with."

Their knowledge of Rebel Empire trade was somewhat short of minuscule, but they'd hit pay dirt looking at the computer records on board this freighter. While the data wasn't going to be useful for specifics, it gave them the appropriate format for such files and recordings of many communications just like this one.

"Sending now," Zia said, adding a somewhat sour note to her tone. "I hope this isn't going to be the same kind of cluster we had a couple of stops back. We just want to see what goods you have available and blow off a little steam. We don't have any cargo destined for Archibald."

The man nodded absently and studied the screen off to his left. "If you're not off-loading, we don't have to bother with a customs inspection. Just the usual ID checks to get on the station. I'll send you parking instructions. Welcome to Archibald."

The screen went dark and Zia sagged a little. "I was afraid that wouldn't be good enough for them. Get us into our spot, Alan. I'll go brief everyone."

The bridge was too small for every interested party to be there. In fact, if they'd had to use the main screen, the presence of any extra people would've seemed odd. That meant Princess Kelsey and the others were in a makeshift conference room nearby.

Zia rose to her feet and quickly made her way back. Everyone looked expectantly toward her as she stepped into the compartment.

"So far, so good. We won't have any customs officials coming our way, and they've given us a parking orbit. They'll be expecting some of us on the station, so we'll see how good our identification is. I'm not expecting them to be all that thorough unless we have to go down to the surface."

Talbot smiled a little at that. "As Carl says, show them what they expect to see, and they won't ask any questions."

"That's not what I say," Carl protested mildly. "Weren't you listening? People see what they expect to see. As long as you don't give them a reason to question their initial impressions, they won't change them."

Veronica frowned at Carl. "That seems like a very unscientific sort of thing to say. Or maybe it's just unusual for a scientist to be saying it."

The young man grinned at her. "I've had some interesting teachers."

Princess Kelsey rapped her knuckles on the table. "Focus, people. This completes step one of our plan. We're in a position to start scouting the station. From there, we have to figure out a way to get over to the shipyard. I'm certain they have some kind of regular transport, but Fleet is going to be paying attention to the people that are on it.

"Some of us are going to have to start looking over the medical research facility too. Based on what Commodore Murdoch said, it's located here on this station. That's going to make it easier to access, but there will undoubtedly be issues with timing between the two operations.

"The people looking into the research facility won't be able to act until we have what we need from the shipyard, but they'll have to know for certain if anything warrants our attention before then. If there's not, then we're not going to break in."

"But we won't know what they have *unless* we break in," Carl objected. "So we kind of have to halfway break in? Break in and then break back out? Something like that."

The princess smiled. "That's going to be up to you to figure out. It's entirely possible that you, Doctor Parker, and her computer specialist can break in remotely and ransack their files. If so, that makes our job a lot easier."

Doctor Parker shook her head. "Research facilities keep their classified data on disconnected systems. We're not going to be able to find out what projects they're working on without getting physical access."

"Maybe. Maybe not. Keep in mind that this isn't like the research you were doing, Doctor. These folks might have communications that mention what their projects are. If we can find any evidence of an advanced regeneration device, then we'll have to proceed. Otherwise, the secondary mission is still discretionary."

Zia smiled at Kelsey. "Since they've seen my face, I think it might be best if I'm one of the ones that goes on board station to get us some temporary housing."

Kelsey nodded. "Take Commander Giguere with you. The two of you can look around for suitable housing and get a read on what we're dealing with."

"We'll make it happen."

She wondered how much gray hair she was going to have by the time this mission was over. Being among the enemy for any kind of extended period of time was going to be nerve-racking. Well, she'd just have to make sure no one slipped up.

20

While Veronica might never have been aboard Archibald Station, she'd visited plenty of orbitals like it over the years. Coming as a civilian, she discovered, was significantly different than how it had been as part of Fleet.

The docking bays in the civilian section were significantly busier than the ones in the military areas she'd visited, the crowds more chaotic, and the people more varied. Especially in the clothing they wore. It seemed every color imaginable was represented in some form.

Including some in eye-searing fluorescent shades that almost hurt to look at.

There was also more shouting than she was used to. People unloading various cargo shuttles all seemingly had something to say to one another at the top of their lungs. It was kind of weird how many emotions could be carried from person to person at maximum volume.

Zia Anderson stepped out and put her hands on her hips as she looked over the bay. "It's just like back home."

Veronica turned her head slightly toward the other woman and raised an eyebrow. "I'm surprised you had this much chaos at your previous job. If it was anything like mine, it was a lot more orderly."

The taller woman laughed. "I had a life before that job, you know. My parents were merchant spacers. I've probably seen a dozen bays just like this before I became an adult. I never would've thought it would be so similar. Where are we going to get housing while we're here? Any ideas?"

Rather than answering the question, Veronica stepped over to a pair of men arguing over a crate. She wasn't sure if they were disputing the ownership or just the disposition, but they were enthusiastic in their posturing.

"Hey, boys," she said. "We're new. Where can some of our crew hole up without spending all our cash? We'd rather be drinking."

The men paused their heated discussion, and one of them pointed down a nearby corridor. "Go straight down that. Past the third cross corridor you'll find Statler's. It's not the bottom of the pile or the top, so it should suit you just fine."

Without waiting for a response from her, they resumed their argument as if she'd never interrupted them.

Zia laughed as the two women stepped into the indicated corridor. "That went a little bit easier than I'd expected. Good thinking."

"Why make it hard?" Veronica asked with a shrug. "Everybody in this bay has been the new guy at some point. Asking for directions isn't going to raise any eyebrows.

"We should keep that in mind going forward. The more we behave like everyone else, the less we'll stand out. The goal is to blend into the crowd so thoroughly that no one remembers us once we've left."

It only took them a couple of minutes to find Statler's. As the man had said, it wasn't much to look at, but it wasn't a dive either.

Veronica took the lead as they stepped inside and headed toward a short, balding man sitting behind a relatively tall counter.

"One room or two?" he asked disinterestedly.

"We're acting as point for our crew, so do you have a dozen rooms available? If so, how much for the block? We like them close together since we're a tight-knit bunch."

The man nodded, showing some interest for the first time, and tapped a couple of keys on the small computer built into the counter. "How long you plan to stay?"

She shrugged. "Depends on how fast we find what we need. Might be a couple of days. Might be as much as a week. Hard to say at this point."

"The weekly rate might suit you better, then. If I charge you by the day and you extend, you're going to pay more for that same stretch of time. If you book the week and leave in a couple of days, I'll cut you a bit of a break."

The price he quoted wasn't too outrageous, so Veronica paid it. Thankfully, the New Terran Empire had a good supply of Rebel Empire money. That was going to come in handy during this mission, she was sure.

People kept wondering why money never went fully digital, but she knew the answer. So that folks could make payments like this without showing up on any electronic record.

If there'd been some kind of digital credit, there'd be a trail to follow. By paying cash, no one would figure out where they'd come from or where they'd gone. Or what they'd paid for while they were here.

They went up to check the rooms after the man had given them the keys. A quick tour of each confirmed that they were of adequate quality. Not top-of-the-line but certainly not the worst she'd ever seen. They'd do.

Their block of rooms sat at the end of a hall, and Zia pointed toward one of the rooms at the very far side. "We'll take that one."

It was a fairly standard sort of place with two smaller beds. They were still larger than what Veronica was used to, though.

"Sounds good," she said. "We'd best go get our bags and signal the rest to start coming over."

Their good luck lasted almost all the way back to the shuttle. A pair of men in security uniforms came out of the bay just as they were about to enter. Veronica thought they were going to walk past and moved to the side, but one of the men intentionally singled her out and blocked her passage.

"Identification," he demanded, his hand extended.

Crap. Well, it looked as if she was about to find out how well the New Terran Empire could forge identity documents. If hers didn't pass muster, this mission was in very deep trouble and so was she.

* * *

Kelsey stared at herself in the mirror, somewhat amazed at her transformation. To match the appearance of the dead Rebel Empire Fleet commander she was impersonating, Kelsey had allowed Angela to cut her hair into a bob and color it an almost midnight black.

She'd also allowed her large friend to apply makeup in the same style as some of the images that they'd found on the wall in the woman's office. Kelsey was no stranger to makeup, but she tended to use it in such a way as to enhance her light complexion and golden hair.

The dead woman had favored a stronger hand. More makeup and in stronger colors to contrast her dark hair. Definitely not Kelsey's style.

To her annoyance, Talbot seemed intrigued. He walked around her, examining her new looks closely.

"I have to say, this is quite a change. You look a bit… dangerous."

"I'm always a bit dangerous, and it's not my looks that are turning you on. It's what you saw in that woman's closet. Which, by the way, I'm *still* not wearing."

Her husband laughed. "It doesn't matter what you wear or, for that matter, don't wear. I'll love you just the same. Still, you can't stop me from imagining you dressed like that. I think you'd be exceptionally sexy. Not that you aren't already exceptionally sexy."

"You're not helping yourself," she growled playfully. "Tell you what. If we get out of this place with everything we need, I'll let you pick something from the stash for me to wear."

"Talk about motivation. Now I'm going to move Heaven and Earth to get what we need. Which, of course, I was going to do anyway."

He stepped back after giving her a quick kiss and examined the uniform hanging from a hook nearby. It was a Rebel Empire Fleet uniform with commander's tabs. They'd had it made special for this mission based on Veronica Giguere's own uniform.

"Do you think you're going to need this? I thought we were leaving the shipyard portion of this to Zia and Veronica."

Kelsey slid an arm around his waist and stared at the uniform. "I'm still not sure. It's possible we'll stay in civilian clothes the entire time. It's better to have it and not need it than to need it and not have it."

She sighed. "I know it's just a disguise, but it feels dirty dressing up like that woman. Not as in the sexy kind of dirty, but the kind you can't scrub off. She was a vile human. How can someone like that have gotten into a senior position inside the Rebel Empire's version of Fleet?"

Talbot squeezed her back for a moment and then released her. "Their version of Fleet isn't really designed the same way ours is. Superficially, it looks the same, but it's not. The New Terran Empire's version is there to protect us from any threat. That woman's version was meant to suppress humanity.

"Even though the lowest ranks don't know what the System Lords really are, the personalities of the senior officers define everything about how Fleet operates. Those people are like a distorted mirror version of the folks you know. Evil."

She almost asked how something like that could operate for even just a little while, but she already knew the answer. She'd heard Olivia West describe the Fleet presence on Harrison's World. Talbot was right. They were oppressors, not defenders.

Not that there weren't some good apples in the bunch. Olivia's dead fiancé, for example, or Captain Black, the man in charge of the Grant Research Facility. But they were the exceptions rather than the rule.

In her Fleet, the percentages were reversed. They had plenty of great people and just a few bad ones like Wallace Breckenridge. Thank God.

She shook off her bad mood. "I'm tired of waiting. We haven't heard anything negative from Zia, so let's go over now."

"I don't think we should do anything until we hear from her," he objected. "No signal might mean that someone's captured them. After all, it's not like they can use their implants without giving themselves away. They're in stealth mode. Any signal at all might blow their covers."

"They have coms," she countered. "All they have to do is signal the shuttle, and it will retransmit something to us. They have a panic button too. If they're about to be captured, they wouldn't hesitate to hit it.

"No. They haven't run into significant trouble at this point, and I'm tired of sitting around doing nothing. If we're not relocating now, we will be shortly. Let's get everyone together and head over. With the enemy warships in the system, we can't afford to waste any time."

"I think this is a really bad idea, but I know that arguing with you isn't going to help," he muttered. "For safety's sake, I think we should take two more of the cargo shuttles over to the orbital. That way if something happens, maybe some of us can get away."

Kelsey knew that wasn't really an option. If the Rebel Empire discovered who they were, the freighter wouldn't escape.

"We can hope," she said softly. "Once we get onto the orbital, I'll send a message to Zia and get a status from her. Make sure that Carl has the special cargo ready to go. I don't want us to have to come back for anything. If we might need it, I'd rather have it with us. Any unnecessary movement could draw unwanted attention."

Following her own advice, Kelsey slipped her uniform into a clothing bag and grabbed what she intended to take with her. If things went badly, it wouldn't matter, so she had to plan for things to go well.

They *had* to go well. She wasn't going to let everyone down like that. She'd make this work or die trying.

21

Zia forced herself not to tense. The Rebel Empire was filled with paranoid people, and identification checks were probably standard procedure.

Veronica dug her forged ID out of her vest pocket and handed it to the security man. His eyes scanned it before looking back up at the other woman.

"I don't recognize your ship's name," he said. "What does *Squared Circle* mean anyway?"

The former Rebel Empire Fleet commander shrugged. "I didn't name the damn ship, so I have no idea. We're just looking for cargo and want to have a good time before we head back out. What needs to happen to make sure our friendly visit stays friendly?"

The security man smiled. "Isn't that what everyone wants? I can arrange for security to leave you and your crew alone, but it's going to cost you."

He named a price. It seemed to be a fairly reasonable rate. Not that Zia was all that familiar with bribes.

She had to admit that she was surprised at how blatant the exchange of money for protection was. It was carried out like a straightforward business transaction.

"What's your name?" Veronica asked as she dug the money out and handed it over. "If someone gets too pushy, I want to know who to refer them to."

"Alden Stoffel. I'll put the word out. If someone gives you trouble, it's because you're doing something you shouldn't. Behave, and everyone will come out of this happy. Understand?"

Veronica nodded. "Pleasure doing business with you."

The two security men resumed their journey into the orbital, and Zia followed Veronica back to their cargo shuttle. Once they were safely inside, she turned to the other woman and raised an eyebrow.

"Is that common? I have to say that's not how things work in the New Terran Empire. At least I hope not."

The news seemed to surprise Veronica. "Really? How do you make sure security doesn't harass you or stick their noses in where they shouldn't?"

"Our security officers stick their noses in the things that are actually business related as opposed to extorting protection money."

"What a strange place your Empire must be," Veronica mused. "It's the cost of doing business here. They have to deliver on the protection, or word gets out, and the payments dry up. The less scrupulous ones get dealt with by their comrades."

Zia didn't know what to say. Their worlds were so different.

"I hope you'll get to find out just how different our world is soon. It's going to be an adjustment, I'd imagine."

"It sure sounds like it. Now that we have the rooms set aside, do we call everyone over?"

Zia nodded. "Shockingly, it seems as if it might be relatively safe to do just that. Especially since you just paid to make sure we weren't harassed. Maybe that'll help us get the gear to the rooms without being searched."

"From what I understand, there are only a few bulky pieces," Veronica said, her tone indicating agreement. "Those might be a little more troublesome but nothing we can't handle so long as we act casually.

"The first step is getting them onto the station and organizing the trip from the bay to Statler's. We'll send out scouts to make sure we don't get stopped by security."

The cargo shuttle's com chimed. Zia hoped it wasn't anything bad as she went to the cockpit and pressed the accept button.

"Zia."

There hadn't been much call to use fake names. It wasn't as if the Rebel Empire knew who they were.

"There you are," Kelsey said. "I got tired of waiting. We have two shuttles making the trip now. We'll be in the bay in a couple of minutes. We brought all the gear we discussed. Did you get us rooms? Better yet, did you find a bar?"

Zia smiled. Some of that was choreographed because they knew that others could be listening in. Probably would be.

"Of course I did. The rooms are all reserved, and we're back at our shuttle. As soon as you land, we'll get everything back to the place we rented, and then we can see about that bar."

"Excellent. You haven't had any trouble, I take it?"

"Nothing we couldn't handle. I let Veronica take lead, and she did a great job. We'll meet you by the bay exit in fifteen minutes. Hope you're ready to relax."

Kelsey laughed. "You have no idea. See you in fifteen."

Zia pressed the button to end the call and headed back to the main part of the cargo shuttle. "Kelsey and the rest will be here in a couple of minutes. I'm not going to feel safe until we have everything in the rooms. Do we need to worry about security searching our quarters? Some of the stuff we're bringing would get a lot of negative attention."

Weapons, high-tech gear to break and enter, specialized computers for hacking, and the small transport ring. Any of that would set security's hair on fire.

"They shouldn't," Veronica said. "We'll just keep our heads down and move forward with the plan."

Fifteen minutes later, Zia spotted Princess Kelsey leading a small crowd of almost two dozen people. A couple of them were moving a trolley with a couple of small crates, and everyone had packs just like the ones Veronica and she had retrieved from the shuttle.

Kelsey looked stunningly different. The shorter, darker hair and more pronounced makeup, combined with a sterner expression on her face, really did make the princess look like a stranger.

That didn't stop the small woman from giving her a hug as soon as they came together. "I was worried you wouldn't get everything set up by the time we arrived. I kind of jumped the gun."

Zia eyed the crates that Carl was hovering near. "We need to get these back to the rooms as soon as possible. Veronica made an arrangement with security to leave us unmolested, but I'm not sure that taking crates into the station won't get someone's attention.

"Veronica and some of our people are going to spread out and keep an eye out for security. If they spot someone, they'll signal us and we'll find a place to loiter until the course is clear. We probably should have someone trail along behind us just to make sure some enthusiastic security team doesn't come running up on us."

"Excellent idea," the princess agreed. "Let's get moving."

Veronica quickly conferred with the people assigned to scout. They spread out and headed into the station. A minute later, the main group moved to follow.

Zia was starting to relax when she spotted movement out of the corner of her eye. A couple of women exiting one of the restaurants near the cargo bay. Both wore lanyards that indicated they worked in the cargo bay.

It seemed as if they would walk into the bay without comment until one of them stopped and glared at Carl. "Hey! Where are you going with that? Has it been checked? Let me see your papers."

Oh crap.

* * *

TALBOT DIDN'T GIVE Carl a chance to respond. Before the young scientist could say a single word, the marine inserted himself between the two women and the crates.

"These were already cleared," he said smoothly. "There's no need for any trouble."

The woman who'd demanded the papers glared up at him. "I decide if there's going to be trouble. No taking cargo out of the bay without the appropriate clearance. Moving anything onto the station itself requires an examination."

He glared at her. "And who exactly are you? So far as I know, you're just some idiot trying to cause me trouble. And good luck talking yourself out of that category."

The woman bristled even more at his words. She grabbed the badge hanging from her lanyard and shoved it into his face.

"Associate Supervisor Marya Franzen, cargo control. You either trot out your paperwork, or I call security. I can tell you right now, your attitude is going to cost you."

He saw that Kelsey was about to step forward and insert herself into the conversation, but Zia beat her to it. The commodore extended some folded paper toward the supervisor.

"Sorry about that," she said, her tone bored. "He's new. Here's the paperwork. I think you'll find everything in order."

To Talbot's amazement, the folded paper turned out to be money. His friend was trying to bribe their way out of trouble. And not subtly, either. Right out there for everyone around them to see!

He waited for the supervisor to start shouting for security, but all she did was count the money and make a gesture for more. "This is light, and your mouthy friend just cost you even more. Take it out of his pay."

Zia counted out more money and handed it over.

The woman pocketed it and gestured for her companion to follow her as they departed toward the cargo bay.

Talbot watch them go in stunned amazement. Then he turned his attention to his friend.

"What the hell was that? Better yet, how could that *possibly* have worked?"

Kelsey waived a hand between Zia and him. "It doesn't matter right now. We need to get these crates out of sight. Pick up the pace a little, but don't be obvious about it."

Even though he was certain security would pounce on them before they arrived at their lodgings, Zia led them to a place called Statler's without trouble.

Only once they had the crates locked up in Carl's room did Talbot start to relax even a little bit. This was crazy. What had just happened? Time for some answers.

He found Zia in one of the rooms at the end of the hall with Veronica, Kelsey, and Doctor Parker. He walked right up to her and fixed her with a scowl.

"Have you gone insane? Offering bribes to an official? She could've turned us in. Second, how the hell do you know how to bribe anyone?"

The flag officer smiled a little and inclined her head toward Veronica. "I have to admit that I was just as skeptical as you were, until I saw Veronica bribe security to leave us alone. Apparently, that's a thing here. If you want to get anything done, you have to be a little free with the cash.

"Thankfully, the behavior is so prevalent that no one bats an eye when you offer them money to bend the rules. In fact, it seems to be expected."

She turned to fully face Veronica. "Is my understanding correct? Even for things that are supposed to be perfectly legal, adding cash to the equation is expected?"

The Rebel Empire Fleet commander nodded. "It's part of the cost of doing business. People along the chain of whatever you're doing expect to get a gratuity for doing their work. If you want them to step outside the bounds of what's normal, the required gratuity gets larger.

"From what I understand, Zia did exactly the right thing. That person wanted money in order to allow a violation to occur. You gave her what she wanted, and she went on her way with no one being the wiser. Excellent work."

Kelsey shook her head. "I don't think I'm ever going to understand the Rebel Empire. Some of this behavior makes my head spin. Still, I have to say I'm glad you were able to think on your feet, Zia. Allow me to second Veronica. Excellent work."

Talbot wasn't sure about that, but what was done was done. He checked the chronometer set into the desk. "It looks like it's fairly late here on the station. We should probably take the opportunity to get something to eat before we get down to really planning out what we need to do tomorrow.

"I'm sure this place is busy during the evenings and night, but we have a better chance going unnoticed if we do what we need to do during normal business hours. Frankly, it's been a stressful couple of days. We need to make sure we stay rested."

Kelsey nodded. "And as usual, I'm starving. Let's see if we can find a place to eat and bring something back for those of us that are staying here to guard the equipment."

Talbot was in favor of food and sleep. The stress of sneaking to Archibald Station and getting aboard had exhausted him. He needed to have his head about him tomorrow. That's when the real fun started.

22

By the time Kelsey led the majority of the team out to find a local eatery, it was what she'd have called deep evening back on Avalon. In fact, most working people they'd seen earlier were probably at home now.

That didn't mean there were no restaurants open. The station had people working in shifts at all hours, and they needed to eat. Finding something interesting was as simple as walking a few hundred meters down the main corridor.

Carmona's purported to be something called Italian food. Kelsey checked her implants and found a reference to a region of old Terra. Apparently, it used to be quite favored in dining. Somehow, it had died off on Avalon, and thus the New Terran Empire had no record of it.

That wasn't to say that things like spaghetti and meatballs were unknown. They just weren't attached to the name 'Italian food.' Or to the other dishes on the menu, most of which meant nothing to her. Thankfully, there were pictures and short descriptions that allowed the diner to determine what they wanted to try.

She settled on something called lasagna. The server suggested fried mozzarella sticks as an appetizer, so Kelsey ordered enough for the entire group.

While they couldn't exactly discuss business out in public, they nibbled around the edges of what their plans would be during the next day.

Zia and Veronica would probe how difficult it was going to be to get over to the shipyard. Talbot, Doctor Parker, and she would scope out the research facility. Carl would be working remotely to see if he could get into the less secure sections of the computer network here on the station.

The fried mozzarella was good, but the lasagna was divine. The meat sauce gave it a spicy flavor that she immediately adored, and who didn't love cheese? Each table had breadsticks with some type of garlic flavoring that perfectly complemented the meal, particularly when dipped into something called alfredo sauce.

Once she'd finished devouring her main dish, she picked up a dessert menu and scanned it. So many options. There was one consisting of some squares of dough fried like donuts that could be dipped into chocolate sauce. It looked as if one order were meant to feed three or four people, but she selfishly ordered one just for herself.

Completely stuffed when she polished off the last square, Kelsey leaned back in her chair. "Somebody make sure Carl gets recipes for all of this stuff. The people back home have no idea what they're missing. We owe it to them to correct that great injustice."

Her husband laughed. "Be truthful. You just want all of this for yourself."

"Hell yes, but don't be petty. Everyone can revel in my victory."

"So in the most general sense, what are we expecting to accomplish tomorrow?" Talbot asked, his smile fading somewhat. "Do we think we'll get access to the medical facility? Will we get aboard the shipyard? How quickly are we expecting to execute?"

Kelsey double-checked to make sure no one was close enough to hear their murmured conversation. She also had her implants tag the locations of all the servers and started keeping a close eye on any coming toward them.

Veronica shook her head. "I don't imagine it's going to be easy to get onto the shipyard, but it's not solely a Fleet installation. It shouldn't be impossible."

"Getting into the computer system on the station shouldn't prove difficult," Carl said, dabbing his napkin at his lips. "The firewalls at the research facility will be another story. Until we get established in the general network, I'm not going to be able to guess at how long it will take to get in, if I can get in at all."

"And we don't dare try to physically enter the medical facility until we know we have to," Talbot said firmly. "A place like that is going to take a very dim view of people just wandering in."

Kelsey didn't disagree, but they were on a relatively tight schedule. With the arrival of the Rebel Empire warships, she really wanted to be gone by the time they finished whatever they were doing.

No matter how well they executed their raid on the shipyard, word was going to get out before their freighter could leave the system. That was an almost certainty. The same was true of an incursion at the medical research facility.

The best they could hope for was to sow enough confusion once they'd completed their initial moves that the locals didn't know what exactly had happened or who was responsible. They'd eventually figure it out, but the more time that took, the better.

Once the locals started going through the records on the battle station, they'd realize the freighter that Kelsey had brought had never actually entered the system. It had simply appeared there, and it was going to vanish in the same way. There was no way they'd miss that, but there was nothing she could do to fix that.

"Tomorrow is scouting day," Kelsey said. "Everyone is going to have to be careful how they approach anyone. Until we're ready to act, I'd rather not raise any suspicions.

"Until then, let's just focus on the pleasant evening ahead of us. We can rest a little easier tonight. Well done, people. And we can even order desserts to take back with us."

That made everyone laugh.

She was still smiling at her own joke—which really wasn't a joke—when a large group of men and women came through the front door to the restaurant and were seated nearby. They looked like a gaggle of low-to-mid-ranking Fleet officers, ranging from a single lieutenant commander down to a trio of ensigns.

Kelsey was about to call for the check when she realized the lieutenant commander was staring at them with a puzzled expression on his face. That's when she saw Veronica Giguere stiffen slightly out of the corner of her eye.

Oh crap. Something was going sideways. That man knew Veronica. Kelsey was certain of it. He hadn't placed her yet, but they'd met.

Things were about to get ugly.

* * *

VERONICA only barely stopped herself from flinching when she recognized Lieutenant Commander Don Sommerville. It was far too late for her to conceal her presence. He was staring *right* at her.

She considered trying to bluff her way out of the situation but instantly rejected the idea. He'd known her for years. There was absolutely no way she was going to fool him. If she tried pretending to be someone else, he'd see through her act and his suspicions would be raised even higher.

Since she couldn't avoid the impending meeting, she decided to embrace it. With a brief prayer to the gods, she deactivated the stealth mode on her implants. If he checked her, she didn't dare turn up blank. That would raise questions they couldn't afford.

With that thought in mind, she sent a message to Princess Kelsey and Zia Anderson.

Activate your implants with your cover identities. Our first test is upon us.

Sommerville was already heading their way, so she rose and came out to meet him.

"Don," she said warmly. "I never expected to see you here. How have you been?"

He took her hand and shook it with a friendly grin. "I could say the same. I've been good. Just transferred in. What brings you to Archibald?"

Veronica smiled but shook her head slightly. "I'm not allowed to get into the details because of operational security. This is a stopping point on the way to where the Lords have tasked us with accomplishing something, so even though I'm not actively on that mission right now, I'm not allowed to talk about it."

A convenient lie. Very convenient.

She turned to face her new friends, pleased to see that no one had stricken looks on their faces. Of course, a few of them looked a little strained, but the main players seemed unruffled.

"Everyone, allow me to introduce Don Sommerville. He was the tactical officer on the heavy cruiser where I was first posted as an executive officer."

Once everyone had murmured their greetings, Veronica gestured toward Princess Kelsey. "Don, this is Captain Diane Delatorre. She's actually in charge of the excursion I was referring to."

They'd decided to give Princess Kelsey's cover identity a promotion. One step in rank would raise no eyebrows if someone checked. People often got promoted, and it took a while for the news to work its way through the system.

Kelsey extended her hand and rose to her feet. "It's a pleasure to meet you, Commander."

"The pleasure's all mine, ma'am," Don responded politely.

"And this is Commander Cordia Kellett, her exec," Veronica finished. "I'm number three this time around."

"Commander," Don said, shaking Zia's hand. "I didn't intend to disrupt your meal, but I was so shocked to see someone I knew. It's always hard when you're posted to a new sector. You never know anyone, so running into a familiar face was unexpected."

"I understand completely," Kelsey said. "It's happened to me too. I wish we had time to stay and talk longer, but even though we aren't in the mission's operation area, we still have a lot of planning to do.

"That said, we'll be here on the station for at least a few days more. You and Veronica could catch up. If, of course, your ship is going to be here for a bit."

Don laughed a little. "My ship isn't going anywhere. I've been assigned to the shipyard to work in the Fleet section. While the yard does mostly civilian work, it has a few of our ships under construction there and others undergoing refit."

He gave Veronica a wide grin. "If you're going to be around for a bit, I'd love to have dinner. Also, if any of you would like a tour of the yard, I'd be happy to act as your guide."

Kelsey smiled even more widely. "We have a little bit of discretion in scheduling, and I'm sure a couple of us would absolutely love to see the yard. In fact, we were talking earlier today about how we could arrange to get over there, so meeting you is a godsend.

"One thing, though. While what we're doing isn't precisely a secret mission, we *are* keeping a low profile. You've noticed that none of us are in uniform and that our associates are civilians. We're working on board a freighter and it would be a favor to both me and the Lords if you would be discreet about who you mentioned us to."

"Absolutely," Don said. "My lips are sealed. Veronica, if you'll give me a call sometime tomorrow, we can work out the details for both dinner and the tour. Everyone, it's been a pleasure meeting you."

With that, her old friend excused himself and returned to his table. His associates immediately started peppering him with questions, and Veronica could tell from their body language that he wasn't explaining things to their liking.

Kelsey gestured and everyone rose to their feet. "I'm stuffed," she said perhaps a tad louder than she needed to. "Let's get back to our rooms and call it a night."

Veronica made a point of waving at Don as she exited the restaurant with the rest of her team. Only when she was outside did she feel her hands starting to shake.

"Oh God. That was so close. Are we screwed?"

Zia put her arm around Veronica's shoulders as they walked toward the hotel. "You did great. No one could possibly anticipate randomly running into someone they knew like that. Your reaction was perfect. No way he saw anything wrong. We're still good."

The other woman's arm steadied her. Veronica took a deep breath and tried not to sag.

"I've been in combat. That was worse in some ways. I don't know if I'm cut out to be a spy."

"You did better than I did the first time," Kelsey said with a laugh. "Not that I've been a spy, but I have done things I'd never expected to do. You were fabulous. I didn't see a hint of tension in you, and neither did your friend.

"You also just solved our problem of getting into the shipyard. We don't have to sneak aboard or steal a cutter now. Obviously, we can't carry out the operation during the middle of the tour, but I'll bet we can make arrangements that will make getting back aboard a second time a lot easier while we're there.

"That's a huge stroke of luck. An opportunity that we can't afford to squander. Come tomorrow morning, I want you to contact him and arrange for Carl and me to accompany you on that tour. Zia can help Talbot."

Kelsey held up a finger toward the scientist. "I understand that you still have a lot of work to do regarding the research facility, but if there's a way to gain access to the shipyard's computer system, we need to take it. And to do that, we need you there in person.

"We're going to have to be fast on our feet to give you the time alone to get into their systems and do what you need to do, but we're not going to get another opportunity like this again. We have to seize it with both hands."

Veronica sighed. "I'm going to have to go out to dinner with him, aren't I? That's going to be a minefield. Probably a couple of hours of conversation where anything I say might trip me up. I feel a headache coming on."

"You'll do fine," Kelsey said. "In fact, you don't have to conceal a single thing. Other than the mission we're currently on, you can tell him the truth, though I'd leave out the mission to Erorsi. He can't check any of the facts in time to do him any good. Don't overcomplicate this. Like I said, you'll do great."

"You can say that all you want, but it's not going to make me feel any better."

She felt awful at playing on Don's friendship. Once they finished, they could leave. He'd face the wrath of the Lords with nowhere to hide. She truly was a traitor now.

Zia gave her shoulder another squeeze. "Don't let this eat at you. Come on. Let's get back to the hotel. Tomorrow is going to come early."

23

Zia awoke to find herself alone in the room. A check of her internal chronometer told her that it was still a bit early. She'd set an internal alarm to wake her in about twenty minutes, so she cancelled it.

There was no sound from the darkened bathroom, and its door was slightly ajar, so she didn't think Veronica was taking a shower. Perhaps she was taking care of other business.

She slipped a robe on before knocking lightly on the bathroom door. When no one answered, she peered inside. Finding it empty, she turned on the main lights and made certain that Veronica was indeed gone. She was.

Dressing quickly, Zia let herself out of the room and went downstairs to see if she could figure out where the other woman had gone. In spite of Fiona having vetted Veronica's loyalty, Zia started to worry.

Her concerns dissipated when the lift doors opened and Veronica stepped inside with two cups of coffee.

The other woman blinked in surprise. "Did I wake you? I'm sorry. I just wanted to slip out and get us some coffee."

Zia took one of the cups and nodded her thanks as Veronica sent the lift back up to their floor. "Did running into your friend keep you up last night?"

The other woman nodded slowly. "I kept tossing and turning, running scenarios through my head. Seeing Don really threw me."

They traveled the rest of the way back to their floor in silence. Only once they were back in their room with the door closed did Zia speak.

"Let's sit over here and talk about it." She gestured toward the two straight-backed chairs. They wouldn't be comfortable, but it was what they had.

As Veronica sat, Zia sipped her coffee, finding the other woman had sweetened it and added creamer. Surprisingly, she'd gotten the mixture right. The woman was observant.

"How would you feel if you hadn't gone through the revelations you had?" Zia asked. "If you just ran across him in the course of your normal life?"

"I'd be happy," Veronica said, her voice sounding tired. "A lot of Fleet officers in the Rebel Empire are power-obsessed scumbags. He was one of the good ones. He *is* one of the good ones. It breaks my heart to stick a knife into his back."

"You're in a hard place," Zia agreed, putting her hand on the other woman's leg sympathetically. "It's one thing to fight back against a system that you completely dislike. It's another thing entirely when the face of that system is a friend.

"I can't pretend to understand what you're going through, but you're not alone. You don't know any of us. It's hard to pick strangers over friends even if you believe in the cause they're fighting for."

Veronica sagged slightly in her chair, setting her untouched coffee on the edge of the desk. "I can't see any way this ends well for Don. I'm using our friendship to start a chain of events that will probably end with his death.

"I have no idea whether he believes in the system or hates it like I do. That's not the kind of thing officers discuss with one another. It's not safe. People disappear when they do things like that, and one learns to keep one's opinions to one's self."

Zia's heart went out to the other woman. Having to choose between friendship and duty was one of the most difficult things a person can do. Veronica was obviously caught on the horns of a dilemma. No matter how things turned out, she'd be scarred.

"I've only been a senior officer for six months," Zia confessed. "After our people found and repaired the ships that we have now, we needed trained, experienced people to man them. And command personnel experienced in the new tech to run them.

"Before that, I was tactical officer on a destroyer. One very similar to the one you commanded, if far less capable. I don't have the depth of experience to even begin advising someone how to navigate the minefield you're walking through.

"What I can say is that if he's a decent man like you say, he would feel just as badly as you do but he'd end up doing what was right. Even if it hurt you. Even if it killed you."

The other woman sat silent for a few minutes, obviously lost in thought. When she finally stirred, she picked up her coffee and took a sip, grimacing at the no doubt cool temperature.

"I'll do what I have to," Veronica said as she set the cup back down. "Maybe I can come up with some way to mitigate what happens to him. You know, stick him in a closet somewhere when push comes to shove. Maybe that will save his life.

"After all, the Lords can't expect him to be omniscient. There is no way he could expect me to betray him like I'm going to do. He's not psychic. It may ruin his career, but if I can save his life, I'm going to try my very best to do so."

She looked up at Zia. "I hope that's not going to be a problem because I'm not willing to negotiate the point. I believe the Rebel Empire has to be brought down, but I'm not going to murder a friend to make it happen."

Zia shrugged. "No one expects you to be a monster, Veronica. I think you can find a way to see your friend spared the worst consequences of our mission, but you're not going to be able to save him completely.

"Don't get so hung up trying to spare him that you put the mission in danger. There are billions of people counting on us. Trillions, if you count all the people in the Rebel Empire. One life is important, but you have to be able to keep your perspective."

Veronica rubbed her face with both hands. "I said I'll do what I have to, and I meant it. The Lords have demanded that I do distasteful things in the past, and I've complied. How can I do any less for the right reasons? That doesn't mean I can't mourn for a betrayed friend."

The two of them sat in silence, sipping at their cooling coffee until it was finally all gone.

She'd put off taking her shower for as long as she could—longer than she should have—so Zia finally rose to her feet. "Everyone else is probably already getting breakfast, but I need to get a shower. It's going to be okay."

Veronica looked up at her. "I'm not looking forward to today, but I think you've made it a little easier for me to do what I need to do. Thanks."

Zia smiled briefly and put her hand on the other woman's shoulder. "The only way any of us get through this is together. It may not feel like it right now, but this isn't necessarily a no-win scenario. If circumstances permit, you'll find a way to save your friend. I know that because it's what friends do."

* * *

Kelsey used her foot to tap on the door where they were holding their morning meeting. Her arms were filled with bags of food and drink from a small place just up the corridor. She'd chosen it because it was so busy that it was unlikely anyone there would remember her presence after the fact.

She also hoped the crowd meant that the food was awesome.

Talbot opened the door, and everyone cleared the way for her to take the food over to the bed. The desk wasn't large enough for everything, so they'd have to spread the containers out on the covers and eat as they stood around talking.

Under any other circumstances, she'd try to find a conference room, but that would draw attention they couldn't afford. They had to stay off of everyone's scanners.

As soon as everyone had piled their plates high with whatever they wanted for breakfast and gotten cups of coffee from the large container she'd brought, she served herself. She ate quickly because she knew she'd be still putting it away once the rest were done.

That used to cause her so much embarrassment. She'd felt like a pig, continually stuffing her face. Now after years of stoking the furnace in her belly, it no longer bothered her. People would think what they thought, and that was no business of hers.

Besides, now that there were new Marine Raiders coming into existence, her appetite would hardly be unusual. If people thought she could eat, they'd be *stunned* over how much food Angela Ellis could put away in one sitting.

About halfway through the meal, the door opened to admit Zia and Veronica. The two women waved and began piling plates high. Their late arrival gave her a little bit more time to finish eating. By the time they finished, everyone else was sipping coffee and Kelsey was wrapping up her own meal.

Everyone put their trash back into the bags. Someone would dispose of it after the meeting.

Kelsey walked over to the desk and rapped her knuckles on the fake wood. "Everyone, if you'll let me have your attention, we'll get this rolling."

Once the various conversations ceased, Kelsey continued. "Veronica, today's work is going to be mainly on your shoulders. I want you to contact your friend and see if he can arrange for us to go out to the shipyard either this morning or afternoon.

"Then have dinner with him tonight, if you can. Any information you can get from him about normal operations at the yard and the situation in this system will be helpful. It's even possible that he might be able to tell us why there are Rebel Empire warships in Archibald's outer system, though we already have our suspicions."

Talbot cleared his throat. "I can shed some light on that. While you were out getting food this morning, I went downstairs and sat in the breakfast room while the other guests were eating. I went so that the management could see that some of us were taking advantage of the free buffet and to listen in on what was being said.

"No one seemed to be aware that there are ships in the outer system, but I did overhear a pair of travelers talking about how they'd been rushed out of a nearby system after some kind of ruckus at one of the system's flip points.

"Apparently there was some kind of fighting in the system next door. Nobody could say exactly who was doing the shooting, but it was serious enough that Fleet was locking everything down. They thought that was peculiar as the system in question only had the one flip point. They were wondering how Fleet had missed the intruders coming in."

Kelsey felt her heart sink a little. "It could be the Clans. Probably has to be."

Zia grimaced. "If that's the case, that one attack is only the beginning. They wouldn't have revealed themselves if they didn't intend to carry out a full-scale invasion of the Rebel Empire. They've had hundreds of years to prepare, with the Singularity building their forces, so they think they can win this fight.

"If the Clans are attacking other nearby systems—and we have to believe that there is more than one incursion—then the possibility of fighting here at Archibald in the very near future can't be ruled out."

Kelsey rubbed the bridge of her nose. "Perfect. That means we have to speed up our timetable as much as humanly possible. It also means that the Rebel Empire Fleet is going to be even more suspicious of anything unusual taking place. We'll have to act faster and be more careful at the same time."

She turned to Carl. "I don't suppose you brought enough equipment to clone yourself?"

"Sadly, no," he said with a shake of his head.

"Then we need you to get into the computer systems on this station as quickly as possible, as well as penetrate the medical research facility, and still be ready to go with us to the shipyard as soon as the opportunity presents itself. Is there anything we can do to help make all that happen?"

"I'm already one step ahead of you," Carl said. "I accessed the station network last night before I went to bed. It wasn't too difficult to get in. The secure areas are still locked away, but I believe that I've worked out which one is the research facility.

"I'm going to have to do a little more work to find a vulnerability that I can exploit to get complete access. Doctor Parker's computer specialist has been a big help. Together, the two of us might manage to do everything we need to do here before I have to go to the shipyard."

"Excellent. Keep it up."

She turned her attention to Talbot. "I want you to conduct an in-person reconnaissance of the area around the research facility. We need to know how we're going to get in. Take anyone you need to help and get the lay of the land."

"I can do that," he agreed. "If you don't need her right now, I'll take Zia."

The flag officer raised an eyebrow. "My schedule is open, but I'm not sure what I can add. I'm not exactly a superspy."

Talbot grinned. "No, but you'll keep me from standing out by being just one dude walking around looking at everything. A couple draws far less attention than a single male. Cain Hopwood and Bill Smith, his security guy, can look at what we record later and help devise an entry plan."

Zia considered his statement with pursed lips and nodded. "I'm in."

"Then let's be about it," Kelsey said. "If we can't get what we need before the Clans come calling, we're all screwed."

24

Talbot and Zia headed for the research facility at a slow stroll. They stopped at a couple of shops and browsed, making certain their progress toward their target didn't show any sign of urgency. Or, frankly, that they had a target at all.

"How's Veronica?" Talbot asked as they were looking at what appeared to be designer women's clothing. What precisely it was designed for, he had no idea. There were a lot of straps and snaps, but he couldn't discern any purpose for them.

"That thing last night really shook her up," Zia said. "But she's solid, and she'll pull through. What's the general plan? I've seen our destination on a map, but we've got no indication of how it's really laid out inside: how many levels, what type of security, that kind of thing. How are we going to get that information without going inside?"

"We *are* going inside. Not to cause any kind of scene but to make an inquiry. We have an injured family member, and we want to know if they have any hope. A child would be best, I think. Everyone has a soft spot for kids."

Zia nodded. "You're hoping we can pull somebody's heartstrings and get them to admit that kind of technology exists or to be very sad in saying that it doesn't. The only problem I see is that we're going to be talking to a receptionist. The odds this person is going to know what research projects are happening is fairly low, isn't it?"

Talbot laughed. "It isn't as if this is a secret military research facility. The different scientists and technicians working here are going to talk about their projects even outside the labs. While they probably won't chat over any classified details, the general thrust of their research is probably going to be mentioned outside the secure areas. Who do they walk past every day when they're leaving work and arriving? The receptionists.

"So, imagine this. A couple of scientists are arriving at work, getting ready to scan their badges and go in. They're already going to be talking about some of the experiments they plan on conducting that day. The receptionist is going to hear all about them.

"Or they've just finished a long day and had some successful or disastrous tests. They're leaving the building but they're not quite done talking work yet. While they're in the lobby, they're getting in that last little bit of discussion about what they're going to need to do the next day. And once again, there's the receptionist to drink it all in."

She gave him a look through narrowed eyes. "Exactly how do you know this?"

He grinned at her. "While I might not be on the market anymore, I've dated a number of receptionists in my time. They've told me quite a bit about things they're not supposed to know about. The people talking just consider them part of the furnishings.

"I have no doubt whatsoever that the receptionists in this building know virtually every single research project being conducted now and over the last few years. They probably have a decent idea of how far along each project is and whether or not they're feasible, just based on what the researchers are saying."

"That seems kind of risky," Zia said cautiously. "They're not involved in the work itself, and if we take their word at face value, we might be completely wrong."

Talbot gestured for them to change direction, and they headed down another corridor. "It's a risk, but we're not going to get the kind of information we need by standing outside the building and staring at it. Carl might get something when he finishes hacking his way in. We're just testing the water.

"If we can get verbal confirmation that something like this exists, we'll know that this mission is a go. If the receptionist doesn't know anything, then the odds of getting something once we get in are low and we might abort. That's going to be up to Kelsey."

They walked in relative silence for another twenty minutes, crossing through a number of larger segments inside the station. People around them hardly glanced at them. Or if they did, they just saw a couple out for a stroll and would barely remember them even one minute after they'd passed.

When they arrived near the research facility, their job became a little bit more difficult. The number of shops had gone down and the area seemed a tad more industrial in nature.

On the plus side, the facility had a large double door made of clear material with "The Michael Anderle Memorial Research Center" printed clearly for everyone to see. They weren't exactly hiding who they were or what they were doing.

Talbot had no idea who the man was or what he'd done to warrant having a research facility named after him, but that hardly mattered.

He raised an eyebrow toward Zia. "Shall we go in?"

"Let's."

Part of him expected the double doors to be locked so that only the receptionist could open it or an individual with a card could unlock it from the outside. Here in the Rebel Empire, the number of people with implants was restricted. Members of the higher orders had them and so did Fleet officers, but most members of society had to get by without them.

To his relief, the doors were unlocked, and they walked in without any issue. The receptionist, a young man with an earnest expression and a shock of dark, curly hair, smiled at them. His name tag indicated that he was Ralph.

"Good morning and welcome to the Michael Anderle Memorial Research Center," he said pleasantly. "How may I assist you today?"

Talbot held back just a little and nudged Zia forward. Since they were dealing with a man, she was more likely to get useful information. Hell, even if they were dealing with a woman, another woman was more likely to get the information they were looking for, now that he thought about it.

Before Zia had a chance to speak, however, the door behind the receptionist's desk opened and an older woman with a hatchet face set in a scowl stalked out. She wasn't wearing a name tag, but if she had, he wouldn't have been surprised to see her name was Helga.

"Take your break, Ralph. I'll handle the desk until you get back." Her voice was gravelly and held a sour note.

The young man rose to his feet with a smile for Zia and walked back the way the woman had come from. His expression held a note of regret or sorrow. Talbot couldn't tell which, but neither bode well for their mission.

Taking a seat, the older woman scowled at Talbot and Zia. "What do you need, and how may we assist you?"

From her tone of voice, Talbot guessed what she'd actually meant to imply was "I don't care what you need, but tell me now so that I can send you packing as quickly as possible."

Talbot hoped Zia was a much better conversationalist than he was, because he suspected that they were about to be unceremoniously tossed out the door.

* * *

Veronica didn't expect Don Sommerville to be available during what would normally be a work day. She was wrong, it seemed, because he said that he was available to meet with her right away.

That made her stomach do a slow roll. She hadn't been expecting to need to start the deception immediately.

"I'm not sure everybody will be ready to take the tour right now," she said. Since Zia was off assisting Talbot, she wouldn't be available to take the tour for a while yet.

"I can probably arrange another tour later, but going now would be perfect," he said with a slight shrug over the com link. "I got delayed on the station, so I'm heading for the Fleet bay in about half an hour. Maybe you could gather a couple of people and I'll give you the grand tour. I can try to arrange a second trip in a day or so. How does that sound?"

"Let me ask," she said and then put him on hold.

She sent an implant message to Princess Kelsey about the situation and received an immediate response.

Tell him we'll go. I'll grab Carl, and it'll just be the three of us.

That sounded exceptionally dangerous to Veronica, but it seemed they didn't have much choice. So, she told Don they'd meet him at the Fleet bay in half an hour.

After she disconnected the call, she went in search of Princess Kelsey. She found the woman already discussing the situation with the scientist.

"I'm not sure what equipment I can sneak through the Fleet bay," Carl was saying. "How thoroughly are they going to scan us?"

Veronica shrugged when Princess Kelsey looked at her. "We're under escort, so it could be no scan at all, or they might decide to examine us more closely. Two of us have Fleet IDs, so it might be better if one of us carries any unusual equipment. We're less likely to be searched."

"What kind of equipment do you think we should take?" Kelsey asked the scientist.

"There are a few pieces of specialized equipment that I can use to directly access the hardwired network inside the shipyard. None of them are very large. I could probably fit everything inside a small pouch. Something that would be concealable underneath normal clothes."

Veronica considered that and nodded slowly. "It might be best if I carry the pouch. Don has known me for years. If it comes down to being searched, I'm going to be the last person they look at. He'll vouch for me."

Knowing that was true made her feel guilty. Don was a decent guy, and she felt bad about the likely outcome of her using him like this.

Princess Kelsey put her hand on Veronica's shoulder. "You like him, and you feel bad?"

She gave the short woman a lopsided smile. "Zia said that your insight goes beyond what one would normally expect, but you continue to surprise me. Yes, I feel bad, but that won't stop me from doing my duty."

Kelsey squeezed her shoulder for a moment and then released it. "Duty can be a hard mistress. I've learned that lesson again and again over the last few years. Our plans are still fluid. There's going to be a lot of chaos when we leave. If we can, I'll try to work things so we take him with us."

"I'm not sure he'll thank either of us for that," Veronica said with a dark chuckle. "Still, with a choice between leaving him to the justice of the System Lords or kidnapping him, I appreciate the effort. Thank you."

"It's not a problem. With everything we've got in the air, what's one more ball?"

While they'd been talking, Carl had been going through his equipment.

He came back over and handed Veronica a small pouch. One that would easily be concealable inside her clothing. So long as she wasn't searched, no one would ever know she was carrying it.

"Most of the hardware is shielded, so they're going to have to be looking exceptionally closely to spot this," he said.

Veronica tucked the pouch away. "Then let's hope they don't look. Shall we go? It wouldn't hurt to be just a little bit early."

She had no idea where the Fleet bay was, so she used her implants to consult with the basic station network and get an overview map. She'd been on a number of similar stations over the years and was quickly able to orient herself and lead them to the lifts that would take them to their destination.

Unlike the cargo bay they'd arrived in, the Fleet bay was segregated from the general areas of the station. The large hatches were closed, and a number of marines stood guard in front of them.

She knew that marines in the Rebel Empire were different than the ones used by the New Terran Empire. None of these men had implants, and their weapons had to be activated by an officer before each shift. The Empire didn't trust them very far.

Also unlike the marines in the New Terran Empire, these men would be more thuggish. Marines were brutes used to assault positions without regard to their own survival, so they tended to view life through the lens of what they could get away with before they died an inevitable and probably gory death.

A large man with a shaved head and what looked like a semipermanent sneer on his face stepped forward and raised his hand. His sleeve had corporal's stripes, and his name tag read Deacon.

"Fleet admittance only."

"We're expected. My name is Veronica Giguere, and this is Diane Delatorre and Carl Owlet. Commander Don Sommerville should have us on the list."

The man didn't bother looking at the clipboard one of his associates held. "You're not on the list. Come back once you are."

Veronica frowned slightly and restrained herself from snapping at him like she would have if she were in uniform. She was pretending not to be a Fleet officer, so she couldn't tear a strip off of him.

"Perhaps you should check the list again," she said firmly. "When the commander gets here, you're not going to like what happens if you continue detaining us."

The corporal grinned. "You want to see detention? We can do that too. Privates, take these three into custody for attempting to gain unauthorized access to a Fleet facility. I'll handle the pat downs myself."

That last was said with a leer toward Veronica.

The other marines smiled and stepped forward, obviously relishing the thought of manhandling two women and a skinny guy.

Oh, hell.

25

Somewhat disconcerted, Zia put on her best smile for the new woman. Her estimation of their chances at getting information plummeted from about fifty percent to around zero, but she was going to try anyway.

"Hi, we have something of an odd question. My sister's little girl had a terrible accident last year that damaged her spine. The doctors told us that they couldn't regenerate it. It's really hard, but we're trying to keep our hopes up. Is the center working on anything that might help her?"

The woman's scowl deepened. "It's against our policy to discuss research projects. The technology being evaluated and developed here is at the very edge of what's possible with Imperial technology.

"Even so, not all projects are successful. We don't want to get anyone's hopes up that a certain technology will be released for general use in the near future or even in the distant future. I hope that it becomes possible for your niece to recover, but I'm not going to be able to answer your question."

Talbot leaned forward, his eyes pleading. "We don't want to know any secret details. We just want to give my sister-in-law something to hold onto. Please. Even a hint that it might be possible would give her the strength to carry on for Rachel."

"I'm sorry," the woman said, her expression becoming fierce. "I'm doubly sorry that a little girl was injured, but that doesn't change the situation. I'm going to have to ask you to leave."

Zia considered pushing one final time, but since the woman had balked at Talbot's plea, she wasn't going to give in to anything Zia said.

"It breaks my heart to see a corporation that won't even say one word to give hope to those they claim they want to help," Zia said with anger that wasn't all that feigned. "We'll go, but you've made our pain worse. Remember that."

She took Talbot's arm and led him back toward the door, her back stiff with actual outrage. Part of her hoped the woman would call out and give them a clue, but she didn't. They exited the building no wiser than when they'd gone inside.

As they were walking away, Talbot grimaced at her. "Well, that was a bust. Not only was access to the building restricted enough that we got no information about what the layout is, the old battle-ax wouldn't even clue us in about any regeneration technology.

"You did good, by the way. If it'd been me, I'd have told you what you wanted to know and damn company policy. We'll just have to let Carl and the other nerds see what they can find out remotely."

She gave the marine officer a smile. "Don't sell yourself short. That last-minute plea of yours was genius. I figured she'd crack for sure."

Zia was about to add more when she saw someone walk around the corner ahead of them. It was the young man who'd been behind the receptionist's desk when they'd arrived.

He came directly to them and smiled a bit sadly. "I'd like to take a moment to apologize for my associate. Regina is somewhat of a stickler for rules. In any case, the company doesn't inform us about the various projects that are underway or their status. I'm sorry about that."

Seeing a second chance being dangled in front of her, Zia tried to pluck it. "I really do understand that confidential information needs to stay inside the company. You wouldn't want your competitors to get details on experiments and hardware and that kind of stuff.

"I'm not looking for any of that. All I want to do is tell my sister that her little girl might one day walk again. Might one day be able to feed herself again. I'm just looking for hope."

The young man glanced up the corridor and back down again before leaning close to her. "While no one has said anything to me directly about the matter, I've heard a couple of our senior researchers discussing a project that *might* lead to something like that.

"It sounds as if it's already in the testing stages, so if it passes the rigorous standards set for general release by the Empire, it might be available for your niece in a year or two. You didn't hear that from me."

Zia smiled widely. "Thank you. *Thank you.* You don't know what a difference you've just made in our lives."

She threw her arms around him and hugged him tightly for a moment before releasing him.

He coughed for a second and smiled at her as he stepped back. "I really hope your niece gets better. Good luck."

With that, the young man turned and walked briskly back the way he'd come. He turned the corner into a side corridor that probably led to another entrance to the facility.

Talbot hurried after the young man and peered around the corner. Zia joined him just in time to see the young man step into a side entrance. A discreet one with no identifying signs.

"Well, that's helpful," Talbot said as he led to Zia away from the area. "Unless he was just selling us sunshine, that means there's something in there that could potentially regenerate a damaged spine."

She raised an eyebrow at him as they mingled with the crowd. "You think he was lying?"

The marine shrugged. "It's possible. In his shoes, if someone came looking for something to hope for, it might be tempting to give them a comforting lie. It won't change the situation for that person, but it might make the near future more bearable. I'd consider doing it. Wouldn't you?"

Probably, now that she thought about it. That was the risk in putting forward a tearjerking story.

"On the plus side," Talbot continued, "we now know of a less obvious entrance to the premises. Better yet, we know someone whose ID card opens it."

Now she gave him a skeptical look. "We know that he can get in, but we don't know who he is or how to get a hold of his card. How do you propose we rectify that?"

He grinned at her. "Now that we know what he looks like, it shouldn't be that hard to put someone in the area to keep an eye out for him and follow him home. Once we know where he lives, I'd wager breaking into his domicile is going to be a lot easier than an assault on a research facility."

"That's not going to be the only security measures they have," Zia warned him. "That's just the first layer. A receptionist won't have access to the classified labs. Even the researchers that can get into the experimental area might not be able to access the specific project area we're looking for.

"In addition, we won't know where to look either. Even if we put that guy to the question, he won't be able to tell us what we need to know, I'd wager. And we don't dare make him disappear. That would raise all kinds of red flags.

"What we need to do is get access to his card and clone it. Then we leave the original with him, and no one will be the wiser. We've got to be subtle."

Talbot looked mildly offended. "I can be subtle."

Zia laughed a little and took his arm. "Only when compared to your wife. Trust me when I say that this operation is going to require a deft hand to pull it off without sounding alarms everywhere across the station."

In spite of their success, she was still worried about how they'd be able to carry out the penetration of the research facility. Getting in was just the first step in a long series of things that had to go right for them to succeed and survive.

That wasn't even counting the mission to the shipyard, which was their primary goal. If the attempt to steal regeneration technology failed, that would be unfortunate for Commodore Murdoch, but they'd have tried.

She was far more concerned about what could go wrong stealing a flip drive or manufacturing replacement parts. And the looming war between the Clans in the Rebel Empire. If, of course, that was really what was happening.

Well, if this kind of thing were easy, anyone could do it. They'd make it work. Somehow.

* * *

KELSEY STEPPED FORWARD, an angry look on her face. The look was mostly manufactured, though part of her was pissed that this idiot was putting them in such danger.

"My name is Diane Delatorre. Captain Delatorre to you. Stand down, or I will *break* you."

Following up on her words, Kelsey pulled her fake ID card out and shoved it into the man's face.

The marines that had been about to seize them stepped back a few paces. Based on the looks they were giving her, this was an extremely unwelcome revelation.

The corporal stared at the badge as if it were a snake that were about to bite him. Then he took a step back too.

"My apologies, Captain," he mumbled.

Kelsey took two steps forward, not allowing the man to increase the space between them.

"That's not good enough, Corporal. What makes you think that Commander Sommerville is going to tolerate your insolence to his guests? Is it your habit to offend officers in general or merely him in specific?"

The man raised his hands as if surrendering. "I meant nothing by this, Captain. I was only doing my duty."

Kelsey laughed, adding a harsh edge to her tone. "If you're going to be an ass, you're going to have to either learn how to lie better or accept the punishment for being a prick."

She jabbed a finger into the man's chest, putting enough force into it to be sure it hurt. "You can rest assured that if Commander Sommerville doesn't put you on report, I will. I'm not the kind of woman you want to cross. I leave my enemies wishing they'd never been born.

"You're hardly worth my attention, so I'll let it go at that. If you trouble me again, I'm going to make you my personal project. I'll be here on this station for another week. That would certainly make my time here more enjoyable."

The man recoiled from her, obviously cowed. "I'm sorry, Captain," he whimpered. "What can I do to make up for my wrongdoing?"

The smile that Kelsey felt creeping onto her face repulsed her, but it was in character for the person she was pretending to be. "Nothing. Now open the hatch and let us pass before I decide it would be more entertaining to start on you now."

The corporal raced to the controls and opened the main hatch. He saluted her rigidly as she strode past him and into the Fleet bay.

Kelsey didn't look behind her, but she knew her companions were following her. Right now she was trying to stop her hands from trembling.

"Remind me never to play poker with you," Veronica said softly. "You scared the hell out of me, and I *know* that wasn't you."

"I can second the thing about not playing poker against her," Carl said, with the wry smile. "I've heard stories. The marines were complaining at the start of the original mission about how she'd cleaned them out. That was years ago, back before everything happened. I'd imagine she's only gotten better."

Kelsey let her breath out and slowed her pace. "I've certainly gotten better at bluffing. What scares me is how easily I stepped into that role. It was almost like being on autopilot. Flip the bitch switch and off I go. Terrifying when you get right down to it."

"One of the things I've discovered in life is that it's easier for a civilized person to be a barbarian than for a barbarian to be civilized," Veronica said. "It's far, far easier to step down to someone else's level than for them rise to yours.

"In this case, that was the absolute right thing to do. When he thought we were civilians and that you were a pushover, he was going to take every advantage he could. Right up to and including sexual assault if he could've gotten away with it. That's how marines are here."

Kelsey sighed. "That would break Talbot's heart. Hell, it breaks my heart. Where are we supposed to go?"

Before Veronica could answer, Kelsey saw Commander Sommerville stepping out of a cutter and waving toward their group.

"Here we go," Kelsey said. "We need to see the manufacturing equipment and give Carl time to do his work, Veronica. Try to angle for something like that, and we'll keep Sommerville distracted while Carl works his magic."

The young scientist took a deep breath and nodded. "If we can find a network junction, it should only take me thirty seconds to install the splice. I brought four, just in case. One will do, but more is better.

"Best of all would be the opportunity to install a splice directly inside the manufacturing equipment. I could read its software and determine if what we're looking for is even here. That would make our lives a lot easier."

Kelsey clapped a hand to her friend's shoulder. "You'll do it. I have complete confidence in you. Now, let's get our game faces on. It's showtime."

26

Talbot finally relaxed when they arrived back at the hotel. He knew the odds of them having raised suspicions in someone this morning were low, but it only took one paranoid bugger to get them all into deep, deep trouble.

He found an empty room and pulled Cain Hopwood and his security guy, Bill Smith, in with them. It only took a few minutes to run down the information they'd gathered and pass along the imagery he'd captured through his implants.

Smith pursed his lips and slowly nodded. "The entry isn't going to be too bad, if we can get our hands on that guy and his badge. That'll get us into the first level of the restricted zone. From there, we'll probably run into segregated rooms, both large and small.

"The computers will be locked down, of course. We'll need to bring along the research hacker just to be sure we can force our way in. The goal is going to be getting all the hardware, reports, and research notes for whatever regeneration equipment we're looking at.

"We'll need to avoid suspicion moving in. Custodial coveralls would be perfect. Unless, of course, we happened to run into some *real* custodians."

"Okay," he said after a moment. "Are you going to be able to get us into the security system, Mr. Smith? Maybe we can make sure we have exactly the right kind of uniforms and possibly even avoid the real custodians."

"Once we're on site, I can physically get into whatever they have for a security system," Smith said. "I'm not a hacker, though. Not of the class we'll need to get in remotely.

"But that's actually fine. You don't realize it, but you're talking about two separate systems. What we need to get access to before we go in isn't the alarms. It's the monitoring side of the equation. That's where our hacker friend will help us."

Talbot nodded. "Have you worked with this guy before?"

Smith shook his head. "No, but Carl vouched for him. Considering how far out of my league Carl is, his word is good enough for me. Unless I miss my guess, the guy has been working on the various computer networks we have access to throughout the station already."

They'd go talk to the man shortly, but Talbot wasn't ready to move on from the planning session just yet.

"We're going to need to find a location in the research facility to set up the large transport ring. We can take everything we steal back to the freighter with no one being the wiser. Then all we have to do is move the small ring back to the cargo shuttle and off to the freighter."

Hopwood shot Talbot a grin. "That thing is *really* handy. Since nobody knows the technology even exists, they'll be scratching their heads wondering how the hell a big pile of boxes just vanished."

"Are you sure it's going to be a large pile?" Zia asked, raising an eyebrow. "It may only be a couple of machines and some files."

"Have you seen Carl's lab?" Hopwood asked with a laugh. "Scientists are like pack rats. There are going to be piles of equipment. Once we get to the lab in question, we won't even be sure what's important, so we're going to have to take *everything*."

The mental image made Talbot chuckle. Carl *was* kind of a pack rat. There was always some kind of experiment going on, and discerning what belonged to which project was never easy.

They'd have Doctor Zoboroski on hand to help them figure that out, but he was a practicing physician rather than a research scientist. They couldn't trust that they'd get everything without taking the whole pile.

"With Princess Kelsey and the rest making a scouting run at the shipyard, we should know by this evening how difficult the task is going to be," Zia said. "I wish that I'd had the chance to go with them and see things for myself, but I'll have an opportunity to go over everything they capture with their implants.

"And Carl knows what he's doing. He's more than capable of taking bold action if the need arises. He'll get the taps put into all of the appropriate computer systems before they come back, I'm sure. That'll give our hacker an opportunity to get us with the research center remotely."

Talbot sighed, rubbing the side of his head. "I wish we didn't have to risk everything on a couple of throws of the dice. It's going to be really easy to roll snake eyes.

"We can start off by seeing what the hacker has been up to. With any luck, he'll have already gotten into the research center's network. If we can tap into the security feed, we'll start mapping the place and devising our plan of attack. We'll know more when Kelsey and the rest get back. Let's hope for the best."

That was going to be the key, Talbot knew. They were going to need a couple of lucky breaks for things to go their way. Otherwise Rebel Empire security would come down on them like a Marine Raider drop capsule.

* * *

VERONICA WAVED as she walked up to Don Sommerville.

"There you are," he said with a smile. "Did you have any trouble?"

Deciding it would be less trouble if she glossed over the events at the main hatch, Veronica shook her head. "Nothing we couldn't handle. Just the usual marine nonsense."

His expression twisted. "I don't get why they put those people in positions over regular people like that. Marines are nothing but trouble."

She considered it ironic how she'd shared her friend's opinion until she'd met the marines of the New Terran Empire. It wasn't the marines that were the problem. It was the Rebel Empire and how they trained them. How they conditioned them to be brutal and then used them up like expendable munitions.

Maybe, with just a little luck, she'd be able to show Don what she'd learned. If they could figure a way to capture him as they were leaving.

"So, what's the plan?" she asked.

He gestured toward the cutter. "This is our ride. It's going directly to the Fleet section of the shipyard and from there I've got about two hours to give you as much of a tour as I can manage. We should be able to see just about everything interesting."

Without further ado, they trooped into the cutter. It was about half filled with Fleet officers of low-to-middle rank. The highest-ranking officer present was a lieutenant sitting in front, reading something on his tablet. He paid them no mind as they sat across from him.

As they sat down and secured themselves, Don turned to Princess Kelsey. "I realize you need to be circumspect in what you say, but I'm wondering if you could tell me anything about what you're doing traveling through here? Does it have anything to do with the Ghost incursion?"

Princess Kelsey, in the guise of the woman she was pretending to be, Veronica thought, scowled. "Tangentially. As I said before, I really can't discuss details. Now in a hypocritical twist, I'm going to ask you what you can tell me about the incursion. All I've heard is public gossip. Can you shed some light on the subject, Commander?"

Don shrugged. "Everything is still pretty confused. Word arrived by fast courier that Balladur was under attack yesterday. It's three flips from here, so we're on alert, but we should get word if there's a force moving toward us.

"Fleet had to withdraw from the system because there were too many ships coming against them. The funny thing is, no one knows where those ships came from. Balladur is a cul-de-sac. One flip point leads in and out. Units in the next system over didn't see anything until the few Fleet ships stationed in Balladur came running through the flip point, screaming for help."

"I don't understand that," Veronica said. "Ships just don't appear from nowhere. Where could they have come from? And if it is the Ghosts, how could they have so many ships?

"Frankly, I kind of thought they were a myth. Every once in a while you'd hear a story about some strange ship being cornered and blown up. Or about supply ships that vanished without a trace. Or even small warships like destroyers disappearing. I really never gave the rumors much credence."

Don nodded. "That's about how I felt too. I guess we can definitely put their existence into the confirmed category at this point. Weirdly, the reports on the kind of ships being used doesn't match up with the few cases Fleet was rumored to have engaged in the past.

"Some of these new vessels are larger than a heavy cruiser and with commensurate weapons. That's scary, and it really has the higher-ups freaked out."

"Is it just Balladur under attack?" Carl asked. "Are other systems being hit too?"

Don shrugged. "We haven't heard of any, but word might come in at any time. The contingency invasion plans that Fleet maintains for each system are being dusted off, and we'll figure out something if they come here.

"We don't have a lot of offensive force, other than the battle stations. If the Ghosts get into the system, we'll evacuate what we can and probably destroy the shipyard. Based on the positioning of the flip points, and the fact that we have scout ships in the adjacent systems, we'll have at least a day's warning."

A tone sounded announcing they were close to docking. Everyone on the cutter began making certain they'd gathered their possessions. None of Veronica's group had taken anything out for the trip so they'd be able to depart quickly once docking was complete.

A few minutes later, the cutter docked, and people began streaming out into the shipyard. Veronica walked with Don out onto the Fleet section of the shipyard.

A trio of people in fleet security uniforms stood near the only hatch leading out of the room. Two large enlisted men with sidearms stood behind a slender woman with strawberry blonde hair and lieutenant's tabs.

Since Veronica wasn't in uniform and expected to have her ID checked, she made certain to look relaxed. In fact, she might as well be proactive.

Smiling, she stepped over to the woman and pulled out her identification. "Commander Veronica Giguere."

The woman took her ID and examined it closely. She then looked up and directly into Veronica's eyes. Moments later, Veronica's implants informed her that they'd just been queried for her identification.

That surprised her. Thankfully it wasn't going to be a problem, but it hinted at a somewhat higher state of readiness than she'd expected.

The woman handed Veronica's ID card back to her. "Thank you, Commander. I'll need to see everyone's identification, please."

Princess Kelsey handed over her ID next.

The woman spent an equal amount of time examining it before looking up at the princess. This time, the woman's gaze seemed a little sharper.

"You might want to see someone about updating your identification photo, Captain. It seems a little out of date."

Princess Kelsey scowled a little. "Did you just say that I'm getting old?"

The security officer smiled without a hint of humor. "Age catches up with us all, Captain. In your case, it's the opposite. Whatever treatments you're getting for your skin and the work you had done on your nose have made you look younger and somewhat different than your photo. My congratulations on finding an excellent cosmetic surgeon."

The woman turned her attention to Carl, her expression showing a little more interest than before. "Identification."

The young scientist handed over his card and waited, his nervousness apparent to Veronica. She hoped it didn't trigger more attention from the security officer.

This time the woman's examination of the ID took almost twice as long and she looked up at Carl twice.

"There may be an irregularity with your identification, Mr. Owlet," she said at last. "I'm going to have to ask you to step aside for enhanced screening." She gestured toward a hatch set off to the side of the compartment.

Dammit.

27

Zia walked down the hall and knocked on the door where the research hacker was working. The man's response was muffled, but she assumed it was an invitation to come in. Hopefully she wasn't about to catch him just coming out of the shower.

To her relief, she found him sitting at the desk, working on a portable computer. It was more substantial than a tablet by a significant margin, and there were extra drives and equipment scattered around the room, probably providing additional resources for his work.

The man bore a striking resemblance to Carl in the fact that he was somewhat scrawny and extremely nerdy. He was also about thirty years older than her friend and wore anachronistic glasses perched on the end of his nose.

He was turned in his seat, facing her as she came in. "Commodore Anderson," he said as he slicked back what was left of the hair on his balding head. "What can I do for you?"

"Doctor Rehnquist, right?"

The man nodded with a slight smile. "That's right. Andy Rehnquist."

"Excellent. You mind if I take a seat?"

Without waiting for his answer, she sat on the edge of his bed. "We've made some progress on identifying potential ingress points at the research facility as well as identifying potential sources for access to the building. I just dropped by to see how you were progressing on getting into their network."

The man smiled widely. "I think I'm ahead of schedule. I've penetrated the outermost layers of the onion, so to speak. In fact, I believe I now have complete access to the nonclassified systems used by them for interfacing with the public."

"That's good news, Doctor. Can you break down exactly what that means for us?"

He nodded briskly. "In effect, I've accessed the systems used by their administrative personnel. That system does interface with more secure areas, but I'm going very slowly. I don't want to trigger any kind of unexpected security response by poking around in a haphazard manner."

"I'm all for caution, Doctor," Zia said with a smile. "In fact, the work you've done thus far might be able to help us get into the building. Do you have access to the service files for the receptionists?"

"As a matter of fact, I've managed to access their version of human resources. Never really liked that term. It makes it sound as if people are property. Of course, in my *particular* case, that wasn't very far from the truth."

"Well here's a chance for you to strike a blow against people like that. I'm looking to identify one of the receptionists I met today. A young man with dark, curly hair. His name tag indicated that he was Ralph.

"I'd like to know where he lives, what his schedule is, and any other juicy details his file might be able to provide for us. The more we know, the better chance we can take him without causing problems."

The scientist spun on his chair and typed on the physical keyboard at what to her was a blinding pace. Data began scrolling up the screen, and what was obviously a file image of the man she'd spoken to appeared.

"Ralph Halstead," the scientist intoned. "He's been with their company for two years. According to HR, he's a diligent worker with no marks against him. His supervisor indicates that he's 'a personable, dedicated young man with a true desire to help people.' I'd say the young man is going to go far in his profession."

"Does it list an address for him?"

"Indeed it does." He rattled off an address that she'd be able to parse later and locate where the man lived.

"There's one more piece of useful information that I think you'll want," the scientist said. "Mr. Halstead is related to one of the research scientists, a Doctor Adriana Lipp. She's listed as his maternal aunt."

That might be useful. If they could use the receptionist to get to his aunt and subvert her access, that might get them very close to their goal when the time came.

"Do you have any idea how long it might take you to find a list of their research projects?" Zia asked.

"In a perfect world, I'd prefer to do that over the next twenty-four hours. I believe with that amount of time I can gain access with no one being the wiser. Better yet, I should be able to access the video from the security feeds at that point. I might not be able to override anything, but I should be able to at least see it in read-only mode."

"What about twelve hours?" Zia countered. "That would put us in the overnight hours. Otherwise, we'll be working during daylight tomorrow, and that's not really the way we want to do this. A late-night heist is exactly the kind of thing we're wanting."

He scratched his chin thoughtfully. "If nighttime is your goal, I suggest that you aim for thirty-six hours as opposed to twelve. That would give us the largest margin for success, in my considered opinion."

She rose to her feet, satisfied. "That sounds good, Doctor. If we can put it off until tomorrow night, we will. The problem is that we don't know what our time frame is going to be. Honestly, if things go poorly enough for Princess Kelsey, we might have to abort this part of the operation entirely. Or we might have to rush it through tonight.

"I suggest you do what you can to gain access without being too overt. Perhaps you'll catch a lucky break and get what we need without having to take too many risks."

He didn't look pleased but nodded. "I'll do what I can and keep you informed of my progress."

That was the best one could ask for.

"In the meantime, Colonel Talbot and I will see if we can get into the young man's apartment. If we can compromise his security system, we'll be able slip in and get his ID card tonight with him none the wiser.

"I'll need an address for his aunt as well. It sounds like she's someone that we need to take captive and question."

The balding man nodded. "You're going to need to be careful. According to her file, she has a husband. If you're expecting to take her, you're going to have to deal with him too."

Zia grunted. "Perfect. I suppose we should also assume the worst about our young man. He's a handsome and polite boy. He might just have a live-in of his own. And pets.

"Unless things go to hell, I have no intention of moving forward tonight. We need to scout these individuals and get an idea of as much of their behavior as we can. When we strike, we're going to have to take them all prisoner."

The doctor nodded. "Then I'd ask that you consider what you're going to do with them when you're finished. When the full scope of what we're doing becomes evident, I have no doubt that security will come down on them hard.

"I doubt very seriously that civilians will be killed for cooperating with armed intruders, but we can't rule that out. The Rebel Empire is an ugly place filled with ugly people. It might be prudent to take them with us so that they can't tell anyone what they've seen. Or so that security doesn't torture them for information they don't possess."

Zia considered that and slowly nodded. "One more complication but a relatively minor one in the scale of things. I'll consider that, Doctor. Get us the access we need while I go talk to a marine about breaking and entering."

* * *

Kelsey was seriously considering going in after Carl. Veronica had subtly shook her head any time she'd looked toward the door. Even though she knew the other woman was undoubtedly correct, that didn't stop her from worrying.

Finally, after what seemed an eternity, Carl came back through the door. He looked shaken, his face pale. Whatever had happened, it hadn't been pleasant.

The female security officer swaggered out behind him and gestured toward her men. "Let them through. Have a pleasant visit."

Commander Sommerville had an expression of mild distaste as he nodded toward the woman and led the three of them into the shipyard.

The corridors beyond the entry point looked like the kind one would see in any station or shipyard. People either dressed in Fleet uniforms or civilian clothes moved about on tasks that Kelsey couldn't begin to guess at.

"I'm sorry about that," the Rebel Fleet officer said. "For what it's worth, Mr. Owlet, I'm sorry you had to go through that."

Carl just nodded, his expression pale. "I understand. Thank you."

Veronica moved up to engage Commander Sommerville in conversation while Kelsey pulled Carl a little behind them.

"What happened?" she asked softly. "Did she hurt you?"

He licked his lips a bit nervously. "I'd rather not discuss the specifics. Imagine whatever humiliating search procedures you like, and let's just say I'm glad Veronica has the gear because I couldn't have hidden it anywhere on me."

A bolt of pure rage shot through Kelsey, and she almost turned on her heel to start back the way they'd come before he grabbed her shoulder.

"Don't," he said softly. "We have too much riding on this mission. People are counting on us. What happened was incredibly demeaning, but I did what I had to do. Let. It. Go."

"I'm so very sorry, Carl," she said at last. "Let's do what we need to do and get the hell out of here. Veronica and I will distract Sommerville when you need us to. Just give me the high sign when you're ready."

He nodded, not saying anything more.

She let the subject drop and moved forward so that she was once again involved in the conversation between Veronica and Commander Sommerville.

He was gesturing toward a cross corridor. "That way goes toward the main viewing area. A lot of construction takes place inside the confines of the shipyard, and they've built a transparent wall so that visitors could see the hulls.

"And up ahead we're going to get into the place where they manufacture the various parts that have to go over to the ships. Everything from the drives to life support. Nothing is imported. Everything is built right here on this shipyard."

Veronica nodded. "Without getting into any classified information, what kind of ships are being built here? Freighters? Destroyers? Maybe even a light cruiser or two?"

"All of that and more," he said. "The civilian side builds just about any kind of ship you can imagine. The Fleet side builds every class of ship we need up to and including heavy cruisers. This is a full-service shipyard. If you need it, we can build it."

Out of the corner of her eye, Kelsey saw Carl raise his hand and meaningfully glance at a junction box on the corridor wall. It was time.

That's when she remembered that Veronica had the equipment that Carl needed. She'd need to distract Commander Sommerville while the other woman slipped the pouch to Carl.

"So, you build flip drives here?" Kelsey asked, stepping between Veronica and Sommerville. "I had a long discussion with one of my engineers about flip drives. There's a lot of rare materials that go into making the damned things. Are they mined locally or imported?"

As she spoke, she walked around him so that Veronica was able to pass the pouch to Carl without Sommerville seeing the act. It only took a moment, and then Carl started working on planting the patch.

"No," Sommerville said. "Those have to be brought in, but luckily the closest source isn't very far away."

Carl's estimate of the time required was conservative. Inside twenty seconds, he had everything closed back up and was listening politely to Sommerville's answer.

One down, three to go.

"You mentioned manufacturing equipment that built all of this stuff, including flip drives," Veronica said, stepping up beside them. "If you don't mind, I'd like to see those next. That sounds fascinating."

Sommerville smiled and gestured for them to continue down the corridor. "It's not very far from here, and it really is an amazing thing to watch. Come on. We'll go take a look at that, and then I'll treat you all to lunch. It's the least I can do."

28

Talbot sat in a small café just down the corridor from where their young target lived. He wasn't alone, but none of his companions were in sight at the moment.

Bill Smith, dressed in nondescript coveralls and wearing a hat that came down over his eyes, was in the building where Ralph Halstead lived. Talbot wasn't certain exactly how the man was going to manage it, but it was his job to figure out if the receptionist lived alone or if they were potentially going to have to deal with a second person.

Rather than communicating by implant, since that might end up being traced back to them, they were using standard com units. Talbot's was linked to an earbud so he could listen without worrying about being overheard. A throat mic meant he could murmur his responses safely.

"It looks like the apartment is empty at the moment," Smith said. "The hall was empty, so I stuck a flexible camera under the door and took a peek. The lights are off, and the unit didn't pick up the sound of any pets."

"So, what's next?" Talbot asked.

"Come on up. I can pick the lock and bypass his security system but not while I'm watching over my shoulder for random passersby."

"I'll be right there."

Talbot left a tip on the table and dropped his disposable coffee cup into a recycle unit. Unhurried, he walked up the corridor and into the residential building. Since he would stand out more than Smith, he made certain to do nothing that would draw anyone's eye.

The building didn't seem to have any cameras in the lobby, but one never knew. The technology could be so small that no one would be able to see it.

Knowing that the elevator would almost certainly have a camera, Talbot used the stairs. Minutes later, he exited onto the target's floor. Smith was standing just down the corridor working on a panel recessed in the wall.

He walked up to the man and looked over his shoulder. "What are you doing?"

"Just passing the time until you showed up. As long as I was working on something, nobody that saw me would give me the slightest bit of attention."

Smith closed up the panel and walked a few doors down to the target's apartment. "I'm going to be focused on the lock in the security system. If anyone pops up, I want you to go ahead and start reading me the riot act for not getting something fixed. Make sure you have something in mind before you start talking."

"Copy that."

Even though he mentally rehearsed a little segment chewing Smith's ass about his toilet not working, no one intruded before the specialist had the lock undone and the door open.

"Inside," Smith said with a hurried gesture.

Already, there was a low beep sounding from an illuminated keypad on the wall. Smith focused on that as soon both were inside and the door was closed.

Rather than ask an idiotic question about whether Smith was going to be able to disarm the alarm before it went off, Talbot reserved his gaze for the apartment itself.

The furniture matched, so young Ralph made enough money to buy his own stuff. It wasn't of the highest quality—in fact, it was somewhat worn—so it might have been hand-me-downs.

Rather than art on the walls, the young man had photographs. A lot of photographs. Not of people but of places. All of nature scenes. He wondered whether the receptionist took them himself or just fancied them.

The beeping stopped. Since there was no alarm blaring, Talbot assumed that Smith had disarmed the security system.

"You're pretty handy," the marine admitted.

"That's what the ladies tell me," Smith said as he tucked his equipment away and relocked the door. "What are we looking for? The guy isn't here, and he's going to have his security badge with him."

"Mainly evidence that he lives alone. We'll be going over everything just in case there's something useful, but I'll be happy if this is just a dry run for breaking in tonight to retrieve his badge."

Talbot had his stunner out. It had been among the equipment they'd smuggled aboard the station. After all, if security found the transport ring it hardly mattered if they found a couple of illegal weapons too.

He didn't need it. There was no one else in evidence. In fact, it seemed their target lived alone and had no pets.

The only thing that stood out as unusual was what would normally have been a spare bedroom. In this case, it seemed to have been converted into a home office. One with a lot of computer equipment and large screens. There was also a VR suite.

Smith looked around with a smile and whistled softly. "My, my. What have we got here?"

The intrusion specialist walked over to the computer—or perhaps Talbot should've said the largest computer—and examined it without turning it on. "I'd have to look inside to be sure, but this is probably a very powerful unit."

"Don't they all look the same from the outside?" Talbot asked. "It's just a computer. The Rebel Empire can make some really small ones, so why would a big one be a shocker? Maybe it's old."

Smith shook his head. "I don't think so. That VR unit and some of the equipment on the shelf beside it make me think this is a gaming computer. Those have to be powerful. In fact, the more powerful they are, the better a player can perform. Gamers tend to have the most advanced equipment in the general population."

Okay, Talbot admitted that was interesting, but it hardly seemed relevant to what they were doing. "If you can stop panting over the equipment, we should finish searching the rest of the place."

The man waved them on. "You go on. I want to call in some computer support. If the hacker can help me get into this system, we might have just hit the jackpot."

Talbot frowned. "I don't follow. How so?"

Running his hand across the top of the computer, Smith grinned. "I'm just following a hunch. I might be wrong, but the thing that gives a gamer the most edge is lots of processing power.

"Our young friend has a relative in a research department with some very serious computing power, I suspect. If he managed to get any kind of access through her—or he's a hacker too—then this computer might be linked into the research facility to use its raw power.

"If we can get into this machine and that is true, our guy can bypass all the stuff that's been keeping him from going through the firewall. Our little hacker might have already done all the work for him."

Talbot considered that. There was a potential for gain, but there was also a risk that someone would catch them in the apartment the longer they stayed. Still, it was a regular workday, so they should be okay.

"Call him. Is this going to be something that requires his physical presence, or can he do it remotely?"

Smith shrugged. "I'm not sure. Let me contact him while you search the rest of the apartment."

Talbot spent fifteen minutes going through the rest of the apartment without finding anything useful. Ralph seemed to be a relatively normal guy living on a fairly regular income, massive computer aside.

He was about to head back to the gaming room to find out what Smith and the hacker had decided when he heard the front door unlock.

* * *

VERONICA HAD to admit that the automated manufacturing setup impressed her. The compartment holding all of the industrial equipment seemed to be as large as her old destroyer, and that was not an exaggeration.

The multilevel room held row after row of massive machines that were being fed raw materials by small automatons, and the finished products were then picked up by those same machines and taken away.

The entire room was visible from the bottom level because the central part of the room had no ceiling. The open space went up seven levels and showed her the entire operation at a glance. It was massive.

The machines seemed to have very little human interaction. Everything was done by computer-controlled machines and seemed to operate at very high speed. Which she supposed was necessary as they were building a number of vessels at the yard and would be continually in need of fresh parts.

Frankly, she couldn't see how they kept everything straight.

"Okay," she said to Don after a few minutes. "This is damned impressive. What I don't understand is how you keep track of everything. That part over there, for example—whatever it is. How does it get to the appropriate ship to be installed? What if there's a delay? Does it get put on a shelf somewhere?"

Her old friend grinned at her. "Everything is tagged so that it can be tracked down. Once a part is on the schedule, it gets built. If the schedule slips, so does the manufacture of the part. If there's some type of short-term holdup, the part gets put into one of the storage rooms for retrieval.

"With computer assistance, it's not hard to keep track of everything that needs to be built for a given project. Or even for a project that is already complete. I could look back at any of the ships previously constructed here and tell you when each and every part for it was made, shipped to the construction site, and installed."

She cocked her head. "If it's so automated, what do they need you for? To stand around and look important?"

He laughed. "It seems like that some days. I spent a lot of time wandering between systems and making sure everything is operating as it should and that all parts are accounted for. I suppose you could say I'm a glorified bean counter and maintenance man."

"That seems like a lot of work for one person," Kelsey said. "Shouldn't there be a team of you?"

"All joking aside, Captain, there *is* a team working on this. We work on different shifts to make sure someone is always here. There are always three of us on shift. It's such a large facility that we occasionally work an entire shift without seeing one another, but we're here."

At that moment, one of the machines one level up began emitting an insistent beep, and a small red light started flashing on top of it.

"And speaking of the devil, there calls my master," Don said with a sigh.

"I'll go see what's wrong with that unit and be right back. It should only take me a couple of minutes to get whatever is out of alignment back on track. Just wait here, I'll take care of it, and we'll go have lunch."

With that, Don set off for a lift serving that side of the compartment.

As soon as he was out of sight, Carl stepped over to one of the machines near them. "Keep an eye out for anybody coming by. I'm going to install a shunt on this machine so I can access the computer system inside the facility."

Veronica watched one way, while Princess Kelsey watched the other. There was no one in sight, but that didn't mean someone couldn't just appear without warning.

The young scientist quickly took off an access panel and dug into the guts of the machine. Sixty seconds later, he had it back together and was standing beside them as if nothing had happened.

"I'm accessing the shunt now just to see what I can get to," he said. "This machine doesn't look like it's set up to manufacture flip drive parts. I need to figure out where exactly the machine we need is located and how to get into its programming."

He closed his eyes for about thirty seconds and then smiled. "Found it. It's on level three just above us. As it's a specialized piece of equipment, I'm going to have to access it directly. I'm not getting much more than the location from here."

"What if Don comes back?" Veronica asked, concerned. "If you're not here, that's going to make him suspicious."

Carl shrugged. "It's not as if we have a choice. If we skip this opportunity, we may never get another one. Tell him I went looking for the bathroom or something."

With that, the young man headed for the lift on this side of the compartment, moving quickly and pressing the button. The doors slid open, he stepped inside, and he was gone.

The next three minutes dragged by with incredible slowness. Veronica willed the scientist to reappear every few seconds, but of course, he didn't.

Instead, the first lift opened, and Don walked out. He grinned at them as he walked over. "Problem solved. Let's go get something to eat."

Then he frowned. "Where's Mr. Owlet? This is a secure facility, he can't just wander around. Technically, I shouldn't have left any of you unescorted."

"He had to go find the bathroom," Princess Kelsey said. "I promise he'll be right back. While we're waiting, can you tell me how this room is broken down? Do specific sections of machines work on specific parts, or is it all random?"

Don hadn't stopped frowning, but he did turn to face the short woman. That put his back toward the lift that Carl had used. With any luck at all, he wouldn't see the young man return.

"It's complicated, but each of these sections holds machines that work on related parts. That simplifies the process of getting the raw materials segregated. I can break down which floors do what kind of work, but I really shouldn't be talking about that level of detail. Which way did he go? We should go find him."

Out of the corner of her eye, Veronica saw the lift doors open. Her relief was short-lived, though. An unknown man in a Fleet uniform stepped out from the lift, pushing Carl in front of him.

They'd been caught.

29

Zia made her way to the receptionist's apartment carefully, being absolutely certain to look casual as she walked down the corridor but keeping an eagle eye out for anything that looked out of place. Ralph Halstead knew what she looked like, so an inopportune meeting would be a very, *very* bad thing.

Doctor Rehnquist followed along behind her, looking completely out of place and somewhat shifty as he attempted to sneak along.

"Just walk, Doctor," she said softly, shooting him a glance. "You look like you're up to something."

"I *am* up to something," he said in something close to a stage whisper. "I've never done anything like this before."

"Talk to me in a soft, but normal, tone of voice," she said firmly. "Don't whisper. That looks suspicious.

"Once we get to the apartment, what are you hoping to find in the computer system? How is it going to help us determine if what we're looking for exists?"

The older man cleared his throat. "If, as Colonel Talbot suspects, the computer system is linked to the research facility to use its computational resources, that means some kind of connection has already been established that bypasses the firewalls. Perhaps not all of them, but it will get us into a better position to assess what needs to happen next.

"From that vantage point, I should be able to get into the files detailing what research projects are currently underway. Perhaps even those that are shelved or completed. Probably not the classified data, but at least summaries of what the research entails."

She nodded as they turned into the apartment building. "What about the security feeds from the classified section of the building? Will you be able to access those from here as well?"

The man shrugged as they entered the stairs. "Perhaps. At a minimum, I should be able to get the security feeds in the nonclassified areas of the building. I hope to also gain control over the side entrance so that I can allow our people access."

No one was in the hallway when they exited the stairwell, so she walked up to the man's apartment briskly and opened the door.

Inside, she found a surprise. Talbot had Ralph Halstead at stunner point. The young man was seated on his own couch with his hands folded in his lap. He looked a little frightened. Understandably so.

"He showed up out of the blue," Talbot said grumpily. "This is probably going to upset our schedule."

"I don't suppose I can ask what's going on," the young man said. "I'm not exactly certain how breaking into my apartment and kidnapping me is going to get your niece medical treatment sooner."

Yes, this was going to severely upset their schedule. They could probably stash the young man for a day and get away with it. If he went incommunicado for longer than that, someone would come looking for him.

"This is a complication we could've done without," Zia agreed with a shake of her head. "Doctor, why don't you head back and see what you can find. Make the most of this opportunity. We may not get one like it again."

She considered what to tell the young man. The truth was definitely off-limits. They needed a lie that made sense but didn't give the Rebel Empire a clue to what they'd *really* been up to.

"Industrial espionage," she said as if she were admitting something she'd rather not. "You discovering us does complicate our schedule, but we'll get what we need and be gone before anyone else on this station is aware of what we're up to.

"If you cooperate, we'll leave you unharmed. If you attempt to cause us trouble, we're going to have to disable you until we get away. I'd much rather not harm you, so I suggest you do the smart thing and cooperate."

His expression was somewhat unreadable, but he nodded. "I'll do whatever you want. Just don't hurt me."

Talbot stepped close to her while still keeping the stunner aimed at the young man. "What the hell do we do now?" he asked softly.

"We play this by ear. Follow my lead."

She raised her voice slightly so that the boy could hear her. "Is your computer system tapped into the research facility computers? Don't bother lying. My compatriot is examining it right now, and he'll be able to tell us the truth in just a couple of minutes."

With a sigh, Ralph nodded. "They have a lot of computer power that they're not using, so I borrowed my aunt's login credentials to get into the external systems without them being aware. It won't get you into the classified research computers, though. Those are isolated."

"I suppose that's the best we can hope for," she said with a sigh. "Why did you come home early?"

The young man looked embarrassed. "Since I live so close to the research center, I often eat lunch at home. It saves me a little bit of money and lets me get away from Regina for little bit. She's something of a pain."

His admission made Zia laugh a little. "I can completely understand that. I really am sorry that you've gotten caught up in this. Honestly, all we were doing was casing your apartment so that we could sneak in tonight and clone your identification. Under other circumstances, you'd never have known we were here."

"I realize you probably can't answer this question," Ralph said slowly, "but I'm not certain why you're so interested in what could only be a specialized kind of regeneration. Normal medical regeneration is good enough for just about any kind of injury. I don't understand why any company would be looking for something so focused."

She raised an eyebrow. "And yet the research center is working on just that."

Ralph shrugged. "The research is funded by the Lords. If we were doing this for profit, that might be a different thing, but our research center is kind of specialized. I can't tell you for certain what use this technology would be put to, if it actually exists, but the Lords won't be pleased at having someone meddle in their affairs."

If only he knew how pissed they'd *really* be if they knew the truth.

Zia was still pondering how to answer his very logical questions when Doctor Rehnquist stepped out into the living room and cleared his throat softly.

"Excuse me," she said as she stepped over to the doctor and drew him back into the hallway. "Have you found something?"

The man nodded, a grin on his face. "Your intrusion specialist and I have been going over the young man's computer closely. He has all the access we desire, though I must confess that he's hidden it rather well. I'm quite impressed with his skills."

She frowned. "I'm not certain I understand. What exactly did you find?"

The research scientist turned so that his back was facing toward the living room. "That's not a gaming computer, though it's certainly meant to look like one. In fact, I suspect our young friend uses it as such, but that's not its true purpose.

"What he has in there is a very powerful machine dedicated to hacking into secure systems. Buried underneath its disguise as a gaming computer, it has a sophisticated array of penetration tools.

"The young man has completely hacked into the research center. Not just the public areas of the system, either. He's penetrated the secure firewalls. We have *complete* access to everything but the labs themselves."

Zia found herself blinking in shock. "Wait a minute. You're telling me that that earnest young man is some kind of criminal and that he's been busy doing exactly what we want to do all this time?"

The scientist nodded energetically. "Indeed."

Well, holy crap.

"Good work, Doctor. Get back in there and make certain we can duplicate that access, just in case we have to run. Also, go through their files and see if they really do have a research project that matches what we're looking for. This is our big chance. Let's not waste it."

Zia walked back into the living room and smiled at Talbot. "You're going to like this."

Before he could respond, the door burst open, and two men came rushing in, weapons in their hands. Their attention zeroed in on Talbot, likely because he was armed.

At the same moment, Ralph Halstead drew a hidden weapon from between the cushions on his couch, raising it to point directly at Zia.

That instant seemed to last an eternity, and then everyone started firing.

* * *

Kelsey forced a relieved smile onto her face. "There you are, Carl! Did you find the restroom?"

He shook his head and gave her a wry smile. "No such luck. I ran into this gentleman and was hoping he'd point me in the right direction, but he's pretty annoyed to find me unescorted."

The man pushed Carl forward as the pair got closer to the group. "I found this guy wandering on level three, Commander. Should I call security?"

Sommerville stared at Veronica for a few seconds. "I don't think that'll be necessary, Jack. I'm sure it was just an honest mistake. Head back to your post."

The man looked unsure about that, but he headed back for the lift.

Once he was gone, Sommerville put his hands on his hips and focused his attention on Carl. "What were you really doing, Mr. Owlet?"

"He was just looking for the—" Kelsey started.

Sommerville held up a finger toward her. "If you don't mind, I'd like to have Mr. Owlet answer for himself, Captain Delatorre. Depending on how satisfied I am with what he says, I might end up calling security after all. Be forewarned, I'm not buying the restroom story."

As Kelsey watched apprehensively, Carl sighed. "You're right. I'm their tech guy. I just wanted to get a closer look at some of the other pieces of equipment to see if they were like the ones down here. I meant no harm, Commander. I have Fleet clearance, and I wouldn't jeopardize our mission. I'm sorry."

Kelsey held her breath wondering if Sommerville was going to believe them or call security. If he seemed doubtful, she was going to have to take him down and then they'd have to go hunt the fellow that had seen Carl. That would screw their primary mission, so she really hoped it wasn't necessary.

The man kept his attention focused on Carl for a long few seconds and then nodded. "It's not very respectful to my position here or me personally, but I can believe that. Unfortunately, it means that our little tour is over. Trust only goes so far. I'm afraid you've abused mine, and I'm going to have to ask you to leave."

Veronica sighed but nodded. "I understand. I'm sorry, Don."

"So am I. I'm afraid that I'm going to have to cancel lunch. I need to perform a walk-through on level three to make certain that nothing has been tampered with."

He turned his attention to Kelsey. "I wish you the best of luck in your mission, Captain Delatorre. If we meet again, I hope it's under more auspicious circumstances."

Fifteen minutes later, Commander Sommerville had escorted them completely out of the Fleet area before turning around and returning to his duty station without a word.

His unspoken message was perfectly clear. They were not welcome in the Fleet section of the shipyard. Kelsey wouldn't be surprised if he'd put a flag on them and would be notified if they attempted to go back inside the Fleet area.

Kelsey led the others to a nearby café, and they ordered some coffee and sweets. The large window nearby had a stunning view of Archibald's red moon as the shipyard orbited around it. She wondered briefly what caused the intense shade of scarlet but set that aside. They had more important things to worry about.

Once the waiter had departed, she leaned in toward Carl. "What happened?"

"It isn't as bad as it looks," he assured her. "I put one shunt into the machine that makes the flip drives and the last into a general computer hookup in the main bulkhead. That one should give us a lot of information about all of the systems and what they've been doing.

"The guy that caught me did so after I'd closed everything up and was headed back for the lift. I didn't have a chance to hide because he was inside it. I gave him my cover story, but he wasn't having any of it. He dragged me downstairs, and you know the rest."

Kelsey turned her attention to Veronica. "Is your friend going to let this go, or is he going to keep digging till he finds something? Is he going to report us?"

Veronica looked uncertain. "I don't think he's going to report us, but that doesn't mean he won't look very closely at everything on level three. It's possible he could find the shunts."

"That's not very likely," Carl said with a shake of his head. "The shunts are designed to look like other components. Nothing he sees will look out of place unless he's *intimately* familiar with what should've been there to begin with."

"We'll just have to hope for the best, then," Kelsey said. "What do we know? Can we do this?"

"It looks like they've already been building a ship that needs a flip drive that might work for our purposes," Carl said. "One of those freighters that Veronica was talking about earlier is about to enter its final trials, or so the construction logs say. I've looked over the design parameters for its flip drive. It's weak for what we need, but if we're cautious, it might work."

"That doesn't sound very promising," Kelsey said with a sigh. "I was hoping we'd be able to get something perfect for what we need, but I suppose that was a long shot. Can't we just have the manufacturing equipment make us a perfectly designed flip drive?"

The young scientist shrugged. "Sure. I can have it build one and put it into storage, but we'd still have to get it out. With Commander Sommerville's suspicions raised, that's probably a lot more dangerous than slipping on board a freighter with a small crew and stealing it during the test flight."

"I have an idea," Veronica said. "Don said something about the system being able to automatically deliver parts where they're needed. Could you have the manufacturing equipment build the perfect flip drive for *Audacious*, deliver it to the target ship, and then erase all traces that you had done so?"

Her young friend pondered that for a moment and then nodded. "I have the plans. I even have updated plans that have the modulator installed that would allow the ship to use multiflip points without risking another burnout.

"The problem is that I'd have to be here to direct things. It's a new drive, and we don't want a problem with it to attract Commander Sommerville's attention. Then comes the order to ship it to the freighter. I can't give it that instruction until the manufacturing is complete."

"How long will it take to build the flip drive?" Kelsey asked.

"Based on what I can see, the machine takes premanufactured parts where it can and puts them together. It only produces unique elements when the design calls for something that's not in storage.

"I think I can have the new flip drive finished in about eight hours. If I then schedule it to be immediately delivered to the ship and placed into one of the storage holds, that means it'll be ready sometime tonight. I'll have to stay here and oversee that though."

Kelsey shook her head slowly. "This is where we take a big risk because I'm not leaving you here where they might pick you up. We'll call for a shuttle to come pick us up and have them bring one of the FTL coms.

"Fiona can direct the construction of the flip drive and see that it's shipped to the right place. She can then erase all evidence it was ever built. If anyone saw those plans, they'd deduce what kind of flip point it's useful for.

"That will also give her some access to the Fleet computer systems. How much access would Fiona have?"

Carl shrugged. "A lot."

Kelsey nodded. "There's undoubtedly a lot of interesting information in there, but that's a bonus. We have to have the right flip drive, and we'll take this risk to make it happen.

"Get things in motion, Carl. We'll need to recover the FTL com when the drive is complete, but we'll figure out that part when the time comes. This means that whether the other team is finished or not, we're getting out of the Archibald system tonight."

30

Talbot had just a moment to bless all the fighting practice he'd had with Kelsey over the last year as he responded to the unexpected attack. Her speed had honed his reflexes to a razor's edge, though she still trashed him every time.

As he had his weapon out, he only had to pivot slightly to fire at the intruders coming through the door. He knew where they were, whereas they hadn't had a firm grasp of where he'd be standing when they rushed in.

Talbot's stunner bolt took the lead attacker in the chest and dropped him to the floor. Even as the second man was firing at him, Talbot was dropping below the shot. A grunt behind him told Talbot that it had still found a target in Zia.

He fired as soon as he hit the floor, taking the second man in the lower torso and dropping him as well.

A stunner bolt struck the carpet right in front of Talbot's face, coming from the couch. Somehow, their prisoner had gotten his hands on a weapon. Perfect.

Even as he was rolling onto his side to return fire, Bill Smith appeared in the doorway leading into the rest of the apartment and shot the young hacker on the couch with his stunner.

Talbot leapt to his feet without waiting to see the results of the shot and threw himself into the hallway. He suspected there would be more intruders waiting to rush into the apartment, and he wasn't disappointed.

Two more people waited in the hall, a man and a woman. The man was armed, so Talbot shot him first. The man's return fire missed the marine by scant centimeters as he gripped his weapon spasmodically.

The woman opened her mouth to say something or maybe to shout, so

Talbot shot her as well. Miraculously, no one else in the building seem to notice all the commotion. At least not yet.

Smith stuck his head out, ready to assist in the fight, so Talbot drafted him into getting the two new prisoners into the apartment.

Moments later, they'd dragged the man inside and dropped him on top of the other two. Talbot was a little gentler with the woman and set her on the couch next to the unconscious hacker.

Smith locked the door again. Talbot had been certain he'd secured it after Zia had arrived, so one of these people undoubtedly had an entry code. This wasn't a random attack.

"Doctor Rehnquist, you need to hurry up," Talbot called out as he made his way to Zia's unconscious form. "Now that we've had visitors, we can assume there'll be more. We need to get out of here. How much longer?"

"I'm wrapping up what I need to do now. Give me three minutes, and I'll have us our own access to the facility computers, independent of this hardware."

"Make it two if you can."

Smith was watching the door, so Talbot holstered his weapon and went to examine the prisoners. He swiftly searched through their pockets and found their identification. Not that they'd mean anything to him.

The woman had an identification badge that indicated she worked at the research center. It showed her name as "Adriana Lipp, PhD." The man from the hall was Kevin Lipp.

"Well, well, well," he muttered. "It looks as if this is a family affair. I certainly wish we could take everyone back to our place for a more detailed questioning, but that seems unlikely considering we'd have to wander through the corridors with them over our shoulders."

"It's not out of the question, if you know what you're doing," Smith said. "Keep an eye on the door, and I'll be right back."

He ducked out into the hallway and was back a minute later pushing a large laundry hamper.

"Where the hell did you find that?" Talbot demanded.

"I saw a sign at the end of the hall. Apparently, this apartment building has a central laundry that the tenants are eligible to use. I tossed out the bags of personal clothing and left the sheets and pillowcases in the cart. We should be able to cover everyone up with those and not suffocate anybody."

Talbot eyed the size of the hamper and slowly nodded. "Maybe. It'll be a tight fit, but I'd rather not leave any witnesses that could describe us later."

Doctor Rehnquist came out and stopped abruptly as he saw all of the bodies lying around the living room. "Good heavens! What happened?"

"You really need to work on your situational awareness skills, Doctor," Talbot said. "These are our young hacker's allies. Did you get everything you needed?"

The scientist nodded. "I physically removed all the storage media. I'll have plenty of time to go over everything the young man has stolen, and I took the time to add another access pathway through the firewalls to allow us to use my equipment for the operation."

"Excellent," Talbot said with a sharp nod. "Smith, you're on lead. We want to make sure nobody raises an eyebrow when we come by. If they do, we're going to have to stun them and make a run for it. I'd rather not do that, but if push comes to shove, that's the plan."

The intrusion specialist signaled his understanding. "Just push that thing like you have every right to do so, and no one will pay you any mind. If anybody asks what you're doing, I'll handle it.

"Doctor Rehnquist, I want you to follow along behind us. Stay back at least thirty meters and pretend you don't know us. Don't even look at us. Just walk back to our hotel."

The scientist raised an eyebrow. "Speaking of our hotel, exactly how are you planning on getting that thing through the front door? I suspect the management is going to object if you try to bring it through the lobby."

Smith smiled. "Our hotel has a freight entrance. I've already taken the liberty of bypassing the security. We'll go in that way and head up the service lift to our floor. If we run into anyone, I'll bribe them to look the other way."

Talbot certainly hoped that worked, but it wasn't as if they had a whole lot of choice in the matter. They needed to get back to their rooms as soon as possible. The research center might not miss their wayward receptionist, but a misplaced research scientist could potentially raise the alarm.

They'd certainly be aware if she failed to show up at work as expected the next day. That pretty much guaranteed they'd have to carry off their intrusion and theft tonight.

"Doctor, did you find anything in the files to indicate they were working on the kind of regeneration equipment we need?" Talbot asked the scientist.

The older man nodded with a smile. "Indeed. As a matter of pure luck, I suppose, Doctor Lipp here is the chief researcher on that project. Sadly for us, her nephew was primarily interested in other projects."

"I'm glad to hear that they have something suitable," Talbot said. "Is there any indication of exactly what projects young Ralph is most interested in?"

The scientist shrugged. "He has a number of files that I haven't had a chance to peruse. I can take care of that once we get back to the hotel. Perhaps by dark I can have a status report for you."

Talbot knew that was the best he was going to get, so he didn't push the matter. He and Smith carefully placed everyone into the cart and covered them with sheets and pillowcases. They then headed down the hallway toward the freight elevator. It took both of them to move the heavy cart.

He crossed his fingers as they walked, praying they didn't run into any trouble. If something went wrong now, it could go very badly for all of them.

"Once we get back to the hotel, I want you to go hit Doctor Lipp's apartment," Talbot told Smith. "We might get lucky, and she'll have copies of her files at home."

"We can't count on that," Smith said with a grunt, "but I suppose it doesn't hurt to try."

Talbot felt better the further away from the apartment building. He hoped Kelsey's side of the operation was going more smoothly than his. It felt as if he were just staying just one step ahead of disaster.

* * *

VERONICA WALKED into chaos as she arrived back at the hotel rooms on the station. It seemed that Colonel Talbot had run into a little more excitement than he'd planned on while scouting out the research center.

They'd apparently gotten into some kind of firefight in the receptionist's apartment and now had five prisoners. That raised a lot of interesting questions about who the receptionist and his aunt were really working for.

Zia wasn't going to be pleased when she woke up either. Stunner headaches were a bitch.

Doctor Zoboroski was monitoring everyone and assured Princess Kelsey that there would be no lasting damage. At his best guess, the everyone would regain consciousness in about two hours.

They'd put Zia in the room she shared with Veronica while the prisoners were cuffed and secured in separate rooms under guard. They'd also put a blocker in the aunt's room. It only had a short range so it didn't affect any of their people.

Unlike her nephew or the others, she'd had implants. They couldn't allow her to wake up and communicate with the station, or she'd call for help. They also couldn't allow others to track her based on those same implants.

Bill Smith had disabled everyone's com units the moment they'd captured them. He'd be overseeing any data extraction when he got back from Doctor Lipp's place.

On the positive side, it seemed they'd gotten information and access into the computers at the research facility. Doctor Rehnquist started cheerfully explaining everything he'd found to Carl Owlet as soon as the young man had walked in the door. Together, the two scientists were firming up their access and knowledge of the facility in preparation for a raid tonight.

Princess Kelsey was closeted with Colonel Talbot and Cain Hopwood discussing the particulars of both missions. They'd invited her to join them, but Veronica decided to do a little bit of scouting on her own.

Something felt off to her about the way people had been behaving on the station since they got back. They seemed a little bit jumpy. More worried. She suspected something had happened, and she needed to find out what that was.

Before heading out, she stopped in her room to change into something more appropriate. Once she'd dressed, she let herself out quietly and made her way down the corridor to a local bar. One that seemed to have a solid Fleet presence.

If anyone knew what was happening in the system, they'd be in this room. The presence of alcohol made it much more likely they'd share something they probably shouldn't too.

The bar was a fairly upscale establishment, not some dark hole where serious drinkers went to drown their sorrows. The lighting was good, the clientele well dressed, and based on the prices, the liquor was of good quality.

A glance around told her that there was a significant amount of serious conversation taking place. Every table seemed to hold people with their heads bent close together, discussing something. There was definitely something afoot.

None of the Fleet officers were seated alone, so Veronica made her way to the bar instead. Bartenders seemed to hear everything. Perhaps she could get the information she needed that way.

She ordered a fairly upscale drink and left enough cash beside it to make for a hefty tip. As the woman was taking it, Veronica leaned forward so that she didn't need to raise her voice too much.

"What's everyone worried about? They all seem so nervous."

The bartender leaned toward her. "You hear those rumors about the Ghosts attacking some system nearby? It seems like they're coming our way. From what I hear, all Fleet elements are being put on alert. They're worried the shipyard might be a target. That Archibald itself might even be a target.

"I don't know about anyone else, but when I get off shift in an hour, I'm headed straight down to the surface. I've already got a ticket on one of the evening shuttles. As soon as I heard about the trouble, I picked it up while I was on break.

"It won't be long before everyone is trying to get off the station, so if you haven't gotten tickets down to the surface, you might want to go ahead and get them now before the rush starts. I wouldn't want to be stuck here if the Ghosts come calling."

Veronica shook her head as the woman moved off to serve someone else. Perfect. Their already tight schedule had just gotten significantly more complicated.

As she finished her drink, Veronica chuckled bitterly. With their luck, it was an almost certainty that the Clans would arrive tonight. She had to get back to the hotel and let Princess Kelsey know.

They'd have to begin preparing to hijack that ship as soon as the new flip drive was delivered. Time was no longer on their side.

31

Zia sat up, clutched her pounding head, and wondering what had happened. Then she remembered the attack in the apartment.

A glance around the room told her she was back at the hotel, so they'd won the fight. Well, that was a pleasant surprise. Considering how abrupt the ambush had been, she'd been afraid they'd lose.

She staggered to the bathroom and washed her face. A small package of painkillers sat beside the sink with a note to take them. That was thoughtful.

It only took a few minutes to find Princess Kelsey and Talbot. They were closeted with Cain Hopwood. Only Veronica was missing.

Kelsey smiled as she came in. "Oh good, you're awake. Feeling okay?"

"That's debatable," Zia grumbled. "My head is beating like a drum. I hate stunners."

Talbot grinned at her. "They beat the heck out of flechettes. As you've already figured out, we won the fight. Our little friend wasn't just a receptionist. It turns out he was an industrial spy or something. He, his aunt, and her husband were stealing technology from the research center. I guess they won't be thrilled with the competition."

"Probably not." Zia sat down and poured herself a glass of water from the handy pitcher. "Did we get what we needed?"

The marine nodded. "We have several bits of good news. First, the project his aunt was working on is indeed an advanced regeneration machine that can probably take care of what we need done for Commodore Murdoch. I realize that we'd be in better shape if we could focus on just one mission, but at least we're past guessing.

"Second, the receptionist had thoroughly penetrated the center's firewalls. He had complete access to the restricted areas and even files from some of the projects. Unless it was on a stand-alone computer, he could get to it. And third, we have both his aunt and uncle stashed in a room nearby under guard.

"I expect they're waking up about now. I'll question them before we make our move. They might be able to give us some clarity about the project. Anything that speeds us along is a good thing."

She nodded in spite of her pounding headache. "That's good news. Tell me the bad news."

"You're a pessimist," Kelsey said gloomily.

"I'm an optimist with a sense of history. The bad news."

"He didn't have any files from his aunt's project," Kelsey said with a chuckle. "Either she has them elsewhere or it's on a stand-alone computer. We have Bill Smith checking her place, but we probably still need to get the files from the center as well as any hardware to be certain we have everything we need.

"Thankfully, Ralph has their security thoroughly penetrated. We don't even need his identification card to get in. Carl said he can create false identities for everyone involved and print up cards that will work if you're confronted. Basically, you should be able to waltz right in, steal everything you need, and waltz back out."

Zia laughed as the door opened and admitted Veronica. "Nothing ever works that easily for us. There will be some major complication along the way."

"I'm not sure what we're talking about," Veronica said as she took a seat, "but I'm here to deliver the mandatory complication. Word is out that the Ghosts are moving toward this system. Fleet is on alert, expecting an intrusion at some point in the next few days.

"We're going to have to move tonight if we expect to get clear before they get here. If I was a betting woman, I'd wager they'll show up at the worst possible moment. For example, while we're busy carrying out our plans tonight."

Kelsey swore. "I wonder what that's going to do to security around the shipyard. Are we still going to be able to slip onto the freighter once our new flip drive is delivered? If we can, are we going to be able to get away without Fleet coming down on us like a ton of bricks? Will Carl be able to retrieve the FTL com?"

Zia cocked her head? "Freighter? FTL com? What did I miss?"

Her short friend shrugged. "We got caught planting Carl's shunts, but they didn't get the shunts themselves. I ordered Carl to hide an FTL com on the shipyard so Fiona could direct the manufacture of the flip drive we need, have it delivered to a freighter we can steal, and plunder their computers for any interesting information.

"The original plan was for Carl to retrieve the com before we leave, but we might have to send a destruct signal to it if we don't have time. Or if we can't get back aboard the yard to get it. We can handle that. I'm worried about getting away when we steal the ship."

"If the ship is in operable condition, then it's going to be ordered to flee as soon as things start looking bad," Veronica said. "If we can get our people on board and ready to secure the vessel ahead of that, we can wait for the real crew to get orders to make a run for it and then take them out."

"What if those orders never come?" Talbot asked. "What if the attack doesn't make it to Archibald?"

"Then the ship will be ordered to do its trials. There's also a good chance it will be used to move critical equipment out of this system. That freighter is a big ship. So long as we hide ourselves well, there's not going to be enough crew on board to find us. We can wait until it gets away from the shipyard to take it over at our leisure."

Cain Hopwood nodded. "If we can get my crew on board, I'd say we have a pretty good chance of taking it over without anyone being the wiser. We can install lockouts on the communication and control systems to make sure.

"Even though the Rebel Empire Fleet might be at a higher state of alert, they'll have their eyes on the flip point. They're not going to expect someone to try stealing a ship right out from under their noses. We can use that to our advantage."

"It sounds as if both plans are advanced enough to execute," Zia said slowly. "What are we going to do at the research center? Sneak inside with the small ring and bring the larger ring through inside the center? Then move everything out to our freighter and walk back out?"

Kelsey nodded. "Something very much like that. Since Carl has access to the security system, he should be able to cancel any calls for help. That's going to be the initial response of anyone that feels like you shouldn't be there. With him watching over your shoulder, you should be able to get the equipment you need and get the hell out of there pretty fast."

Zia certainly hoped it worked out like that, but she'd wager there would be complications. There always were.

"Do we have any idea what *Persephone* is doing?" she asked. "We might have need of the marines on board that ship and even their weapons if things get really hairy. And what about the Rebel Empire Fleet ships at the outer gas giant?"

"We risked contacting Angela. The Rebel Empire ships arrived at the gas giant and haven't left. Our probes say they're sending cutters and pinnaces from all ships down into the atmosphere. I'd wager they're sending crew to the battlecruisers hiding there so they can use them to fight the Clans."

Veronica rubbed her eyes. "I think it's a fair bet that those ships are going to move back toward the flip point or come to Archibald orbit before too much longer. We're going to have to take that into account. If they show up while we're in the process of stealing the freighter, that could get ugly really fast."

Princess Kelsey crossed her arms and nodded. "Both missions have to be carried out tonight."

"I think your best bet is to make the attack at the research center about one in the morning," Cain said. "It's far enough past closing that they won't be expecting trouble, but it gives you enough time to finish everything before the early risers come in the door tomorrow morning. All you'll need to deal with are the researchers and staff there overnight."

"What about our new prisoners?" Talbot asked. "I'm going to hit them up for more information, but they know what Zia and I look like. That might get the Rebel Empire on our trail sooner than we'd like."

Kelsey grimaced. "We'll have to take them with us. Stun them again before you go, and take them with you. Send them through the transport ring to the ship with the equipment. It'll be good to have the aunt with us in any case, since this is her project. If we have questions about the process, we can ask her.

"We'll want to make our move on the freighter around the same time. There are a lot of small craft flitting around the shipyard, so we shouldn't draw undue attention if we don't come too close."

"The ship is ready for trials, so it won't be inside the yard itself," Cain said. "It's going to be orbiting a short distance away. My people can get off the shuttle at range and use suit thrusters to land on its hull and gain access. We should be able to settle ourselves into a hiding place and wait to make our move with no one the wiser."

"There we go," Kelsey said. "That gives us about ten hours before we need to execute both missions. Zia and Talbot, brief your people and get some sleep if you can. Have someone take your noncritical gear back to your shuttles before go time. Leave nothing here at the hotel for the Rebel Empire to find.

"Veronica and I will go with Cain to our freighter. We'll eat and sleep too. Remember, if the Clans attack, we'll be leaving in a hurry. If the Rebel Fleet warships come in, we might have to sneak away a bit more stealthily. If push comes to shove, *Persephone* will have to create a diversion."

Talbot rapped his knuckles on the table. "This is it. We're either going to succeed tonight or go down in flames. Let's make sure we give it our best effort."

"I'm feeling good," Kelsey said. "Only one thing is bothering me. After disguising myself as Delatorre and everything, I never got to blackmail anyone."

Zia laughed. "Maybe next time."

* * *

Kelsey, Talbot, and her team moved back to their cargo shuttle as nonchalantly as they could. They traveled in small groups and did nothing to draw undue attention to themselves.

Even though she expected someone to stop them and try to extort money, everyone arrived at the shuttle without having been harassed. They returned to the freighter without problem.

There was enough time before they were to execute their plan for her to grow nervous and twitchy. With her implants, she didn't require nearly enough sleep to get through until departure time.

Instead, she spent the time going over their scanner readings and refining her thoughts on how they'd get on board the freighter and what they'd do when they did. Cain Hopwood was smarter than she was and was sleeping until just about an hour before they were ready to launch, but she ran what she'd thought about past him as they were making final preparations.

"I think that looks good, as far as it goes, but we're going to have to play this by ear. Once we get on board that freighter, anything can happen. I think it's going to be relatively safe for us until then. Our suits are made to avoid detection so no one is going to see us coming.

"The problem is going to come in once we get inside the ship. There's no telling where the crew is located. I'm hopeful most of them will be in their quarters asleep. Or if we're lucky, not even on board. A skeleton crew would be ideal."

She nodded at him and headed to suit up. "We'll deal with the situation as we find it. Thanks again for your help. You guys have made our successes possible in so many ways. Rest assured that the Empire will remember this when we get home."

A little bit more than an hour later, their shuttle detached from the freighter and headed away from the station. Word from Fiona had come in that the flip drive was complete and had just been delivered to the freighter. One major milestone complete.

Their cargo shuttle wasn't passing close enough to the shipyard to be challenged, though it was at the very edge of what they thought they could get away with. The target freighter was still too far away to be seen visually. Even the shipyard was only a bright speck in the distance.

Thankfully, their stealth suits had overpowered thrusters, and they had no lack of fuel to get to where they needed to go.

Even with all the pressure on them, Kelsey took a moment to admire Archibald after they stepped out into space. The planet was all greens and blues, just rising above the curve of the red moon. Wispy clouds covered a substantial portion of the planet's surface. It was a beautiful world. Perhaps not as pretty as Avalon, but she had to admit she was biased.

"We'd best be on our way," Cain said. "By my best estimate, it'll take us almost an hour to get to the freighter. If everything goes to hell, I'd rather not be floating in space when it happens."

The slow trip to the freighter was rough on her nerves, but Kelsey had gotten much better at dealing with that sort of thing over the last few years. She distracted herself by going over the deck plans that Carl had gotten for them. They needed to find a good hiding place, and she wanted to be sure they were picking the right one.

The final approach was nerve-racking. If anyone observed them visually, they were screwed. She barely breathed until they finally touched down on the ship's hull.

They'd decided not to use even low-powered radio because of the risk of being detected. This was Cain's operation now. He'd get them inside without detection and deal with any unfortunate incidents involving the crew.

She couldn't help feeling a sense of impending doom. This was the part of the mission where things usually went wrong. Often catastrophically wrong.

Five minutes later, Cain's people had the outer airlock door open, and he made a hand gesture for everyone to move into the airlock in groups. This was it.

32

After Kelsey and her people left, Talbot felt like a sword was hanging over his head. He kept expecting a call saying that they'd run into terrible trouble or to hear alarms outside the hotel and see security people rushing around.

That hadn't happened. In fact, the shuttle had made it back to the freighter without any problem, reporting that the drop-off had been smooth and without issue. That didn't stop him from fretting.

He'd distracted himself by interrogating their prisoners. Not that they were being very cooperative. He'd thought the boy would be easier to get information from, but he'd proven exceptionally recalcitrant. He'd smiled and told them nothing.

That impressed Talbot. That level of resistance spoke to either a lot of training or some serious willpower. In either case, he'd had written off getting timely assistance from the young man.

Doctor Lipp was more talkative but still told him nothing. She'd denied everything and claimed she'd received a call for assistance from her nephew.

Neither of them believed that, of course. Any reasonable person would've called security in that set of circumstances, not grabbed her husband and some "friends" to go fight it out in her nephew's apartment.

Bill Smith had gotten back from the woman's dwelling a few minutes ago. He'd gathered a lot of data, but nothing about the project she was working on or the criminal activity she was apparently perpetrating on her employer.

To add to the complexity, the man had also brought back Lipp's cats: a pair of kittens about four months old, both male. One was black and had a stubby tail, and the other was a gray tabby. Both were playful and friendly.

What Talbot was supposed to do with them, he didn't know. Still, the man was right in that he couldn't leave them there. If no one came to check on them, they would die of neglect. Bringing them was the right thing to do.

As far as problems went, they were the least of his worries. Someone would take them back to the cargo shuttles and see them safely on the freighter.

The fact that Lipp had argued with him at least raised the potential that Talbot could get her to tell them something, so he made his way back to her room half an hour before he and Zia would leave for the center.

He entered the room without knocking. It wasn't as if he was going to find her running around loose. She was restrained and under guard. One of the female marines he brought along on this mission even escorted her to the restroom.

When he came in, she was sitting up in bed. Two marines stood against the far wall and the female assigned to watch over her was seated at the small desk.

"My, doesn't this look homey." he said. "How are you feeling, Doctor Lipp?"

She gave him a hard look. "Let me be blunt. I don't know who you are, but you're not going to get any useful information from me, and security is undoubtedly already searching for me and my family. Do yourself a favor and let us go so that you can get the charges against you reduced."

He leaned against the desk and gave her a flat smile. "We both know that's not going to happen. You, your husband, and your nephew were engaged in industrial espionage. If we get caught, you get caught. It's unfortunate for you that we came along and upset your applecart, but your only path out of this as a free woman is in cooperating with us."

She laughed, a bright sound under the circumstances. "You think highly of yourself. If what you said were true—which it isn't—all we have to do is keep our mouths shut until you're gone. It's not as if you're going to take us with you. You're after information, not hostages."

"Maybe. We're after the research project you head at research center, and we need that project to work. Taking you along might suit me fine."

The woman shook her head. "Getting the data I can buy, but you'll never get off the station with the equipment. It's not just a couple of small handheld items. It's easily double the size of a standard regenerator. Not something you're going to put into your pocket and stroll away with, even if you could get access to the lab."

Talbot grinned. "We're not without our tricks, but let's set that aside for the moment. Say you're right and we get caught. We can tell them about you and maybe get a reduced sentence. You're still screwed. Don't forget that we have your nephew's computer access and system as proof."

The woman eyed him for a few seconds. "Just for the sake of this ridiculous discussion, let's say that your fantastic story is true. How does it benefit us to help you? If you succeed, you'll bring all kinds of attention down on the research center. It's going to ruin our operation no matter what."

"Indulge me. It certainly seems as if your nephew has already penetrated the research center's computers quite thoroughly. Why are you still here?"

The woman smiled slightly. "Hypothetically, let's just say that some researchers are more paranoid than others about isolating their research from the network. But, given enough time, they'd have to turn something over to the managers. That gets critical details out into the general research network where a resourceful—if theoretical—thief can access them."

"So, you have some specific project that you need information on that you've been unable to access. We've gotten a basic list of projects from your nephew's computer. Which one are we talking about?"

"Let's pick one at random," she suggested. "Just pulling one out of the air, research project 471DC-3."

"How startlingly specific," Talbot said, amused.

He accessed the list of projects in his implant storage. The receptionist/hacker had picked up a vast amount of data on current and past projects during his intrusion. All of them had the same kind of identifiers. If a project name got out, it wouldn't tell anyone what the researchers were exploring.

Interestingly, there was no data available on the project she named. No indication it even existed.

To avoid hinting at the woman that he had implants, Talbot stepped out of the room for a few minutes and got a cup of coffee before coming back in. He sipped at the hot drink and stared at her.

"Your nephew doesn't have any information on a project like that," he said coolly. "Your hypothetical example might just be too hypothetical."

Doctor Lipp chuckled. "Or perhaps it's so classified that all information revolving around it is kept isolated from even the research network."

"I suspect we're going to need your assistance in using the equipment, and contrary to what you think, we can get you off this station. You're going to be coming with us simply because your knowledge will be helpful. That's happening one way or the other.

"As an incentive, what if we broke into that other research area and stole the data for you? We're already going to be in the facility, so it shouldn't be too much additional trouble to take an extra set of computers."

She raised an eyebrow at him. "That would hardly do me any good if you killed my nephew and me. How do I know that you're not planning something dastardly for us?"

He laughed. "Dastardly. I like that. Look at it this way. We used stunners when you attacked us. Why would we suddenly change to something more lethal?"

"No one had seen your faces at that point," she pointed out somewhat reasonably. "You didn't expect my nephew to come home early, and you certainly didn't expect me and my husband to come after him. Now that you have us, you might decide we've seen too much."

"Want proof we're taking you with us and will let you live? Life doesn't allow for that level of certainty, but we broke into your house and rescued your kittens. A black one and a gray one. They're already off on our ship where you will join them. If we intended to murder you, we probably wouldn't save your cats."

She stared at him with hard eyes but slowly nodded. "I'm inclined to believe you. Since I'm in a bind, I'll take a chance and help you. Getting caught at this point might cost my life, and I no longer have any control over events."

* * *

VERONICA WAITED for her turn through the freighter's airlock a little nervously. Cain Hopwood and his recovery agents had led the way inside and had already reported no contact with any of the crew, but that didn't stop her from feeling on edge.

Princess Kelsey was leading a team to find a hiding place near the bridge. With deck plans provided by Carl Owlet, she had a couple of places in mind that would allow half their force to be ready to seize control of the ship at a moment's notice.

She was in charge of a second team that would seize engineering, but she had one task to perform first. She needed to make certain the flip drive Carl had ordered was safely stored away in the cargo holds.

Team one had already headed out for the bridge, leaving her people waiting for her to give them direction. Veronica consulted the map and pointed down the corridor. Their initial target was a computer interface rather than a hold.

It was positioned on the bulkhead exactly where she'd expected it. Doctor Rehnquist stepped forward and quickly unlocked the interface for her.

Since she had a delivery number, it was a simple matter of consulting the cargo database and having it spit a hold number back at her. Five seconds after she had access, they were on their way to the correct hold.

It was roughly on the way to engineering. In fact, it was close enough that they could wait inside the hold for Princess Kelsey's signal to attack.

The scouts in front kept a close eye out for any randomly encountered crewmen. If someone popped up, they'd have to stun them and that would be bad. Anyone that went suddenly quiet could have their friends looking for them in just a few minutes.

They arrived at the hold without encountering anyone. A different specialist applied her talents to opening the hatch. After a few moments, it slid aside and gave them access.

Half the team entered the hold with their stunners up, searching for trouble. The compartment was unoccupied, and Veronica made her way to join them. The tech closed the hatch behind them.

Veronica quickly realized that the scale of the hold was significantly larger than she'd envisioned. A carrier might be roughly the same size as this ship, but she hadn't seen any open areas this large aboard *Audacious*.

The large hold reminded Veronica of the manufacturing area at the shipyard. The ceiling rose far above their heads and various crates of cargo were strapped to the deck and piled high. It looked somewhat risky to her if the ship had to maneuver, but all the crates were stoutly strapped down.

They spread out looking for the flip drive. Less than a minute later, one of her teammates called her over. She'd found the flip drive.

Only, she hadn't. The order number indicated this was a *different* flip drive.

"Keep looking for our cargo," she ordered, somewhat confused. "It has to be here somewhere."

They found it after another five minutes of searching. It looked *identical* to the first one they'd found. That made Veronica wonder what was going on. Why would someone be shipping a flip drive on this freighter? It was only scheduled to be doing in-system trials.

"Commander Giguere," Jon Paul Olivier said quietly at her shoulder. "I found something I think you need to see."

His expression was unreadable. This probably wasn't good.

The man led her a couple of aisles over, and she stopped dead in her tracks. Stacked on the deck were at least a dozen flip drives. They came in various sizes and configurations, but this was more than just a fluke. What was going on?

Then she saw what was in the row on the other side of the flip drives, and her blood ran cold. Crates and crates of missiles. Based on their size, they looked like Fleet standard munitions.

She walked over and took a closer look. There were several rows of missiles. This cargo hold was filled with weapons.

This didn't make any sense. It had taken days to load all of this cargo. Probably weeks, if other cargo holds held similar load outs. It couldn't be related to evacuating before the Clans attacked.

And, with this amount of equipment stored on the ship, there might be more than just a skeleton crew aboard. In fact, it wouldn't surprise Veronica if there were marines around somewhere and perhaps even a Fleet crew.

The plan called for com silence, but she had to let Princess Kelsey know. The odds were good that there was a lot of trouble waiting just around some corner for them to find.

33

Zia stood in the alley beside the Michael Anderle Memorial Research Center and kept an eye toward the main thoroughfare. Traffic was exceptionally light at this hour, but that didn't mean they were alone in the corridors.

Carl was working on the card reader, if one could call waving a forged card that he'd printed earlier in front of it and having it click open could be called "working."

"Are you sure this isn't going to show up on the security monitors?" she asked in a low voice.

He shook his head. "They're watching a repeated loop of the last two hours. There's been no traffic in or out through this door or inside the corridor housing the research labs. I've blocked the door from logging our entry, so no one is going to be the wiser."

It was about an hour after midnight so she wasn't surprised at the lack of activity. After all, that's why they'd picked this ungodly hour to carry out their raid.

One of the benefits of having penetrated the center's security so thoroughly was that Carl had been able to watch the guards. "Watching the watchers," he'd jokingly said.

It hadn't taken long to figure out the pattern of patrols. At roughly half-hour intervals, a single guard left the security center and tested the exterior doors. Once that was accomplished, the guard returned directly to the security center.

While they could see the long corridor of doors leading to the individual labs in the restricted area, there were no cameras inside the labs themselves, so it was always possible they'd run into unexpected people, but the lack of overt traffic did present them with an opportunity to get in and out without being seen.

Being able to monitor the comings and goings inside the building also allowed their recovery specialists to see the custodial crew in action. They now knew exactly where the cleaners stored their carts and wore coveralls that were identical to the ones in use by the regular workers.

They'd cobbled together a cart of their own to move the small transport ring. It had gotten them a few glances as they'd made their way through the station corridors, but no one really paid them much mind.

Talbot led the way into the research center, his stunner at the ready. Several marines followed him in. Carl was using his implants to monitor all the security feeds, so he'd be able to warn them if security became concerned.

This was Zia's first time on one of these adventures, and she had to admit her adrenaline was really pumping. Her heart thumped in her chest as she led the follow-up group with the cart.

The side entrance to the research facility led into an employee only area that was deserted at this hour. Security had their own break room to make certain no one could easily breach their area at any time. As the rest of the employees were off shift, this section of the building was deserted.

They made it to the single door leading into the research area without incident. Carl's falsified identification got him through. That one door led into a long corridor with four doors on each side that gave no indication of what lay in the labs behind them. Each of the doors had a number on it. Odd numbers on the left, even numbers on the right.

The walls were an unbroken dark gray, as were the doors. No windows. Beside each lab door was a card reader and keypad. Gaining access to an individual lab required both a card and a code, according to Doctor Lipp. Zia was certain that a failure to enter the correct information more than a few times would signal security to come running.

The one they were looking for was lab three. Only once they were certain they had access to the lab they absolutely needed and had set up the large transport ring would they go looking for the second target.

They had Doctor Lipp's identification card, and she'd given them a code, but Zia didn't trust the woman. Carl would probe the system to see if he could get in without it.

Her young friend had brought along a specialized tablet with a series of cables that could plug into various sockets inside this kind of equipment. He carefully pried the keypad apart and examined what he'd found.

To Zia, the electronics would've been indecipherable. If it had been up to her to break in, they'd have been doomed.

Thankfully, Carl was made of sterner stuff. Less than sixty seconds after opening the panel open, the secure door slid aside to admit them. He hadn't entered the code Lipp had given them.

She raised an eyebrow at him as Talbot and his people moved in to sweep the lab. "You're handy to have around. I'm wondering exactly how secure this thing is if you're able to break in so easily."

He grinned at her. "I cheated. Since Doctor Lipp gave us her access code, I was able to double-check it without actually entering it. Systems like this aren't supposed to retain codes, but I've discovered over the years that it rarely works that way in practice.

"People will use parts from other types of equipment when designing something, and they may not always be as secure as they should be. Basically, I used her code to scan all of the electronics to see if I could find a match. Once I'd located it, it was simple enough to verify that the code would open the door and make it do so."

Zia nodded, impressed. "Give you another fifty years, and you're going to be a master criminal. Is this flaw going to be useful at the other lab?"

He shrugged. "Potentially. I started out with a lot of information here, including having cloned Doctor Lipp's identification card. I'm hoping that I can backtrack from a code in the other door to get identification for the user out of the security system. Needless to say, that might be complex, and it's going to take me longer than sixty seconds."

Talbot came back over to the door. "There's nobody in here, and the description of the equipment matches what she told us to expect. We're going to have to go through everything with a fine-toothed comb to be sure, but I think this is the place.

"I'm going to have my folks set up the small transport ring and use it to start bringing in the large ring. Once I get it in place, we'll be able to get everything out of here pretty fast."

"What about the other labs?" she asked. "Just because this lab is empty doesn't mean there aren't people inside them."

"I looked over the feed starting at about five in the afternoon," Carl said. "While I can't see into each lab, I could tally who went into each lab and who came out. If anyone is still working right now, they've been in there since before quitting time."

"I'll keep a couple of marines here in the corridor," Talbot said. "If anyone unexpected pops out, we'll stun them and rush the lab they came from."

Not the most comprehensive plan, but it would have to do.

Zia stepped into the lab as Carl began putting the keypad back together. A quick look around revealed no cameras watching them, so she was fairly confident there would be no record of their presence after they left. Well, except for all the missing equipment and files. People were going to tear out their hair trying to figure out how they'd done it.

"I can oversee this," she told Talbot. "Take Carl and go get what we need from the other laboratory. Be careful. If that project is really hush-hush, there may be extra security measures."

"Relax," he said with a reassuring smile. "We'll make this happen. If you're going to worry about someone, worry about Kelsey. If she can't steal the other freighter, we're screwed."

"You sure know how to make a girl feel better. Get moving."

Zia hoped Kelsey didn't run into trouble. If things went sideways over there, it didn't matter how well she and Talbot did. They'd probably still end up being caught, and that wasn't a fate she wanted to contemplate.

* * *

KELSEY HAD BEEN SEVERELY ANNOYED with Veronica Giguere risking that transmission. At least until she saw the images that went with the warning.

"Holy crap," Kelsey muttered.

Image after image scrolled past her view as she went down the message. There were enough missiles in that hold to completely rearm *Audacious*. There were also a *dozen* flip drives, not including the special one they'd ordered built.

And that was just one hold. There were plenty of others scattered around this ship. What the hell had they stumbled into?

With the time to reflect on it, she realized Veronica had done the right thing in warning her. With this amount of equipment on board, the chances that there were more crew members than she'd planned on were high. They'd be better trained too. If they weren't already on the ship, they might show up at any time.

She turned to Bob Noble, Recovery Incorporated's computer specialist. He'd been working with Jason Young, the company's security specialist, to gain access to the freighter's computer system.

"How is it going?" she asked, hoping her growing worry didn't bleed through into her tone.

"So far, so good," he assured her. "We've got access to the noncritical systems, and Jason is helping me hack our way into the critical systems. Once we have a way to control those, we'll be able to force the bridge hatch open on command and lock down the communication and propulsion systems remotely."

"How long are you anticipating that to take? Can we access the video feeds from the rest of the ship? I'm concerned there may be a larger crew on board the ship than we've anticipated and that they might be more heavily armed too."

Considering that they hadn't anticipated running into armed crewmen at all, even men with stunners would prove problematic. If there were marines aboard, this could turn into a bloodbath very quickly.

"I don't suppose this ship is equipped with anti-boarding weapons," she added. "Just about now I'm thinking it would be a good thing to be able to stun everyone other than ourselves and just sort it out later."

"We won't know until we get into the critical systems, but they aren't standard on a freighter of this class," Young said. "I didn't see any on the way here, but I'll admit I had other things on my mind. Bottom line, don't count on it.

"As far as the time frame for gaining access, we're going slow and careful. I figure another ten or fifteen minutes should give me something. That's for the firewall. After that, each critical system will take more time."

That wasn't the news that Kelsey that had hoped for, but it was what they had to work with. At least Veronica and her people were safe in their cargo hold. Even if someone came into it, they had a lot of space to hide in.

Kelsey and her people were a little bit more constrained. They had to be near the bridge and that ruled out the cargo holds. Instead, they'd secreted themselves into one of the maintenance tubes. She made a mental note to have sensors installed in the maintenance tubes back on their ships because these things were far too convenient for hiding in.

The next fifteen minutes went by so slowly that she thought an hour had passed. Every time she felt like asking if they had made a breakthrough, she'd check her internal chronometer and find out that only a few minutes had passed. It was maddening.

Finally, Bob Noble gave her a thumbs-up. "We've got access to the firewall. I'll start working on getting into the communications and propulsion systems. Jason is working on tapping into the video feeds to see what he can find."

Jason's expression was one of intense concentration as he used his implants to invade the system. "I found the video feeds, and I'm starting to cycle through them now. They aren't even locked down. Sloppy."

Kelsey took a deep breath and forced herself to wait patiently.

"Interesting," he said after a minute. "We have four people on the bridge and one of them is in a Fleet uniform."

"Shunt the feed over to me," Kelsey ordered.

When the image popped up in her implants, she cursed under her breath. It was Lieutenant Commander Don Sommerville.

"What the hell is he doing here?" she asked rhetorically. "This can't be good."

"I've got more bad news," Young said. "I can see a number of people down at the cargo dock. It looks as if we've got an incoming crew. And that's not all. I see some marines in unpowered armor."

Kelsey searched for and found the feed he was watching. There were dozens of crewmen exiting a pair of cargo shuttles. A third shuttle was disgorging what certainly looked like a marine platoon.

What the hell was she going to do now? She couldn't just call everything off. They *needed* that flip drive.

She gritted her teeth. They'd find a way to make it happen. She'd come too far to give up now.

Noble cursed softly. "We've got another problem. A Fleet all-hands notice just came in. There's been an incursion at the flip point. It looks like the Clans have arrived, and they're attacking the battle station. They've come in force."

Perfect.

They needed to take out an armed crew they hadn't expected, steal a ship while the area was under a heightened state of security, and evade an invading hostile force. What could possibly go wrong?

34

Once the small transport ring was set up and the pieces of the larger ring were coming through, Talbot gathered Carl and half a dozen marines to make the side trip to the second laboratory.

Part of him wanted to wait until they'd cleaned out the first lab, but he knew they didn't dare waste the time. If something went wrong on this side mission, they might not complete their primary work before they had to withdraw.

The go-to-hell plan was to barricade themselves in, evacuate through the large ring, and set off explosive charges to destroy the ring past the point of any analysis. They'd rigged plasma grenades all along its circumference.

The blast would wreck not only the lab holding the large transport ring but all of the other labs too. It would probably cause critical damage to the entire building, but the lethal zone should be restricted to the research area.

Destroying the ring would be a terrible loss, but it would get them clear of the station with everything they needed. Security would flip out but wouldn't be able to link this back to his people quickly enough to do anything, he hoped. Best case, he wouldn't need to do that.

He was curious what the medical center could be working on that warranted the level of industrial espionage that Doctor Lipp and her nephew had been engaged in. The woman was either operating under her own name, or her organization had constructed a false identity capable of fooling someone who was undoubtedly very careful about who they hired.

That strongly implied that Doctor Lipp was a real person using her own identity to steal something from a company she'd invested two years of her life insinuating herself into. He had no idea what was worth that amount of commitment, so he wanted to see it for himself. It was like something out of one of the movies that Kelsey favored.

He shook his head and led his people down to lab six. Much like the first target, it had a card reader and keypad. That was something of a relief as Carl wouldn't have to deal with unexpected hardware.

With quick, sure motions, Carl took the reader apart and connected his tablet. He scanned the screen and nodded.

"It looks like the key code is in the same location in this hardware. That's the good news. Now comes the risky part. I can't be certain the last person to access this door was the senior researcher. If I guess the wrong identity, I'll be applying someone else's code and the system will reject it. At best that will earn us one strike for a failed entry attempt. At worst it could set off an alarm."

Talbot nodded. "You have access to the security system. If it signals to the guards, you'll know. Do it."

The scientist tapped a button on his screen and grimaced. "Access rejected. On the plus side, it doesn't look like any kind of alarm went out to the security center. The guards aren't aware of our presence."

"Do you have the names of any other researchers authorized to enter this lab?" Talbot asked as he looked back up the corridor toward the main entrance to the research zone.

"Doctor Lipp gave me a couple of names. Since we can scratch the lead researcher off the list, I'm going to try his chief assistant."

Moments later, Carl cursed under his breath. "Second failure. Still no indication that the system has sent any kind of alarm to the guards. I've got one more name to try. If it's not this one, I'm going to have to figure out a new way to break into this lab and that's almost certain to get us into serious trouble."

Talbot felt his muscles tensing as the young scientist tapped on his tablet a few more times. This could be it.

Instead of an alarm, the hatch unlocked and slid aside. As he already had his stunner out, Talbot stepped into the lab and took a quick look around for potential threats.

To his shock, a pair of men in lab coats were staring at him from one of the many tables set up in the room, their mouths agape.

"Who the hell are you?" one of them demanded. "You're not cleared to be in here! I'm calling security!"

So much for being all alone in the labs.

Talbot shot the man and then took the other one down before the first one had hit the table and collapsed to the floor.

"Spread out," he ordered his marines. "Make sure no one else is hiding in here."

The lab was set up in a pattern similar to the first one and seemed to be of about the same size. Rather than a large piece of equipment resembling a regenerator on steroids, though, this room held rack after rack of computers.

Talbot stepped over to the table where the two men had been working and saw that it was covered with what looked like parts of another computer. The two men had taken this machine apart far beyond what anything Talbot had ever seen.

Or even thought possible. They'd not only disconnected everything that could be disconnected, they'd taken chips off of the board and set them aside. Nonremovable chips, or so it seemed.

"Carl?" he asked. "What the heck are they doing here?"

The scientist took in the contents of the table in at a glance. "Completely disassembling a computer of some kind. They've used specialized equipment to remove the chips from the boards they normally reside on. That's pretty unusual."

"Why are they doing it, and how does it relate to whatever medical research they're doing here?"

His young friend shrugged. "I haven't got the slightest idea. Yet I don't see anything else in the room. This has to be the project they're working on."

Talbot looked at all the computers in the room and shook his head. "It'll take forever to get the files off these things."

One of the marines waived at Talbot. "Colonel, I have something."

He headed over to where the woman was standing and found himself looking at a hatch built into the wall. Based on its location, it led into the lab next door, lab eight. That would be the one at the very end of the corridor on this side of the hall.

This was a very different layout than what they'd seen in the previous laboratory. It had been completely self-contained. Were there even more computers next door that they'd have to worry about?

Or worse, more people. People that could come in at any moment looking for one of the two men he'd stunned.

Unlike the exterior hatch, this one didn't seem to require an access code. Talbot summoned half his marines and triggered the mechanism. With their weapons out, they stepped into the other room.

Unlike the lab they'd just exited, this one looked as if something had exploded inside it. Hunks of debris littered the floor and the smell of burned circuitry and hot metal hung in the air.

Having been around devastation for much of his adult life, Talbot recognized this wasn't fresh damage. Something had blown this equipment apart weeks or months ago. Possibly years.

That made sense. If Doctor Lipp was here looking for information from this lab, all of this had to be here before she was hired. Call it a minimum of two and a half years.

"Carl, I need you to come in here and tell me what I'm looking at again."

Moments later, Carl stepped into the room and goggled. "Holy crap. Someone blew up a computer. A big one. That must be where the pieces parts on the table came from."

"Is this the hardware from a sentient AI?" Talbot asked.

The young scientist stepped over to some of the damaged equipment and began examining it. Moments later, he shook his head.

"While it's big enough for that, this is something different. It matches up with what I was seeing in the other room, though. There are markings on the chips and boards that aren't in Standard. Since the Rebel Empire is just like us linguistically, that implies this hardware comes from outside the Empire."

He looked up at Talbot and patted part of the damaged equipment. "This is made very similarly to Imperial hardware, though I can see some differences even at a glance. Our technology and this share a common ancestor."

Talbot grunted. "The only group we know of like that is the Singularity. If this is one of their computers, it might have critical data we absolutely have to have at some point. They're helping the Clans and this might have come from one of their ships."

He checked his internal chronometer. They probably had four or five hours before people started showing up for work in the labs. These two rooms were absolutely filled with equipment. It would take every second they could beg, borrow, or steal to get the majority of it.

Coming to a decision, he gestured at the damaged hardware. "I'll send as many people over as I can. Have them start taking this and the other computers back to the first lab. Keep an eye out for security. Don't let anyone come and catch us in the corridor with this stuff. We're taking everything we can."

* * *

Veronica covertly monitored the video feeds that Kelsey's associates with Recovery Incorporated had shunted to the cargo hold where she and her people were hiding. Part of her worried that someone on the other side would detect the access, but Jason Young seemed pretty sure they were on safe ground.

The crewmen that had arrived on the cargo shuttles had quickly hurried to various sections of the ship and began making it ready to move. That made sense if they intended to flee.

Yet it still didn't explain what Don Sommerville was up to. He was assigned to the shipyard, yes, but her old friend was obviously taking command of this ship with the expectation that he was going to be leaving in it.

Kelsey had indicated that the third shuttle had held Fleet marines, but Veronica disagreed. Those people were wearing unpowered marine armor, but they were not marines. She'd been around enough Rebel Empire marines to know that these people were too disciplined. Too controlled.

Her suspicions were confirmed when a fourth cargo shuttle docked and disgorged a mixture of crewmen and more individuals in armor. The last one off the shuttle was the female Fleet security officer that had "greeted" them when they'd docked with the yard earlier.

Veronica opened an audio-only communication channel to Princess Kelsey. Hopefully the lower bandwidth would help keep the signal from coming to anyone's attention. It should mix in with any number of other signals going out through the ship right now as the other crewmen spoke to one another.

"I have an update," she said without identifying herself, trusting the other woman to recognize her voice. "Another shuttle has docked, and I see that security officer your friend Carl got to know earlier."

A few seconds of silence greeted her, but she waited, knowing that the princess was probably reviewing the feed right now.

"It looks like you were right," Kelsey conceded. "The people in armor are Fleet security. Which, in its own way, is even more confusing. Why would Fleet security be helping Commander Sommerville take control of this freighter?"

"I haven't got the slightest idea, but I'm not sure we can overpower this many people. I hope you've got a good plan in mind."

"I'm still working on that," the other woman admitted. "Once I figure it out, I'll let you know. Out."

That was fairly brusque coming from Princess Kelsey, but the young woman had a lot to worry about with the Clan warships having just destroyed the battle station at the flip point and begun boosting toward Archibald at maximum acceleration.

Doctor Rehnquist cleared his throat. "I think I might have a few answers to the situation we find ourselves in."

Veronica raised an eyebrow at the scientist. "That sounds refreshing. Do tell."

The older man swiped a hand over his balding head. "I've been reviewing video feeds from other sections of the ship. I think I have a few items that you'll want to see. Why don't we start with feed twenty-seven?"

She accessed the feed in question and frowned. It looked like a small control room. Three people sat in the center of the compartment facing one another over a trio of consoles. Veronica had to admit that she'd never seen anything quite like this particular configuration.

"Do we have any idea what they're doing?" she asked after a few seconds.

"Use the zoom feature and go in close to the consoles. Two of them are visible from this angle."

Veronica did as instructed and then swore. What she was looking at had no business being on a freighter. That was a tactical console. One that indicated it was in control of a dozen missile launchers.

She switched to the other console and saw that it was more defensive in nature. The interface she was examining was designed to manage a heavy warship's battle screens and antimissile defenses. But only cruisers had defenses like that, not freighters.

The third console wasn't in direct view, but it probably had to do with weapons of some kind too. Beams, perhaps? Yet one more impossibility on a freighter.

"You said that you had more than one thing to show me," Veronica told the scientist after a moment. "What else have you found?"

"I've been going over the feed from main engineering. This revelation is less obvious, but the drives seem quite muscular for a freighter. The grav drives in particular seem designed to achieve a level of speed comparable to a much faster vessel. The gravitic compensators are similarly overpowered."

Veronica considered his words for a long stretch of time before finally nodding. "Honestly, I'm not certain if that really affects what we're doing in the slightest. We're already inside the ship so they can't stop us from boarding with those weapons or run away from us with their drives.

"This is all very interesting, but we need to find an edge that'll let us overpower them. I don't suppose you have anything for me in that arena, do you?"

The scientist grinned at her. "As a matter of fact, I have. I've been looking over the manifests from a number of crates in this hold, and I think you'll be pleased to discover some of the things we have to draw upon. Come take a look at this."

He led her across the cargo hold to a series of large crates lined up against one of the bulkheads. "I think these might go quite some way toward evening the odds."

She used her implants to access the manifests built into each crate, and her eyes widened in shock. "That can't be right. These don't have any more business being here than the weapons this ship is apparently armed with. Still, I'm not going to look a gift horse in the mouth."

The row of crates sitting in front of her indicated that they were filled with powered marine armor and all of the associated weapons that went along with those suits. None of the people with her was trained in using them, but they'd be virtually invulnerable to standard weapons inside the things.

If they could use them, of course. She knew the suits were wired with explosives to make certain they didn't get into the wrong hands. Or to put down a rabid marine, if needed.

"Start opening one up," she told the doctor. "I'll see if Princess Kelsey has any idea how we can make them safe to use. Good work, Doctor."

As she stepped back, she considered how this might change the equation. If they could make the suits operational, that just might give them a chance.

35

Zia was relieved when they finished assembling the larger ring and opened the connection to their freighter. The crewmen aboard the ship poured into the lab and began helping to disassemble and move everything in sight.

Even though they had a direct connection, it was still going to take a while to transfer everything. And until they were finished, things could still go terribly wrong.

Just a few minutes after this process had started, Talbot hurried back into the room. From his expression, there was trouble.

"What's wrong?" she asked as her gut started tightening.

"It seems the good doctor was holding out on us," he said as he took in the activity around them. "The lab she wanted us to break into isn't involved with medical research. Unless Carl is gravely mistaken, they have some kind of large computer down there that was blown up a couple of years ago. He thinks it's a Singularity computer."

Zia blinked at him, shocked. "Seriously? How the hell did the Rebel Empire even get their hands on something like that?"

The marine officer shrugged. "I haven't got the slightest idea. The problem is, we're not going to be able to pass it up. Whatever it is, it might be critical to the war with the Clans. We're going to have to take it with us, and that's going to really complicate this raid. They have a lot of equipment down there. Two labs full, in point of fact."

She rubbed her face. "We only have a few hours to get everything that we need. I suggest that you tell Carl to get the most important things first."

"Already done," Talbot said. "He's is going to have everything moved here and queued up for transport through the ring as quickly as possible. He's got one eye on the security officers so we'll stop if they send someone in our direction. If anyone shows up early for work, we're going to have to stun them."

That would work for a little while, Zia knew, but there was going to come a point where too many people were coming into the research area for them to stop them all.

"Have him expedite as much as possible," she finally said. "As soon as they figure out what's going on, they're going to start screaming. We need to be gone by then."

As soon as Talbot headed back toward the other lab, Zia stepped through the ring and into the freighter. Thankfully, there was plenty of room in the massive hold to store everything they were stealing today. Crewmen were already securing pieces of equipment against one of the far bulkheads.

Zia stepped over to one of the communications consoles built into the bulkheads and called the bridge. "This is Anderson. What's the status on the last shuttle from the station?"

"They're on final approach now, Commodore," a young male voice said. "They're not reporting any issues and are less than five minutes out."

"Excellent. Get everyone off it and send it back so the last of the team can use it. Also, have the ship ready for departure on short notice in case we have to expedite. What's the status of the incoming Clan vessels?"

The voice on the other end paused for a moment. "It looks like the incoming hostiles are still about six hours out. The Rebel Empire Fleet ships that went to the gas giant are moving to intercept the incoming vessels, so that time frame might grow.

"It looks like they picked up the four battlecruisers that we suspected might be out there. Even so, they don't really stand a chance, considering that the Clans had more than enough firepower to destroy a battle station. That's pretty brave of them in my book."

"Never fall into the trap of thinking that your enemies are cowards," Zia said. "They may not believe in the same things that you do, but human beings can be gallant and brave even when they're doing the bidding of terrible people. Do the Clans have a force heading toward the other flip point?"

"Yes, ma'am. None of the ships at Archibald are going to be able to escape the system through the usual methods."

She nodded. "They'll come in and take over the station and shipyard, and then start hunting for ships that ran. They're not going to hurry after us as long as we get moving on schedule. Have someone come through the ring and inform me if the situation changes."

Once the man acknowledged her order, Zia headed back through the ring and into the lab.

The hatch to the corridor was open, and Carl was helping to move a cart full of scorched computer parts into the room. He waved a hand at her and stepped over.

"I'll need more of the crewmen from the freighter to come help. We can get a lot of the equipment as long as we have the hands to move it."

"This is risky," she told him. "Every time you move something out into the open, there's a chance that someone will open the hatch at the end of the corridor and see us."

Her young friend shook his head. "Not happening. I've tasked one of the marines with monitoring the video feeds in the corridors leading up to the research area. If anyone shows up, we'll have at least sixty seconds notice before they arrive."

"While that may be true, I'd rather not get into a fight that makes us blow up the rings. They're irreplaceable."

Her friend nodded. "I know. I'd rather not put them at risk, either, but it's not as if we have a choice. Those computers might have information about the Singularity that could make a difference for us in the future.

"It's obvious the Singularity is involved in this war, and it's only a matter of time before they realize the New Terran Empire exists. When they do, they're going to come for us. We have to have these computers and the wreckage that the lab rats were studying."

Zia's implants pinged. It was a message from Talbot. Someone was coming toward the research area. She took a moment to tap into the feed and recognized the lead researcher for the project that Doctor Lipp had been trying to steal. What the heck was he doing here in the middle of the night?

Well, that hardly mattered. They'd have to take him down and hope that no one else came looking for him.

She opened a channel to Talbot. "Let him come to you. Stun him as soon as he comes through the hatch. Put him on the next cart over."

"Copy that. I've got two prisoners that were here when we broke in to send with him."

"Really? You should've mentioned them."

"Sorry. Other things on my mind. I'll handle it. Out."

She sealed the hatch leading out into the corridor and began waiting. Hopefully this was the only interruption they were going to have to deal with.

Inside, she laughed. No, this was probably only the first of a cascading set of complications. Life had a way of throwing curveballs at them, and they were going to have to deal with them.

"Uh-oh," Carl said. "We've got a problem. Two of the security guards are exiting security central and are headed this way. It looks like they're going to arrive about the same time as our guest."

* * *

KELSEY LISTENED with a frown on her face as Veronica explained what she'd found. She wanted this to be a game changer, but she wasn't certain they could make it work.

"You know those suits are booby-trapped and require a specific code to activate, right?" she asked. "Not only do we not have the right tools for the job, the only person we brought that has ever done this successfully is back on the station."

"I'll admit that adds a certain level of complexity to the task," Veronica agreed. "Yet, I don't see that we have a lot of choice. I'm hoping we find some additional weapons that we can use if this doesn't pan out."

Jason Young waved a hand in front of Kelsey's face. She blinked at the distraction and then raised a hand to let him know she'd seen him.

"We can't do anything until we're further away from the shipyard and Archibald," Kelsey said. "Get one uncrated, and we'll see what we can do."

"Copy that," Veronica said. "Out."

Kelsey focused her complete attention on the young security specialist. "What have you got, Jason?"

"The bridge crew is preparing to move the ship. They've received clearance from control to depart the shipyard and try to hide in the outer system. I suppose it's possible. Every hour without pursuit makes it exponentially more likely they can elude detection for as long as their supplies hold out."

"How long do we have and in what direction are they planning on going?"

"Just a couple of minutes, I think. I've tapped into the controls, and it looks like they're headed away from the multiflip point. I'm not sure that's a negative at this point because that will draw any pursuit away."

Kelsey pulled up a map of the system in her implants. This was going to add time to their escape, but it might make it difficult for any of the forces currently here to track them. Jason was right about that.

She checked the current location of the Clan warships and saw they had about five hours remaining before the hostile vessels engaged anything in orbit. The Rebel Empire warships were going to intercept them a couple of hours out. Even with the four battlecruisers, the Clan vessels would be able to take them apart without much trouble.

Tapping into the scanner feed, she watched as the freighter pulled away from the shipyard. She was able to link to the ship's passive scanners and saw that a number of ships were leaving both the station and the shipyard, running in any direction they could. Some smaller Clan vessels were pursuing some of them. Odds were good they'd get one too.

She sat down and gave herself over to thought, checking the scanners every ten minutes or so. Less than an hour later, her fears were confirmed. The freighter was making good time—though not using its full acceleration, she noted—and had drawn what looked like a frigate in pursuit.

While less powerful than a destroyer, a frigate was more than capable of chasing down a freighter and forcing them to stop or be destroyed. Since this vessel was actually a Q-ship—an armed freighter made to look harmless—the fight would be brutally short and certain to give victory to the freighter.

That would draw the Clans' attention. They'd send follow-up ships with more powerful weapons. If the Q-ship went to full acceleration, it might very well elude detection, but they wouldn't just let it go.

More worrisome to her, their original freighter was still in orbit around the station. Talbot and Zia had not yet completed their mission and pulled out.

At this range and lacking the ability to communicate, it would be impossible for her to get an update. She'd just have to hope that her husband and friends managed to get out of there before the enemy arrived in force.

They could call Fiona and *Persephone* if they needed to, but the FTL com she'd intended to use was on the shipyard. The AI was monitoring the situation and would blow it up if it was discovered or when the Clans attacked the shipyard. The damage would then be blamed on them.

The Clan warships had altered course to meet the Rebel Empire warships and were spreading out into a battle formation. That was going to delay their arrival at Archibald, which was a good thing.

Still, Talbot and Zia really needed to speed things up. If they delayed much longer, they were never going to escape the station at all.

If things went really badly, *Persephone* could intervene, but that would cause a whole new set of problems for them. Secrecy was still their best weapon. If they couldn't keep themselves and their mission quiet, the Pandorans would be the ones paying the price.

Well, worrying about her friends wasn't going to help Kelsey do her part. She needed to capture this ship.

She examined the internal video feeds and allowed her combat implants to sort the various enemy personnel inside the deck plans. Her people needed to strike simultaneously and with overwhelming force on the bridge and in engineering when the time came.

Then they'd have to hold those areas against a determined counterattack. How they'd manage that might revolve around the armor Veronica had found. If it could be rendered safe.

That was outside her personal control, so she'd have to pray the other woman figured out a path to success. If not, they were probably screwed.

36

Talbot waited inside the second lab for their unwanted visitors to arrive. He was crouched behind a computer on the right-hand side of the compartment. Everyone was under cover except for two marines who now wore the white lab coats and stood at the worktable with their backs toward the hatch. They were the distraction.

"I've put the corridor feeds back to real time," Carl said over the com. "There's someone in security central monitoring it now."

"Acknowledged," Talbot said. "Be ready to put it back on the loop when we have these people in custody. We'll have to take out security central as soon as we can. They'll be worried if these clowns are too quiet."

"You bet. Our guests are in the main corridor and will be at your location shortly. Good luck."

A minute later, the hatch slid open, and the intruders stepped inside. The security guards didn't have their weapons out, but their hands hovered near them. They were definitely expecting trouble.

"Did anyone come in here half an hour ago?" the project lead demanded. "I was notified about several unsuccessful access attempts."

All three of the men had taken several steps into the lab so Talbot stunned one of the security men. The target dropped without a word. Two other marines took out the remaining hostiles a moment later.

Talbot stepped over to the hatch and closed it. "Start that corridor loop, Carl," he said over the com.

Several of the marines searched the new prisoners and removed the weapons from the security men. They then bound all of them and put them into the corner with the original researchers.

"The loop is playing now," Carl said. "I'll meet you in the corridor."

Getting to the security center wasn't difficult since Carl was able to monitor all the corridors for wandering people and block out any images of them moving through the facility. That didn't make things less tense for Talbot, though. There were still plenty of things that could go wrong.

When they arrived outside the security center, he motioned for Carl to stay to the side. "How many people inside? Where are they located?"

"Two people, both almost directly ahead of you. Since they didn't have any indication of people in the corridor, I suspect the door opening is going to cause them some consternation and surprise. Both are seated but armed."

Talbot nodded and motioned for three marines to join him directly in front of the hatch. "Two of you down on your knees, one of you stand next to me. When the hatch opens, we open fire. If you're on the left, take out the person on the left. You're on the right, take out the person on the right."

As soon as they were ready, Talbot made a gesture to Carl and the young man got to work on the lock. His friend was turning into quite the expert at breaking and entering.

Twenty seconds later, the hatch slid to the side and all four of the ambushers fired at their targets. The security men had barely begun to turn their heads toward the hatch and hadn't even reached for their weapons.

As soon as they were down, Talbot led the marines into the security center, and they spread out to make certain there were no unexpected surprises waiting for them. Sixty seconds later, they were sure the facility was secure.

"Get these two down to the lab with the others," Talbot said as he holstered his stunner. "Let's make them a priority and get them over to the freighter now. If things get chaotic later on, I don't want to have to worry about leaving witnesses behind."

To be certain they weren't surprised again, he stationed two of the marines in the security center to keep an eye on all of the monitors and to handle any incoming calls. He picked two that could wear the security uniforms and had the prisoners stripped.

He didn't anticipate much action this late at night, but with the lead researcher having shown up unexpectedly, he wasn't going to rule it out. Having a few men that looked like security might come in very handy.

Talbot took Carl back to the research area. Zia had been working hard with her people and their primary target was almost cleaned out. He estimated they probably only had another fifteen minutes or so to strip the room bare.

She stepped over to him as he looked into the lab. "Everything taken care of?"

He nodded. "I'm worried that they're going to come and find us, though. We really need to get this done. Moving all of that equipment from one lab to the other is a pain in the ass."

She shook her head and smiled at him. "You're not thinking this through. As soon as we finish clearing this lab out, we can disassemble the large transport ring and move it over to your lab. We'll set it up there and finish cleaning everything out. It'll be faster that way."

Talbot blinked in surprise at the idea and then laughed. "That's thinking outside the box. It's still going to be close, though. I'd like to get every single thing we can out of the other lab, but I don't want to get caught or need to destroy the transport rings. Any word on Kelsey?"

Zia shook her head. "The other freighter left the shipyard over an hour ago. It's making for the outer system. Not exactly in the direction we'd like them to go, but beggars can't be choosers. It looks as if the Rebel Empire warships in the system are going to try to intervene with the Clan warships. I don't think we're going to see anyone here sooner than six hours now.

"With that in mind, I want to be done in four. Sooner, if we can. Let's say it takes another hour after that to get the small transport ring back to the cargo bay, onto the shuttle which is on its way there now, and back out to the freighter. That still gives us an hour to get clear of the station before the Clans arrive in force."

"That doesn't sound like a lot of time," Talbot said with a scowl. "They'll send someone after us."

Zia nodded. "Of course they will. Unfortunately for them, *Persephone* is going to be shadowing us once we get clear of Archibald. The Clans aren't going to send a large ship to chase us down. At most, they'll send a frigate. A Marine Raider strike ship should be able to take it out in one salvo.

"It's not my favorite plan, and it certainly is going to let them know something is wrong, but I don't see that we have a choice. Let's get moving. We've got a lot of work to do if we're going to make that timeline."

* * *

VERONICA EYED the uncrated combat suits uncertainly and then turned toward Doctor Rehnquist with a look of suspicion. "So, let me get this straight, you didn't remove the explosives but you *think* you have them all disabled. Exactly what order of probability would you give to that assertion?"

The older man shrugged. "Nothing in life is certain, Commander. All Princess Kelsey could do is give me a general idea of how the self-destruct system worked. She didn't have plans for exactly what needed to be done to make these absolutely safe. Even if she did, we don't have the tools to disassemble the armor. Or the time."

The scientist and his impromptu assistants had cleared six suits of armor in the last three hours. There was plenty more, but they didn't have time to prep another one. The Clan frigate was almost upon them.

When the confrontation came, her old friend would probably blow it out of space. Based on the weapons she suspected the ship had, he would pretend to surrender to draw the enemy in as closely as possible, then use the beams to eviscerate it. With lightspeed weapons, the frigate would never see what was coming for him.

If the enemy commander was a little more canny, Don would need to use missiles. However, unlike the frigate, this ship had battle screens to protect it while her missiles finished the frigate at knife range.

At that point, Don would go to full acceleration and get as far into the outer system as he could. On a ship this size, he probably had enough supplies to last for many months. Perhaps even years.

All he had to do was outwait the Clans. They'd move on in time, leaving a holding force. Eventually, the Rebel Empire would reclaim the system, or he could find a time to use one of the flip points to get clear.

Princess Kelsey's plan would disrupt everything for him. Of course, timing was everything. They couldn't spring into action until the frigate was no longer a threat. Attacking during the fight would only disrupt the crew defending the ship.

They'd found a few crates of regular flechette weapons, so if they had to fight, they wouldn't be completely reliant on their stunners.

She shook her head, dismissing the worry. "I certainly hope you're right because if they manage to set off any charge you missed, I'll wager the blast would be more than enough to set off all the ones you've disconnected. From what I understand, these make a pretty significant fireball when they go off."

The scientist shrugged slightly. "We've done the best we can, Commander. At this point, we have to trust that we'll come out ahead in the end. If not, I'm certain the princess's ship will come and rescue us. Those of us that survive, that is."

"I'd like to avoid the need for rescue, and we really can't count on anything. We play this straight. Total victory is our goal."

Her com chimed with an incoming call. It was Princess Kelsey.

"Are we ready?" Veronica asked. "I'll need a few minutes to suit up."

"The frigate just demanded the freighter surrender. Commander Sommerville cut acceleration and accepted their terms. Of course, he's powering up his beam weapons. He gave the order, so we can now confirm that the ship has them. We also have battle screens because they're on standby. The missiles are also ready to fly.

"Based on my experience, I think we have maybe twenty minutes before this fight is over. The frigate is only going to have a single pinnace, so they're going to be very careful how they use it. Get suited up and be ready to hit main engineering as soon as the fight is over."

"What about those Fleet security goons?" Veronica asked. "As soon as the attack starts, they're going to come after us. Do we know where on the ship they're congregating?"

"Right now, they're spread out preparing to repel boarders. They're also armed and armored. I think our best bet to deal with them is to wait until this fight is over and they've returned to the area they've set up as their armory and barracks. Once that happens, they'll mostly be gathered in one place and out of armor. Their guards will be down."

That sounded like a solid plan to Veronica. "Which of us is going to deal with them? I can cut aside a group of marines."

"No," Kelsey said. "You need to focus on engineering. It's going to be a much more difficult target than the bridge, so I'll deal with the security forces. You focus on overwhelming everyone in engineering quickly enough that they don't damage this ship. That's the critical part."

"Can do. We'll be ready to go in twenty minutes, just to be safe."

She really hoped she wasn't overpromising with that. None of them had ever used this kind of armor before and getting into it in fifteen minutes might be a challenge.

"I'm thinking more like thirty to forty minutes," Kelsey said firmly. "Getting that armor on isn't something you can rush into, especially if you've never done it before. Also, we need to give the security forces time to stand down. Don't rush this, Veronica. I'll let you know ten minutes before we execute and even if it takes you longer, we have time. Good luck."

Veronica rubbed at her face as the call ended. She wasn't afraid of a fight, but this wasn't what she was used to. Well, she'd rely on Kelsey's marines for guidance and make it work. Or die trying.

37

The next three and a half hours felt like weeks to Zia. They quickly finished emptying the first lab and relocated the transport rings to the second lab to get as much of the computer equipment as possible.

Carl oversaw the removal of the destroyed Singularity computer and all of the support equipment that had been analyzing it like a madman. He rushed from one end of the lab to the other, seeing that the various server towers were removed and hustled through the larger ring as quickly as possible.

As the clock ticked down, Zia made more frequent trips to the freighter to check on the status of the Clan warships. They'd delayed their arrival at Archibald to deal with the Rebel Empire ships, but that wouldn't delay them much longer.

She and her people only had until that fight was done to get everything they could. There were a lot of vessels fleeing the planet, and she didn't want to be the last one out the gate.

By her estimates, they were about half an hour away from emptying the second lab when the research center employees started arriving. They'd run out of time, and she had a hard choice to make. Leave the remaining stuff in the lab with the Singularity computer or destroy the large transport ring.

That was a tough call, but that's why they paid her.

"Carl, finish emptying the lab," she told him. "Then get everyone to the freighter. Send the small ring next because I don't want to leave it here when we go."

He blinked at her. "How will we get the large ring out?"

"We won't," she said harshly. "We're blowing it when we leave."

The scientist grabbed her arm. "No! We can leave what we didn't get.

We still have time to get the large ring out and slip away with the small ring."

Zia shook her head. "We can't afford to lose any of this equipment since we don't know what's important. Stop arguing and get moving. You have ten minutes maximum. Maybe less. Don't waste it."

The young man nodded, his expression filled with anguish, and ran off.

"The marines we left in the security center ran into some trouble," Talbot said, walking over to her. "It seems their replacements have begun arriving for shift change. Thus far they've stunned two new security officers. What are we going to do with them?"

"They'll need to take them to the exit in ten minutes. We're scrapping the plan and blowing the large transport ring."

The marine winced but didn't argue. "Copy that. We need to evacuate the building. The blast will wreck the labs and potentially bring the whole thing down. That means I need to get back to the shuttle with the last of the marines rather than going back with you."

That was an added complication that she hadn't really planned for. Still, she wasn't a terrorist and didn't blow up innocent people. "We do this together. I'm coming with you."

The marine officer scowled at her. "That's a needless risk. I've got this."

"I'm sure you do, but this is my operation, and I'm going to make absolutely certain that everyone gets home."

She could see the calculation in his eyes. He wanted to argue, but he really didn't have any options. Well, she supposed he could stun her and send her back to the freighter with the rest of the prisoners, but even being married to the heir wouldn't save him from that kind of decision.

He must've finally come to the same conclusion because he sighed. "Then I suppose we best get this finished."

Minutes later, everyone except for Talbot, herself, and two marines dressed in security uniforms were back on the freighter, and they'd sent the smaller ring back to the freighter.

"Time to get out of here," Talbot said. "I've armed the plasma grenades and set them for ten minutes. We need to go help move the disabled security people."

As a group, they left the research area and headed for the security center as the fire alarm went off. The marines on guard had triggered it so that they could clear all the workers out of the building.

A minute later, they arrived at the security center and the marines soon had all four unconscious security guards over their shoulders and the group was on the way to the exit.

For this brief window of time, her people weren't going to have any access to the internal video feeds. They were on their own.

They'd almost made it to the exit when an older man in a suit confronted them. He seemingly popped out of nowhere, coming around the corner when the exit door was just in sight.

He scowled at them from under bushy white eyebrows that looked like caterpillars crawling across his face and put his hands on his hips. "What the hell is going on?"

Zia grimaced. They *literally* didn't have time for this.

* * *

KELSEY HAD to admit that she admired how Commander Sommerville had handled the Clan frigate. He'd waited until he was certain the ship was as close as it was going to get before he'd opened fire. His unexpected beams had torn through the other ship in multiple places, crippling it instantly.

Unfortunately for him, his shots hadn't destroyed the ship. It had been able to return fire with its missiles. He'd brought the freighter's battle screens up in time to absorb the hits, though, allowing the Q-ship to strike again.

That time, the frigate had exploded. One of the beams must've hit its fusion plant. The destroyed vessel had already launched its pinnace, but the blast took it out as well. The enemy had been efficiently eliminated.

Sommerville had immediately ordered the freighter to maximum acceleration. He only had a brief window to vanish from the Clan scanners and had been determined not to waste it.

That had been twenty minutes ago, and the Fleet security elements were back in their barracks, presumably stripping off their armor and storing their weapons.

Timing was going to be tricky. She wanted to allow them enough time to disarm but not enough to scatter.

The Clan warships had just engaged the Rebel Fleet elements with crushing force. The fighting wasn't over, but the victor was never in doubt. Only the battlecruisers remained, and they were going down fast. She gave them no more than five minutes more.

It was time to get this party started.

"Tell me that we're into all the command systems," she told Bob Noble.

"Almost all of them. We have access to communications, propulsion, and navigation. We're focusing on the tactical systems next."

"What about scanners? Could we spoof them if we need to?"

He nodded. "With a little warning, yes. What do you have in mind?"

"I'm worried what will happen when *Persephone* turns up. I feel pretty sure Angela is closing in on us. This ship has better scanners than we'd planned for. If they spot her, I'd like to make the sighting look like a scanner ghost. We have to keep them from detecting my ship."

The young man chewed his lip. "That's doable. It would help if we knew where to find her. Can we send them coded instructions?"

Kelsey frowned. "The Clans will detect the transmission. That'll make them wonder who we're talking to."

"It's not as if this ship didn't just paint a huge target on itself by blowing up their friends."

"True enough. I'll code a message for them to come in from behind. This ship is fast for a freighter, but *Persephone* is faster. Once Angela gets the message, she can communicate with us via tight beam, and they'll never know, right?"

Noble nodded. "Sure. We have control of the com system so I can lock out their detection of incoming signals directed at them. It's not as if they're expecting anyone to want to chat."

It only took Kelsey a few minutes to code a brief message explaining everything to Angela. Bob Noble took it and had it sent moments later.

"We're not waiting for her to respond," Kelsey said. "It's time to take this ship. If she gets back to us before then, I'll let you handle the coordination."

"Yes, ma'am."

With that task handled, she turned her attention to the marines and recovery specialists awaiting her orders.

"Cain, you and your people take the bridge. There shouldn't be much resistance there. I didn't see any weapons, and they can't be expecting an attack from inside. Have your people lock out every system they can right before you go in or as soon as the alarm goes up from another group."

"Got it," he said with a nod. "Since Jason and Bob are into the systems, we shouldn't have any problems."

"I'd like to keep the command crew alive," she stressed, "but if they resist too strongly, don't hesitate to use deadly force to protect yourselves."

She gestured for the marines to form up behind her and opened a com channel to Veronica. "Are you ready?"

"My marines are in armor, and we're ready to rock," the former Rebel Empire officer said. "We'll be in engineering in less than five minutes, whether we run into resistance or not."

"Don't get cocky," she warned. "Those suits are powerful, but they don't make you invincible. Mostly."

"Yes, Mother."

Kelsey laughed in spite of the grave situation. "Be glad it's not a case of like mother like daughter. You're go to execute your attack. Everyone, move out."

She killed the com channel and led her forces into the corridor. They had access to the internal video feeds, but that didn't guarantee they'd spot any enemy crewmen before they saw her or her people. They had to plan on an unexpected encounter ruining the element of surprise somewhere along the way.

To her astonishment, her group made it all the way to the Fleet security compartment without running into anyone. So far, Veronica's team and Cain's group had avoided discovery too. This was going to be a devastating surprise for the Rebel Empire forces.

The hatch slid aside just as she approached. Time to make the magic happen. Or to make the donuts. She could never remember which was the correct saying.

It only took a moment to dump Panther into her system, and the world seemed to slow as her cognitive response time raced far faster than a normal human could manage. She was ready for this fight.

Her implants were already in combat mode, but unlike the first time, she now knew how to retain full control of her actions and work in concert with the tactical computer inside her head. No one was going to die if she could help it.

That didn't mean she wouldn't seriously hurt someone. Like that bitch in command of these sadists.

The man coming out of the compartment barely had time to note her presence before she punched him in the diaphragm. His breath exploded out of his lungs as she ghosted past him.

Kelsey drew her stunner with her off hand as she stepped inside. The compartment was filled with people, most of whom were staring at her with shocked expressions.

"Hey there!" she said brightly. "Time to party!"

Her combat computer immediately flagged those who were armed and assisted her in aiming her stunner as she danced between two of the enemy. She had her primary target sighted and wasn't about to let the enemy commander escape retribution for the indignities she'd heaped on her friend.

The marines flooding in behind her made the outcome of this fight a foregone conclusion since no one was armed with anything more than a stunner. Their timing had been excellent.

That didn't stop a few people from bolting toward the compartment where they probably kept the lethal hardware and armor. Odds were good at least a few people were still in there too.

To her credit, the security commander tried to delay Kelsey while her people dove toward the real weapons.

"You!" the woman hissed as she swung at Kelsey's face.

Kelsey leaned her head just far enough to the side for the blow to miss before slamming the heel of her free hand into the woman's face like a hammer.

The woman's nose shattered under the blow, and she somersaulted backward, already unconscious even before she slammed full length into the deck.

Payback was a bitch.

Two men were hauling weapons out of the makeshift armory when Kelsey reached the hatch, but they were far too slow to stop her from stunning them or their friends the security commander had been trying to protect.

By the time she'd made sure the compartment was secure, the fight was over. A few of her people were down but only stunned. They'd knocked out the biggest threat to their dominance and capturing the ship suddenly became a lot more likely.

"All teams, status," Kelsey said over the com.

"We're at engineering," Veronica said. "We had a surprise a few corridors back so expect trouble."

As if summoned by the words, an alarm began hooting over the speakers. Don Sommerville's voice came on a moment later.

"Intruder alert. All hands repel boarders. They're near engineering."

Well, he was a little late for that, but it would still make things more exciting than Kelsey preferred.

"Cain, tell me you're about at the bridge," she said.

"Just got here. The hatch is closed and locked. Jason, can you open it?"

Moments later, the security specialist came on the channel. "Negative. They've manually locked it down. We've cut most of their controls, though. They're deaf and blind in there."

"They'll wait," Kelsey decided. "Veronica, we'll mop up the rest of the ship, but you've got to take engineering intact. We're counting on you."

With that, she killed the com and started directing her people to secure the weapons and to start clearing the ship of hostile crew. That would take a while, but without heavier weapons, the enemy was screwed. The ball was in Veronica Giguere's court now.

38

Talbot spun the old man around. "The fire is spreading, sir! Come on!"

The man tried to resist. "Let go of me! We have to clear out lab seven and eight."

"Can't. That's where the fire is."

Or it would be in a shade over five minutes.

Based on the way the man was dressed, he was an executive here. One that was bound and determined to run in where a bunch of plasma grenades would end him.

When the man made to argue more, Talbot clamped a hand over his mouth, picked him up, and ran for the exit. Awkward to say the least but not impossible when death was racing up behind him.

He didn't stop at the alley either. He kept running toward the cargo bay. He didn't stop until a low thump behind him told him the plasma grenades had detonated. Only then did he release the man.

Thankfully, the man was content with swearing at him and running back toward the now burning research center.

"The clock is ticking," Talbot said he gestured for the marines to set the unconscious security guards down. "We need to be gone before station security gets spun up."

Fifteen minutes later they were at the cargo bay. They got in without issue but found a large cluster of men and women in cargo-handling coveralls trying to bypass the locks on their cargo shuttle.

"Can we help you?" he asked dryly when he and his marines arrived behind them.

The group turned to him almost as one. They each had an expression of fearful despair on their faces.

One woman stepped forward. "Is this your shuttle? Please, take us with you. We can pay!"

He recognized the woman who'd given him a hard time smuggling the small ring onto the station. What had her name been? Associate Supervisor Franzen.

He was about to shut her down when Zia put a hand on his shoulder.

"We're not going to the planet," she said. "We're going to make a run for the outer system in our freighter. We might never get back here if we escape the system."

"We don't care," the woman said hoarsely. "Those Ghosts destroyed all the Fleet ships in the system and are on the way here. We don't want to be here when they arrive. We can work our way. We know cargo better than anyone else you'll ever meet. And we can pay. Whatever you want."

"Step away from the hatch," Talbot ordered, shooting Zia a look that expressed his basic disagreement with what she was doing. Not that he was going to dispute her right to make the call. She was the flag officer, after all.

He let her get inside and head for the shuttle's control area before he allowed the cargo handlers in. Even that was more than he'd bargained for as others came over and joined the first group once it became obvious the shuttle was about to depart the station.

If there'd been more people in the bay, he'd have had to start turning people away. Cargo shuttles could hold a lot, but even so, the large crowd only barely fit.

Talbot noted with some irony that there were a few station security uniforms in the crowd. Even a number of enlisted Fleet crewmen. All told there were probably a hundred people packed into the shuttle.

He entered with the last two marines and sealed the hatch behind him. "Search them. Confiscate anything that could be used as a weapon. We'll off-load them as soon as we get back to the freighter and lock them up."

That done, he joined Zia on the flight deck as she was lifting off. To be safe, he locked the hatch behind them and strapped into the copilot's couch just as she turned the shuttle to face the main bay hatch.

"Did we get clearance?" he asked.

"No one answered," she said as her hands moved across the controls. "I assume control has abandoned their stations because of the impending attack. Let's hope they didn't lock the hatch, or this will be a very short trip."

He felt his gut tighten, but the main hatch began opening before he had a chance to really get worried. It led into a massive airlock so they weren't clear just yet. Still, if one hatch opened, odds were good the other one would too.

A few minutes later they were clear of the station and on their way to the freighter. It had left orbit as soon as Zia signaled they were in space, so it took a bit longer to catch up with it than would be normal. With the incoming ships, it was best to be sure the freighter was one of many others running away, so he understood the need not to delay.

They docked with the freighter half an hour later, and he finally started breathing a bit easier. They still had to get clear of the system, but that was Zia's problem. Nothing he could do from this point forward would make a difference in their escape.

She unstrapped and stood. "I'm heading for the bridge. We'll boost for the outer system, away from the other freighter. The Clans should be busy with conquering Archibald and not worried about the scattering civilians. Get everything secured, including our new passengers. Then get some rest. I'll call you as soon as I get word from Kelsey."

Once Zia had departed, he directed the crew to start unloading the new prisoners. He had no idea what they'd do with these people once they got to Pandora, but that was a problem he could solve later. For now, he wanted a beer and a place to rest while he waited for word on wife and the rest.

* * *

VERONICA RAN behind the marines as they rushed toward main engineering. The crew there knew they were coming, and the hatch was already sliding closed.

The lead marine did the opposite of what Veronica would have expected and sped up, the feet of her powered armor gouging the deck as she launched herself at the shrinking opening. She sailed through the air sideways and bounced through the narrow opening right before the hatch slid shut with a clank reeking of finality.

"Lewandowski?" Zia shouted over the com. "Are you okay?"

"I'm a little busy. Hang on."

The next fifteen seconds dragged by before the hatch began opening. The opening revealed the marine threatening a group of crewmen with her armored fist from beside the hatch controls. They were trying to stun her with zero effect. The thick armor was proof against that.

Since the massive suits were immune to that kind of weapon, they didn't come equipped with them either, so Brenda Lewandowski had no way to stop the people attacking her without maiming or killing them. A standoff of sorts.

The balance of forces changed as the unarmored marines and recovery crew opened fire with their stunners. That quickly cleared the Rebel Empire forces nearest the hatch and got them into engineering.

"Suited marines, dig the enemy out of any pockets of resistance," Veronica ordered. "Everyone else back them up. Clear engineering before someone does something we can't fix."

Veronica led the charge to the drives. She figured the attack had been far too sudden to give anyone the idea of sabotage, but she wasn't going to take any chances when their future depended on it.

A few crewmen tried to use the drives as cover, but an armored marine simply tossed them out into the open where they were stunned. Veronica verified the drives were intact with a sigh. Then she went to make sure the fusion plants were equally secured.

Ten minutes later, she was reporting to Princess Kelsey that engineering was theirs. She'd heard that the bridge was locked down, but without Fleet security and their weapons, clearing the ship would be simple enough, if time consuming.

Of course, any strays might get their hands on a crate filled with weapons, so clearing the freighter quickly was critical.

She left two armored marines inside engineering. Her people would lock the hatch behind her and keep any intruders out. If someone somehow managed to blow the door, the marines would come down on them like an avalanche.

Two other armored marines would secure the Fleet security armory. The final two would join the search for holdouts.

She hoped it didn't come to it, but depressurizing sections of the ship was an effective method of flushing them out. Drop the pressure slowly while calling for anyone hiding to come out. When they couldn't breathe, people tended to see reason.

Her primary task done, Veronica took a couple of unarmored marines to guard her and headed for the bridge.

Princess Kelsey hadn't summoned her, but she owed it to Don to get him out of there alive. His friendship had meant a lot to her back then and she wouldn't allow him to die for the Lords.

She found Jason Young working on the hatch while Princess Kelsey and a team of armed marines and recovery specialists waited impatiently in the corridor nearby.

Veronica didn't have much hope for the man's success. The bridge hatches were designed to keep people out. They'd have to talk Don out or use plasma cutters to burn the hatch off.

"What's your status?" the princess asked as she approached.

"Engineering is secure," Veronica assured her. "I sent some armored marines to guard the Fleet security armory and others to help with the search. I came here to get Don out."

The short woman nodded. "You know him better than I do. Can we end this peacefully? We don't need bridge access right now, but it makes my spine itch to have hostile forces in there, even if all the primary systems are locked out. One never knows how resourceful they are."

"Don is *very* resourceful. We have a bond. Let me use it to save him."

Kelsey's eyebrows rose. "As in a romantic bond? That could prove awkward if he feels betrayed, since you… ah, betrayed him."

Veronica shook her head. "No, not that. He's not my type. I'm more into… well, that's not important right now. What matters is that we were friends. I can get him to surrender."

Princess Kelsey gestured toward the door. "The com at the hatch works. By all means, give it a try."

Veronica walked over to the com and pressed the button. A moment later, her friend's voice came from the speaker.

"We're not opening up."

"I really wish you would, Don. We don't want to hurt you. Quite the opposite, really."

There were a few moments of silence. "What are you doing, Veronica? I never saw you in the role of a traitor."

She leaned her back against the hatch. "Me, either. Then I found out the Lords had been lying to us all along. Enslaving us. Now I'm working with people determined to throw off the yokes of our electronic overlords.

"We've locked you out of all the critical systems. I'm sure you have hopes of regaining control of something. I'll grant that you're resourceful and can probably pull something off. What then? The Ghosts have control of this system, and neither one of us wants them to catch us, trust me on that."

Her friend sighed gustily. "You ruined a perfectly good escape and literally years of hard work and planning. Now you probably have most of my people out of action, and we're both going to pay the price for that. Why?"

"You're not the only one with secrets," she assured him. "We can and will get out of this system, if you don't screw up *our* plan."

When he didn't respond for a minute, she figured she'd failed and the conversation was over, but the hatch slid open. She stood and turned to face the bridge. All four men inside stood there, their hands raised high.

Princess Kelsey wasted no time in sending her marines in to secure them.

Don's eyes never left Veronica. "If you're working against the Lords, I deserve to know who you're working for."

Veronica gestured at Princess Kelsey. "Her. She's a descendant of people that escaped the Lords. They aren't Ghosts. They call themselves the New Terran Empire. There are elements of resistance in our society, and she's working hard with some of them to help us free ourselves.

"We needed this ship because we had to steal something critical. We had no idea you were doing… whatever it is that you're doing here. What *are* you doing with all those flip drives, armored marine suits, and this ship? How did you even get it built?"

He considered Veronica for a few seconds before shaking his head. "I suppose the ship and its contents are more than enough to condemn us if you're working for the Lords, so I might as well take a chance you aren't lying. You know that resistance you mentioned? I work for them. I always have."

Veronica blinked in shock. "I… see. Then I suppose we need to sit down and have a long talk while Princess Kelsey gets us out of this system. We might still be able to be friends after all."

Don frowned at Kelsey. "Princess?"

"That's a *very* long story," the short woman assured him. "Let me get this ship on its way to safety, and we'll have lunch while we tell it. I'm starving."

39

Zia hadn't relaxed until all their ships had eluded the Clan warships in the system. She and her freighter hadn't drawn any pursuit, but Princess Kelsey had drawn the attention of the invaders.

They'd had to go far out into the outer system to be sure they'd escaped pursuit. It had taken more than a day for them to join Zia at the multiflip point with *Persephone* guarding her.

In that time, the Clans had consolidated their control over the Archibald system. More and more ships had continued to pour through the flip point, emphasizing the point that this war had been long planned. Raul Castille might have kicked it off with his unprovoked attack, but it would have happened anyway.

The invading forces had seized control of the station, but the Rebel Empire had chosen to blow up the shipyard just before the Clans reached orbit. At least after the chaos of the attack, no one would put together what they'd done.

Fiona hadn't had to destroy the FTL com. The Rebel Empire had done it for them. Sadly, they'd lost the large transport rings. Carl was despondent, and she wasn't much better.

He'd thrown himself into going over everything they'd stolen. She hoped it was worth the loss they'd suffered.

If Commander Sommerville was to be believed, he was working for the resistance and had stuffed the Q-ship with all kinds of illicit goodies. He wasn't saying where he'd intended to take it all, but he'd seemed fairly certain he could get it out of the system.

She supposed it was possible they knew about the far flip points, but he wasn't saying. Maybe once he laid eyes on *Audacious* he'd be more forthcoming.

They dropped an FTL probe to keep an eye on the Archibald system and flipped back to Pandora. The Q-ship was large, though not as big as her carrier. Carl assured them that this segment of the multiflip point could handle something that size, but she still fretted until they were all safely across and in orbit around the planet.

She virtually snagged Carl by the ear and had him move her ship's new flip drive over to the carrier. Getting it into engineering wasn't a simple task, but a few hours later, her people were maneuvering it into place. They'd had no reason to leave the old one there, so it had been removed while they were gone.

"How long will the installation take?" she asked her chief engineer, Commander Tony Hastert. "Not that we're about to rush off or anything."

"Getting it into the compartment was the difficult part," he assured her. "The unit is basically plug-and-play on a massive scale. We'll have it locked down and fully connected in a shift. I'd prefer to spend another shift testing it before we head to a flip point to make absolutely sure it's working correctly.

"We'll want to flip into an empty system to test out the frequency modulator that Carl built into it. That's unproven. We'll flip once without it and then use the tuner on the way back. At that point, I'll declare us fully fit for action, barring any issues."

Being fully operational in a day sounded excellent to her. "Call me if you run into any problems."

She was about to head for the flag bridge to get an updated tactical briefing when her com chimed with an incoming call. It was Carl.

"What now?" she almost barked. "What else has gone wrong?"

The scientist shook his head sadly. "Someone needs a nap. In fact, we have some good news for a change. Can you come down to my lab?"

Zia considered begging off, but decided she needed to know what he'd found. It might have a bearing on the briefing she'd been planning.

"I'll be right there."

Ten minutes later, she was ensconced in his office. It wasn't much of an office as he didn't have a desk, just more workstations, so she snagged a rolling chair and sat. "Talk to me."

He grabbed an identical chair and settled in across from her. "The researchers have been continuing to work on the FTL anomaly while we were at Archibald. They made a breakthrough right after we got back. It's a big one and has implications on what we do going forward."

When he stopped talking, she gestured for him to continue. "Don't make me drag this out of you. What did they find, and why do I need to know about it right now?"

He smiled widely at her. "They discovered the communications throughput was going down because they'd found a way to enhance the range. That's the tradeoff. Longer range means less bandwidth.

"They tested it by selecting an FTL pair where the other end was far outside our normal transmission range. They couldn't send a message, but they pulsed it to see if they got a status response on the quantumly entangled pairs. They did."

Zia blinked at him. "Are you telling me that we can talk to someone back home? Seriously?"

"Not exactly," he cautioned. "We know the paired com detected its other half, but that end isn't configured correctly to link up with it. I doubt an actual call would be successful without some reconfiguring on the other end.

"The hardest part will be making them aware of us at all. There's likely no indication on that end that we've tagged them for a status. The coms weren't designed to make anyone aware of that sort of thing."

"So, let me see if I understand," Zia said slowly. "We know that we can potentially communicate with home, but we need to somehow make them aware we're out here. They would have no reason to look more deeply because they know we're far too distant and a real call from us would cause their com to signal them."

He nodded. "That's about it. I have a few ideas that might bear fruit, but it's going to be hard going. Also, it's not all the coms at home. It's a single com. We've tried others, but the range limitation is still too great.

"That said, I think you'll be pleased to hear which com we've connected to. The researchers had no luck with the ones on *Audacious*, so they started working the sets aboard *Persephone* as soon as we got back into orbit. They hit pay dirt with the one Admiral Mertz keeps with him that's linked to a special one for Kelsey."

Zia felt her eyes widen. "That's terrific! If anyone can help us get home, it's Admiral Mertz. It's kind of odd that his com is the only one in range, though. What about *Invincible*?"

Carl shook his head. "No dice there. Wherever the admiral is, he isn't aboard *Invincible* or any of the other ships we have FTL coms for. I'd wager, based on the timing, that he's in the captured destroyer giving the report about Harrison's World to the Rebel Empire."

That made sense. It also gave them an opportunity with a limited shelf life. The admiral would deliver his report and go home as quickly as he could.

"Keep working on this," she ordered. "Make it priority one."

"I have everyone working on it," he assured her. "We'll figure this out."

Zia checked her internal chronometer. The briefing could wait. Kelsey would want to hear about this right away.

* * *

Kelsey watched Don Sommerville stare at Derek while Veronica explained where they were and what the New Terran Empire was all about. Since the Rebel Empire had no history with aliens, the man's poleaxed expression made sense.

The Pandoran prince and his human friend Jacob Howell had been waiting for them, and it tickled Kelsey's sense of fancy to have them there for the briefing. They were still curious about their new associates, and it wouldn't hurt to have them see the Rebel Empire was made up of normal people too.

She still hadn't told anyone what the doctor had told her about the Pandoran DNA. It might be a long while before she felt comfortable with the revelation. In any case, at some point they'd be leaving, and it would hardly be worth wrecking the Pandorans' view of themselves before setting off.

Veronica was just finishing her basic overview of the New Terran Empire but hadn't started on how she'd been captured when Zia arrived. Kelsey left her to it when the commodore gestured for her to join her in the corridor.

"What's up?" she asked when they were alone.

Zia proceeded to fill her in on what Carl had told her.

When the other woman finished, Kelsey was grinning. "Carl will figure out how to make contact. We need to start prepping for departure. Even if we don't leave today, it won't be very long."

"I want to go with you," Jacob said from the hatch. He'd slipped up on them quietly and must've overheard most of what they'd said.

She turned to face the man. "We'll be going a long way from here, and I can't say that I'll ever come back, though the Empire might eventually send someone. That could mean a one-way trip. I'm sorry, but no."

"Don't you think that's my decision to make?" he asked seriously. "And I know that Derek will insist that he and some of his people come along. We've heard stories of the Clans for decades. Now those crazy bastards are on the loose. Add in the Rebel Empire, and our people have to know what's going on and do our part to set things right."

Kelsey started to reject him again, but Zia put a hand on her shoulder. "Maybe he has a point. In any case, if his people want to send a group back to the New Terran Empire, we should consider it."

"All I ask is that you consider my words," Jacob said as he bowed his way back into the compartment. "I'll leave you to discuss things without prying ears."

She didn't have to make a decision right this moment. Instead, she turned her head back to Zia.

"How goes the flip drive replacement?"

"So far, so good. We'll know by tomorrow if all this was worth it."

Kelsey laughed. "It was worth it. I've been looking over the master manifest on the Q-ship. Add in the ship itself, and we've come out a lot better than when we started.

"Doctor Zoboroski tells me that he's relatively satisfied that the new regenerator will be effective on Commodore Murdock. Doctor Lipp is helping with that. Not that we can trust her very far, mind you. She's a spy.

"On the positive side, even with the loss of the large transport ring, we have the Singularity computer and its data. That's going to be fascinating. I can't help but wonder what it might tell us that bears on our Singularity prisoner. Or how his tune might change if he knew we had it."

"The next few days should be interesting," Zia agreed.

Kelsey excused herself and sent a message to Veronica that she'd be elsewhere. She needed to get a handle on what they did next. Wherever Jared was, she had to find a path to him via multiflip points and far flip points. The regular network was far too dangerous.

They'd have to start mapping with FTL probes and that meant sending *Persephone*. Now that Angela was a fully operational Marine Raider, Kelsey could pass command of the ship to her.

Not that she really wanted to, but she had to focus on the larger picture. And it was time to start Talbot along the path to being a Marine Raider. Once he was done, they'd expand the program to the rest of the marines he thought were suitable.

So much to do, so little time.

Kelsey found that her feet had taken her to her quarters. Talbot was in there, she knew. She set the door and her implants to "disturb only if something important is on fire" and slipped quietly inside.

Tomorrow's problems would still be there tomorrow. She needed to celebrate their successes today. Besides, once he started the surgeries, Talbot wouldn't feel much like making love. She needed him now and the rest of the universe would have to wait.

* * *

ALSO BY TERRY MIXON

You can always find the most up to date listing of Terry's titles on his Amazon Author Page.

Note: the links below (ebook only, obviously) redirect you to my website where you can click a button to go to Amazon. This allows me to participate in Amazon's associates program and earn a little more. Sorry for any inconvenience.

The Last Hunter

The Last Hunter

Bonds of Blood

Alpha Strike

The Enemy Revealed

Command Authority

The Grand Conspiracy

Shield of Humanity

Fog of War

Ships of the Line

Operation Liberty

The Empire of Bones Saga

Empire of Bones

Veil of Shadows

Command Decisions

Ghosts of Empire

Paying the Price

Recon in Force

Behind Enemy Lines

The Terra Gambit

Hidden Enemies

Race to Terra

Ruined Terra

Victory on Terra

When Luck Runs Out

Gunboat Diplomacy

The Imperial Marines Saga

Spoils of War

Imperial Recruit

Enemy Action

The Humanity Unlimited Saga

Liberty Station

Freedom Express

Tree of Liberty

Blood of Patriots

Single Novels

Scorched Earth

Storm Divers

The Vigilante Series with Glynn Stewart

Heart of Vengeance

Oath of Vengeance

Bound By Law

Bound By Honor

Bound By Blood

Box Sets

The Empire of Bones Saga Volume 1

The Empire of Bones Saga Volume 2

The Empire of Bones Saga Volume 3

The Empire of Bones Saga Volume 4

Humanity Unlimited Publisher's Pack 1

Humanity Unlimited Publisher's Pack 2

ABOUT TERRY

#1 Bestselling Military Science Fiction author Terry Mixon served as a non-commissioned officer in the United States Army 101st Airborne Division. He later worked alongside the flight controllers in the Mission Control Center at the NASA Johnson Space Center supporting the Space Shuttle, the International Space Station, and other human spaceflight projects.

He now writes full time while living in Texas with his lovely wife and a pounce of cats.

TerryMixon.com

amazon.com/author/terrymixon
facebook.com/TerryLMixon
patreon.com/TerryMixon
bookbub.com/authors/terry-mixon
goodreads.com/TerryMixon

www.ingramcontent.com/pod-product-compliance
Lightning Source LLC
Chambersburg PA
CBHW070341030726
47504CB00001B/29

* 9 7 8 1 9 4 7 3 7 6 4 2 7 *